(For more nationwide acclaim, please turn page.)

D0047028

Big Bestsellers from SIGNET

To order these titles,
please use coupon on the
last page of this book.

Fools Die

a novel by

Mario Puzo

A SIGNET BOOK

NEW AMERICAN LIBRARY

TIMES MIRROR

Copyright © 1978 by Mario Puzo

SIGNET, SIGNET CLASSICS, MENTOR, PLUME AND MERIDIAN BOOKS
are published by The New American Library, Inc.,
1301 Avenue of the Americas, New York, New York 10019

First Signet Printing, October, 1979

1 2 3 4 5 6 7 8 9

PRINTED IN THE UNITED STATES OF AMERICA

For Erika

Book I

Chapter 1

"Listen to me. I will tell you the truth about a man's life. I will tell you the truth about his love for women. That he never hates them. Already you think I'm on the wrong track. Stay with me. Really—I'm a master of magic.

"Do you believe a man can truly love a woman and constantly betray her? Never mind physically, but betray her in his mind, in the very 'poetry of his soul.' Well, it's not easy, but men do it all the time.

"Do you want to know how women can love you, feed you that love deliberately to poison your body and mind simply to destroy you? And out of passionate love choose not to love you anymore? And at the same time dizzy you with an idiot's ecstasy? Impossible? That's the easy part.

"But don't run away. This is not a love story.

"I will make you feel the painful beauty of a child, the animal horniness of the adolescent male, the yearning suicidal moodiness of the young female. And then (here's the hard part) show you how time turns man and woman around full circle, exchanged in body and soul.

"And then of course there is TRUE LOVE. Don't go away! It exists or I will make it exist. I'm not a master of magic for nothing. Is it worth what it cost? And how about sexual fidelity? Does it work? Is it love? Is it even human, that perverse passion to be with only one person? And if it doesn't work, do you still get a bonus for trying? Can it work both ways? Of course not, that's easy. And yet—

"Life is a comical business, and there is nothing funnier than love traveling through time. But a true master of magic can make his audience laugh and cry at the same time. Death is another story. I will never make a joke about death. It is beyond my powers.

"I am always alert for death. He doesn't fool me. I spot

• 3 •

him right away. He loves to come in his country-bumpkin disguise; a comical wart that suddenly grows and grows; the dark, hairy mole that sends its roots to the very bone; or hiding behind a pretty little fever blush. Then suddenly that grinning skull appears to take the victim by surprise. But never me. I'm waiting for him. I take my precautions.

"Parallel to death, love is a tiresome, childish business, though men believe more in love than death. Women are another story. They have a powerful secret. They don't take love seriously and never have.

"But again, don't go away. Again; this is not a love story. Forget about love. I will show you all the stretches of power. First the life of a poor struggling writer. Sensitive. Talented. Maybe even some genius. I will show you the artist getting the shit kicked out of him for the sake of his art. And why he so richly deserves it. Then I will show him as a cunning criminal and having the time of his life. Ah, what joy the true artist feels when he finally becomes a crook. It's out in the open now, his essential nature. No more kidding around about his honor. The son of a bitch is a hustler. A conniver. An enemy of society right out in the clear instead of hiding behind his whore's cunt of art. What a relief. What pleasure. Such sly delight. And then how he becomes an honest man again. It's an awful strain being a crook.

"But it helps you to accept society and forgive your fellowman. Once that's done no person should be a crook unless he really needs the money.

"Then on to one of the most amazing success stories in the history of literature. The intimate lives of the giants of our culture. One crazy bastard especially. The classy world. So now we have the poor struggling genius world, the crooked world and the classy literary world. All this laced with plenty of sex, some complicated ideas you won't be hit over the head with and may even find interesting. And finally on to a full-blast ending in Hollywood with our hero gobbling up all its rewards, money, fame, beautiful women. And . . . don't go away—don't go away—how it all turns to ashes.

"That's not enough? You've heard it all before? But remember I'm a master of magic. I can bring all these people truly alive. I can show you what they truly think and feel. You'll weep for them, all of them, I promise you that. Or maybe just laugh. Anyway, we're going to have a lot of fun. And learn something about life. Which is really no help.

"Ah, I know what you're thinking. That conning bastard trying to make us turn the page. But wait, it's only a tale I want to tell. What's the harm? Even if I take it seriously, you don't have to. Just have a good time.

"I want to tell you a story, I have no other vanity. I don't desire success or fame or money. But that's easy, most men, most women don't, not really. Even better, I don't want love. When I was young, some women told me they loved me for my long eyelashes. I accepted. Later it was for my wit. Then for my power and money. Then for my talent. Then for my mind—deep. OK, I can handle all of it. The only woman who scares me is the one who loves me for myself alone. I have plans for her. I have poisons and daggers and dark graves in caves to hide her head. She can't be allowed to live. Especially if she is sexually faithful and never lies and always puts me ahead of everything and everyone.

"There will be a lot about love in this book, but it's not a love book. It's a war book. The old war between men who are true friends. The great 'new' war between men and women. Sure it's an old story, but it's out in the open now. The Women's Liberation warriors think they have something new, but it's just their armies coming out of their guerrilla hills. Sweet women ambushed men always: at their cradles, in the kitchen, the bedroom. And at the graves of their children, the best place not to hear a plea for mercy.

"Ah, well, you think I have a grievance against women. But I never hated them. And they'll come out better people than men, you'll see. But the truth is that only women have been able to make me unhappy, and they have done so from the cradle on. But most men can say that. And there's nothing to be done.

"What a target I've given here. I know—I know—how irresistible it seems. But be careful. I'm a tricky storyteller, not just one of your vulnerable sensitive artists. I've taken my precautions. I've still got a few surprises left.

"But enough. Let me get to work. Let me begin and let me end."

Book II

Chapter 2

On the luckiest day of Jordan Hawley's life he betrayed his three best friends. But yet unknowing, he wandered through the dice pit of the huge gambling casino in the Hotel Xanadu, wondering what game to try next. Still early afternoon, he was a ten-thousand-dollar winner. But he was tired of the glittering red dice skittering across green felt.

He moved out of the pit, the purple carpet sinking beneath his feet, and moved toward the hissing wheel of a roulette table, pretty with red and black boxes, punishing green zero and double zero. He made some foolhardy bets, lost and moved into the blackjack pit.

The small horseshoe blackjack tables ran down in double rows. He walked between them like a captive through an Indian gauntlet. Blue-backed cards flashed on either side. He made it through safely and came to the huge glass doors that led out into the streets of the city of Las Vegas. From here he could see down the Strip sentineled by luxury hotels.

Under the blazing Nevada sun, a dozen Xanadus glittered with million-watt neon signs. The hotels seemed to be melting down into a steely golden haze, a reachable mirage. Jordan Hawley was trapped inside the air-conditioned casino with his winnings. It would be madness to go out to where only other casinos awaited him, with their strange unknown fortunes. Here he was a winner, and soon he would see his friends. Here he was shielded from the burning yellow desert.

Jordan Hawley turned away from the glass door and sat down at the nearest blackjack table. Black hundred-dollar chips, tiny cindered suns, rattled in his hands. He watched a dealer sliding cards from his freshly made shoe, the oblong wooden box that held the cards.

Jordan bet heavy on each of two small circles, playing two hands. His luck was good. He played until the shoe ran out.

The dealer busted often, and when he shuffled up, Jordan moved on. His pockets bulged chips everywhere. But that was no sweat because he was wearing a specially designed Sy Devore Vegas Winner sports coat. It had red crimson trim on sky blue cloth and specially zippered pockets that were optimistically capacious. The inside of the jacket also held special zippered cavities so deep no pickpocket could get at them. Jordan's winnings were safe, and he had plenty of room for more. Nobody had ever filled the pockets of a Vegas Winner jacket.

The casino, lit by many huge chandeliers, had a bluish haze, neon reflected by the deep purple carpeting. Jordan stepped out of this light and into the darkened area of the bar lounge with its lowered ceiling and small platform for performers. Seated at a small table, he could look out on the casino as a spectator looks on a lighted stage.

Mesmerized, he watched afternoon gamblers drift in intricate choreographed patterns from table to table. Like a rainbow flashing across a clear blue sky, a roulette wheel flashed its red, black numbers to match the table layout. Blue-white-backed cards skittered across green felt tables. White-dotted red square dice were dazzling flying fish over the whale-shaped crap tables. Far off, down the rows of blackjack tables, those dealers going off duty washed their hands high in the air to show they were not palming chips.

The casino stage began to fill up with more actors: sun worshipers wandering in from the outdoor pool, others from tennis courts, golf courses, naps and afternoon free and paid lovemaking in Xanadu's thousand rooms. Jordan spotted another Vegas Winner jacket coming across the casino floor. It was Merlyn. Merlyn the Kid. Merlyn wavered as he passed the roulette wheel, his weakness. Though he rarely played because he knew its huge five and a half percent cut like a sharp sword. Jordan from the darkness waved a crimson-striped arm, and Merlyn took up his stride again as if he were passing through flames, stepped off the lighted stage of the casino floor and sat down. Merlyn's zippered pockets did not bulge with chips, nor did he have any in his hands.

They sat there without speaking, easy with each other. Merlyn looked like a burly athlete in his crimson and blue jacket. He was younger than Jordan by at least ten years, and his hair was jet black. He also looked happier, more eager for the coming battle against fate, the night of gambling.

Then from the baccarat pit in the far corner of the casino they saw Cully Cross and Diane step through the elegant royal gray railing and move over the casino floor coming toward them. Cully too was wearing his Vegas Winner jacket. Diane was in a white summer frock, low-cut and cool for her day's work, the top of her breasts dusted pearly white. Merlyn waved, and they came forward through the casino tables without swerving. And when they sat down, Jordan ordered the drinks. He knew what they wanted.

Cully spotted Jordan's bulging pockets. "Hey," he said, "you went and got lucky without us?"

Jordan smiled. "A little." They all looked at him curiously as he paid for the drinks and tipped the cocktail waitress with a red five-dollar chip. He noticed their glances. He did not know why they looked at him so oddly. Jordan had been in Vegas three weeks and had changed fearsomely in that three weeks. He had lost twenty pounds. His ash-blond hair had grown long, whiter. His face, though still handsome, was now haggard; the skin had a grayish tinge. He looked drained. But he was not conscious of this because he felt fine. Innocently, he wondered about these three people, his friends of three weeks and now the best friends he had in the world.

The one Jordan liked best was the Kid. Merlyn. Merlyn prided himself on being an impassive gambler. He tried never to show emotion when he lost or won and usually succeeded. Except that an exceptionally bad losing streak gave him a look of surprised bewilderment that delighted Jordan.

Merlyn the Kid never said much. He just watched everybody. Jordan knew that Merlyn the Kid kept tabs on everything he did, trying to figure him out. Which also amused Jordan. He had the Kid faked out. The Kid was looking for complicated things and never accepted that he, Jordan, was exactly what he presented to the world. But Jordan liked being with him and the others. They relieved his loneliness. And because Merlyn seemed more eager, more passionate, in his gambling, Cully had named him the Kid.

Cully himself was the youngest, only twenty-nine. But oddly enough seemed to be the leader of the group. They had met three weeks ago here in Vegas, in this casino, and they had only one thing in common. They were degenerate gamblers. Their three-week-long debauch was considered extraordinary because the casino percentage should have ground them into the Nevada desert sands in their first few days.

Jordan knew that the others, Cully "Countdown" Cross and Diane, were also curious about him, but he didn't mind. He had very little curiosity about any of them. The Kid seemed young and too intelligent to be a degenerate gambler, but Jordan never tried to nail down why. It was really of no interest to him.

Cully was nothing to wonder about or so it seemed. He was your classical degenerate gambler with skills. He could count the cards in a four-deck blackjack shoe. He was an expert on all the gambling percentages. The Kid was not. Jordan was a cool, abstracted gambler where the Kid was passionate. And Cully professional. But Jordan had no illusions about himself. At this moment he was in their class. A degenerate gambler. That is, a man who gambled simply to gamble and must lose. As a hero who goes to war must die. Show me a gambler and I'll show you a loser, show me a hero and I'll show you a corpse, Jordan thought.

They were all at the end of their bankrolls, they would all have to move on soon, except maybe Cully. Cully was part pimp and part tout. Always trying to work a con to get an edge on the casinos. Sometimes he got a blackjack dealer to go partners against the house, a dangerous game.

The girl, Diane, was really an outsider. She worked as a shill for the house and she was taking her break from the baccarat table. With them, because these were the only three men in Vegas she felt cared about her.

As a shill she played with casino money, lost and won casino money. She was subject not to fate but to the fixed weekly salary she received from the casino. Her presence was necessary to the baccarat table only in slack hours because gamblers shied away from an empty table. She was the flypaper for the flies. She was, therefore, dressed provocatively. She had long jet black hair she used as a whip, a sensuous full mouth and an almost perfect long-legged body. Her bust was on the small side, but it suited her. And the baccarat pit boss gave her home phone number to big players. Sometimes the pit boss or a ladderman would whisper that one of the players would like to see her in his room. She had the option to refuse, but it was an option to be used carefully. When she complied, she was not paid directly by the customer. The pit boss gave her a special chit for fifty or a hundred dollars that she could cash at the casino cage. This she hated to do. So she would pay one of the other girl shills five dollars to cash her chit for her. When Cully heard this, he became her friend. He liked soft women, he could manipulate them.

Jordan signaled the cocktail waitress for more drinks. He felt relaxed. It gave Jordan a feeling of virtue to be so lucky and so early in the day. As if some strange God had loved him, found him good and was rewarding him for the sacrifices he had offered up to the world he had left behind him. And he had this sense of comradeship with Cully and Merlyn.

They ate breakfast together often. And always had this late-afternoon drink before starting their big gambling action that would destroy the night. Sometimes they had a midnight snack to celebrate a win, the lucky man picking up the tab and buying keno tickets for the table. In the last three weeks they had become buddies, though they had absolutely nothing in common and their friendship would die with their gambling lust. But now, still not busted out, they had a strange affection for each other. Coming off a winning day, Merlyn the Kid had taken the three of them into the hotel clothing store and bought their crimson and blue Vegas Winner jackets. That day all three had been winners and had worn their jackets superstitiously ever since.

Jordan had met Diane on the night of her deepest humiliation, the same night he first met Merlyn. The day after meeting her he had bought her coffee on one of her breaks, and they had talked but he had not heard what she was saying. She sensed his lack of interest and had been offended. So there had been no action. He was sorry afterward, sorry that night in his ornately decorated room, alone and unable to sleep. As he was unable to sleep every night. He had tried sleeping pills, but they gave him nightmares that frightened him.

The jazz combo would be coming on soon, the lounge filled up. Jordan noticed the look they had given him when he had tipped the waitress with a red five-dollar chip. They thought he was generous. But it was simply because he didn't want to be bothered figuring out what the tip should be. It amused him to see how his values had changed. He had always been meticulous and fair but never recklessly generous. At one time his part of the world had been scaled and metered out. Everyone earned rewards. And finally it hadn't worked. He was amazed now at the absurdity of having once based his life on such reasoning.

The combo was rustling through the darkness up to the stage. Soon they would be playing too loud for anyone to talk, and this was always the signal for the three men to start their serious gambling.

"Tonight's my lucky night," Cully said. "I got thirteen passes in my right arm."

Jordan smiled. He always responded to Cully's enthusiasm. Jordan knew him only by the name of Cully Countdown, the name he had earned at the blackjack tables. Jordan liked Cully because the man never stopped talking and his talk rarely required answers. Which made him necessary to the group because Jordan and Merlyn the Kid never talked much. And Diane, the baccarat shill, smiled a lot but didn't talk much either.

Cully's small-featured, dark, neat face was glowing with confidence. "I'm going to hold the dice for an hour," he said. "I'm going to throw a hundred numbers and no sevens. You guys get on me."

The jazz combo gave their opening flourish as if to back Cully up.

Cully loved craps, though his best skill was at blackjack where he could count down the shoe. Jordan loved baccarat because there was absolutely no skill or figuring involved. Merlyn loved roulette because it was to him the most mythical, magical game. But Cully had declared his infallibility tonight at craps and they would all have to play with him, ride his luck. They were his friends, they couldn't jinx him. They rose to go to the dice pit and bet with Cully, Cully flexing his strong right arm that magically concealed thirteen passes.

Diane spoke for the first time. "Jordy had a lucky streak at baccarat. Maybe you should bet on him."

"You don't look lucky to me," Merlyn said to Jordan.

It was against the rules for her to mention Jordan's luck to fellow gamblers. They might tap him for a loan or he might feel jinxed. But by this time Diane knew Jordan well enough to sense he didn't care about any of the usual superstitions gamblers worried about.

Cully Countdown shook his head. "I have the feeling." He brandished his right arm, shaking imaginary dice.

The music blared; they could no longer hear each other speak. It blew them out of their sanctuary of darkness into the blazing stage that was the casino floor. There were many more players now, but they could move fluidly. Diane, her coffee break over, went back to the baccarat table to bet the house money, to fill up space. But without passion. As a house shill, winning and losing house money, she was boringly immortal. And so she walked more slowly than the others.

Cully led the way. They were the Three Musketeers in their crimson and blue Vegas Winner sports jackets. He was eager and confident. Merlyn followed almost as eagerly, his gambling blood up. Jordan followed more slowly, his huge winnings making him appear heavier than the other two. Cully was trying to sniff out a hot table, one of his signposts being if the house racks of chips were low. Finally he led them to an open railing and the three lined up so that Cully would get the dice first coming around the stickman. They made small bets until Cully finally had the red cubes in his loving rubbing hands.

The Kid put twenty on the line. Jordan two hundred. Cully Countdown fifty. He threw a six. They all backed up their bets and bought all the numbers. Cully picked up the dice, passionately confident, and threw them strongly against the far side of the table. Then stared with disbelief. It was the worst of catastrophes. Seven out. Wiped. Without even catching another number. The Kid had lost a hundred and forty, Cully a big three fifty. Jordan had gone down the drain for fourteen hundred dollars.

Cully muttered something and wandered away. Thoroughly shaken, he was now committed to playing very careful blackjack. He had to count every card from the shoe to get an edge on the dealer. Sometimes it worked, but it was a long grind. Sometimes he would remember every card perfectly, figure out what was left in the shoe, get a ten percent edge on the dealer and bet a big stack of chips. And even then sometimes with that big ten percent edge he got unlucky and lost. And then count down another shoe. So now, his fantastic right arm having betrayed him, Cully was down to case money. The night before him was a drudgery. He had to gamble very cleverly and still not get unlucky.

Merlyn the Kid also wandered away, also down to his case money, but with no skills to back up his play. He had to get lucky.

Jordan, alone, prowled around the casino. He loved the feeling of being solitary in the crowd of people and the gambling hum. To be alone without being lonely. To be friends with strangers for an hour and never see them again. Dice clattering.

He wandered through the blackjack pit, the horseshoe tables in straight rows. He listened for the tick of a second carder. Cully had taught him and Merlyn this trick. A crooked dealer with fast hands was impossible to spot with the eye. But if you listened very carefully, you could hear the slight rasping tick when he slid out the second card from beneath the top card of his deck. Because the top card was the card the dealer needed to make his hand good.

A long queue was forming for the dinner show though it was only seven. There was no real action in the casino. No big bettors. No big winners. Jordan clicked the black chips in his hand, deliberating. Then he stepped up to an almost empty crap table and picked up the red glittering dice.

Jordan unzipped the outside pocket of his Vegas Winner sports jacket and heaped black hundred-dollar chips into his table rack. He bet two hundred on the line, backed up his number and then bought all the numbers for five hundred dollars each. He held the dice for almost an hour. After the first fifteen minutes the electricity of his hot hand ran through the casino and the table jammed full. He pressed his bets to the limit of five hundred, and the magical numbers kept rolling out of his hand. In his mind he banished the fatal seven to hell. He forbade it to appear. His table rack filled to overflowing with black chips. His jacket pockets bulged to capacity. Finally his mind could no longer hold its concentration, could no longer banish the fatal seven, and the dice passed from his hands to the next player. The gamblers at the table gave him a cheer. The pit boss gave him metal racks to carry his chips to the casino cage. Merlyn and Cully appeared. Jordan smiled at them.

"Did you get on my roll?" he asked.

Cully shook his head. "I got in on the last ten minutes," he said. "I did a little good."

Merlyn laughed. "I didn't believe in your luck. I stayed off."

Merlyn and Cully escorted Jordan to the cashier's cage to help him cash in. Jordan was astonished when the total of the metal racks came to over fifty thousand dollars. And his pockets bulged with still more chips.

Merlyn and Cully were awestricken. Cully said seriously, "Jordy, now's the time for you to leave town. Stay here and they'll get it back."

Jordan laughed. "The night's young yet." He was amused that his two friends thought it such a big deal. But the strain told on him. He felt enormously tired. He said, "I'm going up to my room for a nap. I'll meet you guys and buy a big dinner maybe about midnight. OK?"

The cage teller had finished counting and said to Jordan, "Sir, would you like cash or a check? Or would you like us to hold it for you here in the cage?"

Merlyn said, "Get a check."

Cully frowned with thoughtful greed, but then noticed that Jordan's secret inner pockets still bulged with chips, and he smiled. "A check is safer," he said.

The three of them waited, Cully and Merlyn flanking Jordan, who looked beyond them to the glittering casino pits. Finally the cashier reappeared with the saw-toothed yellow check and handed it to Jordan.

The three men turned together in an unconscious pirouette; their jackets flashed crimson and blue beneath the keno board lights above them. Then Merlyn and Cully took Jordan by the elbows and thrust him into one of the spokelike corridors toward his room.

A plushy, expensive, garish room. Rich gold curtains, a huge silver quilted bed. Exactly right for gambling. Jordan took a hot bath and then tried to read. He couldn't sleep. Through the windows the neon lights of the Vegas Strip sent flashes of rainbow color, streaking the walls of his room. He drew the curtains tighter, but in his brain he still heard the faint roar that diffused through the huge casino like surf on a distant beach. Then he put out the lights in the room and got into bed. It was a good fake, but his brain refused to be fooled. He could not fall asleep.

Then Jordan felt the familiar fear and terrible anxiety. If he fell asleep, he would die. He desperately wanted to sleep, yet he could not. He was too afraid, too frightened. But he could never understand why he was so terribly frightened.

He was tempted to try the sleeping pills again; he had done so earlier in the month and he had slept, but only with night-mares that he couldn't bear. And left him depressed the next day. He preferred going without sleep. As now.

Jordan snapped on the light, got out of bed and dressed. He emptied out all his pockets and his wallet. He unzipped all the outside and inside pockets of his Vegas Winner sports jacket and shook it upside down so that all the black and green and red chips poured down on the silk coverlet. The hundred-dollar bills formed a huge pile, the black and reds forming curious spirals and checkered patterns. To pass the time he started to count the money and sort out the chips. It took him almost an hour.

He had over five thousand dollars in cash. He had eight thousand dollars in black hundred-dollar chips and another six thousand dollars in twenty-five-dollar greens, almost a thousand dollars in five-dollar reds. He was astonished. He took the big jagged-edged Hotel Xanadu check out of his wallet and studied the black and red script and the numbered amount in green. Fifty thousand dollars. He studied it care-fully. There were three different signatures on the check. One of the signatures he particularly noticed because it was so large and the script so clear. Alfred Gronevelt.

And still he was puzzled. He remembered turning in some chips for cash several times during the day, but he hadn't re-alized it was for more than five thousand. He shifted on the bed and all the carefully stacked piles collapsed into each other.

And now he was pleased. He was glad that he had enough money to stay in Vegas, that he would not have to go on to Los Angeles to start his new job. To start his new career, his new life, maybe a new family. He counted all the money again and added the check. He was worth seventy-one thou-sand dollars. He could gamble forever.

He switched off the bedside light so that he could lie there in the darkness with his money surrounding and touching his body. He tried to sleep to fight off the terror that always came over him in this darkened room. He could hear his heart beating faster and faster until finally he had to switch the light back on and get up from the bed.

High above the city in his penthouse suite, the hotel owner, Alfred Gronevelt, picked up the phone. He called the dice pit and asked how much Jordan was ahead. He was told that Jordan had killed the table profits for the night. Then he called back the operator and told her to page Xanadu Five. He held on. It would take a few minutes for the page to cover all the areas of the hotel and penetrate the minds of the players. Idly he gazed out the penthouse window and could see the great thick red and green python of neon that wound down the Las Vegas Strip. And farther off, the dark surrounding desert mountains enclosing, with him, thousands of gamblers trying to beat the house, sweating for those millions of dollars of greenbacks lying so mockingly in cashier cages. Over the years these gamblers had left their bones on that gaudy neon Strip.

Then he heard Cully's voice come over the phone. Cully was Xanadu Five. (Gronevelt was Xanadu One.)

"Cully, your buddy hit us big," Gronevelt said. "You sure he's legit?"

Cully's voice was low. "Yeah, Mr. Gronevelt. He's a friend of mine and he's square. He'll drop it back before he leaves."

Gronevelt said, "Anything he wants, lay it on him. Don't let him go wandering down the Strip, giving our money to other joints. Lay a good broad on him."

"Don't worry," Cully said. But Gronevelt caught something funny in his voice. For a moment he wondered about Cully. Cully was his spy, checking the operation of the casino and reporting the blackjack dealers who were going partners with him to beat the house. He had big plans for Cully when this operation was over. But now he wondered.

"What about that other guy in your gang, the Kid?" Gronevelt said. "What's his angle, what the hell is he doing here three weeks?"

"He's small change," Cully said. "But a good kid. Don't worry, Mr. Gronevelt. I know what I got riding with you."

"OK," Gronevelt said. When he hung up the phone, he was smiling. Cully didn't know that pit bosses had complained about Cully's being allowed in the casino because he was a countdown artist. That the hotel manager had complained about Merlyn and Jordan's being allowed to keep desperately needed rooms for so long despite fresh loaded gamblers who came in every weekend. What no one knew was that Gronevelt was intrigued by the friendship of the three men; how it ended would be Cully's true test.

In his room Jordan fought the impulse to go back down into the casino. He sat in one of the stuffed armchairs and lit a cigarette. Everything was OK now. He had friends, he had gotten lucky, he was free. He was just tired. He needed a long rest someplace far away.

He thought, Cully and Diane and Merlyn. Now his three best friends, he smiled at that.

They knew a lot of things about him. They had all spent hours in the casino lounge together, gossiping, resting between bouts of gambling. Jordan was never reticent. He would answer any question, though he never asked any. The Kid always asked questions so seriously, with such obvious interest, that Jordan never took offense.

Just for something to do he took his suitcase out of the closet to pack. The first thing that hit his eye was the small handgun he had bought back home. He had never told his friends about the gun. His wife had left him and taken the children. She had left him for another man, and his first reaction had been to kill the other man. A reaction so alien to his true nature that even now he was constantly surprised. Of course, he had done nothing. The problem was to get rid of the gun. The best thing to do was to take it apart and throw it away piece by piece. He didn't want to be responsible for anybody's getting hurt by it. But right now he put it to one side and threw some clothes in the suitcase, then sat down again.

He wasn't that sure he wanted to leave Vegas, the brightly lit cave of his casino. He was comfortable there. He was safe there. His not caring really about winning or losing was his magic cloak against fate. And most of all, his casino cave closed out all the other pains and traps of life itself.

He smiled again, thinking about Cully's worrying about his winnings. What, after all, would he do with the money? The best thing would be to send it to his wife. She was a good woman, a good mother, a woman of quality and character. The fact that she had left him after twenty years to marry her lover did not, could not, change those facts. For at this moment, now that the months had passed, Jordan saw clearly the justice of her decision. She had a right to be happy. To live her life to its fullest potential. And she had been suffocating living with him. Not that he had been a bad husband. Just an inadequate one. He had been a good father. He had done his duty in every way. His only fault was that after twenty years he no longer made his wife happy.

His friends knew his story. The three weeks he had spent with them in Vegas seemed like years, and he could talk to them as he could never talk to anyone back home. It had come out over drinks in the lounge, after midnight meals in the coffee shop.

He knew they thought him cold-blooded. When Merlyn asked him what the visitation rights were with his children, Jordan shrugged. Merlyn asked if he would ever see his wife and kids again, and Jordan tried to answer honestly. "I don't think so," he said. "They're OK."

And Merlyn the Kid shot back at him, "And you, are you OK?"

And Jordan laughed without faking it, laughing at the way Merlyn the Kid zeroed in on him. Still laughing, he said, "Yeah, I'm OK." And then just once he paid the Kid off for being so nosy. He looked him right in the eye and said coolly, "There's nothing more to see. What you see is it. Nothing complicated. People are not that important to other people. When you get older, that's the way it is."

Merlyn looked back at him and lowered his eyes and then said very softly, "It's just that you can't sleep at night, right?"

Jordan said, "That's right."

Cully said impatiently, "Nobody sleeps in this town. Just get a couple of sleeping pills."

"They give me nightmares," Jordan said.

"No, no," Cully said. "I mean them." He pointed to three hookers seated around a table, having drinks. Jordan laughed. It was the first time he had heard the Vegas idiom. Now he understood why sometimes Cully broke off gambling with the announcement he was going to take on a couple of sleeping pills.

If there was ever a time for walking sleeping pills, it was

tonight, but Jordan had tried that the first week in Vegas. He could always make it, but he never really felt the relief from tension afterward. One night a hooker, a friend of Cully's, had talked him into "twins," taking her girlfriend with her. Only another fifty and they would really shoot the works because he was a nice guy. And he'd said OK. It had been sort of cheery and comforting with so many breasts surrounding him. An infantile comfort. One girl finally cradled his head in her breast while the other one rode him astride. And at the final moment of tension, as finally he came, surrendering at least his flesh, he caught the girl astride giving a sly smile to the girl on whose breasts he rested. And he understood that now that he was finally out of the way, finished off, they could get down to what they really wanted. He watched while the girl who had been astride went down on the other girl with a passion far more convincing than she had shown with him. He wasn't angry. He'd just as soon they got something out of it. It seemed in some way more natural to be so. He had given them an extra hundred. They thought it was for being so good, but really it was for that sly secret smile—for that comforting, sweetly confirming betrayal. And yet the girl lying back in the final exaltation of her Judas climax had reached out her hand blindly for Jordan to hold, and he had been moved to tears.

And all the walking sleeping pills had tried their best for him. They were the cream of the country, these girls. They gave you affection, they held your hand, they went to a dinner and a show, they gambled a little of your money, never cheated or rolled you. They made believe they truly cared and they fucked your brains out. All for a solitary hundred-dollar bill, a single Honeybee in Cully's phrase. They were a bargain. Ah, Christ, they were a bargain. But he could never let himself be faked out even for the tiny bought moment. They washed him down before leaving him: a sick, sick man on a hospital bed. Well, they were better than the regular sleeping pills, they didn't give him nightmares. But they couldn't put him to sleep either. He hadn't really slept for three weeks.

Wearily Jordan sagged against the headboard of his bed. He didn't remember leaving his chair. He should put out the lights and try to sleep. But the terror would come back. Not a mental fear, but a physical panic that his body could not fight off even as his mind stood by and wondered what was happening. There was no choice. He had to go back down into the casino. He threw the check for fifty thousand into his suitcase. He would just gamble his cash and chips.

Jordan scooped everything off the bed and stuffed his pockets. He went out of the room and down the hall into the casino. The real gamblers were at the tables now, in these early-morning hours. They had made their business deals, finished their dinners in the gourmet rooms, taken their wives to the shows and put them to bed or stuck them with dollar chips at the roulette wheel. Out of traffic. Or they had gotten laid, blown, attended a necessary civic function. All now free to battle fate. Money in hand, they stood in the front rank at crap tables. Pit bosses with blank markers waited for them to run out of chips so they could sign for another grand or two or three. During the coming dark hours men signed away fortunes. Never knowing why. Jordan looked away to the far end of the casino.

An elegantly royal gray railed enclosure nestled the long oval baccarat table from the main casino floor. An armed security guard stood at the gate because the baccarat table dealt mostly in cash, not chips. The green felt table was guarded at each end by high towered chairs. Seated in these chairs were the two laddermen, checking the croupiers and payouts, their hawkish concentration only thinly disguised by the evening dress all casino employees wore inside the baccarat enclosure. The laddermen watched every motion of the three croupiers and pit boss who ran the action. Jordan started walking toward them until he could see the distinct figures of the croupiers in their formal evening dress.

Four Saints in black tie, they sang hosannas to winners, dirges to losers. Handsome men, their motions quick, their charm continental, they graced the game they ruled. But before Jordan could get through the royal gray gate, Cully and Merlyn stepped before him.

Cully said softly, "They only have fifteen minutes to go. Stay out of it." Baccarat closed at 3 A.M.

And then one of the Saints in black tie called out to Jordan, "We're making up the last shoe, Mr. J. A Banker shoe." He laughed. Jordan could see the cards all dumped out on the table, blue-backed, then scooped to be stacked before the shuffle, their inner white pale faces showing.

Jordan said, "How about you two guys coming in with me? I'll put up the money and we'll bet the limit in each chair." Which meant that with the two-thousand limit Jordan would be betting six thousand on each hand.

"Are you crazy?" Cully said. "You can go to hell."

"Just sit there," Jordan said. "I'll give you ten percent of everything your chair wins."

"No," Cully said and walked away from him and leaned against the baccarat railing.

Jordan said, "Merlyn, sit in a chair for me?"

Merlyn the Kid smiled at him and said quietly, "Yeah, I'll sit in the chair."

"You get ten percent," Jordan said.

"Yeah, OK," Merlyn said. They both went through the gate and sat down. Diane had the newly made up shoe, and Jordan sat down in the chair beside her so that he could get the shoe next. Diane bent her head to him.

"Jordy, don't gamble anymore," she said. He didn't bet on her hand as she dealt blue cards out of the shoe. Diane lost, lost her casino's twenty dollars and lost the bank and passed the shoe on to Jordan.

Jordan was busy emptying out all the outside pockets of his Vegas Winner sports jacket. Chips, black and green, hundred-dollar notes. He placed a stack of bills in front of Merlyn's chair six. Then he took the shoe and placed twenty black chips in the Banker's slot. "You too," he said to Merlyn. Merlyn counted twenty hundred-dollar bills from the stack in front of him and placed them on his Banker's slot.

The croupier held up one palm high to halt Jordan's dealing. Looked around the table to see that everyone had made his bet. His palm fell to a beckoning hand, and he sang out to Jordan, "A card for the Player."

Jordan dealt out the cards. One to the croupier, one to himself. Then another one to the croupier and another one to himself. The croupier looked around the table and then threw his two cards to the man betting the highest amount on Player's. The man peeked at his cards cautiously and then smiled and flung his two cards face up. He had a natural, invincible nine. Jordan tossed his cards face up without even looking at them. He had two picture cards. Zero. Bust-out.

Jordan passed the shoe to Merlyn. Merlyn passed the shoe on to the next player. For one moment Jordan tried to halt the shoe, but something about Merlyn's face stopped him. Neither of them spoke.

The golden brown box worked itself slowly around the table. It was chopping. Banker won. Then Player. No consecutive wins, for either. Jordan riding the Banker all the way, pressing, had lost over ten thousand dollars from his own pile, Merlyn still refusing to bet. Finally Jordan had the shoe once again.

He made his bet, the two-thousand-dollar limit. He reached over into Merlyn's money and stripped off a sheaf of bills and threw them onto the Banker's slot. He noticed briefly that Diane was no longer beside him. Then he was ready. He felt a tremendous surge of power, that he could will the cards to come out of the shoe as he wished them to.

Calmly and without emotion Jordan hit twenty-four straight passes. By the eighth pass the railing around the baccarat table was crowded and every gambler at the table was betting Bank, riding with luck. By the tenth pass the croupier in the money slot reached down and pulled out the special five-hundred-dollar chips. They were a beautiful creamy white threaded with gold.

Cully was pressed against the rail, watching, Diane standing with him. Jordan gave them a little wave. For the first time he was excited. Down at the other end of the table a South American gambler shouted, "Maestro," as Jordan hit his thirteenth pass. And then the table became strangely silent as Jordan pressed on.

He dealt effortlessly from the shoe, his hands seemed to flow. Never once did a card stumble or slip as he passed it out from his hiding place in the wooden box. Never did he accidentally show a card's pale white face. He flipped over his own cards with the same rhythmic movement each time, without looking, letting the head croupier call numbers and hits. When the croupier said, "A card for the Player," Jordan slipped it out easily with no emphasis to make it good or bad. When the croupier called, "A card for the Banker," again Jordan slipped it out smoothly and swiftly, without emotion. Finally going for the twenty-fifth pass, he lost to Player's, the Player's hand being played by the croupier because everyone was betting Bank.

Jordan passed the shoe on to Merlyn, who refused it and passed it on to the next chair. Merlyn, too, had stacks of gold five-hundred-dollar chips in front of him. Since they had won on Bank, they had to pay the five percent house commission. The croupier counted out the commission plaques against their chair numbers. It was over five thousand dollars. Which meant that Jordan had won a hundred thousand dollars on that one hot hand. And every gambler around the table had bailed out.

Both laddermen high up in their chairs were on the phone calling the casino manager and the hotel owner with the bad news. An unlucky night at the baccarat table was one of the few serious dangers to the casino profit margin. Not that it meant anything in the long run, but an eye was always kept on natural disasters. Gronevelt himself came down from his penthouse suite and quietly stepped into the baccarat enclosure, standing in the corner with the pit boss, watching. Jordan saw him out of the corner of his eye and knew who he was, Merlyn had pointed him out one day.

The shoe traveled around the table and remained a coyly Banker's shoe. Jordan made a little money. Then he had the shoe in his hand again.

This time effortlessly and easily, his hands balletic, he accomplished every baccarat player's dream. He ran out the shoe with passes. There were no more cards left. Jordan had stack on stack of white gold chips in front of him.

Jordan threw four of the gold and white chips to the head croupier. "For you, gentlemen," he said.

The baccarat pit boss said, "Mr. Jordan, why don't you just sit here and we'll get all this money turned into a check?"

Jordan stuffed the huge wad of hundred-dollar bills into his jacket, then the black hundred-dollar chips, leaving endless stacks of gold and white five-hundred-dollar chips on the table. "You can count them for me," he said to the pit boss. He stood up to stretch his legs, and then he said casually, "Can you make up another shoe?"

The pit boss hesitated and turned to the casino manager standing with Gronevelt. The casino manager shook his head for a no. He had Jordan tabbed as a degenerate gambler. Jordan would surely stay in Vegas until he lost. But tonight was his hot night. And why buck him on *his* hot night? Tomorrow the cards would fall differently. He could not be lucky forever and then his end would be swift. The casino manager had seen it all before. The house had an infinity of nights and every one of them with the edge, the percentage. "Close the table," the casino manager said.

Jordan bowed his head. He turned to look at Merlyn and said, "Keep track, you get ten percent of your chair's win," and to his surprise he saw a look almost of grief in Merlyn's eyes and Merlyn said, "No."

The money croupiers were counting up Jordan's gold chips and stacking them so that the laddermen, the pit boss and the casino manager could also keep track of their count. Finally they were finished. The pit boss looked up and said with reverence, "You got two hundred and ninety thousand dollars here, Mr. J. You want it all in a check?" Jordan nodded. His inside pockets were still lumpy with other chips, paper money. He didn't want to turn them in.

The other gamblers had left the table and the enclosure when the casino manager said there would not be another shoe. Still the pit boss whispered. Cully had come through the railing and stood beside Jordan, as did Merlyn, the three of them looking like members of some street gang in their Vegas Winner sports coats.

Jordan was really tired now, too tired for the physical exertion of craps and roulette. And blackjack was too slow with its five-hundred-dollar limit. Cully said, "You're not playing anymore. Jesus, I never saw anything like this. You can only go down. You can't get that lucky anymore." Jordan nodded in agreement.

The security guard took trays of Jordan's chips and the signed receipts from the pit boss to the cashier's cage. Diane joined their group and gave Jordan a kiss. They were all tremendously excited. Jordan at that moment felt happy. He really was a hero. And without killing or hurting anyone. So easily. Just by betting a huge amount of money on the turning of cards. And winning.

They had to wait for the check to come back from the cashier's cage. Merlyn said mockingly to Jordan, "You're rich, you can do anything you want."

Cully said, "He has to leave Vegas."

Diane was squeezing Jordan's hand. But Jordan was staring at Gronevelt, standing with the casino manager and the two laddermen, who had come down from their chairs. The four men were whispering together. Jordan said suddenly, "Xanadu Number One, how about dealing up a shoe?"

Gronevelt stepped away from the other men, and his face was suddenly in the full glare of the light. Jordan could see that he was older than he had thought. Maybe about seventy, though ruddy and healthy. He had iron gray hair, thick and neatly combed. His face was redly tanned. His figure was sturdy, not yet willowing away with age. Jordan could see that he had reacted only slightly to being addressed by his telephone code name.

Gronevelt smiled at him. He wasn't angry. But something in him responded to the challenge, brought back his youth, when he had been a degenerate gambler. Now he had made his world safe, his life was under control. He had many pleasures, many duties, some dangers but very rarely a pure thrill. It would be sweet to taste one again, and besides, he wanted to see just how far Jordan would go, what made him tick.

Gronevelt said softly, "You have a check for two hundred ninety grand coming from the cage, right?"

Jordan nodded.

Gronevelt said, "I'll have them make up a shoe. We play one hand. Double or nothing. But you have to bet Player's, not Banker's."

Everyone in the baccarat enclosure seemed stunned. The croupiers looked at Gronevelt in amazement. Not only was he risking a huge sum of money, contrary to all casino laws, he was also risking his casino license if the State Gaming Commission got tough about this bet. Gronevelt smiled at them. "Shuffle those cards," he said. "Make up the shoe."

At that moment the pit boss came through the gate of the enclosure and handed Jordan the yellow oblong ragged-edged piece of paper that was the check. Jordan looked at it for just one moment, then put it down on the Player's slot and said smiling to Gronevelt, "You got a bet."

Jordan saw Merlyn back away and lean up against the royal gray railing. Merlyn again was studying him intently. Diane took a few steps to the side in bewilderment. Jordan was pleased with their astonishment. The only thing he didn't like was betting against his own luck. He hated the idea of dealing the cards out of the shoe and betting against his hand. He turned to Cully.

"Cully, deal the cards for me," he said.

But Cully shrank away, horrified. Then Cully glanced at the croupier, who had dumped the cards from the canister under the table and was stacking them for the shuffle. Cully seemed to shudder before he turned to face Jordan.

"Jordy, it's a sucker bet," Cully said softly as if he didn't want anyone to hear. He shot a quick glance at Gronevelt, who was staring at him. But he went on. "Listen, Jordy, the Bank has a two and a half percent edge on the Player all the time. Every hand that's dealt. That's why the guy who bets Bank has to pay five percent commission. But now the house has Bank. On a bet like this the commission doesn't mean anything. It's better to have the two and a half percent edge in the odds on how the hand comes out. Do you understand that, Jordy?" Cully kept his voice in an even tone. As if he were reasoning with a child.

But Jordan laughed. "I know that," he said. He almost said that he had counted on that, but it wasn't really true. "How about it, Cully, deal the cards for me. I don't want to go against my luck."

The croupier shuffled the huge deck in sections, put them all together. He held out the blank yellow plastic card for Jordan to cut. Jordan looked at Cully. Cully backed away without another word. Jordan reached out and cut the deck. Everyone now advanced toward the edge of the table. Gamblers outside the enclosure, seeing the new shoe, tried to get in and were barred by the security guard. They started to protest. But suddenly they fell silent. They crowded around outside the railing. The croupier turned up the first card he slid out of the shoe. It was seven. He slid seven cards out of the shoe, burying them in the slot. Then he shoved the shoe across the table to Jordan. Jordan sat down in his chair. Suddenly Gronevelt spoke. "Just one hand," he said.

The croupier held up his arm and said carefully, "Mr. J., you are betting Player's, you understand? The hand I turn up will be the hand you are betting on. The hand you turn up as the Banker will be the hand you are betting against."

Jordan smiled. "I understand."

The croupier hesitated and said, "If you prefer, I can deal from the shoe."

"No," Jordan said. "That's OK." He was really excited. Not only for the money but because of the power flowing from him to cover the people and the casino.

The croupier said, holding up his palm, "One card to me, one card to yourself. Then one card to me and one card to yourself. Please." He paused dramatically, held up his hand nearest Jordan and said, "A card for the Player."

Jordan swiftly and effortlessly slid the blue-backed cards from the slotted shoe. His hands, again extraordinarily graceful, did not falter. They traveled the exact distance across the green felt to the waiting hands of the croupier, who quickly flipped them face up and then stood stunned by the invincible nine. Jordan couldn't lose. Cully behind him let out a roar, "Natural nine."

For the first time Jordan looked at his two cards before turning them over. He was actually playing Gronevelt's hand and so hoping for losing cards. Now he smiled and turned up his Banker's cards. "Natural nine," he said. And so it was. The bet was a standoff. A draw. Jordan laughed. "I'm too lucky," he said.

Jordan looked up at Gronevelt. "Again?" he asked.

Gronevelt shook his head. "No," he said. And then to the croupier and the pit boss and the laddermen. "Close down the table." Gronevelt walked out of the enclosure. He had enjoyed the bet, but he knew enough not to stretch life to a dangerous limit. One thrill at a time. Tomorrow he would have to square the unorthodox bet with the Gaming Commission. And he would have to have a long talk with Cully the next day. Maybe he had been wrong about Cully.

Like bodyguards, Cully, Merlyn and Diane surrounded Jordan and herded him out of the baccarat enclosure. Cully picked up the yellow jagged-edged check from the green felt table and stuffed it into Jordan's left breast pocket and then zipped it up to make it safe. Jordan was laughing with delight. He looked at his watch. It was 4 A.M. The night was almost over. "Let's have coffee and breakfast," he said. He led them all to the coffee shop with its yellow upholstered booths.

When they were seated, Cully said, "OK, he's got close to four hundred grand. We have to get him out of here."

"Jordy, you have to leave Vegas. You're rich. You can do

anything you want." Jordan saw that Merlyn was watching him intently. Damn, that was getting irritating.

Diane touched Jordan on his arm and said, "Don't play anymore. Please." Her eyes were shining. And suddenly Jordan realized that they were acting as if he had escaped or been pardoned from some sort of exile. He felt their happiness for him, and to repay it he said, "Now let me stake you guys, you too, Diane. Twenty grand apiece."

They were all a little stunned. Then Merlyn said, "I'll take the money when you get on that plane leaving Vegas."

Diane said, "That's the deal, you have to get on the plane, you have to leave here. Right, Cully?"

Cully was not that enthusiastic. What was wrong with taking the twenty grand now, then putting him on the plane? The gambling was over. They couldn't jinx him. But Cully had a guilty conscience and couldn't speak his mind. And he knew this would probably be the last romantic gesture of his life. To show true friendship, like those two assholes Merlyn and Diane. Didn't they know Jordan was crazy? That he could sneak away from them and lose the whole fortune?

Cully said, "Listen, we have to keep him away from the tables. We got to guard him and hogtie him until that plane leaves tomorrow for LA."

Jordan shook his head. "I'm not going to Los Angeles. It has to be farther away. Anyplace in the world." He smiled at them. "I've never been out of the United States."

"We need a map," Diane said. "I'll call the bell captain. He can get us a map of the world. Bell captains can do anything." She picked up the phone on the ledge of the booth and made the call. The bell captain had once gotten her an abortion on ten minutes' notice.

The table became covered with platters of food, eggs, bacon, pancakes and small breakfast steaks. Cully had ordered like a prince.

While they were eating, Merlyn said, "You sending the checks to your kids?" He didn't look at Jordan, who studied him quietly, then shrugged. He really hadn't thought about it. For some reason he was angry with Merlyn for asking the question, but just for a moment.

"Why should he give the money to his kids?" Cully said. "He took care of them pretty good. Next thing you'll be saying he should send the checks to his wife." He laughed as if it were beyond the realm of possibility, and again Jordan was a little angry. He had given a wrong picture of his wife. She was better than that.

Diane lit a cigarette. She was just drinking coffee, and she had a slight reflective smile on her face. For just one moment her hand brushed Jordan's sleeve in some act of complicity or understanding as if he too were a woman and she were allying herself with him. At that moment the bell captain came personally with an atlas. Jordan reached into a pocket and gave him a hundred-dollar bill. The bell captain almost ran away before Cully, outraged, could say anything. Diane started to unfold the atlas.

Merlyn the Kid was still intent on Jordan. "What does it feel like?" he asked.

"Great," Jordan said. He smiled, amused at their passion.

Cully said, "You go near a crap table and we're gonna climb all over you. No shit." He slammed his hand down on the table. "No more."

Diane had the map spread out over the table, covering the messy dishes of half-eaten food. They pored over it, except Jordan. Merlyn found a town in Africa. Jordan said calmly he didn't want to go to Africa.

Merlyn was leaning back, not studying the map with the others. He was watching Jordan. Cully surprised them all when he said, "Here's a town in Portugal I know, Mercedas." They were surprised because for some reason they had never thought of him as living in any place but Vegas. Now suddenly he knew a town in Portugal.

"Yeah, Mercedas," Cully said. "Nice and warm. Great beach. It has a small casino with a fifty-dollar top limit and the casino is only open six hours a night. You can gamble like a big shot and never even get hurt. How does that sound to you, Jordan? How about Mercedas?"

"OK," Jordan said.

Diane began to plan the itinerary. "Los Angeles over the North Pole to London. Then a flight to Lisbon. Then I guess you go by car to Mercedas."

"No," Cully said. "There's planes to some big town near there, I forget which. And make sure he gets out of London fast. Their gambling clubs are murder."

Jordan said, "I have to get some sleep."

Cully looked at him. "Jesus, yeah, you look like shit. Go

up to your room and conk out. We'll make all the arrangements. We'll wake you up before your plane leaves. And don't try coming back down into the casino. Me and the Kid will be guarding the joint."

Diane said, "Jordan, you'll have to give me some money for the tickets." Jordan took a huge wad of hundred-dollar bills from his pocket and put them on the table. Diane carefully counted out thirty of them.

"It can't cost more than three thousand first class all the way, could it?" she asked. Cully shook his head.

"Tops, two thousand," Cully said. "Book his hotels too." He picked the rest of the bills up from the table and stuffed them back into Jordan's pocket.

Jordan got up and said, trying for the last time, "Can I stake you now?"

Merlyn said quickly, "No, it's bad luck, not until you get on the plane." Jordan saw the look of pity and affection on Merlyn's face. Then Merlyn said, "Get some sleep. When we call you, we'll help you pack."

"OK," Jordan said and left the coffee shop and went down the corridor that led to his room. He knew Cully and Merlyn had followed him to where the corridor started, to make sure that he didn't stop to gamble. He vaguely remembered Diane kissing him good-bye, and even Cully had gripped his shoulder with affection. Who would have thought that a guy like Cully had ever been in Portugal.

When Jordan entered his room, he double bolted the door and put the interior chain on it. Now he was absolutely secure. He sat down on the edge of the bed. And suddenly he was terribly angry. He had a headache and his body was trembling uncontrollably.

How dare they feel affection for him? How dare they show him compassion? They had no reason—no reason. He had never complained. He had never sought their affection. He had never encouraged any love from them. He did not desire it. It disgusted him.

He slumped back against the pillows, so tired he could not undress. The jacket, lumpy with chips and money, was too uncomfortable, and he wriggled out of it and let it drop to the carpeted floor. He closed his eyes and thought he would fall asleep instantly, but again that mysterious terror electrified his body, forcing him upward. He couldn't control the violent trembling of his legs and arms.

The darkness of the room began to run with tiny ghosts of dawn. Jordan thought he might call his wife and tell her of the fortune he had won. But knew he could not. And could not tell his children. Or any of his old friends. In the last gray shreds of this night there was not a person in the world he wished to dazzle with his good luck. There was not one person in the world to share his joy in winning this great fortune.

He got up from the bed to pack. He was rich and must go to Mercedas. He began to weep; an overwhelming grief and rage drowned out everything. He saw the gun lying in the suitcase and then his mind was confused. All the gambling he had done in the last sixteen hours tumbled through his brain, the dice flashing winning numbers, the blackjack tables with their winning hands, the oblong baccarat table strewn with the pale white faces of turned dead cards. Shadowing those cards, a croupier, in black tie and dazzling white shirt, held up a palm, calling softly, "A card for the Player."

In one smooth, swift motion Jordan scooped the gun up in his right hand. His mind icily clear. And then, as surely and swiftly as he had dealt his fabulous twenty-four winning hands in baccarat, he swung the muzzle up into the soft line of his neck and pulled the trigger. In that eternal second he felt a sweet release from terror. And his last conscious thought was that he would never go to Mercedas.

Chapter 3

Merlyn the Kid stepped out the casino glass doors. He loved to watch the rising sun while it was still a cold yellow disk, to feel the cool desert air blowing gently from mountains that rimmed the desert city. It was the only time of day he ever stepped out of the air-conditioned casino. They had often planned a picnic in those mountains. Diane had one day appeared with a lunch hamper. But Cully and Jordan refused to leave the casino.

He lit a cigarette, enjoyed it with long, slow puffs, though he rarely smoked. Already the sun was beginning to glow a little redder, a round grill plugged into an infinite neon galaxy. Merlyn turned to go back into the casino, and as he passed through the glass doors, he could spot Cully in his Vegas Winner sports coat hurrying through the dice pit, obviously looking for him. They met in front of the baccarat enclosure. Cully leaned against one of the ladder chairs. His lean dark face was contorted with hatred, fright and shock.

"That son of a bitch, Jordan," Cully said, "he cheated us out of our twenty grand." Then he laughed. "He blew his head off. He beat the house for over four hundred grand and he blew his fucking brains out."

Merlyn didn't even look surprised. He leaned back wearily against the baccarat enclosure, the cigarette slipped out his hand. "Oh, shit," he said. "He never looked lucky."

"We better wait here and catch Diane when she gets back from the airport," Cully said. "We can split the money from the ticket refund."

Merlyn looked at him, not with amazement, but with curiosity. Was Cully that unfeeling? He didn't think so. He saw the sickly smile on Cully's face, a face trying to be tough but filled with dismay that was close to fear. Merlyn sat down at the closed baccarat table. He felt a little dizzy from lack of sleep and from exhaustion. Like Cully, he felt rage, but for a different reason. He had studied Jordan carefully, watched his every movement. Had cunningly led him on to tell his story, his life history. He had sensed that Jordan did not wish to leave Las Vegas. That there was something wrong with him. Jordan had never told them about the gun. And Jordan had always reacted perfectly when he saw Merlyn watching him. Merlyn realized that Jordan had faked him out. Every fucking time. He had faked them out. What made Merlyn dizzy was that he had figured Jordan perfectly all the time they had known each other in Vegas. He'd put all the pieces together but simply through lack of imagination had failed to see the completed picture. Because, of course, now that Jordan was dead, Merlyn knew that there could have been no other ending. From the very beginning Jordan was to have died in Las Vegas.

Only Gronevelt was not surprised. High up in his penthouse suite, long night after night through the years, he never pondered the evil that lurked in the heart of man. He planned against it. Far below his cashier's cage hid a million cash dollars the whole world plotted to steal, and he lay awake night after night, spinning spells to foil those plots. And so coming to know all the boring evil, some hours of the night he pondered other mysteries and was more afraid of the good in the soul of man. That it was the greater danger to his world and even to himself.

When security police reported the shot, Gronevelt immediately called the sheriff's office and let them force entry into the room. But with his own men present. For an honest inventory. There were two casino checks totaling three hundred and forty thousand dollars. And there was close to one hundred thousand in bills and chips stuffed in that ridiculous linen duster jacket Jordan wore. Its zippered pockets held chips not dumped on the bed.

Gronevelt looked out the windows of his penthouse, at the reddening desert sun climbing over the sandy mountains. He sighed. Jordan could never lose his winnings back, the casino had forever lost that particular bankroll. Well, that was the only way a degenerate gambler could ever keep his lucky win. The only way.

But now Gronevelt had to get to work. The papers had to

hush the suicide. How bad it would look, a four-hundred-grand winner blowing his brains out. And he didn't want rumors spreading that there had been a murder so that the casino could recover its losses. Steps had to be taken. He placed the necessary calls to his Eastern offices. A former United States senator, a man of irreproachable integrity, was detailed to bring the sad news to the freshly made widow. And to tell her that her husband had left a fortune in winnings she could collect for the estate when she collected the body. Everyone would be discreet, nobody cheated, justice done. Finally it would only be a tale that gamblers told each other on bust-out nights, in the coffee shops on neon Vegas Strip. But to Gronevelt it was really not that interesting. He had stopped trying to figure out gamblers a long time ago.

The funeral was simple, the burial in a Protestant cemetery surrounded by the golden desert. Jordan's widow flew in and took care of everything. She was also briefed by Gronevelt and his staff as to what Jordan had won. Every cent was meticulously paid. The checks were turned over to her, and all the cash found on the corpse. The suicide was hushed up. With the cooperation of the authorities and the newspapers. It would look so bad for the image of Las Vegas, a four-hundred-grand winner being found dead. Jordan's widow signed a receipt for the checks and money. Gronevelt asked her discretion but had no worries on that score. If this good-looking broad was burying her husband in Vegas, not bringing him home, not letting Jordan's kids come to the funeral, then she had a few jokers to hide.

Gronevelt, the ex-senator and the lawyers escorted the widow out of the hotel to her waiting limousine (Xanadu's courtesy, as everything was its courtesy). The Kid, who had been waiting for her, stepped in front of them. He said to the good-looking woman, "My name is Merlyn, your husband and I were friends. I'm sorry."

The widow saw that he was watching her intently, studying her. She knew immediately he had no ulterior motive, that he was sincere. But he looked just a little too interested. She had seen him in the funeral chapel with a young girl whose face had been swollen with weeping. She wondered why he had not approached her then. Probably because the girl had been Jordan's.

She said quietly, "I'm glad he had a friend here." She was amused by the young man staring at her. She knew she had a special quality that attracted men, not so much her beauty as the intelligence superimposed on that beauty which enough men had told her was a very rare combination. For she had been unfaithful to her husband many times before she had found the one man she had decided she would live with. She wondered if this young man, Merlyn, knew about her and Jordan and what had happened that final night. But she was not concerned, she felt no guilt. His death, she knew, as no one else could know, had been an act of self-will and self-choice. An act of malice by a gentle man.

She felt just a little flattered by the intensity, the obvious fascination with which the young man stared at her. She could not know that he saw not only the fair skin, the perfect bones beneath, the red, delicately sensual mouth, he saw too and would always see, her face as the mask of the angel of death.

Chapter 4

When I told Jordan's widow that my name was Merlyn, she gave me a cool, friendly stare, without guilt or grief. I recognized a woman who had complete control of her life, not from bitchiness or self-indulgence, but out of intelligence. I understood why Jordan had never said a harsh word against her. She was a very special woman, the kind a lot of men love. But I didn't want to know her. I was too much on Jordan's side. Though I had always sensed his coldness, his rejection of all of us beneath his courtesy and seeming friendliness.

The first time I met Jordan I knew there was something out of sync with him. It was my second day in Vegas and I had hit it lucky playing percentage blackjack, so I jumped in for a crack at the baccarat table. Baccarat is strictly a luck game with a twenty-dollar minimum. You were completely in the hands of fate, and I always hated that feeling. I always felt I could control my destiny if I tried hard enough.

I sat down at the long oval baccarat table, and I noticed Jordan at the other end. He was a very handsome guy of about forty, maybe even forty-five. He had this thick white hair but not white from age. A white that he was born with, from some albino gene. There was just me and him and another player, plus three house shills to take up space. One of the shills was Diane, sitting two chairs down from Jordan, dressed to advertise that she was in action, but I found myself watching Jordan.

He seemed to me that day an admirable gambler. He never showed elation when he won. He never showed disappointment when he lost. When he handled the shoe, he did it expertly, his hands elegant, very white. But as I watched him making piles of hundred-dollar bills, it suddenly dawned on me that he really didn't care whether he won or lost.

The third player at the table was a "steamer," a bad gambler who chased losing bets. He was small and thin and would have been bald except that his jet black hair was carefully streaked across his pate. His body was packed with enormous energy. Every movement he had was violent. The way he threw his money down to bet, the way he picked up a winning hand, the way he counted the bills in front of him and angrily scrambled them into a heap to show he was losing. Handling the shoe, he dealt without control so that often a card would flip over or fly past the outstretched hand of the croupier. But the croupier running the table was impassive, his courtesy never varied. A Player card sailed through the air, tilting to one side. The mean-looking guy tried to add another black hundred-dollar chip to his bet. The croupier said, "Sorry, Mr. A., you can't do that."

Mr. A.'s angry mouth got even meaner. "What the fuck, I only dealt one card. Who says I can't?"

The croupier looked up to the ladderman on his right, the one sitting high above Jordan. The ladderman gave a slight nod, and the croupier said politely, "Mr. A., you have a bet."

Sure enough, the first card for the Player was a four, bad card. But Mr. A. lost anyway when Player drew out on him. The shoe passed to Diane.

Mr. A. bet Player's against Diane's Bank. I looked down the table at Jordan. His white head was bowed, he was paying no attention to Mr. A. But I was. Mr. A. put five one-hundred-dollar bills on Player's. Diane dealt out the cards mechanically. Mr. A. got the Player's cards. He squeezed them out and threw the hand down violently. Two picture cards. Nothing. Diane had two cards totaling five. The croupier called, "A card for the Player." Diane dealt Mr. A. another card. It was another picture. Nothing. The croupier sang out, "The Bank wins."

Jordan had bet Bank. I had been about to bet Player's, but Mr. A. pissed me off, so I bet Bank. Now I saw Mr. A. lay down a thousand dollars on Player's. Jordan and I let our money ride on Bank.

She won the second hand with a natural nine over Mr. A.'s seven. Mr. A. gave Diane a malevolent stare as if to scare her out of winning. The girl's behavior was impeccable.

She was very carefully neutral, very carefully a nonparticipant, very carefully a mechanical functionary. But despite all this, when Mr. A. bet a thousand dollars on Player's and Diane threw over a winning natural nine, Mr. A. slammed his fist down on the table and said, "Fucking cunt," and looked at her with hatred. The croupier running the game stood straight up, not a muscle in his face changing. The ladderman leaned forward like Jehovah ducking his head out of the heavens. There was now some tension at the table.

I was watching Diane. Her face crumpled a little. Jordan stacked his money as if unaware of what was happening. Mr. A. got up and went over to the pit boss at the desk used for writing markers. He whispered. The pit boss nodded. Everyone at the table was up to stretch his legs while a new shoe was being assembled. I saw Mr. A. leave through the royal gray gate toward the corridors that led to the hotel rooms. I saw the pit boss go over to Diane and talk to her, and then she too left the baccarat enclosure. It wasn't hard to figure out. Diane was going to turn a trick with Mr. A. and change his luck.

It took the croupiers about five minutes to make up the new shoe. I ducked out to make a few roulette bets. When I got back, the shoe was running. Jordan was still in the same seat, and there were two male shills at the table.

The shoe went around the table three times just chopping before Diane came back. She looked terrible, her mouth sagged, her whole face looked as if it would fall apart, despite the fact that it had been freshly made up. She took a seat between me and one of the money croupiers. He too noticed something wrong. For a moment he bent his head down and I heard him whisper, "You OK, Diane?" It was the first time I heard her name.

She nodded. I passed her the shoe. But her hands dealing the cards out of the shoe were trembling. She kept her head down to hide the tears glistening in her eyes. Her whole face was "shamed," I could think of no other word for it. Whatever Mr. A had done to her in his room was sure enough punishment for her luck against him. The money croupier made a slight motion to the pit boss, and he came over and tapped Diane on the arm. She left her seat at the table and a male shill took her place. Diane sat at one of the seats alongside of the rail, with another girl shill.

The shoe was still chopping from Bank to Player to Bank to Player. I was trying to switch my bets at the right time to catch the chopping rhythm. Mr. A. came back to the table, to the very seat where he had left his money and cigarettes and lighter.

He looked like a new man. He had showered and recombed his hair. He had even shaved. He didn't look that mean anymore. He had on a fresh shirt and trousers and some of his furious energy had been drained away. He wasn't relaxed by any means, but at least he didn't occupy space like one of those whirling cyclones you see in comic strips.

As he sat down, he spotted Diane seated alongside the railing and his eyes gleamed. He gave her a malicious, admonitory grin. Diane turned her head.

But whatever he had done, no matter how terrible, had changed not only his humor but his luck. He bet Player's and won constantly. Meanwhile, nice guys like Jordan and me were getting murdered. That pissed me off, or the pity I felt for Diane, so I deliberately spoiled Mr. A.'s good day.

Now there are guys who are a pleasure to gamble with around a casino table and guys who are a pain in the ass. At the baccarat table the biggest pain in the ass is the guy, Banker or Player, who when he gets his first two cards takes a long drawn-out minute to squeeze them out as the table waits impatiently for the determination of their fate.

This is what I started doing to Mr. A. He was in chair two and I was in chair five. So we were on the same half of the table and could sort of look in each other's eyes. Now I was a head taller than Mr. A. and better built. I looked twenty-one years old. Nobody could guess I was over thirty and had three kids and a wife back in New York that I had run away from. So outwardly I was a pretty soft touch to a guy like Mr. A. Sure, I might be physically stronger, but he was a legitimate bad guy with an obvious rep in Vegas. I was just a dopey kid turning degenerate gambler.

Like Jordan, I nearly always bet Bank in baccarat. But when Mr. A. got the shoe, I went head to head against him and bet Player's. When I got the Player's two cards, I squeezed them out with exquisite care before showing them face up. Mr. A. buzzed his body around in his seat; he won, but he couldn't contain himself and on the next hand said, "Come on, jerk, hurry up."

I kept my cards face down on the table and looked at him calmly. For some reason my eyes caught Jordan down at the other end of the table. He was betting Bank with Mr. A., but he was smiling. I squeezed my cards very slowly.

The croupier said, "Mr. M., you're holding up the game. The table can't make any money." He gave me a brilliant smile, friendly. "They don't change no matter how hard you squeeze."

"Sure," I said and threw the cards face up with the disgusted expression of a loser. Again Mr. A. smiled in anticipation. Then, when he saw my cards, he was stunned. I had an unbeatable natural nine.

Mr. A. said, "Fuck."

"Did I throw up my cards fast enough?" I said politely.

He gave me a murderous look and shuffled his money. He still hadn't caught on. I looked down to the other end of the table and Jordan was smiling, a really delighted smile, even though he too had lost riding with Mr. A. I jockeyed Mr. A. for the next hour.

I could see Mr. A. had juice in the casino. The ladderman had let him get away with a couple of "claim agent" tricks. The croupiers treated him with careful courtesy. This guy was making five-hundred- and thousand-dollar bets. I was betting mostly twenties. So if there was any trouble, I was the one the house'd bounce on.

But I was playing it just right. The guy had called me a jerk and I hadn't got mad or tough. When the croupier told me to turn over my cards faster, I had done so amiably. The fact that Mr. A. was now "steaming" was his gambler's fault. It would be a tremendous loss of face for the casino to take his side. They couldn't let Mr. A. get away with anything outrageous because it would humiliate them as well as me. As a peaceable gambler I was, in a sense, their guest, entitled to protection from the house.

Now I saw the ladderman opposite me reach down the side of his chair to the phone attached to it. He made two calls. While watching him, I missed betting when Mr. A. got the shoe. I stopped betting for a while and just relaxed in the chair. The baccarat chairs were plush and very comfortable. You could sit in them for twelve hours, and many people did.

The tension at the table relaxed when I refused to bet Mr. A.'s shoe. They figured I was being prudent or chickenshit.

The shoe kept chopping. I noticed two very big guys in suits and ties come through the baccarat gate. They went over to the pit boss, who obviously told them the heat was off and they could relax because I could hear them laughing and telling jokes.

The next time Mr. A. got the shoe, I shoved a twenty-dollar bet on Player's. Then to my surprise the croupier receiving the Player's two cards didn't toss them to me but to the other end of the table, near Jordan. That was the first time I ever saw Cully.

Cully had this lean, dark Indian face, yet affable because of his unusually thickened nose. He smiled down the table at me and Mr. A. I noticed he had bet forty dollars on Player's. His bet outranked my twenty, so he got the Player's cards to flip over. Cully turned them over immediately. Bad cards, and Mr. A. beat him. Mr. A. noticed Cully for the first time and smiled broadly.

"Hey, Cully, what you doing playing baccarat, you fucking countdown artist?"

Cully smiled. "Just giving my feet a rest."

Mr. A. said, "Bet with me, you jerkoff. This shoe is ready to turn Bank."

Cully just laughed. But I noticed he was watching me. I put down my twenty bet on Player's. Cully immediately put down forty on Player's to make sure he would get the cards. Again he immediately turned up his cards, and again Mr. A. beat him.

Mr. A. called, "Attaboy, Cully, you're my lucky charm. Keep betting against me."

The money croupier paid off the Banker's slots and then said respectfully, "Mr. A., you're up to the limit."

Mr. A. considered for a moment. "Let it ride," he said.

I knew that I would have to be very careful. I kept my face impassive. The slot croupier running the game had his palm up to halt the dealing of the shoe until all bets had been made. He glanced down inquiringly at me. I didn't make a move. The croupier looked to the other end of the table. Jordan made a bet on the Bank, riding with Mr. A. Cully put a hundred-dollar bet on Player's, watching me all the time.

The slot croupier let his hand fall, but before Mr. A. could get a card out of the shoe, I threw the stack of bills in front of me on Player's. Behind me the buzz of voices of the pit boss and his two friends stopped. Opposite me the ladderman inclined his head from the heavens.

"The money plays," I said. Which meant that the croupier could count it out only after the bet was decided. The Player's cards must come to me.

Mr. A. dealt them to the slot croupier. The slot croupier threw the two cards face down across the green felt. I gave them a quick squeeze and threw them over. Only Mr. A. could see how I made my face fall slightly as if I had lousy cards. But what I turned over was a natural nine. The croupier counted out my money. I had bet twelve hundred dollars and won.

Mr. A. leaned back and lit up a cigarette. He was really steaming. I could feel his hatred. I smiled at him. "Sorry," I said. Exactly like a nice young kid. He glared at me.

At the other end of the table Cully got up casually and sauntered down to my side of the table. He sat in one of the chairs between me and Mr. A. so that he would get the shoe. Cully slapped the box and said, "Hey, Cheech, get on me. I feel lucky. I got seven passes in my right arm."

So Mr. A. was Cheech. An ominous-sounding name. But Cheech obviously liked Cully, and just as obviously Cully was a man who made a science of being liked. Because he now turned to me as Cheech made a bet on the Bank. "Come on, Kid," he said. "Let's all break this fucking casino together. Ride with me."

"You really feel lucky?" I asked, just a little wide-eyed.

"I may run out the shoe," Cully said. "I can't guarantee it, but I may just run out the shoe."

"Let's go," I said. I put a twenty on the Bank. We were all riding together. Me. Cheech, Cully, Jordan down on the other far side of the table. One of the shills had to take the Player's hand and promptly turned up a cold six. Cully turned over two picture cards and on his draw got another picture for a total of zip, zero, the worst hand in baccarat. Cheech had lost a thousand. Cully had lost a hundred. Jordan had lost five hundred. I had lost a measly twenty. I was the only one to reproach Cully. I shook my head ruefully. "Gee," I said, "there goes my twenty." Cully grinned and passed me the shoe. Looking past him, I could see Cheech's face darkening with rage. A jerkoff kid who lost a twenty, daring to bitch. I could read his mind as if it were a deck of cards face up on the green felt.

I bet twenty on my bank, waited to slide the cards out. The croupier in the slot was the young handsome one who had asked Diane if she was OK. He had a diamond ring on the hand he held upraised to halt my deal until all the bets were made. I saw Jordan put down his bet. On the Bank as usual. He was riding with me.

Cully slapped a twenty on Bank. He turned to Cheech and said, "Come on, ride with us. This kid looks lucky."

"He looks like he's still jerking off," Cheech said. I could see all the croupiers watching me. On his high chair the ladderman sat very still and straight. I looked big and strong; they were just a little disappointed in me.

Cheech put three hundred down on Player's. I dealt and won. I kept hitting passes and Cheech kept upping his bet against me. He called for a marker. Well, there wasn't much left of the shoe, but I ran it out with perfect gambling manners, no squeezing of the cards, no joyous exclamations. I was proud of myself. The croupiers emptied the canister and assembled the cards for a new shoe. Everybody paid his commissions. Jordan got up to stretch his legs. So did Cheech, so did Cully. I stuffed my winnings into my pocket. The pit boss brought the marker over to Cheech to sign. Everything was fine. It was the perfect moment.

"Hey, Cheech," I said. "*I'm* a jerkoff?" I laughed. Then I started walking around the table to leave the baccarat pit and made sure to pass close to him. He could no more resist taking a swing at me than a crooked croupier palm a stray hundred-dollar chip.

And I had him cold. Or I thought I did. But Cully and the two big hoods had miraculously come between us. One hood caught Cheech's fist in his big hand as if it were a tiny ball. Cully shoved his shoulder into me, knocking me off stride.

Cheech was screaming at the big guy. "You son of a bitch. Do you know who I am? Do you know who I am?"

To my surprise the big hood let Cheech's hand go and stepped back. He had served his purpose. He was a preventive force, not a punitive one. Meanwhile, nobody was watching me. They were cowed by Cheech's venomous fury, all except the young croupier with the diamond ring. He said very quietly, "Mr. A., you are out of line."

With incredible whiplike fury Cheech struck out and hit the young croupier right smack on the nose. The croupier staggered back. Blood came billowing out onto his frilly white shirtfront and disappeared into the blue-black of his tuxedo. I ran past Cully and the two hoods and hit Cheech a punch that caught him in the temple and bounced him off the floor. And he bounced right up again. I was astonished. It was all going to be very serious. This guy ran on nuclear venom.

And then the ladderman descended from his high chair, and I could see him clearly in the bright lamp of the baccarat table. His face was seamed and parchment pale as if his blood had been frozen white by countless years of air conditioning. He held up a ghostly hand and said quietly, "Stop."

Everybody froze. The ladderman pointed a long, bony finger and said, "Cheech, don't move. You are in very big trouble. Believe me." His voice was quietly formal.

Cully was leading me through the gate, and I was more than willing to go. But I was really puzzled by some of the reactions. There was something very deadly about the young croupier's face even with the blood flowing from his nose. He wasn't scared, or confused, or badly hurt enough not to fight back. But he had never raised a hand. Also, his fellow croupiers had not come to his aid. They had looked on Cheech with a sort of awestricken horror that was not fear but pity.

Cully was pushing me through the casino through the surf-like hum of hundreds of gamblers muttering their voodoo curses and prayers over dice, blackjack, the spinning roulette wheel. Finally we were in the relative quiet of the huge coffee shop.

I loved the coffee shop, with its green and yellow chairs and tables. The waitresses were young and pretty in spiffy short-skirted uniforms of gold. The walls were all glass; you could see the outside world of expensive green grass, the blue-sky pool, the specially grown huge palm trees. Cully led me to one of the large special booths, a table big enough for six people, equipped with phones. He took the booth as a natural right.

As we were drinking coffee, Jordan came walking by us. Cully immediately jumped up and grabbed him by the arm. "Hey, fellah," he said, "have coffee with your baccarat buddies." Jordan shook his head and then saw me sitting in the booth. He gave me an odd smile, amused by me for some reason, and changed his mind. He slid into the booth.

And that's how we first met, Jordan, Cully and I. That day in Vegas when I first saw him, Jordan didn't look too bad, in spite of his white hair. There was an almost impenetrable air of reserve about him which intimidated me, but Cully didn't notice. Cully was one of those guys who would grab the Pope for a cup of coffee.

I was still playing the innocent kid. "What the hell did Cheech get sore about?" I said. "Jesus, I thought we were all having a good time."

Jordan's head snapped up, and for the first time he seemed to be paying attention to what was going on. He was smiling too, as at a child trying to be clever beyond its years. But Cully was not so charmed.

"Listen, Kid," he said. "The ladderman was on to you in two seconds. What the hell do you think he sits way up there for? To pick his fucking nose? To watch pussy walk by?"

"Yeah, OK," I said. "But nobody can say it was my fault. Cheech got out of line. I was a gentleman. You have to admit that. The hotel and the casino have no complaint about me."

Cully gave me an amiable smile. "Yeah, you worked that pretty good. You were really clever. Cheech never caught on and fell right into the trap. But one thing you didn't figure. Cheech is a dangerous man. So now my job is to get you packed and put you on a plane. What the fuck kind of a name is that anyway, Merlyn?"

I didn't answer him. I pulled my sports shirt up and showed him the bare front chest and belly. I had a long, very ugly purple scar on it. I grinned at Cully and said to him, "You know what that is?" I asked him.

He was wary now, alert. His face hawklike.

I gave it to him slow. "I was in the war," I said. "I got hit by machine-gun bullets and they had to sew me up like a chicken. You think I give a shit about you and Cheech both?"

Cully was not impressed. But Jordan was smiling still. Now everything I said was true. I had been in the war, I had been in combat, but I never got hit. What I was showing Cully was my gallbladder operation. They had tried a new way of cutting that left this very impressive scar.

Cully sighed and said, "Kid, maybe you're tougher than you look, but you're still not tough enough to stay here with Cheech."

I remember Cheech bouncing up from that punch so quickly and I started worrying. I even thought for a minute about letting Cully put me on a plane. But I shook my head.

"Look, I'm trying to help," Cully said. "After what happened Cheech will be looking for you, and you're not in Cheech's league, believe me."

"Why not?" Jordan asked.

Cully gave it back very quick. "Because this Kid is human and Cheech ain't."

It's funny how friendships start. At this point we didn't know we were going to be close Vegas buddies. In fact, we were all getting to be slightly pissed off with each other.

Cully said, "I'll drive you to the airport."

"You're a very nice guy," I said. "I like you. We're baccarat buddies. But the next time you tell me you're going to drive me to the airport you'll wake up in the hospital."

Cully laughed gleefully. "Come on," he said. "You hit Cheech a clean shot and he bounced right up. You're not a tough guy. Face it."

At that I had to laugh because it was true. I was out of my natural character. And Cully went on. "You show me where bullets hit you, that doesn't make you a tough guy. That makes you the victim of a tough guy. Now if you showed me a guy who had scars because of bullets *you* put into *him*, I'd be impressed. And if Cheech hadn't bounced up so quick after you hit him, I'd be impressed. Come on, I'm doing you a favor. No kidding."

Well, he was right all the way. But it didn't make any difference. I didn't feel like going home to my wife and my three kids and the failure of my life. Vegas suited me. The casino suited me. Gambling was right down my alley. You could be alone without being lonely. And something was always happening just like now. I wasn't tough, but what Cully missed was that almost literally nothing could scare me because at this particular time of my life I didn't give a shit about anything.

So I said to Cully, "Yeah, you're right. But I can't leave for a couple of days."

Now he really looked me over. Then he shrugged. He

picked up the check and signed it and got up from the table. "See you guys around," he said. And left me alone with Jordan.

We were both uneasy. Neither of us wanted to be with the other. I sensed that we were both using Vegas for a similar purpose, to hide out from the real world. But we didn't want to be rude, Jordan because he was essentially an enormously gentle man. And though I usually had no difficulty getting away from people, there was something about Jordan I instinctively liked, and that happened so rarely I didn't want to hurt his feelings by just leaving him alone.

Then Jordan said, "How do you spell your name?"

I spelled it out for him. M-e-r-l-y-n. I could see his loss of interest in me and I grinned at him. "That's one of the archaic spellings," I said.

He understood right away and he gave me his sweet smile.

"Your parents thought you would grow up to be a magician?" he asked. "And that's what you were trying to be at the baccarat table?"

"No," I said. "Merlyn's my last name. I changed it. I didn't want to be King Arthur, and I didn't want be Lancelot."

"Merlin had his troubles," Jordan said.

"Yeah," I said. "But he never died."

And that's how Jordan and I became friends, or started our friendship with a sort of sentimental schoolboy confidence.

The morning after the fight with Cheech, I wrote my daily short letter to my wife telling her that I would be coming home in a few days. Then I wandered through the casino and saw Jordan at a crap table. He looked haggard. I touched him on the arm, and he turned and gave me that sweet smile that affected me always. Maybe because I was the only one he smiled at so easily. "Let's eat breakfast," I said. I wanted him to get some rest. Obviously he had been gambling all night. Without a word Jordan picked up his chips and went with me to the coffee shop. I still had my letter in my hand. He looked at it and I said, "I write my wife every day."

Jordan nodded and ordered breakfast. He ordered a full meal, Vegas style. Melon, eggs and bacon, toast and coffee. But he ate little, a few bites, and then coffee. I had a rare steak, which I loved in the morning but never had except in Vegas.

While we were eating, Cully came breezing in, his right hand full of red five-dollar chips.

"Made my expenses for the day," he said, full of confidence. "Counted down on one shoe and caught my percentage bet for a hundred." He sat down with us and ordered melon and coffee.

"Merlyn, I got good news for you," he said. "You don't have to leave town. Cheech made a big mistake last night."

Now for some reason that really pissed me off. He was still going on about that. He was like my wife, who keeps telling me I have to adjust. I don't have to do *anything*. But I let him talk. Jordan as usual didn't say a word, just watched me for a minute. I felt that he could read my mind.

Cully had a quick nervous way of eating and talking. He had a lot of energy, just like Cheech. Only his energy seemed to be charged with goodwill, to make the world run smoother. "You know the croupier that Cheech punched in the nose and all that blood? Ruined the kid's shirt. Well, that kid is the favorite nephew of the deputy police chief of Las Vegas."

At that time I had no sense of values. Cheech was a genuine tough guy, a killer, a big gambler, maybe one of the hoods who helped run Vegas. So what was a deputy police chief's nephew? *And* his lousy bloody nose? I said as much. Cully was delighted at this chance to instruct.

"You have to understand," Cully said, "that the deputy police chief of Las Vegas is what the old kings used to be. He's a big fat guy who wears a Stetson and a holster with a forty-five. His family has been in Nevada since the early days. The people elect him every year. His word is law. He gets paid off by every hotel in this town. Every casino begged to have the nephew working for them and pay him top baccarat croupier money. He makes as much as the ladderman. Now you have to understand the chief considers the Constitution of the United States and the Bill of Rights as an aberration of milksop Easterners. For instance, any visitor with any kind of criminal record has to register as soon as he comes to town. And believe me he'd better. Our chief also doesn't like hippies. You notice there's no long-haired kids in this town? Black people, he's not crazy about them. Or bums and panhandlers. Vegas may be the only city in the United States where there are no panhandlers. He likes girls, good for casino business, but he doesn't like pimps. He doesn't mind a dealer living off his girlfriend hustling or stuff like that. But if some wise guy builds up a string of girls, look out. Prostitutes are always hanging themselves in their cells, slashing their wrists. Bust-out gamblers commit suicide in prison. Convicted murderers, bank embezzlers. A lot of people in prison do themselves in. But have you ever heard of a pimp committing suicide? Well, Vegas has the record. Three pimps have committed suicide in our chief's jail. Are you getting the picture?"

"So what happened to Cheech?" I said. "Is he in jail?"

Cully smiled. "He never got there. He tried to get Gronevelt's help."

Jordan murmured, "Xanadu Number One?"

Cully looked at him, a little startled.

Jordan smiled. "I listen to the telephone pages when I'm not gambling."

For just a minute Cully looked a little uncomfortable. Then he went on.

"Cheech asked Gronevelt to cover him and get him out of town."

"Who's Gronevelt?" I asked.

"He owns the hotel," Cully said. "And let me tell you, his ass was in a sling. Cheech isn't alone, you know."

I looked at him. I didn't know what that meant.

"Cheech, he's connected," Cully said significantly. "Still and all Gronevelt had to give him to the chief. So now Cheech is in the Community Hospital. He has a skull fracture, internal injuries, and he'll need plastic surgery."

"Jesus," I said.

"Resisting arrest," Cully said. "That's our chief. And when Cheech recovers, he's barred forever from Vegas. Not only that, the baccarat pit boss got fired. He was responsible for watching out for the nephew. The chief blames him. And now that pit boss can't work in Vegas. He'll have to get a job in the Caribbean."

"Nobody else will hire him?" I asked.

"It's not that," Cully said. "The chief told him he doesn't want him in town."

"And that's it?" I asked.

"That's it," Cully said. "There was one pit boss that sneaked back into town and got another job. The chief happened to walk in and just dragged him out of the casino. Beat the shit out of him. Everybody got the message."

"How the hell can he get away with that shit?" I said.

"Because he's a duly appointed representative of the people," Cully said. And for the first time Jordan laughed. He had a great laugh. It washed away the remoteness and coldness you always felt coming off him.

Later that evening Cully brought Diane over to the lounge where Jordan and I were taking a break from our gambling. She had recovered from whatever Cheech had done to her the night before. It was obvious she knew Cully pretty well. And it became obvious that Cully was offering her as bait to me and Jordan. We could take her to bed whenever we wanted to.

Cully made little jokes about her breasts and legs and her mouth, how lovely they were, how she used her mane of jet black hair as a whip. But mixed in the crude compliments were solemn remarks on her good character, things like: "This is one of the few girls in this town who won't hustle you." And "she never hustles for a free bet. She's such a good kid, she doesn't belong in this town." And then to show his devotion he held out the palm of his hand for Diane to tip her cigarette ash into so that she wouldn't have to reach for the ashtray. It was primitive gallantry, the Vegas equivalent of kissing the hand of a duchess.

Diane was very quiet, and I was a little put out that she was more interested in Jordan than me. After all, hadn't I avenged her like the gallant knight that I was? Hadn't I humiliated the terrible Cheech? But when she left for her tour of duty shilling baccarat, she leaned over and kissed my cheek and, smiling a little sadly, said, "I'm glad you're OK. I was worried about you. But you shouldn't be so silly." And then she was gone.

In the weeks that followed we told each other our stories and got to know each other. An afternoon drink became a ritual, and most of the time we had dinner together at one in the morning, when Diane finished her shift on the baccarat table. But it all depended on our gambling patterns. If one of us got hot, he'd skip eating until his luck turned. This happened most often with Jordan.

But then there were long afternoons when we'd sit around out by the pool and talk under the burning desert sun. Or take midnight walks along the neon-drowned Strip, the glittering hotels planted like mirages in the middle of the desert, or lean against the gray railing of the baccarat table. And so we told each other our lives.

Jordan's story seemed the most simple and the most banal, and he seemed the most ordinary person in the group. He'd had a perfectly happy life and a common ordinary destiny. He was some sort of executive genius and by the age of thirty-five had his own company dealing in the buying and selling of steel. Some sort of middleman, it made him a handsome living. He married a beautiful woman, and they had three children and a big house and everything they wanted. Friends, money, career and true love. And that lasted for twenty years. And then, as Jordan put it, his wife grew out of him. He had concentrated all his energies on making his family safe from the terrors of a jungle economy. It had taken all his will and his energies. His wife had done her duty as a wife and mother. But there came a time when she wanted more out of life. She was a witty woman, curious, intelligent, well read. She devoured novels and plays, went to museums, joined all the town cultural groups, and she eagerly shared everything with Jordan. He loved her even more. Until the day she told him she wanted a divorce. Then he ceased loving her and he ceased loving his kids or his family and his work. He had done everything in the world for his nuclear family. He had guarded them from all the dangers of the outside world, built fortresses of money and power, never dreaming the gates could be opened from within.

Which was not how he told it, but how I listened to it. He just said quite simply that he didn't "grow with his wife." That he had been too immersed in his business and hadn't paid proper attention to his family. That he didn't blame her at all when she divorced him to marry one of his friends. Because that friend was just like her; they had the same tastes, the same kind of wit, the same flair for enjoying life.

So he, Jordan, had agreed to everything his wife wanted. He had sold his business and given her all the money. His lawyer told him he was being too generous, that he would regret it later. But Jordan said it really wasn't generous because he could make a lot more money and his wife and her husband couldn't. "You wouldn't think it to watch me gamble," Jordan said, "but I'm supposed to be a great businessman. I got job offers from all over the country. If my plane hadn't landed in Vegas, I'd be working toward my first million bucks in Los Angeles right now."

It was a good story, but to me it had a phony ring to it. He was just *too* nice a guy. It was all *too* civilized.

One of the things wrong with it was that I knew that he never slept nights. Every morning I went to the casino to work up an appetite for breakfast by throwing dice. And I'd find Jordan at the crap table. It was obvious he'd been gambling all night. Sometimes when he was tired, he'd be in the roulette or blackjack pits. And as the days went by, he looked worse and worse. He lost weight and his eyes seemed to be filled with red pus. But he was always gentle, very low-key. And he never said a word against his wife.

Sometimes, when Cully and I were alone in the lounge or at dinner, Cully would say, "Do you believe that fucking Jordan? Can you believe that a guy would let a dame put him out of whack like that? And can you believe how he talks about her like she's the greatest cunt built?"

"She wasn't a dame," I said. "She was his wife for a lot of years. She was the mother of his children. She was the rock of his faith. He's an old-time Puritan who got a knuckle ball thrown at him."

It was Jordan who got me started talking. One day he said, "You ask a lot of questions, but you don't say much." He paused for a moment as if he were debating whether he was really interested enough to ask the question. Then he said, "Why are you here in Vegas for so long?"

"I'm a writer," I told him. And went on from there. The fact that I had published a novel impressed both of them and that reaction always amused me. But what really amazed them was that I was thirty-one years old and had run away from a wife and three kids.

"I figured you most to be twenty-five," Cully said. "And you don't wear a ring."

"I never wore a ring," I said.

Jordan said kiddingly, "You don't need a ring. You look guilty without it." For some reason I couldn't imagine him making that kind of joke when he was married and living in Ohio. Then he would have felt it rude. Or maybe his mind hadn't been that free. Or maybe it was something his wife would have said and he would let her say and just sit back and enjoy it because she could get away with it and maybe he couldn't. It was fine with me. Anyway, I told them the story about my marriage, and in the process it came out that the scar on my belly I had shown them was the scar of a gallbladder operation, not a war wound. At that point of the story Cully laughed and said, "You bullshit artist."

I shrugged, smiled and went on with my story.

Chapter 5

I have no history. No remembered parents. I have no uncles, no cousins, no city or town. I have only one brother, two years older than me. At the age of three, when my brother, Artie, was five, we were both left in an orphanage outside New York. We were left by my mother. I have no memory of her.

I didn't tell this to Cully and Jordan and Diane. I never talked about those things. Not even to my brother, Artie, who is closer to me than anyone in the world.

I never talk about it because it sounds so pathetic, and it wasn't really. The orphanage was fine, a pleasant, orderly place with a good school system and an intelligent administrator. It did well by me until Artie and I left it together. He was eighteen and found a job and an apartment. I ran away to join him. After a few months I left him too, lied about my age and joined the Army to fight in WW II. And now here in Vegas sixteen years later I told Jordan and Cully and Diane about the war and my life that followed.

The first thing I did after the war was to enroll in writing courses in the New School for Social Research. Everybody then wanted to be a writer, as twenty years later everyone hoped to be a film-maker.

I had found it hard to make friends in the Army. It was easier at the school. I also met my future wife there. Because I had no family, except for my older brother, I spent a lot of time at the school, hanging out in the cafeteria rather than going back to my lonely rooms in Grove Street. It was fun. Every once in a while I got lucky and talked a girl into living with me for a few weeks. The guys I made friends with, all out of the Army and going to school under the GI Bill, talked my language. The trouble was that they were all interested in the literary life and I was not. I just wanted to be a writer because I was always dreaming stories. Fantastic adventures that isolated me from the world.

I discovered that I read more than anyone else, even the guys going for PhD's in English. I didn't really have much else to do, though I always gambled. I found a bookie on the East Side near Tenth Street and bet every day on ball games, football, basketball and baseball. I wrote some short stories and started a novel about the war. I met my wife in one of the short-story classes.

She was a tiny Irish-Scotch girl with a big bust and large blue eyes and very very serious about everything. She criticized other people's stories carefully, politely, but very toughly. She hadn't had a chance to judge me because I had not yet submitted a story to the class. She read a story of her own. And I was surprised because the story was very good and very funny. It was about her Irish uncles who were all drunks.

So when the story was over, the whole class jumped on her for supporting the stereotype that the Irish drank. Her pretty face contorted in hurt astonishment. Finally she was given a chance to answer.

She had a beautiful soft voice, and plaintively she said, "But I've grown up with the Irish. All of them drink. Isn't that true?" She said this to the teacher, who also happened to be Irish. His name was Maloney and he was a good friend of mine. Though he didn't show it, he was drunk at that very moment.

Maloney leaned back in his chair and said solemnly, "I wouldn't know, I'm Scandinavian myself." We all laughed and poor Valerie bowed her head, still confused. I defended her because though it was a good story, I knew she would never be a real writer. Everybody in the class was talented, but only a few had the energy and desire to go a long way, to give up their life for writing. I was one of them. I felt she was not. The secret was simple. Writing was the only thing I wanted to do.

Near the term end I finally submitted a story. Everybody loved it. After class Valerie came up to me and said, "How come I'm so serious and everything I write comes out sounding so funny? And you always make jokes and act as if you're not serious and your story makes me cry?"

She was serious. As usual. She wasn't coming on. So I took her for coffee. Her name was Valerie O'Grady, a name she hated for its Irishness. Sometimes I think she married me just to get rid of the O'Grady. And she made me call her Vallie. I was surprised when it took me over two weeks to get her in bed. She was no freeswinging Village girl and she wanted to be sure I knew it. We had to go through a whole charade of my getting her drunk first so that she could accuse me of taking advantage of a national or racial weakness. But in bed she surprised me.

I hadn't been that crazy about her before. But in bed she was great. I would guess that there are some people who fit sexually, who respond to each other on a primary sexual level. With us I think we were both so shy, so withdrawn into ourselves, that we couldn't relax with other partners sexually. And that we responded to each other fully for some mysterious reason springing out of that mutual shyness. Anyway, after that first night in bed we were inseparable. We went to all the little movie houses in the Village and saw all the foreign films. We'd eat Italian or Chinese and go back to my room and make love, and about midnight I'd walk her to the subway so that she could go home to her family in Queens. She still didn't have the nerve to stay overnight. Until one weekend she couldn't resist. She wanted to be there Sunday to make me breakfast and read the Sunday papers with me in the morning. So she told the usual daughterly lies to her parents and stayed over. It was a beautiful weekend. But when she got home she ran into a clan fire fight. Her family jumped all over her, and when I saw her Monday night, she was in tears.

"Hell," I said. "Let's get married."

She said in surprise, "I'm not pregnant." And was even more surprised when I burst out laughing. She really had no sense of humor, except when she wrote.

Finally I convinced her that I meant it. That I really wanted to marry her, and she blushed and then started to cry.

So on the following weekend I went out to her family's house in Queens for Sunday dinner. It was a big family, father, mother, three brothers and the three sisters, all younger than Vallie. Her father was an old Tammany Hall worker and earned his living with some political job. There were some uncles there and they all got drunk. But in a cheerful happy-go-lucky way. They got drunk as other people stuff themselves at a big dinner. It was no more offensive than that. Though I didn't usually drink, I had a few and we all had a good time.

The mother had dancing brown eyes. Vallie obviously got her sexuality from the mother and lack of humor from her father. I could see the father and uncles watching me with shrewd drunken eyes, trying to judge whether I was just a sharpie screwing their beloved Vallie, kidding her about marriage.

Mr. O'Grady finally got to the point. "When are you two planning to get hitched?" he asked. I knew if I gave the wrong answer, I could get punched in the mouth by a father and three uncles right then and there. I could see the father hated me for screwing his little girl before marrying her. But I understood him. That was easy. Also, I wasn't hustling. I never hustled people, or so I thought. So I laughed and said, "Tomorrow morning."

I laughed because I knew it was an answer that would reassure them but one they could not accept. They could not accept because all their friends would think that Vallie was pregnant. We finally settled on a date two months ahead, so that there would be formal announcements and a real family wedding. And that was OK with me too. I don't know whether I was in love. I was happy and that was enough. I was no longer alone, I could begin my true history. My life would extend outward, I would have a family, wife, children, my wife's family would be my family. I would settle in a portion of the city that would be mine. I would no longer be a single solitary unit. Holidays and birthdays could be celebrated. In short, I would be "normal" for the first time in my life. The Army really didn't count. And for the next ten years I worked at building myself into the world.

The only people I knew to invite to the wedding were my brother, Artie, and some guys from the New School. But there was a problem. I had to explain to Vallie that my real name wasn't Merlyn. Or rather that my original name was not Merlyn. After the war I changed my name legally. I had to explain to the judge that I was a writer and that Merlyn was the name I wanted to write under. I gave him Mark Twain as an example. The judge nodded as if he knew a hundred writers who had done the same thing.

The truth was that at that time I felt mystical about writing. I wanted it to be pure, untainted. I was afraid of being inhibited if anybody knew anything about me and who I really was. I wanted to write universal characters. (My first book was heavily symbolic.) I wanted to be two absolutely separate identities.

It was through Mr. O'Grady's political connections that I got my job as federal Civil Service employee. I became a GS-6 clerk administrator to Army Reserve Units.

After the kids, married life was dull but still happy. Vallie and I never went out. On holidays we'd have dinner with her family or at my brother Artie's house. When I worked nights, she and her friends in the apartment house would visit each other. She made a lot of friends. On weekend nights she'd visit their apartments when they had a little party and I'd stay in our apartment to watch the kids and work on my book. I'd never go. When it was her turn to entertain, I hated it, and I guess I didn't hide that too well. And Vallie resented it. I remember one time I went into the bedroom to look at the kids and I stayed in there reading some pages of manuscript. Vallie left our guests and came looking for me. I'll never forget the hurt look when she found me reading, so obviously reluctant to come back to her and her friends.

It was after one of these little affairs that I got sick for the first time. I woke up at two in the morning and felt an agonizing pain in my stomach and all over my back.

I couldn't afford a doctor so the next day I went to the Veterans Administration hospital, and then they took all kinds of X-rays and made some other tests over a period of a week. They couldn't find anything, but I had another attack and just from the symptoms they diagnosed a diseased gallbladder.

A week later I was back in the hospital with another attack, and they shot me full of morphine. I had to miss two days' work. Then about a week before Christmas, just as I was about to finish up work on my night job, I got a hell of an attack. (I didn't mention that I was working nights in a bank to get extra money for Christmas.) The pain was excruciating. But I figured I could make it to the VA hospital on Twenty-third Street. I took a cab that let me off about a half block from the entrance. It was now after midnight. When the cab pulled away, the pain hit me an agonizing solar plexus blow. I fell to my knees in the dark street. The pain radiated all over my back. I flattened out onto the ice-cold pavement. There wasn't a soul around, no one that could help me. The entrance to the hospital was a hundred feet away. I was so paralyzed by pain I couldn't move. I wasn't even scared. In fact, I was wishing I would just die, so that the pain would go away. I didn't give a shit for my wife or my kids or my brother. I just wanted out. I thought for a moment about the legendary Merlin. Well, I was no fucking magician. I remember rolling over once to stop the pain and rolling off the ledge of the sidewalk and into the gutter. The edge of the curb was a pillow for my head.

And now I could see the Christmas lights decorating a nearby store. The pain receded a little. I lay there thinking I was a fucking animal. Here I was an artist, a book published and one critic had called me a genius, one of the hopes of American literature, and I was dying like a dog in the gutter. And through no fault of my own. Just because I had no money in the bank. Just because I had nobody who really gave a shit about whether I lived or not. That was the truth of the whole business. The self-pity was nearly as good as morphine.

I don't know how long it took me to crawl out of the gutter. I don't know how long it took me to crawl through to the entrance of the hospital, but I was finally in an arc of light. I remember people putting me in a wheelchair and taking me to the emergency room and I answered questions and then magically I was in a warm white bed and feeling blissfully sleepy, without pain, and I knew they had shot me with morphine.

When I awoke, a young doctor was taking my pulse. He had treated me the other time and I knew his name was Cohn. He grinned at me and said, "They called your wife, she'll be down to see you when the kids go to school."

I nodded and said, "I guess I can't wait until Christmas for that operation."

Dr. Cohn looked a little thoughtful and then said cheerily, "Well, you've come this far, why don't you wait until Christmas? I'll schedule it for the twenty-seventh. You can come Christmas night and we'll get you ready."

"OK," I said. I trusted him. He had talked the hospital into treating me as an outpatient. He was the only guy who seemed to understand when I said that I didn't want the operation until after Christmas. I remember his saying, "I don't know what you're trying to do, but I'm with you." I couldn't explain that I had to keep working two jobs until Christmas so my kids would get toys and still believe in Santa Claus. That I was totally responsible for my family and its happiness, and it was the only thing I had.

I'll always remember that young doctor. He looked like your movie actor doctor except that he was so unpretentious and easy. He sent me home loaded up with morphine. But he had his reasons. A few days after the operation he told me, and I could see how happy it made him to tell me, "Listen, you're a young guy to have gallbladder and the tests didn't show anything. We went on your symptoms. But that's all it was, gallbladder, big stones. But I want you to know there was nothing else in there. I took a real good look. When you go home, don't worry. You'll be as good as new."

At that time I didn't know what the hell he meant. In my usual style it only came to me a year later that he had been afraid of finding cancer. And that's why he hadn't wanted to operate before Christmas with just a week to go.

Chapter 6

I told Jordan and Cully and Diane how my brother, Artie, and my wife, Vallie, came to see me every day. And how Artie would shave me and drive Vallie back and forth from the hospital while Artie's wife took care of my kids. I saw Cully smiling slyly.

"OK," I said. "That scar I showed you was my gallbladder scar. No machine guns. If you had any fucking brains you'd know I would never be alive if I got hit like that."

Cully was still smiling. He said, "Did it ever cross your mind that when your brother and your wife left the hospital maybe they fucked before going home? Is that why you left her?"

I laughed like hell, and I knew I'd have to tell them about Artie.

"He's a very good-looking guy," I said. "We look alike, but he's older." The truth is that I'm a sort of charcoal sketch of my brother, Artie. My mouth is too thick. My eye sockets are too hollow. My nose is too big. And I look too strong, but you should see Artie. I told them that the reason I married Vallie was that she was the only one of my girlfriends who didn't fall in love with my brother.

My brother, Artie, is incredibly handsome on a delicate scale. His eyes are like those eyes in the Greek statues. I remember when we both were bachelors how girls used to fall in love with him, cry over him, threaten to kill themselves over him. And how distressed he'd be about that. Because he really didn't know what the hell it was all about. He could never see his beauty. He was a little self-conscious about being small, and his hands and feet were tiny. "Just like a baby's," one girl had said adoringly.

But what distressed Artie was the power he had over them. He finally came to hate it. Ah, how I would have loved it, girls never fell in love with me like that. How I would like it now, that sheer senseless falling in love with externals, the love never earned by qualities of goodness, of character, of intelligence, of wit, of charm, of life-force. In short, how I would like to be loved in a way never earned so that I would never have to keep earning it or work for it. I love that love the way I love the money I win when I get lucky gambling.

But Artie took to wearing clothes that didn't fit. He dressed conservatively in a way that didn't suit his looks. He deliberately tried to hide his charm. He could only relax and be his natural self with people he really cared about and felt safe with. Otherwise he developed a colorless personality that in an inoffensive way kept everyone at a distance. But even so he kept running into trouble. So he married young and was maybe the only faithful husband in the city of New York.

On his job as a research chemist with the federal Food and Drug Administration his female associates and assistants fell in love with him. His wife's best friend and her husband won his trust, and they had a great friendship for about five years. Artie let his guard down. He trusted them. He was his natural self. The wife's best friend fell in love with him and broke up her marriage and announced her love to the world, causing a lot of trouble and suspicion from Artie's wife. Which was the only time I ever saw him angry with her. And his anger was deadly. She accused him of encouraging the infatuation. He said to her in the coldest tone I ever heard any man use to a woman, "If you believe that, get the hell out of my life." Which was so unnatural of him that his wife almost had a breakdown from remorse. I really think she hoped he was guilty so she could get a hold over him. Because she was completely in his power.

She knew something about him that I knew and very few other people knew. He could not bear to inflict pain. On anyone or anything. He could never reproach anyone. That's why he hated women being in love with him. He was, I think, a sensual man, he would have loved a great many women easily and enjoyed it, but he could never have borne the conflicts. In fact, his wife said the one thing she missed in their relationship was that she could use a real fight or two. Not that she never had fights with Artie. They were married after all. But she said that all their fights were one-punch affairs, figuratively, of course. She'd fight and fight and fight, and then he'd wipe her out with one cold remark so devastating she would burst into tears and quit.

But with me he was different; he was older and he treated me as a kid brother. And he knew me, he could read me better than my wife. And he never got angry with me.

It took me two weeks to recover from the operation before I was well enough to go home. On the final day I said goodbye to Dr. Cohn and he wished me luck.

The nurse brought my clothes and told me I'd have to sign some papers before I could leave the hospital. She escorted me to the office. I really felt shitty that nobody had come to take me home. None of my friends. None of my family. Artie. Sure, they didn't know I was going home alone. I was feeling like a little kid, nobody loved me. Was it right that I had to go home after a serious operation, alone, in the subway? What if I got weak? Or fainted? Jesus, I felt shitty. Then I burst out laughing. Because I was really full of shit.

The truth was that Artie had asked who was taking me home, and I said Valerie. Valerie had said she would come down to the hospital, and I told her it was OK, I would take a cab if Artie couldn't make it. So she assumed I had told Artie. My friends had, of course, assumed that somebody in my family would take me home. The fact of the matter is that I wanted to hold a grudge in some funny kind of way. Against everybody.

Except that somebody should have known. I'd always prided myself on being self-sufficient. That I never needed anyone to care about me. That I could live completely alone and inside myself. But this was one time that I wanted some excessive sentimentality that the world dishes out in such abundance.

And so when I got back to the ward and found Artie holding my suitcase, I almost burst into tears. My spirits went way up and I gave him a hug, one of the few times I'd ever done that. Then I asked happily, "How the hell did you know I was leaving the hospital today?"

Artie gave me a sad, tired smile. "You shit, I called Valerie. She said she thought I was picking you up, that's what you told her."

"I never told her that," I said.

"Oh, come on," Artie said. He took my arm, leading the

way out of the ward. "I know your style," he said. "But it's not fair to people who care about you. What you do is not fair to them."

I didn't say anything until we were out of the hospital and in his car. "I told Vallie you might come down," I said. "I didn't want her to bother."

Artie was driving through traffic now, so he couldn't look at me. He spoke quietly, reasonably. "You can't do what you do with Vallie. You can do it with me. But you can't do it with Vallie."

He knew me as no one else did. I didn't have to explain to him how I felt like such a fucking loser. My lack of success as an artist had done me in, the shame of my failure to take care of my wife and kids had done me in. I couldn't ask anyone to do anything for me. I literally couldn't bear to ask anyone to take me home from the hospital. Not even my wife.

When we got home, Vallie was waiting for me. She had a bewildered, scared look on her face when she kissed me. The three of us had coffee in the kitchen. Vallie sat near me and touched me. "I can't understand," she said. "Why couldn't you tell me?"

"Because he wanted to be a hero," Artie said. But he said it to throw her off the track. He knew I wouldn't want her to know how really beat I was mentally. I guess he thought it would be bad for her to know that. And besides, he had faith in me. He knew I'd bounce back. That I'd be OK. Everybody gets a little weak once in a while. What the hell. Even heroes get tired.

After coffee, Artie left. I thanked him and he gave me his sardonic smile, but I could see that he was worried about me. There was, I noticed, a look of strain on his face. Life was beginning to wear him down. When he was out of the house, Vallie made me go to bed and rest. She helped me undress and lay down in bed beside me, naked too.

I fell asleep immediately. I was at peace. The touch of her warm body, her hands that I trusted, her untreacherous mouth and eyes and hair made sleep the sweet sanctuary it could never be with the deep drugs of pharmacology. When I woke up, she was gone. I could hear her voice in the kitchen and the voices of the children home from school. Everything seemed worth it.

Women, for me, were a sanctuary, used selfishly it is true, but making everything else bearable. How could I or any man suffer all the defeats of everyday life without that sanctuary? Jesus, I'd come home hating the day I had just put in on my job, worried to death about the money I owed, sure of my final defeat in life because I would never be a successful writer. And all the pain would vanish because I'd have supper with my family, I'd tell stories to the kids and at night I would make completely confident and trusting love with my wife. And it would seem a miracle. And of course, the real miracle was that it was not just Vallie and me but countless other millions of men with their wives and children. And for thousands of years. When all that goes, what will hold men together? Never mind that it wasn't all love and that sometimes it was even pure hatred. I had a history now.

And then it all goes away anyway.

In Vegas I told all this in fragments, sometimes over drinks in the lounge, sometimes at an after-midnight supper in the coffee shop. And when I was finished, Cully said, "We still don't know why you left your wife." Jordan looked at him with mild contempt. Jordan had already made the rest of the voyage and gone far past me.

"I didn't leave my wife and kids," I said. "I'm just taking a break. I write to her every day. Some morning I'll feel like going home and just get on the plane."

"Just like that?" Jordan asked. Not sardonically. He really wanted to know.

Diane hadn't said anything, she rarely did. But now she patted me on the knee and said, "I believe you."

Cully said to her, "Where do you come off believing in any guy?"

"Most men are shitty," Diane said. "But Merlyn isn't; not yet anyway."

"Thanks," I said.

"You'll get there," Diane said coolly.

I couldn't resist. "How about Jordan?" I knew she was in love with Jordan. So did Cully. Jordan didn't know because he didn't want to know and he didn't care. But now he turned a politely inquiring face toward Diane as if he were interested in her opinion. On that night he really looked like hell. The bones of his face were beginning to show through the skin in sickly white planes.

"No, not you," she said to him. And Jordan turned his head away from her. He didn't want to hear it.

Cully, who was so outgoing and amiable, was the last to tell his story, and then, like all of us, he held back the most important part, which I didn't find out until years later. Meanwhile, he gave an honest picture of his true character, or so it seemed. We all knew that he had some mysterious connection with the hotel and its owner, Gronevelt. But it was also true that he was a degenerate gambler and general lowlife. Jordan was not amused by Cully, but I have to admit that I was. Everything out of the ordinary or caricatures of types interested me automatically. I made no moral judgments. I felt that I was above that. I just listened.

Cully was an education. And an inspiration. Nobody would ever do him in. *He* would do *them* in. He had an instinct for survival. A zest for life, based on immorality and a complete disregard for ethics. And yet he was enormously likable. He could be funny. He was interested in everything, and he could relate to women in a completely unsentimental, realistic way that women loved.

Despite the fact that he was always short of money, he could get to bed with any of the show girls working in the hotel with romantic sweet talk. If she held out, he might pull his fur coat routine.

It was slick. He would bring her to a fur shop farther down the Strip. The owner was a friend of his, but the girl didn't know this. Cully would have the owner show the girl his stock of furs, in fact, have the guy lay all the pelts out on the floor so that he and the girl could pick out the finest. After they made the selection, the furrier would measure the girl and tell her the coat would be ready in two weeks. Then Cully would write out a check for a thousand dollars as a down payment and tell the owner to send him the bill. He'd give the girl the receipt.

That night Cully would take the girl out to dinner and after dinner he'd let her bet a few bucks on roulette, then take her to his room where, as he said, she had to come across because she had the receipt in her pocketbook. Since Cully was so madly in love with her, how could she not? Just the fur coat might not do it. Just Cully's being in love might not do it. But put both of them together and, as Cully explained, you had an ego-greed parlay that was a winner every time.

Of course, the girl never got the fur coat. During the two-week love affair, Cully would pick a fight and they'd break up. And Cully said, not once, never, not one time, had the girl given him back the receipt for the fur coat. In every case she rushed down to the fur store and tried to collect the deposit or even the coat. But of course, the owner blandly told all of them that Cully had already picked up his deposit and canceled the order. His payoff was some of Cully's rejects.

Cully had another trick for the soft hookers in the chorus line. He would have a drink with them a few nights in a row, listen attentively to their troubles and be enormously sympathetic. Never making a bad move or a come-on. Then maybe on the third night he would take out a hundred-dollar bill in front of them, put it in an envelope and put the envelope into the inside pocket of his jacket. Then he would say, "Listen, I don't usually do this, but I really like you. Let's get comfortable in my room and I'll give you this cab fare home."

The girl would protest a little. She wanted that C note. But she didn't want to be thought a hooker. Cully would turn on the charm. "Listen," he would say, "it's gonna be late when you leave. Why should you pay cab fare home? That's the least I can do. And I really like you. What's the harm?" Then he would take out the envelope and give it to her, and she would slip it into her purse. He would immediately escort her to his room and screw her for hours before he let her go home. Then came, he said, the funny part. The girl, on her way down in the elevator, would rip open the envelope for her C note and find a ten-dollar bill. Because naturally, Cully had had two envelopes inside his jacket.

Very often the girl would ride the elevator back up and start hammering on Cully's door. He would go into the bathroom and run a tub to drown out the noise, shave leisurely and wait for her to go away. Or, if she were shyer and less experienced, she would call him from the lobby phone and explain that maybe he had made a mistake, that there was only a ten-dollar bill in the envelope.

Cully loved this. He'd say, "Yeah, right. What can cab fare be, two, three dollars? But I just wanted to make sure, so I gave you ten."

The girl would say, "I saw you put a hundred dollars in the envelope."

Cully would get indignant. "A hundred bucks for cab fare," he'd say. "What the hell are you, a goddamn hooker? I never paid a hooker in my life. Listen, I thought you were a nice girl. I really liked you. Now you pull this shit. Listen, don't call me anymore." Or sometimes, if he thought he could get away with it, he'd say, "Oh no, sweetheart. You're mistaken." And he'd con her for another shot. Some girls believed it was an honest mistake, or as Cully was smart enough to point out, they had to make believe that they had made a mistake not to look foolish. Some even made another date to prove they weren't hookers, that they hadn't gone to bed with him for the hundred dollars.

And yet this was not to save money, Cully gambled his money away. It was the feeling of power, that he could "move" a beautiful girl. He was especially challenged if a girl had a reputation for only putting out for guys she really liked.

If the girls were really straight, Cully got a little more complicated. He would try to get into their heads, pay them extravagant compliments. Complain about his own inability to get sexually aroused unless he had a real interest in or real knowledge of the girl. He would send them little presents, give them twenty-dollar bills for carfare. But still, some smart girls wouldn't let him get his foot in the door. Then he would switch them. He would start talking about a friend of his, a wealthy man who was the best guy in the world. Who took care of girls out of friendship, they didn't even have to come across. This friend would join them for a drink and it would really be a wealthy friend of Cully's, usually a gambler with a big dress business in New York or an auto agency in Chicago. Cully would talk the girl into going to dinner with his friend, the friend being well briefed. The girl had nothing to lose. A free dinner with a likable, wealthy man.

They would have dinner. The man would lay a couple of hundreds on her or send an expensive gift to her the next day. The man would be charming all the way, never pressing. But there were portents of fur coats, automobiles, diamond rings of many karats perceived in the future. The girl would go to bed with the rich friend. And after the rich friend moved on, the beautiful girl who could not be "moved" would fall into Cully's lap for carfare.

Cully had no remorse. His position was that women not married were all soft hustlers, out to hook you with one gimmick or another, including true love, and that you were within your rights to hustle them back. The only time he showed a little pity was when the girls didn't hammer on his door or call him from the lobby. He knew then that the girls were straight, humiliated that they had been tricked. Sometimes he would look them up and if they needed money for rent or to get through the month he would tell them it had been a joke and he would slip them a hundred or two.

And for Cully it was a joke. Something to tell his fellow thieves and hustlers and gamblers. They would all laugh and congratulate him on not getting robbed. These hustlers were all keenly aware of women as an enemy, true, an enemy that had fruits necessary to men, but they were indignant about paying a stickup price, which meant money, time and affection. They needed the company of women, they needed the softness of women around them. They would pay air fare in the thousands to take girls with them from Vegas to London just to have them around. But that was OK. After all, the poor kid had to pack and travel. She was earning the money. And she had to be ready at all times for a quick screw or a before-lunch blow job without preamble or the usual courtesies. No hassles. Above all, no hassles. Here was the cock. Take care of it. Never mind do you love me. Never mind let's eat first. Never mind I want to sightsee first. Never mind a little nap, later, not now, tonight, next week, the day after Christmas. Right now. Quick service all the way down the line. Big gamblers, they wanted first class.

Cully's wooing seemed, to me, profoundly malicious, but women like him a hell of a lot better than other men. It seemed as if they understood him, saw through all his tricks but were pleased that he went to all that trouble. Some of the girls he tricked became good friends, always ready to screw him if he felt lonely. And Jesus, once he got sick, and there was a whole regiment of floozy Nightingales passing through his hotel room, washing him, feeding him and, as they tucked him in, blowing him to make sure he was relaxed enough to get a good night's sleep. Rarely did Cully get angry with a girl, and then he would say with a really deadly loud contempt, "Take a walk," the words having a devastating effect. Maybe it was a switch from complete sympathy and respect he showed them before he became ugly, and maybe it was because to the girl there was no reason for him to turn ugly. Or that he used it quite cruelly for shock when the charm didn't work.

Yet given all this, still Jordan's death affected him. He was terribly angry at Jordan. He took the suicide as a personal affront. He bitched about not having taken the twenty grand, but I could sense that it didn't really bother him. A few days later I came into the casino and found him dealing blackjack for the house. He had taken a job, he had given up gambling. I couldn't believe he was serious. But he was. It was as if he had entered the priesthood as far as I was concerned.

Chapter 7

A week after Jordan's death I left Vegas, forever I thought, and headed back for New York.

Cully took me to the plane and we had coffee in the terminal while I waited to board. I was surprised to see that Cully was really affected by my leaving. "You'll come back," he said. "Everybody comes back to Vegas. And I'll be here. We'll have some great times."

"Poor Jordan," I said.

"Yeah," Cully said. "I'll never in my whole life be able to figure that out. Why did he do it? Why the hell did he do it?"

"He never looked lucky," I said.

We shook hands when my boarding was announced. "If you get jammed up back home, give me a call," Cully said. "We're buddies. I'll bail you out." He even gave me a hug. "You're an action guy," he said. "You'll always be in action. So you'll always be in trouble. Give me a call."

I really didn't believe that he was sincere. Four years later he was a big success, and I was in big trouble appearing before a grand jury looking to indict me. And when I called Cully, he flew to New York to help me.

Chapter 8

Fleeing Western daylight, the huge jet slid into the spreading darkness of the Eastern time zones. I dreaded the moment when the plane would land and I'd have to face Artie and he'd drive me home to the Bronx housing project where my wife and kids were waiting. Craftily I had presents for them, miniature toy slot machines, for Valerie a pearl inset ring which had cost me two hundred dollars. The girl in the Xanadu Hotel gift shop wanted five hundred dollars, but Cully muscled a special discount.

But I didn't want to think about the moment I would have to walk through the door of my home and meet the faces of my wife and three children. I felt too guilty. I dreaded the scene I would have to go through with Valerie. So I thought about what had happened to me in Vegas.

I thought about Jordan. His death didn't distress me. Not now anyway. After all, I had known him for only three weeks, and not really known him. But what, I wondered, had been so touching in his grief? A grief I had never felt and hoped I never would feel. I had always suspected him, studied him as I would a chess problem. Here was a man who had lived an ordinary happy life. A happy childhood. He talked about that sometimes, how happy he had been as a child. A happy marriage. A good life. Everything went right for him until that final year. Then why didn't he recover? Change or die, he said once. That was what life was all about. And he simply couldn't change. The fault was his.

During those three weeks his face became thinner as if the bones underneath were pushing themselves outward to give some sort of warning. And his body began shrinking alarmingly for so short a time. But nothing else betrayed him and his desire. Going back over those days, I could see now that everything he said and did was to throw me off the track. When I refused his offer to stake me and Cully and Diane, it was simply to show my affection was genuine. I thought that might help him. But he had lost the capacity for what Austen called "the blessing of affection."

I guess he thought it was shameful, his despair or whatever it was. He was solid American, it was disgraceful for him to feel it was pointless to stay alive.

His wife killed him. Too simple. His childhood, his mother, his father, his siblings? Even if the scars of childhood heal, you never grow out of being vulnerable. Age is no shield against trauma.

Like Jordan, I had gone to Vegas out of a childish sense of betrayal. My wife put up with me for five years while I wrote a book, never complained. She wasn't too happy about it, but what the hell, I was home nights. When my first novel was turned down and I was heartbroken, she said bitterly, "I knew you would never sell it."

I was stunned. Didn't she know how I felt? It was one of the most terrible days of my life and I loved her more than anyone else in the world. I tried to explain. The book was a good book. Only it had a tragic ending and the publisher wanted an upbeat ending and I refused. (How proud I was of that. And how right I was. I was always right about my work, I really was.) I thought my wife would be proud of me. Which shows how dumb writers are. She was enraged. We were living so poor, I owed so much money, where the fuck did I come off, who the fuck did I think I was, for Christ sake? (Not those words, she never in her life said "fuck.") She was so mad she just took the kids and left the house and didn't come back home until it was time to cook supper. And she had wanted to be a writer once.

My father-in-law helped us out. But one day he ran into me coming out of a secondhand bookstore with an armload of books and he was pissed off. It was a beautiful spring day, sunshiny yellow. He had just come out of his office, and he looked wilted and strained. And there I was walking along, grinning with anticipation at devouring the printed goodies under my arm. "Jesus," he said, "I thought you were writing a book. You're just fucking off." He could say the word pretty well.

A couple of years later the book was published my way,

got great reviews but made just a few grand. My father-in-law, instead of congratulating me, said, "Well, it didn't make any money. Five years' work. Now you concentrate on supporting your family."

Gambling in Vegas, I figured it out. Why the hell *should* they be sympathetic? Why should they give a shit about this crazy eccentricity I had about creating art? Why the fuck should they care? They were absolutely right. But I never felt the same about them again.

The only one who understood was my brother, Artie, and even he, over the last year, I felt, was a little disappointed in me, though he never showed it. And he was the human being closest to me in my life. Or had been until he got married.

Again my mind shied away from going home and I thought about Vegas. Cully had never spoken about himself, though I asked him questions. He would tell you about his present life but seldom anything about himself before Vegas. And the funny thing was that I was the only one who seemed to be curious. Jordan and Cully rarely asked any questions. If they had, maybe I would have told them more.

Though Artie and I grew up as orphans, in an asylum, it was no worse and probably a hell of a lot better than military schools and fancy boarding schools rich people ship their kids just to get them out of the way. Artie was my older brother, but I was always bigger and stronger; physically anyway. Mentally he was stubborn as hell and a lot more honest. He was fascinated by science and I loved fantasy. He read chemistry and math books and worked out chess problems. He taught me chess, but I was always too impatient; it's not a gambling game. I read novels. Dumas and Dickens and Sabatini, Hemingway, Fitzgerald and later on Joyce and Kafka and Dostoevsky.

I swear being an orphan had no effect on my character. I was just like any other kid. Nobody later in life could guess we had never known our mother or father. The only unnatural or warping effect was that instead of being brothers, Artie and I were mother and father to each other. Anyway, we left the asylum in our teens, Artie got a job and I went to live with him. Then Artie fell in love with a girl and it was time for me to leave. I joined the Army to fight the big war, WW II. When I came out five years later, Artie and I had changed back into brothers. He was the father of a family and I was a war veteran. And that's all there was to it. The only time I thought of us as having been orphans was when Artie and I stayed up late in his house and his wife got tired and went to bed. She kissed Artie good-night before she left us. And I thought that Artie and I were special. As children we were never kissed good-night.

But really we had never lived in that asylum. We both escaped through books. My favorite was the story of King Arthur and his Round Table. I read all the versions, all the popularizations, and the original Malory version. And I guess it's obvious that I thought of King Arthur as my brother, Artie. They had the same names, and in my childish mind I found them very similar in the sweetness of their characters. But I never identified with any of the brave knights like Lancelot. For some reason they struck me as dumb. And even as a child I had no interest in the Holy Grail. I didn't want to be Galahad.

But I fell in love with Merlin, with his cunning magic, his turning himself into a falcon or any animal. His disappearing and reappearing. His long absences. Most of all, I loved when he told King Arthur that he could no longer be the king's right hand. And the reason. That Merlin would fall in love with a girl and teach her his magic. And that she would betray Merlin and use his own magic spells against him. And so he would be imprisoned in a cave for a thousand years before the spell wore off. And then he would come back into the world again. Boy, that was some lover, that was some magician. He'd outlive them all. And so as a child I tried to be a Merlin to my brother, Artie. And when we left the asylum, we changed our last name to Merlyn. And we never talked about being orphans again. Between ourselves or to anyone.

The plane was dipping down. Vegas had been my Camelot, an irony that the great Merlin could have easily explained. Now I was returning to reality. I had some explaining to do to my brother and to my wife. I got my packages of presents together as the plane taxied to its bay.

Chapter 9

It all turned out to be easy. Artie didn't ask me questions
about why I had run off from Valerie and the kids. He had a
new car, a big station wagon, and he told me his wife was
pregnant again. That would be the fourth kid. I congratulated
him on becoming a father. I made a mental note to send his
wife flowers in a few days. And then I canceled the note.
You can't send flowers to a guy's wife when you owe that
guy thousands of dollars. And when you might have to borrow more money off him in the future. It wouldn't bother Artie, but his wife might think it funny.

On the way to the Bronx housing project I lived in I asked
Artie the important question: "How does Vallie feel about
me?"

"She understands," Artie said. "She's not mad. She'll be
glad to see you. Look, you're not that hard to understand.
And you wrote every day. And you called her a couple of
times. You just needed a break." He made it sound normal.
But I could see that my running off for a month had
frightened him about me. He was really worried.

And then we were driving through the housing project that
always depressed me. It was a huge area of buildings built in
tall hexagons, erected by the government for poor people. I
had a five-room apartment for fifty bucks a month, including
utilities. And the first few years it had been OK. It was built
by government money and there had been screening
processes. The original settlers had been the hardworking
law-abiding poor. But by their virtues they had moved up in
the economic scale and moved out to private homes. Now we
were getting the hard-core poor who could never make an
honest living or didn't want to. Drug addicts, alcoholics, fa-
therless families on welfare, the father having taken off. Most
of these new arrivals were blacks, so Vallie felt she couldn't

complain because people would think she was a racist. But I knew we had to get out of there soon, that we had to move into a white area. I didn't want to get stuck in another asylum. I didn't give a shit whether anybody thought it was racial. All I knew is I was getting outnumbered by people who didn't like the color of my skin and who had very little to lose no matter what they did. Common sense told me that was a dangerous situation. And that it would get worse. I didn't like white people much, so why should I love blacks? And of course, Vallie's father and mother would put a down payment on a house for us. But I wouldn't take money from them. I would take money only from my brother, Artie. Lucky Artie.

The car had stopped. "Come up and rest and have some coffee," I said.

"I have to get home," Artie said. "Besides, I don't want to see the scene. Go take your lumps like a man."

I reached into the back seat and swung my suitcase out of the car. "OK," I said. "Thanks a lot for picking me up. I'll come over to see you in a couple of days."

"OK," Artie said. "You sure you got some dough?"

"I told you I came back a winner," I said.

"Merlyn the Magician," he said. And we both laughed. I walked away from him down the path that led to my apartment house door. I was waiting for his motor to hum up as he took off, but I guess he watched me until I entered the building. I didn't look back. I had a key, but I knocked. I don't know why. It was as if I had no right to use that key. When Vallie opened the door, she waited until I entered and put my suitcase in the kitchen before she embraced me. She was very quiet, very pale, very subdued. We kissed each other very casually as if it were no big deal having been separated for the first time in ten years.

"The kids wanted to wait up," Vallie said. "But it was too late. They can see you in the morning before they go to school."

"OK," I said. I wanted to go into their bedrooms to see them but I was afraid I would wake them and they'd stay up and wear Vallie out. She looked very tired now.

I lugged the suitcase into our bedroom and she followed me. She started unpacking and I sat on the bed. Watching her. She was very efficient. She sorted out the boxes she knew were presents and put them on the dresser. The dirty clothes she sorted into piles for laundry and dry cleaning. Then took the dirty clothes into the bathroom to throw them into the hamper. She didn't come out, so I followed her in there. She was leaning against the wall, crying.

"You deserted me," she said. And I laughed. Because it wasn't true and because it wasn't the right thing for her to say. She could have been witty or touching or clever, but she had simply told me what she felt, without art. As she used to write her stories at the New School. And because she was so honest, I laughed. And I guess I laughed because now I knew I could handle her and the whole situation. I could be witty and funny and tender and make her feel OK. I could show her that it didn't mean anything, my leaving her and the kids.

"I wrote you every day," I said. "I called you at least four or five times."

She buried her face in my arms. "I know," she said. "I was just never sure you were coming back. I don't care about anything, I just love you. I just want you with me."

"Me too," I said. It was the easiest way to say it.

She wanted to make me something to eat and I said no. I took a quick shower and she was waiting for me in bed. She always wore her nightgown to bed even though we were going to make love and I would have to take it off. That was her Catholic childhood and I liked it. It gave our lovemaking a certain ceremony. And seeing her lying there, waiting for me, I was glad I had been faithful to her. I had plenty of other guilts to handle, but that at least was one I wouldn't have. And it was worth something, in that time and that place. I don't know if it did her any good.

With the lights out, careful not to make noise so as not to wake the children, we made love as we always had for the more than ten years we had known each other. She had a lovely body, lovely breasts, and she was naturally and innocently orgasmic. All the parts of her body were responsive to touch and she was sensibly passionate. Our lovemaking was nearly always satisfying, and so it was tonight. And afterward she fell into a deep sleep, her hand holding mine until she rolled on her side and the connection broke.

But I or my body clock had flown three hours faster in time. Now that I was safe home with my wife and children I could not imagine why I had run away. Why I had stayed nearly a month in Vegas, so solitary and cut off. I felt the relaxation of an animal that has reached sanctuary. I was happy to be poor and trapped in marriage and burdened by children. I was happy to be unsuccessful as long as I could lie in a bed beside my wife, who loved me and would support me against the world. And then I thought, this was how Jordan must have felt before he got the bad news. But I wasn't Jordan. I was Merlyn the Magician, I would make it all come out right.

The trick is to remember all the good things, all the happy times. Most of the ten years had been happy. In fact, at one time I had gotten pissed off because I was too happy for my means and circumstances and my ambitions. I thought of the casino burning brightly in the desert, and Diane gambling as a shill without any chance of winning or losing, of being happy or unhappy. And Cully behind the table in his green apron, dealing for the house. And Jordan dead.

But lying now in my bed, the family I had created breathing around me, I felt a terrible strength. I would make them safe against the world and even against myself.

I was sure I could write another book and get rich. I was sure that Vallie and I would be happy forever, that strange neutral zone that separated us would be destroyed; I would never betray her or use my magic to sleep for a thousand years. I would never be another Jordan.

Chapter 10

In Gronevelt's penthouse suite, Cully stared through huge windows. The red and green python neon Strip ran out to the black desert mountains. Cully was not thinking of Merlyn or Jordan or Diane. He was nervously waiting for Gronevelt to come out of the bedroom, preparing his answers, knowing that his future was at stake.

It was an enormous suite, with a built-in bar for the living room, big kitchen to service the formal dining room; all open to the desert and encircling mountains. As Cully moved restlessly to another window, Gronevelt came through the archway of the bedroom.

Gronevelt was impeccably dressed and barbered, though it was after midnight. He went to the bar and asked Cully, "You want a drink?" His Eastern accent was New York or Boston or Philadelphia. Around the living room were shelves filled with books. Cully wondered if Gronevelt really read them. The newspaper reporters who wrote about Gronevelt would have been astonished to think so.

Cully went over to the bar and Gronevelt made a gesture for him to help himself. Cully took a glass and poured some scotch into it. He noticed Gronevelt was drinking plain club soda.

"You've been doing good work," Gronevelt said. "But you helped that guy Jordan at the baccarat table. You went against me. You take my money and you go up against me."

"He was a friend of mine," Cully said. "It wasn't a big deal. And I knew he was the kind of guy that would take care of me good if he was winners."

"Did he give you anything," Gronevelt asked, "before he knocked himself off?"

"He was going to give us all twenty grand, me and that kid

that hung out with us and Diane, the blonde that shills baccarat."

Cully could see that Gronevelt was interested and didn't seem too pissed off because he had helped Jordan out.

Gronevelt walked over to the huge window and gazed at the desert mountains shining blackly in the moonlight.

"But you never got the money," Gronevelt said.

"I was a jerk," Cully said. "The Kid said he'd wait until we put Jordan on the plane, so me and Diane said we'd wait too. That's a mistake I'll never make again."

Gronevelt said calmly, "Everybody makes mistakes. It's not important unless the mistake is fatal. You'll make more." He finished off his drink. "Do you know why that guy Jordan did it?"

Cully shrugged. "His wife left him. Took him for everything he had, I guess. But maybe there was something wrong with him physically, maybe he had cancer. He looked like hell the last few days."

Gronevelt nodded. "That baccarat shill, she a good fuck?"

Cully shrugged. "Fair."

At that moment Cully was surprised to see a young girl come out of the bedroom area into the living room. She was all made up and dressed to go out. She had her purse slung jauntily over her shoulder. Cully recognized her as one of the seminudes in the hotel stage show. Not a dancer but a show girl. She was beautiful and he remembered that her bare breasts on the stage had been knockouts.

The girl gave Gronevelt a kiss on the lips. She ignored Cully, and Gronevelt did not introduce her. He walked her to the door, and Cully saw him take out his money clip and slip a one-hundred-dollar bill from it. He held the girl's hand as he opened the door and the hundred-dollar bill disappeared. When she was gone, Gronevelt came back into the room and sat down on one of the two sofas. Again he made a gesture and Cully sat down in one of the stuffed chairs facing him.

"I know all about you," Gronevelt said. "You're a countdown artist. You're a good mechanic with a deck of cards. From the work you've done for me I know you're smart. And I've had you checked out all the way down the line."

Cully nodded and waited.

"You're a gambler but not a degenerate gambler. In fact, you're ahead of the game. But you know, all countdown artists eventually get barred from the casinos. The pit bosses here wanted to throw you out long ago. I stopped them. You know that."

Cully just waited.

Gronevelt was staring him straight in the eye. "I've got you all taped except for one thing. That relationship you had with Jordan and the way you acted with him and that other kid. The girl I know you didn't give a fuck about. So before we go any further explain that to me."

Cully took his time and was very careful. "You know I'm a hustler," he said. "Jordan was a strange wacky kind of guy. I had a hunch I could make a score with him. The kid and girl fell into the picture."

Gronevelt said, "That kid, who the hell was he? That stunt he pulled with Cheech, that was dangerous."

Cully shrugged. "Nice kid."

Gronevelt said almost kindly, "You liked him. You really liked him and Jordan or you never would have stood with them against me."

Suddenly Cully had a hunch. He was staring at the hundreds of volumes of books stacked around the room. "Yeah, I liked them. The Kid wrote a book, didn't make much money. You can't go through life never liking anybody. They were really sweet guys. There wasn't a hustler bone in either of them. You could trust them. They'd never try to pull a fast one on you. I figured it would be a new experience for me."

Gronevelt laughed. He appreciated the wit. And he was interested. Though few people knew it, Gronevelt was extremely well read. He treated it as a shameful vice. "What's the Kid's name?" He asked it offhand, but he was genuinely interested. "What's the name of the book?"

"His name is John Merlyn," Cully said. "I don't know the book."

Gronevelt said, "I never heard of him. Funny name." He mused for a while, thinking it over. "That his real name?"

"Yeah," Cully said.

There was a long silence as if Gronevelt were pondering something, and then he finally sighed and said to Cully, "I'm going to give you the break of your life. If you do your job the way I tell you to and if you keep your mouth shut, you'll have a good chance of making some big money and being an executive in this hotel. I like you and I'll gamble on you. But remember, if you fuck me, you're in big trouble. I mean big trouble. Do you have a general idea of what I'm talking about?"

"I do," Cully said. "It doesn't scare me. You know I'm a hustler. But I'm smart enough to be straight when I have to."

Gronevelt nodded. "The most important thing is a tight mouth." And as he said this, his mind wandered back to the early evening he had spent with the show girl. A tight mouth. It seemed to be the only thing that helped him these days. For a moment he had the sense of weariness, a failing of his powers, that had seemed to come more often in the past year. But he knew that just by going down and walking through his casino he would be recharged. Like some mythic giant, he drew power from being planted on the life-giving earth of his casino floor, from all the people working for him, from all the people he knew, rich and famous and powerful who came to be whipped by his dice and cards, who scourged themselves at his green felt tables. But he had paused too long, and he saw Cully watching him intently, with curiosity and intelligence working. He was giving this new employee of his an edge.

"A tight mouth," Gronevelt repeated. "And you have to give up all the cheap hustling, especially with broads. So what, they want presents? So what if they clip you for a hundred here, a thousand here? Remember then they are paid off. You are evened out. You never want to owe a woman anything. *Anything.* You always want to be evened out with broads. Unless you're a pimp or a jerk. Remember that. Give them a Honeybee."

"A hundred bucks?" Cully asked kiddingly. "Can't it be fifty? I don't own a casino."

Gronevelt smiled a little. "Use your own judgment. But if she has anything at all going, make it a Honeybee."

Cully nodded and waited. So far this was bullshit. Gronevelt had to get down to the real meat. And Gronevelt did.

"My biggest problem right now," Gronevelt said, "is beating taxes. You know you can only get rich in the dark. Some of the other hotel owners are skimming in the counting room with their partners. Jerks. Eventually the Feds will catch up with them. Somebody talks and they get a lot of heat. A lot of heat. The one thing I don't like is heat. But skimming is where the real money is. And that is where you are going to help."

"I'll be working in the counting room?" Cully asked.

Gronevelt shook his head impatiently. "You'll be dealing," he said. "At least for a while. And if you work out, you'll move up to be my personal assistant. That's a promise. But you have to prove yourself to me. All the way. You get what I mean?"

"Sure," Cully said. "Any risk?"

"Only from yourself," Gronevelt said. And suddenly he was staring at Cully very quietly and intently and as if he were saying something without words that he wanted Cully to grasp. Cully looked him in the eye and Gronevelt's face sagged a little with an expression of weariness and distaste, and suddenly Cully understood. If he didn't prove himself, if he fucked up, he had a good chance of being buried in the desert. He knew that this distressed Gronevelt, and he felt a curious bond with the man. He wanted to reassure him.

"Don't worry, Mr. Gronevelt," he said. "I won't fuck up. I appreciate what you're doing for me. I won't let you down."

Gronevelt nodded his head slowly. His back was turned to Cully, and he was staring out the huge window to the desert and mountains beyond.

"Words don't mean anything," he said. "I'm counting on your being smart. Come up to see me tomorrow at noon and I'll lay everything out. And one other thing."

Cully made himself look attentive.

Gronevelt said harshly, "Get rid of that fucking jacket you and your buddies always wore. That Vegas Winner shit. You don't know how that jacket irritated me when I saw you three guys walking through my casino wearing it. And that's the first thing you can remind me of. Tell that fucking store owner not to order any more of those jackets."

"OK," Cully said.

"Let's have another drink and then you can go," Gronevelt said. "I have to check the casino in a little while."

They had another drink, and Cully was astonished when Gronevelt clicked their glasses together as if to celebrate their new relationship. It encouraged him to ask what had happened to Cheech.

Gronevelt shook his head sadly. "I might as well give you

the facts of life in this town. You know Cheech is in the hospital. Officially he got hit by a car. He'll recover, but you'll never see him in Vegas again until we get a new deputy police chief."

"I thought Cheech was connected," Cully said. He sipped his drink. He was very alert. He wanted to know how things worked on Gronevelt's level.

"He's connected very big back East," Gronevelt said. "In fact, Cheech's friends wanted me to help him get out of Vegas. I told them I had no choice."

"I don't get it," Cully said. "You have more muscle than the sheriff."

Gronevelt leaned back and drank slowly. As an older and wiser man he always found it pleasant to instruct the young. And even as he did so, he knew that Cully was flattering him, that Cully probably had all the answers. "Look," he said, "we can always handle trouble with the federal government with our lawyers and the courts; we have judges and we have politicians. One way or another we can fix things with the governor or the gambling control commissions. The deputy police chief's office runs the town the way we want it. I can pick up the phone and get almost anybody run out of town. We are building an image of Vegas as an absolute safe place for gamblers. We can't do that without the deputy police chief. Now to exercise that power he has to have it and we have to give it to him. We have to keep him happy. He also has to be a certain kind of very tough guy with certain values. He can't let a hood like Cheech punch his nephew and get away with it. He has to break his legs. And we have to let him. I have to let him. Cheech has to let him. The people back in New York have to let him. A small price to pay."

"The deputy police chief is that powerful?" Cully asked.

"Has to be," Gronevelt said. "It's the only way we can make this town work. And he's a smart guy, a good politician. He'll be chief for the next ten years."

"Why just ten?" Cully asked.

Gronevelt smiled. "He'll be too rich to work," Gronevelt said. "And it's a very tough job."

After Cully left, Gronevelt prepared to go down to the casino floor. It was now nearly two in the morning. He made his special call to the building engineer to pump pure oxygen through the casino air-conditioning system to keep the gamblers from getting sleepy. He decided to change his shirt. For some reason it had become damp and sticky during his talk with Cully. And as he changed, he gave Cully some hard thought.

He thought he could read the man. Cully had believed that the incident with Jordan was a mark against him with Gronevelt. On the contrary, Gronevelt had been delighted when Cully stuck up for Jordan at the baccarat table. It proved that Cully was not just your run-of-the mill, one-shot hustler, that he wasn't one of your fake, scroungy, crooked shafters. It proved that he was a hustler in his heart of hearts.

For Gronevelt had been a sincere hustler all his life. He knew that the true hustler could come back to the same mark and hustle him two, three, four, five, six times and still be regarded as a friend. The hustler who used up a mark in one shot was bogus, an amateur, a waster of his talent. And Gronevelt knew that the true hustler had to have his spark of humanity, his genuine feeling for his fellowman, even his pity of his fellowman. The true genius of a hustler was to love his mark sincerely. The true hustler had to be generous, compassionately helpful and a good friend. This was not a contradiction. All these virtues were essential to the hustler. They built up his almost rocklike credibility. And they were all to be used for the ultimate purpose. When as a true friend he stripped the mark of those treasures which he, the hustler, coveted or needed for his own life. And it wasn't that simple. Sometimes it was for money. Sometimes it was to acquire the other man's power or simply the leverage that the other man's power generated. Of course, a hustler had to be cunning and ruthless, but he was nothing, he was transparent, he was a one-shot winner, unless he had a heart. Cully had a heart. He had shown that when he had stood by Jordan at the baccarat table and defied Gronevelt.

But now the puzzle for Gronevelt was: Did Cully act sincerely or cunningly? He sensed that Cully was very smart. In fact, so smart that Gronevelt knew he would not have to keep a check on Cully for a while. Cully would be absolutely faithful and honest for the next three years. He might cut a few tiny corners because he knew that such liberties would be a reward for doing his job well. But no more than that. Yes, for the next few years Cully would be his right-hand man on an operational level, Gronevelt thought. But after that he would have to keep a check on Cully no matter how hard Cully worked to show honesty and faithfulness and loyalty and even his true affection for his master. That would be the biggest trap. A true hustler, Cully would have to betray him when the time was ripe.

Book III

Chapter 11

Valerie's father fixed it so that I didn't lose my job. My time away was credited as vacation and sick time, so I even got paid for my month's goofing off in Vegas. But when I went back, the Regular Army major, my boss, was a little pissed off. I didn't worry about that. If you're in the federal Civil Service of the United States of America and you are not ambitious and you don't mind a little humiliation, your boss has no power.

I worked as a GS-6 administrative assistant to Army Reserve units. Since the units met only once a week for training, I was responsible for all administrative work of the three units assigned to me. It was a cinch racket job. I had a total of six hundred men to take care of, make out their payrolls, mimeograph their instruction manuals, all that crap. I had to check the administrative work of the units done by Reserve personnel. They made up morning reports for their meetings, cut promotion orders, prepared assignments. All this really wasn't as much work as it sounded except when the units went off to summer training camp for two weeks. Then I was busy.

Ours was a friendly office. There was another civilian named Frank Alcore who was older than I and belonged to a Reserve unit he worked for as an administrator. Frank, with impeccable logic, talked me into going crooked. I worked alongside him for two years and never knew he was taking graft. I found out only after I came back from Vegas.

The Army Reserve of the United States was a great pork barrel. By just coming to a meeting for two hours a week you got a full day's pay. An officer could pick up over twenty bucks. A top-ranking enlisted man with his longevity ten dollars. Plus pension rights. And during the two hours you just went to meetings of instruction or fell asleep at a film.

Most civilian administrators joined the Army Reserve. Except me. My magician hat divined the thousand-to-one-shot kicker. That there might be another war and the Reserve units would be the first guys called into the Regular Army.

Everybody thought I was crazy. Frank Alcore begged me to join. I had been a private in WW II for three years, but he told me he could get me appointed sergeant major based on my civilian experience as an Army unit administrator. It was a ball, doing your patriotic duty, earning double pay. But I hated the idea of taking orders again even if it was for two hours a week and two weeks in the summer. As a working stiff I had to follow my superior's instructions. But there's a big difference between orders and instructions.

Every time I read newspaper reports about our country's well-trained Reserve force I shook my head. Over a million men just fucking off. I wondered why they didn't abolish the whole thing. But a lot of small towns depended on Army Reserve payrolls to make their economies go. A lot of politicians in the state legislatures and Congress were very high-ranking Reserve officers and made a nice bundle.

And then something happened that changed my whole life. Changed it only for a short time but changed it for the better both economically and psychologically. I became a crook. Courtesy of the military structure of the United States.

Shortly after I came back from Vegas the young men in America became aware that enlisting in the newly legislated six months' active duty program would net them a profit of eighteen months' freedom. A young man eligible for the draft simply enlisted in the Army Reserve program and did six months' Regular Army time in the States. After that he did five and a half years in the Army Reserve. Which meant going to one two-hour meeting a week and one two-week summer camp active duty. If he waited and got drafted, he'd serve two full years, and maybe in Korea.

But there were only so many openings in the Army Reserve. A hundred kids applied for each vacancy, and Washington had a quota system put into effect. The units I handled received a quota of thirty a month, first come, first served.

Finally I had a list of almost a thousand names. I controlled the list administratively, and I played it square. My bosses, the Regular Army major adviser and a Reserve lieutenant colonel commanding the units, had the official authority. Sometimes they slipped some favorite to the top. When they told me to do that, I never protested. What did I give a shit? I was working on my book. The time I put into the job was just to get a paycheck.

Things started getting tighter. More and more young men were getting drafted. Cuba and Vietnam were far off in the horizon. About this time I noticed something fishy going on. And it had to be very fishy for me to notice because I had absolutely no interest in my job or its surroundings.

Frank Alcore was older and married with a couple of kids. We had the same Civil Service grade, we operated on our own, he had his units and I had mine. We both made the same amount of money, about a hundred bucks a week. But he belonged to his Army Reserve unit as a master sergeant and earned another extra grand a year. Yet he was driving to work in a new Buick and parking it in a nearby garage which cost three bucks a day. He was betting all the ball games, football, basketball and baseball, and I knew how much that cost. I wondered where the hell he was getting the dough. I kidded him and he winked and told me he could really pick them. He was killing his bookmaker. Well, that was my racket, he was on my ground—and I knew he was full of shit. Then one day he took me to lunch in a good Italian joint on Ninth Avenue and showed his hole card.

Over coffee, he asked, "Merlyn, how many guys do you enlist a month for your units? What quota do you get from Washington?"

"Last month thirty," I said. "It goes from twenty-five to forty depending how many guys we lose."

"Those enlistment spots are worth money," Frank said. "You can make a nice bundle."

I didn't answer. He went on. "Just let me use five of your spaces a month," he said. "I'll give you a hundred bucks a spot."

I wasn't tempted. Five hundred bucks a month was a hundred percent income jump for me. But I just shook my head and told him to forget it. I had that much ego. I had never done anything dishonest in my adult life. It was beneath me to become a common bribe taker. After all, I was an artist. A great novelist waiting to be famous. To be dishonest was to be a villain. I would have muddied my narcissistic image of myself. It didn't matter that my wife and children lived on the edge of poverty. It didn't matter that I had to take an extra job at night to make ends meet. I was a hero born. Though the idea of kids *paying* to get into the Army tickled me.

Frank didn't give up. "You got no risk," he said. "Those lists can be faked. There's no master sheet. You don't have to take money from the kids or make deals. I'll do all that. You just enlist them when I say OK. Then the cash goes from my hand to yours."

Well, if he was giving me a hundred, he had to be getting two hundred. And he had about fifteen slots of his own to enlist, and at the rate of two hundred each that was three grand a month. What I didn't realize was that he couldn't use the fifteen slots for himself. The commanding officers of his units had people to be taken care of. Political bosses, congressmen, United States senators sent kids in to beat the draft. They were taking the bread out of Frank's mouth and he was properly pissed off. He could sell only five slots a month. But still, a grand a month tax-free? Still, I said no.

There are all kinds of excuses you can make for finally going crooked. I had a certain image of myself. That I was honorable and would never tell a lie or deceive my fellowman. That I would never do anything underhanded for the sake of money. I thought I was like my brother, Artie. But Artie was down-to-the-bone honest. There was no way for him ever to go crooked. He used to tell me stories about the pressures brought on him on his job. As a chemical engineer testing new drugs for the federal Food and Drug Administration he was in a position of power. He made fairly good money, but when he ran his tests, he disqualified a lot of the drugs that the other federal chemists passed. Then he was approached by the huge drug companies and made to understand that they had jobs which paid a lot more money than he could ever make. If he were a little more flexible, he could move up in the world. Artie brushed them off. Then finally one of the drugs he had vetoed was approved over his head. A year later the drug had to be recalled and banned because of the toxic effects on patients, some of whom died. The whole thing got into the papers, and Artie was a hero for a while. He was even promoted to the highest Civil Service grade. But he was made to understand that he could never go higher. That he would never become the head of the agency because of his lack of understanding of the political necessities of the job. He didn't care and I was proud of him.

I wanted to live an honorable life, that was my big hang-up. I prided myself on being a realist, so I didn't expect myself to be perfect. But when I did something shitty, I didn't approve of it or kid myself, and usually I did stop doing the same kind of shitty thing again. But I was often disappointed in myself since there was such a great variety of shitty things a person can do, and so I was always caught by surprise.

Now I had to sell myself the idea of turning crook. I wanted to be honorable because I felt more comfortable telling the truth than lying. I felt more at ease innocent than guilty. I had thought it out. It was a pragmatic desire, not a romantic one. If I had felt more comfortable being a liar and a thief, I would have done so. And therefore was tolerant of those who did so behave. It was, I thought, their métier, not necessarily a moral choice. I claimed that morals had nothing to do with it. But I did not really believe that. In essence I believed in good and evil as values.

And then if truth were told, I was always in competition with other men. And therefore, I wanted to be a better man, a better person. It gave me a satisfaction not to be greedy about money when other men abased themselves for it. To disdain glory, to be honest with women, to be an innocent by choice. It gave me pleasure not to be suspicious of the motives of others and to trust them in almost anything. The truth was I never trusted myself. It was one thing to be honorable, another to be foolhardy.

In short, I would rather be cheated than to cheat someone; I would rather be deceived than be a deceiver; I gladly accepted being hustled as long as I did not become a hustler. I would rather be faked out than be a fake-out artist. And I understood that this was an armor I sheathed myself in, that it was not really admirable. The world could not hurt me if it could not make me feel guilty. If I thought well of myself, what did it matter that others thought ill of me? Of course, it didn't always work. The armor had chinks. And I made a few slips over the years.

And yet—and yet—I felt that even this, smugly upright as it sounded, was in a funny kind of way the lowest kind of cunning. That my morality rested on a foundation of cold stone. That quite simply there was nothing in life I desired so much that it could corrupt me. The only thing I wanted to do was create a great work of art. But not the fame or money or power, or so I thought. Quite simply to benefit humanity. Ah. Once as an adolescent, beset with guilt and feelings of unworthiness, hopelessly at odds with the world, I stumbled across the Dostoevsky novel *The Brothers Karamazov*. That book changed my life. It gave me strength. It made me see the vulnerable beauty of all people no matter how despicable they might outwardly seem. And I always remembered the day I finally gave up the book, took it back to the asylum library and then walked out into the lemony sunlight of an autumn day. I had a feeling of grace.

And so all I wished for was to write a book that would make people feel as I felt that day. It was to me the ultimate exercise of power. And the purest. And so when my first novel was published, one that I worked on for five years, one that I suffered great hardship to publish without any artistic compromise, the first review that I read called it dirty, degenerate, a book that should never have been written and once written should never have been published.

The book made very little money. It received some superlative reviews. It was agreed that I had created a genuine work of art, and indeed, I had to some extent fulfilled my ambition. Some people wrote letters to me that I might have written to Dostoevsky. I found that the consolation of these letters did not make up for the sense of rejection that commercial failure gave me.

I had another idea for a truly great novel, my *Crime and Punishment* novel. My publisher would not give me an advance. No publisher would. I stopped writing. Debts piled up. My family lived in poverty. My children had nothing that other children had. My wife, my responsibility, was deprived of all material joys of society, etc., etc. I had gone to Vegas. And so I couldn't write. Now it became clear. To become the artist and good man I yearned to be, I had to take bribes for a little while. You can sell yourself anything.

Still, it took Frank Alcore six months to break me down, and then he had to get lucky. I was intrigued by Frank because he was the complete gambler. When he bought his wife a present, it was always something he could hock in the pawnshop if he ran short of cash. And what I loved was the way he used his checking account.

On Saturdays Frank would go out to do the family shopping. All the neighborhood merchants knew him and they cashed his checks. In the butcher's he'd buy the finest cuts of veal and beef and spend a good forty dollars. He'd give the butcher a check for a hundred and pocket the sixty bucks' change. The same story at the grocery and the vegetable man. Even the liquor store. By noon Saturday he'd have about two hundred bucks' change from his shopping, and he would use that to make his bets on the baseball games. He didn't have a penny in his checking account to cover. If he lost his cash on Saturday, he'd get credit at his bookmaker's to bet the Sunday games, doubling up. If he won, he'd rush to the bank on Monday morning to cover his checks. If he lost, he'd let the checks bounce. Then during the week he would hustle bribes for recruiting young draft dodgers into the six months' program to cover the checks when they came around the second time.

Frank would take me to the night ball games and he'd pay for everything, including the hot dogs. He was a naturally generous guy, and when I tried to pay, he'd push my hand aside and say something like: "Honest men can't afford to be sports." I always had a good time with him, even at work. During lunch hour we'd play gin and I would usually beat him for a few dollars, not because I played better cards but because his mind was on his sports action.

Everybody has an excuse for his breakdown in virtue. The truth is you break down when you are prepared to break down.

I came in to work one morning when the hall outside my office was crowded with young men to be enlisted in the Army six months' program. In fact, the whole armory was full. All the units were busy enlisting on all eight floors. And the armory was one of those old buildings that had been built to house whole battalions to march around in. Only now half of each floor was for storerooms, classrooms and our administrative offices.

My first customer was a little old man who had brought in a young kid of about twenty-one to be enlisted. He was way down on my list.

"I'm sorry, we won't be calling you for at least six months," I said.

The old guy had startlingly blue eyes that radiated power and confidence. "You had better check with your superior," he said.

At that moment I saw my boss, the Regular Army major signaling frantically to me through his glass partition. I got up and went into his office. The major had been in combat in the Korean War and WW II, with ribbons all over his chest. But he was sweating and nervous.

"Listen," I said, "that old guy told me I should talk to you. He wants his kid ahead of everybody on the list. I told him I couldn't do it."

The major said angrily, "Give him anything he wants. That old guy is a congressman."

"What about the list?" I said.

"Fuck the list," the major said.

I went back to my desk where the congressman and his young protégé were seated. I started making out the enlistment forms. I recognized the kid's name now. He would be worth over a hundred million bucks someday. His family was one of the great success stories in American history. And here he was in my office enlisting in the six months' program to avoid doing a full two years' active duty.

The congressman behaved perfectly. He didn't lord it over me, didn't rub it in that his power made me subvert the rules. He talked quietly, friendly, hitting just the right note. You had to admire the way he handled me. He tried to make me feel I was doing him a favor and mentioned that if there was anything he could ever do for me, I should call his office. The kid kept his mouth shut except to answer my questions when I was typing out his enlistment form.

But I was a little pissed off. I don't know why. I had no moral objection to the uses of power and its unfairness. It was just that they had sort of run me over and there was nothing I could do about it. Or just maybe the kid was so fucking rich, why couldn't he do his two years in the Army for a country that had done so well by his family?

So I slipped in a little zinger that they couldn't know about. I gave the kid a critical MOS recommendation. MOS stands for Military Occupational Specialty, the particular Army job he would be trained for. I recommended him for one of the few electronic specialties in our units. In effect I was making sure that this kid would be one of the first guys called up for active duty in case there was some sort of national emergency. It was a long shot, but what the hell.

The major came out and swore the kid in, making him repeat the oath which included the fact that he did not belong to the Communist party or one of its fronts. Then everybody shook hands all around. The kid controlled himself until he and his congressman started out of my office. Then the kid gave the congressman a little smile.

Now that smile was a child's smile when he puts something over on his parents and other adults. It is disagreeable to see it on the faces of children. And was more so now. I understood that the smile didn't really make him a bad kid, but that smile absolved me of any guilt for giving him the booby-trapped MOS.

Frank Alcore had been watching the whole thing from his desk on the other side of the room. He didn't waste any time. "How long are you going to be a jerk?" Frank asked. "That congressman took a hundred bucks out of your pocket. And God knows what he got out of it. Thousands. If that kid had come in to us, I could have milked him for at least five hundred." He was positively indignant. Which made me laugh.

"Ah, you don't take things seriously enough," Frank said. "You could get a big jump on money, you could take care of a lot of your problems if you'd just listen."

"It's not for me," I said.

"OK, OK," Frank said. "But you gotta do me a favor. I need an open spot bad. You notice that red-headed kid at my desk? He'll go five hundred. He's expecting his draft notice any day. Once he gets the notice he can't be enlisted in the six months' program. Against regulations. So I have to enlist him today. And I haven't got a spot in my units. I want you to enlist him in yours and I'll split the dough with you. Just this one time."

He sounded desperate so I said, "OK, send the guy in to see me. But you keep the money. I don't want it."

Frank nodded. "Thanks. I'll hold your share. Just in case you change your mind."

That night, when I went home, Vallie gave me supper and I played with the kids before they went to bed. Later Vallie said she would need a hundred dollars for the kids' Easter clothes and shoes. She didn't say anything about clothes for herself, though like all Catholics, for her buying a new outfit for Easter was almost a religious obligation.

The following morning I went into the office and said to Frank, "Listen, I changed my mind. I'll take my half."

Frank patted me on the shoulder. "That a boy," he said. He took me into the privacy of the men's room and counted out five fifty-dollar bills from his wallet and handed them over. "I'll have another customer before the end of the week." I didn't answer him.

It was the only time in my life I had done anything really dishonest. And I didn't feel so terrible. To my surprise I actually felt great. I was cheerful as hell, and on the way home I bought Vallie and the kids presents. When I got there and gave Vallie the hundred dollars for the kids' clothes, I could see she was relieved that she wouldn't have to ask her father for the money. That night I slept better than I had for years.

I went into business for myself, without Frank. My whole personality began to change. It was fascinating being a crook. It brought out the best in me. I gave up gambling and even gave up writing; in fact, I lost all interest in the new novel I was working on. I concentrated on my government job for the first time in my life.

I started studying the thick volumes of Army regulations, looking for all the legal loopholes through which draft victims could escape the Army. One of the first things I learned was that medical standards were lowered and raised arbitrarily. A kid who couldn't pass the physical one month and was rejected for the draft might easily pass six months later. It all depended on what draft quotas were established by Washington. It might even depend on budget allocations. There were clauses that anyone who had had shock treatments for mental disorders was physically ineligible to be drafted. Also homosexuals. Also if he was in some sort of technical job in private industry that made him too valuable to be used as a soldier.

Then I studied my customers. They ranged in age from eighteen to twenty-five, and the hot items were usually about twenty-two or twenty-three, just out of college and panicked at wasting two years in the United States Army. They were frantic to enlist in the Reserve and just do six months' active duty.

These kids all had money or came from families with money. They all had trained to enter a profession. Someday they would be the upper middle class, the rich, the leaders in many different walks of American life. In wartime they would have fought to get into Officers Candidate School. Now they were willing to settle for being bakers and uniform repair specialists or truck maintenance crewmen. One of them at age twenty-five had a seat on the New York Stock Exchange; another was a securities specialist. At that time Wall Street was alive with new stocks that went up ten points as soon as they were issued, and these kids were getting rich. Money rolled in. They paid me, and I paid my brother, Artie, the few grand I owed him. He was surprised and a little curious. I told him that I had gotten lucky gambling. I was too ashamed to tell him the truth, and it was one of the few times I ever lied to him.

Frank became my adviser. "Watch out for these kids," he said. "They are real hustlers. Stick it to them and they'll respect you more."

I shrugged. I didn't understand his fine moral distinctions.

"They're all a fuckin' bunch of crybabies," Frank said. "Why can't they go and do their two years for their country instead of fucking off with this six months bullshit? You and me, we fought in the war, we fought for our country and we don't own shit. We're poor. These guys, the country did good by them. Their families are all well-off. They have good jobs, big futures. And the pricks won't even do their service."

I was surprised at his anger, he was usually such an easygoing guy, not a bad word for anybody. And I knew his patriotism was genuine. He was fiercely conscientious as a Reserve master sergeant, he was only crooked as a civil servant.

In the following months I had no trouble building up a clientele. I made up two lists: One was the official waiting roster; the other was my private list of bribers. I was careful not to be greedy. I used ten slots for pay and ten slots from the official lists. And I made my thousand a month like clockwork. In fact, my clients began to bid, and soon my going price was three hundred dollars. I felt guilty when a poor kid came in and I knew he would never work his way up the official list before he got drafted. That bothered me so much that finally I disregarded the official list entirely. I made ten guys a month pay, and ten lucky guys got in free. In short, I exercised power, something I had always thought I would never do. It wasn't bad.

I didn't know it, but I was building up a corps of friends in my units that would help save my skin later on. Also, I made another rule. Anybody who was an artist, a writer, an actor or a fledgling theater director got in for nothing. That was my tithe because I was no longer writing, had no urge to write, and felt guilty about that too. In fact, I was piling up guilt as fast as I was piling up money. And trying to expiate my guilts in a classical American way, doing good deeds.

Frank bawled me out for my lack of business instinct. I was too nice a guy, I had to be tougher or everybody would take advantage of me. But he was wrong. I was not as nice a guy as he thought or the rest of them thought.

Because I was looking ahead. Just using any kind of minimum intelligence, I knew that this racket had to blow up someday. There were too many people involved. Hundreds of civilians with jobs like mine were taking bribes. Thousands of reservists were being enlisted in the six months' program only after paying a substantial entrance fee. That was something that still tickled me, everybody paying to get into the Army.

One day a man of about fifty came in with his son. He was a wealthy businessman, and his son was a lawyer just starting his practice. The father had a bunch of letters from politicians. He talked to the Regular Army major, then he came in again on the night of the unit's meeting and met the Reserve colonel. They were very polite to him but referred him to me with the usual quota crap. So the father came over with his son to my desk to put the kid's name down on the official waiting list. His name was Hiller and his son's name was Jeremy.

Mr. Hiller was in the automobile business, he had a Cadillac dealership. I made his son fill out the usual questionnaire and we chatted.

The kid didn't say anything, he looked embarrassed. Mr. Hiller said, "How long does he have to wait on this list?"

I leaned back in my chair and gave him the usual answer. "Six months," I said.

"He'll be drafted before then," Mr. Hiller said. "I'd appreciate it if you could do something to help him."

I gave him my usual answer. "I'm just a clerk," I said. "The only people that can help you are the officers you talked to already. Or you could try your congressman."

He gave me a long, shrewd look, and then he took out his business card. "If you ever buy a car, come to see me, I'll get it for you at cost."

I looked at his card and laughed. "The day I can buy a Cadillac," I said, "I won't have to work here anymore."

Mr. Hiller gave me a nice friendly smile. "I guess that's right," he said. "But if you can help me, I'd really appreciate it."

The next day I had a call from Mr. Hiller. He had the ersatz friendliness of the salesman con artist. He asked after my health, how I was doing and remarked on what a fine day it was. And then he said how impressed he was with my courtesy, so unusual in a government employee dealing with the public. So impressed and overcome with gratitude that when he heard about a year-old Dodge being offered for sale, he had bought it and would be willing to sell it to me at cost. Would I meet him for lunch to discuss it?

I told Mr. Hiller I couldn't meet him for lunch but I would drop over to his automobile lot on my way home from work. He was located out in Roslyn, Long Island, which wasn't more than a half hour away from my housing project in the Bronx. And it was still light when I got there. I parked my car and wandered around the grounds looking at the Cadillacs, and I was smitten by middle-class greed. The Cadillacs were beautiful, long, sleek and heavy; some burnished gold, others creamy white, dark blue, fire engine red. I peeked into the interiors and saw the lush carpeting, the rich-looking seats. I had never cared much about cars, but at that moment I hungered for a Cadillac.

I walked toward the long brick building and passed a robin's-egg blue Dodge. It was a very nice car that I would have loved before I walked through those miles of fucking Cadillacs. I looked inside. The upholstery was comfortable-looking but not rich. Shit.

In short, I was reacting in the style of the classically nouveau riche thief. Something very funny had happened to me the past months. I was very unhappy taking my first bribe. I

had thought I would think less of myself, I had always so
prided myself on never being a liar. Then why was I so enjoying my role as a sleazy small-time bribe taker and hustler?

The truth was that I had become a happy man because I
had become a traitor to society. I loved taking money for be-
traying my trust as a government employee. I loved hustling
the kids who came in to see me. I deceived and dissembled
with the lipsmacking relish of a peasant penny ante Iago.
Some nights, lying awake, thinking up new schemes, I also
wondered at this change in myself. And I figured out that I
was getting my revenge for having been rejected as an artist,
that I was compensating for my worthless heritage as an orphan. For my complete lack of worldly success. And my general uselessness in the whole scheme of things. Finally I had
found something I could do well; finally I was a success as a
provider for my wife and children. And oddly enough I became a better husband and father. I helped the kids with
their homework. Now that I had stopped writing I had more
time for Vallie. We went out to the movies, I could afford a
baby-sitter and the price of admission. I bought her presents.
I even got a couple of magazine assignments and dashed off
the pieces with ease. I told Vallie that I got all this fresh
money from doing the magazine work.

I was a happy, happy thief, but in the back of my mind I
knew there would come a day of reckoning. So I gave up all
thoughts of buying a Cadillac and settled for the robin's-egg
blue Dodge.

Mr. Hiller had a large office with pictures of his wife and
children on his desk. There was no secretary and I hoped it
was because he was smart enough to get rid of her so that
she wouldn't see me. I liked dealing with smart people. I was
afraid of stupid people.

Mr. Hiller made me sit down and take a cigar. Again he
inquired after my health. Then he got down to brass tacks.
"Did you see that blue Dodge? Nice car. Perfect shape. I can
give you a real buy on it. What do you drive now?"

"A 1950 Ford," I said.

"I'll let you use that as a trade-in," Mr. Hiller said. "You
can have the Dodge for five hundred dollars cash and your
car."

I kept a straight face. Taking the five hundred bucks out of
my wallet, I said, "You got a deal."

Mr. Hiller looked just a little surprised. "You'll be able to help my son, you understand." He really was a little worried that I hadn't caught on.

Again I was astonished at how much I enjoyed these little transactions. I knew I could stick him up. That I could get the Dodge just by giving him my Ford. I was really making about a thousand dollars on this deal even by paying him the five hundred. But I didn't believe in a crook driving hard bargains. I still had a little bit of Robin Hood in me. I still thought of myself as a guy who took money from the rich only by giving them their money's worth. But what delighted me most was the worry on his face that I hadn't caught on that this was a bribe. So I said very calmly, without a smile, very matter-of-fact, "Your son will be enlisted in the six months' program within a week."

Relief and a new respect showed on Mr. Hiller's face. He said, "We'll do all the papers tonight, and I'll take care of the license plates. It's all set to go." He leaned over to shake my hand. "I've heard stories about you," he said. "Everybody speaks highly about you."

I was pleased. Of course, I knew what he meant. That I had a good reputation as an honest crook. After all, that was something. It was an achievement.

While the papers were being drawn up by the clerical staff, Mr. Hiller chatted to some purpose. He was trying to find out if I acted alone or whether the major and colonel were in on it. He was clever, his business training, I guess. First he complimented me on how smart I was, how I caught on quickly to everything. Then he started to ask me questions. He was worried that the two officers would remember his son. Didn't they have to swear his son into the Reserve six months' program? Yes, that was true, I said.

"Won't they remember him?" Mr. Hiller said. "Won't they ask about how he jumped so quickly on the list?"

He had a point but not much of one. "Did I ask you any questions about the Dodge?" I said.

Mr. Hiller smiled at me warmly. "Of course," he said. "You know your business. But it's my son. I don't want to see him get in trouble for something I did."

My mind began to wander. I was thinking how pleased Vallie would be when she saw the blue Dodge: Blue was her favorite color and she hated the beat-up old Ford.

I forced myself to think about Mr. Hiller's question. I remembered his Jeremy had long hair and wore a well-tailored suit with vest and shirt and tie.

"Tell Jeremy to get a short haircut and wear sports clothes when I call him into the office," I said. "They won't remember him."

Mr. Hiller looked doubtful. "Jeremy will hate that," he said.

"Then he doesn't have to," I said. "I don't believe in telling people to do what they don't feel like doing. I'll take care of it." I was just a little impatient.

"All right," Mr. Hiller said. "I'll leave it in your hands."

When I drove home with the new car, Vallie was delighted and I took her and the kids for a drive. The Dodge rode like a dream and we played the radio. My old Ford didn't have a radio. We stopped off and had pizza and soda, routine now but something we had rarely done before in our married life because we had had to watch every penny. Then we stopped off in a candy store and had ice-cream sodas and I bought a doll for my daughter and war games for the two boys. And I bought Vallie a box of Schrafft chocolates. I was a real sport, spending money like a prince. I sang songs in the car as we were driving home, and after the kids were in bed, Vallie made love to me as if I were the Aga Khan and I had just given her a diamond as big as the Ritz.

I remembered the days when I had hocked my typewriter to get us through the week. But that had been before I ran away to Vegas. Since then my luck had changed. No more two jobs; twenty grand stashed away in my old manuscript folders on the bottom of the clothes closet. A thriving business which could make my fortune unless the whole racket blew up or there was some worldwide accommodation that made the big powers stop spending so much money on their armies. For the first time I understood how the war industry bigwigs and industrialists and the army generals felt. The threat of a stabilized world could plunge me back into poverty. It was not that I wanted another war, but I couldn't help laughing when I realized that all my so-called liberal attitudes were dissolving in the hope that Russia and the United States didn't get too friendly, not for a while at least.

Vallie was snoring a little, which didn't bother me. She worked hard with the kids and taking care of the house and me. But it was curious that I was always awake late at night no matter how exhausted I was. She always fell asleep before I did. Sometimes I would get up and work on my novel in the kitchen and cook myself something to eat and not go back to bed until three or four in the morning. But now I wasn't working on a novel, so I had no work to do. I thought vaguely that I should start writing again. After all, I had the time and money. But the truth was I found my life too exciting, wheeling and dealing and taking bribes and for the first time spending money on little foolish things.

But the big problem was where to stash my cash permanently. I couldn't keep it in the house. I thought of my brother, Artie. He could bank it for me. And he would if I asked him to do it. But I couldn't. He was so painfully honest. And he would ask me where I got the dough and I'd have to tell him. He had never done a dishonest thing for himself or his wife and kids. He had a real integrity. He would do it for me, but he would never feel the same about me. And I couldn't bear that. There are some things you can't do or shouldn't do. And asking Artie to hold my money was one of them. It wouldn't be the act of a brother or a friend.

Of course, some brothers you wouldn't ask because they'd steal it. And that brought Cully into my mind. I'd ask him about the best way to stash the money the next time he came to town. That was my answer. Cully would know, that was his métier. And I had to solve the problem. I had a hunch the money was going to roll in faster and faster.

The next week I got Jeremy Hiller into the Reserves without any trouble, and Mr. Hiller was so grateful that he invited me to come to his agency for a new set of tires for my blue Dodge. Naturally I thought this was out of gratitude, and I was delighted that he was such a nice guy. I forgot he was a businessman. As the mechanic put new tires on my car, Mr. Hiller in his office gave me a new proposition.

He started off dishing out some nice strokes. With an admiring smile he told me how smart I was, how honest, so absolutely reliable. It was a pleasure to have dealings with me, and if I ever left the government, he would get me a good job. I swallowed it all up, I had had very little praise in my life, mostly from my brother, Artie, and some obscure book reviewers. I didn't even guess what was coming.

"There is a friend of mine who needs your help very badly," Mr. Hiller said. "He has a son who needs desperately to get in the six months' Reserve program."

"Sure," I said. "Send the kid in to see me and have him mention your name."

"There's a big problem," Mr. Hiller said. "This young man has already received his draft notice."

I shrugged. "Then he's shit out of luck. Tell his folks to kiss him good-bye for two years."

Mr. Hiller smiled. "Are you sure there's nothing a smart young man like you can do? It could be worth a lot of money. His father is a very important man."

"Nothing," I said. "The Army regulations are specific. Once a guy receives his draft notice he can no longer be enlisted in the Army Reserve six months' program. Those guys in Washington are not that dumb. Otherwise everybody would wait for his draft notice before enlisting."

Mr. Hiller said, "This man would like to see you. He's willing to do anything, you know what I mean?"

"There is no point," I said. "I can't help him."

Then Mr. Hiller leaned on me a little. "Go see him just for me," he said. And I understood. If I just went to see this guy, even if I turned him down, Mr. Hiller was a hero. Well, for four brand-new tires I could spend a half hour with a rich man.

"OK," I said.

Mr. Hiller wrote on a slip of paper and handed it to me. I looked at it. The name was Eli Hemsi, and there was a phone number. I recognized the name. Eli Hemsi was the biggest man in the garment industry, in trouble with the unions, involved with the mobs. But he also was one of the social lights of the city. A buyer of politicians, a pillar of support to charitable causes, etc. If he was such a big wheel, why did he have to come to me? I asked Mr. Hiller that question.

"Because he's smart," Mr. Hiller said. "He's a Sephardic Jew. They are the smartest of all the Jews. They have Italian, Spanish and Arab blood, and that mixture makes them real killers, besides being smart. He doesn't want his son as a hostage to some politician who can ask him for a big favor. It's a lot cheaper and a lot less dangerous for him to come to you. And besides, I told him how good you were. To be absolutely honest, right now you're the only person who can help him. Those big shots don't dare step in on something like the draft. It's too touchy. Politicians are scared to death of it."

I thought about the congressman who had come in to my office. He'd had balls then. Or maybe he was at the end of his political career and didn't give a shit. Mr. Hiller was watching me carefully.

"Don't get me wrong," he said. "I'm Jewish. But the Sephardic you have to be careful with or they'll just outwit you. So when you go to see him, just use your head." He paused and anxiously asked. "You're not Jewish, are you?"

"I don't know," I said. I thought then how I felt about orphans. We were all freaks. Not knowing our parents, we never worried about the Jews or the blacks, whatever.

The next day I called Mr. Eli Hemsi at his office. Like married men having an affair, my clients' fathers gave me only their office numbers. But they would have my home number, just in case they had to get in touch with me right away. I was already getting a lot of calls which made Vallie wonder. I told her it was gambling and magazine work calls.

Mr. Hemsi asked me to come down to his office during my lunch hour and I went. It was one of the garment center buildings on Seventh Avenue just ten minutes away from the armory. A nice little stroll in the spring air. I dodged guys pushing hand trucks loaded with racks of dresses and reflected a little smugly on how hard they were working for their paltry wages while I collected hundreds for a little dirty paperwork, at the crossroads. Most of them were black guys. Why the hell weren't they out mugging people like they were supposed to? Ah, if they only had the proper education, they could be stealing like me, without hurting people.

In the building the receptionist led me through showrooms that exhibited the new styles for the coming seasons. And then I was ushered through a little grubby door into Mr. Hemsi's office suite. I was really surprised at how plush it was, the rest of the building was so grubby. The receptionist turned me over to Mr. Hemsi's secretary, a middle-aged no-nonsense woman, but impeccably dressed who took me into the inner sanctum.

Mr. Hemsi was a great big guy who would have looked like a Cossack if it had not been for his perfectly tailored suit, rich-looking white shirt and dark red tie. His face was powerfully craggy and had a look of melancholy. He looked almost noble and certainly honest. He rose from his desk and grasped my hands in both of his to greet me. He looked deep into my eyes. He was so close to me that I could see through the thick, ropy gray hair. He said gravely, "My friend is right, you have a good heart. I know you will help me."

"I really can't help. I'd like to, but I can't," I said. And I explained the whole draft board thing to him as I had to Mr. Hiller. I was colder than I meant to be. I don't like people looking deep into my eyes.

He just sat there nodding his head gravely. Then, as if he hadn't heard a word I'd said, he just went on, his voice really melancholy now.

"My wife, the poor woman, she is in very bad health. It will kill her if she loses her son now. He is the only thing she lives for. It will kill her if he goes away for two years. Mr. Merlyn, you must help me. If you do this for me, I will make you happy for the rest of your life."

It wasn't that he convinced me. It wasn't that I believed a word he'd said. But that last phrase got to me. Only kings and emperors can say to a man, "I will make you happy for the rest of your life." What confidence in his powers he had. But then, of course, I realized he was talking about money.

"Let me think about it," I said, "maybe I can come up with something."

Mr. Hemsi was nodding his head up and down very gravely. "I know you will. I know you have a good head and a good heart," he said. "Do you have children?"

"Yes," I said. He asked me how many and how old they were and what sex. He asked me about my wife and how old she was. He was like an uncle. Then he asked me for my home address and phone number so that he could get in touch with me if necessary.

When I left him, he walked me to the elevator himself. I figured I had done my job. I had no idea how I could get his son off the hook with the draft board. And Mr. Hemsi was right, I did have a good heart. I had a good enough heart not to try to hustle him and his wife's anxieties and then not deliver. And I had a good enough head not to get mixed up with a draft board victim. The kid had had his notice and would be in the Regular Army in another month. His mother would have to live without him.

The very next day Vallie called me at work. Her voice was

very excited. She told me that she just received special delivery service of about five cartons of clothing. Clothes for all the kids, winter and fall outfits, and they were beautiful. There was also a carton of clothes for her. All of it more expensive than we could ever buy.

"There's a card," she said. "From a Mr. Hemsi. Who is he? Merlyn, they are just beautiful. Why did he give them to you?"

"I wrote some brochures for his business," I said. "There wasn't much money in it, but he did promise to send the kids some stuff. But I thought he meant a few things."

I could hear the pleasure in Vallie's voice. "He must be a nice man. There must be over a thousand dollars' worth of clothes in the boxes."

"That's great," I said. "I'll talk to you about it tonight."

After I hung up, I told Frank what had happened and about Mr. Hiller, the Cadillac dealer.

Frank squinted at me. "You're on the hook," he said. "That guy will be expecting you to do something for him now. How are you going to come across?"

"Shit," I said, "I can't figure out why I even agreed to go see him."

"It was those Cadillacs you saw on Hiller's lot," Frank said. "You're like those colored guys. They'd go back to those huts in Africa if they could drive around in a Cadillac."

I noticed a little hitch in his speech. He had almost said "niggers" but switched to "colored." I wondered if it was because he was ashamed of saying the ugly word or because he thought I might be offended. As for the Harlem guys liking Cadillacs I always wondered why people got pissed off about that. Because they couldn't afford it? Because they should not go into debt for something not useful? But he was right about those Cadillacs getting me on the hook. That's why I had agreed to see Hemsi and do Hiller the favor. Way back in my head I hoped for a shot at one of those luxurious sleek cars.

That night, when I got home, Vallie put on a fashion show for me with her and the kids. She had mentioned five cartons, but she hadn't mentioned their size. They were enormous, and Vallie and the kids had about ten outfits each. Vallie was more excited than I had seen her in a long time. The kids were pleased, but they didn't care too much about clothes at that age, not even my daughter. The thought flashed through my mind that maybe I'd get lucky and find a toy manufacturer whose kid had ducked the draft.

But then Vallie pointed out that she would have to buy new shoes to go with the outfits. I told her to hold off for a while and made a note to keep an eye out for a shoe manufacturer's son.

Now the curious thing was that I would have felt that Mr. Hemsi was patronizing me if the clothes had been of ordinary quality. There would have been the touch of the poor receiving the hand-me-downs of the rich. But his stuff was top-rate, quality goods I could never afford no matter how much bribe money I raked in. Five thousand bucks, not a thousand. I took a look at the enclosed card. It was a business card with Hemsi's name and title of president and the name of the firm and its address and phone printed on it. There was nothing written. No message of any kind. Mr. Hemsi was smart all right. There was no direct evidence that he had sent the stuff, and I had nothing that I could incriminate him with.

At the office I had thought that maybe I could ship the stuff back to Mr. Hemsi. But after seeing how happy Vallie was, I knew that was not possible. I lay awake until three in the morning, figuring out ways for Mr. Hemsi's son to beat the draft.

The next day, when I went into the office, I made one decision. I wouldn't do anything on paper that could be traced back to me a year or two later. This could be very tricky. It was one thing to take money to put a guy ahead on a list for the six months' program, it was another to get him out of the draft after he had received his induction notice.

So the first thing I did was to call up Hemsi's draft board. I got one of the clerks there, a guy just like me. I identified myself and gave him the story I had thought out. I told him that Paul Hemsi had been on my list for the six months' program and that I had meant to enlist him two weeks ago but that I had sent his letter to the wrong address. That it had been all my fault and I felt guilty about it and also that maybe I could get in trouble on my job if the kid's family started to holler. I asked him if the draft board could cancel the induction notice so that I could enlist him. I would then send the usual official form to the draft board, showing that Paul Hemsi was in the six months' program of the Army

Reserve, and they could take him off their draft rolls. I used what I thought was exactly the right tone, not too anxious. Just a nice guy trying to right a wrong. While I was doing this, I slipped in that if the guy at the draft board could do me this favor, I would help him get a friend of his in the six months' program.

This last gimmick I had thought about while lying awake the previous night. I figured that the clerks at the draft board probably were contacted by kids on their last legs, about to be drafted, and that the draft board clerks probably got propositioned a lot. And I figured if a draft board clerk could place a client of his in the six months' program it could be worth a thousand bucks.

But the guy at the draft board was completely casual and accommodating. I don't even think he caught on that I was propositioning him. He said sure, he'd withdraw the induction notice, that it was no problem, and I suddenly got the impression that smarter guys than I had already pulled this dodge. Anyway, the next day I got the necessary letter from the draft board and called Mr. Hemsi and told him to send his son into my office to be enlisted.

It all went off without a hitch. Paul Hemsi was a nice soft-spoken kid, very shy, very timid, or so it seemed to me. I had him sworn in, stashed his papers until he got his active-duty orders. I drew his supply stuff for him myself, and when he left for his six months' active duty, nobody in his outfit had seen him. I'd turned him into a ghost.

By now I realized that all this action was getting pretty hot and implicating powerful people. But I wasn't Merlyn the Magician for nothing. I put on my star-spangled cap and started to think it all out. Someday it would blow up. I had myself pretty well covered except for the money stashed in my house. I had to hide the money. That was the first thing. And then I had to show another income so I could spend money openly.

I could stash my money with Cully in Las Vegas. But what if Cully got cute or got killed? As for making money legit, I had had offers to do book reviews and magazine work, but I had always turned them down. I was a pure storyteller, a fiction writer. It seemed demeaning to me and my art to write anything else. But what the hell, I was a crook, nothing was beneath me now.

FOOLS DIE

Frank asked me to go to lunch with him and I said OK. Frank was in great form. Happy-go-lucky, top-of-the-world. He'd had a winning week gambling and the money was rolling in. With no sense of what the future could bring, he believed he'd keep winning, the whole bribe scam would last forever. Without even thinking of himself as a magician, he believed in a magic world.

Chapter 12

It was nearly two weeks later that my agent arranged an appointment for me with the editor in chief of Everyday Magazines. This was a group of publications that drowned the American public with information, pseudoinformation, sex and pseudosex, culture and hard-hat philosophy. Movie mags, adventure mags for blue-collar workers, a sports monthly, fishing and hunting, comics. Their "class" leader, top-of-the-line magazine was slanted to swinging bachelors with a taste for literature and avant-garde cinema.

A real smorgasbord. Everyday gobbled up free-lance writers because they had to publish a half million words a month. My agent told me that the editor in chief knew my brother, Artie, and that Artie had called him to prepare the way.

At Everyday Magazines all the people seemed to be out of place. Nobody seemed to belong. And yet they put out profitable magazines. Funny, but in the federal government we all seemed to fit, everybody was happy and yet we all did a lousy job.

The chief editor, Eddie Lancer, had gone to school with my brother at the University of Missouri, and it was my brother who first mentioned the job to my agent. Of course, Lancer knew I was completely unqualified after the first two minutes of the interview. So did I. Hell, I didn't even know what the backyard of a magazine was. But with Lancer this was a plus. He didn't give a shit about experience. What Lancer was looking for was guys touched with schizophrenia. And later he told me that I had qualified highly on that score.

Eddie Lancer was a novelist too; he had published a hell of a book that I loved just a year ago. He knew about my novel and said he liked it and that carried a lot of weight in getting the job. On his bulletin board was a big newspaper headline ripped out of the morning *Times*: ATOM BOMB WAR SEEN BAD FOR WALL STREET.

He saw me staring at the clipping and said, "Do you think you could write a short fiction piece about a guy worrying about that?"

"Sure," I said. And I did. I wrote a story about a young executive worrying about his stocks going down after the atom bombs fall. I didn't make the mistake of poking fun at the guy or being moral. I wrote it straight. If you accepted the basic premise, you accepted the guy. If you didn't accept the basic premise, it was a very funny satire.

Lancer was pleased with it. "You're made to order for our magazine," he said. "The whole idea is to have it both ways. The dummies like it and the smart guys like it. Perfect." He paused for a moment. "You're a lot different from your brother, Artie."

"Yeah, I know," I said. "So are you."

Lancer grinned at me. "We were best friends in college. He's the most honest guy I ever met. You know when he asked me to interview you, I was surprised. It was the first time I ever knew him to ask a favor."

"He does that only for me," I said.

"Straightest guy I ever knew in my life," Lancer said.

"It will be the death of him," I said. And we laughed.

Lancer and I knew we were both survivors. Which meant we were not straight, that we were hustlers to some degree. Our excuse was that we had books to write. And so we had to survive. Everybody had his own particular and valid excuse.

Much to my surprise (but not to Lancer's) I turned out to be a hell of a magazine writer. I could write the pulp adventure and war stories. I could write the soft-porn love stories for the top-of-the-line magazine. I could write a flashy, snotty film review and a sober, snotty book review. Or turn the other way and write an enthusiastic review that would make people want to go out and see or read for themselves what was so good. I never signed my real name to any of this stuff. But I wasn't ashamed of it. I knew it was schlock, but still I loved it. I loved it because all my life I had never had a skill to be proud of. I had been a lousy soldier, a losing gambler. I had no hobby, no mechanical skills. I couldn't fix a car, I couldn't grow a plant. I was a lousy typist, and not a really first-rate bribe taker government clerk. Sure, I was an artist, but that's nothing to brag about. That's just a religion or a hobby. But now I really had a skill, I was an expert schlock writer, and loved it. Especially since for the first time in my life I was making a good living. Legitimately.

The money from the stories averaged four hundred dollars a month and with my regular Army Reserve job brought me to about two hundred bucks a week. And as if work sparked more energy, I found myself starting my second novel. Eddie Lancer was on a new book too, and we spent most of our working time together talking about our novels rather than articles for the magazine.

We finally became such good friends that after six months of free-lance work he offered me a magazine editor slot. But I didn't want to give up the two to three grand a month in graft that I was still making on my Army Reserve job. The bribe-taking scam had been going on for nearly two years without any kind of hitch. I now had the same attitude as Frank. I didn't think anything would ever happen. Also, the truth was that I liked the excitement and the intrigue of being a thief.

My life settled down into a happy groove. My writing was going well, and every Sunday I took Vallie and the kids for rides out in Long Island, where family houses were springing up like weeds, and inspected models. We had already picked out our house. Four bedrooms, two baths and only a ten percent down payment on the twenty-six-thousand-dollar price with a twelve-month wait. In fact, now was the time to ask Eddie Lancer for a small favor.

"I've always loved Las Vegas," I told Eddie. "I'd like to do a piece on it."

"Sure, anytime," he said. "Just make sure you get something in it on hookers." And he arranged for the expenses. Then we talked about the color illustration for the story. We always did this together because it was a lot of fun, and we got a lot of laughs. As usual Eddie finally came up with the effective idea. A gorgeous girl in scanty costume in a wild pelvic dance. And out of her navel rolled red dice showing the lucky eleven. The cover line would read "Get Lucky with Las Vegas Girls."

One assignment had to come first. It was a plum. I was going to interview the most famous writer in America, Osano.

Eddie Lancer gave me the assignment for his flagship magazine, *Everyday Life*, the class magazine of the chain. After that one I could do the Las Vegas piece and trip.

Eddie Lancer thought Osano was the greatest writer in America but was too awed to do the interview himself. I was the only one on the staff not impressed. I didn't think Osano was all that good. Also, I distrusted any writer who was an extrovert. And Osano had appeared on TV a hundred times, been the judge at the Cannes Film Festival, got arrested for leading protest marchers no matter what they were protesting against. And gave blurbs for every new novel written by one of his friends.

Also, he had come up the easy way. His first novel, published when he was twenty-five, made him world-famous. He had wealthy parents, a law degree from Yale. He had never known what it was to struggle for his art. Most of all, I had sent him my first published novel, hoping for a blurb, and he never acknowledged receiving it.

When I went to interview Osano, his stock as a writer was just slipping with editors. He could still command a hefty advance for a book, he still had critics buffaloed. But most of his books were nonfiction. He had not been able to finish a fiction book in the last ten years.

He was working on his masterpiece, a long novel that would be the greatest thing since *War and Peace*. All the critics agreed about that. So did Osano. One publishing house advanced him over a hundred grand and was still whistling for its money and the book ten years later. Meanwhile, he wrote nonfiction books on hot subjects that some critics claimed were better than most novels. He turned them out in a couple of months and picked up a fat check. But each one sold less. He had worn his public out. So finally he accepted an offer to be editor in chief of the most influential Sunday book review section in the country.

The editor before Osano had been in the job twenty years. A guy with great credentials. All kinds of degrees, the best colleges, an intellectual, wealthy family. Class. And a left-handed swinger all his life. Which was OK except that as he aged, he got more outrageous. One sunny, horny afternoon he was caught going down on the office boy behind a ceiling-high stack of books that he had built as a screen in his office. If the office boy had been a famous English author, maybe nothing would have happened. And if the books he used to build that wall had been reviewed, it wouldn't have been so bad. But the books used to build that wall never got out to his staff of readers or to the free-lance reviewers. So he was retired as editor emeritus.

With Osano, the management knew it was home free. Osano was right-handed all the way. He loved women, all sizes and shapes, any age. The smell of cunt turned him on like a junkie. He fucked broads as devotedly as a heroin addict taking a fix. If Osano didn't get his piece of ass that day or at least a blow job, he'd get frantic. But he wasn't an exhibitionist. He'd always lock his office door. Sometimes a bookish teenybopper. Other times a society broad who thought he was the greatest living American writer. Or a starving female novelist who needed some books to review to keep body and soul and ego together. He was shameless in using his leverage as editor, his fame as a world-renowned novelist and what proved to be the busiest bee in his bonnet, a contender for the Nobel Prize in literature. He said it was the Nobel Prize that got the really intellectual ladies. And for the last three years he had mounted a furious campaign for the Nobel with the help of all his literary friends, he could show these ladies articles in classy quarterlies touting him for the prize.

Oddly enough Osano had no ego about his own physical charms—his personal magnetism. He dressed well, spent good money on clothes, yet it was true he was not physically attractive. His face was all lopsided bone, and his eyes were a pale, sneaky green. But he discounted his vibrant aliveness that was magnetic to all people. Indeed, a great deal of his fame rested not on his literary achievement but on his personality, which included a quick, brilliant intelligence that was attractive to men as well as women.

But the women went crazy for him; bright college girls, well-read society matrons, Women's Lib fighters who cursed him out and then tried to get him in the sack so they could have it on him, so they said, the way men used to have it on women in Victorian days. One of his tricks was to address himself to women in his books.

I never liked his work, and I didn't expect to like him. The work is the man. Except that it proved not to be true. After all, there are some compassionate doctors, curious teachers, honest lawyers, idealistic politicians, virtuous women, sane actors, wise writers. And so Osano, despite his fishwife style, the spite in his work, was in reality a great guy to hang out with and not too much of a pain in the ass to listen to, even when he talked about his writing.

Anyway, he had quite an empire as editor of the book review. Two secretaries. Twenty staff readers. And a great outdoors of free-lance critics from top-name authors to starving poets, unsuccessful novelists, college professors and jet-set intellectuals. He used them all and hated them all. And he ran the review like a lunatic.

Page one of the Sunday review is something an author kills for. Osano knew that. He got the first page automatically when he published a book, in all the book reviews in the country. But he hated most fiction writers, he was jealous of them. Or he would have a grudge against the publisher of the book. So he would get a biography of Napoleon or Catherine the Great written by a heavyweight college professor and put it on page one. Book and review usually were both equally unreadable, but Osano was happy. He had infuriated everybody.

The first time I ever saw Osano he lived up to all the literary party stories, all the gossip, all the public images he had ever created. He played the role of the great writer for me with a natural gusto. And he had the props to suit the legend.

I went out to the Hamptons, where Osano took a summer house, and found him ensconced (his word) like an old sultan. At fifty years of age, he had six kids from four different marriages and at that time had not gotten his fifth, sixth and terminal seventh notch. He had on long blue tennis pants and blue tennis jacket specially tailored to hide his bulging beer gut. His face was already craggily impressive, as befitted the next winner of the Nobel Prize for literature. Despite his wicked green eyes, he could be naturally sweet. Today he was sweet. Since he was head of the most powerful Sunday literary review, everybody kissed his ass with the utmost devotion every time he published. He didn't know I was out to kill him, because I was an unsuccessful writer with one flop novel published and the second coming hard. Sure, he'd written one big almost great novel. But the rest of his work was bullshit, and if *Everyday Life* let me, I'd show the world what this guy was really made of.

I wrote the article all right, and I caught him dead to rights. But Eddie Lancer turned it down. They wanted Osano to do a big political story, and they didn't want him to get mad. So it was a day wasted. Except that it really wasn't. Because two years later Osano called me up and offered me a job working for him as assistant on a new big literary review. Osano remembered me, had read the story the magazine killed, and he liked my guts, or so he said. He said it was because I was a good writer and I liked the same things about his work that he liked.

That first day we sat in his garden and watched his kids play tennis. I have to say right now he really loved his kids and he was perfect with them. Maybe because he was so much a child himself. Anyway, I got him talking about women and Women's Lib and sex. And he threw in love with it. He was pretty funny. And though in his writings he was the great all-time left-winger, he could be pretty Texas chauvinistic. Talking about love, he said that once he fell in love with a girl he always stopped being jealous of his wife. Then he put on his big writer-statesman look and said, "No man is allowed to be jealous of more than one woman at a time— unless he's Puerto Rican." He felt he was allowed to make jokes about Puerto Ricans because his radical credentials were impeccable.

The housekeeper came out to yell at the children fighting for a game on the tennis court. She was a pretty bossy housekeeper and pretty snotty with the kids, as if she were their mother. She also was a handsome woman for her age, which was about Osano's. For a moment I wondered. Especially when she gave us both a contemptuous look before she went back into the house.

I got him talking about women, which was easy. He took the cynic's stance, which is always a great stance to take when you're not crazy about some particular lady. He was very authoritative, as befitted a writer who had had more gossip written about him than any novelist since Hemingway.

"Listen, kid," he said, "love is like the little red toy wagon you get for Christmas or your sixth birthday. It makes you deliriously happy and you just can't leave it alone. But sooner or later the wheels come off. Then you leave it in a corner and forget it. Falling in love is great. Being in love is a disaster."

Asking quietly and with the respect he thought due, I said, "What about women, do you think they feel the same way since they claim to think as men think?"

He flashed me a quick look of those surprisingly green eyes. He was on to my act. But it was OK. That was one of the great things about Osano even then. So he went on.

"Women's Lib thinks we have power and control over their lives. In its way that's as stupid as a guy's thinking women are purer sexually than men. Women will fuck anybody, anytime, anyplace, except that they're afraid of talk. Women's Lib bullshits about the fraction of a percent of men who have power. Those guys are not men. They're not even human. That's whose place women have to take. They don't know you have to kill to get there."

I interrupted. "You're one of those men."

Osano nodded. "Yeah. And metaphorically I had to kill. What women will get is what men have. Which is shit, ulcers and heart attacks. Plus a lot of shitty jobs men hate to do. But I'm all for equality. I'll kill those cunts then. Listen, I'm paying alimony to four healthy broads who can earn their own living. All because they are not equal."

"Your affairs with women are almost as famous as your books," I said. "How do you handle women?"

Osano grinned at me. "You're not interested in how I write books."

I said smooth as shit, "Your books speak for themselves."

He gave me another long, thoughtful look, then went on.

"Never treat a woman too good. Women stick with drunks, gamblers, whoremasters and even beater-uppers. They can't stand a sweet, good guy. Do you know why? They get bored. They don't want to be happy. It's boring."

"Do you believe in being faithful?" I asked.

"Sure I do. Listen, being in love means making another person the central thing in your life. When that no longer exists, it's not love anymore. It's something else. Maybe something better, more practical. Love is basically an unfair, unstable, paranoid relationship. Men are worse than women at it. A woman can screw a hundred times, not feel like it once and he holds it against her. But it's true that the first step downhill is when she doesn't want to fuck when you do.

Listen, there's no excuse. Never mind the headaches. No shit. Once a broad starts turning you down in bed it's all over. Start looking for your backer-upper. Never take an excuse."

I asked him about orgasmic women who could have ten orgasms to a man's one. He waved it aside.

"Women don't come like men," he said. "For them it's a little *phitt*. Not like a guy's. Guys really blow their brains with their nuts. Freud was close, but he missed it. Men really *fuck*. Women don't."

Well, he didn't really believe that all the way, but I knew what he was saying. His style was exaggeration.

I switched him on to helicopters. He had this theory that in twenty years the auto would be obsolete, that everybody would have his own chopper. All it needed were some technical improvements. As when auto power steering and brakes enabled every woman to drive and put railroads out of business. "Yeah," he said, "that's obvious." What was also obvious was that on this particular morning he was wound up on women. So he switched back.

"The young guys today are on the right track. They say to their broads, sure you can fuck anybody you want, I'll still love you. They are so full of shit. Listen, any guy who knows a broad will fuck strangers thinks of her as a geek."

I was offended by the comparison and astonished. The great Osano, whose writings women were particularly crazy about. The most brilliant mind in American letters. The most open mind. Either I was missing his point or he was full of shit. I saw his housekeeper slapping some of the little kids around. I said, "You sure give your housekeeper a lot of authority."

Now he was so sharp that he caught everything without even trying. He knew exactly how I felt about what he'd been saying. Maybe that's why he told me the truth, the whole story about his housekeeper. Just to needle me.

"She was my first wife," he said. "She's the mother of my three oldest kids."

He laughed when he saw the look on my face. "No, I don't screw her. And we get along fine. I pay her a damn good salary but no alimony. She's the one wife I don't pay alimony."

He obviously wanted me to ask why not. I did.

"Because when I wrote my first book and got rich, it went to her head. She was jealous of me being famous and getting a lot of attention. *She* wanted attention. So some young guy, one of the admirers of my work, gave her the business, and she fell for it. She was five years older than him, but she was always a sexy broad. She really fell in love, I'll give her that. What she didn't realize was that he was fucking her just to put the great novelist Osano down. So she asked for a divorce and half the money my book made. That was OK with me. She wanted the kids, but I didn't want my kids around that creep she was in love with. So I told her when she married the guy, she'd get the kids. Well, he fucked her brains out for two years and blew all her dough. She forgot about her kids. She was a young broad again. Sure, she came to see them a lot, but she was busy traveling all over the world on my dough and chewing the young guy's cock to shreds. When the money runs out, he takes off. She comes back and wants the kids. But by now she has no case. She deserted them for two years. She puts on a big scene how she can't live without them. So I gave her a job as a housekeeper."

I said coolly, "That's maybe the worst thing I ever heard of."

The startling green eyes flashed for a moment. But then he smiled and said musingly, "I guess it looks that way. But put yourself in my place. I love having my kids around me. How come the father never gets the kids? What kind of bullshit is that? Do you know men never recover from that bullshit? The wife gets tired of being married, so men lose their kids. And men stand still for it because they got their balls chopped off. Well, I didn't stand still for it. I kept the kids and got married again right away. And when that wife started pulling bullshit, I got rid of her too."

I said quietly, "How about her children? How do they feel about their mother being a housekeeper?"

The green eyes flashed again. "Oh, shit. I don't put her down. She's only my housekeeper between wives; otherwise she's more like a free-lance governess. She has her own house. I'm her landlord. Listen, I thought of giving her more dough, of buying her a house and making her independent. But she's a dizzy cunt like all of them. She'd become obnoxious again. She'd go down the drain. Which is OK, but she'd make more trouble for me and I've got books to write. So I control her with money. She has a damn good living from me. And she knows if she gets out of line, she's out on her ass and scratching to make a living. It works out."

"Could it be you're antiwoman?" I said, smiling.

He laughed. "You say that to a guy who's been married four times, he doesn't even have to deny it. But OK. I'm really anti-Women's Lib in one sense. Because right now most women are just full of shit. Maybe it's not their fault. Listen, any broad who doesn't want to fuck two days in a row, get rid of her. Unless she has to go to the hospital in an ambulance. Even if she has forty stitches in her cunt. I don't care whether she enjoys it or not. Sometimes I don't enjoy it and I do it and I have to get a hard-on. That's your job if you love somebody, you gotta fuck their brains out. Jesus, I don't know why I keep getting married. I swore I wouldn't do it anymore, but I always get conned. I always believe it's not getting married that makes them unhappy. They are so full of shit."

"With the proper conditioning don't you think women can become equal?"

Osano shook his head. "They forget they age worse than men. A guy at fifty can get a lot of young broads. A broad of fifty finds it rough. Sure, when they get political power, they'll pass a law so that men of forty or fifty get operated on to look older and equal things out. That's how democracy works. That's full of shit too. Listen, women have it good. They shouldn't complain.

"In the old days they didn't know they had union rights. They couldn't be fired no matter how lousy a job they did. Lousy in bed. Lousy in the kitchen. And who ever had fun with his wife after a couple of years? And if he did, she was a cunt. And now they want to be equal. Let me at 'em. I'll give them equality. I know what I'm talking about; I've been married four times. And it cost me every penny I made."

Osano really hated women that day. A month later I picked up the morning paper and read that he'd married for the fifth time. An actress in a little theater group. She was half his age. So much for the common sense of America's foremost man of letters. I never dreamed that I would be working for him someday and be with him until he died, miraculously a bachelor but still in love with a woman, with women.

I caught it that day through all the bullshit. He was crazy about women. That was his weakness, and he hated it.

Chapter 13

I was finally ready for my trip to Las Vegas to see Cully again. It would be the first time in over three years, three years since Jordan had blown himself away in his room, a four-hundred-grand winner.

We had kept in touch, Cully and I. He phoned me a couple of times a month and sent Christmas presents for me and my wife and kids, stuff I recognized that came from the Xanadu Hotel gift shop, where I knew he got them for a fraction of their selling price or, knowing Cully, even for nothing. But still, it was nice of him to do it. I had told Vallie about Cully but never told her about Jordan.

I knew Cully had a good job with the hotel because his secretary answered his phone with "Assistant to the president." And I wondered how in a few years he had managed to climb so high. His telephone voice and manner of speaking had changed; he spoke in a lower tone; he was more sincere, more polite, warmer. An actor playing a different part. Over the phone it would be just idle chitchat and gossip about big winners and big losers and funny stories about the characters staying in the hotel. But never anything about himself. Eventually one of us would mention Jordan, usually near the end of the call, or maybe the mention of Jordan would end the call. He was our touchstone.

Vallie packed my suitcase. I was going over the weekend so I would only have to miss a day's work at my Army Reserve job. And in the far-off distant future, which I smelled, the magazine story would give me the cover for the cops about why I went to Vegas.

The kids were in bed while Vallie was packing my bag because I was leaving early the next morning. She gave me a little smile. "God, it was terrible the last time you went. I thought you wouldn't come back."

"I just had to get away then," I said. "Things were going bad."

"Everything's changed since," Vallie said musingly. "Three years ago we didn't have money at all. Gee, we were so broke I had to ask my father for some money and I was afraid you'd find out. And you acted as if you didn't love me anymore. That trip changed everything. You were different when you came back. You weren't mad at me anymore and you were more patient with the kids. And you got work with the magazines."

I smiled at her. "Remember, I came back a winner. A few extra grand. Maybe if I'd come back a loser, it would have been a whole different story."

Vallie snapped the suitcase shut. "No," she said. "You were different. You were happier, happier with me and the kids."

"I found out what I was missing," I said.

"Oh, yeah," she said. "With all those beautiful hookers in Vegas."

"They cost too much," I said. "I needed my money to gamble."

It was all kidding around, but part of it was serious. If I told her the truth, that I never looked at another woman, she wouldn't believe me. But I could give good reasons. I had felt so much guilt about being such a lousy husband and father who couldn't give his family anything, who couldn't even make a decent living for them, that I couldn't add to that guilt by being unfaithful to her. And the overriding fact was that we were so lucky in bed together. She was really all I wanted, perfect for me. I thought I was for her.

"Are you going to do some work tonight?" she asked. She was really asking if we were going to make love first so that she could get ready. Then, after we'd made love, usually I would get up to work on my writing and she would fall so soundly asleep she would not stir until morning. She was a great sleeper. I was lousy at it.

"Yes," I said. "I want to work. I'm too excited about the trip to sleep anyway."

It was nearly midnight, but she went into the kitchen to make me a fresh pot of coffee and some sandwiches. I would work until three or four in the morning and then still wake up before she did in the morning.

The worst part about being a writer, anyway for me when I was working well, was the inability to sleep. Lying in bed, I could never turn off the machine in my brain that kept thinking about the novel I was working on. As I lay in the dark, the characters became so real to me that I forgot my wife and my kids and everyday life. But tonight I had another less literary reason. I wanted Vallie to go to sleep so that I could get my big stash of bribe money from its hiding place.

From the bedroom closet way back from its darkest corner I took my old Las Vegas Winner sports jacket and carried it into the kitchen. I had never worn it since I had come home from Las Vegas three years ago. Its bright colors had faded in the darkness of the closet, but it was still pretty garish. I put it on and went into the kitchen. Vallie took one look at it and said, "Merlyn, you're not going to wear that."

"My lucky jacket," I said. "Besides, it's comfortable for the plane ride." I knew she had hidden it way back in the closet so that I would never see it and never think to wear it. She hadn't dared throw it out. Now the jacket would come in handy.

Vallie sighed. "You're so superstitious."

She was wrong. I was rarely superstitious even though I thought I was a magician and it's really not the same thing.

After Vallie kissed me good-night and went to bed, I had some coffee and looked over the manuscript I had taken from my desk in the bedroom. I did mostly editing for an hour. I took a peek into the bedroom and saw Vallie was sound asleep. I kissed her very lightly. She didn't stir. Now I loved it when she kissed me good-night. The simple, dutiful, wifely kiss that seemed to seal us away from all the loneliness and treacherousness of the outside world. And often lying in bed, in the early-morning hours, Vallie asleep and I not able to sleep, I would kiss her lightly on the mouth, hoping she would wake up to make me feel less lonely by making love. But this time I was aware that I had given her a Judas kiss, partly out of affection, but really to make sure she would not awaken when I dug out the hidden money.

I closed the bedroom door and then went to the hall closet which held the big trunk with all my old manuscripts, the carbon copies of my novel and the original manuscript of the book I had worked on for five years and had earned me three thousand dollars. It was a hell of a lot of paper, all the rewrites and carbons, paper I had thought would make me rich and famous and honored. I dug underneath to the big reddish folder with its stringed cover. I pulled it out and brought it into the kitchen. Sipping my coffee, I counted out the money. A little over forty thousand dollars. The money had come rolling in very fast lately. I had become the Tiffany's of bribe takers, with rich, trusting customers. The twenties, about seven thousand dollars' worth, I left in the envelope. There were thirty-three thousand in hundreds. I put these in five long envelopes I had brought from my desk. Then I crammed the money-filled envelopes into the different pockets of the Vegas Winner sports jacket. I zipped up the pockets and hung the coat on the back of my chair.

In the morning, when Vallie hugged me good-bye, she would feel something in the pockets, but I would just tell her it was some notes for the article I was taking with me to Vegas.

Chapter 14

When I got off the plane, Cully was waiting for me at the door of the terminal. The airport was still so small I had to walk from the plane, but construction was underway to build another wing to the terminal—Vegas was growing. And so was Cully.

He looked different, taller and slimmer. And he was smartly dressed in a Sy Devore suit and sports shirt. His hair had a different cut. I was surprised when he gave me a hug and said, "Same old Merlyn." He laughed at the Vegas Winner sports jacket and told me I had to get rid of it.

He had a big suite for me at the hotel with a bar stocked with booze and flowers on the tables. "You must have a lot of juice," I said.

"I'm doing good," Cully said. "I've given up gambling. I'm on the other side of the tables. You know."

"Yeah," I said. I felt funny about Cully now, he seemed so different. I didn't know whether to follow through with my original plan and trust him. In three years a guy could change. And after all, we had only known each other a few weeks.

But as we were drinking together, he said with real sincerity, "Kid, I'm really glad to see you. Ever think about Jordan?"

"All the time," I said.

"Poor Jordan," Cully said. "He went out a four-hundred-grand winner. That's what made me give up gambling. And you know, ever since he died, I've had tremendous luck. If I play my cards right, I could wind up top man in this hotel."

"No shit," I said. "What about Gronevelt?"

"I'm his number one boy," Cully said. "He trusts me with a lot of stuff. He trusts me like I trust you. While we're at it,

I could use an assistant. Anytime you want to move your family to Vegas you got a good job with me."

"Thanks," I said. I was really touched. At the same time I wondered about his affection for me. I knew he was not a man who cared about anyone easily. I said, "About the job I can't answer you now. But I came out here to ask a favor. If you can't do it for me, I'll understand. Just tell me straight, and whatever the answer is, we'll at least have a couple of days together and have a good time."

"You got it," Cully said. "Whatever it is."

I laughed. "Wait until you hear," I said.

For a moment Cully seemed angry. "I don't give a shit what it is. You got it. If I can do it, you got it."

I told him about the whole graft operation. That I was taking bribes and that I had thirty-three grand in my jacket that I had to stash in case the whole operation blew up. Cully listened to me intently, watching my face. At the end he was smiling broadly.

"What the hell are you smiling at?" I said.

Cully laughed. "You sounded like a guy confessing to a priest that he committed murder. Shit, what you're doing everybody does if he ever gets the chance. But I have to admit I'm surprised. I can't picture you telling a guy he has to pay blackmail."

I could feel my face getting red. "I never asked any of those guys for money," I said. "They always come to me. And I never take the money upfront. After I do it for them, they can pay me what they promised or they can stiff me. I don't give a shit." I grinned at him. "I'm a soft hustler, not a hooker."

"Some crook," Cully said. "First thing, I think you're too worried. It sounds like the kind of operation that can go on indefinitely. And even if it blows up, the worst that can happen to you is that you lose your job and get a suspended sentence. But you're right, you have to stash the dough in a good place. Those Feds are real bloodhounds, and when they find it, they'll take it all away from you."

I was interested in the first part of what he said. One of my nightmares was that I would go to jail and Vallie and the kids would be without me. That's why I had kept everything from my wife. I didn't want her to worry. Also, I didn't want her to think less of me. She had an image of me as the pure, uncorrupted artist.

"What makes you think I won't go to jail if I'm caught?" I asked Cully.

"It's a white-collar crime," Cully said. "Hell, you didn't stick up a bank or shoot some poor bastard store owner or defraud a widow. You just took dough from some young punks who were trying to get an edge and cut down their Army time. Jesus, that's some unbelievable scam. Guys paying to get *into* the Army. Nobody would believe it. A jury would laugh themselves sick."

"Yeah, it strikes me funny too," I said.

Cully was all business suddenly. "OK, tell me what you want me to do right now. It's done. And if the Feds nail you, promise you'll call me right away. I'll get you out. OK?" He smiled at me affectionately.

I told him my plan. That I would turn in my cash for chips a thousand dollars at a time and gamble but for small stakes. I'd do that in all the casinos in Vegas, and then, when I cashed in my chips for cash, I would just take a receipt and leave the money in the cashier's cages as a gambling credit. The FBI would never think to look in the casinos. And the cash receipts I could stash with Cully and pick up whenever I needed some ready money.

Cully smiled at me. "Why don't you let me hold your money? Don't you trust me?"

I knew he was kidding, but I handled the crack seriously. "I thought about that," I said. "But what if something happens to you? Like a plane crash. Or you get your gambling bug back? I trust you now. But how do I know you won't go crazy tomorrow or next year?"

Cully nodded his head approvingly. Then he asked, "What about your brother, Artie? You and him are so close. Can't he hold the money for you?"

"I can't ask him to do that for me," I said.

Cully nodded again. "Yeah, I guess you can't. He's too honest, right?"

"Right," I said. I didn't want to go into any long explanation about how I felt. "What's wrong with my plan? Don't you think it's any good?"

Cully got up and began pacing up and down the room. "It's not bad," he said. "But you don't want to have credits in all the casinos. That looks fishy. Especially if the money stays there a long time. That is really fishy. People only leave their money in the cage until they gamble it away or they leave Vegas. Here's what you do. Buy chips in all the casinos and check them into our cage here. You know, about three or four times a day cash in for a few thousand and take a receipt. So all your cash receipts will be in our cage. Now if the Feds do nose around or write to the hotel, it has to go through me. And I'll cover you."

I was worried about him. "Won't that get you into trouble?" I asked him.

Cully sighed patiently. "I do that stuff all the time. We get a lot of inquiries from Internal Revenue. About how much guys have lost. I just send them old files. There's no way they can check me out. I make sure files don't exist that will help them."

"Jesus," I said. "I don't want my cage record to disappear. I won't be able to collect on my receipts."

Cully laughed. "Come on, Merlyn," he said. "You're just a two-bit bribe taker. The Feds don't come in here with a gang of auditors for you. They send a letter or subpoena. Which they will never even think of doing, by the way. Or look at it another way. If you spend the dough and they find out your income exceeded what you earned on your pay, you can say you won it gambling. They can't prove otherwise."

"And I can't prove I did," I said.

"Sure you can," Cully said. "I'll testify for you, and so will a pit boss and a stickman at the crap table. That you had a tremendous roll with the dice. So don't worry about the deal no matter how it falls. Your only problem is where to hide the casino cage receipts."

We both thought that over for a while. Then Cully came up with an answer. "Do you have a lawyer?" he asked.

"No," I said, "but my brother, Artie, has a friend who is a lawyer."

"Then make out your will," Cully said. "In your will you put in that you have cash deposits in this hotel to the amount of thirty-three thousand dollars and you leave it to your wife. No, never mind your brother's lawyer. We'll use a lawyer I know here in Vegas that we can trust. Then the lawyer will mail your copy of the will to Artie in a specially legally sealed envelope. Tell Artie not to open it. That way he won't know.

All you have to tell him is that he is not to open the envelope but hold it for you. The lawyer will send a letter to that effect also. There's no way Artie can get into trouble. And he won't know anything. You just dream up a story why you want him to have the will."

"Artie won't ask me for a story," I said. "He'll just do it and never ask a question."

"That's a good brother you got there," Cully said. "But now what do you do with the receipts? The Feds will sniff out a bank vault if you get one. Why don't you just bury it with your old manuscripts like you did the cash? Even if they get a search warrant, they'll never notice those pieces of paper."

"I can't take that chance," I said. "Let me worry about the receipts. What happens if I lose them?"

Cully didn't catch on or made believe he didn't. "We'll have records in our file," he said. "We just make you sign a receipt certifying that you lost your receipts when you get your money. You just have to sign when you get your cash."

Of course, he knew what I was going to do. That I would tear up the receipts but not tell him so he could never be sure, so that he couldn't mess with the records of the casino owing me money. It meant that I didn't completely trust him, but he accepted that easily.

Cully said, "I've got a big dinner laid on tonight for you with some friends. Two of the nicest-looking ladies in the show."

"No woman for me," I said.

Cully was amazed. "Jesus, aren't you tired of just screwing your wife yet? All these years."

"No," I said. "I'm not tired."

"You think you're going to be faithful to her all your life?" Cully said.

"Yep," I said, laughing.

Cully shook his head, laughing too. "Then you'll really be Merlyn the Magician."

"That's me," I said.

So we went to dinner, just the two of us. And then Cully came around with me to all the casinos in Vegas as I bought chips in thousand-dollar lots. My Vegas Winner sports jacket really came in handy. At the different casinos we had drinks with pit bosses and shift managers of the casinos and the girls from the shows. They all treated Cully like an important man, and they all had great stories to tell about Vegas. It was fun. When we got back to the Xanadu, I pushed my chips into the cashier's cage and got a receipt for fifteen thousand dollars. I tucked it into my wallet. I hadn't made a bet all night. Cully was hanging all over me.

"I have to do a little gambling," I said.

Cully smiled crookedly. "Sure you do, sure you do. As soon as you lose five hundred bucks, I'm going to break your fucking arm."

At the crap table I pulled out five one-hundred-dollar bills and changed them into chips. I made five-dollar bets and bet all the numbers. I won and lost. I drifted into my old gambling patterns, moving from craps to blackjack and roulette. Soft, easy, dreamy gambling, betting small, winning and losing, playing loose percentages. It was one in the morning when I reached into my pocket and took out two thousand dollars and bought chips. Cully didn't say anything.

I put the chips into my jacket pocket and walked over to cashier's cage and turned them in for another cash receipt. Cully was leaning against an empty crap table, watching me. He nodded his head approvingly.

"So you've got it licked," he said.

"Merlyn the Magician," I said. "Not one of your lousy degenerate gamblers." And it was true. I had felt none of the old excitement. There was no urge to take a flyer. I had enough money to buy my family a house and a bankroll for emergencies. I had good sources of income. I was happy again. I loved my wife and was working on a novel. Gambling was fun, that was all. I had lost only two hundred bucks the whole evening.

Cully took me into the coffee shop for a nightcap of milk and hamburgers. "I have to work during the day," he said. "Can I trust you not to gamble?"

"Don't worry," I said. "I'll be busy turning the cash into chips all over town. I'll go down to five-hundred-dollar buys so I won't be so noticeable."

"That's a good idea," Cully said. "This town has more FBI agents than dealers."

He paused for a moment. "You sure you don't want a sleeping partner? I have some beauties." He picked up one of the house phones on the ledge of our booth.

"I'm too tired," I said. And it was true. It was after one in the morning here in Vegas, but New York time was 4 A.M. and I was still on New York time.

"If you need anything, just come up to my office," he said. "Even if you just want to kill some time and bullshit."

"OK, I will," I said.

The next day I woke up about noon and called Vallie. There was no answer. It was 3 P.M. New York time and it was Saturday. Vallie had probably taken the kids to her father and mother's house out on Long Island. So I called there and got her father. He asked a few suspicious questions about what I was doing in Vegas. I explained I was researching an article. He didn't sound too convinced, and finally Vallie got on the phone. I told her I would catch the Monday plane home and would take a cab from the airport.

We had the usual husband and wife bullshit talk with such calls. I hated the phone. I told her I wouldn't call again since it was a waste of time and money, and she agreed. I knew she would be at her parents the next day too, and I didn't want to call her there. And I realized too that her going there made me angry. An infantile jealousy. Vallie and the kids were my family. They belonged to me; they were the only family I had except Artie. And I didn't want to share them with grandparents. I knew it was silly, but still, I wasn't going to call again. What the hell, it was only two days and she could always call me.

I spent the day going through all the casinos in town on the Strip and the sawdust joints in the center of town. There I traded my cash for chips in two- and three-hundred-dollar amounts. Again I'd do a little dollar-chip gambling before moving on to another casino.

I loved the dry, burning heat of Vegas, so I walked from casino to casino. I had a late-afternoon lunch in the Sands next to a table of pretty hookers having their before-going-to-work meal. They were young and pretty and high-spirited. A couple of them were in riding togs. They were laughing and telling stories like teenagers. They didn't pay any attention to me, and I ate my lunch as if I weren't paying any attention to them. But I tried to listen to their conversation. Once I thought I heard Cully's name mentioned.

I took a taxi back to the Xanadu. Vegas cabdrivers are friendly and helpful. This one asked me if I wanted some action, and I told him no. When I left the cab, he wished me a pleasant good day and told me the name of a restaurant where they had good Chinese food.

In the Xanadu casino I changed the other casino chips into a cash receipt, which I stuck into my wallet. I now had nine receipts and only a little over ten thousand in cash to convert. I emptied the cash out of my Vegas Winner sports jacket and put it into a regular suit jacket. It was all hundreds and fitted into two regular long white envelopes. Then I slung the Vegas Winner sports jacket over my arm and went up to Cully's office.

There was a whole wing of the hotel tacked on just for administration. I followed the corridor and took an offshoot corridor labeled "Executive Offices." I came to one of the shingles that read "Executive Assistant to the President." In the outer office was a very pretty young secretary. I gave her my name, and she buzzed the inner office and announced me. Cully came bouncing out with a big handshake and a hug. This new personality of his still threw me off. It was too demonstrative, too outgoing, not what we had been before.

He had a really stylish suite with couch and soft armchairs and low lighting and pictures on the wall, original oil paintings. I couldn't tell if they were any good. He also had three TV screens operating. One showed a corridor of the hotel. Another showed one of the crap tables in the casino in action. The third screen showed the baccarat table. As I watched the first screen, I could see a guy opening his hotel room door in the corridor and leading a young girl in with his hand on her ass.

"Better programs than I get in New York," I said.

Cully nodded. "I have to keep an eye on everything in this hotel," he said. He pushed buttons on a console on his desk, and the three pictures on the TV's changed. Now we saw a view of the hotel parking lot, a blackjack table in action and the cashier in the coffee shop ringing up money.

I threw the Vegas Winner sports jacket on Cully's desk. "You can have it now," I said.

Cully stared at the jacket for a long moment. Then he said absently, "You converted all your cash?"

"Most of it," I said. "I won't need the jacket anymore." I laughed. "My wife hated it as much as you do."

Cully picked up the jacket. "I don't hate it," he said.

"Gronevelt doesn't like to see it around. What do you think happened to Jordan's?"

I shrugged. "His wife probably gave all his clothes to the Salvation Army."

Cully was weighing the jacket in his hand. "Light," he said. "But lucky. Jordan won over four hundred grand wearing it. And then he kills himself. Fucking dumb bastard."

"Foolish," I said.

Cully put the jacket gently down on his desk. Then he sat down and rocked back on his chair. "You know, I thought you were crazy for turning down his twenty grand. And I was really pissed off when you talked me out of taking mine. But it was maybe the luckiest thing that ever happened to me. I would have gambled it away, and then I would have felt like shit. But you know, after Jordan killed himself and I didn't take that money, I got some pride. I don't know how to explain it. But I felt I didn't betray him. And you didn't. And Diane didn't. We were all strangers, and only the three of us cared something about Jordan. Not enough, I guess. Or it didn't mean that much to him. But finally it meant something to me. Didn't you feel that way?"

"No," I said. "I just didn't want his fucking money. I knew he was going to knock himself off."

That startled Cully. "Bullshit you did. Merlyn the Magician. Fuck you."

"Not consciously," I said. "But way down underneath. I wasn't surprised when you told me. Remember?"

"Yeah," Cully said. "You didn't even give a shit."

I passed that one. "How about Diane?"

"She took it real hard," Cully said. "She was in love with Jordan. You know I fucked her the day of the funeral. Weirdest fuck I ever had. She was crazy wild and crying and fucking. Scared the shit out of me."

He sighed. "She spent the next couple of months getting drunk and crying on my shoulder. And then she met this square semi-millionaire, and now she's a straight lady in Minnesota someplace."

"So what are you going to do with the jacket?" I asked him.

Suddenly Cully was grinning. "I'm going to give it to Gronevelt. Come on, I want you to meet him anyway." He got up out of his chair and grabbed the jacket and went out of the office. I followed him. We went down the corridor to another suite of offices. The secretary buzzed us in to Gronevelt's huge private office.

Gronevelt rose from his chair. He looked older than I remembered him. He must be in his late seventies, I thought. He was immaculately dressed. His white hair made him look like a movie star in some character part. Cully introduced us.

Gronevelt shook my hand and then said quietly, "I read your book. Keep it up. You'll be a big man someday. It's very good."

I was surprised. Gronevelt went way back in the gambling business, he had been a very bad guy at one time and he was still a feared man in Vegas. For some reason I never thought he was a man who read books. Another cliché shot.

I knew that Saturdays and Sundays were busy times for men like Gronevelt and Cully who ran big Vegas hotels like the Xanadu. They had customer friends from all over the United States who flew in for weekends of gambling and who had to be entertained in many diverse ways. So I thought I would just say hello to Gronevelt and beat it.

But Cully threw the bright red and blue Vegas Winner sports jacket on Gronevelt's huge desk and said, "This is the last one. Merlyn finally gave it up."

I noticed that Cully was grinning. The favorite nephew teasing the grouchy uncle he knew how to handle. And I noticed that Gronevelt played his role. The uncle who kidded around with his nephew who was the most trouble but in the long run the most talented and the most reliable. The nephew who would inherit.

Gronevelt rang the buzzer for his secretary, and when she came in, he said to her, "Bring me a big pair of scissors." I wondered where the hell a secretary for the president of the Xanadu Hotel would get a big pair of scissors at 6 P.M. on a Saturday night. She was back with them in two minutes flat. Gronevelt took the scissors and started cutting my Vegas Winner sports jacket. He looked at my deadpan and said, "You don't know how much I hated you three guys when you used to walk through my casino wearing these fucking jackets. Especially that night when Jordan won all the money."

I watched him turn my jacket into a huge pile of jagged pieces on his desk, and then I realized he was waiting for me to answer him. "You really don't mind winners, do you?" I said.

"It had nothing to do with winning money," Gronevelt said. "It was so goddamn pathetic. Cully here wearing that jacket and a degenerate gambler in his heart. He still is and always will be. He's in remission."

Cully made a gesture of protest, said, "I'm a businessman," but Gronevelt waved him off, and Cully fell silent, watching the cut patches of material on the desk.

"I can live with luck," Gronevelt said. "But skill and cunning I can't abide."

Gronevelt was working on the cheap fake silk lining of the coat, scissoring it into tiny strips, but it was just to keep his hands busy while he was talking. He spoke directly to me.

"And you, Merlyn, you're one of the worst fucking gamblers I have ever seen and I've been in the business over fifty years. You're worse than a degenerate gambler. You're a romantic gambler. You think you're one of those characters like that Ferber novel where she has the asshole gambler for a hero. You gamble like an idiot. Sometimes you go with percentages, sometimes you go with hunches, another time you go with a system, then you switch to stabbing in thin air, or you're zigging and zagging. Listen, you're one of the few people in this world I would tell to give up gambling completely." And then he put down his scissors and gave me a genuinely friendly smile. "But what the hell, it suits you."

I was really a little hurt, and he had seen it. I thought myself a clever gambler, mixing logic with magic. Gronevelt seemed to read my mind. "Merlyn," he said. "I like that name. It sort of suits you. From what I've read he wasn't that great a magician, and neither are you." He picked up the scissors and started cutting again. "But then why the hell did you pick that fight with that punk hit man?"

I shrugged. "I didn't really pick a fight. But you know how it is. I was feeling lousy about leaving my family. Everything was going bad. I was just looking to take it out on somebody."

"You picked the wrong guy," Gronevelt said. "Cully saved your ass. With a little help from me."

"Thanks," I said.

"I offered him the job, but he doesn't want it," Cully said.

That surprised me. Obviously Cully had talked it over with

Gronevelt before he offered me the job. And then suddenly I realized that Cully would have to tell Gronevelt all about me. And how the hotel would cover me if the Feds came looking.

"After I read your book, I thought we could use you as a PR man," Gronevelt said. "A good writer like you."

I didn't want to tell him that they were two absolutely different things. "My wife wouldn't leave New York, she has her family there," I said. "But thanks for the offer."

Gronevelt nodded. "The way you gamble maybe it's better not living in Vegas. The next time you come into town let's all have dinner together." We took that for our dismissal and left.

Cully had a dinner date with some high rollers from California that he couldn't break, so I was on my own. He had left a reservation for me for the hotel dinner show that night, so I went. It was the usual Vegas stuff with almost nude chorus girls, dancing acts, a star singer and some vaudeville turns. The only thing that impressed me was a trained bear act.

A beautiful woman came out on the stage with six huge bears, and she made them do all kinds of tricks. After each bear completed a trick, the woman kissed the bear on the mouth and the bear would immediately shamble back into his position at the end of the line. The bears were so furry they looked as completely asexual as toys. But why had the woman made the kiss one of her command signals? Bears didn't kiss as far as I knew. And then I realized the kiss was for the audience, some sort of thrust at the onlookers. And then I wondered if the woman had done so consciously, as a mark of her contempt, a subtle insult. I had always hated the circus and refused to take my kids to see it. And so I never really liked animal acts. But this one fascinated me enough to watch it through to the end. Maybe one of the bears would pull a surprise.

After the show was over, I wandered out into the casino to convert the rest of my money into chips and then convert the chips into cash receipts. It was nearly eleven at night.

I started with craps, and instead of betting small to hold down my losses, I was, all of a sudden, making fifty- and hundred-dollar bets. I was losing about three thousand dollars when Cully came up behind me, leading his high rollers to the table and establishing their credit. He took one sardonic look at my green twenty-five-dollar chips and my bets on the green felt in front of me. "You don't have to gamble anymore, huh?" he said to me. I felt like a jerk, and when the dice sevened out, I took the remainder of my chips to the cashier's cage and turned them into receipts. When I turned around, Cully was waiting for me.

"Let's go have a drink," he said. And he led me to the cocktail lounge where we used to booze with Jordan and Diane. From that darkened area we looked out at the brightly lit casino. When we sat down, the cocktail waitress spotted Cully and came over immediately.

"So you fell off the wagon," Cully said. "That fucking gambling. It's like malaria, always coming back."

"You too?" I asked.

"A couple of times," Cully said. "I never got hurt, though. How much did you lose?"

"Just about two grand," I said. "I've turned most of the money into receipts. I'll finish it up tonight."

"Tomorrow's Sunday," Cully said. "The lawyer friend of mine is available, so early in the morning you can make your will and have it mailed to your brother. Then I'm sticking to you like glue until I put you on the afternoon plane to New York."

"We tried something like that once with Jordan," I said jokingly.

Cully sighed. "Why did he do it? His luck was changing. He was going to be a winner. All he had to do was hang in there."

"Maybe he didn't want to push his luck," I said. I had to be kidding, Cully said.

The next morning Cully rang my room, and we had breakfast together. After that he drove me down the Vegas Strip to a lawyer's office, where I had my will drawn up and witnessed. I repeated a couple of times that my brother, Artie, was to be mailed a copy of the will, and Cully finally cut in impatiently. "That's all been explained," he said. "Don't worry. Everything will be done exactly right."

When we left the office, Cully drove me around the city and showed me the new construction going on. The tower building of the Sands Hotel gleamed newly golden in the desert air. "This town is going to grow and grow," Cully said.

The endless desert stretched out to the far outlying mountains. "It has plenty of room," I said.

Cully laughed, "You'll see," he said. "Gambling is the coming thing."

We had a light lunch, and then for old times' sake we went down to the Sands and went partners for two hundred bucks each and hit the crap tables. Cully said self-mockingly, "I have ten passes in my right arm," so I let him shoot the dice. He was as unlucky as ever, but I noticed he didn't have his heart in it. He didn't enjoy gambling. He sure had changed. We drove to the airport, and he waited with me at the gate until boarding time.

"Call me if you run into any trouble," Cully said. "And the next time you come here we'll have dinner with Gronevelt. He likes you and he's a good guy to have on your side."

I nodded. Then I took the cash receipts out of my pocket. The receipts good for thirty thousand dollars in the casino cage of the Xanadu Hotel. My expenses for the trip, gambling and air fare came to about the other three thousand. I handed the receipts to Cully.

"Keep these for me," I said. I had changed my mind.

Cully counted the white slips. There were twelve of them. He checked the amounts. "You trust me with your bankroll?" he asked. "Thirty grand is a big number."

"I have to trust somebody," I said. "And besides, I saw you turn down twenty grand from Jordan when you were flat on your ass."

"Only because you shamed me into it," Cully said. "OK, I'll take care of this. And if things get real hot, I can loan you cash out of my roll and use these as security. Just so you don't leave any traces."

"Thanks, Cully," I said. "Thanks for the hotel room and the meals and everything. And thanks for helping me out." I felt a real rush of affection for him. He was one of my few friends. And yet I was surprised when he hugged me goodbye before I got on the plane.

And on the jet rushing through the light into the darker time zones of the East, fleeing so quickly from the descending sun in the West, as we plunged into darkness, I thought about the affection Cully had for me. We knew each other so little. And I thought it was because we both had so few people we could really get to know. Like Jordan. And we had shared Jordan's defeat and surrender into death.

I called from the airport to tell Vallie I had come home a day early. There was no answer. I didn't want to call her at her father's house, so I just caught a taxi to the Bronx. Vallie still wasn't home. I felt the familiar irritated jealousy that she had taken the kids to visit their grandparents in Long Island. But then I thought, what the hell. Why should she spend the Sunday alone in our project apartment when she could have the company of her happy-go-lucky Irish family, her brothers and sisters and their friends, where the kids could go out and play in fresh air and on country grass?

I would wait up for her. She had to be home soon. While I waited, I called Artie. His wife came to the phone and said Artie had gone to bed early because he wasn't feeling good. I told her not to wake him, it wasn't important. And with a little feeling of panic I asked what was wrong with Artie. She said he just felt tired, he had been working too hard. It wasn't anything even to see the doctor about. I told her I would call Artie at work the next day, and then I hung up.

Chapter 15

The next year was the happiest time in my life. I was waiting for my house to be built. It would be the first time I'd own a house of my own, and I had a funny feeling about it. That now finally I would be just like everybody else. I would be separate and no longer dependent on society and other people.

I think this sprang from my growing distaste for the housing project I was living in. By their very good social qualities blacks and whites moved up in the economic scale and became ineligible to stay in the housing project when they earned too much money. And when they moved out, their places were taken by the not-so-well-adjusted. The blacks and whites moving in were the ones who would live there forever. Junkies, alcoholics, amateur pimps, small-scale thieves and spur-of-the-moment rapists.

Before this new invasion the housing project cops beat a strategic retreat. The new kids were wilder and started taking everything apart. Elevators stopped working; hall windows were smashed and never repaired. When I came home from work, there were empty whiskey bottles in the hallways and some of the men sitting drunk on the benches outside the buildings. There were wild parties that brought in the regular city cops. Vallie made sure she picked up the kids at the bus stop when they came home from school. She even asked me once if we should move to her father's house until our own house was ready. This was after a ten-year-old black girl had been raped and thrown off the roof of one of the project buildings.

I said no, we'd sweat it out. We would stay. I knew what Vallie was thinking, but she was too ashamed to say it out loud. She was afraid of the blacks. Because she had been educated and conditioned as a liberal, a believer in equality, she couldn't bring herself to accept the fact that she feared all the black people moving in around her.

I had a different point of view. I was realistic, I thought, not a bigot. What was happening was that the city of New York was turning its housing projects into black slums, establishing new ghettos, isolating the blacks from the rest of the white community. In effect using projects as a *cordon sanitaire*. Tiny Harlems white-washed with urban liberalism. And all the economic dregs of the white working class were being segregated here, the ones too badly educated to earn a living, too maladjusted to keep the family structure together. Those people with a little something on the ball would run for their lives to the suburbs or private homes or commercial apartments in the city. But the balance of power hadn't shifted yet. The whites still outnumbered the blacks two to one. The socially oriented families, black and white, still had a slim majority. I figured the housing project was safe at least for the twelve months we would have to stay there. I really didn't give a shit about anything else. I had, I guess, a contempt for all those people. They were like animals, without free will, content to live from one day to the other with booze and drugs fucking just to kill time whenever they could find it. It was becoming another fucking orphan asylum. But then how come I was still there? What was I?

A young black woman with four kids lived on our floor. She was solidly built, sexy-looking, full of vibrant good humor and high spirits. Her husband had left her before she moved into the project, and I had never seen him. The woman was a good mother during the day; the kids were always neat, always sent off to school and met by the bus stop. But the mother was not so much on the ball at night. After supper we could see her all dressed up, going out on a date, while the kids were left home alone. Her oldest kid was only ten. Vallie used to shake her head and I told her it was none of her business.

But one night, late, when we were in bed, we heard the scream of fire engines. And we could smell smoke in our apartment. Our bedroom window looked directly across to the black woman's apartment, and like a tableau in a movie, we could see flames dancing in that apartment and the small children running through it. Vallie jumped up in her nightgown, tore a blanket off the bed and ran out of our apartment door. I followed her. We were just in time to see the other apartment door open down the long hallway and four children come running out. Behind them we could see flames in the apartment. Vallie was running down the hallway after them, and I wondered what the hell she was doing. She was running frantically, a blanket in her hand trailing the floor. Then I saw what she had seen. The biggest girl, coming out last, shooing the younger ones before her, had begun to fall. Her back was on fire. Then she was a torch of dark red flame. She fell. As she writhed on the cement floor in agony, Vallie jumped on her and wrapped her in the blanket. Dirty gray smoke rose above them as firemen poured into the hallway with hoses and axes.

The firemen took over, and Vallie was back with me in the apartment. Ambulances were clanging up onto the internal walks of the project. Then suddenly we saw the mother in the apartment opposite us. She was smashing at the glass with her hands and screaming aloud. Blood poured over her finery. I didn't know what the hell she was doing, and then realized that she was trying to impale herself on the glass fragments. Firemen came up behind her, out of the smoke billowing from the dead flames, the charred furniture. They dragged her away from the window, and then we saw her strapped down on a stretcher being carried into the ambulance.

Again these low-income housing projects, built with no thought for profit, had been so made that the fire could not spread or the smoke become a hazard too quickly to other tenants. Just the one apartment was burned out. The little girl who was on fire would, they said, recover, though severely burned. The mother was already out of the hospital.

Saturday afternoon, a week later, Vallie took the kids to her father's house so that I could work on my book in peace. I was working pretty well when there was a knock at the apartment door. It was a timid knock I could barely hear from where I was working on the kitchen table.

When I opened the door, there was this skinny, creamy chocolate black guy. He had a thin mustache and straightened hair. He murmured his name and I didn't catch it, but I nodded. Then he said, "I just wanted to thank you and your wife for what you did for my baby." And I understood that he was the father of the family down the hall, the one that had had the fire.

I asked him if he wanted to come in for a drink. I could see that he was almost close to tears, humiliated and ashamed to be making his thanks. I told him my wife was away, but I would tell her he had come by. He stepped just inside my door, to show that he wouldn't insult me by refusing to come into my house, but he wouldn't take a drink.

I tried my best, but it must have shown that I really hated him. That I had hated him ever since the night of the fire. He was one of the black guys who left their wives and children on welfare to go out and have a good time, to live their own lives. I had read the literature on the broken homes of black families in New York. And how the organization and torments of society made these men leave their wives and children. I understood it intellectually, but emotionally I reacted against it. Who the fuck were they to live their own lives? I wasn't leading my own life.

But then I saw that tears were streaming down that milk chocolate skin. And I noticed he had long eyelashes over soft brown eyes. And then I could hear his words. "Oh, man," he said. "My little girl died this morning. She died in that hospital." He started to fall away and I caught him and he said, "She was supposed to get better, the burns weren't that bad, but she just died anyway. I came to visit her and everybody in that hospital looked at me. You know? I was her father? Where was I? What was I doing? Like they blame me. You know?"

Vallie kept a bottle of rye in the living room for her father and brothers when they came to visit. Neither Vallie nor I drank usually. But I didn't know where the hell she kept the bottle.

"Wait a minute," I said to the man crying before me. "You need a drink." I found the bottle in the kitchen closet and got two glasses. We both drank it straight, and I could see he felt better, he composed himself.

And watching him, I realized that he had not come to give his thanks to the would-be saviors of his daughter. He had come to find someone to pour out his grief and his guilt. So I listened and wondered that he had not seen my judgment of him on my face.

He emptied his glass and I poured him more whiskey. He slumped back on the sofa tiredly. "You know, I never wanted to leave my wife and kids. But she was too lively and too strong. I worked hard. I work two jobs and save my money. I want to buy us a house and bring up my children right. But she wants fun, she wants a good time. She's too strong and I had to leave. I tried to see my kids more, she won't let me. If I give her extra money, she spends it on herself and not on the kids. And then, you know, we got further and further apart and I found a woman who liked to live the way I live and I become a stranger to my own children. And now everybody will blame me because my little girl died. Like I'm one of those flying dudes, who leave their old ladies just to follow their nose."

"Your wife is the one that left them alone," I said.

The man sighed. "Can't blame her. She go crazy if she stay home every night. And she didn't have the money for a baby-sitter. I could have put up with her or I could have killed her, one or the other."

I couldn't say anything, but I watched him and he watched me. I saw his humiliation at telling all this to a stranger and a white stranger. And then I realized that I was the only person to whom he could show his shame. Because I didn't really count and because Vallie had smothered the flames burning his daughter.

"She nearly killed herself that night," I said.

He burst into tears again. "Oh," he said. "She loves her kids. Leaving them alone don't mean nothing. She loves them all. And she ain't ever going to forgive herself, that's what I'm afraid of. That woman is going to drink herself to death, she's going down, man. I don't know what to do for her."

There was nothing I could say to this. In the back of my head I was thinking, a day's work wasted, I'd never even get to go over my notes. But I offered him something to eat. He finished up his whiskey and rose to go. Again that look of shame and humiliation in his face as he thanked me and my wife once again for what we had done for his daughter. And then he left.

When Vallie came home with the kids that night, I told her what had happened, and she went into the bedroom and wept while I made supper for the kids. And I thought of how I had condemned the man before I ever met him or knew anything about him. How I had just put him in a slot whittled out by the books I had read, the drunks and dopers who had come to live in the project with us. I thought of him fleeing from his own people into another world not so poor and black, escaping the doomed circle he had been born in. And left his daughter to die by fire. He would never forgive himself, his judgment far harsher than that I in my ignorance had condemned him with.

Then a week later a lovey-dovey couple across the mall got into a fight and he cut her throat. They were white. She had a lover on the side who refused to stay on the side. But it wasn't fatal, and the errant wife looked dramatically romantic in her huge white neck bandages when she took her little kids to the school bus.

I knew we were getting out at the right time.

Chapter 16

At the Army Reserve office in the armory the bribe business was booming. And for the first time in my Civil Service career I received an "Excellent" rating. Because of my bribe rackets, I had studied all the complicated new regulations, and was finally an efficient clerk, the top expert in the field.

Because of this special knowledge, I had devised a shuttle system for my clients. When they finished their six months' active duty and came back to my Reserve unit for meetings and two weeks summer camp, I vanished them. I devised a perfectly legal system for them to beat it. In effect I could offer them a deal where after they did their six months' active duty, they became names on the Army Reserve inactive rosters to be called up only in case of war. No more weekly meetings, no more yearly summer camps. My price went up. Another plus: When I got rid of them, it opened up a valuable slot.

One morning I opened the *Daily News,* and there on the front page was a big photograph of three young men. Two of them were guys I had just enlisted the day before. Two hundred bucks each. My heart gave a big jump and I felt a little sick. What could it be but an exposé of the whole racket? The caper had blown up. I made myself read the caption. The guy in the middle was the son of the biggest politician in the state of New York. And the caption applauded the patriotic enlistment of the politician's son in the Army Reserve. That was all.

Still, that newspaper photo frightened me. I had visions of going to jail and Vallie and the kids being left alone. Of course, I knew her father and mother would take care of them, but I wouldn't be there. I'd lose my family. But then, when I got to the office and told Frank, he laughed and thought it was great. Two of my paying customers on page one of the *Daily News*. Just great. He cut out the photograph and put it on the bulletin board of his Army Reserve unit. It was a great inside joke for us. The major thought it was up on the board to boost unit morale.

That phony scare threw me off guard in a way. Like Frank, I started to believe that the racket could go on forever. And it might have, except for the Berlin crisis, which made President Kennedy decide to call up hundreds of thousands of Reserve troops. Which proved to be very unlucky.

The armory became a madhouse when the news came out that our Reserve units were being called into the Army for a year's active duty. The draft dodgers who had connived and paid to get into the six months' program went crazy. They were enraged. What hurt the worst was that here they were, the shrewdest young men in the country, budding lawyers, successful Wall Street operators, advertising geniuses, and they had been outwitted by that dumbest of all creatures, the United States Army. They had been bamboozled with the six months' program, tricked, conned, sold, never paying attention to the one little catch. That they could be called up to active duty and be back in the Army again. City slickers being taken by the hicks. I wasn't too pleased by it either, though I congratulated myself for never having become a member of the Reserves for the easy money. Still, my racket was shot to hell. No more tax-free income of a thousand dollars a month. And I was to move into my new house on Long Island very soon. But still, I never realized that this would bring on the catastrophe I had long foreseen. I was too busy processing the enormous paperwork involved to get my units officially on active duty.

There were supplies and uniforms to be requisitioned, all kinds of training orders to be issued. And then there was the wild stampede to get out of the one-year recall. Everybody knew the Army had regulations for hardship cases. Those that had been in the Reserve program for the last three or four years and had nearly finished their enlistment were especially stunned. During those years their careers had prospered, they had gotten married, they made kids. They had the military lords of America beat. And then it all became an illusion.

But remember, these were the sharpest kids in America, the future business giants, judges, show business whizbangs.

They didn't take it lying down. One young guy, a partner in his father's seat on the Wall Street Exchange, had his wife committed to a psychiatric clinic, then put in papers for a hardship discharge on the grounds that his wife had had a nervous breakdown. I forwarded the documents complete with official letters from doctors and the hospital. It didn't work. Washington had received thousands of cases and taken a stand that nobody would get out on hardship. A letter came back saying the poor husband would be recalled to active duty and then the Red Cross would investigate his hardship claim. The Red Cross must have done a good job because a month afterward, when the guy's unit was shipped to Fort Lee, Virginia, the wife with the nervous breakdown came into my office to apply for necessary papers to join him down at camp. She was cheerful and obviously in good health. In such good health that she hadn't been able to go along with the charade and stay in the hospital. Or maybe the doctors wouldn't go that far out on a limb to keep the deception going.

Mr. Hiller called me up about his son, Jeremy. I told him there was nothing I could do. He pressed me and pressed me, and I said jokingly that if his son was a homosexual, he might be discharged from the Army Reserve and not called to active duty. There was a long pause at the other end of the phone, and then he thanked me and hung up. Sure enough, two days later Jeremy Hiller came and filed the necessary papers to get out of the Army on grounds he was a homosexual. I told him that it would always be on his record. That sometime later in life he might regret having such an official record. I could see that he was reluctant, and then he finally said, "My father says it's better than being killed in a war."

I sent the papers through. They were returned from Governors Island, First Army HQ. After Pfc. Hiller was recalled, his case would be evaluated by a Regular Army board. Another strikeout.

I was surprised that Eli Hemsi had not given me a call. The clothing manufacturer's son, Paul, had not even shown his face at the armory since the recall to active duty notices had been sent out. But that mystery was solved when I received papers through the mail from a doctor famous for his book publications on psychiatry. These documents certified that Paul Hemsi had received electric shock treatments for a nervous condition over the past three months and could not be recalled to active duty, it would be disastrous to his health. I looked up the pertinent Army regulation. Sure enough, Mr. Hemsi had found a way out of the Army. He must have been getting advice from people higher up than me. I forwarded the papers on to Governors Island. Sure enough, they finally came back. And with them special orders discharging Paul Hemsi from the United States Army Reserve. I wondered what that deal had cost Mr. Hemsi.

I tried to help everybody who put in for a hardship discharge. I made sure the documents got down to Governors Island HQ and made special calls to check up on them. In other words, I was as cooperative as I could be to all my clients. But Frank Alcore was the opposite.

Frank had been recalled with his unit to active duty. And he felt it a point of honor to go. He made no effort to get a hardship discharge, though with his wife and kids and his old parents he had a good case. And he had very little sympathy for anybody in his units trying to get out of the one-year recall. As chief administrative officer of his battalion, both as a civilian and the battalion sergeant major, he sat on all the requests for hardship discharge. He made it as tough as he could for all of them. None of his men beat the recall to active duty, not even those who had legitimate grounds. And a lot of those guys he sat on were guys who had paid him top dollar to buy their enlistment in the six months' program. By the time Frank and his units left the armory and shipped to Fort Lee there was a lot of bad blood.

I got kidded about not having been caught in the Army Reserve program, that I must have known something. But with that kidding there was respect. I had been the only guy in the armory not to have been sucked in by the easy money and the absence of danger. I was sort of proud of myself. I had really thought it all out years ago. The monetary rewards were not enough to make up for the small percentage of danger involved. The odds were a thousand to one against being called to active duty, but I had still resisted. Or maybe I could see into the future. The irony was that a lot of WW II soldiers had been caught in the trap. And they couldn't believe it. Here they were, guys who had fought three or four years in the old war and now back in green fatigues. True, most of the old-timers would never see combat or be in danger, but still, they were pissed off. It didn't seem fair. Only Frank Alcore didn't seem to mind. "I took the gravy," he said. "Now I have to pay for it." He smiled at me. "Merlyn, I always thought you were a dummy, but you look pretty smart right now."

At the end of the month, when everybody shipped out, I bought Frank a present. It was a wristwatch with all kinds of shit on it to show compass directions and time of day. Absolutely shockproof. It cost me two hundred bucks, but I really liked Frank. And I guess I felt a little guilty because he was going and I wasn't. He was touched by the gift and gave me an affectionate half hug. "You can always hock it when your luck is running bad," I said. And we both laughed.

For the next two months the armory was strangely empty and quiet. Half the units had gone on active duty in the re-call program. The six months' program was dead; didn't look like such a good deal anymore. I was out of business, as far as my racket was concerned. There was nothing to do, so I worked on my novel at the office. The major was out a lot, and so was the Regular Army sergeant. And with Frank on active duty I was in the office all alone most of the time. On one of these days a young guy came in and sat at my desk. I asked him what I could do for him. He asked me if I remembered him. I did, vaguely, and then he said his name, Murray Nadelson. "You took care of me as a favor. My wife had cancer."

And then I remembered the scene. It had happened almost two years ago. One of my happy clients had arranged for me to meet with Murray Nadelson. The three of us had lunch together. The client was a sharpshooting Wasp Wall Street bro-ker named Buddy Stove. A very soft-selling supersalesman. And he had told me the problem. Murray Nadelson's wife had cancer. Her treatment was expensive, and Murray couldn't afford to pay his way into the Army Reserve. Also, he was scared to death of getting inducted for two years and being shipped overseas. I asked why he didn't apply for a hardship deferment based on his wife's health. He had tried that, and it had been refused.

That didn't sound right, but I let it pass. Buddy Stove ex-plained that one of the big attractions of the six months' ac-tive-duty program was that the duty would be done in the States and Murray Nadelson could have his wife come down to live outside whatever training base he would be shipped to. After his six months they also wanted the deal where he would be transferred to the control group so that he wouldn't have to come to meetings. He really had to be with his wife as much as possible.

I nodded my head. OK, I could do it. Then Buddy Stove threw the curveball. He wanted all of it done for free. No charge. His friend Murray couldn't spend a penny.

Meanwhile, Murray couldn't look me in the eye. He kept his head down. I figured it was a hustle except that I couldn't imagine anybody laying that hex on his wife, saying that she had cancer, just to get out of paying some money. And then I had a vision. What if this whole thing blew up someday and the papers printed that I made a guy whose wife had cancer pay a bribe to take care of him? I would look like the worst villain in the world, even to myself. So I said, sure, OK, and said something to Murray about I hoped his wife would be OK. And that ended the lunch.

I had been just a little pissed off. I had made it a policy of enlisting anybody in the six months' program who said he couldn't afford the money. That had happened a good many times. I charged it off to goodwill. But the transfer to a control group and beating five and a half years of Reserve duty was a special deal that was worth a lot of money. This was the first time I had been asked to give that away free. Buddy Stove himself had paid five hundred bucks for that particular favor, plus his two hundred for being enlisted.

Anyway, I had everything necessary done smoothly and efficiently. Murray Nadelson served his six months; then I vanished him into the control group, where he would be just a name on a roster. Now what the hell was Murray Nadelson doing at my desk? I shook his hand and waited.

"I got a call from Buddy Stove," Murray said. "He was recalled from the control group. They need his MOS in one of the units that went on active duty."

"Tough luck for Buddy," I said. My voice wasn't too sympathetic. I didn't want him to get the idea I was going to help.

But Murrary Nadelson was looking me right in the eyes as if he were getting up the nerve to say something he found hard to say. So I leaned back in my chair and tilted it back and said, "I can't do anything for him."

Nadelson shook his head determinedly. "He knows that."

He paused a moment. "You know I never thanked you properly for all the things you did for me. You were the only one who helped. I wanted to tell you that just one time. I'll never forget what you did for me. That's why I'm here. Maybe I can help you."

Now I was embarrassed. I didn't want him offering me money at this late date. What was done was done. And I liked the idea of having some good deeds on the records I kept on myself.

"Forget it," I said. I was still wary. I didn't want to ask how his wife was doing, I never had believed that story. And I felt uncomfortable, his being so grateful for my sympathy when it had been all public relations.

"Buddy told me to come see you," Nadelson said. "He wanted to warn you that there are FBI men all over Fort Lee questioning the guys in your units. You know, about paying to get in. They ask questions about you and about Frank Alcore. And your friend Alcore looks like he's in big trouble. About twenty of the men have given evidence that they paid him off. Buddy says there will be a grand jury in New York to indict him in a couple of months. He doesn't know about you. He wanted me to warn you to be careful about anything you say or do. And that if you need a lawyer, he'll get one for you."

For a moment I couldn't even see him. The world had literally gone dark. I felt so sick that a wave of nausea almost made me throw up. My chair came forward. I had frantic visions of the disgrace, my being arrested, Vallie horrified, her father angry, my brother Artie's shame and disappointment in me. It was no longer a happy lark, my revenge against society. But Nadelson was waiting for me to say something.

"Jesus Christ," I said. "How did they get on to it? There hasn't been any action since the recall. What put them on the track?"

Nadelson looked a little guilty for his fellow bribe givers. "Some of them were so pissed off about getting recalled they wrote anonymous letters to the FBI about paying money to enlist in the six months' program. They wanted to get Alcore into trouble, they blamed him. Some of them were pissed off because he fought them when they tried to beat the recall.

And then down in camp he's a very gung-ho sergeant major, and they don't like that. So they wanted to get him into trouble, and they did."

My mind was racing. It was nearly a year since I had seen Cully in Vegas and stashed my money. Meanwhile, I had accumulated another fifteen thousand dollars. Also, I was due to move into my new house in Long Island very soon. Everything was breaking at the worst possible time. And if the FBI were talking to everybody down at Fort Lee, they would at least be talking to over a hundred guys I had taken money from. How many of them would admit to paying me off?

"Is Stove sure there's going to be a grand jury on Frank?" I asked Nadelson.

"There has to be," Murray said. "Unless the government covers the whole thing up, you know, kicks it under the rug."

"Any chance of that?" I asked.

Murray Nadelson shook his head. "No. But Buddy seems to think you may beat it. All the guys you had dealings with think you're a good guy. You never pushed for money, like Alcore did. Nobody wants to get you in trouble, and Buddy is spreading the word down there not to get you involved."

"Thank him for me," I said.

Nadelson stood up and shook my hand. "I just want to thank you again," he said. "If you should need a character witness to testify for you, or you want to refer the FBI to me, I'll be waiting and do my best."

I shook his hand. I really felt grateful. "Is there anything I can do for you?" I said. "Any chance of your being called up from the control group?"

"No," Nadelson said. "I have a baby son, you remember. And my wife died two months ago. So I'm safe."

I'll never forget his face when he said this. The voice itself was filled with bitter self-loathing. And his face had on it a look of shame and hatred. He blamed himself for being alive. And yet there was nothing he could do except follow the course that life had laid out for him. To take care of his baby son, to go to work in the morning, to obey the request of a friend and come here to warn me and to speak a thanks to me for something I had done for him which he had felt important to him at the time and which really meant nothing to him now. I said I was sorry about his wife, I was a believer now all right, he was the real McCoy all right. I felt like shit for ever thinking that about him. And maybe he had saved that for the last because years ago, when he had kept his head down as Buddy Stove begged for him, he must have known that I thought they were both lying. It was a tiny revenge, and he was very welcome to it.

I spent a jittery week before the ax finally fell. It was on a Monday, and I was surprised when the major came into the office bright and early, for him, on a Monday. He gave me a funny look as he went on into his private office.

Punctually at ten two men walked in and asked for the major. I knew who they were right away. They were almost exactly according to literature and movies; dressed conservatively in suits and ties, wearing deadly Waspish fedoras. The older one was about forty-five with a craggy face that was calmly bored. The other one was just a little out of sync. He was much younger, and he had the tall, stringy physique of a nonathlete. Underneath his padded conservative suit was a very skinny frame. His face was just a little callow but handsome in a very good-natured way. I showed them into the major's office. They were with him for about thirty minutes; then they came out and stood in front of my desk. The older one asked formally, "Are you John Merlyn?"

"Yes," I said.

"Could we talk to you in a private room? We have your officer's permission."

I got up and led them into one of the rooms that served as a Reserve unit HQ on meeting nights. Both of them immediately flipped open their wallets to show green ID cards. The older one introduced himself. "I'm James Wallace of the Federal Bureau of Investigation. This is Tom Hannon."

The guy named Hannon gave me a friendly smile. "We want to ask you a few questions. But you don't have to answer them without consulting a lawyer. But if you do answer us, anything you say can be used against you. OK?"

"OK," I said. I sat down at one end of the table, and they sat down, one on each side of the table so that I was sandwiched.

The older one, Wallace, asked, "Do you have any idea why we're here?"

"No," I said. I had made up my mind that I wouldn't volunteer even one word, that I wouldn't make any wisecracks.

That I wouldn't put on any act. They would know I had an idea of why they were here, but so what?

Hannon said, "Do you of your own personal knowledge have any information you can give about Frank Alcore taking bribes from reservists for any reason whatsoever?"

"No," I said. There was no expression on my face. I had made up my mind not to be an actor. No starts of surprise, no smiles, nothing that could spur additional questions or attacks. Let them think I was covering for a friend. That would be normal even if I were not guilty.

Hannon said, "Have you ever taken money from any reservist for any reason whatsoever?"

"No," I said.

Wallace said very slowly, very deliberately, "You know all about this. You enlisted young men subject to the draft only when they paid you certain sums of money to do so. You know that you and Frank Alcore manipulated those lists. If you deny this, you are lying to a federal officer, and that is a crime. Now I ask you again, have you ever taken money or any other inducement to favor the enlistment of one individual over the other?"

"No," I said.

Hannon laughed suddenly. "We have your buddy Frank Alcore nailed. We have testimony that you two were partners. And that maybe you were in league with other civilian administrators or even officers in this building to solicit bribes. If you talk to us and tell us all you know, it could be a lot better for you."

There hadn't been any question, so I just looked at him and didn't answer.

Suddenly Wallace said in his calm, even voice, "We know you're the kingpin of this operation." And then for the first time I broke my rules. I laughed. It was so natural a laugh that they couldn't take offense. In fact, I saw Hannon smile a little.

The reason I laughed was the word "kingpin." For the first time the whole thing struck me as something right out of a grade B movie. And I laughed because I had expected Hannon to say something like that, he looked callow enough. I had thought Wallace was the dangerous man, maybe because he was obviously in charge.

And I laughed because now I knew they were so obviously

on the wrong track. They were looking for a really sophisticated conspiracy, an organized "ring" with a "mastermind." Otherwise it wouldn't be worth the time of these heavy hitters from the FBI. They didn't know it was just a bunch of small-time clerks hustling to make an extra buck. They forgot and didn't understand that this was New York, where everybody broke a law every day in one form or another. They couldn't conceive of the notion that *everybody* would have the nerve to be crooked on his own. But I didn't want them to get pissed off about my laughing, so I looked Wallace right in the eye. "I wish I were a kingpin of something," I said ruefully, "instead of a lousy clerk."

Wallace looked at me intently and then said to Hannon, "Do you have any more?" Hannon shook his head. Wallace stood up. "Thank you for answering our questions." At the same moment Hannon stood up, and so did I. For a moment we were all there standing close together, and without even thinking about it I stuck out my hand and Wallace shook it. I did the same thing with Hannon. And then we walked out of the room together and down the hall to my office. They nodded good-bye to me as they kept on going to the stairs that would lead them downstairs and out of the building, and I went into my office.

I was absolutely cool, not nervous. Not even a little bit. I wondered about my offering to shake hands. I think it was that act that broke the tension in me. But why did I do it? I think it was out of some sort of gratitude, that they hadn't tried to humiliate me or browbeat me. That they had kept the questioning within civilized limits. And I recognized that they had a certain pity for me. I was obviously guilty but on such a small scale. A poor lousy clerk hustling a few extra bucks. Sure, they would have put me in jail if they could, but their hearts hadn't been in it. Or maybe it was just too small potatoes for them to exert themselves. Or maybe they couldn't help laughing at the crime itself. Guys paying to get *into* the Army. And then I laughed. Forty-five grand wasn't a few lousy bucks. I was letting self-pity carry me away.

As soon as I got back into my office, the major appeared in the doorway of the inner office and motioned me in to join him. The major had all his decorations on his uniform. He had fought in WW II and Korea, and there were at least twenty ribbons on his chest.

"How did you make out?" he asked. He was smiling a little.

I shrugged. "OK, I guess."

The major shook his head in wonderment. "They told me it's been going on for years. How the hell did you guys do it?" He shook his head in admiration.

"I think it's bullshit," I said. "I never saw Frank take a dime off anybody. Just some guys pissed off about being recalled to active duty."

"Yeah," the major said. "But down at Fort Lee they're cutting orders to fly about a hundred of those guys to New York to testify before a grand jury. That's not bullshit." He gazed at me smilingly for a moment. "What outfit were you in against the Germans?"

"Fourth Armored," I said.

"You've got a Bronze Star on your record," the major said. "Not much but something." He had the Silver Star and Purple Heart among the ribbons on his chest.

"No, it wasn't," I said. "I evacuated French civilians under shellfire. I don't think I ever killed a German."

The major nodded. "Not much," he agreed. "But it's more than those kids ever did. So if I can help, let me know. OK?"

"Thanks," I said.

And as I got up to go, the major said angrily almost to himself, "Those two bastards started to ask me questions, and I told them to go fuck themselves. They thought I might be in on that shit." He shook his head. "OK," he said, "just watch your ass."

Being an amateur criminal really doesn't pay. I started reacting to things like a murderer in a film showing the tortures of psychological guilt. Every time the doorbell to my apartment rang at an unusual time my heart really jumped. I thought it was the cops or the FBI. And of course, it was just one of the neighbors, one of Vallie's friends, dropping by to chat or borrow something. At the office the FBI agents dropped by a couple of times a week, usually with some young guy that they were obviously identifying me to. I figured it was some reservist who had paid his way into the six months' program. One time Hannon came in to chat, and I went downstairs to a luncheonette to get coffee and sandwiches for us and the major. As we sat around chatting, Hannon said to me in the nicest way imaginable, "You're a good guy, Merlyn, I really hate the idea of sending you to jail. But you know, I've sent a lot of nice guys to jail. I always think what a shame. If they'd just helped themselves a little bit."

The major leaned back in his chair to watch my reaction. I just shrugged and ate my sandwich. My attitude was that it was pointless to give any answer to such remarks. It would lead to a general discussion about the whole bribe business. In any general discussion I might say something that in some way could help the investigation. So I said nothing. I asked the major if I could have a couple of days off to help my wife with the Christmas shopping. There was not really that much work and we had a new civilian in the office to replace Frank Alcore and he could mind the store while I was out. The major said sure. Also, Hannon had been dumb. His remark about sending a lot of nice guys to jail was dumb. He was too young to have sent a lot of nice guys or bad guys to jail. I had him tabbed for a rookie, a nice rookie, but not the guy that was going to send me to jail. And if he did, I would be his first one.

We chatted a bit and Hannon left. The major was looking at me with a new respect. And then he said, "Even if they can't pin anything on you, I suggest you look for a new job."

Christmas was always a big thing with Vallie. She loved shopping for presents for her mother and father and the kids and me and her brothers and sisters. And this particular Christmas she had more money to spend than she had ever had before. The two boys had bicycles waiting for them in their closet. She had a great imported Irish wool buttoned sweater for her father and an equally expensive Irish lace shawl for her mother. I don't know what she had for me. She always kept that a secret. And I had to keep my present a secret from her. My present for her had been no problem. I had bought, for cash, a small diamond ring, the first piece of real jewelry I'd ever given her. I'd never given her an engagement ring. In those long ago years neither one of us believed in that kind of bourgeois nonsense. After ten years she had changed, and I didn't really give a damn one way or the other. I knew it would make her happy.

So on Christmas Eve the kids helped her decorate the tree while I did some work in the kitchen. Valerie still had no idea of the trouble I was in at my job. I wrote some pages on my novel and then went in to admire the tree. It was all silver with red and blue and golden bells gilded over with rough silvery braiding. On the top was a luminous star. Vallie never used electric lights. She hated them on a Christmas tree.

The kids were all excited, and it took us a long time to get them to bed and stay there. They kept sneaking out, and we didn't dare get tough with them, not Christmas Eve. Finally they wore out and fell asleep. I gave them a final check. They had on their fresh pajamas for Santa Claus, and they had all been bathed and their hair brushed. They looked so beautiful that I couldn't believe they were my kids, that they belonged to me. At that moment I really loved Vallie. I felt that I was really lucky.

I went back into the living room. Vallie was stacking gaily wrapped Christmas packages bright with Christmas seals beneath the tree. There seemed to be an enormous number of them. I went and got my package for her and put it under the tree.

"I couldn't get you much," I said slyly. "Only one little present." I knew she would never suspect that she was getting a real diamond ring.

She smiled at me and gave me a kiss. She never cared really what she got for Christmas, she loved buying presents for others, for the kids especially and then for me and her family. Her father and mother and brothers and sisters. The kids got four or five presents. And there was one super-duper bicycle that I was sorry she had bought. It was a two-wheeled bike for my oldest son, and I was sorry because I would have to put it together. And I didn't have the faintest idea how.

Vallie opened a bottle of wine and made some sandwiches. I opened the huge carton that held the different parts of the bicycle. I spread everything out over the living-room floor, plus three sheets of printed instructions and diagrams. I took one look and said, "I give up."

"Don't be silly," Vallie said. She sat down cross-legged on the floor, sipping wine and studying the diagrams. Then she started to work. I was the idiot helper. I went and got the screwdriver and the wrench and held the necessary parts so that she could screw them together. It was nearly three o'clock in the morning before we finally got the damn thing whole. By that time we had finished the wine and we were nervous wrecks. And we knew the kids would spring out of bed as soon as they woke up. We'd get only about four hours' sleep. And then we would have to drive to Vallie's parents' house for a long day of celebration and excitement.

"We'd better get to bed," I said.

Vallie spread out on the floor. "I think I'll just sleep here," she said.

I lay down beside her, and then we both rolled over on our sides so that we could hug each other tight. We lay there blissfully tired and content. At that moment there was a loud knock on the door. Vallie got up quickly, a look of surprise on her face, and glanced at me questioningly.

In a fraction of a second my guilty mind built a whole scenario. It was, of course, the FBI. They had deliberately waited until Christmas Eve, until I was psychologically off guard. They were here with a search-and-arrest warrant. They would find the fifteen thousand dollars I had hidden in the house and take me away to jail. They would offer to let me spend Christmas with my wife and kids if I confessed. Otherwise I would be humiliated: Vallie would hate me for getting arrested on Christmas. The kids would cry, they would be traumatized forever.

I must have looked sick because Vallie said to me, "What's wrong?" Again there was a loud knocking on the door. Vallie went out of the living room and down the hall to answer it. I could hear her talking to someone, and I went out to take my medicine. She was coming back down the hall and turning into the kitchen. In her arms were four bottles of milk.

"It was the milkman," she said. "He delivered early so that he could get back to his family before his kids woke up. He saw the lights under our door, so he knocked to wish us a Merry Christmas. He's a nice man." She went into the kitchen.

I followed her in and sat weakly in one of the chairs. Vallie sat on my lap. "I'll bet you thought it was some crazy neighbor or crook," she said. "You always think the worst will happen." She kissed me fondly. "Let's go to bed." She gave me a more lingering kiss and so we went to bed. We made love and then she whispered, "I love you." "Me too," I said. And then I smiled in the darkness. I was easily the most chickenshit petty thief in the Western world.

But three days after Christmas a strange man came into my office and asked me if my name was John Merlyn. When I said yes, he handed me a folded letter. As I opened it he walked out. The letter had printed in Old English heavy letters:

UNITED STATES DISTRICT COURT

then in plain capital printing:

SOUTHERN DISTRICT OF NEW YORK

Then in block lines my name and address and off to the far end in capital letters: "GREETING:"

Then it read: "WE COMMAND YOU, that all singular business and excuses being laid aside, you and each of you appear and attend before the GRAND INQUEST of the body of the people of the United States of America"—and went on to give times and place and concluded "alleged violation Title 18, U. S. Code." It went on to say that if I didn't appear, I would be in contempt of court and liable to penalties of the law.

Well, at least now I knew what law I had broken. Title 18, U.S. Code. I'd never heard of it. I read it over again. I was fascinated by the first sentence. As a writer I loved the way it read. They must have taken it from the old English law. And it was funny how clear and concise lawyers could be when they wanted to be, no room for misunderstanding. I read that sentence over again: "WE COMMAND YOU, that all singular business and excuses being laid aside, you and each of you appear and attend before the GRAND INQUEST of the body of the people of the United States of America."

It was great. Shakespeare could have written it. And now that it had finally happened I was surprised that I felt a sort of elation, an urgency to get it over with, win or lose. At the end of the working day I called Las Vegas and got Cully in his office. I told him what had happened and that in a week I would appear before a grand jury. He told me to sit tight, not to worry. He would be flying in to New York the next day and he would call my house from his hotel in New York.

Book IV

Chapter 17

In the four years since Jordan's death, Cully had made himself Gronevelt's right-hand man. No longer a countdown artist, except in his heart, he seldom gambled. People called him by his real name, Cully Cross. His telephone page code was Xanadu Two. And most important of all, Cully now had "The Pencil," that most coveted of Las Vegas powers. With the scribbling of his initials he could bestow free rooms, free food and free liquor to his favored customers and friends. He did not have unrestricted use of "The Pencil," a royal right reserved for hotel owners and the more powerful casino managers, but that too would come.

Cully had taken Merlyn's call on the casino floor, in the blackjack pit, where table number three was under suspicion. He promised Merlyn he would come to New York and help him. Then he went back to watching table three.

The table had been losing money every day for the last three weeks. By Gronevelt's percentage law this was impossible; there must be a scam. Cully had spied from the Eye in the Sky, rerun the videotapes monitoring the table, watched in person, but still couldn't figure out what was happening. And he didn't want to report it to Gronevelt until he had solved the problem. He felt the table was having a run of bad luck, but he knew Gronevelt would never accept that explanation. Gronevelt believed that the house could not lose over the long run, that the laws of percentage were not subject to chance. As gamblers believe mystically in their luck so Gronevelt believed in percentages. His tables could never lose.

After taking Merlyn's call, Cully went by table three again. Expert in all the scams, he made a final decision that the percentages had simply gone crazy. He would give a full report to Gronevelt and let him make the decision on whether to switch the dealers around or fire them.

Cully left the huge casino and took the staircase by the coffee shop to the second floor that led to the executive suites. He checked his own office for messages and then went on to Gronevelt's office. Gronevelt had gone to his living suite in the hotel. Cully called and was told to come down.

He always marveled at how Gronevelt had set himself up a home right there in the Xanadu Hotel. On the second floor was an enormous corner suite, but to get to it, you had to be buzzed into a huge outside terrace that had a swimming pool and a lawn of bright green artificial grass, a green so bright you knew it could never last for more than a week in the Vegas desert sun. There was another huge door into the suite itself, and again you had to be buzzed in.

Gronevelt was alone. He had on white flannels and an open shirt. The man looked amazingly healthy and youthful for his over seventy years. Gronevelt had been reading. His book lay opened on the velvet tan couch.

Gronevelt motioned Cully toward the bar and Cully made himself a scotch and soda and the same for Gronevelt. They sat facing each other.

"That losing table in the blackjack pit is straight," Cully said. "At least as far as I can see."

"Not possible," Gronevelt said. "You've learned a lot in the last four years, but the one thing you refuse to accept is the law of percentages. It's not possible for that table to lose that amount of money over a three-week period without something fishy going on."

Cully shrugged. "So what do I do?"

Gronevelt said calmly, "I'll give the order to the casino manager to fire the dealers. He wants to shift them to another table and see what happens. I know what will happen. It's better to fire them just like that."

"OK," Cully said. "You're the boss." He took a sip from his drink. "You remember my friend Merlyn, the guy who writes books?"

Gronevelt nodded. "Nice kid," he said.

Cully put down his glass. He really didn't like booze, but Gronevelt hated to drink alone. He said, "That chickenshit caper he's involved in blew up. He needs my help. I have to fly into New York next week to see our collection people, so

I thought I'd just go earlier and leave tomorrow if that's OK with you."

"Sure," Gronevelt said. "If there's anything I can do, let me know. He's a good writer." He said this as if he had to have an excuse to help. Then he added, "We can always give him a job out here."

"Thanks," Cully said. "Before you fire those dealers, give me one more shot. If you say it's a scam, then it is. It just pisses me off that I can't figure it out."

Gronevelt laughed. "OK," he said. "If I were your age, I'd be curious too. Tell you what, get the videotapes sent down here and we'll watch them together and go over a few things. Then you can catch the plane for New York tomorrow with a fresh mind. OK? Just have the tapes sent down for the night shifts, covering eight P.M. to two A.M. so we cover the busy times after the shows break."

"Why do you figure those times?" Cully asked.

"Has to be," Gronevelt said. When Cully picked up the phone, Gronevelt said, "Call room service and order us something to eat."

As the two of them ate, they watched the video films of the losing table. Cully couldn't enjoy his meal, he was so intent on the film. But Gronevelt hardly seemed to be glancing at the console screen. He ate calmly and slowly, relishing the half bottle of red wine that came with his steak. The film suddenly stopped as Gronevelt pushed the off button on his console panel.

"You didn't see it?" Gronevelt asked.

"No," Cully said.

"I'll give you a hint," Gronevelt said. "The pit boss is clean. But not the floorwalker. One dealer on that table is clean, but the other two are not. It all happens after the dinner show breaks. Another thing. The crooked dealers give a lot of five-dollar reds for change or payoffs. A lot of times when they could give twenty-five-dollar chips. Do you see it now?"

Cully shook his head. "Paint would show."

Gronevelt leaned back and finally lit one of his huge Havana cigars. He was allowed one a day and always smoked it after dinner when he could. "You didn't see it because it was so simple," he said.

Gronevelt made a call down to the casino manager. Then

he flicked the video switch on to show the suspected black-jack table in action. On the screen Cully could see the casino manager come behind the dealer. The casino manager was flanked by two security men in plain clothes, not armed guards.

On the screen the casino manager dipped his hand into the dealer's money trays and took out a stack of red five-dollar chips. Gronevelt flicked off the screen.

Ten minutes later the casino manager came into the suite. He threw a stack of five-dollar chips on Gronevelt's desk. To Cully's surprise the stack of chips did not fall apart.

"You were right," the casino manager said to Gronevelt.

Cully picked up the round red cylinder. It looked like a stack of five-dollar chips, but it was actually a five-dollar-chip-size cylinder with a hollow case. In the bottom the base moved inward on springs. Cully fooled around with the base and took it off with the scissors Gronevelt handed him. The red hollow cylinder, which looked like a stack of ten five-dol-lar red chips, disgorged five one-hundred-dollar black chips.

"You see how it works," Gronevelt said. "A buddy comes into the game and hands over this five stack and gets change. The dealer puts it in a rack in front of the hundreds, presses it, and the bottom gobbles up the hundreds. A little later he makes change to the same guy and dumps out five hundred dollars. Twice a night, a thousand bucks a day tax-free. They get rich in the dark!"

"Jesus," Cully said. "I'll never keep up with these guys."

"Don't worry about it," Gronevelt said. "Go to New York and help your buddy and get our business finished there. You'll be delivering some money, so come see me about an hour before you catch the plane. And then when you get back here, I have some good news for you. You're finally go-ing to get a little piece of the action, meet some important people."

Cully laughed. "I couldn't solve that little scam at black-jack and I get promoted?"

"Sure," Gronevelt said. "You just need a little more experi-ence and a harder heart."

Chapter 18

On the night plane to New York Cully sat in the first class section, sipping a plain club soda. On his lap was a metal briefcase covered with leather and equipped with a complicated locking device. As long as Cully held the briefcase, nothing could happen to the million dollars inside it. He himself could not open it.

In Vegas Gronevelt had counted the money out in Cully's presence, stacking the case neatly before he locked it and handed it over to Cully. The people in New York never knew how or when it was coming. Only Gronevelt decided. But still, Cully was nervous. Clutching the briefcase beside him, he thought about the last years. He had come a long way, he had learned a lot and he would go further and learn more. But he knew that he was leading a dangerous life, gambling for big stakes.

Why had Gronevelt chosen him? What had Gronevelt seen? What did he foresee? Cully Cross, metal briefcase clutched to his lap, tried to divine his fate. As he had counted down the cards in the blackjack shoe, as he had waited for the strength to flow in his strong right arm to throw countless passes with the dice, he now used all his powers of memory and intuition to read what each chance in his life added up to and what could be left in the shoe.

Nearly four years ago, Gronevelt started to make Cully into his right-hand man. Cully had already been his spy in the Xanadu Hotel long before Merlyn and Jordan arrived and had performed his job well. Gronevelt was a little disappointed in him when he became friends with Merlyn and Jordan. And angry when Cully took Jordan's side in the now-famous baccarat table showdown. Cully had thought his career finished, but oddly enough, after that incident, Gronevelt gave him a real job. Cully often wondered about that.

For the first year Gronevelt made Cully a blackjack dealer, which seemed a hell of a way to begin a career as a right-hand man. Cully suspected that he would be used as a spy all over again. But Gronevelt had a more specific purpose in mind. He had chosen Cully as the prime mover in the hotel skimming operation.

Gronevelt felt that hotel owners who skimmed money in the casino counting room were jerks, that the FBI would catch up with them sooner or later. The counting room skimming was too obvious. The owners or their reps meeting there in person and each taking a packet of money before they reported to the Nevada Gaming Commission struck him as foolhardy. Especially when there were five or six owners quarreling about how much they should skim off the top. Gronevelt had set up what he thought was a far superior system. Or so he told Cully.

He knew Cully was a "mechanic." Not a top-notch mechanic but one who could easily deal seconds. That is, Cully could keep the top card for himself and deal the second card from the top. And so an hour before his midnight-to-morning graveyard shift Cully would report to Gronevelt's suite and receive instructions. At a certain time, either 1 A.M. or 4 A.M. a blackjack player dressed in a certain colored suit would make a certain number of sequence bets starting with one hundred dollars, then five hundred, then a twenty-five-dollar bet. This would identify the privileged customer, who would win ten or twenty thousand dollars in a few hours' gambling. The man would play with his cards face up, not unusual for big players in blackjack. Seeing the player's hand, Cully could save a good card for the customer by dealing seconds around the table. Cully didn't know how the money finally got back to Gronevelt and his partners. He just did his job without asking questions. And he never opened his mouth.

But as he could count down every card in the shoe, he easily kept track of these manufactured player winnings, and over the year he figured that he had on the average lost ten thousand dollars a week to these Gronevelt players. Over the year he worked as a dealer he knew close to the exact figure. It was around a half million dollars, give or take a ten grand. A beautiful scam without a tax bite and without cutting it up with the official point sharers in the hotel and the casino. Gronevelt was also skimming some of his partners.

To keep the losses from being pinpointed, Gronevelt had Cully transferred to different tables each night. He also sometimes switched his shifts. Still, Cully worried about the casino manager's picking up the whole deal. Except that maybe Gronevelt had warned the casino manager off.

So to cover his losses Cully used his mechanic's skill to wipe out the straight players. He did this for three weeks and then one day he received a phone call summoning him to Gronevelt's suite.

As usual Gronevelt made him sit down and gave him a drink. Then he said, "Cully, cut out the bullshit. No cheating the customers."

Cully said, "I thought maybe that's what you wanted, without telling me."

Gronevelt smiled. "A good smart thought. But it's not necessary. Your losses are covered with paperwork. You won't be spotted. And if you are, I'll call off the dogs." He paused for a moment. "Just deal a straight game with the suckers. Then we won't get into any trouble we can't handle."

"Is the second card business showing up on films?" Cully asked.

Gronevelt shook his head. "No, you're pretty good. That's not the problem. But the Nevada Gaming Commission boys might send in a player that can hear the tick and link it up with your sweeping the table. Now true, that could happen when you're dealing to one of my customers, but then they would just assume you're cheating the hotel. So I'm clean. Also I have a pretty good idea when the Gaming Commission sends in their people. That's why I give you special times to dump out the money. But when you're operating on your own, I can't protect you. And then you're cheating the customer for the hotel. A big difference. Those Gaming Commission guys don't get too hot when *we* get beat, but the straight suckers are another story. It would cost a lot in political payoffs to set that straight."

"OK," Cully said. "But how did you pick it up?"

Gronevelt said impatiently, "Percentages. Percentages never lie. We built all these hotels on percentages. We stay rich on the percentage. So all of a sudden your dealer sheet shows you making money when you're dumping out for me.

That can't happen unless you're the luckiest dealer in the history of Vegas."

Cully followed orders, but he wondered about how it all worked. Why Gronevelt went to all the trouble. It was only later, when he had become Xanadu Two that he found out the details. That Gronevelt had been skimming not only to beat the government but most of the point owners of the casino. It was only years later he learned that the winning customers had been sent out of New York by Gronevelt's secret partner, a man named Santadio. That the customers thought that he, Cully, was a crooked dealer fixed by the partner in New York. That these customers thought they were victimizing Gronevelt. That Gronevelt and his beloved hotel were covered a dozen different ways.

Gronevelt had started his gambling career in Steubenville, Ohio, under the protection of the famous Cleveland mob with their control over local politics. He had worked the illegal joints and then finally made his way to Nevada. But he had a provincial patriotism. Every young man in Steubenville who wanted a dealing or croupier job in Vegas came to Gronevelt. If he couldn't place him in his own casino, he would place him in some other casino. You could run across Steubenville, Ohio, alumni in the Bahamas, Puerto Rico, on the French Riviera and even in London. In Reno and Vegas you could count them by the hundreds. Many of them were casino managers and pit bosses. Gronevelt was a green felt Pied Piper.

Gronevelt could have picked his spy from these hundreds; in fact, the casino manager at the Xanadu was from Steubenville. Then why had Gronevelt picked on Cully, a comparative stranger from another part of the country? Cully often wondered about that. And of course, later on, when he came to know the intricacies of the many controls, he understood that the casino manager had to be in on it. And it hit Cully full force. He had been picked because he was expendable if anything went wrong. He would take the rap one way or another.

For Gronevelt, despite his bookishness, had come out of Cleveland into Vegas with a fearsome reputation. He was a man not to be trifled with, cheated or bamboozled. And he had demonstrated that to Cully in the last years. Once in a serious way and another time with high good humor, a special kind of Vegas gambling wit.

After a year Cully was given the office next to Gronevelt and named his special assistant. This involved driving Gronevelt around town and accompanying him to the floor of the casino at night when Gronevelt made his rounds to greet old friends and customers, especially those from out of town. Gronevelt also made Cully an aide to the casino manager so that he could learn the casino ropes. Cully got to know all the shift bosses, the pit bosses, the floorwalkers, the dealers and croupiers in all the pits.

Every morning Cully had breakfast at about ten o'clock in Gronevelt's office suite. Before going up, he would get the win-loss figures for the casino's previous twenty-four hours of play from the cashier cage boss. He would give Gronevelt the little slip of paper as they sat down to breakfast, and Gronevelt would study the figures as he scooped out his first chunk of Crenshaw melon. The slip was made out very simply.

Dice Pit	$400,000 Drop	Hold	$60,000
Blackjack Pit	$200,000 Drop	Hold	$40,000
Baccarat			
Roulette	$100,000 Drop	Hold	$40,000
Others (wheel of fortune, keno included in above)			

The slot machines were totaled up only once a week, and those figures were given to Gronevelt by the casino manager in a special report. The slots usually brought in a profit of about a hundred thousand dollars a week. This was the real gravy. The casino could never get unlucky on slots. It was sure money because the machines were set to pay off only a certain percentage of the money played into them. When the figures on the slots went off there could only be a scam going.

This was not true of the other games, like craps, blackjack and especially baccarat. In those games the house figured to hold sixteen percent of the drop. But even the house could get unlucky. Especially in baccarat, where the heavy gamblers sometimes plunged and caught a lucky streak.

Baccarat had wild fluctuations. There had been nights when the baccarat table lost enough money to wipe out the profits from all the other action in the casino that day. But then there would be weeks when the baccarat table won enormous amounts. Cully was sure that Gronevelt had a skim going on the baccarat table, but he couldn't figure out how it worked. Then he noticed one night when the baccarat table cleaned out heavy players from South America that the next day's figures on the slip were less than they should be.

It was every casino's nightmare that the players would get a hot streak. In Las Vegas history there had been times when crap tables had gotten hot for weeks and the casino was lucky to break even for the day. Sometimes even the black-jack players got smart and beat the house for three or four days running. In roulette it was extremely rare to have even one losing day a month. And the wheel of fortune and keno were straight bust-out operations, the players sitting ducks for the casino.

But these were all the mechanical things to know about running a gambling casino. Things you could learn by the book, that anyone could learn, given the right training and sufficient time. Under Gronevelt, Cully learned a good deal more.

Gronevelt made everybody know he did not believe in luck. That his true and infallible god was the percentage. And he backed it up. Whenever the casino keno game was hit for the big prize of twenty-five thousand dollars, Gronevelt fired all the personnel in the keno operation. Two years after the Xanadu Hotel had begun operating, it got very unlucky. For three weeks the casino never had a winning day and lost nearly a million dollars. Gronevelt fired everybody except the casino manager from Steubenville.

And it seemed to work. After the firings the profits would begin, the losing streak would end. The casino had to average fifty grand a day in winnings for the hotel to break even. And to Cully's knowledge the Xanadu had never had a losing year. Even with Gronevelt skimming off the top.

In the year he had been dealing and skimming for Grone-velt Cully had never been tempted into the error another man might make in his position: skimming on his own. After all, if it was so easy, why could not Cully have a friend of his drop around to win a few bucks? But Cully knew this would be fatal. And he was playing for bigger stakes. He sensed a loneliness in Gronevelt, a need for friendship, which Cully provided. And it paid off.

About twice a month Gronevelt took Cully into Los Ange-les with him to go antique hunting. They would buy old gold watches, gilt-framed photographs of early Los Angeles and

Vegas. They would search out old coffee grinders, ancient toy automobiles, children's savings banks shaped as locomotives and church steeples made in the 1800's, a gold set archaic money clip, into which Gronevelt would put a hundred-dollar black chip *casa* money for the recipient, or a rare coin. For special high rollers he picked up tiny exquisite dolls made in ancient China, Victorian jewel boxes filled with antique jewelry. Old lace scarves silky gray with age, ancient Nordic ale mugs.

These items would cost at least a hundred dollars each but rarely more than two hundred dollars. On these trips Gronevelt spent a few thousand dollars. He and Cully would have dinner in Los Angeles, and sleep over in the Beverly Hills Hotel and fly back to Vegas on an early-morning plane.

Cully would carry the antiques in his suitcase and back in the Xanadu would have them gift-wrapped and delivered to Gronevelt's suite. And Gronevelt every night or nearly every night would slip one in his pocket and take it down to the casino and present it to one of his Texas oil or New York garment center high rollers who were good for fifty or a hundred grand a year at the tables.

Cully marveled at Gronevelt's charm on these occasions. Gronevelt would unwrap the gift package and take out the gold watch and present it to the player. "I was in LA and saw this and I thought about you," he'd say to the player. "Suits your personality. I've had it fixed up and cleaned, should keep perfect time." Then he would add deprecatingly, "They told me it was made in 1870, but who the hell knows? You know what hustlers those antique shops are."

And so he gave the impression that he had given extraordinary care and thought to this one player. He insinuated the idea that the watch was extremely valuable. And that he had taken extra pains to put it in good working condition. And there was a grain of truth in it all. The watch would work perfectly, he had thought about the player to an extraordinary degree. More than anything else was the feeling of personal friendship. Gronevelt had a gift for exuding affection when he presented one of these tokens of his esteem which made it even more flattering.

And Gronevelt used "The Pencil" liberally. Big players were, of course, comped, RFB—free room, food and beverage. But Gronevelt also granted this privilege to five-dollar chip bettors who were wealthy. He was a master at turning these customers into big players.

Another lesson Gronevelt taught Cully was not to hustle young girls. Gronevelt had been indignant. He had lectured Cully severely. "Where the fuck do you come off bullshitting those kids out of a piece of ass? Are you a fucking sneak thief? Would you go into their purses and snatch their small change? What kind of guy are you? Would you steal their car? Would you go into their house as a guest and lift their silverware? Then where do you come off stealing their cunt? That's their only capital, especially when they're beautiful. And remember once you slip them that Honeybee, you're evened out with them. You're free. No bullshit about a relationship. No bullshit about marriage or divorcing your wife. No asking for thousand-dollar loans. Or being faithful. And remember for five of those Honeybees, she'll always be available, even on her wedding day."

Cully had been amused by this outburst. Obviously Gronevelt had heard about his operation with women, but just as obviously Gronevelt didn't understand women as well as he, Cully, did. Gronevelt didn't understand their masochism. Their willingness, their *need* to believe in a con job. But he didn't protest. He did say wryly, "It's not as easy as you make it out to be, even your way. With some of them a thousand Honeybees don't help."

And surprisingly Gronevelt laughed and agreed. He even told a funny story about himself. Early in the Xanadu Hotel history a Texas woman worth many millions had gambled in the casino and he had presented her with an antique Japanese fan that cost him fifty dollars. The Texas heiress, a good-looking woman of forty and a widow, fell in love with him. Gronevelt was horrified. Though he was ten years older than she, he liked pretty young girls. But out of duty to the hotel bankroll he had taken her up to the hotel suite one night and went to bed with her. When she left, out of habit and perhaps out of foolish perversity or perhaps with the cruel Vegas sense of fun, he slipped her a Honeybee and told her to buy herself a present. To this day he didn't know why.

The oil heiress had looked down at the Honeybee and slipped it into her purse. She thanked him prettily. She continued to come to the hotel and gamble, but she was no longer in love with him.

Three years later Gronevelt was looking for investors to
build additional rooms to the hotel. As Gronevelt explained,
extra rooms were always desirable. "Players gamble where
they shit," he said. "They don't go wandering around. Give
them a show room, a lounge show, different restaurants. Keep
them in the hotel the first forty-eight hours. By then they're
banged out."

He had approached the oil heiress. She had nodded and
said of course. She immediately wrote out a check and
handed it to him with an extraordinarily sweet smile. The
check was for a hundred dollars.

"The moral of that story," Gronevelt said, "is never treat a
smart rich broad like a dumb poor cunt."

Sometimes in LA Gronevelt would go shopping for old
books. But usually, when he was in the mood, he would fly to
Chicago to attend a rare books auction. He had a fine collection stored in a locked glass-paneled bookcase in his suite.
When Cully moved into his new office, he found a present
from Gronevelt: a first edition of a book on gambling published in 1847. Cully read it with interest and kept it on his
desk for a while. Then, not knowing what to do with it, he
brought it into Gronevelt's suite and gave it back to him. "I
appreciate the gift, but it's wasted on me," he said. Gronevelt
nodded and didn't say anything. Cully felt that he had disappointed him, but in a curious way it helped cement their relationship. A few days later he saw the book in Gronevelt's
special locked case. He knew then that he had not made a
mistake, and he felt pleased that Gronevelt had tendered him
such a genuine mark of affection, however misguided. But
then he saw another side of Gronevelt that he had always
known must exist.

Cully had made it a habit to be present when the casino
chips were counted three times a day. He accompanied the
pit bosses as they counted the chips on all the tables, blackjack, roulette, craps, and the cash at baccarat. He even went
into the casino cage to count the chips there. The cage manager was always a little nervous to Cully's eyes, but he dismissed this as his own suspicious nature because the cash and
markers and chips in the safe always tallied correctly. And
the casino cage manager was an old trusted member of
Gronevelt's early days.

But one day, on some impulse, Cully decided to have the trays of chips pulled out of the safe. He could never figure out this impulse later. But once the scores of metal racks had been taken out of the darkness of the safe and closely inspected it became obvious that two trays of the black hundred-dollar chips were false. They were blank black cylinders. In the darkness of the safe, thrust far in the back where they would never be used, they had been passed as legitimate on the daily counts. The casino cage manager professed horror and shock, but they both knew that the scam could never have been attempted without his consent. Cully picked up a phone and called Gronevelt's suite. Gronevelt immediately came down to the cage and inspected the chips. The two trays amounted to a hundred thousand dollars. Gronevelt pointed a finger at the cage manager. It was a dreadful moment. Gronevelt's ruddy, tanned face was white, but his voice was composed. "Get the fuck out of this cage," he said. Then he turned to Cully. "Make him sign over all his keys to you," he said. "And then have all the pit bosses on all three of the shifts in my office right away. I don't give a fuck where they are. The ones who are on vacation fly back to Vegas and check in with me as soon as they get here." Then Gronevelt walked out of the cage and disappeared.

As Cully and the casino cage manager were doing the paperwork for signing over the keys, two men Cully had never seen before came in. The casino cage manager knew them because he turned very pale and his hands started shaking uncontrollably.

Both men nodded to him and he nodded back. One of the men said, "When you're through, the boss wants to see you up in his office." They were talking to the cage manager and ignored Cully. Cully picked up the phone and called Gronevelt's office. He said to Gronevelt. "Two guys came down here, they say you sent them."

Gronevelt's voice was like ice. "That's right," he said.

"Just checking," Cully said.

Gronevelt's voice softened. "Good idea," he said. "And you did a good job." There was a slight pause. "The rest of it is none of your business, Cully. Forget about it. Understand?" His voice was almost gentle now, and there was even a note of weary sadness in it.

The cage manager was seen for the next few days around

Las Vegas and then disappeared. After a month Cully learned that his wife had put in a missing persons report on him. He couldn't believe the implication at first, despite the jokes he heard around town that the cage manager was now buried in the desert. He never dared mention anything to Gronevelt, and Gronevelt never spoke of the matter to him. Not even to compliment him upon his good work. Which was just as well. Cully didn't want to think that his good work might have resulted in the cage manager's being buried in the desert.

But in the last few months Gronevelt had shown his mettle in a less macabre way. With typical Vegas nimbleness of foot and quick-wittedness.

All the casino owners in Vegas had started making a big pitch for foreign gamblers. The English were immediately written off, despite their history of being the biggest losers of the nineteenth century. The end of the British Empire had meant the end of their high rollers. The millions of Indians, Australians, South Sea Islanders and Canadians no longer poured money into the coffers of the gambling milords. England was now a poor country, whose very rich scrambled to beat taxes and hold on to their estates. Those few who could afford to gamble preferred the aristocratic high-toned clubs in France and Germany and their own London.

The French were also written off. The French didn't travel and would never stand for the extra house double zero on the Vegas wheel.

But the Germans and Italians were wooed. Germany with its expanding postwar economy had many millionaires, and Germans loved to travel, loved to gamble and loved the Vegas women. There was something in the high-flying Vegas style that appealed to the Teutonic spirit, that brought back memories of *Oktoberfest* and maybe even *Götterdämmerung*. The Germans were also good-natured gamblers and more skillful than most.

Italian millionaires were big prizes in Vegas. They gambled recklessly while getting drunk; they let the soft hustlers employed by casinos keep them in the city a suicidal six or seven days. They seemed to have inexhaustible sums of money because none of them paid income tax. What should have gone into the public coffers of Rome slid into the hold boxes of air-conditioned casinos. The girls of Vegas loved the Italian millionaires because of their generous gifts and because for those six or seven days they fell in love with the same abandon they plunged on the sucker hard-way bets at the crap table.

The Mexican and South American gamblers were even bigger prizes. Nobody knew what was really going on down in South America, but special planes were sent there to bring the pampas millionaires to Vegas. Everything was free to these sporting gentlemen who left the hides of millions of cattle at the baccarat tables. They came with their wives and girlfriends, their adolescent sons eager to become gambling men. These customers too were favorites of the Las Vegas girls. They were less sincere than the Italians, perhaps a little less polished in their lovemaking according to some reports, but certainly with larger appetites. Cully had been in Gronevelt's office one day when the casino manager came with a special problem. A South American gambler, a premier player, had put in a request for eight girls to be sent to his suite, blondes, redheads but no brunettes and none shorter than his own five feet six inches.

Gronevelt took the request coolly. "And what time today does he want this miracle to happen?" Gronevelt asked.

"About five o'clock," the casino manager said. "He wants to take them all to dinner afterward and keep them for the night."

Gronevelt didn't crack a smile. "What will it cost?"

"About three grand," the casino manager said. "The girls know they'll get roulette and baccarat money from this guy."

"OK, comp it," Gronevelt said. "But tell those girls to keep him in the hotel as much as possible. I don't want him losing his dough down the Strip."

As the casino manager started to leave, Gronevelt said, "What the hell is he going to do with eight women?"

The casino manager shrugged. "I asked him the same thing. He says he has his son with him."

For the first time in the conversation, Gronevelt smiled. "That's what I call real paternal pride," he said. Then, after the casino manager left the room, he shook his head and said to Cully, "Remember, they gamble where they shit *and* where they fuck. When the father dies, the son will keep coming here. For three grand he'll have a night he'll never forget.

He'll be worth a million bucks to the Xanadu unless they have a revolution in his country."

But the prize, the champions, the pearl without price that every casino owner coveted were the Japanese. They were hair-raising gamblers, and they always arrived in Vegas in groups. The top echelon of an industrial combine would arrive to gamble tax-free dollars, and their losses in a four-day stay many times went over a million dollars. And it was Cully who snared the biggest Japanese prize for the Xanadu Hotel and Gronevelt.

Cully had been carrying on a friendly go-to-the-movies-and-fuck-afterward love affair with a dancer in the Oriental Follies playing a Strip hotel. The girl was called Daisy because her Japanese name was unpronounceable, and she was only about twenty years old, but she had been in Vegas for nearly five years. She was a terrific dancer, cute as a pearl in its shell, but she was thinking about getting operations to make her eyes Occidental and her bust puffed to corn-fed American. Cully was horrified and told her she would ruin her appeal. Daisy finally listened to his advice only when he pretended an ecstasy greater than he felt for her budlike breasts.

They became such friends that she gave him lessons in Japanese while they were in bed and he stayed overnight. In the mornings she would serve him soup for breakfast, and when he protested, she told him that in Japan everyone ate soup for breakfast and that she made the best breakfast soup in her village outside Tokyo. Cully was astonished to find the soup delicious and tangy and easy on the stomach after a fatiguing night of drinking and making love.

It was Daisy who alerted him to the fact that one of the great business tycoons of Japan was planning to visit Vegas. Daisy had Japanese newspapers airmailed to her by her family; she was homesick and enjoyed reading about Japan. She told Cully that a Tokyo tycoon, a Mr. Fummiro, had given an interview stating that he would come to America to open up overseas branches of his television manufacturing business. Daisy said that Mr. Fummiro was famous in Japan for being an outrageous gambler and would surely come to Vegas. She also told him that Mr. Fummiro was a pianist of great skill, had studied in Europe and would almost certainly have become a professional musician if his father had not ordered his son to take over the family firm.

That day Cully had Daisy come over to his office at the Xanadu and dictated a letter for her to write on the hotel stationery. With Daisy's advice he constructed a letter that observed the, to Occidentals, subtle *politesse* of Japan and would not give Mr. Fummiro offense.

In the letter he invited Mr. Fummiro to be an honored guest at the Xanadu Hotel for as long as he wished and at any time he wished. He also invited Mr. Fummiro to bring as many guests as he desired, his whole entourage, including his business colleagues in the United States. In delicate language Daisy let Mr. Fummiro know that all this would not cost him one cent. That even the theater shows would be free. Before he mailed the letter, Cully got Gronevelt's approval since Cully still did not have the full authority of "The Pencil." Cully had been afraid that Gronevelt would sign the letter, but this did not happen. So now officially these Japanese were Cully's clients, if they came. He would be their "Host."

It was three weeks before he received an answer. And during that time Cully put in some more time studying with Daisy. He learned that he must always smile while talking to a Japanese client. That he always had to show the utmost courtesy in voice and gesture. She told him that when a slight hiss came into the speech of a Japanese man, it was a sign of anger, a danger signal. Like the rattle of a snake. Cully remembered that hiss in the speech of Japanese villains in WW II movies. He had thought it was just the mannerisms of the actor.

When the answer to the letter came, it was in the form of a phone call from Mr. Fummiro's overseas branch office in Los Angeles. Could the Xanadu Hotel have two suites ready for Mr. Fummiro, the president of Japan Worldwide Sales Company and his executive vice-president, Mr. Niigeta? Plus another ten rooms for other members of Mr. Fummiro's entourage? The call had been routed to Cully since he had been specifically asked for, and he answered yes. Then, wild with joy, he immediately called Daisy, and told her he would take her shopping in the next few days. He told her he would get Mr. Fummiro ten suites to make all the members of his entourage comfortable. She told him not to do so. That it would make Mr. Fummiro lose face if the rest of his party had equal accommodations. Then Cully asked Daisy to go out that very day and fly to Los Angeles to buy kimonos that Mr. Fummiro could wear in the privacy of his suite. She told him that this too would offend Mr. Fummiro, who prided himself on being Westernized, though he surely wore the comfortable Japanese traditional garments in the privacy of his own home. Cully, desperately seeking for every angle to get an edge, suggested that Daisy meet Mr. Fummiro and perhaps act as his interpreter and dinner companion. Daisy laughed and said that would be the last thing Mr. Fummiro would want. He would be extremely uncomfortable with a Westernized Japanese girl observing him in this foreign country.

Cully accepted all her decisions. But one thing he insisted on. He told Daisy to make fresh Japanese soup during Mr. Fummiro's three-day stay. Cully would come to her apartment early every morning to pick it up and have it delivered to Mr. Fummiro's suite when he ordered breakfast. Daisy groaned but promised to do so.

Late that afternoon Cully got a call from Gronevelt. "What the hell is a piano doing in Suite Four Ten?" Gronevelt said. "I just got a call from the hotel manager. He said you bypassed channels and caused a hell of a mess."

Cully explained the arrival of Mr. Fummiro and his special tastes. Gronevelt chuckled and said, "Take my Rolls when you pick him up at the airport." This was a car he used only for the richest of Texas millionaires or his favorite clients that he personally "Hosted."

The next day Cully was at the airport with three bellmen from the hotel, the chauffeured Rolls and two Cadillac limos. He arranged for the Rolls and the limousines to go directly onto the flying field so that his clients would not have to go through the terminal. And he greeted Mr. Fummiro as soon as he came down the steps of the plane.

The party of Japanese was unmistakable not only for their features but because of the way they dressed. They were all in black business suits, badly tailored by Western standards, with white shirts and black ties. The ten of them looked like a band of very earnest clerks instead of the ruling board of Japan's richest and most powerful business conglomerate.

Mr. Fummiro was also easy to pick out. He was the tallest of the band, very tall in comparison, a good five feet ten. And he was handsome with wide massive features, broad shoulders and jet black hair. He could have passed for a movie star out of Hollywood cast in an exotic role that made him look falsely Oriental. For a brief second the thought flashed through Cully's mind that this might be an elaborate scam.

Of the others only one stood close to Fummiro. He was slightly shorter than Fummiro, but much thinner. And he had the buckteeth of the caricature Japanese. The remaining men were tiny and inconspicuous. All of them carried elegant black imitation samite briefcases.

Cully extended his hand with utmost assurance to Fummiro and said, "I'm Cully Cross of the Xanadu Hotel. Welcome to Las Vegas."

Mr. Fummiro flashed a brilliantly polite smile. His white teeth were large and perfect, and he said in only slightly accented English, "Very pleased to meet you."

Then he introduced the buck-toothed man as Mr. Niigeta, his executive vice-president. He murmured the names of the others, all of whom ceremoniously shook hands with Cully. Cully took their baggage tickets and assured them all luggage would be delivered to their rooms in the hotel.

He ushered them into the waiting cars. He and Fummiro and Niigeta into the Rolls, the others into the Cadillacs. On the way to the hotel he told his passengers that credit had been arranged. Fummiro patted Niigeta's briefcase and said in his slightly imperfect English, "We have brought you cash money." The two men smiled at Cully. Cully smiled back. He remembered to smile whenever he spoke as he told them all the conveniences of the hotel and how they could see any show in Vegas. For a fraction of a second he thought about mentioning the companionship of women, but some instinct made him hold back.

At the hotel he led them directly to their rooms and had a desk clerk bring up the registration forms for them to sign. All were on the same floor, Fummiro and Niigeta had adjoining suites with a connecting door. Fummiro inspected the living accommodations for his whole party, and Cully saw the glint of satisfaction in his eyes when he noted that his own suite was by far the best. But Fummiro's eyes really lit up when he saw the small piano in his suite. He immediately sat down and fingered the keys, listening. Cully hoped that it was in tune. He couldn't tell, but Fummiro vigorously nodded his head and, smiling broadly and face alight with pleasure, said, "Very good, very kind," and shook Cully's hand effusively.

Then Fummiro motioned to Niigeta to open the briefcase he was carrying. Cully's eyes bulged a little. There were neatly banded stacks of currency filling the case. He had no idea how much it might be. "We would like to leave this on deposit in your casino cage," Mr. Fummiro said. "Then we can just draw the money as we need it for our little vacation."

"Certainly," Cully said. Niigeta snapped the case shut, and the two of them went down to the casino, leaving Fummiro alone in his suite to freshen up.

They went into the casino manager's office, where the money was counted out. It came to five hundred thousand dollars. Cully made sure Niigeta was given the proper receipt and the necessary clerical work done so that the money could be drawn on demand at the tables. The casino manager himself would be on the floor with Cully and would identify Fummiro and Niigeta to the pit bosses and the floorwalkers. Then in every corner of the casino the two Japanese merely had to lift a finger and draw chips, then sign a marker. Without fuss, without showing identification. And they would get the royal treatment, the utmost deference. A deference especially pure since it related only to money.

For the next three days Cully was at the hotel early in the morning with Daisy's breakfast soup. Room service had orders to notify him as soon as Mr. Fummiro called down for his breakfast. Cully would give him an hour to eat and then knock on his door to say good morning. He would find Fummiro already at his piano, playing soulfully, the serving bowl of soup empty on the table behind him. In these morning meetings Cully arranged show tickets and sightseeing trips for Mr. Fummiro and his friends. Mr. Fummiro was always smilingly polite and grateful, and Mr. Niigeta would come through the connecting door from his own suite to greet Cully and compliment him on the breakfast soup, which he had obviously shared. Cully remembered to keep smiling and nodding his head as they did.

Meanwhile, in their three days' gambling in Vegas the band of ten Japanese terrorized the casinos of Vegas. They would travel together and gamble together at the same baccarat table. When Fummiro had the shoe, they all bet the limit with him on the Bank. They had some hot streaks but luckily not at the Xanadu. They only bet baccarat, and they played with a *joie de vivre* more Italian than Oriental. Fummiro would whip the sides of the shoe and bang the table when he dealt himself a natural eight or nine. He was a passionate gambler and gloated over winning a two-thousand-dollar bet. This amazed Cully. He knew Fummiro was worth over half a billion dollars. Why should such paltry (though up to the Vegas limit) gambling excite him?

Only once did he see the steel behind Fummiro's handsome smiling façade. One night Niigeta placed a bet on Player's when Fummiro had the shoe. Fummiro gave him a long look, eyebrows arching, and said something in Japanese. For the first time Cully caught the slight hissing sound that Daisy had warned him against. Niigeta stuttered something in apology through his buckteeth and immediately switched his money to ride with Fummiro.

The trip was a huge success for everybody. Fummiro and his band went back to Japan ahead over a hundred thousand dollars, but they had lost two hundred thousand to the Xanadu. They had made up for their losses at other casinos. And they had started a legend in Vegas. The band of ten men in their shiny black suits would leave one casino for another down the Strip. They were a frightening sight, marching ten strong into a casino, looking like undertakers come to collect the corpse of the casino's bankroll. The baccarat pit boss would learn from the Rolls driver where they were going and call that casino to expect them and give them red-carpet treatment. All the pit bosses pooled their information. It was in this way that Cully learned that Niigeta was a horny Oriental and getting laid by top-class hookers at the other hotels. Which meant that for some reason he didn't want Fummiro to know that he would rather fuck than gamble.

Cully took them to the airport when they left for Los Angeles. He had one of Gronevelt's antique gold fob watches which he presented to Fummiro with Gronevelt's compliments. Gronevelt himself had briefly stopped at the Japanese dining table to introduce himself and show the courtesies of the house.

Fummiro was genuinely effusive in his thanks, and Cully went through the usual rounds of handshakes and smiles before they got on their plane. Cully rushed back to the hotel, made a phone call to get the piano moved out of Fummiro's suite and then went into Gronevelt's office. Gronevelt gave him a warm handshake and a congratulatory hug.

"One of the best 'Host' jobs I've seen in all my years in Vegas," Gronevelt said. "Where did you find out about that soup business?"

"A little girl named Daisy," Cully said. "OK if I buy her a present from the hotel?"

"You can go for a grand," Gronevelt said. "That's a very nice connection you made with those Japs. Keep after them. The special Christmas gifts and invitations. That guy Fummiro is a bust-out gambler if I ever saw one."

Cully frowned. "I was a little leery about laying on broads," he said. "You know Fummiro is a hell of a nice guy, and I didn't want to get too familiar first time out."

Gronevelt nodded. "You were right. Don't worry, he'll be back. And if he wants a broad, he'll ask for one. You don't make his kind of money by being afraid to ask."

Gronevelt as usual was right. Three months later Fummiro was back and at the cabaret show asked about one of the leggy blond dancers. Cully knew she was in action despite being married to a dealer at the Sands. After the show he called the stage manager and asked him if the girl would have a drink with Fummiro and him. It was arranged, and Fummiro asked the girl out for a late-night dinner. The girl looked questioningly at Cully and he nodded. Then he left them alone. He went to his office and called the stage manager to tell him to schedule a replacement for the midnight show. The next morning Cully did not go up to Fummiro's suite after breakfast was delivered. Later in the day he called the girl at her home and told her she could miss all her shows while Fummiro was in town.

On subsequent trips the pattern remained the same. By this time Daisy had taught one of the Xanadu chefs how to make the Japanese soup, and it was officially listed on the breakfast menu. One thing Cully learned was that Fummiro always watched the reruns of a certain long-lasting western TV show. He loved it. Especially the blond ingenue who played a plucky but very feminine, yet innocent dance hall girl. Cully had a brainstorm. Through his movie contacts he got in touch with the ingenue, who was named Linda Parsons. He flew into Los Angeles, had lunch with her and told her about Fummiro's passion for her and her show. She was fascinated by Cully's stories about Fummiro's gambling. How he checked into the Xanadu with briefcases holding a million dollars in cash, which he would sometimes lose in three days of baccarat. Cully could see the childish, innocent greed in her eyes. She told Cully that she would love to come to Vegas the next time Fummiro arrived.

A month later Fummiro and Niigeta checked into the Xanadu Hotel for a four-day stay. Cully immediately told Fummiro about Linda Parsons' wishing to visit him. Fummiro's eyes lit up. Despite being over forty, he had an incredible boyish handsomeness, which his evident joy made even more charming. He asked Cully to call the girl immediately, and Cully said he would, not mentioning that he had already spoken to her and she had promised to come into town the next afternoon. Fummiro was so excited that he gambled like a madman that night and dropped over three hundred thousand dollars.

The next morning Fummiro went shopping for a new blue suit. For some reason he thought blue suits were the height of American elegance, and Cully arranged with the Sy Devore people at the Sands Hotel to measure and fit him out and specially tailor it for him that day. Cully sent one of his Xanadu "Hosts" with Fummiro to make sure everything went smoothly.

But Linda Parsons caught an early plane and arrived in Vegas before noon. Cully met her plane and brought her to the hotel. She wanted to freshen up for Fummiro's arrival, so Cully put her in Niigeta's suite since he assumed that Niigeta was with his chief. It proved to be an almost fatal error.

Leaving her in the suite, Cully went back to his office and tried to locate Fummiro, but he had left the tailor shop and must have stopped off in one of the casinos along the way to gamble. He could not be traced. After about an hour he received a phone call from Fummiro's suite. It was Linda Parsons. She sounded a little upset. "Could you come down?" she said. "I'm having a language problem with your friend."

Cully didn't wait to ask any questions. Fummiro spoke English well enough; for some reason he was pretending not to be able to. Maybe he was disappointed in the girl. Cully had noticed that the ingenue, in person, had more mileage on her than appeared in the carefully photographed TV shows. Or maybe Linda had said or done something that had offended his delicate Oriental sensibilities.

But it was Niigeta who let him into the suite. And Niigeta was preening himself with slightly drunken pride. Then Cully saw Linda Parsons come out of the bathroom clad in a Japanese kimono with golden dragons blazoned all over it.

"Jesus Christ," Cully said.

Linda gave him a wan smile. "You sure bullshitted me," she said. "He's not that shy and he's not that good-looking and doesn't even understand English. I hope he's rich at least."

Niigeta was still smiling and preening, he even bowed toward Linda as she was talking. He had obviously not understood what she was saying.

"Did you fuck him?" Cully asked almost in despair.

Linda made a face. "He kept chasing me around the suite. I thought at least we'd have a romantic evening together with flowers and violins, but I couldn't fight him off. So I figured what the hell. Let's get it over with if he's such a horny Jap. So I fucked him."

Cully shook his head and said, "You fucked the wrong Jap."

Linda looked at him for a moment with a mixture of shock and horror. Then she burst out laughing. It was a genuine laughter that became her. She fell onto the sofa still laughing, her white thigh bared by the flopping of the kimono. For that moment Cully was charmed by her. But then he shook his head. This was serious. He picked up the phone and got Daisy at her apartment. The first thing Daisy said was, "No more soup." Cully told her to stop kidding around and to get down to the hotel. He told her it was terribly important and she had to be fast. Then he called Gronevelt and explained the situation. Gronevelt said he would come right down. Meanwhile, Cully was praying that Fummiro would not appear.

Fifteen minutes later Gronevelt and Daisy were in the suite with them. Linda had made Cully and Niigeta and herself a drink from the suite bar, and she still had a grin on her face. Gronevelt was charming with her. "I'm sorry this happened," he said. "But just be a little patient. We'll get everything sorted out." Then he turned to Daisy. "Explain to Mr.

Niigeta exactly what happened. That he took Mr. Fummiro's woman. That she thought he was Mr. Fummiro. Explain that Mr. Fummiro was madly in love with her and went out to buy a new suit for his meeting with her."

Niigeta was listening intently with the same broad grin he always wore. But now there was a little alarm in his eyes. He asked Daisy a question in Japanese, and Cully noticed the little warning hiss in his speech. Daisy started talking to him rapidly in Japanese. She kept smiling as she talked, but Niigeta's smile kept fading as her words poured out, and when she finished, he fell to the floor of the suite in a dead faint.

Daisy took charge. She grabbed a whiskey bottle and poured some down Niigeta's throat, then helped him up and to the sofa. Linda looked at him pityingly. Niigeta was wringing his hands and pouring out speech to Daisy. Gronevelt asked what he was saying. Daisy shrugged. "He says it means the end of his career. He says that Mr. Fummiro will get rid of him. That he made Mr. Fummiro lose too much face."

Gronevelt nodded. "Tell him to just keep his mouth shut. Tell him I'm going to have him put into the hospital for a day because he's feeling ill, and then he'll fly back to Los Angeles for treatment. We'll make up a story for Mr. Fummiro. Tell him never to tell a soul, and we'll make sure that Mr. Fummiro never finds out what happened."

Daisy translated and Niigeta nodded. His polite smile came back, but it was a ghastly grimace. Gronevelt turned to Cully. "You and Miss Parsons wait for Fummiro. Act as if nothing happened. I'll take care of Niigeta. We can't leave him here; he'll faint again when he sees his boss. I'll ship him out."

And that was how it worked. When Fummiro finally arrived an hour later, he found Linda Parsons, freshly dressed and made up, waiting for him with Cully. Fummiro was immediately enchanted, and Linda Parsons looked smitten with his handsomeness but as innocently as the ingenue of the western TV movie could be.

"I hope you don't mind," she said. "But I took your friend's suite so that I could be right next to you. That way we can spend more time with each other."

Fummiro grasped the implication. She was not just some slut who would move right in with him. She would have to fall in love first. He nodded with a broad smile and said, "Of course, of course." Cully heaved a sigh of relief. Linda was playing her cards just right. He said his good-byes and lingered for a moment in the hall. In a few minutes he could hear Fummiro playing the piano and Linda singing along with him.

In the three days that followed Fummiro and Linda Parsons had the classical, almost geometrically perfect Las Vegas love affair. They were mad for each other and spent each minute together. In bed, at the gambling tables good luck or bad, shopping in the fancy arcades and boutiques of the Strip hotels. Linda loved Japanese soup for breakfast and loved Fummiro's piano playing. Fummiro loved Linda's blond paleness, her milk-white and slightly heavy thighs, the longness of her legs, the soft, drooping fullness of her breasts. But most of all, he loved her constant good humor, her gaiety. He confided to Cully that Linda would have made a great geisha. Daisy told Cully that this was the highest compliment a man like Fummiro could give. Fummiro also claimed that Linda gave him luck when he gambled. When his stay was over, he had lost only two hundred thousand of the million in cash, American, that he had deposited in the casino cage. And that included a mink coat, a diamond ring, a palomino horse and a Mercedes car that he had bought for Linda Parsons. He had gotten away cheap. Without Linda the chances were good he would have dropped at least half a million or maybe even the full million at the baccarat tables.

At first Cully thought of Linda as a high-class soft hooker. But after Fummiro left Vegas, he had dinner with her before she took the night plane to Los Angeles. She was really crazy about Fummiro. "He's such an interesting guy," she said. "I loved that soup for breakfast and the piano playing. And he was just great in bed. No wonder the Japanese women do everything for their men."

Cully smiled. "I don't think he treats his women back home the way he treated you."

Linda sighed. "Yeah, I know. Still, it was great. You know, he took hundreds of pictures of me with his camera. You'd think I'd be tired of that, but I really loved him doing it. I took pictures of him too. He's a very handsome man."

"And very rich," Cully said.

Linda shrugged. "I've been with rich guys before. And I

make good money. But he was just like a little kid. I really don't like the way he gambles, though. God! I could live for ten years on what he loses in one day."

Cully thought, is that so? And immediately made plans for Fummiro and Linda Parsons never to meet again. But he said with a wry smile, "Yeah, I hate to see him get hurt like that. Might discourage him from gambling."

Linda grinned at him. "Yeah, I'll bet," she said. "But thanks for everything. I really had one of the best times of my life. Maybe I'll see you again."

He knew what she was angling for, but instead, he said smoothly, "Anytime you get the yen for Vegas just call me. Everything on the house except chips."

Linda said a little pensively, "Do you think Fummiro will call me the next time he comes in? I gave him my phone number in LA. I even said I'd fly to Japan on my vacation when we finish taping the show, and he said he'd be delighted and to let him know when I was coming. But he was a little cool about that."

Cully shook his head. "Japanese men don't like women to be so aggressive. They're a thousand years behind the times. Especially a big wheel like Fummiro. Your best bet is to lay back and play it cool."

She sighed. "I guess so."

He took her to the airport and kissed her on the cheek before she boarded her plane. "I'll give you a call when Fummiro comes in again," he said.

When he got back to the Xanadu, he went up to Gronevelt's living suite and said wryly, "There's such a thing as being too good to a player."

Gronevelt said, "Don't be disappointed. We didn't want his whole million this early in the game. But you're right. That actress is not the girl to connect with a player. For one thing she's not greedy enough. For another, she's too straight. And worst of all, she's intelligent."

"How do you know?" Cully asked.

Gronevelt smiled. "Am I right?"

"Sure," Cully said. "I'll make sure to tout Fummiro off her when he comes in again."

"You won't have to," Gronevelt said. "A guy like him has too much strength. He doesn't need what she can give him.

Not more than once. Once is fun. But that's all it was. If it were more, he would have taken better care of her when he left."

Cully was a little startled. "A Mercedes, a mink coat and a diamond ring? That's not taking care of her?"

"Nope," Gronevelt said. And he was right. The next time Fummiro came into Vegas he never asked about Linda Parsons. And this time he lost his million cash in the cage.

Chapter 19

The plane flew into morning light and the stewardess came around with coffee and breakfast. Cully kept the suitcase beside him as he ate and drank, and when he had finished, he saw New York's towers of steel on the horizon. The sight always awed him. As the desert stretched away from Vegas, so here the miles of steel and glass rooted and growing thickly toward the sky seemed limitless. And gave him a sense of despair.

The plane dipped and did a slow, graceful tilt to the left as it circled the city and then dropped down, white ceiling to blue ceiling, then to sunlit air with the cement gray runways and scattered green patches that formed the carpet earth. It touched down with a hard enough bump to wake those passengers who were still asleep.

Cully felt fresh and wide-awake. He was anxious to see Merlyn: the thought of it made him feel happy. Good old Merlyn, the original square, the only man in the world he trusted.

Chapter 20

On the day that I was to appear before the grand jury, my oldest son was graduating from the ninth grade and entering high school. Valerie wanted me to take off from work and go with her to the exercises. I told her I couldn't because I had to go to a special meeting on the Army recall program. She still had no clue to the trouble I was in, and I didn't tell her. She couldn't help and she could only worry. If everything went OK, she'd never know. And that was how I wanted it. I really didn't believe in sharing troubles with marriage partners when they couldn't help.

Valerie was proud of her son's graduating day. A few years ago we realized he really couldn't read, yet was getting promoted each semester. Valerie was mad as hell and started teaching him to read, and she did a good job. Now he was getting top grades. Not that I wasn't mad. It was another grudge I had against New York City. We lived in a low-income area, all working stiffs and blacks. The school system didn't give a shit whether the kids learned anything or not. It just kept promoting them on to get rid of them, to get them out of the system without any trouble and with the least amount of effort.

Vallie was looking forward to moving into our new house. It was in a great school district, a Long Island community where the teachers made sure all their students qualified for college. And though she didn't say it, there were hardly any blacks. Her kids would grow up in the same kind of, to her, stable environment she had had as a Catholic schoolchild. That was OK with me. I didn't want to tell her that the problems she was trying to escape were rooted in the illnesses of our entire society and that we wouldn't escape them in the trees and lawns of Long Island.

And besides, I had other worries. I might be going to jail instead. It depended on the grand jury I would appear before today. Everything depended on that. I felt lousy when I got out of bed that morning. Vallie was taking the kids to school herself and staying there for the graduation exercises. I told her that I was going into work late, so they left before me. I got my own coffee, and as I drank it, I figured out all the things I had to do before the grand jury.

I had to deny everything. There was no way they could trace the bribe money I'd taken, Cully had assured me of that. But the thing that worried me was that I had had to fill out a questionnaire as to my assets. One question was did I own a house. And I had walked a thin line on that. The truth was that I had put a down payment on a Long Island home, a deposit, but there had not yet been a "closing" on the house. So I just said no. I figured I didn't own a house and there was nothing said about a deposit. But I wondered if the FBI had found out about that. It seemed it must have.

So one of the questions I could expect the grand jury to ask would be if I had made a deposit on a house. And then I would have to answer yes. Then they would ask me why I hadn't put it down on the sheet and I would have to explain that. Then what if Frank Alcore cracked and pleaded guilty and told them about our dealings when we had been partners? I had already made up my mind to lie about that. It would be Frank's word against mine. He had always handled the deals by himself, nobody could back him up. And now I remembered one day when one of his customers had tried to pay me off with an envelope to deliver to Frank because Frank was not in the office that day. I had refused. And that had been very lucky. Because that customer was one of the guys who had written the anonymous letter to the FBI that started the whole investigation. And that had been pure luck. I had refused simply because I didn't like the guy personally. Well, he would have to testify that I wouldn't take the money and that would be a point in my favor.

And would Frank crack and throw me to the grand jury? I didn't think so. The only way he could save himself would be to give evidence against someone higher up in the chain of command. Like the major or the colonel. And the catch there was that they were not involved at all. And I felt Frank was too decent a guy to cause me grief just because he was caught. Besides, he had too much at stake. If he pleaded guilty, he would lose his government job and pension and his Reserve rank and pension. He had to brazen it out.

My only big worry was Paul Hemsi. The kid I had done the most for and whose father had promised to make me happy for the rest of my life. After I had taken care of Paul, I had never heard from Mr. Hemsi again. Not even a package of stockings. I had expected a big score from that one, at least a couple of grand, but those initial cartons of clothing had been it, the whole thing. And I hadn't pushed it or asked for anything. After all, those cartons of clothes were worth thousands. They wouldn't "make me happy for the rest of my life," but what the hell, I didn't mind being conned.

But when the FBI began its investigation, it got onto the gossip that Paul Hemsi had beaten the draft and been enlisted in the Reserves even after he got an induction notice. I knew that the letter from the draft board rescinding his induction notice had been pulled from our files and sent to higher headquarters. I had to assume that the FBI men had talked to the draft board clerk and that he had told them the story I had given him. Which would still have been OK. Nothing really illegal, a little administrative hocus-pocus that happened every day. But the word was out that Paul Hemsi had cracked under the FBI interrogation and had told them that I received a bribe from other friends of his.

I left the house and drove by my son's school. It had a huge playground with a basketball court of cement, the whole area fenced by high wire-mesh fences. And as I drove by, I could see that the graduation exercises were being held outside in the courtyard. I parked my car and stood outside the fence, clinging to the wire.

Young boys and girls barely in their teens, they stood in orderly rows, all neatly dressed for the ceremony, their hair combed, their faces scrubbed clean, waiting with childish pride for their ceremonial passing into the next step toward adulthood.

Stands had been erected for the parents. And a huge wooden platform for the dignitaries, the principal of the school, a precinct politician, an old grizzled guy wearing the blue braided overseas cap and 1920's-looking uniform of the American Legion. An American flag flew over the platform. I heard the principal saying something about not having enough time to give out the diplomas and honors individually, but that when he announced each class, the members of that class should turn and face the stands.

And so I watched them for a few minutes. After each announcement a row of the young boys and girls swung around to face the stand of mothers and fathers and other relatives to receive their applause. The faces were filled with pride and pleasure and anticipation. They were heroes this day. They had been praised by the dignitaries and applauded now by their elders. Some of the poor bastards still couldn't read. None of them had been prepared for the world or the trouble they would see. I was glad I couldn't see my son's face. I went back to the car and drove to New York and my meeting with the grand jury.

Near the federal courthouse building I put my car in the parking lot and went into the huge marble-floored hallways. I took an elevator to the grand jury room and stepped out of the elevator. And I was shocked to see benches filled with the young men who had been enlisted in our Reserve units. There were at least a hundred of them. Some nodded to me and a few shook my hand and we made jokes about the whole business. I saw Frank Alcore standing by himself near one of the huge windows. I went over to him and shook his hand. He seemed calm. But his face was strained.

"Isn't this a lot of shit?" he said as we shook hands.

"Yeah," I said. Nobody was in uniform except Frank. He wore all his WW II campaign ribbons and his master sergeant stripes and longevity hash marks. He looked like a gung-ho career soldier. I knew he was gambling that a grand jury would refuse to indict a patriot called back to the defense of his country. I hoped it would work.

"Jesus," Frank said. "They flew about two hundred of us up from Fort Lee. All over a bunch of crap. Just because some of these little pricks couldn't take their medicine when they got recalled."

I was impressed and surprised. It had seemed such a little thing we had done. Just taking some money for doing a harmless little hocus-pocus. It hadn't even seemed crooked. Just an accommodation, a meeting in terms of interest between two different parties beneficial to both and harmful to no one. Sure, we had broken a few laws, but we hadn't done anything really bad. And here the government was spending thousands of dollars to put us in jail. It didn't seem fair. We hadn't shot anybody, we hadn't stuck up a bank, we hadn't embezzled funds or forged checks or received stolen goods or committed rape or even been spies for the Russians. What the hell was all the fuss about? I laughed. For some reason I was suddenly in really good spirits.

"What the hell are you laughing about?" Frank said. "This is serious."

There were people scattered all around us, some within earshot. I said to Frank cheerfully, "What the hell do we have to worry about? We're innocent, and we know this is all a bunch of bullshit. Fuck them all."

He grinned back at me, catching on. "Yeah," he said. "But still, I'd like to kill a few of these little pricks."

"Don't even say that kidding." I gave him a warning look. They might have this hall bugged. "You know you don't mean it."

"Yeah, I guess so," Frank said reluctantly. "You'd think these guys would be proud to serve their country. I didn't squawk, and I've been through one war."

Then we heard Frank's name being called out by one of the bailiffs near the two huge doors with the big black and white sign on them that read "Grand Jury Room." As Frank went in, I saw Paul Hemsi coming out. I went up to him and said, "Hi Paul, how you doing?" I held out my hand and he shook it.

He seemed uncomfortable but didn't look guilty. "How's your father?" I said.

"He's OK," Paul said. He hesitated briefly. "I know I'm not supposed to talk about my testimony. You know I can't do that. But my father said to tell you not to worry about anything."

I felt a wild surge of relief. He had been my one real worry. But Cully had said he would fix the Hemsi family, and now it seemed to be done. I didn't know how Cully had managed it and I didn't care. I watched Paul go to the bank of elevators, and then another one of my customers, a young kid who was an apprentice theater director I had enlisted at no charge, came up to me. He was really concerned about me, and he told me that he and his friends would testify that I had never asked for or received money from them. I thanked him and shook hands. I made some jokes and smiled a lot and it wasn't even acting. I was playing the role of the jolly slick bribe taker thereby projecting his all-American innocence. I realized with some surprise that I was enjoying the whole thing. In fact, I was holding court with a lot of my customers, who were all telling me what a bunch of shit the whole business was, caused by a few soreheads. I even felt that Frank might beat the rap. Then I saw Frank come out of the grand jury room and heard my name called. Frank looked a little grim but mad, and I could tell he hadn't cracked, that he was going to fight it out. I went through the two huge doors and into the grand jury room. By the time I went out through the doors I had wiped the smile off my face.

It was nothing like the movies. The grand jury seemed to be a mass of people sitting in rows of folding chairs. Not in a jury box or anything. The district attorney stood by a desk with sheafs of paper he read from. There was a stenotype reporter sitting at a tiny desk with his machine on it. I was directed to sit on a chair that was on a little raised platform so that the jury could see me clearly. It was almost as if I were the ladderman in a baccarat pit.

The district attorney was a young guy dressed in a very conservative black suit with a white shirt and neatly knotted sky blue tie. He had thick black hair and very pale skin. I didn't know his name, and never knew it. His voice was very calm and very detached as he asked me questions. He was just putting information into the record, not trying to impress the jury.

He didn't even come near me when he asked his questions, just stood by his desk. He established my identity and my job.

"Mr. Merlyn," he said, "did you ever solicit money from anyone for any reason whatsoever?"

"No," I said. I looked at him and the jury members right in the eye as I gave my answers. I kept my face serious, though for some reason I wanted to smile. I was still high.

The district attorney said, "Did you receive any money from anyone in order for him to be enlisted in the six months' Army Reserve program?"

"No," I said.

"Do you have any knowledge of any other person's receiving money contrary to law in order to receive preferred treatment in any way?"

"No," I said, still looking at him and the mass of people

sitting so uncomfortably on their small folding chairs. The room was an interior room and dark with bad lighting. I couldn't really make out their faces.

"Do you have any knowledge of any superior officer or anyone else at all using special influence to get someone into the six months' program when his name was not on the waiting lists kept by your office?"

I knew he would ask a question like that. And I had thought about whether I should mention the congressman who had come down with the heir of the steel fortune and made the major toe the line. Or tell how the Reserve colonel and some of the other Reserve officers had put their own friends' sons on the list out of turn. Maybe that would scare off the investigators or divert attention to those higher-ups. But then I realized that the reason the FBI was taking all this trouble was to uncover higher-ups, and if that happened, the investigation would be intensified. Also, the whole affair would acquire more importance to the newspapers if a congressman were involved. So I had decided to keep my mouth shut. If I were indicted and tried, my lawyer could always use that information. So now I shook my head and said, "No."

The district attorney shuffled his papers and then said, without looking at me, "That will be all. You're excused." I got out of my chair and stepped down and left the jury room. And then I realized why I was so cheerful, so high, almost delighted.

I had been a magician, really. All those years when everybody was sailing along, taking bribes without a worry in the world, I had peered into the future and foreseen this day. These questions, this courthouse, the FBI, the specter of prison. And I had cast spells against them. I had hidden my money with Cully. I had taken great pains not to make enemies among all the people I had done illegal business with. I had never explicitly asked for any definite sum of money. And when some of my customers had stiffed me, I had never chased them. Even Mr. Hemsi after promising to make me happy for the rest of my life. Well, he had made me happy just by getting his son not to testify. Maybe that's what had turned the trick, not Cully. Except that I knew better. It was Cully who had got me off the hook. But OK, even if I had needed a little help, I was still a magician. Everything had happened exactly as I knew it would. I was really proud of myself. I didn't care that maybe I was just a slick hustler who took intelligent precautions.

Chapter 21

When Cully got off the plane, he took a taxi to a famous bank in Manhattan. He looked at his watch. It was after 10 A.M. Gronevelt would be making his call right now to the vice-president of the bank that Cully was delivering the money to.

Everything was as planned. Cully was ushered into the vice-president's office, and behind closed, locked doors, he delivered the briefcase.

The vice-president opened it with his key and counted out the million dollars in front of Cully. Then he filled out a bank deposit slip, scribbled his signature on it and gave the slip of paper to Cully. They shook hands and Cully left. A block away from the bank he took a prepared, stamped envelope out of his jacket pocket and put the slip into it and sealed the envelope. Then he dropped it into a mailbox on the corner. He wondered how the whole thing worked, how the vice-president covered the drop and who picked up the money. Someday he would have to know.

Cully and Merlyn met in the Oak Room of the Plaza. They didn't talk about the problem until they had finished lunch and then walked through Central Park. Merlyn told Cully the whole story, and Cully nodded his head and made some sympathetic remarks. From what he could gather it was strictly a small-time grifter's operation that the FBI had stumbled onto. Even if Merlyn were convicted, he would get only a suspended sentence. There wasn't that much to worry about. Except that Merlyn was such a square guy he'd be ashamed of having a conviction on his record. That should be the worst of his worries, Cully thought.

When Merlyn mentioned Paul Hemsi, the name rang a bell in Cully's head. But now, as they walked through Central Park and Merlyn told him about the meeting with Hemsi

Senior in the garment center, everything clicked. One of the many garment center tycoons who came to Vegas for long weekends and the Christmas and New Year holidays, Charles Hemsi was a big gambler and a devoted cunt man. Even when he came to Vegas with his wife, Cully had to arrange for Charlie Hemsi to get a piece. Right on the floor of the casino with Mrs. Hemsi playing roulette, Cully would slip the key, its room-numbered wooden plaque attached, into Charlie Hemsi's hand. Cully would whisper what time the girl would be in the room.

Charlie Hemsi would wander out to the coffee shop to escape his wife's suspicious eye. From the coffee shop he would saunter down the long labyrinth of hotel corridors to the room numbered on the key plaque. Inside the room he would find a luscious girl waiting for him. It would take less than a half hour. Charlie would give the girl a black hundred-dollar chip, then, thoroughly relaxed, saunter down the blue-carpeted corridors into the casino. He would pass by the roulette table and watch his wife gamble, give her a few encouraging words, some chips, never the blacks, then plunge joyfully back into the wild melee of the crap tables. A big, bluff, good-natured guy, a lousy gambler who nearly always lost, a degenerate gambler who never quit when he was ahead. Cully had not remembered him immediately because Charlie Hemsi had been trying to take the cure.

Hemsi had markers out all over Vegas. The Xanadu casino cage alone held fifty grand of Charlie Hemsi's IOU's. Some of the casinos had already sent dunning letters. Gronevelt had told Cully to hold off. "He may bail himself out," Gronevelt said. "Then he'll remember we were nice guys and we'll get most of his action. Money in the bank when that asshole gambles."

Cully doubted it. "That asshole owes over three hundred grand around town," he said. "Nobody has seen him in a year. I think he's going the claim agent route."

"Maybe," Gronevelt said. "He's got a good business in New York. If he has a big year, he'll be back. He can't resist the gambling and the broads. Listen, he's sitting with his wife and kids, going to neighborhood parties. Maybe he hits the hooker in the garment center. But that makes him nervous, too many of his friends know. Here in Vegas it's all so clean. And he's a crap-shooter. They don't leave the table so easy."

"And if his business doesn't have a big year?" Cully asked.

"Then he'll use his Hitler money," Gronevelt said. He took note of Cully's politely inquiring and amused face. "That's what the garment center boys call it. During the war they all made a fortune in black-market deals. When materials were rationed by the government, a lot of money passed beneath the table. Money they didn't have to report to Internal Revenue. Couldn't report. They all got rich. But it's money they can't let show. If you want to get rich in this country, you have to get rich in the dark."

It was that phrase Cully always remembered. "You have to get rich in the dark." The credo of Vegas, not only of Vegas, but of many of the businessmen who came to Vegas. Men who owned supermarkets, cash vending businesses, heads of construction firms, shady church officials of all denominations who collected cash in holy baskets. Big corporations with platoons of legal advisors who created a plain of darkness within the law.

Cully listened to Merlyn with only half an ear. Thank God Merlyn never talked much. It was soon over, and as they walked through the park in silence, Cully sorted everything out in his head. Just to make sure, he asked Merlyn to describe Hemsi Senior again. No, it wasn't Charlie. It must be one of his brothers, a partner in the business and, from the sound of it, the dominant partner. Charlie had never struck Cully as a hardworking executive. Counting down in his head, Cully could see all the steps he would have to take. It was beautiful, and he was sure Gronevelt would approve. He had only three days before Merlyn appeared before the grand jury, but that would be enough.

So now Cully could enjoy the walk through the park with Merlyn. They talked about old times. They asked the same old questions about Jordan. Why had he done it? Why would a man who had just won four hundred grand blow his brains out? Both of them were too young to dream of the emptiness of success, though Merlyn had read about it in novels and textbooks. Cully didn't buy that bullshit. He knew how happy "The Pencil," the complete one, would make him. He would be an emperor. Rich and powerful men, beautiful women would be his guests. He could fly them from the ends of the world free, the Xanadu Hotel would pay. Just by his, Cully's, use of "The Pencil." He could bestow luxurious suites, the richest foods, fine wines, beautiful women one at a time, two at a time, three at a time. And really beautiful. He could transport the ordinary mortal into paradise for three, four, five days, even a week. All free.

Except, of course, that they had to buy chips, the greens and blacks, and they had to gamble. A small price to pay. They could win, after all, if they got lucky. If they gambled intelligently, they would not lose too much. Cully thought benevolently that he would use "The Pencil" for Merlyn. Merlyn could have anything he wanted whenever he came to Vegas.

And now Merlyn was crooked. Or at least bent. Yet it was plain to Cully that it was a temporary aberration. Everybody gets bent at least one time in his life. And Merlyn showed his shame, at least to Cully. He had lost some of his serenity, some of his confidence. And this touched Cully. He had never been innocent and he treasured innocence in others.

So when he and Merlyn said their good-byes, Cully gave him a hug. "Don't worry, I'll fix it. Go into that grand jury room and deny everything. OK?"

Merlyn laughed. "What else can I do?" he said.

"And when you come out to Vegas, everything is on the house," Cully said. "You're my guest."

"I don't have my lucky Winner jacket," Merlyn said, smiling.

"Don't worry," Cully said. "If you sink too deep, I'll deal you a little blackjack personally."

"That's stealing, not gambling," Merlyn said. "I gave up stealing ever since I got that notice to the grand jury."

"I was only kidding," Cully said. "I wouldn't do that to Gronevelt. If you were maybe a beautiful broad, yes, but you're too ugly." And he was surprised to see Merlyn flinch again. And it struck him that Merlyn was one of those people who thought of themselves as ugly. A lot of women felt that, but not men, he thought. Cully said his final good-bye by asking Merlyn if he needed some of his black cash stashed at the hotel, and Merlyn said not yet. And so they parted.

Back in his Plaza Hotel suite Cully made a series of calls to the casinos in Vegas. Yes, Charles Hemsi's markers were still outstanding. He made a call to Gronevelt to outline his plan and then changed his mind. Nobody in Vegas knew how many taps the FBI had around town. So he just mentioned casually to Gronevelt that he would stay in New York for a few days and ask for some markers from New York customers who were behind, a little late. Gronevelt was laconic. "Ask them nice," he said. And Cully said of course, what else could he do? They both understood they were talking for the FBI record. But Gronevelt had been alerted and would expect an explanation later in Vegas. Cully would be in the clear, he had not tried to throw a fastball by Gronevelt.

The next day Cully got in touch with Charles Hemsi, not at the garment center office, but on a golf course in Roslyn, Long Island. Cully rented a limo and got out there early. He had a drink at the clubhouse and waited.

It was two hours before he saw Charles Hemsi come off the links. Cully got up from his chair and strolled outside, where Charles was chatting with his partners before going into the lockers. He saw Hemsi hand over some money to one of the players; the sucker had just been hustled in golf, he lost everywhere. Cully sauntered up to them casually.

"Charlie," he said with sincere Vegas "Host" pleasure. "Good to see you again." He held out his hand and Hemsi shook it.

He could see that funny look on Hemsi's face which meant he recognized Cully but couldn't place him. Cully said, "From the Xanadu Hotel. Cully. Cully Cross."

Hemsi's face changed again. Fear mixed with irritation, then the salesman grimace. Cully gave his most charming smile, and slapping Hemsi on the back, he said, "We've missed you. Haven't seen you in a long time. Jesus, what are the odds of me running into you like this? Like betting a number on the roulette wheel straight up."

The golf partners were drifting into the clubhouse, and Charlie started to follow them. He was a big man, much bigger than Cully, and he just brushed past. Cully allowed it. Then he called after Hemsi, "Charlie, give me a minute. I'm here to help." He made his voice fill with sincerity, without pleading. And yet the notes of his words were strong, rang like iron.

The other man hesitated and Cully was quickly at his side. "Charlie, listen, this will not cost you a dime. I can square all your markers in Vegas. And you don't pay a cent. All your brother has to do is a small favor."

Charlie Hemsi's big bluff face went pale, and he shook his head. "I don't want my brother to know about those markers. He's murder. No way you can tell my brother."

Cully said softly, almost sorrowfully, "The casinos are tired of waiting, Charlie. The collectors are going to be in the picture. You know how they operate. They go down to your place of business, make scenes. They scream for their money. When you see two seven-foot three-hundred-pound guys screaming for their money, it can be a little unnerving."

"They can't scare my brother," Charlie Hemsi said. "He's tough and he has connections."

"Sure," Cully said. "I don't mean they can make you pay if you don't want to. But your brother will know and he'll get involved and the whole thing will be messy. Look, I'll make you a promise. Get your brother to see me and I'll put a hold on all your markers at the Xanadu. And you can come there and gamble, and I'll comp you all the way just like before. You won't be able to sign markers, you'll have to pay cash. If you win, you can make a little payment on the markers as you go along. That's a good deal. No?" Here Cully made a little gesture almost of apology.

He could see Charlie's light blue eyes get interested. The guy hadn't been to Vegas for a year. He must be missing the action. Cully recalled that in Vegas he had never asked to be comped for the golf course. Which meant that he wasn't that crazy about golf. Because a lot of degenerate gamblers liked to put in a morning on the great golf course of the Xanadu Hotel. This guy was bored stiff. Still, Charlie hesitated.

"Your brother is going to know anyway," Cully said. "Better from me than the collectors. You know me. You know I'll never go over the line."

"What's the small favor?" Charlie asked.

"Small, small," Cully said. "He'll do it once he hears the proposition. I swear to you. He won't mind. He'll be glad to do it."

Charlie smiled a sad smile. "He won't be glad," he said. "But come on into the clubhouse and we'll have a drink and talk."

An hour later Cully was on his way back to New York. He had stood over Charlie when Charlie made the phone call to his brother and arranged the appointment. He had conned and hustled and charmed Charlie Hemsi a dozen different ways. That he would square all the markers in Vegas, that nobody would ever bother him for the money. That the next time Charlie came to Vegas he would have the best suite and be comped all the way. And also as a bonus, that there was a girl, tall, long-legged, blond, from England with that great English accent, and the loveliest ass you ever saw, the best-looking dancer in the line at the Xanadu Hotel cabaret show. And Charlie could have her all night. Charlie would love her. And she would love Charlie.

So they had made arrrangements for Charlie's trip at the end of the month. By the time Cully got through with him Charlie thought he was eating honey rather than getting castor oil poured down his throat.

Cully went back to the Plaza first to wash up and change. He got rid of the limousine. He would walk down to the garment center. In his room he put on his best Sy Devore suit, silk shirt and conservative brown plaid tie. He put cuff links into his shirt sleeves. He had a pretty good picture of Eli Hemsi from brother Charles, and he didn't want to make a bad first impression.

Walking through the garment center, Cully felt disgust at the dirtiness of the city and the pinched, haggard faces walking its streets. Hand trucks, loaded with brightly colored dresses gallowed from metal racks, were being pushed by black men or old-timers with the seamed red faces of alcoholics. They pushed the hand trucks through the streets like cowboys, stopping traffic, almost knocking down pedestrians. Like sand and tumbleweed of a desert, the garbage of discarded newspapers, remnants of food, empty pop bottles caught in the truck wheels, washed over their shoes and trouser cuffs. The sidewalks were so clogged with people you could hardly breathe, even in the open air. The buildings looked cancerous, gray tumors rising to the sky. Cully regretted for a moment his affection for Merlyn. He hated this city. He was amazed that anyone chose to live in it. And people made cracks about Vegas. And gambling. Shit. At least gambling kept the city clean.

The entranceway of the Hemsi building seemed neater than others; the skin of the foyer that held the elevator seemed to have a thinner coat of grime over the usual white tiles. Jesus, Cully thought, what a crummy business. But when he got off on the sixth floor, he had to change his mind. The receptionist and secretary were not up to Vegas standards, but Eli Hemsi's suite of offices was. And Eli Hemsi, Cully saw at a glance, was a man not to be fucked around with in any way.

Eli Hemsi was dressed in his usual dark silk suit with a pearly gray tie sitting on his startlingly white shirt. His massive head bowed in alert attention as Cully spoke. His deep-socketed eyes seemed sad. But his energy and force could not be contained. Poor Merlyn, Cully thought, getting mixed up with this guy.

Cully was brief as could be under the circumstances, gravely businesslike. Charm would be wasted on Eli Hemsi. "I've come here to help two people," Cully said. "Your brother, Charles, and a friend of mine named Merlyn. Believe me when I tell you that is my sole purpose. For me to help them you have to do a small favor. If you say no, there is nothing more I can do to help. But even if you say no, I will do nothing to hurt anyone. Everything will remain the same." He paused for a moment to let Eli Hemsi say something, but that great buffalolike head was frozen with wary attention. The somber eyes did not even flicker.

Cully went on. "Your brother, Charles, owes my hotel in Vegas, the Xanadu, over fifty thousand dollars. He owes another two hundred and fifty thousand scattered around Vegas. Let me say right now that my hotel will never press him for his markers. He's been too good a customer and he's too nice a man. The other casinos may make things a little unpleasant for him, but they can't really make him pay if you use your connections, which I know you have. But then you owe your connections a favor which eventually may cost you more than what I ask."

Eli Hemsi sighed and then asked in his soft but powerful voice, "Is my brother a good gambler?"

"Not really," Cully said. "But that doesn't make any difference. Everybody loses."

Hemsi sighed again. "He's not much better in the business. I am going to buy him out, get rid of him, fire my own brother. He's nothing but trouble with his gambling and his women. When he was young, he was a great salesman, the

best, but he's too old now and he's not interested. I don't
know if I can help him. I know I won't pay his gambling
debts. I don't gamble, I don't take that pleasure. Why should
I pay for his?"

"I'm not asking you to," Cully said. "But here's what I can
do. My hotel will buy all his markers from the other casinos.
He won't have to pay for them unless he comes and gambles
and wins at our casino. We won't give him any more credit,
and I'll make sure no other casino in Vegas gives him credit.
He can't get hurt if he just plays for cash. That's strength.
For him. Just like letting people sign markers is our strength
in our operation. I can give him that protection."

Hemsi was still watching him very intently. "But my
brother keeps gambling?"

"You'll never be able to stop him," Cully said simply.
"There are many men like him, very few men like yourself.
Real life is not that exciting to him anymore, he's not inter-
ested. Very common."

Eli Hemsi nodded, thinking that over, rolling it around his
buffalolike head. "But this isn't too bad a business deal for
you," he said to Cully. "Nobody can collect my brother's
debts, you said that yourself, so you're giving away nothing.
And then my foolish brother comes with ten, twenty thousand dollars in his pocket and you win it from him. So you
gain. No?"

Cully said very carefully, "It could go another way. Your
brother could sign more markers and owe a great deal more
money. Enough money to make certain people think it worthwhile to collect them or try harder to collect them. Who
knows how foolish a man can get? Believe me when I tell
you that your brother won't be able to stay away from Vegas.
It's in his blood. Men like him come from all over the world.
Three, four, five times a year. I don't know why, but they
come. It means something to them that you and I can't understand. And remember, I have to buy up his markers; that
will cost me something." As he said this, he wondered how he
could make Gronevelt accept the proposition. But he would
worry about that later.

"And what is the favor?" The question was finally asked in
that same soft, yet powerful voice. It was really the voice of
a saint, the voice seemed to give off a spiritual serenity. Cully

was impressed and for the first time a little worried. Maybe this wouldn't work.

Cully said, "Your son, Paul. He gave testimony against my friend Merlyn. You remember Merlyn. You promised to make him happy for the rest of his life." And Cully let the steel come into his voice. He was annoyed by the power given off by this man. A power born of his tremendous success with money, the rise from poverty to millions in an adverse world, from the victorious wars of his life while carrying a foolish brother.

But Eli Hemsi did not rise to the bait of this ironic reproach. He did not even smile. He was still listening.

"Your son's testimony is the only evidence against Merlyn. Sure I understand, Paul was frightened." Suddenly there was a dangerous flicker in those dark eyes watching him. Anger at this stranger knowing his son's first name and using it so familiarly and almost contemptuously. Cully gave back a sweet smile. "A very nice boy you have, Mr. Hemsi. Everybody is certain he was tricked, threatened, to make his statement to the FBI. I've consulted some very good lawyers. They say he can back off in the grand jury room, give his testimony in such a way so that he will not convince the jury and still not get in trouble with the FBI. Maybe he can retract the testimony altogether." He studied the face opposite him. There was nothing to read. "I assume your son has immunity," Cully said. "He won't be prosecuted. I also understand you probably have it arranged so he won't have to do his Army duty. He'll come out of it a hundred percent OK. I figure you have that all set. But if he does this favor, I promise you nothing will change."

Eli Hemsi spoke now in a different voice. It was stronger, not so soft, yet persuasive, a salesman selling. "I wish I could do that," he said. "That boy, Merlyn, he's a very nice boy. He helped me, I will be grateful to him forever." Cully noted that here was a man who used the word "forever" pretty often. No halfway gestures for him. He had promised Merlyn he would make him happy for the rest of his life. Now he was going to be grateful forever. A real fucking claim agent weaseling out of his obligations. For the second time Cully felt some anger that this guy was treating Merlyn like such a schmuck. But he continued to listen with an agreeable smile on his face.

"There is nothing I can do," Hemsi said. "I can't endanger my son. My wife would never forgive me. He is her whole life to her. My brother is a grown man. Who can help him? Who can guide him, who can make his life now? But my son has to be cared for. He is my first concern. Afterward, believe me, I will do anything for Mr. Merlyn. Ten, twenty, thirty years from now I will never forget him. Then, when this is all over, you can ask me anything." Mr. Hemsi rose from his desk and put out his hand, his powerful frame bent over with grateful solicitousness. "I wish my son had a friend like you."

Cully grinned at him, shook his hand. "I don't know your son, but your brother is my friend. He's coming out to visit me in Vegas at the end of the month. But don't worry, I'll take care of him. I'll keep him out of trouble." He saw the pondering look on Eli Hemsi's face. He might as well sock it to him all the way.

"Since you can't help me," Cully said, "I have to get Merlyn a really good lawyer. Now the district attorney has probably told you that Merlyn will plead guilty and get a suspended sentence. And everything will blow away so that your son not only will get immunity but will never have to go back into the Army. That may be. But Merlyn will not plead guilty. There will be a trial. Your son will have to appear in an open court. Your son will have to testify. There will be a lot of publicity. I know that won't bother you, but the newspapers will get to know where your son, Paul, is and what he is doing. I don't care who promised you what. Your son will have to go into the Army. The newspapers will just put on too much pressure. And then, besides all that, you and your son will have enemies. To use your phrase, 'I'll make you unhappy for the rest of your life.'"

Now that the threat was out in the open Hemsi leaned back in the chair and stared at Cully. His face, heavy and cragged, was more sad in its somberness than angry. So Cully gave it to him again. "You have connections. Call them and listen to their advice. Ask about me. Tell them I work for Gronevelt at the Xanadu Hotel. If they agree with you and call Gronevelt, there is nothing I can do. But you'll be in their debt."

Hemsi leaned back in his chair. "You say everything will come out right if my son does what you ask?"

"I guarantee it," Cully said.

"He won't have to go back into the Army?" Hemsi asked again.

"I guarantee that too," Cully said. "I have friends in Washington, as you have. But my friends can do things your friends can't do, even if only because they can't be connected to you."

Eli Hemsi was ushering Cully to the door. "Thank you," he said. "Thank you very much. I have to think over everything you said. I'll be in touch with you."

They shook hands again as he walked Cully to the door of his suite. "I'm at the Plaza," Cully said. "And I'm leaving for Vegas tomorrow morning. So if you could call me tonight, I'd be grateful."

But it was Charlie Hemsi who called him. Charlie was drunk and gleeful. "Cully, you smart little bastard. I don't know how you did it, but my brother told me to tell you that everything is OK. He agrees with you completely."

Cully relaxed. Eli Hemsi had made his phone calls to check him out. And Gronevelt must have backed the play. He felt an enormous affection and gratitude for Gronevelt. He said to Charlie, "That's great. See you in Vegas at the end of the month. You'll have the time of your life."

"I wouldn't miss it," Charlie Hemsi said. "And don't forget that dancer."

"I won't," Cully said.

After that he dressed and went out for dinner. In the restaurant lobby he used the pay phone to call Merlyn. "Everything is OK, it was all a misunderstanding. You're going to be all right."

Merlyn's voice seemed faraway, almost abstracted and not as grateful as Cully would have liked it to be. "Thanks," Merlyn said. "See you in Vegas soon." And he hung up.

Chapter 22

Cully Cross squared everything for me, but poor patriotic Frank Alcore was indicted, released from active duty to civilian status, tried and convicted. A year in prison. A week later the major called me into his office. He wasn't mad at me or indignant; in fact, he had an amused smile on his face.

"I don't know how you did it, Merlyn," he told me. "But you beat the rap. Congratulations. And I don't give a shit, the whole business is a fucking joke. They should have put those kids in jail. I'm glad for you, but I've got my orders to handle this business and make sure it doesn't happen again. Now I'm talking to you as a friend. I'm not pressing. My advice is, resign from the government service. Right away."

I was shocked and a little sick. I thought I was home free and here I was out of a job. How the hell would I meet all my bills? How would I support my wife and kids? How would I pay the mortgage on the new house on Long Island I would be moving into in just a few months?

I tried to keep a poker face when I said, "The grand jury cleared me. Why do I have to quit?"

The major must have read me. I remember Jordan and Cully in Las Vegas kidding me about how anybody could tell what I was thinking. Because the major had a look of pity when he said, "I'm telling you for your own good. The brass will have their CID people all over this armory. The FBI may keep snooping around. All the kids in the Reserve will still try to use you, try to get you into deals. They'll keep the pot stirring. But if you quit, everything should blow over pretty quick. The investigators will cool off and go away with nothing to focus on."

I wanted to ask about all the other civilians who had been taking bribes, but the major anticipated me. "I know of at least ten other advisers like you, unit administrators, who are going to resign. Some have already. Believe me, I'm on your side. And you'll be OK. You're wasting your time on this job. You should have done better for yourself at your age."

I nodded. I was thinking that too. That I hadn't done much with my life so far. Sure, I'd had a novel published, but I was making a hundred bucks a week take-home pay from Civil Service. True, I earned another three or four hundred a month with free-lance articles for the magazines, but with the illegal gold mine closed down, I had to make a move.

"OK," I said. "I'll write a letter giving two weeks' notice."

The major nodded and shook his head. "You have some paid sick leave coming," he said. "Use it up in those two weeks and look for a new job. I'll stand still for it. Just come in a couple of times a week to keep the paperwork going."

I went back to my desk and wrote out my letter of resignation. Things weren't as bad as they looked. I had about twenty days of vacation pay coming to me, which was about four hundred dollars. I had, I figured, about fifteen hundred dollars in my government pension fund, which I could draw out, though I'd forfeit my rights to a pension when I was sixty-five. But that was more than thirty years away. I could be dead by then. A total of two grand. And then there was the bribe money I had stashed with Cully in Vegas. Over thirty grand there. For a moment I had an overwhelming sense of panic. What if Cully reneged on me and didn't give me my money? There would be nothing I could do about that. We were good friends, he had bailed me out of my troubles, but I had no illusions about Cully. He was a Vegas hustler. What if he said he had my money coming to him for the favor he had done me? I couldn't dispute it. I would have paid the money to keep out of jail. Christ, would I have paid it!

But the thing I dreaded most was having to tell Valerie I was out of a job. And having to explain to her father. The old man would ask around and get the truth anyway.

I didn't tell Valerie that night. The next day I took off from work and went to see Eddie Lancer at his magazines. I told him everything and he sat there, shaking his head and laughing. When I finished, he said, almost wonderingly, "You know, I'm always getting surprised. I thought you were the straightest guy in the world next to your brother, Artie."

I told Eddie Lancer about how taking the bribes, becoming a half-assed criminal had made me feel better psychologically. That in some way I had discharged a lot of the bitterness I felt. The rejection of my novel by the public, the drabness of my life, its basic failure, how I'd always really been unhappy.

Lancer was looking at me with that little smile on his face. "And I thought you were the least neurotic guy I ever met," he said. "You're happily married, you have kids, you live a secure life, you earn a living. You're working on another novel. What the hell more do you want?"

"I need a job," I told him.

Eddie Lancer thought that one over for a moment. Oddly enough I didn't feel embarrassed appealing to him.

"Just between you and me I'm leaving this place in about six months," he said. "They'll move another editor up to my place. I'll be recommending my successor and he'll owe me a favor. I'll ask him to give you enough free-lance to live on."

"That would be great," I said.

Eddie said briskly, "I can load you up with work until then. Adventure stories, some of the love fiction crap and some book reviews I usually do. OK?"

"Sure," I said. "When do you figure you'll finish your book?"

"In a couple of months," Lancer said. "How about you?"

It was a question I always hated. The truth was that I had only an outline of a novel I wanted to write about a famous criminal case in Arizona. But I hadn't written anything. I had submitted the outline to my publisher, but he had refused to give me an advance. He said it was the kind of novel that wouldn't make money because it involved the kidnapping of a child who was murdered. There wouldn't be any sympathy for the kidnapper, the hero of the book. I was aiming at another *Crime and Punishment*, and that had scared the publisher off.

"I'm working on it," I said. "Still a long way to go."

Lancer smiled sympathetically. "You're a good writer," he said. "You'll make it big someday. Don't worry."

We talked awhile longer about writing and books. We both agreed we were better novelists than most of the famous novelists making their fortunes on the best-seller lists. When I left, I was in a confident mood. I always left Lancer that way. For some reason he was one of the few people I felt easy with, and because I knew he was smart and gifted, his good opinion of my talent cheered me up.

And so everything had turned out for the best. I was now a full-time writer, I would lead an honest life, I had escaped jail and in a few months I would move into my very own house, for the first time in my life. Maybe a little crime does pay.

Two months later I moved into my newly built house on Long Island. The kids all had their own bedrooms. We had three bathrooms and a special laundry room. I would no longer have to lie in my bath while newly washed clothes dripped down into my face. No longer have to wait for the kids to finish. I had the almost excruciating luxury of privacy. My own den to write in, my own garden, my own lawn. I was separate from other people. It was Shangri-La. And yet it was something so many people took for granted.

Most important of all, I felt that now my family was safe. We had left the poor and desperate behind us. They would never catch up; their tragedies would never cause ours. My children would never be orphans.

Sitting on my suburban back porch one day, I realized I was truly happy, maybe happier than I would ever be in my life again. And that made me a little pissed off. If I was an artist, why was I so happy with such ordinary pleasures, a wife I loved, children who delighted me, a cheap tract house in the suburbs? One thing sure, I was no Gauguin. Maybe that was why I wasn't writing. I was too happy. And I felt a twinge of resentment against Valerie. She had me trapped. Jesus.

Except even this couldn't keep me feeling content. Everything was going so well. And the pleasure you took in children was so commonplace. They were so disgustingly "cute." When my son was five years old, I had taken him for a walk through the streets of the city and a cat had jumped out of a cellar and almost literally sailed in front of us. My son had turned to me and said, "Is that a scaredy-cat?" When I told Vallie about it, she was delighted and wanted to send it in to one of those magazines that pay money for cute little stories. I'd had a different reaction. I wondered if one of his friends had taunted him with being a scaredy-cat and he had been puzzled by what the phrase meant rather than insulted. I thought of all the mysteries of language and experience my son was encountering for the first time. And I envied him the innocence of childhood as I envied him the luck he had in having parents he could say that to and then have them make a fuss over him.

And I remembered one day when we had gone out for a family Sunday-afternoon walk on Fifth Avenue, Valerie window-shopping for dresses she could never afford. Coming towards us was a woman about three feet tall but dressed elegantly in suede jerkin and white frilly blouse and dark tweed skirt. My daughter tugged at Valerie's coat and pointed to the dwarf lady and said, "Mommy, what's that?"

Valerie was horrified with embarrassment. She was always terrified about hurting anyone's feelings. She shushed my daughter until the woman was safely past. Then she explained to our daughter that the woman was one of those people who had never grown taller. My daughter didn't really grasp the idea. Finally she asked, "You mean she didn't grow up. You mean she's an old lady like you?"

Valerie smiled at me. "Yes, dear," she said. "Now don't think about it anymore. It only happens to very few people."

At home that night, when I told my kids a story before sending them to bed, my daughter seemed to be lost in thought and not listening. I asked her what was wrong. Then, her eyes very wide, she said, "Daddy, am I really a little girl or am I just an old lady who didn't grow up?"

I knew that there were millions of people who had stories like this to tell about their kids. That it was all terribly commonplace. And yet I couldn't help the feeling that sharing a part of my children's lives made me richer. That the fabric of my life was made up of these little things that seemed to have no importance.

Again my daughter. One evening at dinner she had infuriated Valerie by continuingly misbehaving. She threw food at her brother, deliberately spilled a drink and then knocked over a gravy boat. Finally Valerie screamed at her, "You do one more thing and I'll kill you."

It was, of course, a figure of speech. But my daughter stared at her very intently and asked, "Do you have a gun?"

It was funny because she so obviously believed that her mother couldn't kill her unless she had a gun. She knew nothing yet of wars and pestilence, of rapists and molesters, of automobile accidents and plane crashes, clubbings, cancer, poison, getting thrown out of a window. Valerie and I both laughed, and Valerie said, "Of course I haven't got a gun, don't be silly." And the knot of worried concentration disappeared from my daughter's face. I noticed that Valerie never made that kind of irritated remark again.

And Valerie astonished me too sometimes. She had become more and more Catholic and conservative with the years. She was no longer the bohemian Greenwich Village girl who had wanted to become a writer. In the city housing project pets had been forbidden, and Vallie never told me she loved animals. Now that we owned a house Valerie bought a puppy and a kitten. Which didn't make me too happy, even though my son and daughter made a pretty picture playing with their pets on the lawn. The truth is that I had never liked house dogs and cats; they were caricatures of orphans.

I was *too* happy with Valerie. I had no idea then how rare this was and how valuable. And she was the perfect mother for a writer. When the kids fell and had to get stitched up, she never panicked or bothered me. She didn't mind doing all the work a man usually does around the house and which I had no patience for. Her parents now lived only thirty minutes away, and often in the evenings and on weekends she took the car and the kids and went there without even asking me if I wanted to go. She knew I hated that kind of visit and that I could use time alone to work on my book.

But for some reason she had nightmares, maybe because of her Catholic upbringing. During the night I would have to wake her up because she gave little cries of despair and wept even while sound asleep. One night she was terribly frightened and I held her close in my arms and asked her what was wrong, what she'd dreamed about and she whispered to me, "Never tell me that I'm dying."

Which scared the hell out of me. I had visions of her having gone to the doctor and receiving bad news. But the next morning, when I questioned her about it, she didn't remember anything. And when I asked her if she had been to see the doctor, she laughed at me. She said, "It's my religious upbringing. I guess I just worry about going to hell."

For two years I wrote free-lance articles for the magazines, watched my kids grow up, so happily married that it almost disgusted me. Valerie did a lot of visiting with her family, and I spent a lot of time in my basement writing den, so we really didn't see that much of each other. I had at least three assignments from the magazines every month, while working on a novel I hoped would make me rich and famous. The kidnapping and murder novel was my plaything; the magazines were my bread and butter. I figured I had another three years to go before I finished the book, but I didn't care. I read through the growing pile of manuscript whenever I became lonely. And it was lovely watching the kids grow older and Valerie happier and more content and less afraid of dying. But nothing lasts. It doesn't last because you don't want it to last, I think. If everything is perfect, you go looking for trouble.

After two years of living in my suburban house, writing ten hours every day, going to a movie once a month, reading everything in sight, I welcomed a call from Eddie Lancer asking me to have dinner with him in the city. For the first time in two years I would see New York at night. I had gone in during the day to talk over my magazine assignments with the editors, but I always drove home for dinner. Valerie had become a great cook, and I didn't want to miss the evening with my kids and my final nightcap of work in my den.

But Eddie Lancer was just back from Hollywood, and he promised me some great stories and some great food. And as usual he asked me how my novel was coming. He always treated me as if he knew I was going to be a great writer, and I loved that. He was one of the few people I knew who seemed to have a genuine kindness untouched by self-interest. And he could be very funny in a way I envied. He reminded me of Valerie when she had been writing stories at the New School. She had it in her writing and sometimes in everyday life. It flashed out every once in a while even now. And so I told Eddie I had to go into the magazines the next day to get an assignment and we could have dinner afterward.

He took me to a place called Pearl's that I had never heard of. I was so dumb that I didn't know it was New York's "in" Chinese restaurant. It was the first time I had ever eaten Chinese food, and when I told Eddie that, he was amazed. He did a whole routine introducing me to different Chinese dishes while pointing out the celebrities and even opening up my fortune cookie and reading it for me. He also stopped me from eating the fortune cookie. "No, no, you never eat them," he said. "That's terribly unsophisticated. If there's one valuable thing you'll get out of this night, it's learning never to eat your fortune cookie in a Chinese restaurant."

It was a whole routine that was only funny between two friends in the context of their relationship with each other. But months later I read a story of his in *Esquire* in which he used that incident. It was a touching story, making fun of himself making fun of me. I knew him better after that story, how his good humor masked his essential loneliness and estrangement from the world and the people around him. And I got a hint of what he really thought about me. He painted a picture of me as a man in control of life and knowing where he was going. Which amused the hell out of me.

But he was wrong about the fortune cookie business being the only valuable thing I would get out of that night. Because after dinner he talked me into going to one of those New York literary parties, where again I met the great Osano.

We were having our dessert and coffee. Eddie made me order chocolate ice cream. He told me that it was the only dessert that went with Chinese food. "Remember that," he said. "Never eat your fortune cookie and always order chocolate ice cream for dessert." Then offhandedly he asked me to come to the party with him. I was a little reluctant. I had an hour and a half drive out to Long Island, and I was anxious to get home and maybe get in an hour's work before I went to bed.

"Come on," Eddie said. "You can't always be an uxurious hermit. Make a night out of it. There'll be some great booze, good talk and some nice-looking broads. And you might make some valuable contacts. It's harder for a critic to knock the shit out of you if he knows you personally. And your stuff may read better to some publisher if he's met you at a party and he thinks you're a nice guy." Eddie knew that I had no publisher for my new book. The publisher of my first book never wanted to see me again because it had sold only two thousand copies and never got a paperback.

So I went to the party and met Osano. He never let on that he remembered that interview, and neither did I. But a week later I got a letter from him asking me if I would come in to see him and have lunch about a job he had to offer me.

Chapter 23

I took the job with Osano for many different reasons. The job was interesting and prestigious. Since Osano had been appointed the editor of the most influential literary supplement in the country a few years ago, he had trouble with people working for him and so I would be his assistant. The money was good, and the work wouldn't interfere with my novel. And then I was too happy at home; I was becoming too much of a bourgeois hermit. I was happy, but my life was dull. I craved some excitement, some danger. I had vague fleeting memories of my running away to Vegas and how I had actually relished the loneliness and despair I felt then. Is that so crazy, to remember unhappiness with such delight and to despise happiness you hold in your hand?

But most of all, I took the job because of Osano himself. He was, of course, the most famous writer in America. Praised for his string of successful novels, notorious for his scrapes with the law and his revolutionary attitude toward society. Infamous for his scandalous sexual misbehavior. He fought against everybody and everything. And yet at the party where Eddie Lancer had taken me to meet him he charmed and fascinated everyone. And the people at the party were the cream of the literary world and no slouches at being charming and difficult in their own right.

And I have to admit Osano charmed me. At the party he got into a furious argument with one of the most powerful literary critics in America, who was also a close friend and supporter of his work. But the critic had dared voice the opinion that nonfiction writers were creating art and that some critics were artists. Osano swarmed all over him. "You bloodsucking cocksucker," he shouted, drink balanced in one hand, his other hand poised as if ready to throw a punch. "You have the fucking nerve to make a living off real writers and then say you're the artist? You don't even know what art is. An artist creates out of nothing but himself, do you understand that, you fucking asshole? He's like a fucking spider, the cobwebs are packed away in his body. And you pricks just come along and blow them away with your fucking housewife brooms after he spins them out. You're good with a broom, you fucking jerkoff, that's all you are." His friend was stunned because he had just praised Osano's nonfiction books and said they were art.

And Osano walked away to a group of women who were waiting to lionize him. There were a couple of feminists in the group, and he wasn't with them two minutes before his group again became the center of attention. One of the women was shouting at him furiously as he listened to her with amused contempt, his sneaky green eyes glowing like a cat's. Then he was off.

"You women want equality and you don't even understand power plays," he said. "Your hole card is your cunt, and you show it to your opponents face up. You give it away. And without your cunts you have no power at all. Men can live without affection but not without sex. Women have to have affection and can do without sex." At this last statement the women swarmed over him with furious protests.

But he stood them off. "Women are complaining about marriage when they are getting the best bargain they will ever get in their lives. Marriage is like those bonds you buy. There is inflation and there is devaluation. The value keeps going down and down for men. You know why? Women become less and less valuable as they grow older. And then we're stuck with them like an old car. Women don't age as well as men. Can you imagine a fifty-year-old broad being able to con a twenty-year-old kid into bed? And very few women have the economic power to buy youth as men do."

One woman shouted, "I have a twenty-year-old lover." She was a good-looking woman of about forty.

Osano grinned at her wickedly. "I congratulate you," he said. "But what about when you're fifty? With the young girls giving it away so easily you'll have to catch them coming out of grammar school and promise them a ten-speed bike. And do you think your young lovers fall in love with you as young women do with men? You haven't got that old Freudian father image working for you as we do. And I must repeat, a man at forty looks more attractive than he does at twenty. At fifty he can still be very attractive. It's biological."

"Bullshit," the attractive forty-year-old woman said. "Young girls make fools out of you old guys and you believe their bullshit. You're not any more attractive, you just have more power. And you have all the laws on your side. When we change that, we'll change everything."

"Sure," Osano said. "You'll get laws passed so that men will have to get operations to make themselves look uglier when they get older. In the name of fair play and equal rights. You may even get our balls cut off legally. That doesn't change the truth now." He paused and said, "You know the worst line of poetry? Browning. 'Grow old along with me! The best is yet to be. . . .' "

I just hung around and listened. What Osano was saying struck me as mostly bullshit. For one thing we had different ideas about writing. I hated literary talk, though I read all the critics and bought all the critical reviews.

What the hell was being an artist? It was not sensitivity. It was not intelligence. It was not anguish. Not ecstasy. That was all bullshit.

The truth was that you were like a safecracker fiddling with the dial and listening to the tumblers click into place. And after a couple of years the door might swing open and you could start typing. And the hell of it was that what was in the safe was most times not all that valuable.

It was just fucking hard work and a pain in the ass in the bargain. You couldn't sleep at night. You lost all your confidence with people and the outside world. You became a coward, a malingerer in everyday living. You ducked the responsibilities of your emotional life, but after all, it was the only thing you could do. And maybe that was why I was even proud of all the junk I wrote for pulp magazines and book reviews. It was a skill I had, finally a craft. I wasn't just a lousy fucking artist.

Osano never understood that. He had always striven to be an artist and turned out some art and near art. Just as years later he never understood the Hollywood thing, that the movie business was young, like a baby not yet toilet-trained, so you couldn't blame it for shitting all over everybody.

One of the women said, "Osano, you have such a great track record with women. What's the secret of your success?"

Everybody laughed, including Osano. I admired him even more, a guy with five ex-wives who could afford to laugh.

Osano said, "I tell them it has to be a hundred percent my way and no percent their way before they move in with me. They understand their position and they accept. I always tell them that when they are no longer satisfied with the arrangement to just move out. No arguments, no explanations, no negotiations, just leave. And I can't understand it. They say yes when they move in, and then they break the rules. They try to get it ten percent their way. And when they don't get it, they start a fight."

"What a marvelous proposition," another woman said. "And what do they get in return?"

Osano looked around, and with a perfectly straight face he said, "A fair fuck." Some of the women began to boo.

When I decided to take the job with him, I went back and read everything he'd written. His early work was first-rate, with sharp, precise scenes like etchings. The novels held together glued by character and story. And a lot of ideas working. His later books became deeper, more thoughtful, the prose more pompous. He was like an important man wearing his decorations. But all his novels invited the critics in, gave them a lot of material to work on, to interpret, to discuss, to stab around. But I thought his last three books were lousy. The critics didn't.

I started a new life. I drove to New York every day and worked from 11 A.M. to all hours. The offices of the review were huge, part of the newspaper which distributed it. The pace was hectic: books came in literally by the thousands every month, and we had space for only about sixty reviews each week. But all the books had to be at least skimmed. On the job Osano was genuinely kind to everybody who worked for him. He always asked me about my novel and volunteered to read it before publication and give me some editorial advice, but I was too proud to show it to him. Despite his fame and my lack of it, I thought I was the better novelist.

After long evenings working on the schedule of books to be reviewed and whom to give them to, Osano would drink from the bottle of whiskey he kept in his desk and give me long lectures on literature, the life of a writer, publishers, women and anything else that was bugging him at that particular time. He had been working on his big novel, the one that he thought would win him the Nobel Prize, for the last five years. He had already collected an enormous advance on it, and the publisher was getting nervous and pushing him. Osano was really pissed off about that. "That prick," he said. "He told me to read the classics for inspiration. That ignorant fuck. Have you ever tried to read the classics over again? Jesus, those old fuckers like Hardy and Tolstoy and Galsworthy had it made. They took forty pages to let out a fart. And you know why? They had their readers trapped. They had them by the balls. No TV, no radio, no movies. No traveling unless you wanted cysts over your asshole from bouncing around on stagecoaches. In England you couldn't even get fucked. Maybe that's why the French writers were more disciplined. The French at least were into fucking, not like those English Victorian jerkoffs. Now I ask you why should a guy with a TV set and a beach house read Proust?"

I'd never been able to read Proust, so I nodded. But I had read everybody else and couldn't see TV or a beach house taking their place.

Osano kept going. "*Anna Karenina*, they call it a masterpiece. It's a full-of-shit book. It's an educated upper-class guy condescending to women. He never shows you what that broad really feels or thinks. He gives us the conventional outlook of that time and place. And then he goes on for three hundred pages on how to run a Russian farm. He sticks that right in there as if anybody gives a shit. And who gives a shit about that asshole Vronsky and his soul? Jesus, I don't know who's worse, the Russians or the English. That fucking Dickens and Trollope, five hundred pages were nothing to them. They wrote when they had time off from tending their garden. The French kept it short at least. But how about that fucking Balzac? I defy! I defy! anybody to read him today."

He took a slug of whiskey and gave out a sigh. "None of them knew how to use language. None of them except Flaubert, and he's not that great. Not that Americans are that much better. That fuck Dreiser doesn't even know what words mean. He's illiterate, I mean that. He's a fucking aborigine. Another nine-hundred-page pain in the ass. None of those fucking guys could get published today, and if they did, the critics would murder them. Boy, those guys had it made then. No competition." He paused and sighed wearily. "Merlyn, my boy, we're a dying breed, writers like us. Find another racket, hustle TV shit, do movies. You can do that stuff with your finger up your ass." Then, exhausted, he would lie on the couch he kept in his office for his afternoon snooze. I tried to cheer him up.

"That could be a great idea for an *Esquire* article," I told him. "Take about six classics and murder them. Like that piece you did on modern novelists."

Osano laughed. "Jesus, that was fun. I was kidding and just using it for a power play to give myself more juice and everybody got pissed off. But it worked. It made me bigger and them smaller. And that's the literary game, only those poor assholes didn't know it. They jerked themselves off in their ivory towers and thought that would be enough."

"So this should be easy," I said. "Except that the professor critics will jump on you."

Osano was getting interested. He got up from the couch and went to his desk. "What classic do you hate most?"

"*Silas Marner*," I said. "And they still teach it in schools."

"Old dykey George Eliot," Osano said. "The schoolteachers love her. OK, that's one. I hate *Anna Karenina* most. Tolstoy is better than Eliot. Nobody gives a shit about Eliot anymore, but the profs will come out screaming when I hit Tolstoy."

"Dickens?" I said.

"A must," Osano said. "But not *David Copperfield*. I gotta admit I love that book. He was really a funny guy, that Dickens. I can get him on the sex stuff, though. He was some fucking hypocrite. And he wrote a lot of shit. Tons of it."

We started making the list. We had the decency not to molest Flaubert and Jane Austen. But when I gave him Goethe's *Young Werther*, he clapped me on the back and howled. "The most ridiculous book ever written," he said. "I'll make German hamburger out of it."

Finally we had a list:

> *Silas Marner*
> *Anna Karenina*
> *Young Werther*
> *Dombey and Son*
> *The Scarlet Letter*
> *Lord Jim*

Moby Dick
Proust (Everything)
Hardy (Anything)

"We need one more for an even ten," Osano said.

"Shakespeare," I suggested.

Osano shook his head. "I still love Shakespeare. You know it's ironic; he wrote for money, he wrote fast, he was an ignorant lowlife, yet nobody could touch him. And he didn't give a shit whether what he wrote was true or not just so long as it was beautiful or touching. How about 'Love is not love which alters when it alteration finds'? And I could give you tons. But he's too great. Even though I always hated that fucking phony Macduff and that moron Othello."

"You still need one more," I said.

"Yeah," said Osano, grinning with delight. "Let's see. *Dostoevsky*. He's the guy. How about *Brothers Karamazov*?"

"I wish you luck," I said.

Osano said thoughtfully, "Nabokov thinks he's shit."

"I wish him luck too," I said.

So we were stuck, and Osano decided to go with just nine. That would make it different from the usual ten of anything anyway. I wondered why we couldn't get up to ten.

He wrote the article that night and it was published two months later. He was brilliant and infuriating, and all through it he dropped little hints how his great novel in progress would have none of the faults of these classics and would replace them all. The article started a furious uproar, and there were articles all over the country attacking him and insulting his novel in progress, which was just what he wanted. He was a first-rate hustler, Osano. Cully would be proud of him. And I made a note that the two of them should meet someday.

In six months I became Osano's right-hand man. I loved the job. I read a lot of books and gave notes on them to Osano so that he could assign them for review to the freelancers we used. Our offices were an ocean of books; you were swamped with them, you tripped over them, they covered our desks and chairs. They were like those masses of ants and worms covering a dead carcass. I had always loved and revered books, but now I could understand the contempt and disdain of some intellectual reviewers and critics; they served as valets to heroes.

But I loved the reading part, especially novels and biographies. I couldn't understand the science books or philosophy or the more erudite critics, so Osano shoveled them off to other specialized assistants. It was his pleasure to take on the heavyweight literary critics who came out with books, and he usually murdered them. When they called or wrote to protest, he told them that he "umpired the ball, not the player," which lowbrow chatter inflamed them the more. But always keeping his Nobel Prize in mind, he treated some critics very respectfully, gave a lot of space for their articles and books. There were very few exceptions. He especially hated English novelists and French philosophers. And yet as time went on, I could see that he hated the job and goofed off from it as much as he could.

And he used his position shamelessly. The publishers' public relations girls soon learned that if they had a "hot" book they wanted to get reviewed, they had only to take Osano out to lunch and lay a big line of bullshit on him. If the girls were young and pretty, he would kid around and make them understand in a nice way that he would trade space for a piece of ass. He was that upfront about it. Which to me was shocking. I thought that happened only in the movie business. He used the same bargaining techniques on reviewers looking for free-lance work. He had a big budget and we commissioned a lot of reviews that we would pay for but never use. And he always kept his bargains. If they came across, he came across. By the time I arrived he had a nice long string of girlfriends who had access to the most influential literary review in America on the strength of their sexual generosity. I loved the contrast of this with the high intellectual and moral tone of the review.

I often stayed late with him in the office on our deadline nights and we would go out for dinner and a drink together, after which he would go get shacked. He would always want to fix me up, but I kept telling him I was happily married. This developed into a standing joke. "You still not tired of fucking your *wife*?" he would ask. Just like Cully. I wouldn't answer, just ignore him. It was none of his business. He would shake his head and say, "You're the tenth wonder. Married a hundred years and still like fucking your wife."

Sometimes I would give him an irritated look, and he'd say, quoting from some writer I'd never read, "No villain need be. Time is the enemy." It was his favorite quote. He used it often.

And working there, I got a taste of the literary world. I had always dreamed about being part of it. I thought of it as a place where no one quarreled or bargained about money. That since these were the people who created the heroes you loved in their books, the creators were like them. And of course, I found out that they were the same as anybody else, only crazier. And I found out that Osano hated all these people too. He'd give me lectures.

"The only special person is the novelist," Osano would say. "Not like your fucking short story writers and screenwriters and poets and playwrights and those fucking flyweight literary journalists. All fancy dress. All thin. Not a heavy bone in them. You have to have heavy bones in your work when you write a novel." He mused about that and then wrote it on a piece of paper, and I knew there would be an essay about heavy bones in next Sunday's review.

Then other times he would rant about the lousy writing in the review. Circulation was going down, and he blamed the dullness of the critical profession.

"Sure, those fuckers are smart, sure, they have interesting things to say. But they can't write a decent sentence. They're like guys who stutter. They break your feet as you try to hang on to every word coming out between those clenched teeth."

Every week Osano had his own essay on the second page. His writing was brilliant, witty and slanted to make as many enemies as possible. One week he published an essay in favor of the death penalty. He pointed out that in any national referendum the death penalty would be approved by an overwhelming vote. That it was only the elitist class like the readers of the review that had managed to bring the death penalty to a standstill in the United States. He claimed this was a conspiracy of the upper echelons of government. He claimed that it was government policy to give the criminal and poverty-stricken elements a license to steal, assault, burglarize, rape and murder the middle class. That this was an outlet provided for the lower classes so that they would not turn revolutionary. That the higher echelons of government had estimated the cost to be less this way. That the elitists lived in safe neighborhoods, sent their children to private schools, hired private security forces and so were safe from the revenge of the misled proletariat. He mocked the liberals who claimed that human life was sacred and that a government policy of putting citizens to death had a brutalizing effect on humanity in general. We were only animals, he said, and should be treated no better than the rogue elephants executed in India when they killed a human being. In fact, he asserted, the executed elephant had more dignity and would go to a higher heaven than the heroin-crazed murderers who were allowed to live in a comfortable prison for five or six years before they were let out to murder more middle-class citizens. When he dealt with whether the death penalty was a deterrent, he pointed out that the English were the most law-abiding people on earth, policemen didn't even carry guns. And he attributed this solely to the fact that the English had executed eight-year-old children for stealing lace handkerchiefs as late as the nineteenth century. Then he admitted that though this had wiped out crime and protected property, it had finally turned those more energetic of the working classes into political animals rather than criminal ones and so had brought socialism to England. One Osano line particularly enraged his readers. "We don't know if capital punishment is a deterrent, but we know that men we execute will not murder again."

He finished the essay by congratulating the rulers of America for having the ingenuity to give their lower classes a license to steal and kill so that they would not become political revolutionists.

It was an outrageous essay, but he wrote it so well that the whole thing appeared logical. Letters of protest rolled in by the hundreds from the most famous and important social thinkers of our liberal intellectual readership. A special letter composed by a radical organization and signed by the most important writers in America was sent to the publisher asking that Osano be removed as editor of the review. Osano printed it in the next issue.

He was still too famous to be fired. Everybody was waiting for his "great" novel to be finished. The one that would assure him of the Nobel Prize. Sometimes when I went into his office, he would be writing on long yellow sheets, which he would put into a desk drawer when I entered and I knew this was the famous work in progress. I never asked him about it and he never volunteered anything.

A few months later he got into trouble again. He wrote a page two essay in the review in which he quoted studies to show that stereotypes were perhaps true. That Italians were born criminals, that Jews were better at making money than anybody else and better violin players and medical students, that worst of all, more than any other people they put their parents into old folks' homes. Then he quoted studies to show that the Irish were drunks owing perhaps to some unknown chemical deficiency or diet or the fact that they were repressed homosexuals. And so on. That really brought the screams. But it didn't stop Osano.

In my opinion he was going crazy. One week he took the front page for his own personal review of a book on helicopters. That crazy bee in his bonnet was still buzzing. Helicopters would replace the automobile, and when that happened, all the millions of miles of concrete highways would be torn up and replaced by farmland. The helicopter would help return families to their nuclear structure because then it would be easy for people to visit far-flung relatives. He was convinced the automobile would become obsolete. Maybe because he hated cars. For his weekends in the Hamptons he always took a seaplane or a helicopter specially chartered.

He claimed that only a few more technical inventions would make the helicopter as easy to handle as the automobile. He pointed out that the automatic shift had made millions of women drivers who couldn't handle shifting gears. And this little aside brought down the wrath of Women's Liberation groups. What made it worse, in that very same week a serious study of Hemingway had been published by one of the most respected literary scholars in America. This scholar had a powerful network of influential friends, and he had spent ten years on the study. It got front-page reviews in every publication but ours. Osano gave it page five and three columns instead of the full page. Later that week the publisher sent for him, and he spent three hours in the big office suite on the top floor, explaining his actions. He came down, grinning from ear to ear, and said to me cheerfully, "Merlyn, my boy, I'll put some life in this fucking rag yet. But I think you should start looking for another job. I don't have to worry, I'm nearly finished with my novel and then I'll be home free."

By that time I had been working for him for nearly a year and I couldn't understand how he got any work done at all. He was screwing everything he could get his hands on, plus he went to all the New York parties. During that time he had knocked out a quickie short novel for a hundred grand advance. He wrote it in the office on the review's time, and it took him two months. The critics were crazy about it, but it didn't sell very much though it was nominated for the National Book Award. I read the book, and the prose was brilliantly obscure, the characterizations ridiculous, the plotting lunatic. To me it was a foolish book despite some complicated ideas. He had a first-rate mind, no question of that. But to me the book was a total failure as a novel. He never asked if I had read it. He obviously didn't want my opinion. He knew it was full of shit, I guess. Because one day he said, "Now that I've got a bankroll I can finish the big book." A sort of apology.

I got to like Osano, but I was always just a little afraid of him. He could draw me out as nobody else could. He made me talk about literature and gambling and even women. And then, when he had measured me, he would lay me out. He had a keen eye for pretentiousness in everyone else but himself. When I told him about Jordan's killing himself in Vegas and everything that had happened afterward and how I felt it had changed my life, he thought that over for a long time and then he gave me his insights combined with a lecture.

"You hold on to that story, you always go back to it, do you know why?" he asked me. He was wading through the piles of books in his office, waving his arms around. "Because you know that's the one area you're not in danger. You'll never knock yourself off. You'll never be that shattered. You know I like you, you wouldn't be my right-hand man if I didn't. And I trust you more than anybody I know. Listen, let me confess something to you. I had to redraw my will last week because of that fucking Wendy." Wendy had been his third wife and still drove him crazy with her demands though she had remarried since their divorce. When he just mentioned her, his eyes went a little crazy. But then he calmed down. He gave me one of his sweet smiles that made him look like a little kid, though he was well into his fifties by now.

"I hope you don't mind," he said. "But I've named you as my literary executor."

I was stunned and pleased, and with all that I shrank away from the whole thing. I didn't want him to trust me that much or like me that much. I didn't feel that way about him. I had come to enjoy his company, indeed, to be fascinated by how his mind worked. And though I tried to deny it, I was impressed by his literary fame. I thought of him as rich and famous and powerful, and the fact that he had to trust me so much showed me how vulnerable he was, and that dismayed me. It shattered some of my illusions about him.

But then he went on about me. "You know, underneath everything, you have a contempt for Jordan you don't dare admit to yourself. I've listened to that story of yours I don't know how many times. Sure, you liked him, sure, you felt sorry for him; maybe you even understood him. Maybe. But you can't accept the fact that a guy that had so much going for him knocked himself off. Because you know you had a ten times worse life than he had and you would never do such a thing. You're even happy. You're living a shitty life, you never had anything, you knocked your balls off working, you've got a limited bourgeois marriage and you're an artist with half your life gone and no real success. And you're basically happy. Christ, you still enjoy fucking your wife and you've been married—what?—ten, fifteen years. You're either the most insensitive prick I ever met or the most together. One thing I know, you're the toughest. You live in your own world, you do exactly what you want to do. You control your life. You never get into trouble, and when you do, you don't panic; you get out of it. Well, I admire you, but I don't envy you. I've never seen you do or say a really mean thing, but I don't think you really give a shit about anybody. You're just steering your life."

And then he waited for me to react. He was grinning, the sneaky green eyes challenging. I knew he was having fun just laying it on, but I also knew he meant it a little and I was hurt.

There were a lot of things I wanted to say. I wanted to tell him how it was growing up an orphan. That I had missed what was basic, the core of almost every human being's experience. That I had no family, no social antennae, nothing to bind myself to the rest of the world. I had only my brother, Artie. When people talked about life, I couldn't really grasp what they meant until after I had married Vallie. That was why I had volunteered to fight in the war. I had understood that war was another universal experience, and I hadn't wanted to be left out of it. And I had been right. The war had been my family, no matter how dumb that sounds. I was glad now I hadn't missed it. And what Osano missed or didn't bother saying because he assumed I knew it was that it wasn't that easy to exercise control over your own life. And what he couldn't know was that the coin of happiness was a currency I could never understand. I had spent most of my early life being unhappy purely because of external circumstance. I had become relatively happy again because of external circumstance. Marrying Valerie, having kids, having a skill or art or the ability to produce written matter that earned me a living made me happy. It was a controlled happiness built on what I had gained from a dead loss. And so, very valuable to me. I knew I lived a limited life, what seemed to be a life that was bare, bourgeois. That I had very few friends, no sociability, little interest in success. I just wanted to make it through life, or so I thought.

And Osano, watching me, was still smiling. "But you're the toughest son of a bitch I've ever seen. You never let anybody get near you. You never let anybody know what you really think."

At this I had to protest. "Listen, you ask me my opinion about anything and I'll give it to you. Don't even ask. Your last book was a piece of shit, and you run this review like a lunatic."

Osano laughed. "I don't mean that kind of stuff. I never said you weren't honest. But let it go. You'll know what I'm talking about someday. Especially if you start chasing broads and wind up with somebody like Wendy."

Wendy came around to the review offices once in a while. She was a striking brunette with crazy eyes and a body loaded with sexual energy. She was very bright, and Osano would give her books to review. She was the only one of his ex-wives who was not afraid of him, and she had made his life miserable ever since they were divorced. When he fell behind in his alimony payments, she went to court to get her child support and alimony raised. She had taken a twenty-year-old writer into her apartment and supported him. The writer was heavy on drugs, and Osano worried about what he might do to the kids.

Osano told stories about their marriage that were to me incredible. That once, going to a party, they had gotten into the elevator and Wendy refused to tell him the floor the party was on simply because they had quarreled. He became so infuriated that he had started to choke her to make her tell him, playing a game, as he called it, of "choke the chicken." A game that was his fondest memory of the marriage. Her face turning black, she shook her head, still refusing to answer his question about where the party was being held. He had to release her. He knew she was crazier than he was.

Sometimes when they had minor arguments, she would call the police to have him thrown out of the apartment and the police would come and be stunned by her unreasonableness. They would see Osano's clothes scissored to pieces on the floor. She admitted doing it, but that didn't give Osano a right to hit her. What she left out was that she had sat on the pile of scissored suits and shirts and ties and masturbated over them with a vibrator.

And Osano had stories to tell about the vibrator. She had gone to a psychiatrist because she could not achieve orgasms. After six months she had admitted to Osano that the psychiatrist was fucking her as part of the therapy. Osano wasn't jealous; by this time he really loathed her, "loathe" he said, "not hate. There's a difference."

But Osano would get furious every time he got the bill from the psychiatrist and he would rage to her, "I pay a guy a hundred dollars a week to fuck my wife and they call that modern medicine?" He told the story when his wife gave a cocktail party, and she was so mad that she stopped going to the psychiatrist and bought a vibrator. Every evening before dinner she locked herself into the bedroom to shut out the kids and masturbated with the machine. She always achieved orgasm. But she laid down the strict rule that she was never to be disturbed during that hour, by the children or her husband. The whole family, even the children, referred to it as "The Happy Hour."

What made Osano finally leave her, as he told the story,

was when she started carrying on about how F. Scott Fitzgerald had stolen all his best stuff from his wife, Zelda. That she would have become a great novelist if her husband had not done this. Osano grabbed her by the hair of her head and shoved her nose into *The Great Gatsby*.

"Read this, you dumb cunt," he said. "Read ten sentences, then read his wife's book. Then come and tell me that shit."

She read both and came back to Osano and told him the same thing. He punched her in the face and blackened both her eyes and then left for good.

Just recently Wendy had won another infuriating victory over Osano. He knew she was giving the child-support payments to her young lover. But one day his daughter came to him and asked for money for clothes. She explained that her gynecologist had told her not to wear jeans anymore because of a vaginal infection, and when she had asked her mother for money for dresses, her mother said, "Ask your father." This was after they had been divorced for five years.

To avoid an argument, Osano gave his daughter's support money to her directly. Wendy didn't object. But after a year she took Osano to court for the year's money. The daughter testified for her father. Osano had been sure he would win when the judge knew all the circumstances. But the judge told him sternly not only to pay the money directly to the mother but also to pay the support money for the past year in a lump sum. So in effect he paid twice.

Wendy was so delighted with her victory that she tried to be friendly with him afterward. In front of their children he brushed off her affectionate advances and said coldly, "You are the worst cunt I've ever seen." The next time Wendy came around to the review he refused her entrance to his office and cut off all the work he had given her. And what amazed him was that she couldn't understand why he loathed her. She raged about him to her friends and spread the word that he had never satisfied her in bed, that he couldn't get it up. That he was a repressed homosexual who really liked little boys. She tried to keep him from having the kids for the summer, but Osano won that battle. Then he published a maliciously witty short story about her in a national magazine. Maybe he couldn't handle her in life, but in fiction he painted a truly terrible portrait, and since everybody in the literary world of New York knew her, she was recognized immediately. She was crushed, as much as it was possible for her to be, and she left Osano alone after that. But she rankled in him like some poison. He couldn't bear to think about her without his face flushing and his eyes going a little crazy.

One day he came into the office and told me that the movies had bought one of his old novels to make into a picture and he had to go out there for a conference on the script, all expenses paid. He offered to take me along. I said OK but that I would like to drop off in Las Vegas to visit an old friend for a day or two while we were out there. He said that would be OK. He was between wives and he hated to travel alone or be alone and he felt he was going into enemy territory. He wanted a friend along with him. Anyway, that was what he said. And since I'd never been to California and I'd get paid while I was away, it looked like a good deal. I didn't know that I would more than earn my way.

Chapter 24

I was in Vegas when Osano finished up on the conferences for that movie script of his book. So I took the short flight to LA to fly home with him, keep him company from LA to New York. Cully wanted me to bring Osano to Vegas just to meet him. I couldn't talk Osano into it, so I went to LA.

In his suite at the Beverly Hills Hotel Osano was more pissed off than I had ever seen him. He felt the movie industry had treated him like shit. Didn't they know that he was world-famous, the darling of literary critics from London to New Delhi, from Moscow to Sydney, Australia? He was famous in thirty languages, including the different variations of the Slavic. What he left out was that every movie made from one of his books had lost money for some strange reason.

And Osano was pissed off about other things. His ego couldn't stand the director of the film's being more important than the writer. When Osano tried to get a girlfriend of his a small part in the film, he couldn't swing it, and that pissed him off. It pissed him even more when the cameraman and the supporting actor got their girlfriends into the movie. The fucking cameraman and a lousy supporting actor had more clout than the great Osano. I just hoped I could get him on the plane before he went crazy and started tearing the whole studio apart and wound up in the clink. And we had a whole day and night to wait in LA for the plane the next morning. To quiet him down, I brought him around to his West Coast agent, a very hip, tennis-playing guy who had a lot of clients in show business. He also had some of the best-looking girlfriends I had ever seen. His name was Doran Rudd.

Doran did his best, but when disaster waits, nothing helps. "You need a night out," Doran said, "a little relaxation, a good dinner with a beautiful companion, a little tranquilizer so you can sleep tonight. Maybe a blow job pill." Doran was absolutely charming with women. But alone with men he insulted the female species.

Well, Osano had to go into a little act before he gave the OK. After all, a world-famous writer, a future Nobel literary prizewinner, doesn't want to be fixed up like some teenage kid. But the agent had handled guys like Osano before. Doran Rudd had fixed up a secretary of state, a President, the biggest evangelist in America who drew millions of believers to the Holy Tabernacle and was the horniest bigcocked son of a bitch in the world, so Doran said.

It was a pleasure to watch the agent smooth Osano's ruffled ego. This wasn't a Vegas operation, where girls were sent to your room like a pizza. This was class.

"I've got a really intelligent girl who's dying to meet you," Doran told Osano. "She's read all your books. She thinks you're the greatest writer in America. No shit. And she's not one of your starlets. She has a psychology degree from the University of California, and she takes bit parts in movies so that she can make contacts to write a script. Just the girl for you."

Of course, he didn't fool Osano. Osano knew the joke was on him, that he was to be conned into what he really wanted. So he couldn't resist saying as Doran picked up the phone, "That's all very well, but do I get to fuck her?"

The agent was already dialing with a gold-headed pencil.

"You got a ninety percent chance," he said.

Osano said quickly, "How do you get that figure?" He always did that whenever somebody pulled a statistic on him. He hated statistics. He even believed the New York *Times* made up its stock market quotations just because one of his IBM stocks had been listed at 295 and, when he tried to sell it, he could get only 290.

Doran was startled. He stopped dialing. "I sent her out with five guys since I've known her. Four of them scored."

"That's eighty percent," Osano said. Doran started dialing again. When a voice answered, he leaned back in his swivel chair and gave us a wink. Then he went into his dance.

I admired it. I really admired it. He was so good. His voice was so warm, his laugh so infectious.

"Katherine," the agent crooned. "My favorite, favorite client. Listen, I was talking to the director who's going to make that western with Clint Eastwood. Would you believe he remembered you from that one interview last year? He said you gave the best reading of anybody, but he had to go with a name and after the picture he was sorry he did. Anyway, he wants to see you tomorrow at eleven or three. I'll call you later to get the exact time. OK? Listen I have a really good feeling about this one. I think this is the big break. I think your time has come. No, no kidding."

He listened for a while. "Yeah, yeah, I think you'd be great in that. Absolutely marvelous." He rolled his eyes at us comically which made me dislike him. "Yeah, I'll sound them out and get back to you. Hey, listen, guess who I've got in my office right now. Nope. Nope. Listen, it's a writer. Osano. Yeah, no kidding. No, honest. Yes, he really is. And believe it or not he happened to mention you not by name, but we were talking about movies and he mentioned that part you did, that cameo role, in *City Death*. Isn't that funny? Yeah, he's a fan of yours. Yeah, I told him you love his work. Listen, I've got a great idea. I'm going out to dinner with him tonight, Chasen's, why don't you come beautify our table? Great. I'll have a limo pick you up at eight. OK, sweetheart. You're my baby. I know he'll like you. He doesn't want to meet any starlets. He doesn't like the starlet type. He needs conversation and I just realized that you two were made for each other. Right, good-bye, honey."

The agent hung up and leaned back and gave us his charming smile. "She's really a nice cunt," he said.

I could see Osano was a little depressed by the whole scene. He really liked women, and he hated to see them hustled. He often said he'd rather be hustled by a woman than hustle her. In fact, he once gave me his whole philosophy about being in love. How it was better to be the victim.

"Look at it this way," Osano had said. "When you're in love with a broad, you're getting the best of it even though she's hustling you. You're the guy who's feeling great, you're the guy who's enjoying every minute. She's the one who's having a lousy time. She's working . . . you're playing. So why complain when she finally dumps you and you know you've been conned?"

Well, his philosophy was put to the test that night. He got home before midnight and called my room and then came in for a drink to tell me what happened with Katherine. Katherine's percentage for scores had gone down that night. She had been a charming vibrant little brunette and swarmed all over Osano. She loved him. She adored him. She was thrilled to death that she was having dinner with him. Doran got the message and disappeared after coffee. Osano and Katherine were having a final loosening-up bottle of champagne before going back to the hotel to get down to business. That's when Osano's luck turned bad, though he could still have bailed out if it hadn't been for his ego.

What screwed it up was one of the most unusual actors in Hollywood. His name was Dickie Sanders, and he had won an Oscar and had been in six successful movies. What made him unique was that he was a dwarf. That's not as bad as it sounds. He just missed being a very short man. And he was a very handsome guy, for a dwarf. You could say he was a miniature James Dean. He had the same sad, sweet smile which he used with devastating and calculated effect on women. They couldn't resist him. And as Doran said later, all bullshit aside, what balling broad could resist going to bed with a handsome dwarf?

So when Dickie Sanders walked into the restaurant, it was no contest. He was alone and he stopped at their table to say hello to Katherine; it seemed they knew each other, she'd had a bit part in one of his movies. Anyway, Katherine adored him twice as much as she adored Osano. And Osano got so pissed off he left her with the dwarf and went back to the hotel alone.

"What a fucking town," he said. "A guy like me loses out to a fucking dwarf." He was really sore. His fame didn't mean anything. The Nobel Prize coming didn't mean anything. His Pulitzers and National Book Awards cut no ice. He came second to a dwarf actor, and he couldn't stand it. I had to carry him to his room finally and pour him into his bed. My final words of consolation to him were: "Listen, he's not a dwarf, he's just a very short guy."

Next morning, when Osano and I got on that 747 to New York, he was still depressed. Not only because he'd brought Katherine's average down, but because they'd botched the movie version of his book. He knew it was a lousy script, and he was right. So he was really in a bad mood on the plane and bullied a scotch off the stewardess even before takeoff.

We were in the very front seats near the bulkhead, and in

the two seats across the aisle were one of those middle-aged couples, very thin, very elegant. The man had a beaten-down, unhappy look on his face that was sort of appealing. You got the impression that he was living in a private hell, but one that he deserved. Deserved because of his outward arrogance, the richness of his dress, the spitefulness of his eyes. He was suffering, and by Christ he was going to make everybody else around him suffer too, if he thought they would stand for it.

His wife looked like the classic spoiled woman. She was obviously rich, richer than her husband, though possibly they were both rich. The stamp was on them in the way they took the menu from the stewardess. The way they glanced at Osano sipping his technically illegal drink.

The woman had that bold handsomeness preserved by top-notch plastic surgery and glossed over with the even tan of daily sunlamps and Southern sun. And had that discontented mouth that is perhaps the ugliest thing in any woman. At her feet and up against the bulkhead wall was a wire-mesh box which held maybe the prettiest French poodle in the whole world. It had curly silver fur which fell into ringlets over its eyes. It had a pink mouth and pink ribbon bow over its head. It even had a beautiful tail with a pink bow on it that wagged around. It was the happiest little dog you ever saw and the sweetest-looking. The two miserable human beings that owned it obviously took pleasure from owning such a treasure. The man's face softened a little as he looked at the poodle. The woman didn't show pleasure, but a proprietary pride, like an older ugly woman in charge of her beautiful virginal daughter that she is preparing for the marketplace. When she reached out her hand for the poodle to lick lasciviously, it was like a Pope extending his ring to be kissed.

The great thing about Osano was that he never missed anything even when he seemed to be looking the other way. He had paid strict attention to his drink, slouched down in his seat. But now he said to me, "I'd rather get a blow job from that dog than that broad." The jet engines made it impossible for the woman across the aisle to hear, but I felt nervous anyway. She gave us a coldly dirty look, but maybe that's the way she always looked at people.

Then I felt guilty at having condemned her and her husband. They were, after all, two human beings. Where did I come off putting them down on sheer speculation? So I said to Osano, "Maybe they're not as bad as they look."

"Yes, they are," he said.

That wasn't worthy of him. He could be chauvinistic, racist and narrow-minded but only off the top of his head. It really didn't mean anything. So I let it go, and as the pretty stewardess imprisoned us in our seats for dinner, I told him stories about Vegas. He couldn't believe I had once been a degenerate gambler.

Ignoring the people across the aisle, forgetting about them, I said to him, "You know what gamblers call suicide?"

"No," Osano siad.

I smiled. "They call it the Big Ace."

Osano shook his head. "Isn't that marvelous?" he said dryly.

I saw he was a little contemptuous of the melodrama of the phrase, but I kept on. "That's what Cully said to me that morning when Jordan did it. Cully came down and he said, 'You know what that fucking Jordy did? He pulled the Big Ace out of his sleeve. The prick used his Big Ace.'" I paused, remembering it more clearly now years later. It was funny. I had never remembered that phrase before or Cully using it that night. "He capitalized it in his voice, you know. The Big Ace."

"Why do you think he really did it?" Osano asked. He was not too interested, but he saw I was upset.

"Who the hell knows?" I said. "I thought I was so smart. I thought I had him figured. I nearly had him figured, but then he faked me out. That's what kills me. He made me disbelieve in his humanity, his tragic humanity. Never let anybody make you disbelieve in anybody's humanity."

Osano grinned, nodded his head at the people across the aisle. "Like them?" he said. And then I realized that this was what made me tell him the story.

I glanced at the woman and man. "Maybe."

"OK," he said. "But sometimes it goes against the grain. Especially rich people. You know what's wrong with rich people? They think they're as good as anybody else just because they got lots of dough."

"They're not?" I asked.

"No," Osano said. "They're like hunchbacks."

"Hunchbacks are not as good as anybody else?" I asked. I nearly said dwarfs.

"No," Osano said. "Nor are people with one eye, basket cases, and critics and ugly broads and chickenshit guys. They gotta work at being as good as other people. Those two people didn't work at it. They never got there."

He was being a little irrational and illogical, not at his most brilliant. But what the hell, he'd had a bad week. And it's not everybody who gets his love life ruined by a dwarf. I let it ride.

We finished our dinner, Osano drinking the lousy champagne and eating the lousy food that even in first class you would trade in for a Coney Island hot dog. As they lowered the movie screen, Osano bolted out of his chair and went up the steps to the 747 dome lounge. I finished my coffee and followed him up there.

He was seated in a long-backed chair and had lit up one of his long Havana cigars. He offered me one and I took it. I was developing a taste for them, and that delighted Osano. He was always generous but a little careful with his Havanas. If you got one from him, he watched you closely to see if you enjoyed it enough to deserve it. The lounge was beginning to fill up. The stewardess on duty was busy making drinks. When she brought Osano his martini, she sat on the arm of his lounge chair and he put one hand in her lap to hold her hand.

I could see that one of the great things about being as famous as Osano was that you get away with stuff like that. In the first place, you had the confidence. In the second place, the young girl, instead of thinking you a dirty old man, is usually enormously flattered that somebody so important could think her that attractive. If Osano wanted to screw her, she must be something special. They didn't know that Osano was so horny he would screw anything with skirts. Which is not as bad as it sounds since a lot of guys like him screwed anything in pants and skirts.

The young girl was charmed by Osano. Then a good-looking woman passenger started coming on to him, an older woman with a crazy, interesting face. She told us about how she had just recovered from heart surgery and hadn't fucked for six months and was now ready to go. That's the kind of things women always told Osano. They felt they could tell him anything because he was a writer and so would understand anything. Also, because he was famous and that would make them interesting to him.

Osano took out his heart-shaped Tiffany pillbox. It was filled with white tablets. He took one and offered the box to the heart lady and the stewardess. "Come on," he said. "It's an upper. We'll really be flying high." Then he changed his mind. "No, not you," he said to the heart lady. "Not in your condition." That's when I knew the heart lady was out of it.

Because the pills were really penicillin pills Osano always took before sexual contact so that he would be immunized against VD. And he always used this trick to make a prospective partner take them to double the insurance. He popped one in his mouth and washed it down with scotch. The stewardess laughingly took one, and Osano watched her with a cheerful smile. He offered me the box and I shook my head.

The stewardess was really a pretty young thing, but she couldn't handle Osano and the heart lady. Trying to get the attention back to her, she said sweetly to Osano, "Are you married?"

Now she knew, as everybody knew, that not only was Osano married, but he had been married at least five times. She didn't know that a question like that irritated Osano because he always felt a little guilty about cheating—on all his wives, even the ones he'd divorced. Osano grinned at the stewardess and said coolly, "I'm married, I got a mistress and I got a steady girlfriend. I'm just looking for a dame I can have some fun with."

It was insulting. The young girl flushed and took off to serve the other passengers drinks.

Osano settled down to enjoy the conversation with the heart lady, giving advice on her first fuck. He was putting her on a little.

"Listen," he said. "You don't want to straight fuck for the first time out. It won't be a good fuck for the guy because you'll be a little scared. The thing to do is have the guy go down on you while you're half asleep. Take a tranquilizer and then, just as you're dozing off, he eats you up, you know? And get a guy who's good at it. A real gentleman blow job artist."

The woman turned a little red. Osano grinned. He knew what he was doing. I got a little embarrassed too. I always fall a little in love with strange women who hit me right. I could see her thinking how she could get Osano to do the job for her. She didn't know that she was too old for him and he was just playing his cards very coolly to nail the young stewardess.

There we were speeding along at six hundred miles an hour and not feeling a thing. But Osano was getting drunker, and things started going bad. The heart lady was boozy maudlin about dying and how to find the right guy to go down on her the right way. That made Osano nervous. He said to her, "You can always play the Big Ace." Of course, she didn't know what he was talking about. But she knew she was being dismissed, and the hurt look on her face irritated Osano even more. He ordered another drink, and the stewardess, jealous and pissed off that he had ignored her, gave him the drink and slipped away in the cool, insulting way the young can always use to put older people down. Osano showed his age that day.

At that moment the couple with the poodle came up the steps into the lounge. Well, she was one woman I would never fall in love with. The discontented mouth, that artificially tinted nut-brown face with all the lines of life excised by a surgeon's knife, were too repellent, no fantasies could be spun around them unless you were into sadomaso stuff.

The man carried the beautiful little poodle, the dog's tongue hanging out with happiness. Carrying the poodle gave the sour-faced man a touching air of vulnerability. As usual Osano seemed not to notice them, though they gave him glances that showed they knew who he was. Probably from TV. Osano had been on TV a hundred times and always making himself interesting in a foolish way that lessened his real worth.

The couple ordered drinks. The woman said something to the man and he obediently dropped the poodle to the floor. The poodle stayed close to them, then wandered around a bit, sniffing at all the people and at all the chairs. I knew Osano hated animals, but he didn't seem to notice the poodle sniffing at his feet. He kept talking to the heart lady. The heart lady leaned over to fix the pink ribbon over the poodle's head and get her hand licked by the poodle's little pink tongue. I never could understand the animal thing, but this poodle was, in a funny kind of way, sexy. I wondered what went on with that sour-faced couple. The poodle pattered around the lounge, wandered back to its owners and sat on the feet of the woman. She put on dark glasses, which for some reason seemed ominous, and when the stewardess brought her drink, she said something to the young girl. The stewardess looked at her in astonishment.

I guess it was at this moment that I got a little nervous. I knew Osano was all jazzed up. He hated being trapped in a plane, he hated being trapped in a conversation with a woman he didn't really want to screw. What he was thinking about was how to get the young stewardess into a toilet and give her a quick, savage fuck. The young stewardess came to me with my drink and leaned over to whisper in my ear. I could see Osano getting jealous. He thought the girl was coming on to me, and that was an insult to his fame more than anything else. He could understand the girl wanting a younger, better-looking guy, but not turning down his fame.

But the stewardess was whispering a different kind of trouble. She said, "That woman wants me to tell Mr. Osano to put out his cigar. She says it's bothering her dog."

Jesus Christ. The dog wasn't even supposed to be up in the lounge running around. It was supposed to be in its box. Everybody knew that. The girl whispered worriedly, "What should I do?"

I guess what happened next was partly my fault. I knew Osano could go crazy at any time and that this was a prime time. But I was always curious about how people react. I wanted to see if the stewardess would really have the nerve to tell a guy like Osano to put out one of his beloved Havana cigars because of a fucking dog. Especially when Osano had paid for a first class ticket just to smoke it in the lounge. I also wanted to see Osano put the hard-faced snotty woman in her place. I would have ditched my cigar and let it ride. But I knew Osano. He would send the plane down into hell first.

The stewardess was waiting for an answer. I shrugged. "Whatever your job makes you do," I said. And it was a malicious answer.

I guess the stewardess felt the same way. Or maybe she just wanted to humiliate Osano because he was no longer paying any attention to her. Or maybe, because she was just a kid, she took what she thought was the easy way out.

Osano, if you didn't know him, looked easier to handle than the bitch lady.

Well, we all made a bad mistake. The stewardess stood next to Osano and said, "Sir, would you mind putting out your cigar? That lady says the smoke is bothering her dog."

Osano's startling green eyes went cold as ice. He gave the stewardess a long, hard look.

"Let me hear that again," he said.

Right then I was ready to jump out of the plane. I saw the look of maniacal rage form over Osano's face. It was no longer a joke. The woman was staring at Osano with distaste. She was dying for an argument, a real uproar. You could see she'd love a fight. The husband glanced out the window, studying the limitless horizon. Obviously this was a familiar scene and he had every confidence that his wife would prevail. He even had a slight, satisfied smile. Only the sweet-looking poodle was distressed. It was gasping for air and giving delicate little hiccups. The lounge was smoky but not from just Osano's cigar. Nearly everybody had cigarettes going, and you got the feeling that the poodle owners would make everybody stop smoking.

The stewardess, frightened by Osano's face, was paralyzed—she couldn't speak. But the woman was not intimidated. You could see that she just loved seeing that look of maniacal rage on Osano's face. You could also see that she never in her life had been punched in the mouth, that she had never gotten a few teeth knocked out. The thought had never occurred to her. So she even leaned toward Osano to speak to him, putting her face in range. I almost closed my eyes. In fact, I did close my eyes for a fraction of a second and I could hear the woman in her cultured, cold voice saying very flatly to Osano, "Your cigar is distressing my dog. Could you please just stop?"

The words were snotty enough, but the tone was insulting beyond any mere words. I could see she was waiting for an argument about her dog's not being allowed in the lounge, how the lounge was for smoking. How she realized that if she had said the smoke was distressing her personally, Osano would get rid of the cigar. But she wanted him to put out the cigar for her dog. She wanted a scene.

Osano grasped all this in a second. He understood everything. And I think that was what drove him crazy. I saw that smile come over his face, a smile that could be infinitely charming but for the cold green eyes that were pure maniac.

He didn't yell at her. He didn't punch her in the face. He gave her husband one look to see what he would do. The husband smiled faintly. He liked what his wife was doing, or so it seemed. Then with a deliberate motion Osano put out his cigar in the welled tray of his seat. The woman watched him with contempt. Then Osano reached out his arm across the table and you could see the woman thought he was going to pet the poodle. I knew better. Osano's hand went down over the poodle's head and around its neck.

What happened next was too quick for me to stop. He lifted the poor dog up, rising up out of his seat, and strangled it with both hands. The poodle gasped and choked, its pink-beribboned tail wagging in distress. Its eyes started bulging out of its mattress of silky ringed fur. The woman screamed and sprang up and clawed at Osano's face. The husband didn't move out of his seat. At that moment the plane hit a small air pocket and we all lurched. But Osano, drunk, all his balance concentrated on strangling the poodle, lost his footing and went sprawling down the aisle, his hands still tight around the dog's throat. To get up he had to turn the dog loose. The woman was screaming something about killing him. The stewardess was screaming out of shock. Osano, standing straight up, smiled around the lounge and then advanced toward the woman, still screaming at him. She thought that now he would be ashamed of what he had done, that she could abuse him. She didn't know that he had already made up his mind to strangle her as he had the dog. Then she caught on. . . . She shut up.

And Osano said with maniacal quiet, "You cunt, now you get it." And he lunged for her. He was really crazy. He hit her in the face. I ducked in front and grabbed him. But he had his hands around her throat and she screamed. And then it became a madhouse. The plane must have had security guards in plain clothes because two men took Osano very professionally by the arms and peeled his coat back to form a straitjacket. But he was wild and he was throwing them around anyway. Everybody watched, horrified. I tried to quiet Osano down, but he couldn't hear anything. He was berserk. He was screaming curses at the woman and her husband. The two security men were trying to gentle him down, addressing him by name, and one, a good-looking strong boy, was asking him if they let him go would he behave. Osano still fought. Then the strong boy lost his temper.

Now Osano was in an uncontrollable rage because partly it was his nature and partly because he was famous and knew he would be insulated against any retaliations for his rage. The young strong boy understood this by instinct, but now he was affronted that Osano didn't respect his superior youthful strength. And he got mad. He took a handful of Osano's hair and yanked his head back so hard he nearly snapped his neck. Then he put his arm around Osano's neck and said, "You son of a bitch, I'll break it." Osano went still.

Jesus, it was a mess after that. The captain of the plane wanted to put Osano in a straitjacket, but I talked him out of it. The security cleared out the lounge, and Osano and I sat there with them for the rest of the trip. They didn't let us off in New York until the plane was empty, so we never saw the woman again. But that last glimpse of her was enough. They had washed the blood off her face, but she had one eye almost shut and her mouth was mashed to pulp. The husband carried the poodle, still alive, wagging its tail desperately for affection and protection. Later there were some legal complaints that the lawyers handled. Of course, it got in all the papers. The great American novelist and prime candidate for the Nobel Prize had almost murdered a little French poodle. Poor dog. Poor Osano. The cunt had turned out to be a large stockholder in the airline plus having millions of other dollars, and of course, she couldn't even threaten never to fly that airline again. As for Osano he was perfectly happy. He had no feeling about animals. He said, "As long as I can eat them, I can kill them." When I pointed out that he had never eaten dog meat, he just shrugged and said, "Cook it right and I'll eat it."

One thing Osano missed. That crazy woman had her humanity too. OK, she was crazy. OK, she deserved a bloody mouth, it might even have done her good. But she really didn't deserve what Osano did to her. She really couldn't help the kind of person she was, I thought then. The earlier Osano would have seen all that. For some reason he couldn't now.

Chapter 25

The sexy poodle didn't die, so the lady didn't press charges. She didn't seem to mind getting her face smashed or it wasn't important to her or to her husband. She might even have enjoyed it. She sent Osano a friendly note, leaving the door open for them to get together. Osano gave a funny little growl and tossed the note into the wastepaper basket. "Why don't you give her a try?" I said. "She might be interesting."

"I don't like hitting women," Osano said. "That bitch wants me to use her as a punching bag."

"She could be another Wendy," I said. I knew Wendy always had some sort of fascination for him despite their being divorced all these years and despite all the aggravation she caused him.

"Jesus," Osano said. "That's all I need." But he smiled. He knew what I meant. That maybe beating women didn't displease him that much. But he wanted to show me I was wrong.

"Wendy was the only wife I had that made me hit her," he said. "All my other wives, they fucked my best friends, they stole my money, they beat me for alimony, they lied about me, but I never hit them, I never disliked them. I'm good friends with all my other wives. But that fucking Wendy is some piece of work. A class by herself. If I'd stayed married to her, I'd have killed her."

But the poodle strangling had got around in the literary circles of New York. Osano worried about his chances of getting the Nobel Prize. "Those fucking Scandinavians love dogs," he said. He fired up his active campaign for the Nobel by writing letters to all his friends and professional acquaintances. He also kept publishing articles and reviews on the most important critical works to appear in the review. Plus essays on literature which I always thought were full of shit. Many times when I went into his office he would be working on his novel, filling yellow lined sheets. His great novel, because it was the only thing he wrote in longhand. The rest of his stuff he banged out with two fingers on the typewriter he could swivel to from his executive desk piled with books. He was the fastest typist I have ever seen even with just two fingers. He sounded like a machine gun literally. And with that machine-gun typing he wrote the definition of what the great American novel should be, explained why England no longer produced great fiction, except in the spy genre, took apart the latest works and sometimes the body of work of guys like Faulkner, Mailer, Styron, Jones, anybody who could give him competition for the Nobel. He was so brilliant, the language so charged, that he convinced you. By publishing all that crap, he demolished his opponents and left the field clear for himself. The only trouble was that when you went to his own work, he had only his first two novels published twenty years ago that could give him serious claim to a literary reputation. The rest of his novels and nonfiction work were not that good.

The truth was that over the last ten years he had lost a great deal of his popular success and his literary reputation. He had published too many books done off the top of his head, made too many enemies with the high-handed way he ran the review. Even when he did some ass kissing by praising powerful literary figures, he did it with such arrogance and condescension, did it with himself mixed up with it in some way (as his Einstein article had been as much about himself as about Einstein) that he made enemies of the people he was stroking. He wrote one line that really caused an uproar. He said the huge difference between French literature of the nineteenth century and English literature was that French writers had plenty of sex and the English didn't. Our review clientele boiled with rage.

On top of this his personal behavior was scandalous. The publishers of the review had learned of the airplane incident, and it had leaked into the gossip columns. On one of his lectures at a California college he met a young nineteen-year-old literary student who looked more like a cheerleader or starlet than a lover of books, which she really was. He brought her to New York to live with him. She lasted about six months, but during that time he took her to all the literary parties. Osano was in his middle fifties, not yet gray but definitely paunchy. When you saw them together, you got a little uncomfortable. Especially when Osano was drunk and she had to carry him home. Plus he was drinking while he was working in the office. Plus he was cheating on his nineteen-year-old girlfriend with a forty-year-old female novelist who had just published a best-seller. The book wasn't really that good, but Osano wrote a full-page essay in the review hailing her as a future great of American literature.

And he did one thing I really hated. He would give a quote to any friend who asked. So you saw novels coming out that were lousy but with a quote from Osano saying something like: "This is the finest Southern novel since Styron's *Lie Down in Darkness*." Or, "A shocking book that will dismay you," which was kind of sly because he was trying to play both ends against the middle, doing his friend the favor and yet trying to warn the reader off the book with an ambiguous quote.

It was easy for me to see that he was coming apart in some way. I thought maybe he was going crazy. But I didn't know from what. His face looked unhealthy, puffy; his green eyes had a glitter that was not really normal. And there was something wrong with his walk, a hitch in his stride or a little waver to the left sometimes. I worried about him. Because despite my disapproval of his writings, his striving for the Nobel with all his cutthroat maneuvers, his trying to screw every dame he came into contact with, I had an affection for him. He would talk to me about the novel I was working on, encourage me, give me advice, try to lend me money though I knew he was in hock up to his ears and spent money at an enormous rate supporting his five ex-wives and eight or nine children. I was awestricken by the amount of work he published, flawed though it was. He always appeared in one of the monthlies, sometimes in two or three; every year he published a nonfiction book on some subject the publishers thought was "hot." He edited the review and did a long essay for it every week. He did some movie work. He earned enormous sums, but he was always broke. And I knew he owed a fortune. Not only from borrowing money but drawing advances on future books. I mentioned this to him, that he was digging a hole he'd never get out of, but he just waved the idea away impatiently.

"I've got my ace in the hole," he said. "I got the big novel nearly finished. Another year maybe. And then I'll be rich again. And then on to Scandinavia for the Nobel Prize. Think of all those big blond broads we can fuck." He always included me on the trip to the Nobel.

The biggest fights we had were when he'd ask me about what I thought of one of his essays on literature in general. And I would infuriate him with my by now familiar line that I was just a storyteller. "You're an artist with divine inspiration," I'd tell him. "You're the intellectual, you've got a fucking brain that could squirt out enough bullshit for a hundred courses on modern literature. I'm just a safecracker. I put my ear to the wall and wait to hear the tumblers fall in place."

"You and your safecracker bullshit," Osano said. "You're just reacting away from me. You have ideas. You're a real artist. But you like the idea of being a magician, a trickster, that you can control everything, what you write, your life in general, that you can beat all the traps. That's how you operate."

"You have the wrong idea of a magician," I told him. "A magician does magic. That's all."

"And you think that's enough?" Osano asked. He had a slightly sad smile on his face.

"It's enough for me," I said.

Osano nodded his head. "You know, I was a great magician once, you read my first book. All magic, right?"

I was glad that I could agree. I had an affection for that book. "Pure magic," I said.

"But it wasn't enough," Osano said. "Not for me."

Then too bad for you, I thought. And he seemed to read my mind. "No, not how you think," he said. "I just couldn't do it again because I don't want to do it or I can't do it maybe. I wasn't a magician anymore after that book. I became a writer."

I shrugged a little unsympathetically, I guess. Osano saw it and said, "And my life went to shit, but you can see that. I envy you your life. Everything is under control. You don't drink, you don't smoke, you don't chase broads. You just write and gamble and play the good father and husband. You're a very unflashy magician, Merlyn. You're a very safe magician. A safe life, safe books; you've made despair disappear."

He was pissed off at me. He thought he was driving into the bone. He didn't know he was full of shit. And I didn't mind, that meant my magic was working. That was all he could see, and that was fine with me. He thought I had my life under control, that I didn't suffer or permit myself to, that I didn't feel the bouts of loneliness that drove him on to different women, to booze, to his snorts of cocaine. Two things he didn't realize. That he was suffering because he was actually going crazy, not suffering. The other was that everybody else in the world suffered and was lonely and made the best of it. That it was no big deal. In fact, you could say that life itself wasn't a big deal, never mind his fucking literature.

And then suddenly I had troubles from an unexpected quarter. One day at the review I got a call from Artie's wife, Pam. She said she wanted to see me about something important, and she wanted to see me without Artie. Could I come over right away? I felt a real panic. In the back of my mind I was always worried about Artie. He was really frail and always looked tired. His fine-boned handsomeness showed stress more clearly than most. I was so panicky I begged her to tell me what it was over the phone, but she wouldn't. She did tell me that there was nothing physically wrong, no medical reports of doom. It was a personal problem she and Artie were having, and she needed my help.

Immediately, selfishly, I was relieved. Obviously she had a problem, not Artie. But still I took off early from work and drove out to Long Island to see her. Artie lived on the North Shore of Long Island and I lived on the South Shore. So it really wasn't much out of my way. I figured I could listen to her and be home for dinner, just a little late. I didn't bother to call Valerie.

* * *

I always liked going to Artie's house. He had five kids, but they were nice kids who had a lot of friends who were always around and Pam never seemed to mind. She had big jars of cookies to feed them and gallon jugs of milk. There were kids watching television and other kids playing on the lawn. I said hi to the kids, and they gave me a brief hi back. Pam took me into the kitchen with its huge bay window. She had coffee ready and poured some. She kept her head down and then suddenly looked up at me and said, "Artie has a girlfriend."

Despite her having had five kids, **Pam** was still very young-looking with a fine figure, tall, slender, lanky before the kids, and one of those sensual faces that had a Madonna kind of look. She came from a Midwest town. Artie had met her in college and her father was president of a small bank. Nobody in the last three generations of her family had ever had more than two kids, and she was a hero-martyr to her parents because of the five births. They couldn't understand it, but I did. I had once asked Artie about it and he said, "Behind that Madonna face is one of the horniest wives on Long Island. And that suits me fine." If any other husband had said that about his wife, I would have been offended.

"Lucky you," I had said.

"Yeah," Artie said. "But I think she feels sorry for me, you know, the asylum business. And she wants to make sure I never feel lonely again. Something like that."

"Lucky, lucky you," I had said.

And so now, when Pam made her accusation, I was a little angry. I knew Artie. I knew it wasn't possible for him to cheat on his wife. That he would never endanger the family he had built up or the happiness it gave him.

Pam's tall form was drooping; tears were in her eyes. But she was watching my face. If Artie were having an affair, the only one he would ever tell was me. And she was hoping I would give away the secret by some expression on my face.

"It's not true," I said. "Artie always had women running after him and he hated it. He's the straightest guy in the world. You know I wouldn't try to cover for him. I wouldn't rat on him, but I wouldn't cover for him."

"I know that," Pam said. "But he comes home late at least three times a week. And last night he had lipstick on his shirt. And he makes phone calls after I go up to bed, late at night. Does he call you?"

"No," I said. And now I felt shitty. It might be true. I still didn't believe it, but I had to find out.

"And he's spending extra money he never spent before," Pam said. "Oh, shit." She was crying openly now.

"Will he be home for dinner tonight?" I asked. Pam nodded. I picked up the kitchen phone and called Valerie and told her I was eating at Artie's house. I did that once in a while on the spur of the moment when I had an urge to see him, so she didn't ask any questions. When I hung up the phone, I said to Pam, "You got enough to feed me?"

She smiled and nodded her head. "Of course," she said.

"I'll go down and pick him up at the station," I said. "And we'll have this all straightened out before we eat dinner." I burlesqued it a bit and said, "My brother is innocent."

"Oh, sure," Pam said. But she smiled.

Down at the station, as I waited for the train to come in, I felt sorry for Pam and Artie. There was a little smugness in my pity. I was the guy Artie always had to bail out and finally I was going to bail him out. Despite all the evidence, the lipstick on the shirt, the late hours and phone calls, the extra money, I knew that Artie was basically innocent. The worst it could be was some young girl being so persistent that he finally weakened a little, maybe. Even now I couldn't believe it. Mixed with the pity was the envy I always felt about Artie's being so attractive to women in a way I could never be. With just a touch of satisfaction I felt it was not all that bad being ugly.

When Artie got off the train, he wasn't too surprised to see me. I had done this before, visiting him unexpectedly and meeting his train. I always felt good doing it, and he was always glad to see me. And it always made me feel good to see that he was glad to see me waiting for him. This time, watching him carefully, I noticed he wasn't quite that glad to see me today.

"What the hell are you doing here?" he said, but he gave me a hug and he smiled. He had an extraordinarily sweet smile for a man. It was the smile he had as a child and it had never changed.

"I came to save your ass," I said cheerfully. "Pam finally got the goods on you."

He laughed. "Jesus, not that shit again." Pam's jealousy was always good for a laugh.

"Yep," I said. "The late hours, the late phone calls and now, finally, the classic evidence: lipstick on your shirt." I was feeling great because just by seeing Artie and talking to him I knew it was all a mistake.

But suddenly Artie sat down on one of the station benches. His face looked very tired. I was standing over him and beginning to feel just a little uneasy.

Artie looked up at me. I saw a strange look of pity on his face. "Don't worry," I said. "I'll fix everything."

He tried to smile. "Merlyn the Magician," he said. "You'd better put on your fucking magic hat. At least sit down." He lit up a cigarette. I thought again that he smoked too much. I sat down next to him. Oh, shit, I thought. And my mind was racing on to how to square things between him and Pam. One thing I knew, I didn't want to lie to her or have Artie lie to her.

"I'm not cheating on Pam," Artie said. "And that's all I want to tell you."

There was no question about my believing him. He would never lie to me. "Right," I said. "But you have to tell Pam what's going on or she'll go crazy. She called me at work."

"If I tell Pam, I have to tell you," Artie said. "You don't want to hear it."

"So tell me," I said. "What the hell's the difference? You always tell me everything. How can it hurt?"

Artie dropped his cigarette to the stone cement floor of the train platform. "OK," he said. He put his hand on my arm and I felt a sudden sense of dread. When we were children alone together, he always did that to comfort me. "Let me finish, don't interrupt," he said.

"OK," I said. My face was suddenly very warm. I couldn't think of what was coming.

"For the last couple of years I've been trying to find our mother," Artie said. "Who she is, where she is, what we are. A month ago I found her."

I was standing up. I pulled my arm away from his. Artie stood up and tried to hold me again. "She's a drunk," he said. "She wears lipstick. She looks pretty good. But she's all alone in the world. She wants to see you, she says that she couldn't help—"

I broke in on him. "Don't tell me any more," I said. "Don't ever tell me any more. You do what you want, but I'll see her in hell before I'll see her alive."

"Hey, come on, come on," Artie said. He tried to put his hand on me again and I broke away and walked toward the car. Artie followed me. We got in and I drove him to the house. By this time I was under control and I could see that Artie was distressed, so I said to him, "You'd better tell Pam."

Artie said, "I will."

I stopped in the driveway of the house. "You coming in for dinner?" Artie asked. He was standing by my open window, and again he reached in to put his hand on my arm.

"No," I said.

I watched him as he went into the house, shooing the last of the kids still playing on the lawn into the house with him. Then I drove away. I drove slowly and carefully, I had trained myself all my life to be more careful when most people became more reckless. When I got home, I could see by Vallie's face that she knew about what happened. The kids were in bed, and she had dinner for me on the kitchen table. While I ate, she ran her hand over the back of my head and neck when she went by to the stove. She sat opposite, drinking coffee, waiting for me to open the subject. Then she remembered. "Pam wants you to call her."

I called. Pam was trying to make some apology for having gotten me into such a mess. I told her it was no mess, and did she feel better now that she knew the truth? Pam giggled and said, "Christ, I think I'd rather it were a girlfriend." She was cheerful again. And now our roles were reversed. Early that day I had pitied her, she was the person in terrible danger and I was the one who would rescue or try to help her. Now she seemed to think it was unfair that the roles were reversed. That was what the apology was about. I told her not to worry.

Pam stumbled over what she wanted to say next. "Merlyn, you didn't really mean it, about your mother, that you won't see her?"

"Does Artie believe me?" I asked her.

"He says he always knew it," Pam said. "He wouldn't have told you until he'd softened you up. Except for me causing the trouble. He was teed off at me for bringing it all on."

I laughed. "See," I said, "it started off as a bad day for you and now it's a bad day for him. He's the injured party. Better him than you."

"Sure," Pam said. "Listen, I'm sorry for you, really."

"It has nothing at all to do with me," I said. And Pam said OK and thanks and hung up.

Valerie was waiting for me now. She was watching me intently. She'd been briefed by Pam and maybe even by Artie on how to handle this, and she was being careful. But I guess she hadn't really grasped it. She and Pam were really good women, but they didn't understand. Both their parents had made trouble and objections about them marrying orphans with no traceable lineage. I could imagine the horror stories told about similar cases. What if there had been insanity or degeneracy in our family? Or black blood or Jewish blood or Protestant blood, all that fucking shit. Well, now here was a nice piece of evidence turned up when it was no longer needed. I could figure out that Pam and Valerie were not too happy about Artie's romanticism, his digging up the lost link of a mother.

"Do you want her here to the house so that she can see the children?" Valerie asked.

"No," I said.

Valerie looked troubled and a little terrified. I could see how she was thinking what if her children rejected her someday.

"She's your mother," Valerie said. "She must have had a very unhappy life."

"Do you know what the word 'orphan' means?" I said. "Have you looked it up in the dictionary? It means a child who has lost both parents through death. Or a young animal that has been deserted or has lost its mother. Which one do you want?"

"OK," Valerie said. She looked terrified. She went to look in on the kids and then went into our bedroom. I could hear her going into the bathroom and preparing for bed. I stayed up late reading and making notes, and when I went to bed, she was sound asleep.

It was all over in a couple of months. Artie called me up one day and told me his mother had disappeared again. We arranged to meet in the city and have dinner together so that we could talk alone. We could never talk about it with our wives present, as if it were too shameful for their knowledge. Artie seemed cheerful. He told me she had left a note. He told me that she drank a lot and always wanted to go to bars and pick up men. That she was a middle-aged floozy but that he liked her. He had made her stop drinking, he had bought her new clothes, he had rented her a nicely furnished apartment, given her an allowance. She had told him everything that had happened to her. It hadn't really been her fault. I stopped him there. I didn't want to hear about that.

"Are you going to look for her again?" I asked him.

Artie smiled his sad, beautiful smile. "No," he said. "You know, I was a pain in the ass to her even now. She really didn't like having me around. At first, when I found her, she played the role I wanted her to play, I think out of a sense of guilt that maybe she could make things up to me by letting me take care of her. But she really didn't like it. She even made a pass at me one day, I think just to get some excitement." He laughed. "I wanted her to come to the house, but she never would. It's just as well."

"How did Pam take the whole business?" I asked.

Artie laughed out loud. "Jesus, she was even jealous of my mother. When I told her it was all over, you should have seen the look of relief on her face. One thing I have to say for you, brother, you took the news without cracking a muscle."

"Because I don't give a shit one way or the other," I said.

"Yeah," Artie said. "I know. It doesn't matter. I don't think you would have liked her."

Six months later Artie had a heart attack. It was a mild one, but he was in the hospital for weeks and off from work another month. I went to see him in the hospital every day, and he kept insisting that it had been some sort of indigestion, that it was a borderline case. I went down to the library and read everything I could about heart attacks. I found out that his reaction was a common one with heart attack victims and that sometimes they were right. But Pam was panic-stricken. When Artie came out of the hospital, she put him on a strict diet, threw all the cigarettes out of the house and stopped smoking so that Artie could quit. It was hard for him, but he did. And maybe the heart attack did scare him because now he took care of himself. He took the long walks the doctors prescribed, ate carefully and never touched to-bacco. Six months later he looked better than he had ever looked in his life and Pam and I stopped giving each other panicky looks whenever he was out of the room. "Thank God, he's stopped smoking," Pam said. "He was up to three packs a day. That's what did him in."

I nodded, but I didn't believe it. I always believed it was that two months he spent trying to claim his mother that did him in.

And as soon as Artie was OK, I got into trouble. I lost my job on the literary review. Not through any fault of mine but because Osano got fired and as his right-hand man I was fired with him.

Osano had weathered all the storms. His contempt of the most powerful literary circles in the country, the political intelligentsia, the culture fanatics, the liberals, the conservatives, Women's Liberation, the radicals, his sexual escapades, his gambling on sports, his use of his position to lobby for the Nobel Prize. Plus a nonfiction book he published in defense of pornography, not for its redeeming social value, but as antielitist pleasure of the poor in intellect. For all these things the publishers would have liked to fire him, but the circulation of the review had doubled since he became editor.

By this time I was making good money. I wrote a lot of Osano's articles for him. I could imitate his style pretty well, and he would start me off with a fifteen-minute harangue on how he felt about a particular subject, always brilliantly crazy. It was easy for me to write the article based on his fifteen minutes of ranting. Then he'd go over and put in a few of his masterful touches and we'd split the money. Just half his money was twice what I got paid for an article.

Even that didn't get us fired. It was his ex-wife Wendy who did us in. Though that's maybe unfair; Osano did us in, Wendy handed him the knife.

Osano had spent four weeks in Hollywood while I ran the review for him. He was completing some sort of movie deal, and during the four weeks we used a courier to fly out and give him review articles to OK before I ran it. When Osano finally came back to New York, he gave a party for all his friends to celebrate his home-coming and the big chunk of money he had earned in Hollywood.

The party was held at his East Side brownstone which his latest ex-wife used with their batch of three kids. Osano was living in a small studio apartment in the Village, the only thing he could afford, but too small for the party.

I went because he insisted that I go. Valerie didn't come. She didn't like Osano and she didn't like parties outside her family circle. Over the years we had come to an unspoken agreement. We excused each other from each other's social lives whenever possible. My reason was that I was too busy working on my novel, my job and free-lance writing assignments. Her excuse was that she had to take care of the kids and didn't trust baby-sitters. We both enjoyed the arrangement. It was easier for her than it was for me since I had no social life except for my brother, Artie, and the review.

Anyway, Osano's party was one of the big events of the literary set in New York. The top people of the *New York Times Book Review* came, the critics for most of the magazines and novelists that Osano was still friendly with. I was sitting in a corner talking with Osano's latest ex-wife when I saw Wendy come in and I thought immediately, Jesus, trouble, I knew she had not been invited.

Osano spotted her at the same time and started walking toward her with the peculiar lurching gait he'd acquired in the last few months. He was a little drunk, and I was afraid he might lose his temper and cause a scene or do something crazy, so I got up and joined them. I arrived just in time to hear Osano greet her.

"What the fuck do you want?" he said. He could be frightening when he was angry, but from what he had told me about Wendy I knew she was the one person who enjoyed making him mad. But I was still surprised at her reaction.

Wendy was dressed in jeans and sweater and a scarf over her head. It made her thin dark face Medea-like. Her wiry black hair escaped from the scarf like thin black snakes.

She looked at Osano with a deadly calm which held malevolent triumph. She was consumed with hatred. She took a long look around the room as if drinking in what she now no longer could claim any part of, the glittering literary world of Osano that he had effectively banished her from. It was a look of satisfaction. Then she said to Osano, "I have something very important to tell you."

Osano downed his glass of scotch. He gave her an ugly grin. "So tell me and get the fuck out."

Wendy said very seriously, "It's bad news."

Osano laughed uproariously and genuinely. That really tickled him. "You're always bad news," he said and laughed again.

Wendy watched him with quiet satisfaction. "I have to tell you in private."

"Oh, shit," Osano said. But he knew Wendy, she would delight in a scene. So he took her up the stairs to his study. I figured later that he didn't take her to one of the bedrooms because deep down he was afraid he would try to fuck her, she still had that kind of hold on him. And he knew she would delight in refusing him. But it was a mistake to bring her into the study. It was his favorite room, still kept for him as a place to work. It had a huge window which he loved to stare out of while he was writing and watch the goings-on in the street below.

I hung around at the bottom of the stairs. I really don't know why, but I felt that Osano was going to need help. So I was the first one to hear Wendy scream in terror and the first one to act on that scream. I ran up the stairs and kicked in the door of the study.

I was just in time to see Osano reach Wendy. She was flailing her thin arms at him, trying to keep him away. Her bony hands were curled, the fingers extended like claws to scratch his face. She was terrified, but she was enjoying it too. I could see that. Osano's face was bleeding from two long furrows on his right cheek. And before I could stop him, he had hit Wendy in the face so that she swayed toward him. In one terrible swift motion he picked her up as if she were a weightless doll and threw her through the picture window with tremendous force. The window shattered, and Wendy sailed through it to the street below.

I don't know whether I was more horrified by the sight of Wendy's tiny body breaking through the window or Osano's completely maniacal face. I ran out of the room and shouted, "Call an ambulance." I snatched up a coat from the hallway and ran out in the street.

Wendy was lying on the cement like an insect whose legs had been broken. As I came out of the house, she was teetering up on her arms and legs but had only gotten to her knees. She looked like a spider trying to walk, and then she collapsed again.

I knelt beside her and covered her with the coat. I took off my jacket and folded it beneath her head. She was in pain, but there was no blood trickling out of her mouth or ears and there was not that deadly film over the eyes that long ago during the war I had recognized as a danger signal. Her face finally was calm and at peace with itself. I held her hand, it was warm, and she opened her eyes. "You'll be OK," I said. "An ambulance is coming. You'll be OK."

She opened her eyes and smiled at me. She looked very

beautiful, and for the first time I understood Osano's being fascinated by her. She was in pain but actually grinning, "I fixed that son of a bitch this time," she said.

When they got her to the hospital, they found that she had suffered a broken toe and a fracture of the shoulder clavicle. She was conscious enough to tell what had happened, and the cops went looking for Osano and took him away. I called Osano's lawyer. He told me to keep my mouth shut as much as I possibly could and that he would straighten everything out. He had known Osano and Wendy a long time and he understood the whole thing before I did. He told me to stay where I was until he called.

Needless to say, the party broke up after detectives questioned some of the people, including myself. I said I hadn't seen anything except Wendy falling through the window. No, I hadn't seen Osano near her, I told them. And they left it at that. Osano's ex-wife gave me a drink and sat next to me on the sofa. She had a funny little smile on her face. "I always knew this would happen," she said.

It took almost three hours for the lawyer to call me. He said he had Osano out on bail but that it would be a good idea for someone to be with him a couple of days. Osano would be going to his studio apartment in the Village. Could I go down there to keep him company and keep him from talking to the press? I said I would. Then the lawyer briefed me. Osano had testified that Wendy had attacked him and that he had flung her away from him and she had lost her balance and went through the window. That was the story given to the newspapers. The lawyer was sure that he could get Wendy to go along with the story out of her own self-interest. If Osano went to jail, she would lose out on alimony and child support. It would all be smoothed over in a couple of days if Osano could be kept from saying something outrageous. Osano should be at his apartment in an hour, the lawyer would bring him there.

I left the brownstone and took a taxi down to the Village. I sat on the stoop of the apartment house until the lawyer's chauffeured limo rolled up. Osano got out.

He looked dreadful. His eyes were bulging out of his head, and his skin was dead white with strain. He walked right past me, and I got into the elevator with him. He took his keys out, but his hands were shaking and I did it for him.

When we were in his tiny studio apartment, Osano flopped down on the couch that opened out into a bed. He still hadn't said a word to me. He was lying there now, his face covering his hands out of weariness, not despair. I looked around the studio apartment and thought, here was Osano, one of the most famous writers in the world and he lived in this hole. But then I remembered that he rarely lived here. That he was usually living in his house in the Hamptons or up in Provincetown. Or with one of the rich divorced women he would have a love affair with for a few months.

I sat down in a dusty armchair and kicked a pile of books into a corner. "I told the cops I didn't see anything," I said to Osano.

Osano sat up and his hands were away from his face. To my amazement I could see that wild grin on his face.

"Jesus, how did you like the way she sailed through the air. I always said she was a fucking witch. I didn't throw her that hard. She was flying on her own."

I stared at him. "I think you're going fucking crazy," I said. "I think you'd better see a doctor." My voice was cold. I couldn't forget Wendy lying in the street.

"Shit, she's going to be OK," Osano said. "And you don't ask why. Or do you think I throw all my ex-wives out the window?"

"There's no excuse," I said.

Osano grinned. "You don't know Wendy. I'll bet twenty bucks when I tell you what she said to me, you'll agree you'd have done the same thing."

"Bet," I said. I went into the bathroom and wet a facecloth and threw it to him. He wiped his face and neck and sighed with pleasure as the cold water refreshed his skin.

Osano hunched forward on the couch. "She reminded me how she had written me letters the last two months begging for money for our kid. Of course, I didn't send her any money, she'd spend it on herself. Then she said that she hadn't wanted to bother me while I was busy in Hollywood but that our youngest boy had gotten sick with spinal meningitis and because she didn't have enough money she had to put him in the charity ward in the city hospital, Bellevue no less. Can you imagine that fucking cunt? She didn't call me that he was sick because she wanted to lay all that shit on me, all that guilt on me."

I knew how Osano loved all his kids from his different wives. I was amazed at this capacity in him. He always sent them birthday presents and always had them with him for the summers. And he dropped in to see them sporadically to take them to the theater or to dinner or a ball game. I was astonished now that he didn't seem worried about his kid being sick. He understood what I was feeling.

"The kid only had a high fever, some sort of respiratory infection. While you were being so gallant about Wendy, I was calling the hospital before the cops came. They told me there was nothing to worry about. I called my doctor and he's having the kid taken to a private hospital. So everything's OK."

"Do you want me to hang around?" I asked him.

Osano shook his head. "I have to go see my kid and take care of the other kids now that I've deprived them of their mother. But she'll be out tomorrow, that bitch."

Before I left him, I asked Osano one question. "When you threw her out that window, did you remember that it was really only two stories above the street?"

He grinned at me again. "Sure," he said. "And besides, I never figured she'd sail that far. I tell you she's a witch."

All the New York newspapers had front-page stories the next day. Osano was still famous enough for that kind of treatment. At least Osano didn't go to jail because Wendy didn't press charges. She said that maybe she had stumbled and gone through the window. But that was the next day and the damage had been done. Osano was made to resign gracefully from the review and I resigned with him. One columnist, trying to be funny, speculated that if Osano won the Nobel Prize, he would be the first one to win who had ever thrown his wife out of the window. But the truth was that everybody knew that this little comedy would end all Osano's hopes in that direction. You couldn't give the sober respectable Nobel to a sordid character like Osano. And Osano didn't help matters much when a little later he wrote a satirical article on the ten best ways to murder your wife.

But right now we both had a problem. I had to earn a living free lance without a job. Osano had to lie low someplace where the press couldn't keep hounding him. I could solve

Osano's problem. I called Cully in Las Vegas and explained what had happened. I asked Cully if he could stash Osano in the Xanadu Hotel for a couple of weeks. I knew nobody would be looking for him there. And Osano was agreeable. He had never been to Las Vegas.

Chapter 26

With Osano safely stashed in Vegas I had to fix my other problem. I had no job, so I took on as much free-lance work as I could get. I did book reviews for *Time* magazine, the New York *Times*, and the new editor of the review gave me some work. But for me it was too nerve-racking. I never knew how much money was going to come in at any particular time. And so I decided that I would go all-out to finish my novel and hope that it would make a lot of money. For the next two years my life was very simple. I spent twelve to fifteen hours a day in my workroom. I went with my wife to the supermarket. I took my kids to Jones Beach in the summer, on Sundays, to give Valerie a rest. Sometimes at midnight I took Dexamyls to keep me awake so that I could work until three or four in the morning.

During that time I saw Eddie Lancer for dinner a few times in New York. Eddie had become primarily a screenwriter in Hollywood, and it was clear that he would no longer write novels. He enjoyed the life out there, the women, the easy money, and swore he would never write another novel again. Four of his screenplays had become hit movies and he was much in demand. He offered to get me a job working with him if I was willing to come out there, and I told him no. I couldn't see myself working in the movie business. Because despite the funny stories Eddie told me, what was very clear was that being a writer in the movies was no fun. You were no longer an artist. You were just a translator of other people's ideas.

During those two years I saw Osano about once a month. He had stayed a week in Vegas and then disappeared. Cully called me to complain that Osano had run away with his favorite girlfriend, a girl named Charlie Brown. Cully hadn't been mad. He had just been astonished. He told me the girl was beautiful, was making a fortune in Vegas under his guidance and was living a great life, and she had abandoned all this to go with a fat old writer who not only had a beer gut but was the craziest guy Cully had ever seen.

I told Cully that that was another favor I owed him and if I saw the girl with Osano in New York, I would buy her a plane ticket back to Vegas.

"Just tell her to get in touch with me," Cully said. "Tell her I miss her, tell her I love her, tell her anything you want. I just want to get her back. That girl is worth a fortune to me in Vegas."

"OK," I said. But when I met Osano in New York for dinner, he was always alone and he didn't much look like anybody who could hold the affections of a young, beautiful girl with the advantages that Cully had described.

It's funny when you hear of somebody's success, of his fame. That fame, like a shooting star that has appeared out of nowhere. But the way it happened to me was surprisingly tame.

I lived the life of a hermit for two years and at the end the book was finished and I turned it into my publisher and I forgot about it. A month later my editor called me into New York and told me they had sold my novel to a paperback house for reprint for over half a million dollars. I was stunned. I really couldn't react. Everybody, my editor, my agent, Osano, Cully, had warned me that a book about kidnapping a child where the kidnapper is a hero would not appeal to a mass public. I expressed my astonishment to my editor, and he said, "You told such a great story that it doesn't matter."

When I went home to Valerie that night and told her what had happened, she seemed not to be surprised either. She merely said calmly, "We can buy a bigger house. The kids are getting bigger, they need more room." And then life simply went on as before, except that Valerie found a house only ten minutes from her parents and we bought it and moved in.

By that time the novel was published. It made all the best-seller lists all over the country. It was a big best-seller, and yet it really didn't seem to change my life in any way. In thinking about this I realized that it was because I had such few friends. There was Cully, there was Osano, there was

Eddie Lancer and that was it. Of course, my brother, Artie, was terribly proud of me and wanted to give a big party until I told him he could give the party but I wouldn't come. What really touched me was a review of the book by Osano which appeared on the front page of the literary review. He praised me for the right reasons and pointed out the true flaws. In his usual fashion he overrated the book because I was a friend of his. And then, of course, he went on and talked about himself and his novel in progress.

I called his apartment, but there was no answer. I wrote him a letter and got a letter in return. We had dinner together in New York. He looked terrible, but he had a great-looking young blonde who rarely spoke but ate more than Osano and I put together. He introduced her as "Charlie Brown," and I realized she was Cully's girl, but I never gave her Cully's message. Why should I hurt Osano?

There was one funny incident I always remembered. I told Valerie to go out shopping and buy herself some new clothes, whatever she wanted, and that I would mind the kids for that day. She went with some of her girlfriends and came back with an armful of packages.

I was trying to work on a new book but really couldn't get into it, so she showed me what she had bought. She unwrapped a package and showed me a new yellow dress.

"It cost ninety dollars," Valerie said. "Can you imagine ninety dollars for a little summer dress?"

"It looks beautiful," I said dutifully. She was holding it against her neck.

"You know," she said, "I really couldn't make up my mind whether I liked the yellow one or the green one. Then I decided on the yellow. I think I look better in the yellow, don't you?"

I laughed. I said, "Honey, didn't it occur to you that you could buy both?"

She looked at me stunned for a moment, and then she too laughed. And I said, "You can buy a yellow and a green and a blue and a red."

And we both smiled at each other, and for the first time we realized, I think, that we had entered some sort of new life. But on the whole I found success not to be as interesting or as satisfying as I had thought it would be. So, as I usually did, I read up on the subject and I found that my case was not unusual, that in fact, many men who had fought all their lives to reach the top of their professions immediately celebrated by throwing themselves out of a high window.

It was wintertime, and I decided to take the whole family down to Puerto Rico for a vacation. It would be the first time in our married life that we had been able to afford to go away. My kids had never even been to summer camp.

We had a great time swimming, enjoying the heat, enjoying the strange streets and food, the delight of leaving the cold winter one morning and that afternoon being in the broiling sun, enjoying the balmy breezes. At night I took Valerie to the hotel gambling casino while the children dutifully sat in the great wicker chairs of the lobby, waiting for us. Every fifteen minutes or so Valerie would run down and see if they were OK, and finally she took them all to our suite of rooms and I gambled until four o'clock in the morning. Now that I was rich, naturally I was lucky, and I won a few thousand dollars and in a funny way I enjoyed winning in the casino more than the success and the huge sums of money I had made so far on the book.

When we got back home, there was an even greater surprise waiting for me. A movie studio, Malomar Films, had spent a hundred thousand dollars for the film rights to my book and another fifty thousand dollars plus expenses for me to go out to Hollywood to write the screenplay.

I talked it over with Valerie. I really didn't want to write movie scripts. I told her I would sell the book but turn down the screen-writing contract. I thought she would be pleased, but instead, she said, "I think it would be good for you to go out there. I think it would be good for you to meet more people, to know more people. You know I worry about you sometimes because you're so solitary."

"We could all go out," I said.

"No," Valerie said. "I'm really happy here with my family and we can't take the children out of school and I wouldn't want them to grow up in California."

Like everybody else in New York, Valerie regarded California as an exotic outpost of the United States filled with drug addicts, murderers and mad preachers who would shoot a Catholic on sight.

"The contract is for six months," I said, "but I could work for a month and then go back and forth."

"That sounds perfect," Valerie said, "and besides, to tell you the truth we could use a rest from each other."

That surprised me. "I don't need a rest from you," I said.

"But I need a rest from you," Valerie said. "It's nerve-racking to have a man working at home. Ask any woman. It just upsets the whole routine of my keeping house. I never could say anything before because you couldn't afford an outside studio to work in, but now that you can, I wish you wouldn't work at home anymore. You can rent a place and leave in the morning and come home at night. I'm sure you'd work better."

I don't know even now why her saying this offended me so much. I had been happy staying and working at home, and I was really hurt that she didn't feel the same way, and I think it was this that made me decide to do the screenplay of my novel. It was a childish reaction. If she didn't want me home, I'd leave and see how she liked it. At that time I swear that Hollywood was a nice place to read about, but I didn't even want to visit it.

I realized a part of my life was over. In his review Osano had written, "All novelists, bad and good, are heroes. They fight alone, they must have the faith of saints. They are more often defeated than victorious and they are shown no mercy by a villainous world. Their strength fails (that's why most novels have weak spots, are an easy target for attack); the troubles of the real world, the illness of children, the betrayal by friends, the treacheries of wives must all be brushed aside. They ignore their wounds and fight on, calling on miracles for fresh energy."

I disapproved of his melodramatics, but it was true that I felt as if I were deserting the company of heroes. I didn't give a damn if that was a typical writer's sentimentality.

Book V

Chapter 27

Malomar Films, though a subsidiary of Moses Wartberg's Tri-Culture Studios, operated on a completely independent basis, creatively, and had its own small lot. And so Bernard Malomar had free rein for his planned picture of the John Merlyn novel.

All Malomar wanted to do was make good movies, and that was never easy, not with Wartberg's Tri-Culture Studios hovering over his every move. He hated Wartberg. They were acknowledged enemies, but Wartberg, as an enemy, was interesting, fun to deal with. Also, Malomar respected Wartberg's financial and management genius. He knew that moviemakers like himself could not exist without it.

Malomar in his plush suite of offices nestled in a corner of his own lot had to put up with a bigger pain in the ass than Wartberg, though a less deadly one. If Wartberg was cancer of the rectum, as Malomar jokingly said, Jack Houlinan was hemorrhoids and, on a day-to-day basis, far more irritating.

Jack Houlinan, vice-president in charge of creative public relations, played his role of the number one PR genius with a killing sincerity. When he asked you to do something outrageous and was refused, he acknowledged with violent enthusiasm your right to refuse. His favorite line was: "Anything you say is OK with me. I would never, never try to persuade you to do anything you don't want to do. I only asked." This would be after an hour's pitch of why you had to jump off the Empire State Building to make sure your new picture got some space in the *Times*.

But with his bosses, like the VP in charge of production at Wartberg's Tri-Culture International Studios, with this Merlyn picture for Malomar Films and his own personal client, Ugo Kellino, he was much more frank, more human. And now he was talking frankly to Bernard Malomar, who really didn't have time for bullshit.

"We're in trouble," Houlinan said. "I think this fucking picture can be the biggest bomb since Nagasaki."

Malomar was the youngest studio chief since Thalberg and liked to play a dumb genius role. With a straight face he said, "I don't know that picture, and I think you're full of shit. I think you're worried about Kellino. You want us to spend a fortune just because that prick decided to direct himself and you want to get him insurance."

Houlinan was Ugo Kellino's personal PR rep with a retainer of fifty grand a year. Kellino was a great actor but almost certifiably insane with ego, a not uncommon disease in top actors, actresses, directors and even script girls who fancied themselves screenplay writers. Ego in movie land was like TB in a mining town. Endemic and ravaging but not necessarily fatal.

In fact, their egos made many of them more interesting than they would otherwise be. This was true of Kellino. His dynamism on screen was such that he had been included in a list of the fifty most famous men in the world. The laminated news story hung in his den and his own legend in red crayon that said, "For fucking." Houlinan always said, his voice emphatic, admiring, "Kellino would fuck a *snake*." Accenting the word as if the phrase were not an old macho cliché but coined now especially for his client.

A year ago Kellino had insisted on directing his next picture. He was one of the few stars who could get away with such a demand. But he had been put on a strict budget, his upfront money and percentages pledged for a completion bond. Malomar Films was in for a top two million and then off the hook. Just in case Kellino went crazy and started shooting a hundred takes of each scene with his latest girlfriend opposite him or his latest boyfriend under him. Both of which he had proceeded to do with no visible harm to the picture. But then he had fucked around with the script. Long monologues, the lights soft and shadowy on his despairing face, he had told the story of his tragic boyhood in excruciating flashbacks. To explain why he was fucking boys and girls on the screen. The implication was that if he had had a decent childhood, he would never have fucked anybody. And he had final cut, the studio couldn't doctor up the picture in the editing room legally. Except that they would anyway if necessary. Malomar wasn't too worried. A Kellino starrer would get the studio's two million back. That was certain. Everything else was gravy. And if worse came to worst, he could bury the picture in distribution; nobody would see it. And he had come out of the deal with his main objective. That Kellino would star in John Merlyn's blockbuster bestselling novel that Malomar felt in his bones would make the studio a fortune.

Houlinan said, "We have to get a special campaign. We have to spend a lot of money. We have to sell it on its class."

"Jesus Christ," Malomar said. He was usually more polite. But he was tired of Kellino, he was tired of Houlinan and he was tired of motion pictures. Which didn't mean anything. He was tired of beautiful women and charming men. He was tired of California weather. To divert himself he studied Houlinan. He had a long-standing grudge against him and Kellino.

Houlinan was beautifully dressed. Silk suit, silk tie, Italian shoes, Piaget watch. His eyeglass frames were specially made, black and gold-flecked. He had the benign sweet Irish face of the leprechaun preachers that filled the California TV screens on Sunday mornings. It was hard to believe he was a blackhearted son of a bitch and proud of it.

Years ago Kellino and Malomar had quarreled in a public restaurant, a vulgar shouting match that had become a humiliating story in the columns and trades. And Houlinan had masterminded a campaign to make Kellino come out of the argument as the hero and Malomar the craven villain, the weakling studio chief bending to the heroic movie star. Houlinan was a genius all right. But a little shortsighted. Malomar had made him pay ever since.

For the last five years not a month had gone by that the papers had not carried a story about Kellino's helping somebody less fortunate than himself. Did a poor girl with leukemia need a special blood transfusion from a donor who lived in Siberia? Page five of any newspaper would tell you Kellino had sent his private jet to Siberia. Did a black go to a Southern jail for protesting? Kellino posted bail. When an Italian policeman with seven kids got chopped down by a Black Panther ambush in Harlem, did not Kellino send a check for ten thousand dollars to the widow and set up a scholarship for all seven children? When a Black Panther was accused of murdering a cop, Kellino sent ten thousand dollars to his defense fund. Whenever a famous old-time movie star became ill, the papers noted that Kellino picked up his hospital tab and assured him of a cameo role in his next film so that the old codger would have something to live for. One of the old codgers with ten million stashed and a hatred for his profession gave an interview insulting Kellino's generosity, spitting on it in fact, and it was so funny that even the great Houlinan couldn't get it squashed.

And Houlinan had more hidden talents. He was a pimp whose fine nose for new fresh starlets made him the Daniel Boone of Hollywood's celluloid wilderness. Houlinan often boasted of his technique. "Tell any actress she was great in her bit part. Tell her that three times in one evening and she pulls down your pants and tears your cock off by the roots." He was Kellino's advance scout, many times testing the girl's talents in bed before passing her on. Those who were too neurotic, even by the lenient industry standards, never got past him to Kellino. But as Houlinan often said, "Kellino's rejects are worth picking up options on."

Malomar said with the first pleasure he had felt that day, "Forget about any big advertising budgets. It's not that kind of picture."

Houlinan looked at him thoughtfully. "How about doing a little private promoting with some of the more important critics? You have a couple of big ones that owe you a favor."

Malomar said dryly, "I'm not wasting it on this." He didn't say that he was going to call in all his IOU's on the big picture next year. He already had that one mapped out, and Houlinan was not going to run that show. He wanted the next picture to be the star, not Kellino.

Houlinan looked at him thoughtfully. Then said, "I guess I'll have to build my own campaign."

Malomar said wearily, "Just remember it's still a Malomar Films' production. Clear everything with me. OK?"

"*Of course*," Houlinan said with his special emphasis as if it had never occurred to him to do anything else.

Malomar said evenly, "Jack, remember there's a line you don't go over with me. No matter who you are."

Houlinan said with his dazzling smile, "I never forget that. Have I ever forgotten that? Listen, there's a great looking broad from Belgium. I got her stashed in the Beverly Hills Hotel bungalow. Shall we have a breakfast conference tomorrow?"

"Another time," Malomar said. He was tired of women flying in from all over the world to be fucked. He was tired of all the slender, beautiful, chiseled faces, the thin, elegant bodies perfectly dressed, the beauties he was constantly photographed with at parties and restaurants and premieres. He was famous not only as the most talented producer in Hollywood, but as the one who had the most beautiful women. Only his closest friends knew he preferred sex with plump Mexican maids who worked in his mansion. When they kidded him about his perverseness, Malomar always told them that his favorite relaxation was going down on a woman and that those beautiful women in the magazines had nothing to go down on but bone and hair. The Mexican maid had meat and juice. Not that all this was always true; it was just that Malomar, knowing how elegant he looked, wanted to show his distaste for that elegance.

At this time in his life all Malomar wanted to do was make a good movie. The happiest hours for him were after dinner when he went into the cutting room and worked until the early-morning hours editing a new film.

As Malomar ushered Houlinan out of the door, his secretary murmured that the writer of the novel was waiting with his agent, Doran Rudd. Malomar told her to bring them in. He introduced them to Houlinan.

Houlinan gave both men a quick appraisal. Rudd he knew. Sincere, charming, in short a hustler. He was a type. The writer also was a type. The naïve novelist who comes out to work on his film script, gets dazzled by Hollywood, faked out of his shoes by producers, directors and studio heads and then falls for a starlet and wrecks his life by divorcing his wife of twenty years for a broad who had screwed every casting director in town just for openers. And then gets indignant at the way his half-assed novel gets mutilated on the screen. This one was no different. He was quiet and obviously shy and dressed like a slob. Not fashionable slob, which was the new fad even among producers like Malomar and stars who sought specially patched and faded blue jeans that were exquisitely fitted by top tailors—but real slob. And ugly to boot like that fucking French actor who grossed so high in Europe. Well, he, Houlinan, would do his little bit to grind this guy into sausage right now.

Houlinan gave the writer, John Merlyn, a big hello and told him that his book was the very best book he had ever read in his life. He hadn't read it.

Then he stopped at the door and turned around and said to the writer, "Listen, Kellino would love to have his picture taken with you this afternoon. We have a conference with Malomar later, and it would be great publicity for the movie. OK for about three o'clock? You should be through here, right?"

Merlyn said OK. Malomar grimaced. He knew Kellino wasn't even in town, that he was sunning himself in Palm Springs and wouldn't arrive until six. Houlinan was going to make Merlyn hang around for a no-show just to teach him where the muscle was in Hollywood. Well, he might as well learn.

Malomar, Doran Rudd and Merlyn had a long session on the writing of the movie. Malomar noted that Merlyn seemed reasonable and cooperative rather than the usual pain in the ass. He gave the agent the usual bullshit about bringing in the picture for a million when everybody knew that eventually they'd have to spend five. It was only when they left that Malomar got his surprise. He mentioned to Merlyn that he could wait for Kellino in the library. Merlyn looked at his watch and said mildly, "It's ten after three. I never wait more than ten minutes for anybody, not even my kids." Then he walked out.

Malomar smiled at the agent. "Writers," he said. But he often said, "Actors," in the same tone of voice. And "Directors" and "Producers." He never said it about actresses because you couldn't put down a human being who had to contend with a menstrual cycle and wanting to be an actress both. That made them fucking crazy just for openers.

Doran Rudd shrugged. "He doesn't even wait for doctors. We both had to take a physical together, and we had ten A.M. appointments. You know doctor's offices. You gotta wait a few minutes. He told the receptionist, 'I'm on time, why isn't the doctor on time?' Then he walked out."

"Jesus," Malomar said.

He was getting pains in his chest. He went into the bathroom and swallowed an angina pill and then went to take a nap on the couch as his doctor had ordered. One of his secretaries would wake him up when Houlinan and Kellino arrived.

"The Stone Woman *is Kellino's debut as director. As an actor he is always marvelous; as a director he is less than competent; as a philosopher he is pretentious and despicable. This is not to say that* Stone Woman *is a bad film. It isn't really trashy, merely hollow.*

"Kellino dominates the screen, we always believe the character he plays, but here the character he plays is a man we do not care about. How can we care about a man who throws away his life for an empty-headed doll like Selina Denton whose personality appeals to men satisfied with women whose breasts and rear are extravagantly rounded in the cliché style of male chauvinistic fantasy? Selina Denton's acting, her usual wooden-Indian style, insipid face contorted in grimaces of ecstasy, is just plain embarrassing. When will Hollywood casting directors learn that the audience is interested in seeing real women on the screen? An actress like Billie Stroud with her commanding presence, her intelligent and forceful technique, her striking appearance (she is truly beautiful if one can forget all the deodorant commercial stereotypes the American male has idolized since the invention of television) might have salvaged the film, and it is surprising that Kellino, whose acting is so intelligent and intuitive, did not realize this when he was casting. Presumably he has enough clout as star and director and co-producer to call this shot, at least.

"The script by Hascom Watts is one of those pseudoliterary exercises that read well on paper but don't make any sense at all on film. We are expected to feel a sense of tragedy for a man to whom nothing tragic happens, a man who finally commits suicide because his comeback as an actor fails (everyone fails) and because an empty-headed, selfish woman uses her beauty (all in the eyes of the beholder) to betray him in the most banal fashion since the heroines of Dumas the Younger.

"The counterpoint of Kellino trying to save the world by being on the right side of every social question is goodhearted but essentially fascist in concept. The embattled liberal hero evolves into the fascist dictator, as Mussolini did.

The treatment of women in this film is also basically fascist; they do nothing except manipulate men with their bodies. When they do take part in political movements, they are shown as destroyers of men striving to better the world. Can't Hollywood believe for a moment that there is a relationship between men and women in which sex does not play a part? Can't it show just one goddamn time that women have the 'manly' virtues of a belief in humanity and its terrible struggle to go forward? Don't they have the imagination to foresee that women might, just might, love a movie that portrays them as real human beings, rather than those familiar rebellious puppets that break the strings men attach to them?

"Kellino is not a gifted director; he is less than competent. He places the camera where it should be; the only trouble is that he never gets the lead out of it. But his acting saves the film from the complete disaster the whoremongering script dooms it to be. Kellino's directing doesn't help, but it doesn't destroy the film. The rest of the cast is simply dreadful. It's not fair to dislike an actor because of his looks, but George Fowles is physically too slimy even for the slimy role he plays here. Selina Denton is too empty-looking even for the empty woman she plays here. It's not a bad idea sometimes to cast against the role, and maybe that's what Kellino should have done in this film. But maybe it wasn't worth the trouble. The fascist philosophy of the script, its male chauvinistic conception of what constitutes a 'lovable' woman, doomed the whole project before they loaded film into the camera."

"That fucking cunt," Houlinan said not in anger but with bewildered helplessness. "What the fuck does she want from a movie anyway? And Jesus Christ, why does she keep going on about Billie Stroud being a good-looking broad? In all my forty years in movies I've never seen an uglier movie star. It's beyond me."

Kellino said thoughtfully, "All those other fucking critics follow her. We can forget about this movie."

Malomar listened to both of them. A matched pair of pain in the asses. What the hell did it matter what Clara Ford said? The picture with Kellino as star would make its money back and help pay some studio overhead. That's all he'd ever expected from it. And now he had Kellino on the hook for the important picture, from the novel by John Merlyn. And

Clara Ford, brilliant as she was, didn't know that Kellino had a backup director doing all the work without credit.

The critic was a particular hate of Malomar's. She spoke with such authority, she wrote so well, she was so influential but she had no idea at all about what went into the making of a movie. She complained about casting. Didn't she know that it depended on whom Kellino was fucking in the major female role and then it depended on who was fucking the casting director for the smaller parts? Didn't she know these were the jealously guarded prerogatives of many people in power in certain movies? There were a thousand broads for each bit part and you could fuck half of them without even giving them anything, just letting them read for it and saying you might call them back for another read. And all those fucking directors building up their own private harems, more powerful than the greatest money-makers in the world as far as beautiful, intelligent women were concerned. Not that you even bothered to do that. Even that was too much trouble and not worth it. What amused Malomar was that the critic was the only one who got the unflappable Houlinan upset.

Kellino was angry about something else. "What the hell does she mean it's fascist? I've been antifascist all my life."

Malomar said tiredly, "She's just a pain in the ass. She uses the word 'fascist' the way we use the word 'cunt.' She doesn't mean anything by it."

Kellino was mad as hell. "I don't give a shit about my acting. But nobody compares me with fascists and gets away with it."

Houlinan paced up and down the room, almost dipped into Malomar's box of Monte Cristo cigars, then thought better of it. "That broad is killing us," he said. "She's always killing us. And your barring her from previews doesn't help, Malomar."

Malomar shrugged. "It's not supposed to help, I do it for my bile."

They both looked at him curiously. They knew what bile meant but knew it wasn't in character for him to say it. Malomar had read it in a script that morning.

Houlinan said, "No shit, it's too late for this picture, but what the hell are we going to do about Clara on the next one?"

Malomar said, "You're Kellino's personal press agent, do what you want. Clara's your baby."

He was hoping to end this conference early. If it had been just Houlinan, it would have ended in two minutes. But Kellino was one of the truly great stars, and his ass had to be kissed with infinite patience and extreme shows of love.

Malomar had the rest of the day and evening scheduled for the cutting room. His greatest pleasure. He was one of the greatest film editors in the business and he knew it. And besides, he loved cutting a film so that all the starlet heads dropped on the floor. It was easy to recognize them. The unnecessary close-ups of a pretty girl watching the main action. The director had banged her, and that was his payoff. Malomar in his cutting room chopped her right out unless he liked the director or the one-in-a-million times the shot worked. Jesus, how many broads had put out to see themselves up there on the screen for one split second, thinking that one split second would send them on the way to fame and fortune. That their beauty and talent would flash out like lightning. Malomar was tired of beautiful women. They were a pain in the ass, especially if they were bright. Which didn't mean he didn't get hooked once in a while. He'd had his share of disastrous marriages, three, all with actresses. Now he was looking for any broad who wasn't hustling him for something. He felt about pretty girls as a lawyer feels hearing his phone ring. It can mean only trouble.

"Get one of your secretaries in here," Kellino said. Malomar rang the buzzer on his desk, and a girl appeared in the door as if by magic. As she better had. Malomar had four secretaries: two guarding the outer door of his offices and another two guarding the inner sanctum door, one on each side like dragons. No matter what disasters happened—when Malomar rang his buzzer, somebody appeared. Three years ago the impossible had happened. He had pressed the buzzer and nothing happened. One secretary was having a nervous breakdown in a nearby executive office, and a free-lance producer was curing her with some head. Another had dashed upstairs to accounting to get some figures on the grosses of a film. The third was out sick that day. The fourth and last had been overcome with a painful desire to take a leak, and gambled. She established a woman's record for taking a leak, but it was not enough. In that fatal few seconds Malomar rang his buzzer and four secretaries were not insurance enough. Nobody appeared. All four were fired.

Now Kellino dictated a letter to Clara Ford. Malomar admired his style. And knew what he was getting to. He didn't bother to tell Kellino that there was no chance.

"Dear Miss Ford," Kellino dictated. "Only my admiration for your work impels me to write this letter and point out a few areas where I disagree with you in your review of my new film. Please don't think this is a complaint of any kind. I respect your integrity enough and revere your intelligence too much to voice an idle complaint. I just want to state that the failure of the film, if indeed it is a failure, is entirely due to my inexperience as a director. I still think it was a beautifully written script. I think the people who worked with me in the film were very good and handicapped by me as a director. That is all I have to say except that I am still one of your fans and maybe someday we can get together for lunch and a drink and really talk about film and art. I feel that I have a great deal to learn before I direct my next film (which won't be for quite a long time, I assure you) and what better person to learn from than you? Sincerely, Kellino."

"It won't work," Malomar said.

"Maybe," Houlinan said.

"You'll have to go after her and fuck her brains out," Malomar said. "And she's too smart a broad to fall for your line of bullshit."

Kellino said, "I really admire her. I really want to learn from her."

"Never mind that," Houlinan almost yelled. "Fuck her. Jesus. That's the answer. Fuck her brains out."

Malomar suddenly found them both unbearable. "Don't do it in my office," he said. "Get out of here and let me work."

They left. He didn't bother to walk them to the door.

The next morning in his special suite of offices in Tri-Culture Studios, Houlinan was doing what he liked to do best. He was preparing press releases that would make one of his clients look like God. He had consulted Kellino's contract to make sure that he had the legal authority to do what he had to do, and then he wrote:

FOOLS DIE

TRI-CULTURE STUDIOS & MALOMAR FILMS PRESENT

A MALOMAR-KELLINO PRODUCTION
STARRING
UGO KELLINO
FAY MEADOWS
IN A UGO KELLINO FILM
"JOYRIDE"
DIRECTED BY BERNARD MALOMAR

. . . also starring, and then he scribbled a few names very small to indicate the small type. Then he put: "Executive Producers Ugo Kellino and Hagan Cord." Then: "Produced by Malomar and Kellino." And then he indicated much smaller type: "Screenplay by John Merlyn from the novel by John Merlyn." He leaned back in his chair and admired his work. He buzzed his secretary to type it up and then asked his secretary to bring in the Kellino obituary file.

He loved to look at that file. It was thick with the operations that would be put into effect on Kellino's death. He and Kellino had worked for a month up in Palm Springs perfecting the plan. Not that Kellino expected to die, but he wanted to make sure that when he did, everybody would know what a great man he had been. There was a thick folder which contained all the names of everybody he knew in show business who would be called for quotes upon his death. There was a complete outline on a television tribute. A two-hour special.

All his movie star friends would be asked to appear. There were specific clips of film in another folder of Kellino in his best roles to be shown on that special. There was a film clip of him accepting his two Academy Awards as best actor. There was a fully written comedy sketch in which friends of his would poke fun at his aspirations to be a director.

There was a list of everybody Kellino had helped so that some of them could tell little anecdotes about how Kellino had rescued them from the depths of despair on condition they never let anyone know.

There was a note on those ex-wives who would be approached for a quote and those who would not be. There were plans for one wife in particular: to fly her out of the country to a safari in Africa on the day Kellino died so no one in the media could get in touch with her. There was an ex-President of the United States who had already given his quote.

In the file was a recent letter to Clara Ford asking for a contribution to Kellino's obituary. It was written on the letterhead of the Los Angeles *Times* and was legitimate but inspired by Houlinan. He had gotten his copy of Clara Ford's reply but never showed it to Kellino. He read it again. "Kellino is a gifted actor who has done some marvelous work in films, and it's a pity that he passed away too soon to achieve the greatness that might have been in store for him with the proper role and the proper direction."

Every time that Houlinan read that letter he had to have another drink. He didn't know whom he hated more, Clara Ford or John Merlyn. Houlinan hated snotty writers on sight, and Merlyn was one of them. Who the fuck was that son of a bitch he couldn't wait to have his picture taken with Kellino? But at least he could fix Merlyn's wagon, Ford was beyond his reach. He tried getting her fired by organizing a campaign of hate mail from fans, by using all the pressure of Tri-Culture Studios, but she was simply too powerful. He hoped Kellino was having better luck but he would soon know. Kellino had been on a date with her. He'd taken her to dinner the night before and was sure to call him and report everything that happened.

Chapter 28

In my first weeks in Hollywood I began to think of it as the Land of Empidae. An amusing conceit, at least to me, even if a bit condescending.

The empid is an insect. The female is cannibalistic, and the act of sex whets her appetite so that in the last moment of the male's ecstasy he finds himself without a head.

But in one of those marvelous evolutionary processes the male empid learned to bring a tiny bit of food wrapped in a web spun from his own body. While the murderous female peels away the web, he mounts her, copulates and makes his getaway.

A more highly developed male empid figured out that all he had to do was spin a web around a tiny stone or pebble, any little bit of junk. In a great evolutionary jump the male empid fly became a Hollywood producer. When I mentioned this to Malomar, he grimaced and gave me a dirty look; then he laughed.

"OK," he said, "do you want to get your fucking head bit off for a piece of ass?"

At first nearly everyone I met struck me as a person who would eat off somebody's foot to become successful. And yet, as I stayed on, I was struck by the passion of people involved in filmmaking. They really loved it. Script girls, secretaries, studio accountants, cameramen, propmen, the technical crews, the actors and actresses, the directors and even the producers. They all said, "the movie I made." They all considered themselves artists. I noticed that the only ones concerned with films that did not speak this way were usually screenwriters. Maybe that was because everyone rewrote their scripts. Everybody put his fucking two cents in. Even the script girl would change a line or two, or a character actor's wife would rewrite her husband's part, and he'd bring it in the next day and say that was the way he thought it should be played. Naturally the rewrite showed off his talents rather than forwarded the movie's purpose. It was an irritating business for a writer. Everyone wanted his job.

It occurred to me that moviemaking is a dilettante art form to an extreme degree and this innocently enough because the medium itself is so powerful. By using a combination of photographs, costumes, music and a simple story line, people with absolutely no talent could actually create works of art. But maybe that was going too far. They could at least produce something good enough to give themselves a sense of importance, some value.

Movies can give you great pleasure and move you emotionally. But they can teach you very little. They couldn't plumb the depths of a character the way a novel could. They couldn't teach you as books could teach you. They could only make you feel; they could not make you understand life. Film is so magical it can give some value to almost anything. For many people it could be a form of drug, a harmless cocaine. For others it could be a form of valuable therapy. Who doesn't want to record his past life or future traits as he would want them to be so that he could love himself?

Anyway, that was as close as I could figure the movie world out, at that time. Later on, bitten a little by the bug myself, I felt that it was maybe a too cruel and snobbish view.

I wondered about the powerful hold making films seemed to have on everyone. Malomar passionately loved making films. All the people who worked in films struggled to control them. The directors, the stars, the chief photographers, the studio wheels.

I was aware that cinema was the most vital art of our time, and I was jealous. On every college campus students, instead of writing novels, were making their own films. And suddenly it occurred to me that maybe the use of film was not even an art. That it was a form of therapy. Everyone wanted to tell his own life story, his own emotions, his own thoughts. Yet how many books had been published for that reason? But the magic was not that strong in books or painting or music. Movies combined all the arts; movies should be irresistible. With that powerful arsenal of weapons it should be impossible to make a bad movie. You could be the biggest asshole

FOOLS DIE

in the world and still make an interesting film. No wonder
there was so much nepotism in moviemaking. You literally
could let a nephew write a screenplay, take a girlfriend and
make her a star, make your son the head of a studio. Movies
could make a successful artist out of anyone. Mute Miltons
no longer.

And how come no actor had ever murdered a director or a
producer? Certainly over the years there had been plenty of
cause, financial and artistic. How come a director had never
murdered the head of a studio? How come a writer had never
murdered a director? It must be that the making of a film
purged people of violence, was therapeutic.

Could it be that someday one of the most effective treatments for the emotionally disturbed would be to let them
make their own motion pictures? Christ, think of all the professional people in films who were crazy or near crazy anyway. Actors and actresses were certifiable certainly.

So that would be it. In the future everybody would stay
home and watch films his friends made to keep from going
crazy. The films would save his life. Think of it that way.
And finally every asshole could be an artist. Certainly, if the
people in this business could turn out good pictures, anybody
could. Here you had bankers, garment makers, lawyers, etc.,
deciding what movies would be made. They didn't even have
that craziness which might help create art. So what would be
lost if every asshole made a film? The only problem was to
get the cost down. You wouldn't need psychiatrists anymore
or talent. Everybody could be an artist.

All those people, unlovable, never understood you had to
work at being loved, yet despite their narcissism, infantilism,
their self-love, they could now project their internal image of
themselves to a lovable exterior on the screen. Make themselves lovable as shadows. Without having earned it in real
life. And of course, you could say that all artists do that;
think of the image of the great writer as a self-indulgent
prick in his personal life, Osano. But at least they had to
have some gift, some talent in their art that gave pleasure or
learning or deeper understanding.

But with film everything was possible without talent, without any gift. You could get a really rich prick making the
story of his life, and without the help of a great director,
great writer, great star, etc., etc., just with the magic of film

make himself a hero. The great future of film for all these people was that it could work with no talent, which didn't mean that talent could not make it better.

Because we were working so closely on the script, Malomar and I spent a lot of time together, sometimes late at night in his movie mogul home where I felt uncomfortable. It was too much for one person, I thought. The huge, heavily furnished rooms, the tennis court, the swimming pool and the separate house that held the screening room. One night he offered to screen a new movie, and I told him I wasn't that crazy about movies. I guess my snottiness showed because he got a little pissed off.

"You know we'd be doing a lot better on this script if you didn't have such contempt for the movie business," he said.

That stung me a little. For one thing I prided myself that my manners were too good to show such a thing. For another I had a professional pride in my work and he was telling me I was fucking off. For still another I had come to respect Malomar. He was the producer-director and he could have ridden right over me while we were working together, but he never did. And when he made a suggestion to change the script, he was usually right. When he was wrong and I could prove it by argument, he deferred to me. In short, he did not fit all my preconceived notions of the Land of Empidae.

So instead of watching the movie or working on the script, we fought that night. I told him how I felt about the movie business and the people in it. The more I talked, the less angry Malomar became, and finally he was smiling.

"You talk like some cunt who can't get guys anymore," Malomar said. "Movies are the new art form, you worry your racket is becoming obsolete. You're just jealous."

"Movies can't compare with novels," I said. "Movies can never do what books do."

"That's irrelevant," Malomar said. "Movies are what people want now and in the future. And all your bullshit about producers and the empid fly. You came here for a few months and you pass judgment on everybody. You put us all down. But every business is the same, they all wave that carrot on a stick. Sure, movie people are fucking crazy, sure, they hustle, sure, they use sex like barter beads, but so what? What you ignore is, all of them, producers and writers, direc-

tors and actors, go through a lot of pain. They study their
trade or craft for years and work harder than any people I
know. They are truly dedicated, and no matter what you say,
it takes talent and even genius to make a good movie. Those
actors and actresses are like the fucking infantry. They get
killed. And they don't get the important roles by fucking.
They have to be proven artists, they have to know their craft.
Sure there are assholes and maniacs in this business that ruin
a five-million-dollar picture by casting their boyfriend or
girlfriend. But they don't last long. And then you go on about
producers and directors. Well, directors I don't have to defend. It's the toughest job in the business. But producers have
a function too. They're like lion tamers in a zoo. You know
what it is to make a picture? First you have to kiss ten asses
on the financial board of a studio. Then you have to be
mother and father to some crazy fucking stars. You have to
keep the crews happy or they murder you with malingering
and overtime. And then you have to keep them all from murdering each other. Look, I hate Moses Wartberg, but I recognize that he has a financial genius that helps keep the movie
business going. I respect that genius as much as I despise his
artistic taste. And I have to fight him all the time as a producer and a director. And I think even you will admit that a
couple of my movies could be called art."

"That's at least half bullshit," I said.

Malomar said, "You keep putting down producers. Well,
they are the guys who get pictures together. And they do it
by spending two years kissing a hundred different babies, financial babies, actor babies, director babies, writer babies.
And producers have to change their diapers, get tons of shit
up their nose into their brain. Maybe that's why they usually
have such lousy taste. And yet a lot of them believe in art
more than the talent. Or in its fantasy. You never see a producer not appear at the Academy Awards to pick up his Oscar."

"That's just ego," I said, "not a belief in art."

"You and your fucking art," Malomar said. "Sure, only
one movie out of a hundred is worth something, but what
about books?"

"Books have a different function," I said defensively.
"Movies can only show the outside."

Malomar shrugged. "You really are a pain in the ass."

"Movies are not art," I said. "It's magic tricks for kids." I only half believed that.

Malomar sighed. "Maybe you have the right idea. In every form, it's all magic, not art. It's a fake-out so that people forget about dying."

That wasn't true, but I didn't argue. I knew Malomar had trouble since his heart attack and I didn't want to say that this was what influenced him. For my money it was art that made you understand how to live.

Well, OK, he didn't convince me, but after that I did look around me in a less prejudiced way. But he was right in one thing. I was jealous of the movies. The work was so easy, the rewards so rich, the fame dizzying. I hated the idea of going back to writing novels alone in a room. Underneath all my contempt was a childish envy. It was something I could never really be a part of; I didn't have the talent or the temperament. I would always in some way despise it but for reasons more snobbish than moral.

I had read all about Hollywood, and by Hollywood I really mean the movie business. I had heard writers, especially Osano, come back East and curse the studios, call the producers the worst cocksucking meddlers in the world, the studio chiefs the crudest, rudest men this side of the apes, the studios so crooked, overbearing and criminal that they made the Black Hand look like the Sweet Sisters of Charity. Well, how they came back from Hollywood, that's how I went in.

I had all the confidence in the world that I could handle it. When Doran took me into my first meeting with Malomar and Houlinan, I spotted them right away. Houlinan was easy. But Malomar was more complicated than I expected. Doran, of course, was a caricature. But to tell the truth I liked Doran and Malomar. I detested Houlinan on sight. And when Houlinan told me to have my picture taken with Kellino, I almost told him to go fuck himself. When Kellino didn't show up on time, I had my out. I hate waiting for anybody. I don't get mad at them for being late, so why should they get mad at me for not waiting?

What made Hollywood fascinating was all the different species of empid fly.

Young guys with vasectomy cards, cans of film under their

arms, scripts and cocaine in their studio apartments, hoping to make movies, searching for talented young girls and guys to read for parts and fuck to pass time. Then there were the bona fide producers with offices on the studio lots and a secretary, plus a hundred thousand dollars in development money. They called agents and casting agencies to send people over. These producers had at least one picture to their credit. Usually a low-budget dumb picture that never made back the cost of the negative and wound up being shown on airplanes or at drive-ins. These producers paid off a California weekly for a quote that called their film one of the ten best pictures of the year. Or a planted *Variety* report that the picture had outgrossed *Gone with the Wind* in Uganda, which really meant *Gone with the Wind* had never played there. These producers usually had signed pictures of big stars on their desks inscribed with "LOVE." They spent the day interviewing beautiful, struggling actresses who were deadly serious about their work and had no idea that for the producers it was just a way to kill an afternoon and maybe get lucky with a blow job that would give them a better appetite for dinner. If they were really hot for a particular actress, they would take her for lunch in the studio commissary and introduce her to the heavyweights who went by. The heavyweights, having gone through the same routine in their salad days, stood still for this if you didn't push it too far. The heavyweights had outgrown this kid stuff. They were too busy unless the girl was something special. Then she might get a shot.

The girls and boys knew the game, knew it was partly a fixed wheel, but they also knew that you could get lucky. So they took their chances with a producer, a director, a star, but if they really knew their stuff and had some brains, they would never pin their hopes on a writer. I realized now how Osano must have felt.

But again I always understood this was part of the trap. Along with the money and the plush suites and the flattery and heady atmosphere of studio conferences and the feeling of importance in making a big film. So I never really got hooked. If I got a little horny, I flew to Vegas and gambled it cold. Cully would always try to send a class hooker to my room. But I always refused. Not that I was priggish, and of course, I was tempted. But I liked gambling more and had too much guilt.

I spent two weeks in Hollywood playing tennis, going out to dinner with Doran and Malomar, going to parties. The parties were interesting. At one I met a faded star who had been my masturbation fantasy when I was a teenager. She must have been fifty, but she still looked pretty good with face-lifts and all kinds of beauty aids. But she was just a little fat and her face was puffy with alcohol. She got drunk and tried to fuck every male and female at the party but couldn't find a taker. And this was a girl that millions of young red-blooded Americans had fantasized about. I found that sort of interesting. I guess the truth is that it depressed me too. The parties were OK. Familiar faces of actors and actresses. Agents brimming over with confidence. Charming producers, forceful directors. I have to say they were a hell of a lot more charming and interesting than I ever was at a party.

And then I loved the balmy climate. I loved the palm tree streets of Beverly Hills, and I loved goofing around Westwood with all its movie theaters and young college kids who were film afficionados with really great-looking girls. I understood why all those 1930 novelists had "sold out." Why spend five years writing a novel that made two grand when you could live this life and make the same money in a week?

During the day I would work in my office, have conferences on the script with Malomar, lunch in the commissary, wander over to a set and watch a picture being shot. On the set the intensity of the actors and actresses always fascinated me. One time I was really awed. A young couple played a scene in which the boy murdered his girlfriend while they made love. After the scene the two of them fell into each other's arms and wept as if they had been part of a real tragedy. They walked off the set hugging each other.

Lunch at the commissary was fun. You met all the people acting in films, and it seemed as if everybody had read my book, at least they said they did. I was surprised that actors and actresses really didn't talk much. They were good listeners. Producers talked a lot. Directors were preoccupied, usually accompanied by three or four assistants. The crew seemed to have the best time. But to watch the shooting of a picture was boring. It wasn't a bad life, but I missed New York. I missed Valerie and the kids, and I missed my dinners with Osano. Those were nights I'd hop a plane to Vegas for the evening, sleep over and come back in the early morning.

Then one day at the studio, after I had been back and forth a few times, NY to LA, LA to NY, Doran asked me to come to a party at his rented house in Malibu. A goodwill party where movie critics, scriptwriters and production people mixed it up with actors and actresses and directors. I didn't have anything better to do, I didn't feel like going to Vegas, so I went to Doran's party, and there I met Janelle for the first time.

Chapter 29

It was one of those Sunday informal gatherings thrown in a Malibu house that had a tennis court plus a big pool, with steaming hot water. The house was divided from the ocean by only a thin strip of sand. Everybody was dressed casually. I noticed that most of the men threw their car keys on the table in the first receiving room, and when I asked Eddie Lancer about that, he told me that in Los Angeles male trousers were tailored so perfectly that you couldn't put anything into your pockets.

As I moved through the different rooms, I heard interesting conversations. A tall, thin, aggressive-looking dark woman was falling all over a handsome producer type wearing a yachting cap. A very short little blonde rushed up to them and said to the woman, "Lay another hand on my husband and I'll punch you right in the cunt." The man in the yachting cap had a stutter and very deadpan said, "Th-th-that's OK. She doesn't use it mu-u-u-ch anyway."

Going through a bedroom, I saw a couple head to toe and I heard a woman's very schoolmarm voice say, "Get *up* here."

I heard a guy I recognized as a New York novelist saying, "The movie business. If you make a reputation as a great dentist, they'll let you do brain surgery." And I thought, another pissed-off writer.

I wandered out into the parking area near the Pacific Coast Highway and I saw Doran with a group of friends admiring a Stutz Bearcat. Somebody had just told Doran the car cost sixty thousand dollars. Doran said, "For that kind of money it should be able to give head." And everybody laughed. Then Doran said, "How do you get the nerve to just park it? It's like having a night job while being married to Marilyn Monroe."

I really went to the party just to meet Clara Ford, for my money the best American film reviewer who ever lived. She was smart as hell, wrote great sentences, read a lot of books, saw every movie and agreed with me on ninety-nine films out of a hundred. When she praised a film, I knew I could go see it and probably love it, or at the very least would be able to sit through the damn thing. Her reviews were the closest a critic could come to being an artist, and I liked the fact that she never claimed to be creative. She was content to be a critic.

At the party I didn't get much chance to talk to her, which was OK with me. I just wanted to see what kind of lady she really was. She came with Kellino, and he kept her busy. And since most of the people clustered around Kellino, Clara Ford got a lot of attention. So I sat in the corner and just watched.

Clara Ford was one of those small, sweet-looking women who are usually called plain, but her face was so alive with intelligence that, in my eyes anyway, she was beautiful. What made her fascinating was that she could be both tough and innocent at the same time. She was tough enough to take on all the other major movie critics in New York and show them up as top-notch assholes. She did it A-B-C, like a prosecuting DA with an airtight case. She showed up as an idiot one guy whose humorous Sunday columns on movies were embarrassing. She took on the voice of the Greenwich Village avant-garde movie buffs and showed him for the dull bastard he was, yet she was smart enough to see him as an idiot savant, the dumbest guy who ever put words on paper, with a real feeling for certain movies. By the time she was through she had all their balls in her unfashionable J. C. Penny handbag.

I could see she was having a good time at the party. And that she was aware that Kellino was conning her with his romancing. Through the uproar I could hear Kellino say, "An agent is an idiot savant *manqué*." That was an old trick of his with critics, male and female. In fact, he had scored a great success with an astringent male critic by calling another critic a fag *manqué*.

Now Kellino was being so fucking charming with Clara Ford that it was a scene in a movie. Kellino showed his dimples like muscles and Clara Ford, for all her intelligence, was beginning to wilt and hang on to him a little.

Suddenly a voice next to me said, "Do you think Kellino will let her fuck him on the first date?"

The voice came from a really good-looking blond girl, or rather a woman because she wasn't a kid. I guessed she was about thirty. Like Clara Ford, what gave her face some of its beauty was its intelligence.

She had great sharp-planed bones in her face with lovely white skin over those bones, you couldn't notice the skin owed something to makeup. She had vulnerable brown eyes that could be delighted as a child's and tragic as a Dumas heroine. If this sounds like a lover's description out of Dumas, that's OK. Maybe I didn't feel this way when I first saw her. That came later. Right now the brown eyes looked mischievous. She was having a good time standing outside the party storm center. What she had, which was unusual in beautiful women, was the delighted, happy air that children have when they are being left alone, doing what is to them amusing. I introduced myself and she said her name was Janelle Lambert.

I recognized her now. I'd seen her in small parts in different movies and she'd always been good. She gave her part second effort. You always liked her on screen, but you never thought of her as great. I could see she admired Clara Ford and had hoped the critic would say something to her. She hadn't, so now Janelle was being funny malicious. In another woman it would have been a catty remark about Ford, but with her it was OK.

She knew who I was and said the usual things about the book that people say. And I put on my usual absentminded act as if I had barely heard the compliment. I liked the way she dressed, modest, yet stylish as hell without being high fashion.

"Let's go over," she said. I thought she wanted to meet Kellino, but when we got there, I saw her trying to get Clara Ford into a conversation. She said intelligent things, but you could see Ford putting the ice on because she was so beautiful, or so I thought then.

Suddenly Janelle turned and walked away from the group. I followed her. She had her back to me, but when I caught her at the door, I found that she was crying.

Her eyes were magnificent with tears in them. They were golden brown flecked with black dots that were maybe just darker brown (later I found out they were contact lenses), and the tears made the eyes bigger, with more gold. They also betrayed the fact that she'd given the eyes a little help with makeup that was now running.

"You're beautiful when you cry," I said. I was imitating Kellino in one of his charming roles.

"Oh, fuck you, Kellino," she said.

I hate women using words like "fuck" and "cunt" and "mother-fucker." But she was the only woman I ever heard who made the word "fuck" sound humorous and friendly. The *f* and the *k* were Southern slurry soft.

Maybe it was obvious that she had never said the word until lately. Maybe it was because she grinned at me to let me know she knew I was imitating Kellino. She had a great grin, not a charming smile.

"I don't know why I'm so silly," she said. "But I never go to parties. I just came because I knew she'd be here. I admire her so much."

"She's a good critic," I said.

"Oh, she's so smart," Janelle said. "She once wrote something nice about me. And you know, I thought she'd like me. Then she put me down. For no reason."

"She had plenty of reason," I said. "You're beautiful and she's not. And she's got plans for Kellino tonight, and she was not going to have him distracted by you."

"That's silly," she said. "I don't like actors."

"But you're beautiful," I said. "Also, you were talking intelligently. She has to hate you."

For the first time she looked at me with something like real interest. I was way ahead of her. I liked her because she was beautiful. I liked her because she never went to parties. I liked her because she didn't go for actors like Kellino, who were so goddamn handsome and charming and dressed so beautifully in exquisitely tailored suits, with haircut by a scissored Rodin. And because she was intelligent. Also, she could cry over a critic putting her down at a party. If she was that tenderhearted, maybe she wouldn't kill me. It was the vulnerability finally that made me ask her to have dinner and a movie. I didn't know what Osano could have told me. A vulnerable woman will kill you all the time.

The funny thing is, I didn't see her sexually. I just liked her a hell of a lot. Because despite the fact that she was beautiful and had that wonderfully happy grin even with tears, she was not really a sexy woman at first glance. Or I was too inexperienced to notice. Because later, when Osano met her, he said he felt the sexuality in her like an exposed electric wire. When I told Janelle about Osano, she said that must have happened to her after I met her. Because before she met me, she had been off sex. When I kidded her about that and didn't believe her, she gave me that happy grin and asked if I had ever heard about vibrators.

It's funny that a grown woman telling you that she masturbated with a vibrator can turn you on to her. But it's easy to figure out. The implication is that she is not promiscuous, though she is beautiful and lives in a milieu where men are after women as quickly as a cat after a mouse and mostly for the same reason.

We went out with each other for two weeks, about five times, before we finally got to bed. And maybe we had a better time before we slept together than we did afterward.

I would go to work at the studio during the day and work on the script and have some drinks with Malomar and then go back to the suite at the Beverly Hills Hotel and read. Sometimes I'd go to a movie. On the nights I'd have a date with Janelle she'd meet me at the suite, and then she would drive me around to the movies and a restaurant and then back to the suite. We'd have a few drinks and talk, and she'd go home about one in the morning. We were buddies, not lovers.

She told me why she divorced her husband. When she was pregnant, she'd been horny as hell, but he didn't care for her pregnant. Then when the baby came, she'd loved nursing it. She was delighted by the milk flowing from her breast and the baby enjoying it. She wanted her husband to taste the milk, to suck her breast and feel the flow. She thought it would be so great. Her husband turned away in disgust. And that finished him for her.

"I've never told anybody that before," she said.

"Jesus," I said. "He was crazy."

Late one night in the suite she sat beside me on the sofa. We necked like kids and I got her panties down around her legs and then she balked and stood up. By this time I had my pants down in anticipation, and she was laughing and half crying, and she said, "I'm sorry. I'm an intelligent woman. But I just can't." We looked at each other and we both started laughing. We just looked too funny, both of us, with our bare legs and crotches and her white panties over her bare feet. Me with my pants and shorts snagging my ankles.

By that time I liked her too much to get mad. And oddly enough I didn't feel rejected. "It's OK," I said. I pulled up my trousers. She pulled up her panties and we hugged each other on the sofa again. When she left, I asked her if she would come around the next night. When she said she would, I knew she would go to bed with me.

The next night she came into the suite and kissed me. Then she said, with a shy smile, "Shit, guess what happened."

I knew enough, innocent as I was, that when a prospective bed mate says something like that, you're out in the cold. But I wasn't worried.

"My period started," she said.

"That doesn't bother me if it doesn't bother you," I said. I took her by the hand and led her to the bedroom. In two seconds we were naked in bed except for her panties and I could feel the pad underneath. "Take all that stuff off," I said. She did. We kissed and just held each other.

We weren't in love that first night. We just liked each other a hell of a lot. We made love like kids. Just kissing and fucking straight. And holding each other and talking and feeling comfortable and warm. She had satiny skin and a lovely soft ass that wasn't mushy. Her small breasts had a really great feel to them and big red nipples. We made love twice in the space of an hour, and it had been a long time since I had done that. Finally we got thirsty, and I went into the other room to open a bottle of champagne I had waiting. When I got back into the bedroom, she had her panties back on. She was sitting cross-legged on the bed with a wet towel in her hand, and she was scrubbing out the dark bloodstains on the white sheets. I stood watching her, naked, champagne glasses in my hand, and it was then I first got that overwhelming feeling of tenderness that is the signal of doom. She looked up and smiled at me, her blond hair tousled, her huge brown eyes myopically serious.

"I don't want the maid to see," she said.

"No, we don't want her to know what we did," I said.

Very seriously she kept scrubbing, peering nearsightedly at

the sheets to make sure that she hadn't missed any spots. Then she dropped the wet towel on the floor and took a glass of champagne from my hand. We sat on the bed together, drinking and smiling foolishly at each other in a delighted sort of way. As if we had both made the team, passed some sort of important test. But we still weren't in love with each other. The sex had been good but not great. We were just happy to be together, and when she had to go home, I asked her to sleep over but she said she couldn't and I didn't question her. I thought maybe she was living with a guy and she could stay out late on him but not stay overnight. And it didn't bother me. That was the great thing about not being in love.

One good thing about Women's Lib is that maybe it will make falling in love less corny. Because, of course, when we did fall in love, it was in the corniest tradition. We fell in love by having a fight.

Before that we had a little trouble. One night in bed I couldn't quite get there. Not that I was impotent, but I couldn't finish. And she was trying like hell for me to make it. Finally she started to yell and scream that she would never have sex again, that she hated sex and why did we ever start. She was crying with frustration and failure. I laughed her out of it. I explained to her that it was no big deal. That I was tired. That I had a lot of things on my mind like a five-million-dollar movie, plus all the usual guilts and hang-ups of a conditioned twentieth-century American male who had led a square life. I held her in my arms and we talked for a while and then after that we both came—no sweat. Still not great but good.

OK. There came a time when I had to go back to New York to take care of family business, and then, when I came back to California, we had a date for my first night back. I was so anxious that on the way to the hotel in my rented car I went through a red light and got smashed by another car. I didn't get hurt, but I had to get a new car and I guess I was in a mild sort of shock. Anyway, when I called Janelle, she was surprised. She had misunderstood. She thought it was for the next night. I was mad as hell. I'd nearly gotten myself killed so I could see her, and she was pulling this routine on me. But I was polite.

I told her I had some business the next night, but I would

call her later on in the week when I knew I would be free. She had no idea I was angry, and we chatted for a while. I never called her. Five days later she called me. Her first words were: "You son of a bitch, I thought you really liked me. And then you pulled that old Don Juan shit of not calling me. Why the hell didn't you just come out and say you don't like me anymore."

"Listen," I said. "You're the phony one. You knew goddamn well we had a date that night. You canceled out because you had something better to do."

She said very quietly, very convincingly, "I misunderstood, or you made the mistake."

"You're a goddamn liar," I said. I couldn't believe the infantile rage I felt. But maybe it was more than that. I'd trusted her. I thought she was great. And she had pulled one of the oldest female tricks. I knew, because before I married, I'd been on the other end when girls broke their dates that way to be with me. And I hadn't thought much of those girls.

That was that. It was over and I really didn't give a shit. But two nights later she called me.

We said hello to each other, and then she said, "I thought you really liked me."

And I found myself saying, "Honey, I'm sorry." I don't know why I said "honey." I never use that word. But it loosened her all up.

"I want to see you," she said.

"Come on over," I said.

She laughed. "Now?" It was one in the morning.

"Sure," I said.

She laughed again. "OK," she said.

She got there about twenty minutes later. I had a bottle of champagne ready and we talked and then I said, "Do you want to go to bed?"

She said yes.

Why is it so hard to describe something that is completely joyful? It was the most innocent sex in the world and it was great. I hadn't felt so happy since I was a kid playing ball all day in the summer. And I realized that I could forgive Janelle everything when I was with her and forgive her nothing when I was away from her.

I had told Janelle once before that I loved her, and she had told me not to say something like that, that she knew that

I didn't mean it. I wasn't sure I meant it, so I said OK. I didn't say it now. But sometime during the night we both woke up and we made love and she said very seriously in the darkness, "I love you."

Jesus Christ. The whole business is so goddamn cornball. It's so much bullshit that they use to make you buy a new kind of shaving cream or fly a special airline. But then why is it so effective? After that everything changed. The act of sex became special. I literally never even saw another woman. And it was enough just to see her to get sexually excited. When she met me at the plane, I'd grab her behind the cars in the parking lot to touch her breasts and legs and kiss her twenty times before we drove to the hotel.

I couldn't wait. Once, when she protested laughingly, I told her about the polar bears. About how a male polar bear could react only to the scent of one particular female polar bear and sometimes had to wander over a thousand square miles of Arctic ice before he could fuck her. And that was why there were so few polar bears. She was surprised at that, and then she caught on that I was kidding and punched me. But I told her really that was the effect she had on me. That it was not love or that she was so great-looking and smart and everything that I had ever dreamed about in a woman since I was a kid. It was not that at all. I was not vulnerable to that corny bullshit of love and soul mates and all that. It was quite simply that she had the right smell; her body gave off the right odor for me. It was simple and nothing to brag about.

The great thing was that she understood. She knew I wasn't being cute. That I was rebelling against my surrender to her and to the cliché of romantic love. She just hugged me and said, "OK, OK," and when I said, "Don't take too many baths," she just hugged me again and said, "OK."

Because really it was the last thing in the world I wanted. I was happily married. I loved my wife more than anyone else in the world at one time, and still liked her better than any female I ever met even when I started being unfaithful. So now for the first time I felt guilty with both of them. And stories about love had always irritated me.

Well, we were more complicated than polar bears. And the catch in my fairy tale, which I didn't point out to Janelle, was that the female polar bear did not have the same problem as the male.

And then, of course, I pulled the usual shitty things that people in love do. I slyly asked around about her. Did she date producers and stars to get parts? Did she have other affairs? Did she have another boyfriend? In other words, was she a cunt and fucking a million other guys at the drop of a hat? It's funny the things you do when you fall for a woman. You would never do it with a guy you liked. There you always trusted your own judgment, your own gut feeling. With women you were always mistrustful. There is something really shitty about being in love.

And if I had gotten some real dirt on her, I wouldn't have fallen in love. How is that for a shitty romanticism? No wonder so many women hate men now. My only excuse was that I had been a writing hermit so many years and not smart about women to begin with. And then I couldn't get any scandal on her. She didn't go out to parties. She wasn't linked with any actors. In fact, for a girl who had appeared and worked in movies pretty often very little was known about her. She didn't run with any of the movie crowds or go to any of the eating places where everybody went. She never appeared in the gossip columns. In short, she was the girl of a square hermit's dream. She even liked to read. What more could I want?

Asking around, I found out to my surprise that Doran Rudd had grown up with her in some hick town in Tennessee. He told me she was the straightest girl in Hollywood. He also told me not to waste my time, that I'd never get laid. This delighted me. I asked him what he thought of her, and he said she was the best woman he had ever known. It was only later, and it was Janelle who told me, that I learned that they had been lovers, had lived together, that it was Doran who had brought her to Hollywood.

Well, she was very independent. Once I tried to pay for the gas when we were riding around in her car. She laughed and refused. She didn't care how I dressed and she liked it when I didn't care how she dressed. We went to movies together in jeans and sweaters and even ate in some of the fancy joints that way. We had enough status for that. Everything was perfect. The sex became great. As good as when you're a kid, and with innocent foreplay that was more erotic than any porno jazz.

Sometimes we'd talk about getting her fancy undergarments, but we never got around to it. A couple of times we tried to use the mirrors to catch any reflections, but she was too nearsighted and she was too vain to put on her glasses. Once we even read a book on anal sex together. We got all excited and she said OK. We worked very carefully, but we didn't have any Vaseline. So we used her cold cream. It was really funny because to me it felt lousy, as if the temperature had gone down. As for her, the cold cream didn't work and she screamed bloody murder. And then we quit. It was not for us, we were too square. Giggling like kids, we took a bath; the book had been very stern about cleaning up after anal sex. What it came down to was that we didn't need any help. It was just great. And so we lived happily ever after. Until we became enemies.

And during that happy time, a blond Scheherazade, she told me the story of her life. And so I lived not two but three lives. My family life in New York with my wife and children, with Janelle in Los Angeles and Janelle's life before she met me. I used the 747 planes like magic carpets. I was never so happy in my life. Working on movies was like shooting pool or gambling, relaxing. Finally I had found the crux of what life should be. And I was never more charming. My wife was happy, Janelle was happy, my kids were happy. Artie didn't know what was going on, but one night, when we were having dinner together, he said suddenly, "You know for the first time in my life I don't worry about you anymore."

"When did that start?" I said, thinking it was because of my success with the book and my working in movies.

"Just now," Artie said. "Just this second."

I was instantly on the alert. "What does that mean exactly?" I said.

Artie thought it over. "You were never really happy," he said. "You were always a grim son of a bitch. You never had any real friends. All you did was read books and write books. You couldn't stand parties, or movies, or music, or anything. You couldn't even stand it when our families had holiday dinners together. Jesus, you never even enjoyed your kids."

I was shocked and hurt. It wasn't true. Maybe I seemed

that way, but it wasn't really true. I felt a sick feeling in my stomach. If Artie thought of me this way, what did other people think? I had that familiar feeling of desolation.

"It's not true," I said.

Artie smiled at me. "Of course it's not. I just mean that now you show things more to other people besides me. Valerie says you're a hell of a lot easier to live with."

Again I was stung. My wife must have complained all these years and I never knew it. She never reproached me. But at this moment I knew I had never really made her happy, not after the first few years of our marriage.

"Well, she's happy now," I said.

And Artie nodded. And I thought how silly that was, that I had to be unfaithful to my wife to make her happy. And I realized suddenly that I loved Valerie more now than I ever had. That made me laugh. It was all very convenient, and it was in the textbooks I had been reading. Because as soon as I found myself in the classical unfaithful-husband position, I naturally started to read all the literature on it. "Valerie doesn't mind my going out to California so much?" I asked.

Artie shrugged. "I think she likes it. You know I'm used to you, but you are a tough guy on the nerves."

Again I was a little stunned, but I could never get mad at my brother.

"That's good," I said. "I'm leaving for California tomorrow to work on the movie again."

Artie smiled. He understood what I was feeling. "As long as you keep coming back," he said. "We can't live without you." He never said anything so sentimental, but he'd caught on that my feelings were hurt. He still babied me.

"Fuck you," I said but I was happy again.

It seems incredible that only twenty-four hours later I was three thousand miles away, alone with Janelle, in bed, and listening to her life story.

One of the first things she told me was that she and Doran Rudd were old friends, had grown up in the same Southern town of Johnson City, Tennessee, together. And that finally they had become lovers and moved to California, where she became an actress and Doran Rudd an agent.

Chapter 30

When Janelle went to California with Doran Rudd, she had one problem. Her son. Only three years old and too young to cart around. She left him with her ex-husband. In California she lived with Doran. He promised her a start in movies and did get her a few small parts or thought he did. Actually he made the contacts, and Janelle's charm and wit did the rest. During that time she remained faithful to him, but he obviously cheated with anyone in sight. Indeed, once he tried to talk her into going to bed with another man and him at the same time. She was repelled by the idea. Not because of any morality but because it was bad enough to feel used by one man as a sexual object and the thought of two men feasting off her body was repugnant to her. At that time, she said, she was too unsophisticated to realize that she would get a chance to watch the two men making love together. If she had, she might have considered it—just to see Doran get it up the ass, as he richly deserved.

She always believed the California climate was more responsible for what happened to her life than anything else. People there were weird, she said to Merlyn often, when telling him stories. And you could see she loved their being weird no matter how much damage they had done to her.

Doran was trying to get his foot in the door as a producer, trying to put a package together. He had bought a terrible script from an unknown writer, whose only virtue was that he agreed to take a net percentage instead of cash upfront. Doran persuaded a former big-time director to direct it and a washed-up male star to play the lead.

Of course, no studio would touch the project. It was one of those packages that sounded good to innocents. Doran was a terrific salesman and hunted outside money. One day he brought home a good prospect, a tall, shy, handsome man of about thirty-five. Very soft-spoken. No bullshitter. But he was an executive in a solid financial institution that dealt with investments. His name was Theodore Lieverman, and he fell in love with Janelle over the dinner table.

They dined in Chasen's. Doran picked up the check and then left early for an appointment with his writer and director. They were working on the script, Doran said, frowning with concentration. Doran had given Janelle her instructions.

"This guy can get us a million dollars for the movie. Be nice to him. Remember you play the second female lead."

That was Doran's technique. He promised the second female lead so he could have some bargaining power. If Janelle became difficult, he would up the ante to the first female lead. Not that that meant anything. He would, if necessary, renege on both promises.

Janelle had no intention of being nice in Doran's sense. But she was surprised to find that Theodore Lieverman was a very sweet guy. He didn't make leering jokes about starlets. He didn't come on to her. He was genuinely shy. And he was overcome by her beauty and her intelligence, which gave her a heady feeling of power. When he took her home to Doran's and her apartment after dinner, she invited him in for a drink. Again he was the perfect gentleman. So Janelle liked him. She was always interested in people, found everybody fascinating. And she knew from Doran that Ted Lieverman would inherit twenty million dollars someday. What Doran had not told her was that he was married and had two children. Lieverman told her. Quite diffidently he said, "We're separated. Our divorce is being held up because her lawyers are asking too much money."

Janelle grinned, her infectious grin which always disarmed most men except Doran. "What's too much money?"

Theodore Lieverman said, grimacing, "A million dollars. That's OK. But she wants it in cash, and my lawyers feel this is the wrong time to liquidate."

Janelle said laughingly, "Hell, you have twenty million. What's the difference?"

For the first time Lieverman became really animated. "You don't understand. Most people don't. It's true I'm worth about sixteen, maybe eighteen million, but my cash flow isn't too good. You see, I own real estate and stocks and corporations, but you have to keep the money reinvesting. So I really have very little liquid capital. I wish I could spend money like Doran. And you know, Los Angeles is a terribly expensive place to live."

Janelle realized she had met that familiar type in literature, the stingy millionaire. And since he was not witty, not charming, not sexually magnetic, since, in short, he had no bait except his sweetness and his money, which he made clear he didn't part with easily, she got rid of him after the next drink. When Doran came home that night, he was angry.

"Goddamn, that could have been our meal ticket," Doran told her. It was then she decided to leave him.

The next day she found a small apartment in Hollywood near the Paramount lot and on her own got a bit part in a movie. After her few days' work was done, homesick for her child and Tennessee, she went back for a visit of two weeks. And that was all she could stand of Johnson City.

She debated bringing her son back with her, but that would be impossible, so she left him with her ex-husband again. She felt miserable leaving him, but she was determined to make some money and some sort of career before setting up a household.

Her ex-husband was still obviously smitten by her charm. Her looks were better, more sophisticated. She turned him on deliberately and then brushed him off when he tried to get her to bed. He left in an ugly mood. She was contemptuous of him. She had truly loved him, and he had betrayed her with another woman when she was pregnant. He had refused the milk from her breast that she had wanted him to share with the baby.

"Wait a minute," Merlyn said. "Give me that again."

"What?" Janelle said. She grinned. Merlyn waited.

"Oh, I had great tits when I had the baby. And I was fascinated by the milk. I wanted him to taste it. I told you about it once."

When she filed for divorce, she refused to accept alimony out of sheer contempt.

When she got back to her apartment in Hollywood, she found two messages on her phone service. One from Doran and the other from Theodore Lieverman.

She called Doran first and got him in. He was surprised that she had gone back to Johnson City but didn't ask a single question about their mutual friends. He was too intent, as usual, on what was important to him.

"Listen," he said. "That Ted Lieverman is really gone on you. I'm not kidding. He's madly in love, not just after your ass. If you play your cards right, you can marry twenty million dollars. He's been trying to get in touch with you and I gave him your number. Call him back. You can be a queen."

"He's married," Janelle said.

"The divorce comes through next month," Doran said. "I checked him out. He's a very straight square guy. He gets one taste of you in bed and you got him and his millions forever." All this was off the top of his head. Janelle was just one of his cards.

"You're disgusting," Janelle said.

Doran was at his most charming. "Ah, honey, come on. Sure we split. Still, you are the best piece of ass I ever had in my life. Better than all those Hollywood broads. I miss you. Believe me, I understand why you split. But that doesn't mean we can't stay friends. I'm trying to help, you have to grow up. Give this guy a chance, that's all I ask."

"OK, I'll call him," Janelle said.

She had never been concerned about money in the sense that she wanted to be rich. But now she thought about what money could do. She could bring her son to live with her and have servants to take care of him when she was working. She could study with the best teachers of drama. Gradually she had come to love acting. She knew finally that it was what she wanted to do with her life.

The love for acting was something she had not even told Doran, but he sensed it. She had taken countless plays and books on drama and film from the library and read them all. She enrolled in a little theater workshop whose director gave himself such airs of importance that she was amused, yet charmed. When he told her she was one of the best natural talents he had ever seen, she almost fell in love with him and quite naturally went to bed with him.

Charmless, stingy, rich, Theodore Lieverman held a golden key to so many doors that she called him. And arranged to meet him that night for dinner.

Janelle found Lieverman sweet, quiet and shy; she took the initiative. Finally she got him to talk about himself. Little things came out. He had had twin sisters, a few years younger than he, who had both died in a plane crash. He had had a nervous breakdown from that tragedy. Now his wife wanted a divorce, a million dollars in cash and part of his holdings. Gradually he bared an emotionally deprived life—an economically rich boyhood which had left him weak and vulnerable. The only thing he was good at was making money. He had a scheme to finance Doran's movie that was foolproof. But the time had to be ripe, the investors played like fish. He, Lieverman, would throw in the pump-priming cash, the development money.

They went out nearly every night for two or three weeks, and he was always so nice and shy that Janelle finally became impatient. After all, he sent her flowers after each date. He bought her a pin from Tiffany's, a lighter from Gucci's and an antique gold ring from Roberto's. And he was madly in love with her. She tried to get him into bed and was astonished when he proved reluctant. She could only show her willingness, and then finally he asked her to go to New York and Puerto Rico with him. He had to go on a business trip for his firm. She understood that for some reason he could not make love to her, initially, in Los Angeles. Probably because of guilt feelings. Some men were like that. They could only be unfaithful when they were a thousand miles from their wives. The first time anyway. She found this amusing and interesting.

They stopped in New York, and he brought her to his business meetings. She saw him negotiating for the movie rights for a new novel coming out and a script written by a famous writer. He was shrewd, very low-key, and she saw here was his strength. But that first night they finally got to bed together in their suite at the Plaza and she learned one of the truths about Theodore Lieverman.

He was almost totally impotent. She was angry at first, feeling the lack in herself. She did everything she could and finally she made him get there. The next night was a little better. In Puerto Rico he was a little better still. But he was easily the most incompetent and boring lover she had ever had. She was glad to get back to Los Angeles. When he dropped her off at her apartment, he asked her to marry him. She said she'd think it over.

She had no intention of marrying him until Doran gave her a tongue-lashing. "Think it over? Think it over? Use your head," he said. "The guy is crazy about you. You marry him. So you stick with him for a year. You come out with at least a million and he'll still be in love with you. You'll call your own shots. Your career has a hundred times better chance of going. Besides, through him, you'll meet other rich guys. Guys that you'll like better and maybe love. You can change your whole life. Just be bored for a year, hell, that's not suffering. I wouldn't ask you to suffer."

It was like Doran to think that he was being very clever. That he was really opening Janelle's eyes to the verities of life every woman knows or is taught from her cradle. But Doran recognized that Janelle really hated to do anything like that not because it was immoral but because she could not betray another human being in such a fashion. So cold-bloodedly. And also because she had such a zest for life that she couldn't bear being bored for a year. But as Doran quickly pointed out, the chances were good that she would be bored that year even without Theodore to bring her down. And also she would really make poor Theodore happy for that year.

"You know, Janelle," Doran said, "having you around on your worst day is better than having most people around on their best day." It was one of the very few things he had said since his twelfth birthday that was sincere. Though self-serving.

But it was Theodore acting with uncommon aggressiveness who tipped the balance. He bought a beautiful two-hundred-fifty-thousand-dollar house in Beverly Hills, with swimming pool, tennis court, two servants. He knew Janelle loved to play tennis, she had learned to play in California, had had a brief affair as a matter of course with her tennis teacher, a slim, beautiful blond young man who had to her astonishment billed her for his teaching. Later other women told her about California men. How they would have drinks in a bar, let you pay for your own drinks and then ask you to go to their apartments for the night. They wouldn't even spring for the cab fare home. She enjoyed the tennis pro in bed and on the tennis court, and he had improved her performance in both areas. Eventually she tired of him because he dressed better than she did. Also, he batted right and left and he vamped her male as well as her female friends, which even Janelle, open-minded as she was, felt was stretching it.

She had never played tennis with Lieverman. He had casually mentioned once that he had beaten Arthur Ashe in high school, so she assumed he was out of her class and like most good tennis players would rather not play with hackers. But when he persuaded her to move into the new house, they gave an elaborate tennis party.

She loved the house. It was a luxurious Beverly Hills mansion with guest rooms, a den, a cabana for the pool, an outdoor heated whirlpool. She and Theodore went over plans to decorate and put in some special wood paneling. They went shopping together. But now in bed he was a complete bust, and Janelle didn't even try him anymore. He promised her that when his divorce came through next month and they married, he would be OK. Janelle devoutly hoped so because feeling guilty, she had decided the least she could do, since she was going to marry him for his money, was to be a faithful wife. But going without sex was getting on her nerves. It was on the day of the tennis party that she knew it was all down the drain. She had felt there was something fishy about the whole deal. But Theodore Lieverman inspired so much confidence in her, her friends and even the cynical Doran that she thought it was her guilty conscience looking for a way out.

On the day of the tennis party, Theodore finally got on the court. He played well enough, but he was a hacker. There was no way he could beat Arthur Ashe even in his bassinet. Janelle was astonished. The one thing she was sure of was that her lover was not a liar. And she was no innocent. She had always assumed lovers were liars. But Theodore never bullshitted, never bragged, never mentioned his money or his high standing in investment circles. He never really talked to other people except Janelle. His low key approach was extremely rare in California, so much so that Janelle had been surprised that he had lived his whole life in that state. But seeing him on the tennis court, she knew he had lied in one respect. And lied well. A casual deprecatory remark that he had never repeated, never lingered on. She had never doubted him. As she had never doubted anything he said really. There was no question that he loved her. He had shown that in every way, which of course didn't mean too much when he couldn't get it up.

That night after the tennis party was over he told her that she should get her little boy from Tennessee and move him to the house. If it had not been for his lie about beating Arthur

Ashe, she would have agreed. It was well she did not. The next day when Theodore was at work she received a visitor.

The visitor was Mrs. Theodore Lieverman, the heretofore invisible wife. She was a pretty little thing, but frightened and obviously impressed by Janelle's beauty, as if she couldn't believe her husband had come up with such a winner. As soon as she announced who she was, Janelle felt an overwhelming relief and greeted Mrs. Lieverman so warmly the woman was further confused.

But Mrs. Lieverman surprised Janelle too. She wasn't angry. The first thing she said was startling. "My husband is nervous, very sensitive," she said. "Please don't tell him I came to see you."

"Of course," Janelle said. Her spirits were soaring. She was elated. The wife would demand her husband and she would get him back so fast her head would swim.

Mrs. Lieverman said cautiously, "I don't know how Ted is getting all this money. He makes a good salary. But he hasn't any savings."

Janelle laughed. She already knew the answer. But she asked anyway. "What about the twenty million dollars?"

"Oh, God. Oh, God," Mrs. Lieverman said. She put her head down in her hands and started to weep.

"And he never beat Arthur Ashe in tennis in high school," Janelle said reassuringly.

"Oh, God, God," Mrs. Lieverman wailed.

"And you're not getting divorced next month," Janelle said.

Mrs. Lieverman just whimpered.

Janelle went to the bar and mixed two stiff scotches. She made the other woman drink through the sniffles.

"How did you find out?" Janelle asked.

Mrs. Lieverman opened her purse as if looking for a handkerchief for her sniffles. Instead, she brought out a sheaf of letters and handed them to Janelle. They were bills. Janelle looked at them thoughtfully. And she got the whole picture. He had written a twenty-five-thousand-dollar check as down payment on the beautiful house. With it was a letter requesting that he be allowed to move in until the final closing. The check had bounced. The builder was now threatening to put him in jail. The checks for hired help had bounced. The caterer's check for the tennis party had bounced.

"Wow," Janelle said.

"He's too sensitive," Mrs. Lieverman said.

"He's sick," Janelle said.

Mrs. Lieverman nodded.

Janelle said thoughtfully, "Is it because of his two sisters who died in the plane crash?"

There was a scream from Mrs. Lieverman, a shriek finally of outrage and exasperation. "He never had any sisters. Don't you understand? He's a pathological liar. He lies about everything. He has no sisters, he has no money, he's not divorcing me, he used the firm's money to take you to Puerto Rico and New York and to pay the expenses of this house."

"Then why the hell do you want him back?" Janelle asked.

"Because I love him," Mrs. Lieverman said.

Janelle thought that over for at least two minutes, studying Mrs. Lieverman. Her husband was a liar, a cheat, had a mistress, couldn't get it up in bed, and that's only what *she* knew about him, plus the fact, of course, that he was a lousy tennis player. Then what the hell was Mrs. Lieverman? Janelle patted the other woman on the shoulder, gave her another drink and said, "Wait here for five minutes."

That's all it took her to throw all her things into two Vuitton suitcases Theodore had bought her, probably with bum checks. She came down with the suitcases and said to the wife, "I'm leaving. You can wait here for your husband. Tell him I never want to see him again. And I'm truly sorry for the pain I've caused you. You have to believe me when I tell you that he said you had left him. That you didn't care."

Mrs. Lieverman nodded miserably.

Janelle left in the bright new baby blue Mustang Theodore had bought her. No doubt it would be repossessed. She could have it driven back to the house. Meanwhile, she had no place to go. She remembered the director and costume designer Alice De Santis, who had been so friendly, and she decided to drive to her house and ask her advice. If Alice was not at home, she would go to Doran. She knew he would always take her in.

Janelle loved the way Merlyn enjoyed the story. He didn't laugh. His enjoyment was not malicious. He just smiled, closing his eyes, savoring it. And he said the right thing—wonderingly, almost admiringly.

"Poor Lieverman," he said. "Poor, poor Lieverman."

"What about me, you bastard?" Janelle said with mock rage. She flung herself naked on his naked body and put her hands around his neck. Merlyn opened his eyes and smiled.

"Tell me another story."

She made love to him instead. She had another story to tell him, but he wasn't ready for it yet. He had to fall in love with her first, as she was in love with him. He couldn't take more stories yet. Especially about Alice.

Chapter 31

I had come to the point now that lovers always come to. They are so happy they can't believe they deserve it. And so they start thinking that maybe it's all a fake. So with me jealousy and suspicion haunted the ecstasies of our lovemaking. Once she had to read for a part and couldn't meet my plane. Another time I understood she would spend the night and she had to go home to sleep because she had to get up for an early-morning call at the studio. Even when she made love to me in the early afternoon so that I wouldn't be disappointed and I would believe her, I thought she lied. And now, expecting she would lie, I said to her, "I had lunch with Doran this afternoon. He says you had a fourteen-year-old lover when you were just a Southern belle."

Janelle raised her head slightly and gave the sweet, tentative smile that made me forget how I hated her.

"Yes," she said. "That was a long time ago."

She bowed her head then. Her face had an absentminded, amused look as she remembered that love affair. I knew she always remembered her love affairs with affection, even when they ended very badly. She looked up again.

"Does that bother you?" she said.

"No," I said. But she knew it did.

"I'm sorry," she said. She looked at me for a moment, then turned her head away. She reached out with her hands, slid them under my shirt and caressed my back. "It was innocent," she said.

I didn't say anything, just moved away because the remembered touch made me forgive her everything.

Again expecting her to lie, I said, "Doran told me because of the fourteen-year-old kid you stood trial for impairment of the morals of a minor."

With all my heart I wanted her to lie. I didn't care if it

was true. As I would not blame or reproach her if she were an alcoholic or hustler or murderess. I wanted to love her, and that was all. She was watching me with that quiet, contemplative look as if she would do anything to please me.

"What do you want me to say?" she asked, looking directly into my face.

"Just tell me the truth," I said.

"Well, then it's true," she said. "But I was acquitted. The judge dismissed the case."

I felt an enormous relief. "Then you didn't do it."

"Do what?" she asked.

"You know," I said.

She gave me that sweet half-smile again. But it was touched with a sad mockery.

"You mean, did I make love to a fourteen-year-old boy?" she asked. "Yes, I did."

She waited for me to walk out of the room. I remained still. Her face became more mocking. "He was very big for his age," she said.

That interested me. It interested me because of the boldness of the challenge. "That makes all the difference," I said dryly. And watched her when she gave a delighted laugh. We had both been angry with each other. Janelle because I dared judge her. I was going to leave, so she said, "It's a good story, you'll like it." And she saw me bite. I always loved a story almost as much as making love. Many nights I'd listened to her for hours, fascinated as she told her life story, making guesses at what she left out or edited for my tender male ears as she would have edited a horror story for a child.

It was the thing she loved me most for, she told me once. The eagerness for stories. And my refusal to make judgments. She could always see me shifting it around in my head, how I would tell it or how I would use it. And I had never really condemned her for anything she'd done. As she knew now I would not when she told her story.

After her divorce Janelle had taken a lover, Doran Rudd. He was a disc jockey on the local radio station. A rather tall man, a little older than Janelle. He had a great deal of energy, was always charming and amusing and finally got

Janelle a job as the weather girl of the radio station. This was a fun job and well paid for a town like Johnson City.

Doran was obsessed with being the town character. He had an enormous Cadillac, bought his clothes in New York and swore he would make it big someday. He was awed and enchanted by performers. He went to see all the road companies of all the Broadway plays and always sent notes back to one of the actresses, followed up by flowers, followed up by offers of dinner. He was surprised to find how easy it was to get them to bed. He gradually realized how lonely they were. Glamorous onstage, they were a little pathetic-looking back in their second-rate hotel rooms stocked with old-model refrigerators. He would always tell Janelle about his adventures. They were more friends than lovers.

One day he got his break. A father and son duo were booked into the town concert hall. The father was a pickup piano player who had earned a steady living unloading freight cars in Nashville until he discovered his nine-year-old son could sing. The father, a hardworking Southern man who hated his job, immediately saw his son as the impossible dream come true. He might escape from a life of dull, backbreaking toil.

He knew his son was good, but he didn't really know how good. He was quite content with teaching the young boy all the gospel songs and making a handsome living touring the Bible Belt. A young cherub praising Jesus in pure soprano was irresistible to that regional audience. The father found his new life extremely agreeable. He was gregarious, had an eye for a pretty girl and welcomed vacations from his already worn-out wife, who, of course, remained home.

But the mother too dreamed of all the luxuries her son's pure voice would bring her. They were both greedy but not greedy as the rich are greedy, as a way of life, but greedy as a starving man on a desert island who is suddenly rescued and can finally realize all his fantasies.

So when Doran went backstage to rave about the lad's voice, then proposition the parents, he found a willing audience. Doran knew how good the boy was and soon realized that he was the only one. He reassured them that he did not want any percentage of the gospel-singing earnings. He would manage the boy and take only thirty percent of anything the boy earned over twenty-five thousand dollars a year.

It was, of course, an irresistible offer. If they got twenty-five thousand dollars a year, an incredible sum, why worry if Doran got thirty percent of the rest? And how could their boy, Rory, make more than that amount? Impossible. There was not that much money. Doran also assured Mr. Horatio Bascombe and Mrs. Edith Bascombe that he would not charge them for any expenses. So a contract was prepared and signed.

Doran immediately went into furious action. He borrowed money to produce an album of gospel songs. It was an enormous hit. In that first year the boy Rory earned over fifty thousand dollars. Doran immediately moved to Nashville and made connections in the music world. He took Janelle with him and made her administrative assistant in his new music company. The second year Rory made more than a hundred thousand dollars, most of it on a single of an old religious ballad Janelle found in Doran's disc jockey files. Doran had absolutely no creative taste in any sense; he would never have recognized the worth of the song.

Doran and Janelle were living together now. But she didn't see that much of him. He was traveling to Hollywood for a movie deal or to New York to get an exclusive contract with one of the big recording companies. They would all be millionaires. Then the catastrophe. Rory caught a bad cold and seemed to lose his voice. Doran took him to the best specialist in New York. The specialist cured Rory completely but then casually, just in passing, said to Doran, "You know his voice will change as he goes into puberty."

It was something that Doran had not thought of. Maybe because Rory was big for his age. Maybe because Rory was a totally innocent young boy, unworldly. He had been shielded from girlfriends by his mother and father. He loved music and was indeed an accomplished musician. Also, he had always been sickly until his eleventh year. Doran was frantic. A man who has the location of a secret gold mine and misplaced the map. He had plans to make millions out of Rory; now he saw it all going down the drain. Millions of dollars at stake. Literally millions of dollars!

Then Doran got one of his greater ideas. He checked it out medically. After he had all the dope, he tried his scheme out on Janelle. She was horrified.

"You are a terrible son of a bitch," she said, almost in tears.

Doran couldn't understand her horror. "Listen," he said, "the Catholic Church used to do it."

"They did it for God," Janelle said. "Not for a gold album."

Doran shook his head. "Please stick to the point. I have to convince the kid and his mother and father, that's going to be a hell of a job."

Janelle laughed. "You really are crazy. I won't help you, and even if I did, you'll never convince one of them."

Doran smiled at her. "The father is the key. I was thinking you could be nice to him. Soften him up for me."

It was before Doran had acquired the creamy, sunlit, extra smoothness of California. So when Janelle threw the heavy ashtray at him, he was too surprised to duck. It chipped one of his teeth and made his mouth bleed. He didn't get angry. He just shook his head at Janelle's squareness.

Janelle would have left him then, but she was too curious. She wanted to see if Doran could really pull it off.

Doran was, in general, a good judge of character, and he was really sharp on finding the greed threshold. He knew one key was Mr. Horatio Bascombe. The father could swing his wife and son. Also, the father was the most vulnerable to life. If his son failed to make money, it was back to going to church for Mr. Bascombe. No more traveling around the country, playing piano, tickling pretty girls, eating exotic foods. Just his worn-out wife. The father had most at stake; the loss of Rory's voice was more important to him than anyone.

Doran softened Mr. Bascombe up with a pretty little singer from a sleazy Nashville jazz club. Then a fine dinner with cigars the following evening. Over cigars he outlined Rory's career. A Broadway musical, an album with special songs written by the famous Dean brothers. Then a big role in a movie that might turn Rory into another Judy Garland or Elvis Presley. You wouldn't be able to count the money. Bascombe was drinking it all in, purring like a cat. Not even greedy because it was all there. It was inevitable. He was a millionaire. Then Doran sprang it on him.

"There's only one thing wrong," Doran said. "The doctors say his voice is about to change. He's going into puberty."

Bascombe was a little worried. "His voice will get a little deeper. Maybe it will be better."

Doran shook his head. "What makes him a superstar is that high, clear sweetness. Sure he might be better. But it will take him five years to train it and break through with a new image. And then it's a hundred to one shot he'll make it big. I sold him to everybody on the voice he has now."

"Well, maybe his voice won't change," Bascombe said.

"Yeah, maybe it won't," Doran said and left it at that.

Two days later Bascombe came around to his apartment. Janelle let him in and gave him a drink. He looked her over pretty carefully, but she ignored him. And when he and Doran started talking, she left the room.

That night in bed, after making love, Janelle asked Doran, "How is your dirty little scheme coming?"

Doran grinned. He knew Janelle despised him for what he was doing, but she was such a great broad she had still given him her usual great piece of ass. Like Rory, she still didn't know how great she was. Doran felt content. That's what he liked, good service. People who didn't know their value.

"I've got the greedy old bastard hooked," he said. "Now I've got to work on the mother and the kid."

Doran, who thought he was the greatest salesman east of the Rockies, attributed his final success to those powers. But the truth was that he was lucky. Mr. Bascombe had been softened up by the extremely hard life he had led before the miracle of his son's voice. He could not give up the golden dream and go back to slavery. That was not so unusual. Where Doran got really lucky was with the mother.

Mrs. Bascombe had been a small-town Southern belle, mildly promiscuous in her teens and swept off her feet into matrimony by Horatio Bascombe's piano playing and Southern small-town charm. As her beauty faded year by year, she succumbed to the swampy miasma of Southern religiosity. As her husband became more unlovable, Mrs. Bascombe found Jesus more attractive. Her son's voice was her love offering to Jesus. Doran worked on that. He kept Janelle in the room while he talked to Mrs. Bascombe, knowing the delicate subject matter would make the older woman nervous if she were alone with a male.

Doran was respectfully charming and attentive to Mrs. Bascombe. He pointed out that in the years to come a hundred million people all over the world would hear her son, Rory, singing the glories of Jesus. In Catholic countries, in Moslem countries, in Israel, in the cities of Africa. Her son would be the most powerful evangelist for the Christian religion since Luther. He would be bigger than Billy Graham, bigger than Oral Roberts, two of Mrs. Bascombe's saints on earth. And her son would be saved from the most grievous and easiest-to-fall-into sin on this earth. It was clearly the will of God.

Janelle watched them both. She was fascinated by Doran. That he could do such a thing without being evil, merely mercenary. He was like a child stealing pennies from his mother's pocket book. And Mrs. Bascombe after an hour of Doran's feverish pleading was weakening. Doran finished her off.

"Mrs. Bascombe, I just know you'll make this sacrifice for Jesus. The big problem is your son, Rory. He's just a boy, and you know how boys are."

Mrs. Bascombe gave him a grim smile. "Yes," she said. "I know." She darted a quick venomous look at Janelle. "But my Rory is a good boy. He'll do what I say."

Doran heaved a sigh of relief. "I knew I could count on you."

Then Mrs. Bascombe said coolly, "I'm doing this for Jesus. But I'd like a new contract drawn up. I want fifteen percent of your thirty percent as his co-manager." She paused for a moment. "And my husband needn't know."

Doran sighed. "Give me some of that old-time religion all the time," he said. "I just hope you can swing it."

Rory's mama did swing it. Nobody knew how. It was all set. The only one who didn't like the idea was Janelle. In fact, she was horrified, so horrified she stopped sleeping with Doran, and he considered getting rid of her. Also, Doran had one final problem. Getting a doctor who would cut off a fourteen-year-old kid's balls. For that was the idea. What was good enough for the old Popes was good enough for Doran.

It was Janelle who blew the whole thing up. They were all gathered in Doran's apartment. Doran was working out how to screw Mrs. Bascombe out of her co-manager's fifteen percent, so he wasn't paying attention. Janelle got up, took Rory by the hand and led him to the bedroom.

Mrs. Bascombe protested, "What are you doing with my boy?"

Janelle said sweetly, "We'll be right out. I just want to show him something." Once inside the bedroom she locked the door. Then very firmly she led Rory to the bed, unbuckled his belt, stripped down his trousers and shorts. She put his hand between her legs and his head between her now bare breasts.

In three minutes they were finished, and then the boy surprised Janelle. He pulled on his trousers, forgetting his shorts. He unlocked the bedroom door and flew into the living room. His first punch caught Doran square in the mouth, and then he was throwing punches like a windmill until his father restrained him.

Naked on the bed, Janelle smiled at me. "Doran hates me, even though it's six years later. I cost him millions of dollars."

I was smiling too. "So what happened at the trial?"

Janelle shrugged. "We had a civilized judge. He talked to me and the kid in chambers, and then he dismissed the case. He warned the parents and Doran they were subject to prosecution but advised everybody to keep their mouths shut."

I thought that over. "What did he say to you?"

Janelle smiled again. "He told me that if he were thirty years younger, he'd give anything if I were his girl."

I sighed. "Jesus, you make everything sound right. But now I want you to answer truthfully. Swear?"

"Swear," Janelle said.

I paused for a moment, watching her. Then I said, "Did you enjoy fucking that fourteen-year-old kid?"

Janelle didn't hesitate. "It was terrific," she said.

"OK," I said. I was frowning with concentration, and Janelle laughed. She loved these times best when I was really interested in figuring her out. "Let's see," I said. "He had curly hair and a great build. Great skin, no pimples yet. Long eyelashes and choirboy virginity. Wow." I thought a little longer.

"Tell me the truth. You were indignant, but deep down you knew here was your excuse to fuck a fourteen-year-old kid. You couldn't have done it otherwise, even though that was what you really wanted to do. That the kid turned you on from the beginning. And so you could have it both ways. You saved the kid by fucking him. Great. Right?"

"No," Janelle said, smiling sweetly.

I sighed again and then laughed. "You're such a phony." But I was licked and I knew it. She had performed an unselfish act, she had saved the manhood of a budding boy. That she had a hell of a thrill along the way was, after all, a bonus the virtuous deserved. Down South everybody serves Jesus—in his own way.

And Jesus, I really loved her more.

Chapter 32

Malomar had had a hard day and a special conference with Moses Wartberg and Jeff Wagon. He had fought for Merlyn's and his movie. Wartberg and Wagon had hated it after he had shown them a first draft. It became the usual argument. They wanted to turn it into schlock, put in more action, coarsen the characters. Malomar stood fast.

"It's a good script," he said. "And remember this is just a first draft."

Wartberg said, "You don't have to tell us. We know that. We've judged it on that basis."

Malomar said coolly, "You know I'm always interested in your opinions and I weigh them very carefully. But everything you've said so far strikes me as irrelevant."

Wagon said appeasingly, with his charming smile, "Malomar, you know we believe in you. That's why we gave you your original contract. Hell, you have full control over your pictures. But we have to back our judgment with advertising and publicity. Now we've let you project a million dollars over budget. That gives us, I think, a moral right to have some say in the final shape of this picture."

Malomar said, "That was a bullshit budget to begin with and we all knew it and we all admitted it."

Wartberg said, "You know that in all our contracts, when we go over budget, you start losing your points in the picture. Are you willing to take that risk?"

"Jesus," Malomar said. "I can't believe that if this makes a lot of money, you guys would invoke that clause."

Wartberg gave his shark grin. "We may or may not. That's the chance you will have to take if you insist on your version of the film."

Malomar shrugged. "I'll take that risk," he said. "And if

that's all you guys have to say, I'll get back to the cutting room."

When he left Tri-Culture Studios to be driven back to his lot, Malomar felt drained. He thought of going home and taking a nap, but there was too much work to be done. He wanted to put in at least another five hours. He felt the slight pains in his chest starting again. Those bastards will kill me yet, he thought. And then he suddenly realized that since his heart attack Wartberg and Wagon had been less afraid of him, had argued with him more, had harried him about costs more. Maybe the bastards *were* trying to kill him.

He sighed. The fucking things he had to put up with, and that fucking Merlyn always bitching about producers and Hollywood and how they all weren't artists. And here he was risking his life to save Merlyn's conception of the picture. He felt like calling Merlyn up and making him go to the arena with Wartberg and Wagon to do his own fighting, but he knew that Merlyn would just quit and walk away from the picture. Merlyn didn't believe as he, Malomar, did. Didn't have his love for film and what film could do.

Well, the hell with it, Malomar thought. He'd make the picture his way and it would be good and Merlyn would be happy, and when the picture made money, the studio would be happy, and if they tried to take away his percentage because of the overbudget, he'd take his production company elsewhere.

As the limousine pulled up to a stop, Malomar felt the elation he'd always felt. The elation of an artist coming to his work knowing that he would fashion something beautiful.

He labored with his film editors for almost seven hours, and when the limousine dropped him at his home, it was nearly midnight. He was so tired he went directly to bed. He almost groaned with weariness. The pains in his chest came and spread to his back, but after a few minutes they went away and he lay there quietly, trying to fall asleep. He was content. He had done a good day's work. He had fought off the sharks and he had cut film.

Malomar loved to sit in the cutting room with the editors and the director. He loved to sit in the dark and make decisions on what the tiny flickering images should do and not do. Like God, he gave them a certain kind of soul. If they were "good," he made them physically beautiful by telling the editor to cut an unflattering image so that a nose was not too bony; a mouth not too mean. He could make a heroine's eyes more doelike with a better lighted shot, her gestures more graceful and touching. He would not send the good down to despair and defeat. He was more merciful.

Meanwhile, he kept a sharp eye on the villains. Did they wear the right color tie and the right cut of jacket to enhance their villainy? Did they smile too trustingly? Were the lines in their faces too decent? He blotted out that image with the cutting machine. Most of all, he refused to let them be boring. The villain had to be interesting. Malomar in his cutting room truly watched every feather that fell from the tail of the sparrow. The world he created must have a sensible logic, and when he finished with that particular world, you usually were glad to have seen it exist.

Malomar had created hundreds of these worlds. They lived in his brain forever and ever as the countless galaxies of God must exist in His brain. And Malomar's feat was as astounding to him. But it was different when he left the darkened cutting room and emerged into the world created by God which made no sense at all.

Malomar had suffered three heart attacks over the past few years. From overwork, the doctor said. But Malomar always felt that God had fucked up in the cutting room. He, Malomar, was the last man who should have a heart attack. Who would oversee all those worlds to be created? And he took such good care of himself. He ate sparingly and correctly. He exercised. He drank little. He fornicated regularly but not to excess. He never drugged. He was still young, handsome; he looked like a hero. And he tried to behave well, or as well as possible in the world God was shooting. In Malomar's cutting room a character like Malomar would never die from a heart attack. The editor would excise the frame, the producer call for a rewrite of the script. He would command the directors and all the actors to the rescue. Such a man would not be allowed to perish.

But Malomar could not excise the chest pains. And often at night, very late, in his huge house, he popped angina pills in his mouth. And then he would lie in bed petrified with fear. On really bad nights he called his personal physician. The doctor would come and sit with him through the night, examine him, reassure him, hold his hand until dawn broke. The doctor would never refuse him because Malomar had written the script for the doctor's life. Malomar had given him access to beautiful actresses so that he could become their doctor and sometimes their lover. When Malomar in his early days indulged in more strenuous sex, before his first heart attack, when his huge home was filled with overnight guests of starlets and high-fashion models, the doctor had been his dinner companion and they had sampled together the smorgasbord of women prepared for the evening.

Now on this midnight, Malomar alone in his bed, in his home, phoned the doctor. The doctor came and examined him and assured him the pains would go away. That there was no danger. That he should let himself fall asleep. The doctor brought him water for his angina pills and tranquilizers. And the doctor measured his heart with his stethoscope. It was intact; it was not breaking into pieces as Malomar felt it was. And after a few hours, resting more easily, Malomar told the doctor he could go home. And then Malomar fell asleep.

He dreamed. It was a vivid dream. He was at a railroad station, enclosed. He was buying a ticket. A small but burly man pushed him aside and demanded his ticket. The small man had a huge dwarf's head and screamed at Malomar. Malomar reassured him. He stepped aside. He let the man buy his ticket. He told the man, "Look, whatever is bothering you is OK with me." And as he did so, the man grew taller, his features more regular. He was suddenly an older hero, and he said to Malomar, "Give me your name; I'll do something for you." He loved Malomar. Malomar could see that. They were both very kind to each other. And the railroad agent selling the tickets now treated the other man with enormous respect.

Malomar came awake in the vast darkness of his huge bedroom. His eye lenses narrowed down, and with no peripheral vision, he fixed on the white rectangular light from the open bathroom door. For just a moment he thought the images on the cutting-room screen had not ended, and then he realized it had only been a dream. At that realization his heart broke away from his body in a fatal arhythmic gallop. The electrical impulses of his brain snarled together. He sat up, sweating.

His heart went into a final thundering rush, shuddered. He fell back, eyes closing, all light fading on the screen that was his life. The last thing he ever heard was a scraping noise like celluloid breaking against steel, and then he was dead.

Chapter 33

IT was my agent, Doran Rudd, who called me with the news of Malomar's death. He told me there was going to be a big conference on the picture at Tri-Culture Studios the next day. I had to fly out and he would meet my plane.

At Kennedy Airport I called Janelle to tell her I was coming into town, but I got her answering machine with her French-accented machine voice, so I left a message for her.

Malomar's death shocked me. I had developed an enormous respect for him during the months we had worked together. He never gave out any bullshit, and he had an eagle eye for any bullshit in a script or a piece of film. He tutored me when he showed me films, explaining why a scene didn't play or what to watch for in an actor who might be showing talent even in a bad role. We argued a lot. He told me that my literary snobbishness was defensive and that I hadn't studied film carefully enough. He even offered to teach me how to direct a film, but I refused. He wanted to know why.

"Listen," I said, "just by existing, just by standing still and not bothering anybody, man is a fate-creating agent. That's what I hate about life. And a movie director is the worst fate-creating agent on earth. Think of all those actors and actresses you make miserable when you turn them down. Look at all the people you have to give orders to. The money you spend, the destinies you control. I just write books, I never hurt anybody, I only help. They can take it or leave it."

"You're right," Malomar said. "You'll never be a director. But I think you're full of shit. Nobody can be that passive." And of course, he was right. I just wanted to control a more private world.

But still I felt saddened by his death. I had some affection for him though we did not really know each other well. And then too I was a little worried about what was going to happen to our movie.

Doran Rudd met me at the plane. He told me that Jeff Wagon would now be the producer and that Tri-Culture had swallowed up Malomar Studios. He told me to expect a lot of trouble. On the way over to the studio he briefed me on the whole Tri-Culture operation. On Moses Wartberg, on his wife, Bella, on Jeff Wagon. Just for openers he told me that though they were not the most powerful studio in Hollywood, they were the most hated, often called "Tri-Vulture Studios." That Wartberg was a shark and the three VP's were jackals. I told him that you couldn't mix up your symbols like that, that if Wartberg was a shark, the others had to be pilot fish. I was kidding around, but my agent wasn't even listening. He just said, "I wish you were wearing a tie."

I looked at him. He was in his slick black leather jacket over a turtleneck sweater. He shrugged.

"Moses Wartberg could have been a Semitic Hitler," Doran said. "But he would have done it a little differently. He would have sent all the adult Christians to the gas chamber and then set up college scholarships for their children."

Comfortably slouched down in Doran Rudd's Mercedes 450SL, I barely listened to Doran's chatter. He was telling me that there was going to be a big fight over the picture. That Jeff Wagon would be producer and Wartberg would be taking a personal interest in it. They had killed Malomar with their harassment, Doran said. I wrote that off as typical Hollywood exaggeration. But the essence of what Doran was telling me was that the fate of the picture would be decided today. So in the long ride to the studio I tried to remember everything I knew or had heard about Moses Wartberg and Jeff Wagon.

Jeff Wagon was the essence of a schlock producer. He was schlock from the top of his craggy head to the tiptoes of his Bally shoes. He had made his mark in TV, then muscled his way into feature films by the same process with which a blob of ink spreads on a linen tablecloth and with the same aesthetic effect. He had made over a hundred TV feature films and twenty theatrical films. Not one of them had had a touch of grace, of quality, of art. The critics, the workers and artists in Hollywood had a classic joke that compared Wagon with Selznick, Lubitsch, Thalberg. They would say of one of his pictures that it had the Dong imprint because a young malicious actress called him the Dong.

A typical Jeff Wagon picture was loaded with stars a bit frayed by age and celluloid wear and tear, desperate for a paycheck. The talent knew it was a schlock picture. The directors were handpicked by Wagon. They were usually run-of-the-mill with a string of failures behind them so that he could twist their arms and make them shoot the picture his way. The odd thing was that though all the pictures were terrible, they either broke even or made money simply because the basic idea was good in a commercial way. It usually had a built-in audience, and Jeff Wagon was a fierce bulldog on cost. He was also terrific on contracts that screwed everybody out of his percentage if the picture became a big hit and made a lot of cash. And if that didn't work, he would have the studio start litigation so that a settlement could be made on percentages. But Moses Wartberg always said that Jeff Wagon came up with sound ideas. What he presumably didn't know was that Wagon stole even these ideas. He did this by what could only be called seduction.

In his younger days Jeff Wagon had lived up to his nickname by knocking over every starlet on the Tri-Culture lot. He was very much on the line with his approach. If they came across, they became girls in TV movies who were bartenders or receptionists. If they played their cards right, they could get enough work to carry them through the year. But when he went into feature films, this was not possible. With three-million-dollar budgets you didn't fuck around handing out parts for a piece of ass. So then he got away with letting them read for a part, promising to help them, but never a firm commitment. And of course, some were talented, and with his foot in the door, they got some nice parts in feature films. A few became stars. They were often grateful. In the Land of Empidae, Jeff Wagon was the ultimate survivor.

But one day out of the northern rain forests of Oregon a breathtaking beauty of eighteen appeared. She had everything going for her. Great face, great body, fiery temperament, even talent. But the camera refused to do right by her. In that idiotic magic of film her looks didn't work.

She was also a little crazy. She had grown up as a woodsman and hunter in the Oregon forests. She could skin a deer and fight a grizzly bear. She reluctantly let Jeff Wagon fuck her once a month because her agent gave her a little heart-to-heart talk. But she came from a place where the people were straight shooters, and she expected Jeff Wagon to keep his word and get her the part. When it didn't happen, she went to bed with Jeff Wagon with a deer-skinning knife and, at the crucial moment, stuck it into one of Jeff Wagon's balls.

It didn't turn out badly. For one thing she only took a nick off his right ball, and everybody agreed that with his big balls a little chip wouldn't do him any harm. Jeff Wagon himself tried to cover up the incident, refused to press charges. But the story got out. The girl was shipped home to Oregon with enough money for a log cabin and a new deer-hunting rifle. And Jeff Wagon had learned his lesson. He gave up seducing starlets and devoted himself to seducing writers out of their ideas. It was both more profitable and less dangerous. Writers were dumber and more cowardly.

And so he seduced writers by taking them to expensive lunches. By dangling jobs before their eyes. A rewrite of a script in production, a couple of thousand dollars for a treatment. Meanwhile, he let them talk about their ideas for future novels or screenplays. And then he would steal their ideas by switching them to other locales, changing the characters, but always preserving the central idea. And then it was his pleasure to screw them by giving them nothing. And since writers did not usually have a clue to the worthiness of their ideas, they never protested. Not like those cunts who gave you a piece of their ass and expected the moon.

It was the agents that got on to Jeff Wagon and forbade their writer clients to go to lunch with him. But there were fresh young writers coming into Hollywood from all over the country. All hoping for that one foot in the door that would make them rich and famous. And it was Jeff Wagon's genius that he could let them see the door crack open just enough to jam toes black and blue when he slammed the door shut.

Once when I was in Vegas, I told Cully that he and Wagon mugged their victims the same way. But Cully disagreed.

"Listen," Cully said. "Me and Vegas are after your money, true. But Hollywood wants your balls."

He didn't know that Tri-Culture Studios had just bought one of the biggest casinos in Vegas.

Moses Wartberg was another story. On one of my early visits to Hollywood I had been taken to Tri-Culture Studios to pay my respects.

I met Moses Wartberg for a minute. And I knew who he was right away. There was that sharklike look to him that I had seen in top military men, casino owners, very beautiful and very rich women and top Mafia bosses. It was the cold steel of power, the iciness that ran through the blood and brain, the chilling absence of mercy or pity in all the cells of the organism. People who were absolutely dedicated to the supreme drug power. Power already achieved and exercised over a long period of time. And with Moses Wartberg it was exercised down to the smallest square inch.

That night, when I told Janelle that I had been to Tri-Culture Studios and met Wartberg, she said casually, "Good old Moses. I know Moses." She gave me a challenging look, so I took the bait.

"OK," I said. "Tell me how you know Moses."

Janelle got out of bed to act out the part. "I had been in town for about two years and wasn't getting anyplace, and then I was invited to a party where all the big wheels would be, and like a good little would-be star, I went to make contacts. There were a dozen girls like me. All walking around, looking beautiful, hoping that some powerful producer would be struck by our talent. Well, I got lucky. Moses Wartberg came over to me, and he was charming. I didn't know how people could say such terrible things about him. I remember his wife came up for a minute and tried to take him away, but he didn't pay any attention to her. He just kept on talking to me and I was at my most fascinating Southern belle best and, sure enough, by the end of the evening I had an invitation from Moses Wartberg to have dinner at his house the next night. In the morning I called up all my girlfriends and told them about it. They congratulated me and told me I would have to fuck him and I said of course I would not, not on my first date and I also thought he'd respect me more if I held him off a little."

"That's a good technique," I said.

"I know," she said. "It worked with you, but that's the way

I felt. I hadn't ever gone to bed with a man unless I really liked him. I'd never gone to bed with a man just to make him do something for me. I told my girlfriends that, and they told me I was crazy. That if Moses Wartberg was really in love with me or really liked me, I would be on my way to being a star."

For a few minutes she gave a charming pantomime of false virtue arguing itself into honest sinning.

"And so what happened?" I said.

Janelle stood proud, her hands on her hips, her head tilted dramatically. "At five o'clock that afternoon I made the greatest decision of my life. I decided I would fuck a man I didn't know just to get ahead. I thought I was so brave and I was delighted that finally I had made a decision that a man would make."

She came out of her role for just a moment.

"Isn't that what men do?" she said sweetly. "If they can make a business deal, they'd give anything, they demean themselves. Isn't that business?"

I said, "I guess so."

She said to me, "Didn't you have to do that?"

I said, "No."

"You never did anything like that to get your books published, to get an agent or to get a book reviewer to treat you better?"

I said, "No."

"You have a good opinion of yourself, don't you?" Janelle said. "I've had affairs with married men before, and the one thing I have noticed is that they all want to wear that big white cowboy hat."

"What does that mean?"

"They want to be fair to their wives and girlfriends. That's the one impression they want to make, so you can't blame them for anything, and you do that too."

I thought that over a minute. I could see what she meant. "OK," I said. "So what?"

"So what?" Janelle said. "You tell me you love me, but you go back to your wife. No married man should tell another woman he loves her unless he's willing to leave his wife."

"That's romantic bullshit," I said.

For a moment she became furious. She said, "If I went to

your house and told your wife you loved me, would you deny me?"

I laughed and I really laughed. I pressed my hand across my chest and said, "Would you say that again?"

And she said, "Would you deny me?"

And I said, "With all my heart."

She looked at me a moment. She was furious, and then she started to laugh. She said, "I regressed with you, but I won't regress anymore."

And I understood what she was saying.

"OK," I said. "So what happened with Wartberg?"

She said, "I took a long bath with my turtle oil. I anointed myself, dressed in my best outfit and drove myself to the sacrificial altar. I was let into the house and there was Moses Wartberg and we sat down and had a drink and he asked about my career and we were talking for about an hour and he was being very clever, letting me know that if the night turned out OK, he would do a lot of things for me and I was thinking, the son of a bitch isn't going to fuck me, he's not even going to feed me."

"That's something I never did to you," I said.

She gave me a long look, and she went on. "And then he said, 'There's dinner waiting upstairs in the bedroom. Would you like to go up?' And I said, in my Southern belle voice, 'Yes, I think I'm a little hungry.' He escorted me up the stairs, a beautiful staircase just like the movies, and opened the bedroom door. He closed it behind me, from the outside, and there I was in the bedroom with a little table set up with some nice snacks on it."

She struck another pose of the innocent young girl, bewildered.

"Where's Moses?" I said.

"He's outside. He's in the hallway."

"He made you eat alone?" I said.

"No," Janelle said. "There was Mrs. Bella Wartberg in her sheerest negligee waiting for me."

I said, "Jesus Christ."

Janelle went into another act. "I didn't know I was going to fuck a woman. It took me eight hours to decide to fuck a man, and now I find out I had to fuck a woman. I wasn't ready for that."

I said I wasn't ready for that either.

She said, "I really didn't know what to do. I sat down and Mrs. Wartberg served some sandwiches and tea and then she pushed her breasts out of her gown and said, 'Do you like these, my dear?' And I said, 'They're very nice.'"

And then Janelle looked me in the eye and hung her head, and I said, "Well, what happened? What did she say after you said they're nice?"

Janelle made her eyes look wide open, startled. "Bella Wartberg said to me, 'Would you like to suck on these, my dear?'"

And then Janelle collapsed on the bed with me. She said, "I ran out of the room, I ran down the stairs, out of the house, and it took me two years to get another job."

"It's a tough town," I said.

"Nay," Janelle said. "If I had talked to my girlfriends another eight hours, that would have been OK too. It's just a matter of getting your nerve up."

I smiled at her, and she looked me in the eye, challengingly. "Yeah," I said, "what's the difference?"

As the Mercedes sped over the freeways, I tried to listen to Doran.

"Old Moses is the dangerous guy," Doran was saying, "watch out for him." And so I thought about Moses.

Moses Wartberg was one of the most powerful men in Hollywood. His Tri-Culture Studios was financially sounder than most but made the worst movies. Moses Wartberg had created a money-making machine in a field of creative endeavor. And without a creative bone in his body. This was recognized as sheer genius.

Wartberg was a sloppily fat man, carelessly tailored in Vegas-style suits. He spoke little, never showed emotion, he believed in giving you everything you could take away from him. He believed in giving you nothing you could not force from him and his battery of studio lawyers. He was impartial. He cheated producers, stars, writers and directors out of their percentages of successful films. He was never grateful for a great directing job, a great performance, a great script. How many times had he paid big money for lousy stuff? So why should he pay a man what his work was worth if he could get it for less?

Wartberg talked about movies as generals talk about making war. He said things like: "You can't make an omelet without breaking eggs." Or when a business associate made claims to their social relationship, when an actor told him how much they loved each other personally and why was the studio screwing him, Wartberg gave a thin smile and said coldly, "When I hear the word 'love,' I reach for my wallet."

He was scornful of personal dignity, proud when accused of having no sense of decency. He was not ambitious to be known as a man whose word was his bond. He believed in contracts with fine print, not handshakes. He was never too proud to cheat his fellowman out of an idea, a script, a rightful percentage of a movie's profits. When reproached, usually by an overwrought artist (producers knew better), Wartberg would simply answer, "I'm a moviemaker," in the same tone that Baudelaire might have answered a similar reproach with "I am a poet."

He used lawyers as a hood used guns, used affection as a prostitute used sex. He used good works as the Greeks used the Trojan Horse, supported the Will Rogers home for retired actors, Israel, the starving millions of India, Arab refugees from Palestine. It was only personal charity to individual human beings that went against his grain.

Tri-Culture Studios had been losing money when Wartberg took charge. He immediately put it on a strict computer with a bottom-line basis. His deals were the toughest in town. He never gambled on truly creative ideas until they had been proved at other studios. And his big ace in the hole was small budgets.

When other studios were going down the drain with ten-million-dollar pictures, Tri-Culture Studios never made one that went over three million. In fact, over two million and Moses Wartberg or one of his three assistant vice-presidents was sleeping with you twenty-four hours a day. He made producers post completion bonds, directors pledge percentages, actors swear their souls away, to bring in a picture on budget. A producer who brought a picture in on budget or below budget was a hero to Moses Wartberg and knew it. It didn't matter if the picture just made its cost. But if the picture went over budget, even if it grossed twenty million and made the studio a fortune, Wartberg would invoke the penalty clause in the producer's contract and take away his percentage of the profits. Sure, there would be lawsuits, but the studio had twenty salaried lawyers sitting around on their asses who needed practice in court. So a deal could usually be made. Especially if the producer or actor or writer wanted to make another picture at Tri-Culture.

The one thing everybody agreed upon was that Wartberg was a genius at organization. He had three vice-presidents who were in charge of separate empires and competing with each other for Wartberg's favor and the day when one would succeed him. All three had palatial homes, big bonuses and complete power within their own spheres subject only to Wartberg's veto. So the three of them hunted down talent, scripts, thought out special projects. Always knowing that they had to keep the budget low, the talent tractable, and to stamp out any spark of originality before they dared bring it up to Wartberg's suite of offices on the top floor of the studio building.

His sexual reputation was impeccable. He never had fun and games with starlets. He never put pressure on a director or producer to hire a favorite in a film. Part of this was his ascetic nature, a low sexual vitality. The other was his own sense of personal dignity. But the main reason was that he had been happily married for thirty years to his childhood sweetheart.

They had met in a Bronx high school, married in their teens and lived together forever after.

Bella Wartberg had lived a fairy-tale life. A zaftig teenager in a Bronx high school, she had charmed Moses Wartberg with the lethal combination of huge breasts and excessive modesty. She wore loose heavy wool sweaters, dresses, a couple of sizes too large, but it was like hiding a glowing radioactive piece of metal in a dark cave. You knew they were there, and the fact that they were hidden made them even more aphrodisiacal. When Moses became a producer, she didn't really know what it meant. She had two children in two years and was quite willing to have one a year for the rest of her fertile life, but it was Moses who called a halt. By that time he had channeled most of his energy into his career, and also, the body that he thirsted for was marred by childbirth scars, the breasts he had suckled had drooped and become veined. And she was too much the good little Jewish housewife for his taste. He got her a maid and forgot about her. He still valued her because she was a great laundress, his white shirts were impeccably starched and ironed. She was a fine housekeeper. She kept track of his Vegas suits and gaudy ties, rotating them to the dry cleaner's at exactly the right time, not so often as to wear them out prematurely, not too seldom as to make them appear soiled. Once she had bought a cat that sat on the sofa, and Moses had sat down on that sofa, and when he rose, his trouser leg had cat hairs on it. He picked up the cat and threw it against the wall. He screamed at Bella hysterically. She gave away the cat the next day.

But power flows magically from one source to another. When Moses became head of Tri-Culture Studios, it was as if Bella Wartberg had been touched by the magic wand of a fairy. The California-bred executive wives took her in hand. The "in" hairdresser shaped her a crown of black curls that made her look regal. The exercise class at the Sanctuary, a spa to which all the show people belonged, punished her body unmercifully. She went down from a hundred and fifty pounds to a hundred and ten. Even her breasts shrank, shriveled. But not enough to conform to the rest of her body. A plastic surgeon cut them down into two small perfectly proportioned rosebuds. While he was at it, he whittled down her thighs and took a chunk out of her ass. The studio fashion experts designed a wardrobe to fit her new body and her new status. Bella Wartberg looked into her mirror and saw there, not a zaftig Jewish princess lushly fleshed, vulgarly handsome, but a slim, Waspy, forty-year-old ex-debutante, peppy, vivacious, brimming full of energy. What she did not see mercifully was that her appearance was a distortion of what she had been, that her old self, like a ghost, persisted through the bones of her body, the structure of her face. She was a skinny fashionable lady built on the heavy bones she had inherited. But she believed she was beautiful. And so she was quite ready when a young actor on the make pretended to be in love with her.

She returned his love passionately, sincerely. She went to his grubby apartment in Santa Monica and for the first time in her life was thoroughly fucked. The young actor was virile, dedicated to his profession and threw himself into his role so wholeheartedly that he almost believed he was in love. So much so that he bought her a charm bracelet from Gucci's that she would treasure the rest of her life as proof of her first great passion. And so, when he asked for her help in getting a role in one of Tri-Culture's big feature films, he was thoroughly confounded when she told him she never interfered in her husband's business. They quarreled bitterly, and the actor disappeared from her life. She missed him, she missed the grubby apartment, his rock records, but she had been a level-headed girl and had grown to be a levelheaded woman. She would not make the same mistake. In the future she would pick her lovers as carefully as a comedian picks his hat.

In the years that followed she became an expert negotiator in her affairs with actors, discriminating enough to seek out talented people rather than untalented ones, and indeed, she enjoyed the talented ones more. It seemed that general intelligence went with talent. And she helped them in their careers. She never made the mistake of going directly to her husband. Moses Wartberg was too Olympian to be concerned with such decisions. Instead, she went to one of the three vice-presidents. She would rave about the talent of an actor she had seen in a little art group giving Ibsen and insist that she didn't know the actor personally but she was sure he would be an asset to the studio. The vice-president would put the name down and the actor would get a small part. Soon enough the word got around. Bella Wartberg became so notorious for fucking anybody, anywhere, that whenever she stopped by one of the vice-president's offices, that VP would make sure that one of his secretaries was present, as a gynecologist would make sure a nurse was present when examining a patient.

The three VP's jockeying for power had to accommodate Wartberg's wife, or felt they had to. Jeff Wagon became good friends with Bella and would even introduce her to some especially upstanding young fellow. When all this failed, she prowled the expensive shops of Rodeo for women, took long lunches with pretty starlets at exclusive restaurants, wearing ominously huge macho sunglasses.

Because of his close relationship with Bella, Jeff Wagon was the odds-on favorite to get Moses Wartberg's spot when he retired. There was one catch. What would Moses Wartberg do when he learned that his wife, Bella, was the Messalina of Beverly Hills? Gossip columnists planted Bella's

affairs as "blind items" Wartberg couldn't fail to see. Bella
was notorious.

As usual Moses Wartberg surprised everyone. He did so by
doing absolutely nothing. Only rarely did he take his revenge
on the lover; he never took reprisals against his wife.

The first time he took his revenge was when a young rock
and roll star boasted of his conquest, called Bella Wartberg
"a crazy old cunt." The rock and roll star had meant it as a
supreme compliment, but to Moses Wartberg it was as insulting as one of his vice-presidents coming to work in blue
jeans and turtleneck sweater. The rock and roll star made ten
times as much money from a single album as he was being
paid for the featured part in his movie. But he was infected
with the American dream; the narcissism of playing himself
on film entranced him. On the night of the first preview he
had assembled his entourage of fellow artists and girlfriends
and taken them to the Wartberg private screening room
crammed with the top stars of Tri-Culture Studios. It was one
of the big parties of the year.

The rock and roll star sat and sat and sat. He waited and
waited and waited. The film ran on and on. And on screen he
was nowhere to be seen. His part was on the cutting-room
floor. He had immediately gotten stoned out of his mind and
had to be taken home.

Moses Wartberg had celebrated his transformation from
producer to head of a studio with a great coup. Over the
years he had noticed that the studio moguls were furious with
all the attention given actors, writers, directors and producers
at the Academy Awards. It infuriated them that their employees were the ones who received all the credit for the
movies that they had created. It was Moses Wartberg who
years before first supported the idea for an Irving Thalberg
award to be given at the Academy ceremonies. He was clever
enough to have included in the plan that the award would
not be a yearly one. That it would be given to a producer for
constantly high quality over the years. He was also clever
enough to have the clause put in that no one would be eligible to receive the Thalberg Award more than once. In effect
many producers, whose pictures never won Academy
Awards, but who had a lot of clout in the movie industry, got
their share of publicity by winning the Thalberg. But still,
this left out the actual studio heads and the real money-mak-

ing stars whose work was never good enough. It was then that Wartberg supported a Humanitarian Award to be given to the person in the movie industry of the highest ideals, who gave of himself for the betterment of the industry and mankind. Finally, two years ago, Moses Wartberg had been given this award and accepted it on television in front of one hundred million admiring American *viewers*. The award was presented by a Japanese director of international renown for the simple reason that no American director could be found who could give the award with a straight face. (Or so Doran said when telling me this particular story.)

On the night when Moses Wartberg received his award, two screenwriters had heart attacks from outrage. An actress threw her television set out of the fourth-floor suite of the Beverly Wilshire Hotel. Three directors resigned from the Academy. But that award became Moses Wartberg's most prized possession. One screen writer commented that it was like members of a concentration camp voting for Hitler as their most popular politician.

It was Wartberg who developed the technique of loading a rising star with huge mortgage payments on a Beverly Hills mansion to force him to work hard in lousy movies. It was Moses Wartberg whose studio continually fought in the courts to the bitter end to deprive creative talent of the monies due them. It was Wartberg who had the connections in Washington. Politicians were entertained with beautiful starlets, secret funds, paid-for expensive vacations at the studio facilities all over the world. He was a man who knew how to use lawyers and the law to do financial murder; to steal and cheat. Or so Doran said. To me he sounded like any red-blooded American businessman.

Apart from his cunning, his fix in Washington was the most important asset that Tri-Culture Studios possessed.

His enemies spread many scandalous stories about him that were not true because of his ascetic life. They started rumors that with careful secrecy he flew to Paris every month to indulge himself with child prostitutes. They spread the rumor that he was a voyeur. That he had a peephole to his wife's bedroom when she entertained her lovers. But none of this was true.

Of his intelligence and force of character there could be no doubt. Unlike the other movie moguls, he shunned the publicity limelight, the one exception being his seeking the Humanitarian Award.

When Doran drove into the Tri-Culture Studios lot, it was hate at second sight. The buildings were concrete, the grounds landscaped like those industrial parks that make Long Island look like benign concentration camps for robots. When we went through the gates, the guards didn't have a special parking spot for us, and we had to use the metered lot with its red-and-white-striped wooden arm that raised automatically. I didn't notice that I would need a quarter coin to get out through the exit arm.

I thought this was an accident, a secretarial slipup, but Doran said it was part of the Moses Wartberg technique to put talent like me in its place. A star would have driven right back off the lot. They would never put it over with directors or even a big featured player. But they wanted writers to know that they were not to get delusions of grandeur. I thought Doran was paranoid and I laughed, but I guess it irritated me, just a little.

In the main building our identities were checked by a security guard, who then made a call to make sure we were expected. A secretary came down and took us up in the elevator to the top floor. And that top floor was pretty spooky. Classy but spooky.

Despite all this, I have to admit I was impressed with Jeff Wagon's charm and movie business bottom line. I knew he was a phony and hustler, but that seemed natural somehow. As it is not unnatural to find an exotic-looking inedible fruit on a tropical island. We sat down in front of his desk, my agent and I, and Wagon told his secretary to stop all calls. Very flattering. But he obviously had not given the secret code word really to stop all calls because he took at least three during our conference.

We still had a half hour to wait for Wartberg before the conference would start. Jeff Wagon told some funny stories, even the one about how the Oregon girl took a slice out of his balls. "If she'd done a better job," Wagon said, "she would have saved me a lot of money and trouble these past years."

Wagon's phone buzzed, and he led me and Doran down

the hall to a luxurious conference room that could serve as a movie set.

At the long conference table sat Ugo Kellino, Houlinan and Moses Wartberg chatting easily. Farther down the table was a middle-aged guy with a head of fuzzy white hair. Wagon introduced him as the new director for the picture. His name was Simon Bellfort, a name I recognized. Twenty years ago he had made a great war film. Right afterward he had signed a long-term contract with Tri-Culture and become the ace schlockmaster for Jeff Wagon.

The young guy with him was introduced as Frank Richetti. He had a sharp, cunning face and was dressed in a combo Polo Lounge-rock star-California hippie style. The effect was stunning to my eyes. He fitted perfectly Janelle's description of the attractive men who roamed Beverly Hills as Don Juan-hustler-semipimps. She called them Slime City. But maybe she just said that to cheer me up. I didn't see how any girl could resist a guy like Frank Richetti. He was Simon Bellfort's executive producer on the film.

Moses Wartberg wasted no time on any bullshit. His voice laden with power, he put everything right on the line.

"I'm not happy with the script Malomar left us," he said. "The approach is all wrong. It's not a Tri-Culture film. Malomar was a genius, he could have shot this picture. We don't have anybody on this lot in his class."

Frank Richetti broke in, suave, charming. "I don't know, Mr. Wartberg. You have some fine directors here." He smiled fondly at Simon Bellfort.

Wartberg gave him a very cold look. We would hear no more from Richetti. And Bellfort blushed a little and looked away.

"We have a lot of money budgeted for this picture," Wartberg went on. "We have to insure that investment. But we don't want the critics jumping all over us, that we ruined Malomar's work. We want to use his reputation *for* the picture. Houlinan is going to issue a press release signed by all of us here that the picture will be made as Malomar wanted it to be made. That it will be Malomar's picture, a final tribute to his greatness and his contribution to the industry."

Wartberg paused as Houlinan handed out copies of the press release. Beautiful letterhead, I noticed, with the Tri-Culture logo in slashing red and black.

Kellino said easily, "Moses, old boy, I think you'd better mention that Merlyn and Simon will be working with me on the new script."

"OK, it's mentioned," Wartberg said. "And, Ugo, let me remind you that you can't fuck with the production or the directing. That's part of our deal."

"Sure," Kellino said.

Jeff Wagon smiled and leaned back in his chair. "The press release is our official position," he said, "but, Merlyn, I must tell you that Malomar was very sick when he helped you with this script. It's terrible. We'll have to rewrite it, I have some ideas. There's a lot of work to be done. Right now we fill up the media with Malomar. Is that OK with you, Jack?" he asked Houlinan. And Houlinan nodded.

Kellino said to me very sincerely, "I hope you'll work with me on this picture to make it the great movie that Malomar wanted it to be."

"No," I said. "I can't do that. I worked on the script with Malomar, I think it's fine. So I can't agree to any changes or rewriting, and I won't sign any press release to that effect."

Houlinan broke in smoothly. "We all know how you feel. You were very close to Malomar in this picture. I approve of what you just said, I think it's marvelous. It's rare that there's such loyalty in Hollywood, but remember, you have a percentage in the film. It's in your interest to make the film a success. If you are not a friend of the picture, if you are an enemy of the picture, you're taking money out of your pocket."

I really had to laugh when he said that line. "I'm a friend of the picture. That's why I don't want to rewrite it. You're the guys that are the enemy of this picture."

Kellino said abruptly, harshly, "Fuck him. Let him go. We don't need him."

For the first time I looked directly at Kellino, and I remembered Osano's description of him. As usual, Kellino was dressed beautifully, perfectly cut suit, a marvelous shirt, silky brown shoes. He looked beautiful, and I remembered Osano's use of the Italian peasant word *cafone*. "A *cafone*," he said, "is a peasant who had risen to great riches and great fame and tries to make himself a member of the nobility. He does everything right. He learns his manners, he improves his speech and he dresses like an angel. But no matter how beautiful he dresses, no matter how much care he takes, no matter how much time he cleans, there clings to his shoe one tiny piece of shit."

And looking at Kellino, I thought how perfectly he fitted this definition.

Wartberg said to Wagon, "Straighten this out," and he left the room. He couldn't be bothered fucking around with some half-assed writer. He had come to the meeting as a courtesy to Kellino.

Wagon said smoothly, "Merlyn is essential to this project, Ugo. I'm sure when he thinks it over, he'll join us. Doran, why don't we all meet again in a few days?"

"Sure," Doran said. "I'll call you."

We got up to leave. I handed my copy of the press release to Kellino. "There's something on your shoe," I said. "Use this to wipe it off."

When we left Tri-Culture Studios, Doran told me not to worry. He told me he could get everything straightened out within the week, that Wartberg and Wagon could not afford to have me as an enemy of the picture. They would compromise. And not to forget my percentage.

I told him that I didn't give a shit and I told him to drive faster. I knew that Janelle would be waiting for me at the hotel, and it seemed as if the thing I wanted most in the world was to see her again. To touch her body and kiss her mouth and lie with her and hear her tell me stories.

I was glad to have an excuse to stay in Los Angeles for a week to be with her for six or seven days. I really didn't give a shit about the picture. With Malomar dead I knew it would just be another piece of schlock from Tri-Culture Studios.

When Doran left me off at the Beverly Hills Hotel, he put his hand on my arm and said, "Wait a minute. There's something I have to talk to you about."

"OK," I said impatiently.

Doran said, "I've been meaning to tell you for a long time, but I felt maybe it wasn't my business."

"Jesus," I said. "What the hell are you talking about? I'm in a hurry."

Doran smiled a little sadly, "Yeah, I know. Janelle is waiting for you, right? It's Janelle I want to talk to you about."

"Look," I said to Doran, "I know all about her and I don't

care what she did, what she was. It doesn't make any difference to me."

Doran paused for a moment. "You know that girl, Alice, she lives with?"

"Yeah," I said. "She's a sweet girl."

"She's a little dykey," Doran said.

I felt a strange sense of recognition as if I were Cully counting down a shoe. "Yeah," I said. "So what?"

"So is Janelle," Doran said.

"You mean she's a lesbian?" I said.

"Bisexual is the word," Doran said. "She likes men and women."

I thought that over for a moment, and then I smiled at him and said, "Nobody's perfect." And I got out of the car and went up to my suite, where Janelle was waiting for me, and we made love together before going out to supper. But this time I didn't ask her for any stories. I didn't mention what Doran said. There was no need. I had caught on a long time ago and made my peace with it. It was better than her fucking other men.

Book VI

Chapter 34

Over the years Cully Cross had counted down the shoe perfectly and finally caught the loaded winning hand. He was really Xanadu Two, loaded with "juice," and had full power of "The Pencil." A "Gold Pencil." He could comp everything, not only room, food and beverage, the standard RFB, but air fares from all over the world, top-price call girls, the power to make customer markers disappear. He could even dispense free gambling chips to the top-rank entertainers who played the Xanadu Hotel.

During those years Gronevelt had been more like a father to him than a boss. Their friendship had become stronger. They had battled against hundreds of scams together, repelled the pirates, inside and out, who tried to buccaneer the Hotel Xanadu's sacred bankroll. Claim agents reneging on markers, magnet toters trying to empty slot machines against all the laws of chance, junket masters who sneaked in bad-credit artists with phony ID's, house dealers dumping out, keno ticket forgers, computer boys at blackjack tables, dice switchers by the thousand. Cully and Gronevelt had fought them off.

During those years Cully had won Gronevelt's respect with his flair for attracting new customers to the hotel. He had organized a worldwide backgammon tournament to be held at the Xanadu. He had kept a million-dollar-a-year customer by giving him a new Rolls-Royce every Christmas. The hotel charged the car off to public relations, a tax deduction. The customer was happy to receive a sixty-thousand-dollar car which would have cost him a hundred eighty thousand dollars in tax dollars, a twenty percent cut of his losses. But Cully's finest coup had been with Charles Hemsi. Gronevelt bragged about his protégé's cunning for years after that.

Gronevelt had had his reservations about Cully's buying up all of Hemsi's markers around Vegas for ten cents on the dollar. But he had given Cully his head. And sure enough, Hemsi came to Vegas at least six times a year and always stayed at the Xanadu. On one trip he had had a fantastic roll at the crap table and won seventy thousand dollars. He used that money to pay off some of his markers, and so the Xanadu was already ahead of the game. But then Cully showed his genius.

On one trip Charlie Hemsi mentioned that his son was being married to a girl in Israel. Cully was overjoyed for his friend and insisted on the Hotel Xanadu's picking up the whole tab for the wedding. Cully told Hemsi that the Hotel Xanadu jet plane (another Cully idea, the plane bought to steal business from the junkets) would fly the whole wedding party to Israel and pay for their hotels there. The Xanadu would pay for the wedding feast, the orchestra, all expenses. There was only one catch. Since the wedding guests were from all over the United States, they would have to board the plane in Las Vegas. But no sweat, they could all stay at the Xanadu, free of charge.

Cully calculated the cost to the hotel at two hundred thousand dollars. He convinced Gronevelt that it would pay off, and if it didn't, they at least would have Charlie Hemsi and son as players for life. But it proved to be a great "Host" coup. Over a hundred wedding guests came to Vegas, and before they left for the wedding in Israel, they left nearly a million dollars in the hotel's cashier cage.

But today Cully planned to present Gronevelt with an even greater money-making scheme, one that would force Gronevelt and his partners to name him general manager of the Hotel Xanadu, the most powerful open official position next to Gronevelt. He was waiting for Fummiro. Fummiro had piled up markers in his last two trips; he was having trouble paying. Cully knew why and Cully had the solution. But he knew that he had to let Fummiro take the initiative, that he would shy away if Cully himself suggested the solution. Daisy had taught him that.

Fummiro finally came to town, played his piano in the morning and drank his soup for breakfast. He wasn't interested in women. He was intent on gambling, and in three days he had lost all his cash and signed another three hundred thousand in markers. Before he left, he summoned

Cully to his hotel room. Fummiro was very polite and just a little nervous. He didn't want to lose face. He was afraid that Cully would think that he did not wish to pay his gambling debts, but very carefully he explained to Cully that though he had plenty of money in Tokyo and the million dollars was a mere trifle to him, the problem was getting the cash out of Japan, turning the Japanese yen into American dollars.

"So, Mr. Cross," he said to Cully, "if you could come to Japan, I will pay you there in yen, and then I'm sure that you can find a way to get the money to America."

Cully wanted to assure Fummiro of the hotel's complete trust and faith in him. "Mr. Fummiro," he said, "there's really no rush, your credit is good. The million dollars can wait until the next time you can come to Vegas. It's really no problem. We're always delighted to have you here. Your company is such a pleasure to us. Please don't concern yourself. Just let me put myself at your service, and now, if there's anything you would like, please tell me and I will arrange anything you wish. It's an honor for us to have you owe us this money."

Fummiro's handsome face relaxed. He was not dealing with a barbarian American, but one who was almost as polite as a Japanese. He said, "Mr. Cross, why don't you come to visit me? We will have a wonderful time in Japan. I will take you to a geisha house, you will have the best of food, the best of liquor, the best of women. You will be my personal guest and I can repay you for some of the hospitality you have always shown me and I can give you the million dollars for the hotel."

Cully knew that the Japanese government had a tough law about smuggling yen out of the country. Fummiro was proposing a criminal act. He waited and just nodded his head, remembering to smile continuously.

Fummiro went on. "I would like to do something for you. I trust you with all my heart, and that is the only reason I am saying this to you. My government is very strict on the exporting of yen. I would like to get my own money out. Now when you pick up a million for the Hotel Xanadu, if you could take one million out for me and deposit it in your cage, you receive fifty thousand dollars."

Cully felt the sweet satisfaction of counting down the shoe perfectly. He said sincerely, "Mr. Fummiro, I will do it out of my friendship for you. But of course, I must speak to Mr. Gronevelt."

"Of course," Fummiro said. "I will also speak to him."

Immediately afterward Cully called Gronevelt's suite and was told by his special operator that Gronevelt was busy and not taking any calls that afternoon. He left a message that the matter was urgent. He waited in his office. Three hours later the phone rang, and it was Gronevelt telling him to come down to the suite.

Gronevelt had changed a great deal over the last few years. The red had drained from his skin, leaving it a ghostly white. His face was like that of a fragile hawk. He had very suddenly become old, and Cully knew that he rarely had a girl to while away his afternoons. He seemed more and more immersed in his books and left most of the detail of running the hotel to Cully. But every evening he still made his tour of the casino floor, checking all the pits, watching the dealers and the stickmen and the pit bosses with his hawklike eyes. He still had that capacity to draw the electric energy of the casino into his small-framed body.

Gronevelt was dressed to go down to the casino floor. He fiddled with the control panel that would flood the casino pits with pure oxygen. But it was still too early in the evening. He would push the button sometime in the early-morning hours when the players were tiring and thinking of going to bed. Then he would revive them as if they were puppets. It was only in the past year that he had the oxygen controls wired directly to his suite.

Gronevelt ordered dinner to be brought up to the suite. Cully was tense. Why had Gronevelt kept him waiting for three hours? Had Fummiro spoken to him first? And he knew instantly that this was what had happened. He felt resentment; the two of them were so strong, he was not yet at their eminence and so they had consulted together without him.

Cully said smoothly, "I guess Fummiro told you about his idea. I told him I'd have to check it out with you."

Gronevelt smiled at him. "Cully, my boy, you're a wonder. Perfect. I couldn't have done better myself. You let that Jap come to you. I was afraid you might get impatient with all those markers piling up in the cage."

"That's my girlfriend Daisy," Cully said. "She made a Japanese citizen out of me."

Gronevelt frowned a little. "Women are dangerous," he said. "Men like you and I can't afford to let them get too close. That's our strength. Women can get you killed over nothing. Men are more sensible and more trustworthy." He sighed. "Well, I don't have to worry about you in that area. You spread the Honeybees around pretty good." He sighed, gave his head a little shake and returned to business.

"The only trouble with this whole deal is that we've never found a safe way to get our money out of Japan. We have a fortune in markers there, but I wouldn't give a nickel for them. We have a whole set of problems. One, if the Japanese government catches you, you'll do years in the clink. Two, once you pick up the money you'll be a target for hijackers. Japanese criminals have very good intelligence. They'll know right away when you pick up the money. Three, two million dollars in yen will be a big, big suitcase. In Japan they X-ray baggage. How do you get it turned into U.S. dollars once you get it out? How do you get into the United States, and then, though I think I can guarantee you it won't happen, how about hijackers on this end? People in this hotel will know we are sending you there to pick up the money. I have partners, but I can't guarantee the discretion of all of them. Also, by sheer accident, you could lose the money. Cully, here's the position you will be in. If you lose the money, we will always suspect you of being guilty unless you get killed."

Cully said, "I thought of all that. I checked the cage, and I see we have at least another million or two million dollars in markers with other Japanese players. So I would be bringing out four million dollars."

Gronevelt laughed. "In one trip that would be an awful gamble. Bad percentage."

Cully said, "Well, maybe one trip, maybe two trips, maybe three trips. First I have to find out how it could be done."

Gronevelt said, "You're taking all the risk in every way. As far as I can see, you're getting nothing out of it. If you win, you win nothing. If you lose, you lose everything. If you take a position like that, then the years I've spent teaching you have been wasted. So why do you want to do this? There's no percentage."

Cully said, "Look, I'll do it on my own without help, I'll take all the blame if it goes wrong. But if I bring back four million dollars, I would expect to be named general manager of the hotel. You know that I'm your man. I would never go against you."

Gronevelt sighed, "It's an awful gamble on your part. I hate to see you do it."

"Then it's OK?" Cully asked. He tried to keep the jubilation out of his voice. He didn't want Gronevelt to know how eager he was.

"Yeah," Gronevelt said. "But just pick up Fummiro's two million, never mind the money the other people owe us. If something goes wrong, then we only lose the two million."

Cully laughed, playing the game. "We only lose one million, the other million is Fummiro's. Remember?"

Gronevelt said completely serious, "It's all ours. Once that money is in our cage, Fummiro will gamble it away. That's the strength of this deal."

The next morning Cully took Fummiro to the airport in Gronevelt's Rolls-Royce. He had an expensive gift for Fummiro, an antique coin bank made in the days of the Italian Renaissance. The bulk was filled with gold coins. Fummiro was ecstatic, but Cully sensed a sly amusement beneath his effusions of delight.

Finally Fummiro said, "When are you coming to Japan?"

"Between two weeks and a month from now," Cully said. "Even Mr. Gronevelt will not know the exact day. You understand why."

Fummiro nodded. "Yes, you must be very careful. I will have the money waiting."

When Cully got back to the hotel, he put in a call to Merlyn in New York. "Merlyn, old buddy, how about keeping me company on a trip to Japan, all expenses paid and geisha girls thrown in?"

There was a long pause on the other end, and then he heard Merlyn's voice say, "Sure."

Chapter 35

Going to Japan struck me as a good idea. I had to be in Los Angeles the following week to work on the movie anyway, so I'd be partway there. And I was fighting so much with Janelle that I wanted to take a break from her. I knew she would take my going to Japan as a personal insult, and that pleased me.

Vallie asked me how long I would be in Japan and I said about a week. She didn't mind my going, she never did mind. In fact, she was always happy to see me leave, I was too restless around the house, too nerve-racking. She spent a lot of time visiting her parents and other members of her family, and she took the kids with her.

When I got off the plane in Las Vegas, Cully met me with the Rolls-Royce, right on the landing field, so that I wouldn't have to walk through the terminal. That set off alarm bells in my head.

A long time ago Cully had explained to me why he sometimes met people right on the landing field. He did this to escape FBI camera surveillance of all incoming passengers.

Where all the gate corridors converged into the central waiting room of the terminal there was a huge clock. Behind this clock, in a specially constructed booth, were movie cameras that recorded the throngs of eager gamblers rushing to Las Vegas from every part of the world. At night the FBI team on duty would run all the film and check it against their wanted lists. Happy-go-lucky bank robbers, on-the-run embezzlers, counterfeit money artists, successful kidnappers and extortionists were astonished when they were picked up before they had a chance to gamble away their ill-gotten gains.

When I asked Cully how he knew about this, he told me he had a former top FBI agent working as chief of security for the hotel. It was that simple.

Now I noticed that Cully had driven the Rolls himself. There was no chauffeur. He guided the car around the terminal to the baggage area, and we sat in the car while we waited for my luggage to come down the chute. While we waited, Cully briefed me.

First he warned me not to tell Gronevelt that we were going to Japan the following morning. To pretend that I had come in just for a gambling holiday. Then he told me about our mission, the two million dollars in yen he'd have to smuggle out of Japan and the hazards involved. He said very sincerely, "Look, I don't think there's any danger, but you may not feel the same way. So if you don't want to go, I'll understand."

He knew there was no way I could refuse him. I owed him the favor; in fact, I owed him two favors. One for keeping me out of jail. The other for handing me back my thirty-thousand-dollar stash when the troubles were all over. He had given me back my thirty grand in cash, twenty-dollar bills, and I had put the money in a savings bank account in Vegas. The cover story would be that I had won it gambling, and Cully and his people were prepared to back the cover. But it never came to that. The whole Army Reserve scandal died away.

"I always wanted to see Japan," I said. "I don't mind being your bodyguard. Do I carry a gun?"

Cully was horrified. "Do you want to get us killed? Shit, if they want to take the money away from us, let them take it. Our protection is secrecy and moving very fast. I have it all worked out."

"Then why do you need me?" I asked him. I was curious and a little wary. It didn't make sense.

Cully sighed. "It's a hell of long trip to Japan," Cully said. "I need some company. We can play gin on the plane and hang out in Tokyo and have some fun. Besides, you're a big guy, and if some small-time snatch-and-run artists luck onto us, you can scare them off."

"OK," I said. But it still sounded fishy.

That night we had dinner with Gronevelt. He didn't look well, but he was in great form telling stories about his early days in Vegas. How he had made his fortune in tax-free dollars before the federal government sent an army of spies and accountants to Nevada.

"You have to get rich in the dark," Gronevelt said. It was the bee in his bonnet, buzzing around as crazily as Osano's Nobel Prize hornet. "Everybody in this country has to get rich in the dark. Those thousands of little stores and business firms skimming off the top, big companies creating a legal plain of darkness." But none of them was so plentiful in opportunity as Vegas. Gronevelt tapped the edge of his Havana cigar and said with satisfaction, "That's what makes Vegas so strong. You can get rich in the dark here easier than anyplace else. That's the strength."

Cully said, "Merlyn is just staying the night. I figure I'll go into Los Angeles with him tomorrow morning and pick up some antiques. And I can see some of those Hollywood people about their markers."

Gronevelt took a long puff on his Havana. "Good idea," he said, "I'm running out of presents." He laughed. "Do you know where I got that idea about giving presents? From a book published in 1870 about gambling. Education is a great thing." He sighed and rose, a signal for us to leave. He shook my hand and then courteously escorted us to the door of his suite. As we went out the door, Gronevelt said gravely to Cully, "Good luck on your trip."

Outside on the false green grass of the terrace, I stood with Cully in the desert moonlight. We could see the Strip with its millions of red and green lights, the dark desert mountains far away. "He knows we're going," I said to Cully.

"If he does, he does," Cully said. "Meet me for breakfast at eight A.M. We have to get an early start."

The next morning we flew from Las Vegas to San Francisco. Cully carried a huge suitcase of rich brown leather, its corners made of dull shining brass. Strips of brass bound the case. The locking plate was also heavy. It was formidable-looking and strong. "It won't bust open," Cully said. "And it will be easy for us to keep track of it on the baggage trucks."

I had never seen a suitcase like it and said so. "Just an antique I picked up in LA," Cully said smugly.

We jumped on a Japan Airlines 747 with just fifteen minutes to spare. Cully had deliberately timed it very close. On the long flight we played gin, and when we landed in Tokyo, I had him beaten for six thousand dollars. But Cully didn't seem to mind; he just slapped me on the back and said, "I'll get you on the trip home."

We took a taxi from the airport to our Tokyo hotel. I was eager to see the fabulous city of the Far East. But it looked like a shabbier and smokier New York. It also seemed smaller in scale, the people shorter, the buildings flatter, the dusky skyline a miniaturization of the familiar and overpowering skyline of New York City. When we entered the heart of the city, I saw men wearing white surgical gauze masks. It made them look eerie. Cully told me that the Japanese in urban centers wore these masks to guard against lung infections from the heavily polluted air.

We passed buildings and stores that seemed to be made of wood, as if they were sets on a movie lot, and intermingled with them were modern skyscrapers and office buildings. The streets were full of people, many of them in Western dress, others, mainly women, in some sort of kimono outfit. It was a bewildering collage of styles.

The hotel was a disappointment. It was modern and American. The huge lobby had a chocolate-colored rug and a great many black leather armchairs. Small Japanese men in black American business suits sat in most of these chairs clutching briefcases. It could have been a Hilton hotel in New York.

"This is the Orient?" I said to Cully.

Cully shook his head impatiently. "We're getting a good night's snooze. Tomorrow I'll do my business, and tomorrow night I'll show you what Tokyo is really made of. You'll have a great time. Don't worry."

We had a big suite together, a two-bedroom suite. We unpacked our suitcases and I noticed that Cully had very little in his brassbound monster. We were both tired from the trip, and though it was only six o'clock Tokyo time, we went to bed.

The next morning there was a knock at the door of my bedroom and Cully said, "Come on, time to get up." Dawn was just breaking outside my window.

He ordered breakfast in the suite, which disappointed me. I began to get the idea that I wasn't going to see much of Japan. We had eggs and bacon, coffee and orange juice and even some English muffins. The only thing Oriental were some pancakes. The pancakes were huge and twice as thick as a pancake should be. They were more like huge slabs of bread, and they were a very funny sickly yellow color rather than brown. I tasted one and I could swear that it tasted like fish.

I said to Cully, "What the hell are these?"

He said, "They're pancakes but cooked in fish oil."

"I'll pass," I said, and I pushed the dish over to him.

Cully finished them off with gusto. "All you have to do is get used to it," he said.

Over our coffee I asked him, "What's the program?"

"It's a beautiful day out," Cully said. "We'll take a walk and I'll lay it out for you."

I understood that he didn't want to talk in the room. That he was afraid it might be bugged.

We left the hotel. It was still very early in the morning, the sun just coming up. We turned down a side street and suddenly I was in the Orient. As far as the eye could see there were little ramshackle houses, small buildings and along the curb stretched huge piles of green-colored garbage so high that it formed a wall.

There were a few people out in the streets, and a man went by us riding a bicycle, his black kimono floating behind him. Two wiry men in khaki work pants and khaki shirts, white gauze masks covering their faces, suddenly appeared before us. I gave a little jump and Cully laughed as the two men turned into another side street.

"Jesus," I said, "those masks are spooky."

"You'll get used to them," Cully said. "Now listen close. I want you to know everything that's going on, so you don't make any mistakes."

As we walked along the wall of gray-green garbage, Cully explained to me that he was smuggling out two million dollars in Japanese yen and that the government had very strict laws about exporting the national currency.

"If I get caught, I go to jail," Cully said. "Unless Fummiro can put the fix in. Or unless Fummiro goes to jail with me."

"How about me?" I said. "If you get caught, don't I get caught?"

"You're an eminent writer," Cully said. "The Japanese have a great respect for culture. You'll just get thrown out of the country. Just keep your mouth shut."

"So I'm just here to have a good time," I said. I knew he was full of shit and I wanted him to know I knew it.

Then another thing occurred to me. "How the hell do we get through customs in the States?" I said.

"We don't," Cully said. "We dump the money in Hong Kong. It's a free port. The only people who have to go through customs there are the ones traveling on Hong Kong passports."

"Jesus," I said. "Now you tell me we're going to Hong Kong. Where the fuck do we go after that, Tibet?"

"Be serious," Cully said. "Don't panic. I did this a year ago with a little money, just for a trial run."

"Get a gun for me," I said. "I got a wife and three kids, you son of a bitch. Give me a fighting chance." But I was laughing. Cully had really roped me in.

But Cully didn't know I was kidding. "You can't carry a gun," he said. "Every Japanese airline has their electronic security check of your person and your hand luggage. And most of them X-ray any baggage you check in." He paused for a moment and then said, "The only airline that doesn't X-ray checked baggage is the Cathay. So if something happens to me, you know what to do."

"I can just picture myself alone in Hong Kong with two million bucks," I said. "I'd have a million fucking hatchets in my neck," I said.

"Don't worry," Cully said soothingly. "Nothing's going to happen. We'll have a ball."

I was laughing, but I was also worried. "But if something does happen," I said, "what do I do in Hong Kong?"

Cully said, "Go to the Futaba Bank and ask for the vice-president. He'll take the money and change it into Hong Kong dollars. He'll give you a receipt and charge you maybe twenty grand. Then he'll change the Hong Kong dollars into American dollars and charge you another fifty thousand dollars. The American dollars will be sent to Switzerland and you'll get another receipt. A week from now the Hotel Xanadu will receive a draft from the Swiss bank for two million minus the Hong Kong bank charges. See how simple it is?"

I thought this over as we walked back to the hotel. Finally I came back to my original question. "Why the hell do you need me?"

"Don't ask me any more questions, just do what I tell you," Cully said. "You owe me a favor, right?"

"Right," I said. And I didn't ask any more questions.

When we got back to the hotel, Cully made some phone calls, talking Japanese, and then told me he was going out. "I should be back around five P.M.," he said. "But I may be a little late. Just wait in this room for me. If I'm not back tonight, you hop the morning plane for home. OK?"

"OK," I said.

I tried reading in the bedroom of the suite and then imagined noises in the living room, so I went there to read. I ordered lunch in the suite, and after I had finished eating, I called the States. The connection went through in only a few minutes, which surprised me. I thought it would take at least a half hour.

Vallie picked up the phone right away, and I could tell from her voice that she was pleased that I'd called.

"How is the mysterious Orient?" she asked. "Are you having a good time? Have you gone to a geisha house yet?"

"Not yet," I said. "So far all I've seen is the morning Tokyo garbage. Since then I've been waiting for Cully. He's out doing business. At least I've got him beat for six grand in gin."

"Good," Valerie said. "You can buy me and the kids some of those fabulous kimonos. Oh, by the way, you got a call yesterday from some man who claimed he was a friend of yours in Vegas. He said he expected to see you out there. I told him you were in Tokyo."

My heart stopped a little. Then I said casually, "Did he give his name?"

"No," Valerie said. "Don't forget our presents."

"I won't," I said.

I spent the rest of the afternoon worrying. I called the airline for a reservation back to the States for the next morning. Suddenly I wasn't so sure that Cully would be back. I checked his bedroom. The big brassbound suitcase was gone.

Darkness was beginning to fall when Cully came into the suite. He was rubbing his hands, excited and happy. "Everything is all set," he said. "Nothing to worry about. Tonight we have fun and tomorrow we wind things up. The day after that we'll be in Hong Kong."

"I called my wife," I said. "We had a nice little chat. She told me some guy called from Vegas and asked where I was. She told him Tokyo."

That cooled him off. He thought about it. Then shrugged.

"That sounds like Gronevelt," Cully said. "Just making sure his hunch was right. He's the only one who has your phone number."

"Do you trust Gronevelt on a deal like this?" I asked Cully. And right away I knew I had stepped over the line.

"What the hell do you mean?" Cully said. "That man has been like a father to me all these years. He made me. Shit, I'd trust him over anybody, even you."

"OK," I said. "Then why didn't you let him know we were leaving? Why did you give him that bullshit about buying antiques in Los Angeles?"

"Because that's the way he taught me to operate," Cully said. "Never tell anybody anything he doesn't have to know. He'll be proud of me for that, even though he found out. I did it the right way." Then he eased up. "Come on," he said. "Get dressed. Tonight I'm going to show you the best time of your life." For some reason that reminded me of Eli Hemsi.

Like everybody who has seen films about the Orient, I had fantasized about a night in a geisha house: beautiful talented women devoting themselves to my pleasure. When Cully told me that we were going to be entertained by geishas, I expected to be taken to one of those crazy-cornered, gaily ornamented houses I had seen in movies. So I was surprised when the chauffeured car stopped in front of a small restaurant housed in a canopied storefront on one of the main streets of Tokyo. It looked like any Chinese joint in the lower part of Manhattan. But a maître d' led us through the crowded restaurant to a door that led to a private dining room.

The room was lavishly furnished in Japanese style. Colored lanterns were suspended from the ceiling; a long banquet table, raised only a foot above the floor, was decorated with exquisitely colored dishes, small drinking cups, ivory chopsticks. There were four Japanese men, all in kimonos. One of them was Mr. Fummiro. He and Cully shook hands, the other men bowed. Cully introduced me to all of them. I had seen Fummiro gambling in Vegas but had never met him.

Seven geisha girls came into the room, running with tiny steps. They were beautifully dressed in heavy brocade kimonos embroidered with startlingly colored flowers. Their faces were heavily made up with a white powder. They sat on cushions around the banquet table, a girl for each man.

Following Cully's lead, I sat down on one of the cushions around the banquet table. Serving women brought in huge platters of fish and vegetables. Each geisha girl fed her assigned male. They used the ivory chopsticks, picking up bits of fish, little strands of green vegetables. They wiped our mouths and faces with countless tiny napkins that were like washcloths. These were scented and wet.

My geisha girl was very close to me, leaning her body against mine, and, with a charming smile and entreating gestures, make me eat and drink. She kept filling my cup with some sort of wine, the famous sake, I guessed. The wine tasted great, but the food was too fishy until they brought out platters of heavily marbled Kobe beef, cut into cubes and drenched in a delicious sauce.

Seeing her close, I knew that my charming geisha had to be at least forty. Though her body was pressed against mine, I could feel nothing except the heavy brocade of her kimono; she was swathed like an Egyptian mummy.

After dinner the girls took turns entertaining us. One played a musical instrument that was like a flute. By this time I had drunk so much wine that the unfamiliar music sounded like bagpipes. Another girl recited what must have been a poem. The men all applauded. Then my geisha got up. I was rooting for her. She proceeded to do some astonishing somersaults.

In fact, she scared the hell out of me by somersaulting right over my head. Then she did the same somersault over Fummiro's head, but he caught her in midair and tried to give her a kiss or something like a kiss. I was too drunk to see really well. But she eluded him, tapped him lightly on the cheek in reproach, and they both laughed gaily.

Then the geisha girls organized the men into playing games. I was astonished to see that it was a game involving an orange on a stick, that we had to bite the orange with our hands behind our backs. As we did so, a geisha would try the same thing from the other side of the stick. As the orange bobbed between male and female, the two faces would brush each other with a caress which made the geishas giggle.

Cully, behind me, said in a low voice, "Jesus, the next thing we'll be playing spin the bottle." But he smiled hugely at Fummiro, who seemed to be having a great time, shouting at the girls in Japanese and trying to grab them. There were other games involving sticks and balls and juggling acts, and I was so drunk that I was enjoying them as much as Fummiro. At one point I fell down into a pile of cushions and my geisha cradled my head in her lap and wiped my face off with a hot scented napkin.

The next thing I knew I was in the chauffeured car with Cully. We were moving through dark streets, and then the car stopped in front of a mansion in the suburbs. Cully led through the gate and the door opened magically. And then I saw we were in a real Oriental house. The room was bare except for sleeping mats. The walls were really sliding doors of thin wood.

I fell down on one of the mats. I just wanted to sleep. Cully knelt down beside me. "We're spending the night here," he whispered. "I'll wake you up in the morning. Stay here, go to sleep. You'll be taken care of." Behind him I could see Fummiro's smiling face. I registered that Fummiro was no longer drunk, and that set off some alarm bell in my mind. I tried to struggle up off the mat, but Cully pushed me down. And then I heard Fummiro's voice say, "Your friend needs some company." I sank back down on the mat. I was too tired. I didn't give a damn. I fell asleep.

I don't know how long I slept. I was awakened by the slight hiss of sliding doors. In the dim light of the shaded lanterns I saw two young Japanese girls in light blue and yellow kimonos come through the open wall. They carried a small redwood tub filled with steaming water. They undressed me and washed me from head to foot, kneading my body with their fingers, massaging every muscle. While they were doing this, I got an erection and they giggled and one of them gave it a little pat. Then they picked up the redwood tub and disappeared.

I was awake enough to wonder where the hell Cully was but not sober enough to get up and look for him. It was just as well. The wall fell apart as the doors slid back again. This time there was a single girl, a new one, and just by looking at her, I could tell what her function would be.

She was dressed in a long flowing green kimono that hid her body. But her face was beautiful and highlighted exotically with makeup. Her rich jet black hair was piled high on her head and was topped with a brilliant comb that seemed made out of precious stones. She came to me, and before she knelt, I could see that her feet were bare, small and beautifully formed. The toenails were painted dark red.

The lights seemed to become dimmer, and suddenly she was naked. Her body was a pure milky white, the breasts small but full. The nipples were startling light pink, as if they had been rouged. She bent over, took the comb out of her hair and shook her head. Long black tresses poured down endlessly over my body, covering it, and then she started kissing and licking my body, her head giving little determined shakes, the silky thick black hair whipping over my thighs. I lay back. Her mouth was warm, her tongue rough. When I tried to move, she pressed me back. When she was finished, she lay down beside me and put my head against her breast. At some time during the night I woke up and made love to her. She locked her legs behind mine and thrust fiercely as if it were a battle between our two sexual organs. It was a fierce fuck, and when we climaxed, she gave a thin scream and we fell off the mat. Then we fell asleep in each other's arms.

The wall sliding back woke me up again. The room was filled with early-morning light. The girl was gone. But through the open wall, in the adjoining room, I saw Cully sitting on the huge brassbound suitcase. Though he was far away, I could see him smiling. "OK, Merlyn, rise and shine," he said. "We're flying to Hong Kong this morning."

* * *

The suitcase was so heavy that I had to carry it out to the car, Cully couldn't manage it. There was no chauffeur, Cully drove. When we got to the airport, he just left the car parked outside the terminal. I carried the suitcase inside, Cully walking ahead to clear a path and lead me to the baggage check-in desk. I was still groggy, and the huge case kept hitting me in the shins. At the check-in the stub was put on my ticket. I figured it didn't make any difference, so I didn't say anything when Cully didn't notice.

We walked through the gate onto the field to the plane. But we didn't board. Cully waited until a loaded baggage truck came around the terminal building. We could see our huge brassbound case sitting on top. We watched while the laborers loaded it into the belly of the plane. Then we boarded.

It was over four hours' ride to Hong Kong. Cully was nervous and I beat him for another four thousand in gin. While we were playing I asked him some questions.

"You told me we were leaving tomorrow," I said.

"Yeah, that's what I thought," Cully said. "But Fummiro got the money ready sooner than I figured."

I knew he was full of shit. "I loved that geisha party," I said.

Cully grunted. He pretended to study his cards, but I knew his mind wasn't on the game. "Fucking high school cunt teasing party," he said. "That geisha stuff is bullshit, I'll take Vegas."

"I don't know," I said. "I thought it was charming. But I have to admit that little treat I got afterward was better."

Cully forgot about his cards. "What treat?" he said.

I told him about the girls in the mansion. Cully grinned. "That was Fummiro. You lucky son of a bitch. And I was out running around all night." He paused for a moment. "So you finally broke. I'll bet that's the first time you've been unfaithful to that broad you got in LA."

"Yeah," I said. "But what the hell, anything over three thousand miles away doesn't count."

When we landed in Hong Kong, Cully said, "You go on to the baggage area and wait for the case. I'll stick by the plane until they unload. Then I'll follow the luggage truck. That way no sneak thief can pinch it."

I walked quickly through the terminal to the baggage carousel. The terminal was thronged, but the faces were different from those in Japan though still mostly Oriental. The carousel started to turn and I watched intently for the brassbound case to come down the chute. After ten minutes I wondered why Cully had not appeared. I glanced around, thankful that none of the people were wearing gauze masks; those things had spooked me. But I didn't see anybody who looked dangerous.

Then the brassbound suitcase shot out of the chute. I grabbed it as it went by. It was still heavy. I checked it to make sure it had not been knifed open. As I did so, I noticed a tiny square name tag attached to the handle. It bore the legend "John Merlyn," and under the name my home address and passport number. I finally knew why Cully asked me to come to Japan. If anybody went to jail, it would be me.

I sat on the case and about three minutes later Cully appeared. He beamed with satisfaction when he saw me. "Great," he said. "I have a cab waiting. Let's get to the bank." And this time he picked up the case and without any trouble carried it out of the terminal.

The cab went down winding side streets thronged with people. I didn't say anything. I owed Cully a big favor and now I'd evened him out. I felt hurt that he had deceived me and exposed me to such risk, but Gronevelt would have been proud of him. And out of the same tradition I decided not to tell Cully what I knew. He must have anticipated I would find out. He'd have a story ready.

The cab stopped in front of a ramshackle building on a main street. The window had gold lettering which read "Futaba International Bank." On both sides of the door were two uniformed men with submachine guns.

"Tough town, this Hong Kong," Cully said, nodding at the guards. He carried the case into the bank himself.

Inside, Cully went down the hall and knocked on a door, and then we went in. A small Eurasian with a beard beamed at Cully and shook his hand. Cully introduced me, but the name was a strange combination of syllables. Then the Eurasian led us farther down the hall into a huge room with a long conference table. Cully threw the case on the table and unlocked it. I have to admit the sight was impressive. It was filled with crisp Japanese currency, black print on gray-blue paper.

The Eurasian picked up a phone and barked out some orders in, I guess, Chinese. A few minutes later the room was filled with bank clerks. Fifteen of them, all in those black shiny suits. They pounced on the suitcase. It took all of them over three hours to count and tabulate the money, recount it and check it again. Then the Eurasian took us back into his office and made out a sheaf of papers, which he signed, stamped with official seals and then handed over to Cully. Cully looked the papers over and put them in his pocket. The packet of documents was the "little" receipt.

Finally we were standing in the sunlit street outside the bank. Cully was tremendously excited. "We've done it," he said. "We're home free."

I shook my head. "How could you take such a risk?" I said. "It's a crazy way to handle so much money."

Cully smiled at me. "What the hell kind of business do you think it is running a Vegas casino? It's all risk. I've got a risky job. And on this I had a big percentage going with me."

When we got into a cab, Cully instructed the driver to take us to the airport. "Jesus," I said, "we go halfway across the world and I don't even get to eat a meal in Hong Kong?"

"Let's not press our luck," Cully said. "Somebody may think we still have the money. Let's just get the hell home."

On the long plane ride back to the States, Cully got very lucky and won back seven of the ten grand he owed me. He would have won it all back if I hadn't quit. "Come on," he said. "Give me a chance to get even. Be fair."

I looked at him straight in the eye. "No," I said, "I want to outsmart you just once on this trip."

That shook him up a little and he let me sleep the rest of the way back to Los Angeles. I kept him company while he was waiting for his flight to Vegas. While I was sleeping, he had been thinking things over and he must have figured I saw the name plate on the case.

"Listen," he said. "You have to believe me. If you had gotten into trouble on this trip, me and Gronevelt and Fummiro would have gotten you out. But I appreciate what you did. I couldn't have made the trip without you, I didn't have the nerve."

I laughed. "You owe me three grand from the gin," I said. "Just put it in the Xanadu cage and I'll use it for a baccarat stake."

"Sure thing," Cully said. "Listen," he said. "Is that the only way you can cheat on your broads and feel safe, with three thousand miles between them? The world isn't big enough to cheat more than two more times."

We both laughed and shook hands before he got on the plane. He was still my buddy, old Countdown Cully, I just couldn't trust him all the way. I had always known what he was and accepted his friendship. How could I be angry when he was true to his character?

I walked through the LA terminal of Western Airlines and stopped by the phones. I had to call Janelle and tell her I was in town. I wondered if I should tell her I had been in Japan, but I decided not to. I would act in the Gronevelt tradition. And then I remembered something else. I didn't have any presents from the Orient for Valerie and the kids.

Chapter 36

In a way it's interesting being crazy about somebody who's no longer crazy about you. You go sort of blind and deaf. Or choose to. It was nearly a year before I heard the almost inaudible tick of Janelle dealing seconds, and yet I had had plenty of warnings, plenty of hints.

On one of my trips back to Los Angeles my plane got in a half hour early. Janelle always met me, but she wasn't there and I walked through the terminal and waited outside. In the back of my head, way back, I was thinking I would catch her at something. I didn't know what. Maybe a guy she had picked up for a drink while waiting for the plane. Maybe dropping off another boyfriend catching a plane out of Los Angeles, anything. I was not your trusting lover.

And I did catch her, but not in the way I thought. I saw her come out of the parking lot and cross the wide double streets to the terminal. She was walking very slowly, very reluctantly. She wore a long gray skirt and a white blouse, and her long blond hair was pinned up around her head. At that moment I had almost a sense of pity for her. She looked so reluctant, as if she were a child going to a party her parents had made her go to. On the other side of the continent I had been an hour early for my plane. I had rushed through the terminal to meet her. I was dying to see her, but she, obviously, was not dying to see me. As I was thinking this, she lifted her head and saw me and her face became radiant and then she was hugging and kissing me and I forgot what I had seen.

During this visit she was rehearsing days for a play that was to open in a few weeks. Since I was working at the studio this was fine. We saw each other at night. She would call me at the studio to tell me what time she would be through rehearsing. When I asked her for a number where I could call her, she told me there was no phone in the theater.

Then one evening, when her rehearsal ran late, I went to the theater to pick her up. As we were about to leave, a girl came out of the backstage office and said to her, "Janelle, Mr. Evarts is calling you," and she led the way to the phone.

When Janelle came out of the office, her face was rosy and flushed with pleasure, but then she took one look at me and said, "That's the first time he called. I didn't even know they could get me on the phone in the theater."

I heard that tick of the second card being dealt. I still had so much pleasure with her company, with her body, in just looking at her face. I still loved the expression that went across her eyes and mouth. I loved her eyes. They could get such a hurt look and yet be so gay. I thought her mouth the most beautiful in the world. Hell, I was really still a kid. It didn't matter that I knew she was deceiving me. She really hated to lie and did it badly. In a funny kind of way she told you she was lying. Even that was a fake-out.

And it didn't matter. It didn't matter. I suffered, sure, but it was still a good bargain. Yet as time went on, I enjoyed her less and she made me suffer more.

I was sure she and Alice were lovers. One week, when Alice was out of town on a movie production job, I went to Janelle's and Alice's apartment to spend the night. Alice called Janelle long distance to chat with her. Janelle was very short with her, almost angry. A half hour later, when we were making love, the phone rang again. Janelle reached over, took the phone off the hook and threw the receiver under the bed.

One of the things I liked about her was that she hated to be interrupted while making love. Sometimes, at the hotel, she wouldn't let me answer the phone or even answer the door if a waiter was bringing in food or drinks when we were on our way to bed.

A week later in my hotel on a Sunday morning I called Janelle at her apartment. I knew she usually slept late, so I didn't call until eleven o'clock. I got a busy signal. I waited a half hour and called again. I got a busy signal. Then I called every ten minutes for an hour and kept getting a busy signal, and suddenly I got a flash of Janelle and Alice in bed, the phone off its hook. When I finally did get through, it was Alice who answered the phone, her voice soft and happy. I was sure they were lovers.

Another day we were planning a trip to Santa Barbara when she got a rush call to go to a producer's office to read for a part. She said it would take only one-half hour, so I went to the studio with her. The producer was an old friend of hers, and when he came into the office, he made a tender, affectionate gesture, brushing his fingers along her face, and she smiled at him. I read the gesture immediately. It was the tenderness of a former lover, now a dear friend.

When we were on our way to Santa Barbara, I asked Janelle if she had ever been to bed with the producer. She turned to me and said, "Yes." And I didn't ask her any more questions.

One night we had a date for dinner and I went to her apartment. She was getting dressed. Alice opened the door for me. I always liked her and in a funny kind of way I didn't mind that she was Janelle's lover. I still wasn't really sure. Alice always kissed me on the lips, a very sweet kiss, she always seemed to enjoy my company. We got along fine. But you could sense the lack of femininity in her. She was very thin, wore tight shirts that showed that she had surprisingly full breasts but was very businesslike. She gave me a drink and put on an Edith Piaf record and we waited until Janelle came out of the bathroom.

Janelle kissed me and said, "Merlyn, I'm sorry, I tried to call you at the hotel. I have to rehearse tonight. The director's going to come by and pick me up."

I was stunned. Again I heard the tick of the second card. She was smiling at me radiantly, but there was a little quiver to her mouth which made me think she was lying. She was searching my face intently with her eyes. She wanted me to believe her and she saw that I didn't. She said, "He's coming here to pick me up. I'll try and get through by eleven."

"That's OK," I said. Over her shoulder I could see Alice looking down in her glass, not watching us, pointedly trying not to hear what we were saying.

So I waited around, and sure enough, the director came up. He was a young guy but already almost bald, and he was very businesslike and efficient. He didn't have time for a drink. He said patiently to Janelle, "We're rehearsing at my place. I want you absolutely perfect for this dress rehearsal tomorrow. Evarts and I have changed some lines and some business."

He turned to me. "I'm sorry I spoiled your evening, but that's show business." He parodied the cliché.

He seemed like a nice guy. I gave him and Janelle a cold smile. "It's OK," I said. "Take as long as you like."

At this Janelle became a little panicky. She said to the director, "Do you think we can get through by ten?"

And the director said, "If we really work hard, maybe."

Janelle said, "Why don't you wait here with Alice and I'll get back by ten and we can still go to dinner? Is that all right?"

I said, "Sure."

So I waited with Alice after they left and we talked to each other. She said she had redecorated the apartment and she took me by the hand and led me through the rooms. It was really charming. The kitchen was fixed up with special shutters, the cupboards were decorated with some sort of inlaid patterns. Copper pots and pans were hanging on the ceiling.

"It's lovely," I said. "I can't imagine Janelle doing all this."

Alice laughed. "No," she said. "I'm the homebody."

Then she led me through the three bedrooms. One was obviously a child's bedroom.

"That's for Janelle's son when he comes to visit us."

Then she led me to the master bedroom, which had a huge bed. She had really changed it. It was utterly feminine with dolls against the walls, big pillows on a sofa and a television at the foot of the bed.

And then I said, "Whose bedroom is this?"

Alice said, "Mine."

We went to the third bedroom, which was a shambles. It was obviously used as a small storeroom for the apartment. All kinds of odds and ends of furniture scattered all over the room. The bed was small with a quilt on it.

"And whose bedroom is this?" I said mockingly, a hairy Goldilocks.

"Janelle's," Alice said. As she said this, she let go of my hand and turned her head away.

I knew she was lying and that she and Janelle shared the huge bedroom. We went back into the sitting room and we waited.

At ten thirty the phone rang. It was Janelle. "Oh, God!" she said. Her voice was as dramatic as if she had a fatal illness. "We're not finished. We won't be finished for another hour. Do you want to wait?"

I laughed. "Sure," I said. "I'll wait."

"I'll call you again," Janelle said. "As soon as I know we're through. Is that OK?"

"Sure," I said.

I waited with Alice until twelve o'clock. She wanted to make me something to eat, but I wasn't hungry. By this time I was enjoying myself. There is nothing so funny as to be made an utter fool of.

At midnight the phone rang again and I knew what she would say and she said it. They weren't through yet. They didn't know what time they would be through.

I was very cheerful with her. I knew that she would be tired. That I wouldn't see her that night and I would call her the next day from home.

"Darling, you're sweet, you're so sweet. I'm really sorry," Janelle said. "Call me tomorrow afternoon."

I said good-night to Alice and she kissed me at the door and it was a sisterly kiss and she said, "You're going to call Janelle tomorrow, aren't you?"

I said, "Sure. I'll call her from home."

The next morning I caught the early plane to New York, and at the terminal in Kennedy Airport I called Janelle. She was delighted to hear from me. "I was afraid you wouldn't call."

I said, "I promised I'd call."

She said, "We worked until three this morning and the dress rehearsal isn't until nine o'clock tonight. I could come over to the hotel for a couple of hours if you want to see me."

I said, "Sure I want to see you. But I'm in New York. I told you I'd call you from home."

There was a long pause on the other side of the phone.

"I see," she said.

"OK," I said. "I'll call you when I'm coming to Los Angeles again. OK?"

There was another long pause on the phone and she said,

"You've been incredibly good for me, but I can't let you hurt me anymore."

And then she hung up the phone.

But on my next trip to California we made up and started all over again. She wanted to be completely honest with me; there were to be no more misunderstandings. She swore she hadn't been to bed with Evarts and the director. That she was always completely honest with me. That she would never lie to me again. And to prove it, she told me about Alice and her. It was an interesting story, but it didn't prove anything, not to me anyway. Still, it was nice to know the truth for sure.

Chapter 37

Janelle lived with Alice De Santis for two months before she realized that Alice was in love with her. It took that long because during the day they both worked so hard, Janelle constantly hustling around to interviews arranged by her agent, Alice working long hours as costume designer on a big-budget film.

They had separate bedrooms. But late at night Alice came into Janelle's room and sat on her bed to gossip. Alice would prepare something to eat and a hot chocolate drink to help them sleep. Usually they talked about their work. Janelle told stories about the subtle and not so subtle passes made at her through the day and they would both laugh. Alice never pointed out that Janelle encouraged these passes with her Southern belle charm.

Alice was a striking-looking, tall woman, very businesslike and hard to the outside world. But she was very soft and gentle with Janelle. She would give Janelle a sisterly kiss before they went to bed in their separate rooms. Janelle admired her for her intelligence, her competent efficiency in her field of costume design.

Alice finished work on her picture at the same time that Janelle's son, Richard, came up to spend part of his summer vacation with Janelle. Usually, when her son came to visit, Janelle would devote all her time to taking him around Los Angeles, to shows, to a skating rink, to Disneyland. Sometimes she would rent a small apartment on the beach for a week. She always enjoyed her son's visit and was always happy for the month he was with her. This one summer, as luck would have it, she got a small part in a TV series which would keep her busy most of the time but would also pay her living for a year. She started to write a long letter to her ex-husband to explain why Richard could not visit her this summer, and then she put her head down on the table and began to weep. It seemed to her as if now she were truly giving up her child.

It was Alice who saved her. She told Janelle to let Richard come. Alice would take him around. She would bring him to visit Janelle on the set to watch her work and whisk him away before he got on the director's nerves. Alice would take care of him during the day. Then Janelle could be his buddy at night. Janelle felt enormously grateful to Alice.

And when Richard came for his month, they had a great time together. After work Janelle would come back to the apartment and Alice had Richard all scrubbed up for a night on the town. They would all three go to the movies and then have a late snack. It was so comfortable and easy. Janelle realized that she and her former husband had never had such a good time with Richard as she and Alice were having. It was almost a perfect marriage. Alice never quarreled or reproached her. Richard never got sulky or disobedient. He lived in what perhaps was a dream of children. A life with two adoring mothers and no father. He loved Alice because she spoiled him in some things and was strict with him only rarely. She took him for tennis lessons during the day and they played together. She taught him Scrabble and how to dance. Alice, in fact, was the perfect father. She was athletic and coordinated, yet with none of a father's harshness, nothing of male domination. Richard responded extremely well to her. He helped Alice serve Janelle her dinner after work and then watched both women pretty themselves up to go out on the town with him. He loved dressing up too in white slacks and dark blue coat and white frilly shirt and no tie. He loved California.

When the day came for him to go home, Alice and Janelle both brought him to the midnight plane, and then, finally alone again, Janelle and Alice held hands, breathing the sigh of relief a married couple might breathe on the departure of a houseguest. Janelle felt so enormously touched that she gave Alice a tight hug and kiss. Alice turned her head to receive the kiss on her soft, delicately thin mouth. For the fraction of a second she held Janelle's mouth on hers.

Back in the apartment they had their cocoa together as if nothing had happened. They went to their bedrooms. But Janelle was restless. She knocked on Alice's bedroom door and went in. She was surprised to find Alice undressed in her lingerie. Though thin, Alice had a full bosom restrained by a very tight bra. They had, of course, seen each other in various stages of undress. But now Alice took off her bra to let her breasts free and then looked at Janelle with a slight smile.

At the sight of the nippled breasts Janelle felt a surge of sexual lust. She could feel herself blushing. It had not occurred to her that she could be attracted to another woman. Especially after Mrs. Wartberg. So when Alice slid under the covers, Janelle sat casually on the edge of her bed, and they talked about the good time they had had with Richard, just the three of them. Suddenly Alice burst into tears.

Janelle patted her dark hair and said, "Alice, what is it?" in a very concerned voice. Yet at the moment both knew they were acting a play that would enable them to do what they both wanted to do.

Alice said, sobbing, "I don't have anyone to love. I don't have anyone to love me."

There was just one moment when Janelle someplace in her mind kept an ironic distance. This was a scene she had played with male lovers. But her warm gratitude to Alice for the past month, the moment of lust that had been sparked by her heavy breasts were far more promising than the rewards of irony. And she too loved to play scenes. She pulled the covers down from Alice and touched her breasts and curiously watched the nipples rise. Then she bent her golden head and covered a nipple with her mouth. The effect on her was extraordinary.

She felt an enormous liquid peace flow through her body as she sucked on the nipple of Alice's breast. She felt almost like a child. The breast was so warm, it tasted so richly sweet to her mouth. She slipped her body next to Alice now, but she refused to give up the nipple, though Alice's hands began a steadily increasing pressure on her neck to force her down lower. Finally Alice let her stay on the breast. Janelle was murmuring as she sucked, the murmurs of an erotic child, and Alice caressed the golden head, only stopping for a moment to put out the light beside her bed so that they could be in darkness. Finally, a long time later, with a soft sigh of satisfied pleasure Janelle stopped sucking on Alice's breast and let her head fall between the other woman's legs. A long time later she fell into an exhausted sleep. When she woke up, she found that she had been undressed and was now naked in the bed beside Alice. They were sleeping in each other's arms with complete trust, like two innocent infants, and with the same peace.

So started what was to Janelle the most satisfying sexual partnership she had experienced up to then. Not that she was in love, she was not. Alice was in love with her. That was partly the reason it was so satisfying. Also, quite simply she loved sucking a full breast, it was a blazing new discovery. And she was completely uninhibited with Alice, and her complete lord and master. Which was great. She didn't have to play her Southern belle role.

The curious part of the relationship was that Janelle, sweet and soft and feminine, was the butch, the sexual aggressor. Alice, who looked a little dykey in a very sweet way, was really the woman of the pair. It was Alice who turned their bedroom (they now shared the same bed) into a frilly woman's chamber with dolls hanging on walls, specially made shutters on the windows and all other kinds of knickknacks. Janelle's bedroom, which they kept up for the sake of appearance, was untidy and messy as a child's.

Part of the thrill of the relationship for Janelle was that she could act the role of a man. Not only sexually but in everyday life, the small details of routine day-to-day living. Around the house she was sloppy in a masculine way. A slob, in fact, while Alice always took care to look attractive to Janelle. Janelle would even do the lustful groping of the male, grabbing Alice by the crotch as she went by in the kitchen, squeezing her breasts. Janelle loved acting the role of the man. She would force Alice to make love. At those times she felt more lust than she could ever feel with a man. Then, although they still both had dates with men, inevitable in their professions where social and business obligations intermingled, it was only Janelle who still enjoyed spending an evening with a male. It was only Janelle who still occasionally stayed out all night. To come back the next morning to find Alice literally sick with jealousy. In fact, so ill that Janelle became frightened and considered moving out. Alice never stayed away all night. And when she was out late, Janelle never worried about whether she was shacking up with a guy. She didn't care. To her mind one thing had nothing to do with another.

But gradually it came to be understood that Janelle was a free agent. That she could do what she pleased. That she was not accountable. Partly because Janelle was so beautiful that it was difficult to avoid attentions and phone calls from all the men she came into contact with: actors, assistant directors, agents, producers, directors. But gradually, during the year they were living together, Janelle lost interest in having sex with men. It became unsatisfying. Not so much physically but because the power relationship was different. She could sense, or imagined she sensed, how they felt they had something on her after they had gotten her to bed. They became too sure of themselves, too sleek with satisfaction. They expected too many attentions. Attentions she did not feel like giving. Also, she found in Alice something she had never felt in any man. An absolute trust. She never felt that Alice gossiped about her or held her cheap. Or that Alice would betray her with another woman or man. Or that Alice would cheat her out of material possessions or break a promise. Many of the men she met were lavish with promises that they never kept. She was truly happy with Alice, who took care to keep her happy in every way.

One day Alice said, "You know, we could have Richard live with us permanently."

"Oh, God, I wish I could," Janelle said. "We just haven't got the time to take care of him."

"Sure we do," Alice said. "Look, we rarely work at the same time. He'll be in school. On vacations he can go to camp. If there's a pinch, we can hire a woman. I think you'd be much happier if you had Richard with you."

Janelle was tempted. She realized that their ménage would become more permanent with Richard living with them. But that didn't seem a bad idea. She was getting enough movie work now to live well. They could even get a larger apartment and really fix it up. "OK," she said. "I'll write Richard and see how he feels about it."

She never did. She knew her ex-husband would reject her. And also she did not want Alice to become too important to her.

Chapter 38

When I knew for sure that Janelle went both ways, that Alice was also her lover, I was relieved. What the hell. Two women making love together was like two women knitting together. I told that to Janelle to make her angry. Then too, her arrangement was a bailout for me. I was in the position of a guy with a married mistress whose husband was understanding and female, a great combination.

But nothing is simple. Gradually I came to realize that Janelle loved Alice at least as much as she did me. What was worse, I came to realize that Alice loved Janelle better than I did; in a way that was less selfish and much less damaging to Janelle Because I knew by this time that I wasn't doing Janelle much good emotionally. Never mind that it was a hopeless trap. That no guy would ever solve her problems. But I was using her as an instrument of my pleasure. OK again. But I expected her to accept a strictly subordinate place in my life. After all, I had my wife and kids and my writing Yet I expected her to place me in a primary position.

Everything is a bargain to some degree. And I was getting a better bargain than she was. It was that simple.

But here's where the gravy came in, having a bisexual girlfriend. Janelle became sick on one of my visits. She had to go to the hospital to get a cyst removed from her ovary. What with that and some complications she was in the hospital for ten days. Sure, I sent flowers, tons and tons of flowers, the usual bullshit that women love and so let men get away with murder. Sure, I went to see her every night for about an hour. But Alice ran all her errands, stayed with her all day. Sometimes Alice was there when I came, and she always left the room a little while so Janelle and I could be alone. Maybe she knew that Janelle would want me to hold her bare breasts when I was talking to her. Not sexy but because that was comforting to her. Jesus, how much of sex is just comforting, like a hot bath, a great dinner, good wine. And if only you could come at sex just that way without love and other complications.

Anyway, just this one time Alice stayed in the room with us. I was always struck by how sweet a face Alice had. In fact, the two women looked like sisters, two very sweet-looking women, soft and feminine. Alice had a small, almost thin mouth, which rarely looks generous, but hers did. I liked her enormously. And why the hell shouldn't I? She was doing all the dirty work I should have been doing. But I was a busy guy. I was married. I had to leave for New York the next day. Maybe if Alice weren't there, I would have done all the things she had done, but I don't think so.

I had sneaked in a bottle of champagne to celebrate our last night together. But I didn't mind sharing it with Alice. Janelle had three glasses stashed. Alice opened the bottle. She was very capable.

Janelle had on a pretty frilled lace nightgown, and as always, she looked somehow dramatic lying there on the bed. I knew that she had deliberately not used makeup for my visit so as to look the part. Wan, pale, another Camille. Except that she really was in great shape and bursting with vitality. Her eyes were dancing with pleasure as she sipped the champagne. She had trapped in this room the two people she loved best. They were not allowed to be mean to her in any way, or hurt her feelings in any way, not even stop her from being mean to them. And maybe it was this that made her reach out and take my hand in hers as Alice sat there watching.

Ever since I had known about them, I had been careful not to act like a lover in front of Alice. And Alice never betrayed her sexual relationship with Janelle. Watching them, you would swear that they were two sisters or two comrades. They were absolutely casual with one another. Their relationship was indicated only by Janelle, who sometimes bossed Alice around like a domineering husband.

Now Alice moved her chair back so that it tilted her against the far wall, away from Janelle's bed, away from us. As if she were giving us the official status of lovers. For some reason this gesture of hers affected me painfully, it was so generous.

I guess I envied them both. They were so comfortable with

each other that they could afford to indulge me, my privileged position as an official lover. Janelle played with the fingers on my hand. And now I realized it was not perversity on her part but a genuine desire to make me happy, so I smiled at her. In the next hour we would finish the champagne and I would leave and catch my plane to New York and they would be alone and Janelle would make it up to Alice. And Alice knew that. As she knew that Janelle must have this moment with me. I resisted the impulse to pull my hand away. That would be ungenerous, and the male mystique has it that men are basically more generous than women. But I knew that my generosity was forced. I couldn't wait to leave.

Finally I could kiss Janelle good-bye. I promised to call her the next day. We hugged each other as Alice discreetly left the room. But Alice was waiting outside for me and kept me company down to the car. She gave me another of her soft kisses on the mouth.

"Don't worry," she said. "I'll spend the night with her." Janelle had told me that after her operation Alice spent the whole night curled up on the armchair in her room, so I was not surprised.

I just said, "Take care of yourself, thanks," and got into my car and drove to the airport.

It was dark before the plane started its journey east. I could never sleep on a plane.

And so I could think of Alice and Janelle comfortable with each other in the hospital bedroom, and I was glad Janelle was not alone. And I was glad that early in the dawn I would be having breakfast with my family.

Chapter 39

One of the things I never admitted to Janelle was that my jealousy was not merely romantic, but pragmatic. I searched the literature of romantic novels, but in no novel could I find the admission that one of the reasons a married man wants his mistress to be faithful is that he fears catching the clap or worse and then transmitting it to his wife. I guess one of the reasons this couldn't be admitted to the mistress at least is that the married man usually lied and said he was no longer sleeping with his wife. And since he was already lying to his wife and since if he did infect her, if he was human at all, he'd have to tell both. He was caught in the double horn of guilt.

So one night I told Janelle about that and she looked at me grimly and said, "How about if you caught it from your wife and gave it to me? Or don't you think that's possible?"

We were playing our usual game of fighting but not really fighting. really a duel of wits in which humor and truth were allowed and even some cruelty but no brutality.

"Sure." I said, "But the odds are less. My wife is a pretty strict Catholic. She's virtuous." I held up my hand to stop Janelle's protest. "And she's older and not as beautiful as you are and has less opportunity."

Janelle relaxed a bit. Any compliment to her beauty could soften her up.

Then I said, grinning a little, "But you're right. If my wife gave it to me and I gave it to you, I wouldn't feel guilty. That would be OK. That would be a kind of justice since you and I are both criminals together."

Janelle couldn't resist any longer. She was almost jumping up and down. "I can't believe you said something like that. I just can't believe it. I may be a criminal," she said, "but you're just a coward."

Another night in the early-morning hours, when as usual we couldn't sleep because we were so excited by each other after we had made love a couple of times and drunk a bottle of wine, she was finally so persistent that I told her about when I was a kid in the asylum.

As a child I used books as magic. In the dormitory late at night, separate and alone, a greater loneliness than I have ever felt since, I could spirit myself away and escape by reading and then weave my own fantasies. The books I loved best at that early age of ten, eleven or twelve were the romantic legends of Roland, Charlemagne, the American West, but especially of King Arthur and his Round Table and his brave knights Lancelot and Galahad. But most of all, I loved Merlin because I thought myself like him. And then I would weave my fantasies, my brother, Artie, was King Arthur and that was right too, and that was because Artie had all the nobility and fairness of King Arthur, the honesty and true purpose, the forgiving lovingness which I did not have. As a child I fantasized myself as cunning and far-seeing and was firmly convinced that I would rule my own life by some sort of magic. And so I came to love King Arthur's magician, Merlin, who had lived through the past, could foresee the future, who was immortal and all-wise.

It was then I developed the trick of actually transferring myself from the present into the future. I used it all my life. As a child in the asylum I would make myself into a young man with clever bookish friends. I could make myself live in a luxurious apartment and on the sofa of that apartment make love to a passionate, beautiful woman.

During the war on tedious guard or patrol duty I would project myself into the future when I would be on leave to Paris, eating great food and bedding down with luscious whores. Under shellfire I could magically disappear and find myself resting in the woods by a gentle brook, reading a favorite book.

It worked, it really worked. I magically disappeared. And I would remember in later actual time, when I was really doing those great things, I remembered these terrible times and it would seem as if I had escaped them altogether, that I had never suffered. That they were only dreams.

I remember my shock and astonishment when Merlin tells

King Arthur to rule without his help because he, Merlin, will be imprisoned in a cave by a young enchantress to whom he has taught all his secrets. Like King Arthur, I asked why. Why would Merlin teach a young girl all his magic simply so he could become her prisoner and why was he so cheerful about sleeping in a cave for a thousand years, knowing the tragic ending of his king? I couldn't understand it. And yet, as I grew older, I felt that I too might do the same thing. Every great hero, I had learned, must have a weakness, and that would be mine.

I had read many different versions of the King Arthur legend, and in one I had seen a picture of Merlin as a man with a long gray beard wearing a conical duncelike cap spangled with stars and signs of the zodiac. In the shop class of the asylum school I made myself such a hat and wore it around the grounds. I loved that hat. Until one day one of the boys stole it and I never saw it again and I never made another one. I had used that hat to spin magic spells around myself, of the hero that I would become; the adventures I would have, the good deeds I would perform and the happiness I would find. But the hat really wasn't necessary. The fantasies wove themselves anyway. My life in that asylum seems a dream. I never was there. I was really Merlin as a child of ten. I was a magician, and nothing could ever harm me.

Janelle was looking at me with a little smile. "You really think you're Merlin, don't you?" she said.

"A little bit," I said.

She smiled again and didn't say anything. We drank a little wine, and then she said suddenly, "You know, sometimes I'm a little kinky and I'm afraid, really, to be that way with you. Do you know what's a lot of fun? One of us ties the other up and then makes love to whoever is tied up. How about it? Let me tie you up and then I'll make love to you and you'll be helpless. It's really a great kick."

I was surprised because we had tried to be kinky before and failed. One thing I knew: Nobody would ever tie me up. So I told her, "OK, I'll tie you up, but you're not tying me up."

"That's not fair," Janelle said. "That's not fair play."

"I don't give a shit," I said. "Nobody's tying me up. How

do I know when you have me tied up you won't light matches under my feet or stick a pin in my eye? You'll be sorry afterward, but that won't help me."

"No, you dope. It would be a symbolic bond. I'll just get a scarf and tie you up. You can break loose anytime you want. It can be like a thread. You're a writer, you know what 'symbolic' means."

"No," I said.

She leaned back on the bed, smiling at me very coolly, "And you think you're Merlin," she said. "You thought I'd be sympathetic about poor you in the orphanage imagining yourself as Merlin. You're the toughest son of a bitch I ever met and I just proved it to you. You'd never let any woman put you under a spell or put you in a cave or tie a scarf around your arms. You're no Merlin, Merlyn."

I really hadn't seen that coming, but I had an answer for her, an answer I couldn't give. That a less skillful enchantress had been before her. I was married, wasn't I?

The next day I had a meeting with Doran and he told me that negotiations for the new script would take awhile. The new director, Simon Bellfort, was fighting for a bigger percentage. Doran said tentatively, "Would you consider giving up a couple of your points to him?"

"I don't even want to work on the picture," I told Doran. "That guy Simon is a hack, his buddy Richetti is a fucking born thief. At least Kellino is a great actor to excuse his being an asshole. And that fucking prick Wagon is the prize creep of them all. Just get me off the picture."

Doran said smoothly, "Your percentage of the picture depends on your getting screenplay credit. That's in the contract. If you let those guys go on without you, they'll work it so you won't get the credit. You'll have to go to arbitration before the Writers Guild. The studio proposes the credits, and if they don't give you partial credit, you gotta fight it."

"Let them try," I said. "They can't change it that much."

Doran said soothingly, "I have an idea. Eddie Lancer is a good friend of yours. I'll ask to have him assigned to work with you on the script. He's a savvy guy and he can run interference for you against all those other characters. OK? Trust me this once."

"OK," I said. I was tired of the whole business.

Before he left, Doran said, "Why are you pissed off at those guys?"

"Because not one of them gave a shit about Malomar," I said. "They're glad he's dead." But it wasn't really true. I hated them because they tried to tell me what to write.

I got back to New York in time to see the Academy Awards presented on television. Valerie and I always watched them every year. And this year I was watching particularly because Janelle had a short, a half hour film, she had made with her friends that had been nominated.

My wife brought out coffee and cookies, and we settled down to watching. She smiled at me and said, "Do you think someday you'll be there picking up an Oscar?"

"No," I said. "My picture will be lousy."

As usual, in the Oscar presentations they got all the small stuff out of the way first, and sure enough, Janelle's film won the prize as the Best Short Subject and there was her face on the screen. Her face was rosy and pink with happiness and she was sensible enough to make it short and she was guilty enough to make it gracious. She just simply said, "I want to thank the women who made this picture with me, especially Alice De Santis."

And it brought me back to the day when I knew that Alice loved Janelle more than I ever could.

Janelle had rented a beach house in Malibu for a month, and on weekends I would leave my hotel and spend my Saturday and Sunday with her at the house. Friday night we walked on the beach, and then we sat on the porch, the tiny porch under the Malibu moon and watched the tiny birds, Janelle told me they were sandpipers. They scampered out of the reach of the water whenever the waves came up.

We made love in the bedroom overlooking the Pacific Ocean. The next day, Saturday, when we were having lunch instead of breakfast, Alice came out to the house. She had breakfast with us, and then she took a rectangular tiny piece of film out of her purse and gave it to Janelle. The piece of film was no more than an inch wide and two inches long.

Janelle asked, "What's this?"

"It's the director's credit on the film," Alice said. "I cut it out."

"Why did you do that?" Janelle said.

"Because I thought it would make you happy," Alice said.

I was watching both of them. I had seen the film. It had been a lovely little piece of work. Janelle and Alice had made it with three other women as a feminist venture. Janelle had screen credit as star. Alice had a credit as director, and the other two women had credits appropriate to the work they had done on the film.

"We need a director's credit. We just can't have a picture without a director's credit," Janelle said.

Just for the hell of it I put my two cents in. "I thought Alice directed the film," I said.

Janelle looked at me angrily. "She was in charge of directing," she said. "But I made a lot of the director suggestions and I felt I should get some credit for that."

"Jesus," I said. "You're the star of the film. Alice has to get some credit for the work she did."

"Of course she does," Janelle said indignantly. "I told her that. I didn't tell her to cut out her credit on the negative. She just did it."

I turned to Alice and said, "How do you really feel about it?"

Alice seemed very composed. "Janelle did a lot of work on the directing," she said. "And I really don't care for the credit. Janelle can have it. I really don't care."

I could see that Janelle was very angry. She hated being put in such a false position, but I sensed that she wasn't going to let Alice have full credit for directing the film.

"Damn you," Janelle said to me. "Don't look at me like that. I got the money to have this film made and I got all the people together and we all helped write the story and it couldn't have been made without me."

"All right," I said. "Then take credit as the producer. Why is the director's credit so important?"

Then Alice spoke up. "We're going to be showing this film in competition for the Academy and Filmex, and on films like this, people feel the only thing that's important is the directorship. The director gets most of the credit for the picture. I think Janelle's right." She turned to Janelle. "How do you want the director's credit to read?"

Janelle said, "Have both of us being given credit and you put your name first. Is that OK?"

Alice said, "Sure, anything you want."

After having lunch with us, Alice said she had to leave even though Janelle begged her to stay. I watched them kiss each other good-bye and then I walked Alice out to her car.

Before she drove away, I asked her, "Do you really not mind?"

Her face perfectly composed, beautiful in its serenity, she said, "No, I really don't mind. Janelle was hysterical after the first showing when everybody came up to me to congratulate me. She's just that way and making her happy is more important to me than getting all that bullshit. You understand that, don't you?"

I smiled at her and kissed her cheek good-bye. "No," I said. "I don't understand stuff like that." I went back into the house and Janelle was nowhere in sight. I figured she must have gone for a walk down the beach and she didn't want me with her, and sure enough, an hour later I spotted her coming up the sand walking by the water. And when she came into the house, she went up to the bedroom, and when I found her up there, I saw that she was in bed with the covers over her and she was crying.

I sat down on the bed and didn't say anything. She reached out to hold my hand. She was still crying.

"You think I'm such a bitch, don't you?" she said.

"No," I said.

"And you think Alice is so marvelous, don't you?"

"I like her," I said. I knew I had to be very careful. She was afraid that I would think Alice was a better person than she was.

"Did you tell her to cut out that piece of negative?" I said.

"No," Janelle said. "She just did that on her own."

"OK," I said. "Then just accept it for what it is and don't worry about who behaved better and who seems like a better person. She wanted to do that for you. Just accept it. You know you want it."

At this she started to cry again. In fact, she was hysterical, so I made her some soup and fed her one of her blue ten-milligram Valiums and she slept from that afternoon till Sunday morning.

That afternoon I read; then I watched the beach and the water until dawn broke.

Janelle finally woke up. It was about ten o'clock, a beautiful day in Malibu. I knew immediately that she wasn't comfortable with me, that she didn't want me around for the rest of the day. That she wanted to call Alice and have Alice come out and spend the rest of the day. So I told her I had gotten a call and had to go to the studio and couldn't spend the rest of the day with her. She made the usual Southern belle protestations, but I could see the light in her eyes. She wanted to call Alice and show her love for her.

Janelle walked me out to the car. She was wearing one of those big floppy hats to protect her skin from the sun. It was really a floppy hat. Most women would have looked ugly in it. But with her perfect face and complexion she was quite beautiful. She had on her specially tailored, secondhand, specially weathered jeans that fitted on the body like skin. And I remembered that one night I had said to her when she was naked in bed that she had a real great woman's ass, that it takes generations to breed an ass like that. I said it to make her angry because she was a feminist, but to my surprise she was delighted. And I remembered that she was partly a snob. That she was proud of the aristocratic lineage of her Southern family.

She kissed me good-bye and her face was all rosy and pink. She wasn't a bit desolated that I was leaving. I knew that she and Alice would have a happy day together and that I would have a miserable day in town at my hotel. But I figured, what the hell? Alice deserved it and I really didn't. Janelle had once said that she, Janelle, was a practical solution to my emotional needs but I was not a practical solution to hers.

The television kept flickering. There was a special tribute in memory of Malomar. Valerie said something to me about it. Was he a nice person? and I answered yes. We finished watching the awards, and then she said to me, "Did you know any of the people that were there?"

"Some of them," I said.

"Which ones?" Valerie asked me.

I mentioned Eddie Lancer who had won an Oscar for his contribution to a film script, but I didn't mention Janelle. I

wondered for just a moment if Valerie had set a trap for me
to see if I would mention Janelle and then I said I knew the
blond girl who won a prize at the beginning of the program.
Valerie looked at me and then turned away.

Chapter 40

A week later Doran called me to go out to California for more conferences. He said he had sold Eddie Lancer to Tri-Culture. So I went out and hung around and went to meetings and picked up with Janelle again. I was a little restless now. I didn't love California that much anymore.

One night Janelle said to me, "You always tell how great your brother, Artie, is. Why is he so great?"

"Well," I said, "I guess he was my father as well as my brother."

I could see she was fascinated by the two of us growing up, as orphans. That it appealed to her dramatic sense. I could see her spinning all kinds of movies, fairy tales in her head, about how life had been. Two young boys. Charming. One of your real Walt Disney fantasies.

"So, you really want to hear another story about orphans?" I said. "Do you want a happy story or a true story? Do you want a lie or do you want the truth?"

Janelle pretended to think it over. "Try me with the truth," she said. "If I don't like it, you can tell me the lie."

So I told her how all the visitors to the asylum wanted to adopt Artie but never wanted to adopt me. That's how I started off the story.

And Janelle said mockingly, "Poor you." But when she said it, though her face smiled, she let her hand fall along the side of my body and rest there.

It was on a Sunday when I was seven and Artie was eight that we were made to dress up in what was called our adoption uniforms. Light blue jackets, white starched shirt, dark blue tie and white flannel trousers with white shoes. We were brushed and combed and brought to the head matron's reception room, where a young married couple waited to inspect us. The procedure was that we were introduced and shook hands and showed our best manners and sat around talking and became acquainted. Then we would all take a walk through the grounds of the asylum, past the huge garden, past the football field and the school buildings. The thing I remember most clearly is that the woman was very beautiful. That even as a seven-year-old boy I fell in love with her. It was obvious that her husband was also in love with her but wasn't too crazy about the whole idea. It also became obvious during that day that the woman was crazy about Artie, but not about me. And I really couldn't blame her. Even at eight, Artie looked handsome in almost a grown-up way. Also, the features in all of the planes of his face were perfectly cut, and though people said to me we looked alike and always knew we were brothers, I knew that I was a smudged version of him as if he were the first out of the mold. The impression was clear. As a second impression I had picked up little pieces of wax on the mold, lips thicker, nose bigger. Artie had the delicacy of a girl, the bones in my face and my body were thicker and heavier. But I had never been jealous of my brother until that day.

That night we were told that the couple would return the next Sunday to make their decision on whether to adopt both of us or one of us. We were also told that they were very rich and how important it was for at least one of us to be taken.

I remember the matron gave us a heart-to-heart talk. It was one of those heart-to-heart talks adults give to children warning them against the evil emotions such as jealousy, envy, spitefulness and urging us on to a generosity of spirit that only saints could achieve, much less children. As children we listened without saying a word. Nodding our heads and saying, "Yes, Ma'am." But not really knowing what she was talking about. But even at the age of seven I knew what was going to happen. My brother next Sunday would go away with the rich, beautiful lady and leave me alone in the asylum.

Even as a child Artie was not vain. But the week that followed was the only week in our lives that we were estranged. I hated him that week. On Monday after classes, when we had our touch football game, I didn't pick him to be on my team. In sports I had all the power. For the sixteen years we were in the asylum I was the best athlete of my age and a natural leader. So I was always one of the captains who picked their teams, and I always picked Artie to be on my team as my first choice. That Monday was the only time in sixteen years that I didn't pick him. When we played the game, though he was a year older than I was, I tried to hit him as hard as I could when he had the ball. I can still remember thirty years later the look of astonishment and hurt on his face that day. At evening meals I didn't sit next to him at the dinner table. At night I didn't talk to him in the dormitory. On one of those days during the week I remember clearly that after the football game was over and he was walking away across the field I had the football in my hand and I very coolly threw a beautiful twenty-yard spiral pass and hit him in the back of the head and knocked him to the ground. I had just thrown it. I really didn't think I could hit him. For a seven-year-old boy it was a remarkable feat. And even now I wonder at the strength of the malice that made my seven-year-old arm so true. I remember Artie's getting off the ground and my yelling out, "Hey, I didn't mean it." But he just turned and walked away.

He never retaliated. It made me more furious. No matter how much I snubbed him or humiliated him he just looked at me questioningly. Neither of us understood what was happening. But I knew one thing that would really bother him. Artie was always a careful saver of money. We picked up pennies and nickels by doing odd jobs around the asylum, and Artie had a glass jar filled with these pennies and nickels that he kept hidden in his clothes locker. On Friday afternoon I stole the glass jar, giving up my daily football game, and ran out into a wooded area of the grounds and buried it. I didn't even count the money. I could see the copper and silver coins filled the jar almost to the brim. Artie didn't miss the jar until the next morning and he looked at me unbelievingly, but he didn't say anything. Now he avoided me.

The following day was Sunday and we were to report to the matron to be dressed in our adoption suits. I got up early Sunday morning before breakfast and ran away to hide in the wooded area behind the asylum. I knew what would happen that day. That Artie would be dressed in his suit, that the beautiful woman I loved would take him away with her and that I would never see him again. But at least I would have his money. In the thickest part of the woods I lay down and went to sleep and I slept the whole day through. It was almost dark before I awoke and then I went back. I was brought to the matron's office and she gave me twenty licks with a wooden ruler across the legs. It didn't bother me a bit.

I went back to the dormitory, and I was astonished to find Artie sitting in his bed waiting for me. I couldn't believe that he was still there. In fact, if I remember, I had tears in my eyes when Artie punched me in the face and said, "Where's my money?" And then he was all over me, punching me and kicking me and screaming for his money. I tried to defend myself without hurting him, but finally I picked him up and threw him off me. We sat there staring at each other.

"I haven't got your money," I said.

"You stole it," Artie said. "I know you stole it."

"I didn't," I said. "I haven't got it."

We stared at each other. We didn't speak again that evening. But when we woke up the next morning, we were friends again. Everything was as it was before. Artie never asked me again about the money. And I never told him where I had buried it.

I never knew what happened that Sunday until years later when Artie told me that when he had found out I had run away, he had refused to put on his adoption suit, that he had screamed and cussed and tried to hit the matron, that he had been beaten. When the young couple that wanted to adopt him insisted on seeing him, he had spit on the woman and called her all the dirty names an eight-year-old boy could think of. It had been a terrible scene and he took another beating from the matron.

* * *

When I finished the story, Janelle got up from the bed and went to get herself another glass of wine. She came back into the bed, leaning up against me, and said, "I want to meet your brother, Artie."

"You never will," I said. "Girls I brought around fell in love with him. In fact, the only reason I married my wife was that she was the only girl who didn't."

Janelle said, "Did you ever find the glass jar with the money?"

"No," I said. "I never wanted to. I wanted it to be there for some kid who came after me, some kid might dig in that wood and it would be a piece of magic for him. I didn't need it anymore."

Janelle drank her wine and then said jealously, as she was jealous of all my emotions, "You love him, don't you?"

And I really couldn't answer that. I couldn't think of that word of "love" as a word that I would use for my brother or any man. And besides, Janelle used the word "love" too much. So I didn't answer.

On another night Janelle argued with me about women having the right to fuck as freely as men. I pretended to agree with her. I was feeling coolly malicious from suppressed jealousy.

All I said was: "Sure they do. The only trouble is that biologically women can't handle it."

At this, Janelle became furious. "That's all bullshit," she said. "We can fuck just as easily as you do. We don't give a shit. In fact, it's you men who make all the fuss about sex being so important and serious. You're so jealous and so possessive we're your property."

It was just the trap I hoped she would fall into. "No, I didn't mean that," I said. "But did you know that a man has a twenty to fifty percent chance of catching gonorrhea from a woman, but a woman has a fifty to eighty percent chance of catching gonorrhea from a man?"

She looked astounded for a moment and I loved that look of childish astonishment on her face. Like most people, she didn't know a damn thing about VD or how it worked. As for myself, as soon as I had started cheating on my wife, I had read up on the whole subject. My big nightmare was catching VD, gonorrhea or syphilis, and infecting Valerie, which is one of the reasons that it distressed me when Janelle told me about her love affairs.

"You're just making it up to scare me," Janelle said. "I know you when you sound so sure of yourself and so professorial; you're just making stories up."

"No," I said. "It's true. A male has a thin, clear discharge from within one to ten days, but women most of the time never even know they have gonorrhea. Fifty to eighty percent of women have no symptoms for weeks or months or they have a green or yellow discharge. Also, women get a mushroom odor from their genitals."

Janelle collapsed on the bed, laughing, and threw her bare legs up in the air. "Now I know you're full of shit."

"No, it's true," I said. "No kidding. But you're OK. I can smell you from here." Hoping the joke would hide my malice. "You know usually the only way you know you have it is if your male partner tells you."

Janelle straightened up primly. "Thanks a lot," she said. "Are you getting ready to tell me you have it and, therefore, I must have it?"

"No," I said. "I'm straight, but if I do get it, I know it's either from you or my wife."

Janelle gave me a sarcastic look. "And your wife is above suspicion, right?"

"That's right," I said.

"Well, for your information," Janelle said, "I go to my gynecologist every month and get a complete checkup."

"That's full of shit," I said. "The only way that you can tell is to take a culture. And most gynecologists do not. They take it in a thin glass with light brown jelly from your cervix. The test is very tricky and it's not always a positive test."

She was fascinated now, so I threw her a zinger. "And if you think you can beat the rap by just going down on a guy, the percentages are much greater for a woman getting a venereal disease from going down on a man than a man has from going down on a woman."

Janelle sprang up from the bed. She was giggling, but she yelled, "Unfair! Unfair!"

We both laughed.

"And gonorrhea is nothing," I said. "Syphilis is the real *bad* part. If you go down on a guy, you can get a nice chancre on your mouth or your lips or even your tonsils. It would hurt your acting career. What you have to look out for on a chancre is if it's dull red and breaks down into a dull red sore that does not bleed easily. Now, here's what's tricky about it. The symptoms can vanish in one to five weeks, but the disease is still in your body and you can infect somebody after this point. You may get a second lesion or the palms and soles of your feet may develop red bumps." I picked up one of her feet and said, "Nope, you haven't got them."

She was fascinated now, and she hadn't caught on either to why I was lecturing her.

"What about men? What do you bastards get out of all this?"

"Well," I said, "we get swelling of the lymph glands in the groin, and that's why sometimes you tell a guy he's got two pairs of balls, or sometimes you lose your hair. That's why in the old days the slang for syphilis was 'haircut.' But still, you're not in too bad a shape. Penicillin can wipe it all out. Again, as I said, the only trouble is men know they got it, but women don't and that's why women are not biologically equipped to be promiscuous."

Janelle looked a little stunned. "Do you find this fascinating? You son of a bitch." She was beginning to catch on.

I continued very blandly. "But it's not as terrible as it sounds. Even if you don't find out that you have syphilis or, as it happens with most women, you have no symptoms of any kind unless some guy tells you out of the goodness of his heart. In one year you won't be infectious. You won't infect anyone." I smiled at her. "Unless you're a pregnant woman and then your child is born with syphilis."

I could see her shrink away from the thought. "Now after that one year, two-thirds of those infected will live with no ill effects. They are home free. They are OK."

I smiled at her.

Janelle said suspiciously, "And the other one-third?"

"They're in a lot of trouble," I said. "Syphillis injures the heart, it injures the blood vessels. It can lie low for ten to twenty years, and then it can cause insanity, it can cause paralysis, make you a paralytic. It can also affect your eyes, lungs and liver. So you see, my dear, you're shit out of luck."

Janelle said, "You're just telling me this to keep me from going out with other men. You're just trying to scare me just like my mother did when I was fifteen by telling me I'd be pregnant."

"Sure," I said. "But I'm backing it up with science. I have no moral objection. You can fuck whoever you want. You don't belong to me."

"You're such a smart-ass," Janelle said. "Maybe they'll come up with a pill just like the birth control pill."

I made my voice sound very sincere. "Sure," I said. "They have that already. If you take a tablet of five hundred milligrams of penicillin one hour before you have contact, it knocks out the syphilis completely. But sometimes it doesn't work and it just reaches the symptoms and then ten or twenty years later you can be really screwed. If you take it too early or too late, these spirochetes multiply. Do you know what spirochetes are? They're like corkscrews and they fill up your blood and get into the tissues and there's not enough blood in your tissues to fight it off. There is something about the drug that keeps the cell from increasing and blocking off the infection, and then the disease becomes resistant to penicillin in your body. In fact, the penicillin helps them grow. But there is another thing you can use. There is a female gel, Proganasy, that's used as a contraceptive and they found that it destroys VD bacteria as well, so you can kill two birds with one stone. Come to think of it, my friend Osano uses those penicillin pills whenever he thinks he's going to get lucky with a girl."

Janelle laughed scornfully. "That's all right for men. You men will fuck anything, but women never know who or when they are going to fuck until an hour or two hours beforehand."

"Well," I said very cheerfully, "let me give you some advice. Never fuck anybody between the ages of fifteen and twenty-five. They have about ten times more VD than any other age bracket. Another thing is before you go to bed with a guy, give him a short arm."

Janelle said, "That sounds disgusting. What is that?"

"Well," I said, "you strip down his penis, you know, like you're masturbating him, and if there's a yellow fluid coming out like a drippage, you know he's infected. That's what prostitutes do."

When I said that, I knew I had gone too far. She gave me a cold look, so I went on hastily. "Another thing is herpes virus. It isn't really a venereal disease and is usually transmitted by uncircumcised men. It can give women cervical cancer. So you see what the score is. You can get cancer from screwing, syphilis from screwing and never even know you're infected. And that's why women can't fuck as freely as men."

Janelle clapped her hands, "Bravo, Professor. I think I'll just fuck women."

"That's not a bad idea," I said.

It was easy for me to say. I wasn't jealous of her women lovers.

Chapter 41

On my next trip back a month later I called Janelle, and we decided to have dinner and go to the movies together. There was something a little cold in her voice, so I was wary, which prepared me for the shock of seeing her when I picked her up at her apartment.

Alice opened the door and I kissed her and I asked Alice how Janelle was and Alice rolled her eyes up in her head, which meant I could expect Janelle to be a little crazy. Well, it wasn't crazy, but it was a little funny. When Janelle came out of the bedroom, she was dressed as I had never seen her before.

She had on a white fedora with a red ribbon in it. The brim snapped over her dark brown gold-flecked eyes. She was wearing a perfectly tailored man's suit of white silk, or what looked like silk. The trouser legs were strictly tailored straight as any man's. She had on a white silk shirt and the most beautiful red-and-blue-striped tie, and to top it off, she was carrying a delicately slender cream-colored Gucci cane, which she proceeded to stab me in the stomach with. It was a direct challenge, I knew what she was doing; she was coming out of the closet and without words she was telling the world of her bisexuality.

She said, "How do you like it?"

I smiled and said, "Great." The most dapper dyke I ever met. "Where do you want to eat?"

She leaned on her cane and watched me very cooly. "I think," she said, "we should eat at Scandia and that for once in our relationship you might take me to a nightclub."

We had never eaten at the fancy places. We had never gone to a nightclub. But I said OK. I understood, I think, what she was doing. She was forcing me to acknowledge to the world that I loved her despite her bisexuality, testing me to see if I could bear the dyke jokes and snickers. Since I had already accepted the fact myself, I didn't care what anybody else thought.

We had a great evening. Everybody stared at us in the restaurant, and I must admit that Janelle looked absolutely smashing. In fact, she looked like a blonder and fairer version of Marlene Dietrich, Southern belle style, of course. Because, no matter what she did, that overwhelming femininity came off her. But I knew that if I told her that, she would hate it. She was out to punish me.

I really enjoyed her playing the dyke role simply because I knew how feminine she was in bed. So it was a sort of double joke on whoever was watching us. I also enjoyed it because Janelle thought she was making me angry and was watching my every move and was disappointed and then pleased that I obviously didn't mind.

I drew the line at going to a nightclub, but we went and had drinks at the Polo Lounge, where for her satisfaction I submitted our relationship to the stares of her friends and mine. I saw Doran at one table and Jeff Wagon at another, and they both grinned at me. Janelle waved to them gaily and then turned to me and said, "Isn't it wonderful to go somewhere for a drink and see all your old dear friends?"

I grinned back at her and I said, "Great."

I got her home before midnight and she tapped me on the shoulder with her cane and she said, "You did very well."

And I said, "Thank you."

She said, "Will you call me?"

And I said, "Yes." It had been a nice night anyway. I had enjoyed the double takes of the maître d', the doorman, even the guys who did the valet parking, and at least now Janelle was out of the closet.

There came a time soon after this when I loved Janelle as a person. That is, it wasn't that I just wanted to fuck her brains out; or look into her dark brown eyes and faint; or eat up her pink mouth. And all the rest of it, the staying up all night telling her stories, Jesus, telling her my whole life, and her telling me all her life. In short, there came a time when I realized it was her sole function to make me happy, to make me delight in her. I saw that it was my job to make her a little happier than she was and not to get pissed off when she didn't make me happy.

I don't mean I became one of those guys who are in love with a girl because it makes them unhappy. I never understood that really. I always believed in getting my share of any bargain, in life, in literature, in marriage, in love, even as a father.

And I don't mean I learned to make her happy by giving her a gift, that was my pleasure. Or to cheer her when she was down, which was just clearing obstacles out of the way so that she could get on with the job of making me happy.

Now what was curious was that after she had "betrayed" me, after we started to hate each other a little, after we had the goods on each other, I came to love her as a person.

She was really such a good guy. She used to say like a child sometimes, "I'm a good person," and she really was. She was really so straight in all the important things. Sure she fucked other guys and women too, but what the hell, nobody's perfect. She still loved the same books I did, the same movies, the same people. When she lied to me, it was to keep from hurting me. And when she told me the truth, it was partly to hurt me (she had a nice vengeful streak and I even loved that too), but also because she was terrified I'd learn the truth in a way that would hurt me more.

And of course, as time went on, I had to understand that she led a hurtful life in many ways. A complicated life. As who indeed does not.

So finally all the falseness and illusion had gone out of our relationship. We were true friends and I loved her as a person. I admired her courage, her indestructability with all the disappointments of her professional life, all the treacheries of her personal life. I understood it all. I was for her all the way.

Then why the hell didn't we have those deliriously good times we had before? Why wasn't the sex as good as it had been, though still better than anyone else? Why weren't we as ecstatic with each other as we used to be?

Magic-magic, black or white. Sorcery, spells, witches and alchemy. Could it really be true that spinning stars decide our destiny and moon blood makes lives wax and wane? Could it be true that the innumerable galaxies decide our fate day by day on earth? Is it quite simply true that we cannot be happy without false illusions?

There comes a point in every love affair when, so it seems, the woman gets pissed off at her lover's being too happy. Sure she knows it's her making him happy. Sure she knows that it's her pleasure, even her job. But finally she comes to the conclusion that in some way, the son of a bitch is getting away with murder. Especially with the man married and the woman not. For then the relationship is an answer to his problem but does not solve hers.

And there comes a time when one of the partners needs a fight before making love. Janelle had come to that stage. I usually managed to sidetrack her, but sometimes I felt like fighting too. Usually when she was pissed off that I stayed married and didn't make any promises for a permanent commitment.

We were in her house in Malibu after the movies. It was late. From our bedroom we could look over the ocean, which wore a long streak of moonlight like a lock of blond hair.

"Let's go to bed," I said. I was dying to make love to her. I was always dying to make love to her.

"Oh, Christ," she said, "you always want to fuck."

"No," I said. "I want to make love to you." I had become that sentimental.

She looked at me coldly, but her liquid brown eyes were flashing with anger. "You and your fucking innocence," she said. "You're like a leper without his bell."

"Graham Greene," I said.

"Oh, fuck you," she said, but she laughed.

And what had led to all this was that I never lied. And she wanted me to lie. She wanted me to give her all the bullshit married men give to girls they screw. Like "My wife and I are getting a divorce." Like "My wife and I haven't screwed in years." Like "My wife and I don't share the same bedroom." Like "My wife and I have an understanding." Like "My wife and I are unhappy together." Since none of this was true for me, I wouldn't say it. I loved my wife, we shared the same bedroom, we had sex, we were happy. I had the best of two worlds and I wasn't going to give it up. So much the worse for me.

Once Janelle laughed she was OK for a while. So now she went and drew a tub full of hot water. We always took a bath together before we went to bed. She would wash me and I would wash her and we'd fool around a little and then jump out and dry each other, with big towels. Then we'd wind ourselves around each other, naked under the covers.

But now she lit a cigarette before getting into bed. That was a danger signal. She wanted to fight. A bottle of energy pills had spilled out of her purse and that had pissed me off, so I was a little ready too. I was no longer in so loving a mood. Seeing that bottle of energy pills had set off a whole train of fantasies. Now that I knew she had a woman lover, now that I knew she slept with other men when I was away back with my family in New York, I no longer loved her as much, and the energy pills made me think that she needed them to make love to me because she was fucking other people. So now I didn't feel like it. She sensed this.

"I didn't know you read Graham Greene," I said. "That crack about the leper without his bell, that's very pretty. You saved that one up just for me."

She squinted her brown eyes over the cigarette smoke. The blond hair was loose down over her delicately beautiful face. "It's true, you know," she said. "You can go home and screw your wife and that's OK. But because I have other lovers, you think I'm just a cunt. You don't even love me anymore."

"I still love you," I said.

"You don't love me as much," she said.

"I love you enough to want to make love to you and not just fuck you," I said.

"You're really sly," she said. "You're innocent sly. You just admitted you love me less as if I tricked you into it. But you wanted me to know that. But why? Why can't women have other lovers and still love other men? You always tell me you still love your wife and you just love me more. That it's different. Why can't it be different for me? Why can't it be different for all women? Why can't we have the same sexual freedom and men still love us?"

"Because you know for sure whether it's your kid and men don't," I said. I was kidding, I think.

She threw back the covers dramatically and sprang up so that she was standing in bed. "I don't believe you said that," she said incredulously. "I can't believe that you said such an incredibly male chauvinistic thing."

"I was kidding," I said. "Really. But you know, you're not

realistic. You want me to adore you, to be really in love with you, to treat you like a virginal queen. As they did in the old days. But you reject those values that surrendering love is built on. You want us to love you like the Holy Grail, but you want to live like a liberated woman. You won't accept that if your values change, so must mine. I can't love you as you want me to. As I used to."

She started to cry. "I know," she said. "God, we loved each other so much. You know I used to fuck you when I had blinding headaches, I didn't care, I just took Percodan. And I loved it. I loved it. And now sex isn't as good, is it, now that we're honest?"

"No, it isn't," I said.

That made her angry again. She started to yell and her voice sounded like a duck quacking.

It was going to be a long night. I sighed and reached over to the table for a cigarette. It's very hard to light a cigarette when a beautiful girl is standing so that her cunt is right over your mouth. But I managed it and the tableau was so funny that she collapsed back onto the bed, laughing.

"You're right," I said. "But you know the practical arguments for women being faithful. I told you women most of the time don't know that they have venereal disease. And remember, the more guys you screw, the more chance you have of getting cervical cancer."

Janelle laughed. "You liaaarr," she drawled out.

"No kidding," I said. "All the old taboos have a practical basis."

"You bastards," Janelle said. "Men are lucky bastards."

"That's the way it is," I said smugly. "And when you start yelling, you sound just like Donald Duck."

I got hit with a pillow and had the excuse to grab and hug her and we wound up making love.

Afterward, when we were smoking a cigarette together, she said, "But I'm right, you know. Men are not fair. Women have every right to have as many sexual partners as they want. Now be serious. Isn't that true?"

"Yes," I said just as seriously as she and more. I meant it. Intellectually I knew she was right.

She snuggled up to me. "That's why I love you," she said. "You really do understand. Even at your male chauvinistic pig worst. When the revolution comes, I'm going to save your life. I'm going to say you were a good male, just misguided."

"Thanks a lot," I said.

She put out the light and then her cigarette. Very thoughtfully she said, "You really don't love me less because I sleep with others, do you?"

"No," I said.

"You know I love you really and truly," she said.

"Yeah," I said.

"And you don't think I'm a cunt for doing that, do you?" Janelle said.

"Nope," I said. "Let's go to sleep." I reached out to hold her. She moved away a little.

"Why don't you leave your wife and marry me? Tell me the truth."

"Because I have it both ways," I said.

"You bastard." She poked me in the balls with her finger.

It hurt. "Jesus," I said. "Just because I'm madly in love with you, just because I like to talk to you better than anybody, just because I like fucking you better than anybody, what gives you the balls to think I'd leave my wife for you?"

She didn't know whether I was serious or not. She decided I was kidding. It was a dangerous assumption to make.

"Very seriously," she said. "Honestly I just want to know. Why do you still stay married to your wife? Give me just one good reason."

I rolled up into a protective ball before I answered. "Because she's not a cunt," I said.

One morning I drove Janelle to the Paramount lot, where she had a day's work shooting a tiny part in one of its big pictures.

We were early, so we took a walk around what was to me an amazingly lifelike replica of a small town. It even had a false horizon, a sheet of metal rising to the sky that fooled me momentarily. The fake fronts were so real that as we walked past them, I couldn't resist opening the door of a bookstore, almost expecting to see the familiar tables and shelves covered with bright-jacketed books for sale. When I opened the door, there was nothing but grass and sand beyond the doorsill.

Janelle laughed as we kept walking. There was a window

filled with medicine bottles and drugs of the nineteenth century. We opened that door and again saw the grass and sand beyond. As we kept walking, I kept opening doors and Janelle didn't laugh anymore. She only smiled. And finally we came to a restaurant with a canopy leading to the street and beneath the canopy a man in work clothes sweeping. And for some reason the man sweeping really faked me out. I thought that we had left the sets and come into the Paramount commissary area. I saw a menu pasted in the window and I asked the workman if the restaurant was open yet. He had an old actor's rubbery face. He squinted at me. Gave a huge grin then almost closed his eyes and winked.

"Are you serious?" he said.

I went to the restaurant door and opened it, and I was really astonished. Really surprised to see again the sand and grass beyond. I closed the door and looked at the workman's face. It was almost maniacal with glee as if he had arranged this trip for me. As if he were some sort of God and I had asked him "Is life serious?" and that's why he had answered me, "Are you serious?"

I walked Janelle to the sound stage where she was shooting and she said to me, "They're so obviously fake. How could they fool you?"

"They didn't fool me," I said.

"But you so obviously expected them to be real," Janelle said. "I watched your face as you opened the doors. And I know that the restaurant fooled you."

She gave my arm a playful tug.

"You really shouldn't be let out alone," she said. "You're so dumb."

And I had to agree. But it wasn't so much that I believed. It wasn't that really. What bothered me was that I had wanted to believe that there was something beyond those doors. That I could not accept the obvious fact that behind those painted sets was nothing. That I really thought I was a magician. When I opened those doors, real rooms would appear and real people. Even the restaurant. Just before I opened the door, I saw in my mind red tablecloths and dark wine bottles and people standing silently waiting to be seated. I was really surprised when there was nothing there.

I realized it had been some kind of aberration that had made me open those doors, and yet I was glad I had done so.

I didn't mind Janelle laughing at me and I didn't mind working with that crazy actor. God, I had just wanted to be sure; and if I had not opened those doors, I would have always wondered.

Chapter 42

Osano came to LA for a movie deal and called me to have dinner. I brought Janelle along because she was dying to meet him. When dinner was over and we were having our coffee, Janelle tried to draw me out about my wife. I shrugged her off.

"You never talk about that, do you?" she said.

I didn't answer. She kept on. She was a little flushed with wine and a little uncomfortable that I had brought Osano with me. She became angry. "You never talk about your wife because you think that's dishonorable."

I still didn't say anything.

"You still have a good opinion of yourself, don't you?" Janelle said. She was now very coldly furious.

Osano was smiling a little, and just to smooth things over he played the famous brilliant writer role, caricaturing it ever so slightly. He said, "He never talks about being an orphan too. All adults are orphans really. We all lose our parents when we grow into adulthood."

Janelle was instantly interested. She had told me she admired Osano's mind and his books. She said, "I think that's brilliant. And it's true."

"It's full of shit," I said. "If you're both going to use language to communicate, use words for their meaning. An orphan is a child who grows up without parents and many times without any blood relationships in the world. An adult is not an orphan. He's a fucking prick who's got no use for his mother and father because they are a pain in the ass and he doesn't need them anymore."

There was an awkward silence, and then Osano said, "You're right, but also you don't want to share your special status with everybody."

"Yeah, maybe," I said. Then I turned to Janelle. "You and your girlfriends call each other 'sister.' Sisters mean female children born of the same parents who have usually shared the same traumatic experiences of childhood, who have imprints of their same experiences in their memory banks. That's what a sister is; good, bad or indifferent. When you call a girlfriend 'sister,' you're both full of shit."

Osano said, "I'm getting divorced again. More alimony. One thing, I'll never marry again. I've run out of alimony money."

I laughed with him. "Don't say that. You're the institution of marriage's last hope."

Janelle lifted her head and said, "No, Merlyn. You are."

We all laughed at that, and then I said I didn't want to go to to a movie. I was too tired.

"Oh, hell," Janelle said. "Let's go for a drink at Pips and play some backgammon. We can teach Osano."

"Why don't you two go?" I said coolly. "I'll go back to the hotel and get some sleep."

Osano was watching me with a sad smile on his face. He didn't say anything. Janelle was staring at me as if daring me to say it again. I made my voice as cold and loveless as possible. And yet understanding. Very deliberately I said, "Look, really I don't mind. No kidding. You two are my best friends, but I really feel like just going to sleep. Osano, be a gentleman and take my place." I said this very straight-faced.

Osano guessed right away I was jealous of him. "Whatever you say, Merlyn," he said. And he didn't give a shit about what I felt. He thought I was acting like a jerk. And I knew he would take Janelle to Pips and take her home and screw her and not give me another thought. As far as he was concerned, it was none of my business.

But Janelle shook her head. "Don't be silly. I'll go home in my car and you two can do what you want."

I could see what she was thinking. Two male chauvinistic pigs trying to divvy her up. But she also knew that if she went with Osano, it would give me the excuse never to see her again. And I guess I knew what I was doing. I was looking for a reason really to hate her, and if she went with Osano, I could do it and be rid of her.

Finally Janelle went back to the hotel with me. But I could

feel her coldness, though our bodies were warm against each other. A little later she moved away, and as I fell asleep, I could hear the rustle of the springs as she left our bed. I murmured drowsily, "Janelle, Janelle."

Chapter 43

JANELLE

I'm a *good* person. I don't care what anybody thinks, I'm a good person. All my life the men I really loved always put me down, and they put me down for what they said they loved in me. But they never accepted the fact I could be interested in other human beings, not just them. That's what screws everything up. They fall in love with me at first and then they want me to become something else. Even the great love of my life, that son of a bitch, Merlyn. He was worse than any of them. But he was the best too. He understood me. He was the best man I ever met and I really loved him and he really loved me. And he tried as hard as he could. And I tried as hard as I could. But we could never beat that masculine thing. If I even liked another man, he got sick. I could see that sick look on his face. Sure, I couldn't stand it if he even got into an interesting conversation with another woman. So what? But he was smarter than I was. He covered up. When I was around, he never paid any attention to other women even though they did to him. I wasn't that smart or maybe I felt it was too phony. And what he did was phony. But it worked. It made me love him more. And my being honest made him love me less.

I loved him because he was so smart in almost everything. Except women. He was really dumb about women. And he was dumb about me. Maybe not dumb, just that he could live only with illusions. He said that to me once and he said that I should be a better actress, that I should give him a better illusion that I loved him. I really loved him, but he said that wasn't as important as the illusion that I loved him. And I understood that and I tried. But the more I loved him the less I could do it. I wanted him to love the true me. Maybe nobody can love the true me or the true you or the true it. That's the truth—nobody can love truth. And yet I can't live without trying to be true to what I really am. Sure I lie, but only when it's important, and later, when I think the time is right, I always admit I told a lie. And that screws it up.

I always tell everybody how my father ran away when I was a little girl. And when I get drunk, I tell strangers how I tried to commit suicide when I was only fifteen, but I never tell them why. The true why. I let them think it was because my father went away, and maybe it was. I admit a lot of things about myself. That if a man I like buys me a real boozy dinner and makes me like him, I'll go to bed with him even if I'm in love with somebody else. Why is that so horrible? Men do that all the time. It's OK for them. But the man I loved the most in the whole world thought I was just a cunt when I told him that. He couldn't understand that it wasn't important. That I just wanted to get fucked. Every man does the same thing.

I never deceived a man about important things. About material things maybe I mean. I never pulled the cheap tricks some of my best friends pull on their men. I never accused a guy of being responsible when I got pregnant just to make him help me. I never tricked men like that. I never told a man I loved him when I didn't, not at the beginning anyway. Sometimes after, when I stopped loving him and he still loved me and I couldn't bear to hurt him, I'd say it. But I couldn't be that loving afterward and they'd catch on and things would cool off and we wouldn't see each other again. And I never really hated a man once I loved him no matter how hateful he was to me afterward. Men are so spiteful to women they no longer love, most men anyway, or to me anyway. Maybe because they still love me and I never love them afterward or love them a little, which doesn't mean anything. There's a big difference between loving somebody a little and loving somebody a lot.

Why do men always doubt that you love them? Why do men always doubt you are true to them? Why do men always leave you? Oh, Christ, why is it so painful? I can't love them anymore. It hurts me so and they are such pricks. Such bastards. They hurt you as carelessly as children, but you can forgive children, you don't mind. Even though they both make you cry. But not anymore, not men, not children.

Lovers are so cruel, more loving, more cruel. Not the Casanovas, Don Juans, the "cunt men" as men always call them. Not those creeps. I mean the men who truly love you. Oh, you really love and they say they do and I know it's true. And I know how they will hurt me worse than any other man in the world. I want to say, "Don't say you love me." I want to say, "I don't love you."

Once when Merlyn said he loved me, I wanted to cry because I truly loved him and I knew that he would be so cruel later when we both really knew each other, when all the illusions were gone, and when I loved him most, he would love me so much less.

I want to live in a world where men will never love women as they love them now. I want to live in a world where I will never love a man as I love him now. I want to live in a world where love never changes.

Oh, God, let me live in dreams; when I die, send me to a paradise of lies, undiscoverable and self-forgiven, and a lover will love me forever or not at all. Give me deceivers so sweet they will never cause me pain with true love, and let me deceive them with all my soul. Let us be deceivers never discovered, always forgiven. So that we can believe in each other. Let us be separated by wars and pestilence, death, madness but not by the passing of time. Deliver me from goodness, let me not regress into innocence. Let me be free.

I told him once that I had fucked my hairdresser and you should have seen the look on his face. The cool contempt. That's how men are. They fuck their secretaries, that's OK. But they put down a woman who fucks her hairdresser. And yet it's more understandable, what we do. A hairdresser does something personal. He has to use his hands on us and some of them have great hands. And they know women. I fucked my hairdresser only once. He was always telling me how good he was in bed and one day I was horny and I said OK and he came up that night and he fucked me just that once. While he was fucking me, I saw him watching me turn on. It was a power thing with him. He did all his little tricks with his tongue and his hands and special words, and I have to say it was a good fuck. But it was such a coldhearted fuck. When I came, I expected him to hold up a mirror to see how he did the back of my head. When he asked me if I liked it, I said it was terrific. He said we had to do it again sometime and I said sure. But he never asked me again even though I would have said no. So I guess I wasn't too great either.

Now what the hell is the harm in that? Why do men when they hear a story like that just put a woman down as a cunt? They would do it in a shot, every son of a bitch. It didn't mean a thing. It didn't make me any less a person. Sure, I fucked a creep. How many men, the best of them, fuck creepy women and not just once either?

I have to fight against regressing into innocence. When a man loves me, I want to be faithful to him and never fuck anybody else for the rest of my life. I want to do everything for him, but I know now that it never lasts with him or me. They start putting you down, they start making you love them less. In a million different ways.

The love of my life, the son of a bitch, I really loved him and he really loved me, I'll give him that. But I hated the way he loved me. I was his sanctuary, I was where he ran when the world was too much for him. He always said he felt safe with me alone in our hotel rooms, our different suites like different landscapes. Different walls, strange beds, prehistoric sofas, rugs with different colored bloods, but always our naked bodies the same. But that's not even true and this is funny. Once I surprised him and it was really funny. I had the big tit operation. I always wanted bigger tits—nice and round and standing up—and I finally did it. And he loved them. I told him I did it especially for him and it was partly true. But I did it so I would be less shy when I read for a part that required some nudity. Producers sometimes look at your tits. And I guess I did it for Alice too. But I told him I did it just for him and the bastard had better appreciate them. And so he did. And so he did. I always loved the way he loved me. That was always the best part of it. He really loved me—my flesh—and always told me it was special flesh, and finally I believed he couldn't possibly make love to anyone else but me. I regressed into that innocence.

But it was never true. It is, finally, never true. Nothing is. Even my reasons. Like another reason. I love women's tits and why is that unnatural? I love to suck another woman's tits and why does that disgust men? They find it so comforting—don't they think women do? We were all babies once together. Infants.

Is that why women cry so much? That they can never be

that again? Infants? Men can be. That's true, that's really true. Men can be infants again. Women can't. Fathers can be infants again. Mothers can't.

He always said that he felt safe. And I knew what he meant. When we were alone together, I could see the strain go out of his face. His eyes became softer. And when we were lying down together warm and naked, soft skin touching, and I put my arms around him and truly loved him, I could hear him sigh like a cat purring. And I knew that for that short time he was truly happy. And that I could do that was truly magical. And that I was the only human being in the world who could make him feel like that made me feel so worthwhile. That I really meant something. I wasn't just a cunt to fuck. I wasn't just somebody to talk to and be intelligent with. I was truly a witch, a love witch, a good witch, and it was terrific. At that moment we both could die happy, literally, truly die happy. We could face death and not be afraid. But only for that short time. Nothing lasts. Nothing ever will. And so we deliberately shorten it, make the end come faster, I can see that now. One day he just said, "I don't feel safe anymore," and I never loved him again.

I'm no Molly Bloom. That son of a bitch Joyce. While she was saying yes, yes, yes, her husband was saying no, no, no. I won't fuck any man who says no. Never, not anymore.

Merlyn was sleeping. Janelle got out of bed and pulled an armchair up to the window. She lit a cigarette and stared out. As she was smoking, she heard Merlyn thrash around the bed in a restless dreaming sleep. He was muttering something, but she didn't care. Fuck him. And every other man.

MERLYN

Janelle had on boxing gloves, dull red with white laces. She stood facing me, in the classic boxing stance, left extended, right hand cocked for the knockout punch. She wore white satin trunks. On her feet were black sneakers, slip-ons, no laces. Her beautiful face was grim. The delicately cut, sensuous mouth was pressed tight, her white chin tucked against her shoulder. She looked menacing. But I was fascinated by her bare breasts, creamy white and round nipples red, taut with an adrenaline that came not from love but the desire for combat.

I smiled at her. She didn't smile back. Her left flicked out and caught me on the mouth and I said, "Ah, Janelle." She hit me with two more hard lefts. They hurt like hell, and I could feel blood filling the gap beneath my tongue. She danced away from me. I put my hands out and they too had red gloves on them. I slid forward on sneakered feet and hitched up my trunks. At that moment Janelle darted in on me and hit me with a solid right hand. I actually saw green and blue stars as if I were in a comic strip. She danced away again, her breasts bobbing, the dancing red nipples mesmerizing.

I stalked her into a corner. She crouched down, her red-gloved tiny hands protecting her head. I started to throw a left hook into her delicately rounded belly, but the navel I had licked so many times repelled my hand. We went into a clinch and I said, "Ah, Janelle, cut it out. I love you, honey." She danced away and hit me again. It was like a cat ripping my eyebrow with its claw and blood started dripping down. I was blinded and I heard myself saying, "Oh, Christ."

Brushing away the blood, I saw her standing in the middle of the ring, waiting for me. Her blond hair was pulled tightly back into a bun and the rhinestone clip that held it glittered like a hypnotic charm. She hit me with two more lightning jabs, the tiny red gloves flicking in and out like tongues. But now she left an opening and I could hit the finely boned face. My hands wouldn't move. I knew that the only thing that could save me was a clinch. She tried to dance around me. I grabbed her around the waist as she tried to slip away and spun her around. Defenseless now except that the trunks did not go all the way around her body and I could see her back and her beautiful buttocks, so rounded and full, that I had always pressed against in our bed together. I felt a sharp pain in my heart and wondered what the hell she was fighting me for. I grabbed her around the waist and whispered in her ear, tiny filaments of gold hair remembered on my tongue. "Lie on your stomach," I said. She spun quickly. She hit me with a straight right I never saw coming and then I was tumbling in slow motion, upended in the air and floating down on the canvas. Stunned, I managed to get to one knee and I could hear her counting to ten in her lovely warm voice that she used to make me come. I stayed on one knee and stared up at her.

She was smiling and then I could hear her saying, "Ten, ten, ten, ten," frantically, urgently, and then a gleeful smile broke over her face and she raised both hands in the air and jumped for joy. I heard the ghostly roar of millions of women screaming in ecstatic glee; another woman, heavyset, was embracing Janelle. This woman wore a heavy turtleneck sweater with "CHAMP" stenciled across two enormous breasts. I started to cry.

Then Janelle came over to me and helped me. "It was a fair fight," she kept saying. "I beat you fair and square," and through my tears I said, "No, no, you didn't."

And then I woke up and reached out for her. But she was not in bed beside me. I got up and, naked, went into the living room of the suite. In the darkness I could see her cigarette. She was sitting in a chair, watching the foggy dawn come up over the city.

I went over and reached down and traced my hands over her face. There was no blood, her features were unbroken and she reached one velvety hand up to touch mine as it covered her naked breast.

"I don't care what you say," I said. "I love you whatever the hell that means."

She didn't answer me.

After a few minutes she got up and led me back to the bed. We made love and then fell asleep in each other's arms. Half asleep, I murmured, "Jesus, you nearly killed me."

She laughed.

Chapter 44

Something was waking me out of a deep sleep. Through the cracks of the shutters of the hotel room I could see the rose light of early California dawn, and then I heard the phone ringing. I just lay there for a few seconds. I saw Janelle's blond head snuggled almost under the covers. She was sleeping far apart from me. As the phone kept on ringing, I got a panicky feeling. It must be early in the morning here in Los Angeles, so the call had to be from New York and it had to be from my wife. Valerie never called me except in an emergency, something had happened to one of my kids. There was also the feeling of guilt that I would be receiving this call with Janelle in bed beside me. I hoped she wouldn't wake up as I picked up the phone.

The voice on the other end said, "Is that you, Merlyn?"

And it was a woman's voice. But I couldn't recognize it. It wasn't Valerie.

I said, "Yes, who is it?"

It was Artie's wife, Pam. There was a tremor in her voice. "Artie had a heart attack this morning."

And when she said it, I felt a lessening of anxiety. It wasn't one of my kids. Artie had had a heart attack before and for some reason in my mind I thought of it as something not really serious.

I said, "Oh, shit. I'll get on a plane and come back right away I'll be back today. Is he in the hospital?"

There was a pause at the other end of the phone, and then I heard her voice finally break.

She said, "Merlyn, he didn't make it."

I really didn't understand what she was saying. I really didn't. I still wasn't surprised or shocked, and then I said, "You mean he's dead?"

And she said, "Yes."

I kept my voice very controlled. I said, "There's a nine

o'clock plane and I'll be on it and I'll be in New York at five and I'll come right to your house. Do you want me to call Valerie?"

And she said, "Yes, please."

I didn't say I was sorry, I didn't say anything. I just said, "Everything will be all right. I'll be there tonight. Do you want me to call your parents?"

And she said, "Yes, please."

And I said, "Are you all right?"

And she said, "Yes, I'm all right. Please come back."

And then she hung up the phone.

Janelle was sitting up in bed and staring at me. I picked up the phone and got long distance and got Valerie. I told her what had happened. I told her to meet me at the plane and she wanted to talk about it, but I told her I had to pack and get on the plane. That I didn't have any time and I would talk to her when she met me. And then I got the operator again and I called Pam's parents. Luckily I got the father and explained to him what had happened. He said he and his wife would catch the next plane to New York and he would call Artie's wife.

I hung up the phone and Janelle was staring at me, studying me very curiously. From the phone conversations she knew, but she didn't say anything. I started hitting the bed with my fist and kept saying, "No, *no, no, no.*" I didn't know I was shouting it. And then I started to cry, my body flooded with an unbearable pain. I could feel myself losing consciousness. I took one of the bottles of whiskey that was on the dresser in the room and drank. I couldn't remember how much I drank, and after that all I could remember was Janelle's dressing me and taking me down through the lobby of the hotel and putting me on a plane. I was like a zombie. It was only much later, when I had come back to Los Angeles, that she told me she had to throw me in the bath to sober me up and bring me back to consciousness and then she had dressed me, she had made the reservations and accompanied me onto the plane and told the stewardess and chief flight attendant to look out for me. I don't even remember the plane ride, but suddenly I was in New York and Valerie was waiting for me and by that time I was OK.

We drove right to Artie's house. I took charge of everything and made all the arrangements. Artie and his wife had agreed that he would be buried as a Catholic with a Catholic ceremony and I went to the local church and arranged for services. I did everything I could do and I was OK. I didn't want him lying aboveground alone in the mortuary, so I made sure the services would be next day and he would be buried right afterward. The wake would be this night. And as I went through the rituals of death, I knew I could never be the same again. That my life would change and the world around me; my magic fled.

Why did my brother's death affect me so? He was quite simple, quite ordinary, I guess. But he was truly virtuous. And I cannot think of anyone else that I have met in my life that I can say this of.

Sometimes he told me of battles on his job against its corruption and administrative pressures to soften reports on additives his tests showed were dangerous. He always refused to be pressured. But his stories were never a pain in the ass in the way of some people who always tell you how they refuse to be corrupted. Because he told them without indignation, with complete coolness. He was not unpleasantly surprised that rich men with money would insist on poisoning their fellowmen for profit. Again he was never pleasantly surprised that he could resist such corruption; he made it very clear that he felt no obligation to do battle for the right.

And he had no delusions of grandeur about how much good his fighting did. They could go around him. I remembered the stories he told me about how other agency chemists made official tests and gave favorable reports. But my brother never did. He always laughed when he told me these stories. He knew the world was corrupt. He knew his own virtue was not valuable. He did not prize it.

He just simply refused to give it up. As a man would refuse to give up an eye, a leg; if he had been Adam, he would have refused to give up a rib. Or so it seemed. And he was that way in everything. I knew that he had never been unfaithful to his wife, though he was really a handsome man and the sight of a very pretty girl made him smile with pleasure; and he rarely smiled. He loved intelligence in a man or a woman, yet never was seduced by that either, as many people are. He never accepted money or favors. He never asked for mercy to his feelings or his fate. And yet he would never judge others, outwardly at least. He rarely spoke, always listened, because that was his pleasure. He demanded the barest minimum of life.

And Christ, what breaks my heart now is that I remember he was virtuous even as a kid. He never cheated in a ball game, never stole from a store, was never insincere with a girl. He never bragged or lied. I envied his purity then and I envy it now.

And he was dead. A tragic, defeated life, so it seemed, and I envied him his life. For the first time I understood the comfort people get from religion, those people who believe in a just God. That it would comfort me to believe now that my brother could not be refused his just reward. But I knew that was all shit. I was alive. Oh, that I should be alive and rich and famous, enjoying all the pleasures of the flesh on this earth, that I should be victorious and not anywhere near the man he was, and he so ignominiously put to death.

Ashes, Ashes, Ashes, I wept as I had never wept for my lost father or my lost mother, for lost loves and all other defeats. And so at least I had that much decency, to feel anguish at his death.

Tell me, anyone, why all this should be? I cannot bear to look at my brother's dead face. Why was I not lying in that casket, devils dragging me to hell? My brother's face had never looked so strong, so composed, so at rest, but it was gray as if powdered over with the dust of granite. And then his five children came, dressed in neat funerality, and knelt before his coffin to say their final prayers. I could feel my heart break, tears came against my will. I left the chapel.

But anguish is not important enough to last. In the fresh air I knew that I was alive. That I would dine well the next day, that in time I would have a loving woman again, that I would write a story and walk along the beach. Only those we most love can cause our death, and only of them we must beware. Our enemies can never harm us. And at the core of my brother's virtue was that he feared neither his enemies nor those he loved. So much the worst for him. Virtue is its own reward and fools are they who die.

But then weeks later I heard other stories. How early in his marriage, when his wife became ill, he had gone to her parents weeping and begged for money to get his wife well.

How, when the final heart attack came and his wife tried to give him mouth-to-mouth resuscitation, he waved her wearily away the moment before he died. But what had that final gesture really meant? That life had become too much for him, his virtue too heavy to bear? I remember Jordon again, was he too a virtuous man?

Eulogies for suicides condemn the world and blame it for their deaths. But could it be that those who put themselves to death believed there was no fault anywhere, some organisms must die? And they saw this more clearly than their bereaved lovers and friends?

But all this was too dangerous. I extinguished my grief and my reason and put my sins forward as my shield. I would sin, beware and live forever.

Book VII

Chapter 45

A week later I called Janelle to thank her for getting me on the plane. I got her answering machine voice disguised in a French accent, asking me to leave a message.

When I spoke, her real voice was there, breaking in.

"Who are you ducking?" I said.

Janelle was laughing. "If you knew how your voice sounded," she said. "So sour. . . ."

I laughed too.

"I was ducking your friend Osano," she said. "He keeps calling me."

I felt a sick feeling in my stomach. I wasn't surprised. But I liked Osano so much and he knew how I felt about Janelle. I hated the idea that he would do that to me. And then I didn't really give a shit. It was no longer important.

"Maybe he was just trying to find out where I was," I said.

"No," Janelle said. "After I put you on the plane, I called him and told him what happened. He was worried about you, but I told him you were OK. Are you?"

"Yes," I said.

She didn't ask me any questions about what had happened when I got home. I loved that about her. Her knowing I wouldn't want to talk about it. And I knew she would never tell Osano about what happened that morning when I got the news about Artie, how I fell apart.

I tried to act cool. "Why are you ducking him? You enjoyed his company at dinner when we were together. I'd think you'd jump at the chance of meeting him again."

There was a pause at the other end, and then I heard a tone in her voice that showed she was angry. It became very calm. The words were precise. As if she were pulling back a bow to send her words like arrows.

"That's true," she said, "and the first time he called I was delighted and we went out to dinner together. He was great fun."

Not believing the answer I would get, I asked out of some remaining jealousy, "Did you go to bed with him?"

Again there was the pause. I could almost hear the bow's twang as she sent off the arrow.

"Yes," she said.

Neither of us said anything. I felt really lousy, but we had our rules. We could never reproach each other anymore, just take our revenge.

Very shittily but automatically I said, "So how was it?"

Her voice was very bright, very cheery as if she were talking about a movie. "It was fun. You know he makes such a big deal out of going down on you that it builds up your ego."

"Well," I said casually, "I hope he's better at it than I am."

Again there was the long pause. And then the bow snapped and the voice was hurt and rebellious. "You have no right to be angry," she said. "You have no goddamn right to be angry about what I do with other people. We settled that before."

"You're right," I said. "I'm not angry." And I wasn't. I was more than that. At that moment I gave her up as someone I loved. How many times had I told Osano how much I loved Janelle? And Janelle knew how I cared about Osano. They had both betrayed me. There was no other word for it. The funny thing was that I wasn't angry with Osano. Just with her.

"You are angry," she said, as if I were being unreasonable.

"No, really I'm not," I said. She was paying me off for my being with my wife. She was paying me off for a million things, but if I hadn't asked her that specific question about going to bed, she wouldn't have told me. She wouldn't have been that cruel. But she wouldn't lie to me anymore. She had told me that once, and now she was backing it up. What she did was none of my business.

"I'm glad you called," she said. "I've missed you. And don't be mad about Osano. I won't see him again."

"Why not?" I said. "Why shouldn't you?"

"Oh, shit," she said. "He was fun, but he couldn't keep it up. Oh, shit, I promised myself I wouldn't tell you that." She laughed.

Now, being a normal jealous lover, I was delighted to hear that my dearest friend was partially impotent. But I just said carelessly, "Maybe it was you. He's had a lot of devoted females in New York."

Her voice was gay and bright. "God," she said, "I worked hard enough. I could have brought a corpse back to life." She laughed cheerfully.

So now, as she meant me to, I had a vision of her ministering to an invalid Osano, kissing and sucking at his body, her blond hair flying. I felt very sick.

I sighed. "You hit too hard," I said. "I quit. Listen, I want to thank you again for taking care of me. I can't believe you got me in that tub."

"That's my gym class," Janelle said. "I'm very strong, you know." Then her voice changed. "I'm awfully sorry about Artie. I wish I could have gone back with you and taken care of you."

"Me too," I said. But the truth was that I was glad that she couldn't. And I was ashamed that she had seen me break down. I felt in a curious way that she could never feel the same way about me again.

Her voice came very quietly over the phone. "I love you," she said.

I didn't answer.

"Do you still love me?" she said.

Now it was my turn. "You know I'm not allowed to say things like that."

She didn't answer.

"You're the one that told me that a married man should never tell a girl he loves her unless he's ready to leave his wife. In fact, he's not allowed to tell her that unless he's left his wife."

Finally Janelle's voice came over the phone. It was all choked with angered breaths.

"Fuck you," she said, and I could hear the phone slamming down.

I would have called her back, but then she could let that

phony French-accented voice answer. "Mademoiselle Lambert isn't at home. Could you please leave your name?" So I thought, Fuck you, too. And I felt great. But I knew we weren't through yet.

Chapter 46

When Janelle told me about her screwing Osano, she couldn't know how I felt. That I had seen Osano make a pass at every woman he met unless she was absolutely ugly. That she had fallen for his sweeping approach, that she had been so easy for him, made her seem less in my eyes. She had been a pushover, like so many women. And I felt that Osano felt some contempt for me. That I had been so madly in love with a girl he had been able to push over in just one evening.

So I wasn't heartbroken, just depressed. An ego thing, I guess. I thought of telling Janelle all this, and then I saw that that would be just a cheap shot. To make her feel trampy. And then too I knew she would fight back. Why the hell shouldn't she be a pushover? Weren't men pushovers for girls who fucked everybody? Why should she take into account that Osano's motives were not pure? He was charming, he was intelligent, he was talented, he was attractive and he wanted to fuck her. Why shouldn't she fuck him? And where was it any of my business? My poor male ego had its nose out of joint, that's all. Of course, I could tell her Osano's secret, but that would be a cheap, irrelevant revenge.

Still, I was depressed. Fair or not, I liked her less.

On the next trip West, I didn't call Janelle. We were in the final stages of complete alienation, which is classic in affairs of this kind. Again, as I always did in anything I was involved with, I had read the literature and I was a leading expert on the ebb and flow of the human love affair. We were in the stage of saying good-bye to each other but coming back together once in a while to ward off the blow of final separation. And so I didn't call her because it was really all over, or I wanted it to be.

Meanwhile, Eddie Lancer and Doran Rudd had talked me into going back to the picture. It was a painful experience.

Simon Bellfort was just a tired old hack doing the best he could and scared shitless of Jeff Wagon. His assistant, "Slime City" Richetti, was really a gopher for Simon but tried to give us some of his own ideas on what should be in the script. Finally one day after a particular asshole idea I turned to Simon and Wagon and said, "Get that guy out of here."

There was an awkward silence. I'd made up my mind. I was going to walk out and they must have sensed it, because finally Jeff Wagon said quietly, "Frank, why don't you wait for Simon in my office?" Richetti left the room.

There was an awkward silence and I said, "I'm sorry, I didn't mean to be rude. But are we serious about this fucking script or not?"

"Right," Wagon said. "Let's get on with it."

On the fourth day, after working at the studio, I decided to see a movie. I had the hotel call me a taxi and had the taxi drive me to Westwood. As usual, there was a long line waiting to get in and I took my place in it. I had brought a paperback book along with me to read while waiting in line. After the movie I planned to go to a restaurant nearby and call a taxi to take me back to the hotel.

The line was at a standstill, all young kids talking about movies in a knowledgeable way. The girls were pretty and the young men with their beards and long hair prettier in a Christlike way.

I sat down on the curb of the sidewalk to read and nobody paid any attention to me. Here in Hollywood this was not eccentric behavior. I was intent on my book when I became conscious of a car horn honking insistently and I looked up. There was a beautiful Phantom Rolls-Royce stopped in front of me, and I saw Janelle's bright rosy face in the driver's seat.

"Merlyn," Janelle said, "Merlyn, what are you doing here?"

I got up casually and said, "Hi, Janelle." I could see the guy in the Rolls-Royce passenger seat. He was young, handsome and beautifully dressed in a gray suit and gray silk tie. He had beautifully cut hair, and he didn't seem to mind stopping so that Janelle could talk to me.

Janelle introduced us. She mentioned that he was the owner of the car. I admired the car and he said how much he admired my book and how eagerly he was waiting for the picture. Janelle said something about his working at a studio in some executive position. She wanted me to know that she wasn't just going out with a rich guy in a Rolls-Royce, that he was part of the movie business.

Janelle said, "How did you get down here? Don't tell me you're finally driving."

"No," I said. "I took a taxi."

Janelle said, "How come you're waiting in line?"

I looked by her and said I didn't have beautiful friends with me with their Academy cards to get in.

She knew I was kidding. Whenever we had to go to a movie, she would always use her Academy card to get ahead. "You wouldn't use the card even if you had it," he said.

She turned to her friend and said, "That's the kind of dope he is." But there was a little bit of pride in her voice. She really loved me for not doing things like that, even though she did.

I could see that Janelle was stricken, pitied me having to take a taxi to go to the movies alone, forced to wait in line like any peasant. She was building a romantic scenario. I was her desolate, broken husband, looking in through the window and seeing his former wife and happy children with a new husband. There were tears in her gold-flecked brown eyes.

I knew I had the upper hand. This handsome guy in the Rolls-Royce didn't know that he was going to lose out. But then I got to work on him. I got him in a conversation about his work and he started chatting away. I pretended to be very interested and he went on and on with the usual Hollywood bullshit and I could see Janelle getting very nervous and irritated. She knew he was a dummy, but she didn't want me to know he was a dummy. And then I started admiring his Rolls-Royce and the guy really became animated. In five minutes I knew more about a Rolls-Royce than I wanted to know. I kept admiring the car and then I used Doran's old joke that Janelle knew and I repeated it word for word. First I made the guy tell me how much it cost and then I said, "For that kind of money this car should give head." She hated that joke.

The guy started to laugh and laugh, and he said, "That's the funniest thing I ever heard."

Janelle's face was flushed. She looked at me and then I saw the line moving and I had to get into my place. I told the guy it was very nice meeting him and told Janelle that it was great to see her again.

Two and a half hours later I walked out of the movie and I saw Janelle's familiar Mercedes parked in front of the theater. I got in.

"Hi, Janelle," I said. "How did you get rid of him?"

She said, "You son of a bitch."

And I laughed and I reached over and she gave me a kiss and we drove to my hotel and spent the night.

She was very loving that night. She asked me once, "Did you know I would come back to get you?"

And I said, "Yes."

And she said, "You bastard."

It was a wonderful night, but in the morning it was as if nothing had happened. We said good-bye.

She asked me how long I would be in town. I said I had three days more and then I would be back in New York.

She said, "Will you call me?"

I said I didn't think I would have time.

She said, "Not to meet me, just call me."

I said, "I will."

I did, but she wasn't in. I got her French-accented voice on the machine. I left a message and then I went back to New York.

The last time I ever saw Janelle was really an accident. I was in my Beverly Hills Hotel suite and I had an hour to kill before going out to dinner with some friends and I couldn't resist the impulse to call her. She agreed to meet me for a drink at the La Dolce Vita bar, which was only about five minutes away from the hotel. I went right over there and in a few minutes she came in. We sat at the bar and had a drink and talked casually as if we were just acquaintances. She swung around on the barstool to get her cigarette lit by the bartender, and as she did so, her foot hit my leg slightly, not even enough to dirty the trousers, and she said, "Oh, I'm sorry."

And for some reason that broke my heart, and when she lifted her eyes after lighting her cigarette, I said, "Don't do that."

And I could see the tears in her eyes.

It was in the literature on breaking up, the last tender moments of sentiment, the last flutters of a dying pulse, the last flush of a rosy cheek before death. I didn't think of it then.

We held hands, left the bar and went to my hotel suite. I called my friends to cancel my appointment. Janelle and I had dinner in the suite. I lay back on the sofa, and she took her favorite position with legs tucked underneath her and her upper body leaning on mine so that we were always in touch with each other. In that way she could look down at my face and look into my eyes and see if I lied to her. She still thought that she could read somebody's face. But also from my position, looking up, I could see the lovely line that her neck made between her chin and neck and the perfect triangulation of her face.

We just held each other for a while, and then, looking deep into my eyes, she said, "Do you still love me?"

"No," I said, "but I find it painful to be without you."

She didn't say anything for a while, and then she repeated with a peculiar emphasis, "I'm serious, really I am serious. Do you still love me?"

And I said seriously, "Sure," and it was true, but I said it in that way to tell her that even though I loved her, it didn't make any difference, that we could never be the same again and that I would never be at her mercy again, and I saw that she recognized that immediately.

"Why do you say it like that?" she said. "You still don't forgive me for the quarrels we had?"

"I forgive you for everything," I said, "except for going to bed with Osano."

"But that didn't mean anything," she said. "I just went to bed with him and then it was all over. It really didn't mean anything."

"I don't care," I said, "I'll never forgive you for that."

She thought that over and went to get another glass of wine, and after she had drunk a bit, we went to bed. The magic of her flesh still had its power. And I wondered if out of the silly romanticism of love stories there could be a basis of scientific fact. It could be true, that in the many millions of disparate cells a person met with a person of the opposite sex who had those very same cells and those cells responded to each other. That it had nothing to do with power or class or intelligence, nothing to do with virtue or sin. It was quite simply a scientific response of similar cells. How easy it would be then to understand.

We were in bed naked, making love, when suddenly Janelle sat up and withdrew from me.

"I have to go home," she said.

And it wasn't one of her deliberate acts of punishment. I could see that she could no longer bear to be here. Her body seemed to shrivel up, her breasts became flatter, her face gaunt with tension as if she had suffered some frightful blow, and she looked me directly in the eyes without any attempt of apology or excuses, without any attempt to reassure me for my hurt ego. She said again as simply as before, "I have to go home."

I didn't dare touch her to reassure her. I started to dress and I said, "It's OK. I understand. I'll go downstairs with you to get your car."

"No," she said. She was dressed now. "You don't have to."

And I could see she couldn't bear to be with me, that she wanted me out of her sight. I let her out of the suite. We didn't attempt to kiss each other good-bye. She tried to smile at me before she turned away but could not.

I closed and locked the door and went to bed. Despite the fact that I had been interrupted in mid-course, I found that I had no sexual excitement left. The repulsion she had for me had killed any sexual desire, but my ego wasn't hurt. I really felt I understood what had happened, and I was as relieved as she was. I fell asleep almost immediately without dreams. In fact, it was the best sleep I had had in years.

Chapter 47

Cully, making his final plans to depose Gronevelt, could not think of himself as a traitor. Gronevelt would be taken care of, receive a huge sum of money for his interest in the hotel, be allowed to keep his living quarters suite. Everything would be as it had been before except that Gronevelt would no longer have any real power. Certainly Gronevelt would have "The Pencil." He still had many friends who would come to the Xanadu to gamble. But since Gronevelt "Hosted" them, that would be a profitable courtesy.

Cully thought he would never have done this had Gronevelt not had his stroke. Since that stroke the Xanadu Hotel had slid downhill. Gronevelt had simply not been strong enough to act quickly and make the right decisions when necessary.

But still Cully felt some guilt. He remembered the years he had spent with Gronevelt. Gronevelt had been like a father to him. Gronevelt had helped him ascend to power. He had spent many happy days with Gronevelt listening to his stories, making the rounds of the casino. It had been a happy time. He had even given Gronevelt first shot at Carole, beautiful "Charlie Brown." And for a moment he wondered where Charlie Brown was now, why she had run off with Osano, and then he remembered how he had met her.

Cully had always loved to accompany Gronevelt on his casino rounds, which Gronevelt would usually make around midnight, after dinner with friends or after a private dinner with a girl in his suite. Then Gronevelt would come down to the casino and tour his empire. Searching for signs of betrayal, spotting traitors or outside hustlers all trying to destroy his god, percentage.

Cully would walk beside him, noting how Gronevelt

seemed to become stronger, more upright, the color in his cheeks better as if he took strength through the casino's carpeted floor.

One night in the dice pit Gronevelt heard a player ask one of the dice croupiers what time it was. The dice croupier looked at his wristwatch and said, "I don't know, it stopped."

Gronevelt was immediately alert, staring at the croupier. The man had on a wristwatch with a black face, very large, very macho with chronometers in it, and Gronevelt said to the croupier, "Let me see your watch."

The croupier looked startled for a moment and then thrust out his arm. Gronevelt held the croupier's hand in his, looking at the watch, and then with the quick fingers of the born card mechanic he worked the wristwatch off the man's arm. He smiled at the croupier. "I'll hold this for you up in my office," he said. "In an hour you can come up for it or you can be out of this casino. If you come up for it, I'll give you an apology. Five hundred bucks' worth." Then Gronevelt turned away, still holding the watch.

Up in Gronevelt's suite Gronevelt had shown Cully how the watch worked. That it was hollow and there was a slot in its top through which a chip could be slipped. Gronevelt easily took the watch apart with some little tools in his desk, and when it was open, there was a single solitary gold-flecked hundred-dollar black chip.

Gronevelt said musingly, "I wonder if he just used this watch himself or whether he rented it out to other shift workers. It's not a bad idea, but it's small potatoes. What could he take out on the shift? Three hundred, four hundred dollars." Gronevelt shook his head. "Everybody should be like him. I'd never have to worry."

Cully went back down to the casino. The pit boss told him that the croupier had resigned and already left the hotel.

That was the night that Cully met Charlie Brown. He saw her at the roulette wheel. A beautiful, slender blond girl with a face so innocent and young that he wondered if she was legally of age to gamble. He saw that she was dressed well, sexily but without any real flair. So he guessed that she was not from New York or Los Angeles, but from one of the Midwest cities.

Cully kept an eye on her as she played roulette. And then, when she wandered over to one of the blackjack tables, he followed her. He went into the pit behind the dealer. He saw she didn't know how to play the percentages in blackjack, so he chatted with her, telling her when to hit and when to stick. She started making money, her pile of chips growing higher. She gave Cully plenty of encouragement when he asked if she was alone in town. She said no, she was with a girlfriend.

Cully gave her his card. It read, "Vice-president, Xanadu Hotel." "If you want anything," he said, "just call me. Would you like to go to our show tonight and have dinner as my guest?"

The girl said that would be marvelous. "Could it be for me and my girlfriend?"

Cully said, "OK." He wrote something on the card before he gave it to her. He said, "Just show that to the maître d' before the dinner show. If you need anything else, give me a call." Then he walked away.

Sure enough, after the dinner show he heard himself being paged. He picked up the call and he heard the girl's voice.

"This is Carole," the girl said.

Cully said, "I'd know your voice anywhere, Carole, you were the girl at the blackjack table."

"Yes," she said. "I just wanted to call and thank you. We had a marvelous time."

"I'm glad," Cully said. "And whenever you come into town, please call me and I'll be happy to do anything I can for you. In fact, if you can't get reservations for a room, call me and I'll fix it for you."

"Thank you," Carole said. Her voice sounded a little disappointed.

"Wait a minute," Cully said. "When are you leaving Vegas?"

"Tomorrow morning," Carole said.

"Why don't you let me buy you and your girlfriend a farewell drink?" Cully said. "It would be my pleasure."

"That would be wonderful," the girl said.

"OK," Cully said. "I'll meet you by the baccarat table."

Carole's friend was another pretty girl with dark hair and pretty breasts, dressed a little more conservatively than her friend. Cully didn't push it. He bought them drinks at the casino lounge, found out that they came from Salt Lake City and, though they were not yet working at any job, they hoped to be models.

"Maybe I can help you," Cully said. "I have friends in the business in Los Angeles and maybe we can get you two girls a start. Why don't you call me in the middle of next week and I'm sure I'll have something for you two either here or in Los Angeles?" And that's how they left it for that night.

The next week, when Carole called him, he gave her the phone number of a modeling agency in Los Angeles where he had a friend, and told her she would almost surely get some kind of a job. She said she was coming into Vegas the following weekend, and Cully said, "Why don't you stay at our hotel? I'll comp you. It won't cost you a penny." Carole said she would be delighted.

That weekend everything fell into place. When Carole checked in, the desk called his office. He made sure there were flowers and fruit in her room, and then he called her and asked if she would like to have dinner with him. She was delighted. After dinner he took her to one of the shows on the Strip and to some of the other casinos to gamble. He explained to her he could not gamble at the Xanadu because his name was on the license. He gave her a hundred dollars to play blackjack and roulette. She squealed with delight. He kept a sharp eye on her and she didn't try to slip any chips into her handbag, which meant she was a straight girl. He made sure that she would be impressed with the greetings he got from the maître d' at the hotel and pit bosses at the casinos. By the time the night was through Carole had to know that he was a very important man in Vegas. When they got back to the Xanadu, he said to her, "Would you like to see what a vice-president's suite looks like?"

She gave him an innocent grin and said, "Sure." And when they got up to the suite, she made the proper nods of exclamations of delight and then flopped down on the sofa in an exaggerated sprawled show of tiredness. "Wow," she said. "Vegas is sure different from Salt Lake City."

"You ever think of living here?" Cully said. "A girl as beautiful as you could have a great time. I'd introduce you to all the best people."

"Would you?" Carole said.

"Sure," Cully said. "Everybody would love to know a beautiful girl like you."

"Uh-uh," she said. "I'm not beautiful."

"Sure you are," Cully said. "You know you are."

By this time he was sitting beside her on the sofa. He placed one hand on her stomach, bent over and kissed her on the mouth. She tasted very sweet, and as he kissed her, he made his hand go into her skirt. There was no resistance. She kissed him back, and Cully, thinking of his expensive sofa covering, said, "Let's go into the bedroom."

"OK," she said. And holding hands, they went into the bedroom. Cully undressed her. She had one of the most beautiful bodies he had ever seen. Milk white. A golden blond bush to match her hair, and her breasts sprang out as soon as she took her clothes off. And she wasn't shy. When Cully undressed, she ran her hands over his belly and his crotch and leaned her face against his stomach. He touched her head downward and with that encouragement she did what she wanted to do. He let her for a moment and then took her into the bed.

They made love, and when it was over, she buried her face in his neck with her arms around him and sighed contentedly. They rested and Cully thought about it and evaluated her charms. Well, she was great-looking and not a bad cocksucker, but she wasn't that great. He had a lot to teach her and now his mind was working. She really was one of the most beautiful girls he had ever seen, and the innocence of her face was an extra charm set off by the lushness of her slim body. In clothes she looked slender. Without clothes she was a delightful surprise. She was classically voluptuous, Cully thought. The best body he had ever seen and, though no virgin, still inexperienced, still uncynical, still very sweet. And Cully had a flash of inspiration. He would use this girl as a weapon. As one of his tools for power. There were hundreds of good-looking girls in Vegas. But they were either too dumb or too hard or they didn't have the right mentors. He would make her into something special. Not a hooker. He would never be a pimp. He would never take a penny from her. He would make her the dream woman of every gambler that came to Vegas. But first, of course, he would have to fall in love with her and make her fall in love with him. And after that was out of the way, they could get down to business.

Carole never went back to Salt Lake City. She became Cully's mistress and hung out in his suite although she lived in an apartment house next to the hotel. Cully made her take tennis lessons, dancing lessons. He got one of Xanadu's classiest show girls to teach her how to use makeup and dress properly. He arranged modeling jobs in Los Angeles and pretended to be jealous of her. He'd question her about how she spent nights in Los Angeles when she stayed over night and question her relationship with the photographers at the agency.

Carole would smother him with kisses and say, "Honey, I couldn't make love with anybody but you now."

And as far as he could tell, she was sincere. He could have checked on her, but it wasn't important. He let the love affair go for three months, and then one night, when she was in his suite, he said to her, "Gronevelt is really feeling low tonight. He's had some bad news. I tried to get him to come out for a drink with us, but he's up in his suite all by himself." Carole had met Gronevelt in her comings and goings in the hotel and one night had had dinner with him and Cully. Gronevelt had been charming with her in his courtly way. Carole liked him.

"Oh, how sad," Carole said.

Cully smiled. "I know whenever he sees you, it cheers him up. You're so beautiful," he said. "With that great face of yours. Men love an innocent face." And it was true. Her eyes were spaced wide in a face sprinkled with tiny freckles. She looked like a piece of candy. Her blond hair, tawny yellow, was tousled like a child's.

"You look just like that kid in the comic strip," Cully said. "Charlie Brown." And that became her name in Vegas. She was delighted.

Charlie Brown said, "Older men always liked me. Some of my father's friends would make passes at me."

Cully said, "Sure they did. How do you feel about that?"

"Oh, I never got mad," she said. "I was sort of flattered and I never told my father. They were really nice. They always brought me presents and they never really did anything bad."

"I've got an idea," Cully said. "Why don't I call Gronevelt and you go up there and keep him company? I have some things to do down in the casino. Do your best to cheer him up." He smiled at her, and she looked at him gravely.

"Okay," she said.

Cully gave her a fatherly kiss. "You know what I mean, don't you?" he said.

"I know what you mean." And for a moment Cully, looking at that angelic face, felt a tiny arrow of guilt.

But she gave him a brilliant smile. "I don't mind," she said. "I really don't, and I like him. But are you sure he wants me to?"

And then Cully was reassured. "Honey," he said, "don't worry. You just go up and I'll give him a call. He'll be expecting you, and you just be your natural self. He'll absolutely love you. Believe me." And as he said that, he reached for the phone.

He called Gronevelt's suite and heard Gronevelt's amused voice say, "If you're sure she wants to come up, by all means. She's a lovely girl."

And Cully hung up the phone and said, "Come on, honey. I'll take you up there."

They went to Gronevelt's suite. Cully introduced her as Charlie Brown and could see Gronevelt was delighted with the name. Cully made them all drinks and they sat around and talked. Then Cully excused himself, and said that he had to go down to the casino and left them together.

He didn't see Charlie Brown that night at all and knew she had spent it with Gronevelt. The next day, when he saw Gronevelt, he said, "Was she OK?"

And Gronevelt said, "She was fine. Lovely, lovely girl. Sweet girl. I tried to give her some money, but she wouldn't take it."

"Well," Cully said, "you know she's a young girl. She's a little new at this. But was she OK with you?"

Gronevelt said, "Fine."

"Should I make sure that you could see her whenever you want to?"

"Oh, no," Gronevelt said. "She's a little too young for me, I'm a little uncomfortable with girls that young, especially when they don't take money. In fact, why don't you buy her a present for me in the jewelry shop?"

When Cully got back to his office, he called Charlie Brown's apartment. "Did you have a good time?" Cully said.

"Oh, he was just great," Charlie Brown said. "He was such a gentleman."

Cully began to be a little worried. "What do you mean he was such a gentleman? Didn't you do anything?"

"Oh, sure we did," Charlie Brown said. "He was great. You wouldn't think someone that old could be so great. I'll cheer him up anytime he wants."

Cully made a date with her to have dinner that night, and when he hung up the phone, he leaned back his chair and tried to think it out. He had hoped Gronevelt would fall in love and he could use her as a weapon against Gronevelt. But somehow Gronevelt had sensed all this. There was no way to get to Gronevelt through women. He had had too many of them. He had seen too many of them corrupted. He did not know the meaning of virtue and so could not fall in love. He could not fall in love with lust because it was too easy. "You don't have a percentage going with you against women," Gronevelt said. "You should never give away your edge."

And so Cully thought, well, maybe not with Gronevelt, but there were plenty of other wheels in town that Charlie could wreck. At first he had thought that it was her lack of technical facility. After all, she was a young girl and not an expert. But in the past few months he had taught her a few things and she was much better than when he had first had her. OK. He couldn't get Gronevelt, which would have been ideal for all of them, and now he would have to use her in a more general way. So in the months that followed Cully "turned her out." He fixed her up with weekend dates with the biggest high rollers that came to Vegas, and he taught her never to take money from them and not always to go to bed with them. He explained his reasoning to her. "You're looking for the big shot only. Someone who's going to fall in love with you and going to lay plenty of money on you and going to buy you plenty of presents. But they won't do that if they think they can lay a couple of hundred on you just for screwing you. You're going to have to play it like a soft, soft hustler. In fact, it could be a good idea sometimes not to screw them the first night. Just like the old days. But if you do, just make believe it's because they óverpowered you."

He was not surprised that Charlie agreed to do everything that he told her. He had on the first night detected the masochism so often found in beautiful women. He was familiar with that. The lack of self-worth, the desire to please someone that they thought really cared about them. It was, of course, a pimp's trick, and Cully was no pimp, but he was doing this for her good.

Charlie Brown had another virtue. She could eat more than any person he had ever met. The first time she had let herself go Cully had been amazed. She had eaten a steak with a baked potato, a lobster with french fried potatoes, cake, ice cream, then helped polish off Cully's plate. He would show off her eating qualities, and some of the men, some of the high rollers, were infatuated by this quality in her. They would love to take her to dinner and watch her eat enormous quantities of food, which never seemed to distress her or make her less hungry and never added an inch of fat to her frame.

Charlie acquired a car, some horses to ride; she bought the town house in which she was renting an apartment and she gave her money to Cully to bank for her. Cully opened up a special guardian account. He had his own tax adviser do her taxes. He put her on the casino payroll of the hotel so that she could show a source of income. He never took a penny from her. But in a few years she fucked every powerful casino manager in Vegas, plus some of the hotel owners. She fucked high rollers from Texas, New York and California, and Cully was thinking of springing her on Fummiro. But when he suggested that to Gronevelt, Gronevelt, without giving any reason, said, "No, not Fummiro."

Cully asked him why, and Gronevelt said to him. "There's something a little flaky about that girl. Don't risk her with the real top rollers." And Cully accepted that judgment.

But Cully's biggest coup with Charlie Brown was fixing her up with Judge Brianca, the federal judge in Las Vegas. Cully arranged the rendezvous. Charlie would wait in one of the hotel's rooms, the judge would come in the back entrance of Cully's suite and the judge would enter Charlie's room. Faithfully, Judge Brianca came every week. And when Cully started asking him for favors, they both knew what the score would be.

He duplicated this setup with a member of the Gaming Commission, and it was Charlie's special qualities that made it all work. Her loving innocence, her great body. She was great fun. Judge Brianca took her on his vacation trips fishing. Some of the bankers took her on business trips to screw them when they weren't busy. When they were busy, she went shopping, and when they were horny, she fucked them. She didn't need to be courted with tender words, and she would take money only for shopping. She had the quality of making them believe that she was in love with them, that she found them wonderful to be with and to make love with, and this without making any demands. All they had to do was call her up or call Cully.

The only trouble with Charlie was that she was a slob at home. By this time her friend Sarah had moved from Salt Lake City to her apartment and Cully had "turned her out" too after a period of instruction. Sometimes when he went to their apartment, he was disgusted by the way they kept it, and one morning he was so enraged after looking around the kitchen he kicked them both out of bed, made them wash and clean up the black pots in the sink and hang up new curtains. They did it grouchily, but when he took them both out to dinner, they were so affectionate that all three of them wound up together in his suite that night.

Charlie Brown was the Vegas dream girl, and then, finally, when Cully needed her, she vanished with Osano. Cully never understood that. When she came back, she seemed to be the same, but Cully knew that if ever Osano called for her, she would leave Vegas.

For a long time Cully was Gronevelt's loyal and devoted right-hand man. Then he started thinking of replacing Gronevelt.

The seed of betrayal had been sown in Cully's mind when he had been made to buy ten points in the Xanadu Hotel and its casino.

Summoned to a meeting in Gronevelt's suite, he had met Johnny Santadio. Santadio was a man of about forty, soberly but elegantly dressed in the English style. His bearing was erect, soldierly. Santadio had spent four years at West Point. His father, one of the great Mafia leaders in New York, used political connections to secure his son, Johnny, an appointment to the military academy.

Father and son were patriots. Until the father had been forced to go into hiding to avoid a congressional subpoena. The FBI had flushed him out by holding his son, Johnny, as a hostage and sending out word that the son would be harassed until the father gave himself up. The elder Santadio had done so and had appeared before a congressional committee, but then Johnny Santadio resigned from West Point.

Johnny Santadio had never been indicted or convicted of any crime. He had never even been arrested. But merely by being his father's son, he had been denied a license to own points in the Xanadu Hotel by the Nevada Gaming Commission.

Cully was impressed by Johnny Santadio. He was quiet, well spoken and could even have passed for an Ivy League graduate from an old Yankee family. He did not even look Italian. There were just the three of them in the room, and Gronevelt opened the conversation by saying to Cully, "How would you like to own some points in the hotel?"

"Sure," Cully said. "I'll give you my marker."

Johnny Santadio smiled. It was a gentle, almost sweet smile. "From what Gronevelt has told me about you," Santadio said, "you have such a good character that I'll put up the money for your points."

Cully understood at once. He would own the points as a front for Santadio. "That's OK with me," Cully said.

Santadio said, "Are you clean enough to get a license from the Gaming Commission?"

"Sure," Cully said. "Unless they've got a law against screwing broads."

This time Santadio did not smile. He just waited until Cully had finished speaking, and then he said, "I will loan you money for the points. You'll sign a note for the amount that I put up. The note will read that you pay six percent interest and you will pay. But you have my word that you won't lose anything by paying that interest. Do you understand that?"

Cully said, "Sure."

Gronevelt said, "This is an absolutely legal operation we're doing here, Cully, I want to make that clear. But it's important that nobody know that Mr. Santadio holds your note. The Gaming Commission just on its own can veto your being on our license for that."

"I understand," Cully said. "But what if something happens to me? What if I get hit by a car or I go down in a plane? Have you thought that out? How does Santadio get his points?"

Gronevelt smiled and patted his back and said, "Haven't I been just like a father to you?"

"You really have," Cully said sincerely. And he meant it. And the sincerity was in his voice and he could see that Santadio approved of it.

"Well then," Gronevelt said, "you make out your will and you leave me the points in your will. If something should happen to you, Santadio knows I'll get the points or his money back to him. Is that OK with you, Johnny?"

Johnny Santadio nodded. Then he said casually to Cully, "Do you know of any way that I could get on the license? Can the Gaming Commission pass me despite my father?"

Cully realized that Gronevelt must have told Santadio that he had one of the gaming commissioners in his pocket. "It would be tough," Cully said, "and it would take time and it would cost money."

"How much time?" Santadio said.

"A couple of years," Cully said. "You do mean that you want to be directly on the license?"

"That's right," Santadio said.

"Will the Gaming Commission find anything on you when they investigate you?" Cully asked.

"Nothing, except that I'm my father's son," Santadio said. "And a lot of rumors and reports in the FBI files and New York police files. Just raw material. No proof of anything."

Cully said, "That's enough for the Gaming Commission to turn you down."

"I know," Santadio said. "That's why I need your help."

"I'll give it a try," Cully said.

"That's fine," Gronevelt said. "Cully, you can go to my lawyer to have your will made out so that I'll get a copy, and Mr. Santadio and I will take care of all the other details."

Santadio had shaken Cully's hand and Cully left them.

It was a year after that Gronevelt suffered his stroke, and while Gronevelt was in the hospital, Santadio came to Vegas and met with Cully. Cully assured Santadio that Gronevelt would recover and that he was still working on the Gaming Commission.

And then Santadio said, "You know the ten percent you have is not my only interest in this casino. I have other friends of mine who own a piece of the Xanadu. We're very concerned about whether Gronevelt can run the hotel after this stroke. Now, I want you to take this the right way. I have enormous respect for Gronevelt. If he can run the hotel, fine. But if he can't, if the place starts going down, I'll want you to let me know."

At that moment Cully had to make his decision to be faithful to Gronevelt to the end or to find his own future. He operated purely on instinct. "Yes, I will," he said to Santadio. "Not only for your interest and mine, but also for Mr. Gronevelt."

Santadio smiled. "Gronevelt is a great man," he said. "Anything we can do for him I would want to do. That's understood. But it's no good for any of us if the hotel goes down the drain."

"Right," Cully said. "I'll let you know."

When Gronevelt came out of the hospital, he seemed to be completely recovered and Cully reported directly to him. But after six months he could see that Gronevelt really did not have the strength to run the hotel and the casino, and he reported this to Johnny Santadio.

Santadio flew in and had a conference with Gronevelt and asked Gronevelt if he had considered selling his interest in the hotel and relinquishing control.

Gronevelt, much frailer now, sat quietly in his chair and looked at Cully and Santadio. "I see your point," he said to Santadio. "But I think with a little time I can do the job. Let me say this to you. If in another six months things don't get better, I'll do as you suggest, and of course, you get first crack at my interest. Is that good enough for you, Johnny?"

"Sure," Santadio said. "You know that I trust you more than any man I know and have more confidence in your ability. If you say you can do it in six months, I believe you, and when you say that you'll quit in six months if you can't do it, I believe you. I leave it all in your hands."

And so the meeting ended. But that night, when Cully took Santadio to get his plane back to New York, Santadio said, "Keep a close eye on things. Let me know what's happening. If he gets really bad, we can't wait."

It was then that Cully had to pause in his betrayal because in the next six months Gronevelt did improve, did get a greater grasp. But the reports that Cully gave to Santadio did not indicate this. The final recommendation to Santadio was that Gronevelt should be removed.

It was only a month later that Santadio's nephew, a pit boss in one of the hotels on the Strip, was indicted for tax evasion and fraud by a federal grand jury and Johnny Santadio flew to Vegas to have a conference with Gronevelt. Ostensibly the meeting was to help the nephew, but Santadio started on another tack.

He said to Gronevelt, "You have about three months to go. Have you come to any decision about selling me your interest?"

Gronevelt looked at Cully, who saw his face was a little sad, a little tired. And then Gronevelt turned to Santadio and said, "What do you think?"

Santadio said, "I'm more concerned about your health and the hotel. I really think that maybe the business is too much for you now."

Gronevelt sighed. "You may be right," he said. "Let me think it over. I have to go see my doctor next week, and the report he gives me will probably make it tough for me no matter what I want. But what about your nephew?" he said to Santadio. "Is there anything we can do to help?"

For the first time since Cully had known him Santadio looked angry. "So stupid. So stupid and unnecessary. I don't give a damn if he goes to jail, but if he gets convicted, it's another black mark on my name. Everybody will think I was behind him or had something to do with it. I came out here to help, but I really haven't got any ideas."

Gronevelt was sympathetic. "It's not all that hopeless," he said. "Cully here has a lock on the federal judge who will try the case. How about it, Cully? Do you still have Judge Brianca in your pocket?"

Cully thought it over. What the advantages would be. This would be a tough one to spring with the judge. The judge would have to go out on a limb, but Cully, if he had to, would make him. It would be dangerous, but the rewards might be worth it. If he could do this for Santadio, then Santadio would surely let him run the hotel after Gronevelt sold out. It would cement his position. He would be ruler of the Xanadu.

Cully looked at Santadio very intently, he made his voice

very serious, very sincere. "It would be tough," he said. "It will cost money, but if you really must have it, Mr. Santadio, I promise you your nephew won't go to jail."

"You mean he'll be acquitted?" Santadio said.

"No, I can't promise that," Cully said. "Maybe it won't go that far. But I promise you if he is convicted, he will only get a suspended sentence, and the odds are good the judge will handle the trial and charge the jury so that maybe your nephew can get off."

"That would be great," Santadio said. He shook his hand warmly. "You do this for me and you can ask me for anything you want."

And then suddenly Gronevelt was in between them, placing his hand like a benediction on both of theirs locked together.

"That's great," Gronevelt said. "We have solved all the problems. Now let's go out and have a good dinner and celebrate."

It was a week later that Gronevelt called Cully into his office. "I got my doctor's report," Gronevelt said. "He advised me to retire. But before I go, I want to try something. I've told my bank to put a million dollars into my checking account and I'm going to take my shot at the other tables in town. I'd like you to hang out with me either till I go broke or double the million."

Cully was incredulous. "You're going to go against the percentage?" he said.

"I'd like to give it one more shot," Gronevelt said. "I was a great gambler when I was a kid. If anybody can beat the percentage, I can. If I can't beat the percentage, nobody can. We'll have a great time, and I can afford the million bucks."

Cully was astonished. Gronevelt's belief in the percentage had been unshakable in all the years he had known him. Cully remembered one period in the history of the Xanadu Hotel when three months straight the Xanadu dice tables had lost money every night. The players were getting rich. Cully was sure there was a scam going on. He had fired all of the dice pit personnel. Gronevelt had had all the dice analyzed by scientific laboratories. Nothing helped. Cully and the casino manager were sure somebody had come up with a new scientific device to control the roll of the dice. There could be no other explanation. Only Gronevelt held fast.

"Don't worry," he said. "The percentage will work."

And sure enough, after three months the dice had swung just as wildly the other way. The dice pit had winning tables every night for over three months. At the end of the year it had all evened out. Gronevelt had had a congratulatory drink with Cully and said, "You can lose faith in everything, religion and God, women and love, good and evil, war and peace. You name it. But the percentage will always stand fast."

And during the next week, when Gronevelt gambled, Cully always kept that in mind. Gronevelt gambled better than any man he had ever seen. At the crap table he made all the bets that cut down the percentage of the house. He seemed to divine the ebb and flow of luck. When the dice ran cold, he switched sides. When the dice got hot, he pressed every bet to the limit. At baccarat he could smell out when the shoe would turn Banker and when the shoe would turn Player and ride the waves. At blackjack he dropped his bets to five dollars when the dealer hit a lucky streak and brought it up to the limit when the dealer was cold.

In the middle of the week Gronevelt was five hundred thousand dollars ahead. By the end of the week he was six hundred thousand dollars ahead. He kept going. Cully by his side. They would eat dinner together and gamble only until midnight. Gronevelt said you had to be in good shape to gamble. You couldn't push, you had to get a good night's sleep. You had to watch your diet and you should only get laid once every three or four nights.

By the middle of the second week Gronevelt, despite all his skill, was sliding downhill. The percentages were grinding him into dust. And at the end of two weeks he had lost his million dollars. When he bet his last stack of chips and lost, Gronevelt turned to Cully and smiled. He seemed to be delighted, which struck Cully as ominous. "It's the only way to live," Gronevelt said. "You have to live going with the percentage. Otherwise life is not worthwhile. Always remember that," he told Cully. "Everything you do in life use percentage as your god."

Chapter 48

On my last trip to California to do the final rewrite on Tri-Culture's film I ran into Osano at the Beverly Hills Hotel lounge. I was so shocked by his physical appearance that at first I didn't notice he had Charlie Brown with him. Osano must have put on about thirty pounds, and he had a huge gut that bulged out of an old tennis jacket. His face was bloated, it was speckled with tiny white fat dots. The green eyes that had once been so brilliant had faded into pale colorlessness that looked gray, and as he walked toward me, I could see that the curious lurch in his gait had become worse.

We had drinks in the Polo Lounge. As usual, Charlie drew the eyes of all the men in the room. This was not only because of her beauty and her innocent face. There were plenty of those in Beverly Hills, but there was something in her dress, something in the way she walked and glanced around the room that signaled an easy availability.

Osano said, "I look terrible, don't I?"

"I've seen you worse," I said.

"Hell, I've seen myself worse," Osano said. "You, you lucky bastard, can eat anything you want and you never put on an ounce."

"But I'm not as good as Charlie," I said. And I smiled at her and she smiled back.

Osano said, "We're catching the afternoon plane. Eddie Lancer thought he could fix me up with a script job, but it fell through, so I might as well get the hell out of here. I think I'll go to a fat farm, get in shape and finish my novel."

"How's the novel coming?" I asked.

"Great," Osano said. "I got over two thousand pages, just five hundred more to go."

I didn't know what to say to him. By this time he had acquired a reputation for not delivering with magazine publishers, even on his nonfiction books. His novel was his last hope.

"You should just concentrate on the five hundred pages," I said, "and get the goddamn book finished. That will solve all your troubles."

"Yeah, you're right," Osano said. "But I can't rush it. Even my publisher wouldn't want me to do that. This is the Nobel Prize for me, kid, when this is finished."

I looked at Charlie Brown to see if she was impressed, and it struck me that she didn't even know what the Nobel Prize was.

"You're lucky to have such a publisher," I told Osano. "They've been waiting ten years for that book."

Osano laughed. "Yeah, the classiest publishers in America. They've given me over a hundred grand and they haven't seen a page. Real class, not like these fucking movie people."

"I'll be leaving for New York in a week," I said. "I'll call you for dinner there. What's your new phone number?"

Osano said, "It's the same one."

I said, "I've called there and nobody ever answered."

"Yeah," Osano said. "I've been down in Mexico working on my book, eating those beans and tacos. That's why I got so goddamn heavy. Charlie Brown here, she didn't put on an ounce and she ate ten times as much as I did." He patted Charlie Brown on the shoulder, squeezing her flesh. "Charlie Brown," he said, "if you die before me, I'm going to have them dissect your body and find out what you got that keeps you skinny."

She smiled back at him. "That reminds me, I'm hungry," she said.

So just to cheer things up I ordered lunch for us. I had a plain salad and Osano had an omelet and Charlie Brown ordered a hamburger with french fried potatoes, a steak with vegetables, a salad and a three-scoop ice-cream desert on top of apple pie. Osano and myself enjoyed the people watching Charlie eat. They couldn't believe it. A couple of men in the next booth made audible comments, hoping to draw us into a conversation so they would have an excuse to talk to Charlie. But Osano and Charlie ignored them.

I paid the tab, and when I left, I promised to call Osano when I got to New York.

Osano said, "That would be great. I've agreed to talk in

front of that Women's Lib convention next month, and I'll need some moral support from you, Merlyn. How about if we have dinner that night and then go on to the convention?"

I was a little doubtful. I wasn't really interested in any kind of convention, and I was a little worried about Osano's getting into trouble and I'd have to bail him out again. But I said OK, that I would.

Neither one of us had mentioned Janelle. I couldn't resist saying to Osano, "Have you seen Janelle in town?"

"No," Osano said, "have you?"

"I haven't seen her for a long time," I said.

Osano stared at me. The eyes for just one second became their usual sneaky pale green. He smiled a little sadly. "You should never let a girl like that go," he said. "You just get one of them in a lifetime. Just like you get one big book in your lifetime."

I shrugged and we shook hands again. I kissed Charlie on the cheek and then I left.

That afternoon I had a story conference at Tri-Culture Studios. It was with Jeff Wagon, Eddie Lancer, and the director, Simon Bellfort. I had always thought the Hollywood legends of a writer being rude to his director and producer in a story conference were shitty no matter how funny. But for the first time, at this story conference, I could see why such things had happened. In effect, Jeff Wagon and his director were ordering us to write their story, not my novel. I let Eddie Lancer do most of the arguing, and finally Eddie, exasperated, said to Jeff Wagon, "Look, I'm not saying I'm smarter than you, I'm just saying I'm luckier. I've written four hit pictures in a row. Why not ride with my judgment?"

To me this seemed like a superbly clever argument, but Jeff Wagon and the director had puzzled looks on their faces. They didn't know what Eddie was talking about, and I could see there was no way to change their minds.

Finally Eddie Lancer said, "I'm sorry, but if that's the way you guys want to go, I have to leave this picture."

"OK," Jeff said. "How about you, Merlyn?"

"I don't see any point in my writing it your way," I said. "I don't think I'd do a good job with it."

"That's fair enough," Jeff Wagon said. "I'm sorry. Now is there any writer you know that could work on this picture with us and could have some consultations with you guys since you already have done most of the work? It would be very helpful?"

The thought flashed through my mind that I could get Osano this job. I knew he needed the money desperately and I knew that if I said I would work with Osano he would get the assignment. But then I thought of Osano in a story conference like this taking directions from men like Jeff Wagon and the director. Osano was still one of the great men in American literature, and I thought these guys would humiliate him and then fire him. So I didn't speak up.

It was only when trying to go to sleep that I realized maybe I had denied Osano the job to punish him for sleeping with Janelle.

The next morning I got a call from Eddie Lancer. He told me that he had had a meeting with his agent and his agent said that Tri-Culture Studios and Jeff Wagon were offering him a fifty-thousand-dollar extra fee to stay on the picture, and what did I think?

I told Eddie that it was perfectly OK with me, whatever he did, but that I wasn't going back on. Eddie tried to persuade me. "I'll tell them I won't go back unless they take you back and pay you twenty-five thousand dollars," Eddie Lancer said. "I'm sure they'll go for it."

Again I thought of helping Osano, and again I just couldn't do it. Eddie was going on, "My agent told me if I didn't go back on this picture, the studio would put more writers on and then try to get the new writers the credit on the picture. Now, if we don't get script credit, we lose our Writers Guild contract and TV gross points when the picture is sold to television. Also, we both have some net points which we will probably never see. But it's just an off chance the picture may be a big hit, and then we'll be kicking our asses in. It could wind up to be a sizable chunk of dough, Merlyn, but I won't go back on it if you think we should stick together and try to save our story."

"I don't give a shit about the percentage," I said, "or the credits, and as far as the story goes, what the fuck kind of story it is? It's schlock, it's not my book anymore. But you go ahead. I really don't care. I mean that."

"'OK," Eddie said, "and while I'm on, I'll try to protect your credit as much as I can. I'll call you when I'm in New York and we'll have dinner."

"Great," I said. "Good luck with Jeff Wagon."

"Yeah," Eddie said, "I'll need it."

I spent the rest of the day moving out of my office at Tri-Culture Studios and doing some shopping. I didn't want to go back on the same plane as Osano and Charlie Brown. I thought of calling Janelle, but I didn't.

A month later, Jeff Wagon called me in New York. He told me that Simon Bellfort thought that Frank Richetti should get a writing credit with Lancer and me.

"Is Eddie Lancer still with the picture?" I asked him.

"Yes," Jeff Wagon said.

"OK," I said. "Good luck."

"Thank you," Wagon said. "And we'll keep you posted on what happens. We'll all see each other at the Academy Awards dinner." And he hung up.

I had to laugh. They were turning the picture into a piece of schlock and Wagon had the nerve to talk about Academy Awards. That Oregon beauty should have taken a bigger piece out of his balls. I felt a sense of betrayal that Eddie Lancer had remained on the picture. It was true what Wagon had once said. Eddie Lancer was a natural-born screenwriter, but he was also a natural-born novelist and I knew he would never write a novel again.

Another funny thing was that though I had fought with everybody and the script was getting worse and worse and I had intended to leave, I still felt hurt. And I guess, too, in the back of my head I still hoped that if I went to California again to work on the script, I might see Janelle. We hadn't seen or spoken to each other for months. The last time I had called her up just to say hello and we had chatted for a while and at the end she had said, "I'm glad you called me," and then she waited for an answer.

I paused and said, "Me too." At that she started to laugh and mimicked me.

She said, "Me too, me too," and then she said, "Oh, it doesn't matter," and laughed gaily. She said, "Call me when you come out again."

And I said, "I will." But I knew that I would not.

A month after Wagon called, I got a call from Eddie Lancer. He was furious. "Merlyn," he said, "they're changing the script to screw you out of your credit. That guy Frank

Richetti is writing all new dialogue, just paraphrasing your words. They're changing incidents just enough so that it will seem different from your scenes and I heard them talking, Wagon and Bellfort and Richetti, about how they're going to screw you out of your credit and your percentage. Those bastards don't even pay any attention to me."

"Don't worry," I told him. "I wrote the novel and I wrote the original screenplay and I checked it with the Writers Guild, and there's no way I can get screwed out of at least a partial credit and that saves my percentage."

"I don't know," Eddie Lancer said. "I'm just warning you about what they're going to do. I hope you'll protect yourself."

"Thanks," I told him. "What about you? How are you coming on the picture?"

He said, "That fucking Frank Richetti is a fucking illiterate, and I don't know who's the bigger hack, Wagon or Bellfort. This may become one of the worst pictures ever made. Poor Malomar must be spinning in his grave."

"Yeah, poor Malomar," I said. "He was always telling me how great Hollywood was, how sincere and artistic the people there could be. I wish he were alive now."

"Yeah," Eddie Lancer said. "Listen, next time you come to California call me and we'll have dinner."

"I don't think I'll be coming to California again," I said. "If you come to New York, call me."

"OK, I will," Lancer said.

* * *

A year later the picture came out. I got credit for the book but no credit as the screenwriter. Screenwriting credit was given to Eddie Lancer and Simon Bellfort. I asked for an arbitration at the Writers Guild, but I lost. Richetti and Bellfort had done a good job changing the script, and so I lost my percentage. But it didn't matter. The picture was a disaster, and the worst of it was Doran Rudd told me that in the industry the novel was blamed for the failure of the film. I was no longer a salable product in Hollywood, and that was the only thing about the whole business that cheered me up.

One of the most scathing reviews of the film was by Clara

Ford. She murdered it from A to Z. Even Kellino's performance. So Kellino hadn't done his job too well with Clara Ford. But Houlinan took a last shot at me. He placed a story on one of the wire services headlined MERLYN NOVEL FAILS AS MOVIE. When I read that, I just shook my head with admiration.

Chapter 49

Shortly after the picture came out I was at Carnegie Hall attending the Women's National Liberation Conference with Osano and Charlie Brown. It featured Osano as the only male speaker.

Earlier we all had dinner at Pearl's, where Charlie Brown astonished the waiters by eating a Peking duck, a plate of crabs stuffed with pork, oysters in black bean sauce, a huge fish and then polished off what Osano and me had left on our plates without even smearing her lipstick.

When we got out of the cab in front of Carnegie Hall, I tried to talk Osano into going on ahead and letting me follow with Charlie Brown on my arm so that the women would think she was with me. She looked so much like the legendary harlot she would enrage the left-wingers of the convention. But Osano, as usual, was stubborn. He wanted them all to know that Charlie Brown was his woman. So when we walked down the aisle to the front, I walked behind them. As I did so, I studied the women in the hall. The only thing odd about them was that they were all women and I realized that many times in the Army, in the orphan asylum, at ball games I was used to seeing either all men or mostly men. Seeing all women this time was a shock, as if I were in an alien country.

Osano was being greeted by a group of women and led up to the platform. Charlie Brown and I sat down in the first row. I was wishing we were in the back, so I could get the hell out fast. I was so worried I hardly heard the opening speeches, and then suddenly Osano was being led to the lectern and being introduced. Osano stood for a moment waiting for the applause which did not come.

Many of the women there had been offended by his male chauvinistic essays in the male magazines years ago. Some were offended because he was one of their generation's most important writers and they were jealous of his achievement. And then there were some of his admirers who applauded very faintly just in case Osano's speech met with disfavor from the convention.

Osano stood at the lectern, a vast hulk of a man. He waited a long moment; then he leaned against the lectern arrogantly and said slowly, enunciating every word, "I'll fight you or fuck you."

The hall reverberated with boos, catcalls and hisses. Osano tried to go on. I knew he had used that phrase just to catch their attention. His speech would be in favor of Women's Liberation, but he never got a chance to make it. The boos and hisses got louder and louder, and every time Osano tried to speak they started again until Osano made an elaborate bow and marched down off the stage. We followed him up the aisle and out the doors of Carnegie Hall. The boos and hisses turned to cheers and applause, to tell Osano that he was doing what they wanted him to do. Leave them.

Osano didn't want me to go home with him that night. He wanted to be alone with Charlie Brown. But the next morning I got a call from him. He wanted me to do him a favor.

"Listen," Osano said. "I'm going down to Duke University in North Carolina to their rice diet clinic. It's supposed to be the best fat farm in the United States and they also get you healthy. I have to lose weight and the doctor seems to think that maybe my arteries are clogged and that's what the rice diet cures. There's only one thing wrong. Charlie wants to come down with me. Can you imagine that poor girl eating rice for two months? So I told her she can't come. But I have to bring my car down and I'd like you to drive it for me. We could both bring it down and hang around together for a few days and maybe have some laughs."

I thought it over for a minute and then I said, "Sure." We made a date for the following week. I told Valerie I would be gone for only three or four days. That I would drive Osano's car down with him, just spend a few days with Osano until he got set, then fly back.

"But why can't he drive the car himself?" Valerie said.

"He really doesn't look good," I said. "I don't think he's in shape to make that kind of drive. It's at least eight hours."

That seemed to satisfy Valerie, but there was one thing

that was still bothering me. Why didn't Osano want to use Charlie as his driver? He could have shipped her out as soon as they got down there, so the excuse he gave me about not wanting her to eat rice was a phony one. Then I thought maybe he was tired of Charlie and this was his way of getting rid of her. I didn't worry too much about her. She had plenty of friends who would take care of her.

So I drove Osano down to the Duke University clinic in his four-year-old Cadillac, and Osano was in great form. He even looked a little better physically. "I love this part of the country," Osano said when we were in the Southern states. "I love the way they run the Jesus Christ business down here, it's almost like every small town has its Jesus Christ store, they have Mom-and-Pop Jesus Christ stores and they make a good living and a lot of friends. One of the greatest rackets in the world. When I think about my life, I think only if I had been a religious leader instead of a writer. What a better time I would have had."

I didn't say anything. I just listened. We both knew that Osano could not have been anything but a writer and that he was just following a private flight of fantasy.

"Yeah," Osano said. "I would have got together a great hillbilly band and I would have called them Shit Kickers for Jesus. I love the way they're humble in their religion and so fierce and proud in their everyday life. They're like monkeys in a training den. They haven't correlated the action to its consequence, but I guess you could say that about all religions. How about those fucking Hebes in Israel? They won't let the buses and trains run on holy days and here they are fighting the Arabs. And then those fucking Ginzos in Italy with their fucking Pope. I sure wish I was running the Vatican. I'd put a logo, 'Every priest is a thief.' That would be our motto. That would be our goal. The trouble with the Catholic Church is that there are a few honest priests left and they fuck everything up."

He went on about religion for the next fifty miles. Then he switched to literature, then he took on the politicians and finally, near the end of our journey, he talked about Women's Liberation.

"You know," he said, "the funny thing is that I'm really all for them. I've always thought women got a shitty deal, even when I was the one handing it out to them, and yet those cunts, they didn't even let me finish my speech. That's the trouble with women. They have absolutely no sense of humor. Didn't they know I was making a joke, that I would turn it around for them afterward?"

I said to him, "Why don't you publish the speech and that way they will know? *Esquire* magazine would take it, wouldn't they?"

"Sure," Osano said. "Maybe when I'm staying down the fat farm I'll work it over so it will look good in print."

I wound up spending a full week with Osano at the Duke University clinic. In that week I saw more fat people, and I'm talking about your two-hundred-fifty- to three-hundred-fifty-pounders, then I have ever seen in my whole life together. Since that week I have never trusted a girl who wore a cape because every fat girl who is over two hundred pounds thinks she can hide it by draping some sort of Mexican blanket over her or a French gendarme's cloak. What it really made them look like was this huge, threatening mass coming down the street, some hideously engorged Superman or Zorro.

The Duke Medical Center was by no means a cosmetic-oriented reducing operation. It was a serious endeavor to repair the damage done to the human body by long periods of overweight. Every new client was put through days of all kinds of blood tests and X-rays. So I stayed with Osano and made sure he went to restaurants that served the rice diet.

For the first time I realized how lucky I was. That no matter how much I ate I never put on a pound. The first week was something I'll never forget. I saw three three-hundred-pound girls bouncing on a trampoline. Then a guy who was over five hundred pounds being taken down to the railroad station and getting weighed on the freight-weighing machine. There was something genuinely sad about that huge form shambling into the dusk like some elephant wandering toward the graveyard where he knew he had to die.

Osano had a suite of rooms at the Holiday Inn close by the Duke Medical Center building. Many of the patients stayed there and got together for walks or card games or just sat together trying to start an affair. There was a lot of gossip. A two-hundred-fifty-pound boy had taken his three-hundred-fifty-pound girl to New Orleans for a shack-up date for the weekend. Unfortunately the restaurants in New Orleans were so great they spent the two days eating and came back ten pounds heavier. What struck me as funny is that the gaining of the ten pounds was treated as a greater sin than their supposed immorality.

Then one evening Osano and I, at four o'clock in the morning, were startled by the screams of a man in mortal agony. Stretched on the lawn outside our bedroom windows was one of the male patients who had finally gotten himself down to two hundred pounds. He was obviously dying or sounded like it. People were rushing to him and a clinic doctor was already there. He was taken away in an ambulance. The next day we found out what had happened. The patient had emptied all the chocolate bar machines in the hotel. They counted the wrappers on the lawn, there were a hundred and sixteen. Nobody seemed to think this was peculiar, and the guy recovered and continued on the program.

"You're going to have a great time here," I told Osano. "Plenty of material."

"Naw," Osano said. "You can write a tragedy about skinny people, but you can never write a tragedy about fat people. Remember how popular TB was? You could cry over Camille, but how could you cry over a bag encased in three hundred pounds of fat? It's tragic, but it wouldn't look right. There's only so much that art can do."

The next day was the final day of Osano's tests and I planned to fly back that night. Osano had behaved very well. He had stayed strictly on the rice diet and he was feeling good because I had kept him company. When Osano went over to the Medical Center for the results of his tests, I packed my bags while waiting for him to come back to the hotel.

Osano didn't show until four hours later. His face was alive with excitement. His green eyes were dancing and had their old sparkle and color.

"Everything came out OK?" I said.

"You bet your ass," Osano said.

For just a second I didn't trust him. He looked too good, too happy.

"Everything is perfect, couldn't be better. You can fly home tonight and I have to say you are a real buddy. No one would do what you did, eating that rice day after day, and worse still, watching those three-hundred-pound broads go by shaking their asses. Whatever sins you have committed against me I forgive you." And for a moment his eyes were kind, very serious. There was a gentle expression on his face. "I forgive you," he said. "Remember that, you're such a guilty fuck I want you to know that."

And then for one of the few times since we knew each other he gave me a hug. I knew he hated to be touched except by women and I knew he hated being sentimental. I was surprised, but I didn't wonder about what he meant by forgiving me because Osano was so sharp. He was really so much smarter than anyone else I had ever known that in some way he knew the reason why I had not gotten him the job on the Tri-Culture-Jeff Wagon script. He had forgiven me and that was fine, that was like Osano. He was really a great man. The only trouble was I had not yet forgiven myself.

I left Duke University that night and flew to New York. A week later I got a call from Charlie Brown. It was the first time I had ever spoken to her over the phone. She had a soft, sweet voice, innocent, childlike, and she said, "Merlyn, you have to help me."

And I said, "What's wrong?"

And she said, "Osano is dying, he's in the hospital. Please, please come."

Chapter 50

Charlie had already taken Osano to St. Vincent's Hospital, so we agreed to meet there. When I got there, Osano was in a private room and Charlie was with him, sitting on the bed where Osano could put his hand in her lap. Charlie let her hand rest on Osano's stomach, which was bare of covers or top shirt. In fact, Osano's hospital nightgown lay in shreds on the floor. That act must have put him in good humor because he was sitting up cheerfully in bed. And to me he really didn't look that bad. In fact, he seemed to have lost some weight.

I checked the hospital room quickly with my eyes. There were no intravenous settings, no special nurses on duty, and I had seen walking down the corridor that it was not in any way an intensive care unit. I was surprised at the amount of relief I felt, that Charlie must have made a mistake and that Osano wasn't dying after all.

Osano said coolly, "Hi, Merlyn. You must be a real magician. How did you find out I was here? It's supposed to be a secret."

I didn't want any fooling around or any kind of bullshit, so I said straight out, "Charlie Brown told me." Maybe she wasn't supposed to tell me, but I didn't feel like lying.

Charlie just smiled at Osano's frown.

Osano said to her, "I told you it was just me and you, or just me. However you like it. Nobody else."

Charlie said almost absently, "I know you wanted Merlyn."

Osano sighed. "OK," he said. "You've been here all day, Charlie. Why don't you go to the movies or get laid or have a chocolate ice-cream soda or ten Chinese dishes? Anyway, take the night off and I'll see you in the morning."

"All right," Charlie said. She got up from the bed. She stood very close to Osano and he, with a movement not really lecherous, but as if he were reminding himself of what it felt like, put his hand under her dress and caressed her inner thighs and then she leaned her head over the bed to kiss him.

And on Osano's face as his hand caressed that warm flesh beneath the dress came a look of peace and contentment as if reassured in some holy belief.

When Charlie left the room, Osano sighed and said, "Merlyn, believe me. I wrote a lot of bullshit in my books, my articles and my lectures. I'll tell you the only real truth. Cunt is where it all begins and where it all ends. Cunt is the only thing worth living for. Everything else is a fake, a fraud and just shit."

I sat down next to the bed. "What about power?" I said. "You always liked power and money pretty good."

"You forgot art," Osano said.

"OK," I said. "Let's put art in there. How about money, power and art?"

"They're OK," Osano said. "I won't knock them. They'll do. But they're not really necessary. They're just frosting on the cake."

And then I was right back to my first meeting with Osano and I thought I knew the truth about him then, when he didn't know it. And now he's telling it to me and I wonder if it's true because Osano had loved them all. And what he was really saying was that art and money and fame and power were not what he regretted leaving.

"You're looking better than when I saw you last," I told Osano. "How come you're in the hospital? Charlie Brown says it's really trouble this time. But you don't look it."

"No shit?" Osano said. He was pleased. "That's great. But you know I got the bad news down the fat farm when they took all those tests. I'll give it to you short and sweet. I fucked up when I took those dosages of penicillin pills every time I got laid, so I got syphilis and the pills masked it, but the dosage wasn't strong enough to wipe it out. Or maybe those fucking spirochetes figured out a way to bypass the medicine. It must have happened about fifteen years ago. Meantime, those old spirochetes ate away at my brain, my bones and my heart. Now they tell me I got six months or a year before going cuckoo with paresis, unless my heart goes out first."

I was stunned. I really couldn't believe it. Osano looked so cheerful. His sneaky green eyes were so brilliant. "There's nothing that can be done?" I asked him.

"Nothing," Osano said. "But it's not so terrible. I'll rest up here for a couple of weeks and they'll shoot me up a lot and then I'll have at least a couple of months on the town and that's where you come in."

I didn't know what to say. I really didn't know whether to believe him. He looked better than I had seen him look in a long time. "OK," I said.

"Here's my idea," Osano said. "You visit me in the hospital once in a while and help take me home. I don't want to take the chance of becoming senile, so when I think the time is right, I check out. The day I decide to do that I want you to come down to my apartment and keep me company. You and Charlie Brown. And then you can take care of all the fuss afterward."

Osano was staring at me intently. "You don't have to do it," Osano said.

I believed him now. "Sure, I'll do it," I said. "I owe you a favor. Will you have the stuff you need?"

"I'll get it," Osano said. "Don't worry about that."

I had some conferences with Osano's doctors, and they told me he wouldn't leave the hospital for a long time. Maybe never. I felt a sense of relief.

I didn't tell Valerie about anything that had happened or even that Osano was dying. Two days later I went to visit Osano at the hospital. He'd ask me if I would bring him in a Chinese dinner the next time I came. So I had brown paper bags full of food when I went down the corridor and heard yelling and screaming coming from Osano's room. I wasn't surprised. I put the cartons down on the floor outside another patient's private bedroom and ran down the corridor.

In the room was a doctor, two nurses and a nursing supervisor. They were all screaming at Osano. Charlie stood watching in a corner of the room. Her beautiful face freckles startling against the pallor of her skin, tears in her eyes. Osano was sitting on the side of the bed, completely naked and yelling back at the doctor, "Get me my clothes! I'm getting the fuck out of here."

And the doctor was almost yelling at him, "I won't be responsible if you leave this hospital. I will not be responsible."

Osano said to him, laughing, "You dumb shit, you were never responsible. Just get me my clothes."

The nursing supervisor, a formidable-looking woman, said angrily, "I don't give a damn how famous you are, you don't use our hospital as a whorehouse!"

Osano stared at her, "Fuck you," he said. "Get the fuck out of this room." And stark naked, he got up off the bed, and then I could see how really sick he was. He took a lurching step and his body fell sideways. The nurse immediately went to help him, quiet now, moved to pity, but Osano struggled erect. Finally he saw me standing at the doorway and he said very quietly, "Merlyn, get me out of here." I was struck by their indignation. Surely they had caught patients fucking before. Then I studied Charlie Brown. She had on a short tight skirt with obviously nothing underneath. She looked like a child harlot. And Osano's gross rotting body. Their outrage unconsciously was aesthetic, not moral.

The others now noticed me too. And I said to the doctor, "I'll check him out and I'll take the responsibility."

The doctor started to protest, almost pleading, then turned to the supervisor and said, "Get him his clothes." He gave Osano a needle and said, "That will make you more comfortable for the trip."

And it was that simple. I paid the bill and checked Osano out. I called up a limousine service and we got Osano home. Charlie and I put him to bed and he slept for a while and then he called me into the bedroom and told me what had happened in the hospital. That he had made Charlie undress and get into bed with him because he felt so bad that he thought he was dying.

Osano turned his head away a bit. "You know," he said, "the most terrible thing in modern life is that we all die alone in bed. In the hospital with all our family around us, nobody offers to get in bed with somebody dying. If you're at home, your wife won't offer to get in bed when you're dying."

Osano turned his head back to me and gave me that sweet smile he sometimes had. "So that's my dream. I want Charlie in bed with me when I die, at the very moment, and then I'll feel that I've gotten an edge, that it wasn't a bad life and certainly not a bad end. And symbolic as hell, right? Proper for a novelist and his critics."

"When can you know that final moment?" I said.

"I think it's about time," Osano said. "I really don't think I should wait anymore."

Now I was really shocked and horrified. "Why don't you wait a day?" I said. "You'll feel better tomorrow. You still have some more time. Six months is not bad."

Osano said, "Do you have any qualms about what I'm going to do? The usual moral prejudices?"

I shook my head. "Just what's the rush?"

Osano looked at me thoughtfully. "No," he said. "that fall when I tried to get out of bed gave me the message. Listen, I've named you as my literary executor, your decisions are final. There's no money left, just copyrights and those go to my ex-wives, I guess, and my kids. My books still sell pretty well, so I don't have to worry about them. I tried to do something for Charlie Brown, but she won't let me and I think maybe she's right."

I said something I would not ordinarily say. "The whore with the heart of gold," I said. "Just like in the literature," I said.

Osano closed his eyes. "You know, one of the things I liked best about you, Merlyn, is that you never said the word 'whore' and maybe I've said it, but I never thought it."

"OK," I said. "Do you want to make some phone calls or do you want to see some people? Or do you want to have a drink?"

"No," Osano said. "I've had enough of all that bullshit. I've got seven wives, nine kids, I got two thousand friends and millions of admirers. None of them can help and I don't want to see a fucking one of them." He grinned at me. "And mind you, I've led a happy life." He shook his head. "The people you love most do you in."

I sat down beside the bed and we talked for hours about different books that we had read. He told me about all the women he had made love to, and for a few minutes Osano tried to remember fifteen years ago, the girl who infected him. But he couldn't track it down. "One thing," he said, "they were all beauties. They were all worth it. Ah, hell, what difference does it make? It's all an accident."

Osano held out a hand and I shook it and pressed it and Osano said, "Tell Charlie to come in here and you wait outside." Before I left, he called after me, "Hey, listen. An artist's life is not a fulfilling life. Put that on my fucking tombstone."

I waited a long time in the living room. Sometimes I could hear noises and once I thought I heard weeping and then I didn't hear anything. I went into the kitchen and made some coffee and set two cups on the kitchen table. Then I went into the living room and waited some more. Then not a scream, not a call for help, not even grief-stricken I heard Charlie's voice, very sweet and clear, call my name.

I went into the bedroom. On the night table was the gold Tiffany box he used to keep his penicillin pills in. It was open and empty. The lights were on, and Osano was lying on his back, eyes staring at the ceiling. Even in death his green eyes seemed to glitter. Nestled beneath his arm, pressed against his chest, was Charlie's golden head. She had drawn the covers up to cover their nakedness.

"You'll have to get dressed," I said to her.

She rose up on one elbow and leaned over to kiss Osano on his mouth. And then she stood staring down at him for a long time.

"You'll have to get dressed and leave," I said. "There's going to be a lot of fuss and I think it's one thing Osano wanted me to do. To keep you out of any fuss."

And then I went to the living room. I waited. I could hear the shower going, and then, fifteen minutes later, she came into the room.

"Don't worry about anything," I said. "I'll take care of everything." She came over to me and put herself into my arms. It was the first time I had ever felt her body and I could partly understand why Osano had loved her for so long. She smelled beautifully fresh and clean.

"You were the only one he wanted to see," Charlie said. "You and me. Will you call me after the funeral?"

I said yes, I would, and then she went out and left me alone with Osano.

I waited until morning, and then I called the police and told them that I had found Osano dead. And that he had obviously committed suicide. I had considered for a minute hiding the suicide, hiding the pillbox. But Osano wouldn't care even if I could get the press and authorities to cooperate. I told them how important a man Osano was so that an ambu-

lance would get there right away. Then I called Osano's lawyers and gave them the responsibility of informing all the
wives and all the children. I called Osano's publishers because
I knew they would want to give out a press release and publish an ad in the New York *Times*, in memoriam. For some
reason I wanted Osano to have that kind of respect.

The police and district attorney had a lot of questions to
ask as if I were a murder suspect. But that blew over right
away. It seemed that Osano had sent a suicide note to his
publisher telling him that he would not be able to deliver his
novel owing to the fact that he was planning on killing himself.

There was a great funeral out in the Hamptons. Osano was
buried in the presence of his seven wives, nine children, literary critics from the New York *Times*, *New York Review of
Books*, *Commentary*, *Harper's* magazine and the *New
Yorker*. A bus load of people came direct from Elaine's in
New York. Friends of Osano and knowing that he would approve, they had a keg of beer and a portable bar on the bus.
They arrived drunk for the funeral. Osano would have been
delighted.

In the following weeks hundreds of thousands of words
were written about Osano as the first great Italian literary figure in our cultural history. That would have given Osano a
pain in the ass. He never thought of himself as Ital-
ian/American. But one thing would have pleased him. All the
critics said that if he had lived to publish his novel in
progress, he would have surely won the Nobel Prize.

* * *

A week after Osano's funeral I got a telephone call from
his publisher with a request that I come to lunch the following week. And I agreed.

Arcania Publishing House was considered one of the
classy, most literary publishing houses in the country. On its
backlist were a half dozen Nobel Prize winners and dozens
of Pulitzer and NBA winners. They were famous for being
more interested in literature than best-sellers. And the editor
in chief, Henry Stiles, could have passed for an Oxford don.
But he got down to business as briskly as any Babbitt.

"Mr. Merlyn," he said, "I admire your novels very much. I hope someday we can add you to our list."

"I've gone over Osano's stuff," I said, "as his executor."

"Good," Mr. Stiles said. "You may or may not know, since this is the financial end of Mr. Osano's life, that we advanced him a hundred thousand dollars for his novel in progress. So we do have first claim to that book. I just wanted to make sure you understood that."

"Sure," I said. "And I know it was Osano's wish that you publish it. You did a great job publishing his books."

There was a grateful smile on Mr. Stiles's face. He leaned back. "Then there's no problem?" he said. "I assume you've gone through his notes and papers and you found the manuscript."

I said, "Well, that's the problem. There is no manuscript; there is no novel, only five hundred pages of notes."

Stiles had a stunned, horrified look on his face and behind that exterior I know what he thought: Fucking writers, hundred-thousand-dollar advance, all those years and all he has is notes! But then he pulled himself together. "You mean there's not one page of manuscript?" he said.

"No," I said. I was lying, but he would never know. There were six pages.

"Well," Mr. Stiles said, "it's not something we usually do, but it has been done by other publishing houses. We know that you helped Mr. Osano with some of his articles, under his by-lines, that you imitated his style very well. It would have to be secret, but why couldn't you write Mr. Osano's book in a six-month period and publish it under Mr. Osano's name? We could make a great deal of money. You realize that couldn't show in any contract between us, we could sign a separate very generous contract for your future books."

Now he had surprised me. The most respectable publishing house in America doing something that only Hollywood would do, or a Vegas hotel? Why the fuck was I surprised?

"No," I told Mr. Stiles. "As his literary executor I have the power and authority to keep the book from being published from those notes. If you would like to publish the notes themselves, I'll give you permission."

"Well, think it over," Mr. Stiles said. "We'll talk about it again. Meanwhile, it's been a pleasure to meet you." He shook his head sadly. "Osano was a genius. What a pity."

I never told Mr. Stiles that Osano had written some pages of his novel, the first six. With them was a note addressed to me.

MERLYN:
Here are the six pages of my book. I give them to you. Let's see what you can make of them. Forget the notes, they're bullshit.

OSANO

I had read the pages and decided to keep them for myself. When I got home, I read them over again very slowly, word by word.

"Listen to me. I will tell you the truth about a man's life. I will tell you the truth about his love for women. That he never hates them. Already you think I'm on the wrong track. Stay with me. Really—I'm a master of magic.

"Do you believe a man can truly love a woman and constantly betray her? Never mind physically, but betray her in his mind, in the very 'poetry of his soul.' Well, it's not easy, but men do it all the time.

"Do you want to know how women can love you, feed you that love deliberately to poison your body and mind simply to destroy you? And out of passionate love choose not to love you anymore? And at the same time dizzy you with an idiot's ecstasy? Impossible? That's the easy part.

"But don't run away. This is not a love story.

"I will make you feel the painful beauty of a child, the animal horniness of the adolescent male, the yearning suicidal moodiness of the young female. And then (here's the hard part) show you how time turns man and woman around full circle, exchanged in body and soul.

"And then of course, there is TRUE LOVE. Don't go away! It exists or I will make it exist. I'm not a master of magic for nothing. Is it worth what it costs? And how about sexual fidelity? Does it work? Is it love? Is it even human, that perverse passion to be with only one special person? And if it doesn't work, do you still get a bonus for trying? Can it work both ways? Of course not, that's easy. And yet—

"Life is a comical business, and there is nothing funnier than love traveling through time. But a true master of magic

can make his audience laugh and cry at the same time. Death is another story. I will never make a joke about death. It is beyond my powers.

"I am always alert for death. He doesn't fool me. I spot him right away. He loves to come in his country-bumpkin disguise; a comical wart that suddenly grows and grows; the dark, hairy mole that sends its roots to the very bone; or hiding behind a pretty little fever blush. Then suddenly that grinning skull appears to take the victim by surprise. But never me. I'm waiting for him. I take my precautions.

"Parallel to death, love is a tiresome, childless business, though men believe more in love than death. Women are another story. They have a powerful secret. They don't take love seriously and never have.

"But again, don't go away. Again, this is not a love story. Forget about love. I will show you all the stretches of power. First the life of a poor struggling writer. Sensitive. Talented. Maybe even some genius. I will show you the artist getting the shit kicked out of him for the sake of his art. And why he so richly deserves it. Then I will show him as a cunning criminal and having the time of his life. Ah, what joy the true artist feels when he finally becomes a crook. It's out in the open now, his essential nature. No more kidding around about his honor. The son of a bitch is a hustler. A conniver. An enemy of society right out of the clear instead of hiding behind his whore's cunt of art. What a relief. What pleasure. Such sly delight. And then how he becomes an honest man again. It's an awful strain being a crook.

"But it helps you to accept society and forgive your fellow-man. Once that's done no person should be a crook unless he really needs the money.

"Then on to one of the most amazing success stories in the history of literature. The intimate lives of the giants of our culture. One crazy bastard especially. The classy world. So now we have the poor struggling genius world, the crooked world, and the classy literary world. All this laced with plenty of sex, some complicated ideas you won't be hit over the head with and may even find interesting. And finally on to a full-blast ending in Hollywood with our hero gobbling up all its rewards, money, fame, beautiful women. And . . . don't go away—don't go away—how it all turns to ashes.

"That's not enough? You've heard it all before? But

remember I'm a master of magic. I can bring all these people truly alive. I can show you what they truly think and feel. You'll weep for them, all of them I promise you that. Or maybe just laugh. Anyway, we're going to have a lot of fun. And learn something about life. Which is really no help.

"Ah, I know what you're thinking. That conning bastard trying to make us turn the page. But wait, it's only a tale I want to tell. What's the harm? Even if I take it seriously, you don't have to. Just have a good time.

"I want to tell you a story, I have no other vanity. I don't desire success or fame or money. But that's easy, most men, most women don't, not really. Even better, I don't want love. When I was young, some women told me they loved me for my long eyelashes. I accepted. Later it was for my wit. Then for my power and money. Then for my talent. Then for my mind—deep. OK, I can handle all of it. The only woman who scares me is the one who loves me for myself alone. I have plans for her. I have poisons and daggers and dark graves in caves to hide her head. She can't be allowed to live. Especially if she is sexually faithful and never lies and always puts me ahead of everything and everyone.

"There will be a lot about love in this book, but it's not a love book. It's a war book. The old war between men who are true friends. The great 'new' war between men and women. Sure it's an old story, but it's out in the open now. The Women's Liberation warriors think they have something new, but it's just their armies coming out of their guerrilla hills. Sweet women ambushed men always: at their cradles, in the kitchen, the bedroom. And at the graves of their children, the best place not to hear a plea for mercy.

"Ah well, you think I have a grievance against women. But I never hated them. And they'll come out better people than men, you'll see. But the truth is that only women have been able to make me unhappy, and they have done so from the cradle on. But most men can say that. And there's nothing to be done.

"What a target I've given here. I know—I know—how irresistible it seems. But be careful. I'm a tricky storyteller; not just one of your vulnerable sensitive artists. I've taken my precautions. I've still got a few surprises left.

"But enough. Let me get to work. Let me begin and let me end."

And that was Osano's great novel, the book that would cinch the Nobel Prize, restore his greatness. I wish he had written it.

That he was a great con artist, as those pages showed, was irrelevant. Or maybe part of his genius. He wanted to share his inner worlds with the outside world, that was all. And now as his final joke he had given me his last pages. A joke because we were such different writers. He so generous. And, I, I realized now, so ungenerous.

I was never crazy about his work. And I don't know whether I really loved him as a man. But I loved him as a *writer*. And so I decided, maybe for luck, maybe for strength, maybe just for the con, to use his pages as my own. I should have changed one line. Death has always surprised me.

Chapter 51

I have no history. That is the thing Janelle never understood. That I started with myself. That I had no grandparents or parents, uncles and aunts, friends of the family or cousins. That I had no childhood memories of a special house, or a special kitchen. That I had no city or town or village. That I began my history with myself and my brother, Arthur. And that when I extended myself with Valerie and the kids and her family and lived with her in a house in the city, when I became a parent and a husband, they became my reality and my salvation. But I don't have to worry about Janelle anymore. I haven't seen her for over two years and it's three years since Osano died.

I can't bear to remember about Artie, and when I even think of his name, I find tears coming from my eyes, but he is the only person I have ever wept for.

For the last two years I have sat in a working study in my home, reading, writing and being the perfect father and husband. Sometimes I go to dinner with friends, but I like to think that finally I have become serious, dedicated. That I will now live the life of a scholar. That my adventures are over. In short, I am praying that life holds no more surprises. Safely in this room, surrounded by my books of magic, Austen, Dickens, Dostoevsky, Joyce, Hemingway, Dreiser and finally, Osano, I feel the exhaustion of an animal who has escaped many times before reaching its haven.

Beneath me in the house below, the house that is now my history, I knew my wife was busy in the kitchen preparing Sunday dinner. My children were watching TV and playing cards in the den, and because I knew they were there, sadness was bearable in this room.

I read all Osano's books again and he was a great writer at the beginning. I tried to analyze his failure in later life, his inability to finish his great novel. He started off amazed by the wonderment of the world around him and the people in it. He ended writing about the wonderment of himself. His concern, you could see, was to make a legend of his own life. He wrote to the world rather than to himself. In every line he screamed for attention to Osano rather than to his art. He wanted everyone to know how clever, how brilliant he was. He even made sure that the characters he created would not get credit for his brilliance. He was like a ventriloquist getting jealous of the laughs his dummy earned. And it was a shame. Yet I think of him as a great man. His terrifying humanity, his terrifying love of life, how brilliant he was and what fun to be with.

How could I say that he was a failed artist when his achievements, flawed though they were, seemed much greater than mine? I remembered going through his papers, as his literary executor, and the astonishment growing upon me when I could find no trace of his novel in progress. I could not believe he was such a fake, that he had been pretending to write it all those years and that had just been fucking around with notes. Now I realized that he had been burned out. And that part of the joke had not been malicious or cunning, but simply a joke that delighted him. And the money.

He had written some of the most beautiful prose, created some of the most powerful ideas, of his generation, but he had delighted in being a scoundrel. I read all his notes, over five hundred pages of them on long yellow sheets. They were brilliant notes. But notes are nothing.

Knowing this made me think about myself. That I had written mortal books. But more unfortunate than Osano, I had tried to live without illusions and without risk. That I had none of his love for life and his faith in it. I thought about Osano's saying that life was always trying to do you in. And maybe that's why he lived so wildly, struggled so hard against the blows and the humiliations.

Long ago Jordan had pulled the trigger of the gun against his head. Osano had lived life fully and ended that life when there was no other choice. And I, I tried to escape wearing a magical conical hat. I thought about another thing Osano had said: "Life is always getting in the way." And I knew what he meant. The world to a writer is like one of those pale ghosts who with age become paler and paler, and maybe that's the reason Osano gave up writing.

The snow was falling heavily outside the windows of my workroom. The whiteness covered the gray, bare limbs of the trees, the moldy brown and green of the winter lawn. If I were sentimental and so inclined, it would be easy to conjure up the faces of Osano and Artie drifting smilingly through those swirling snowflakes. But this I refused to do. I was neither so sentimental nor so self-indulgent nor so self-pitying. I could live without them. Their death would not diminish me, as they perhaps hoped it would do.

No, I was safe here in my workroom. Warm as toast. Safe from the raging wind that hurled the snowflakes against my window. I would not leave this room, this winter.

Outside, the roads were icy, my car could skid and death could mangle me. Viral poisonous colds could infect my spine and blood. Oh, there were countless dangers besides death. And I was not unaware of the spies death could infiltrate into the house and even into my own brain. I set up defenses against them.

I had charts posted around the walls of my room. Charts for my work, my salvation, my armor. I had researched a novel on the Roman Empire to retreat into the past. I had researched a novel in the twenty-fifth century if I wanted to hide in the future. Hundreds of books stacked up to read, to surround my brain.

I pulled a big soft chair up to windows so that I could watch the falling snow in comfort. The buzzer from the kitchen sang. Supper was ready. My family would be waiting for me, my wife and children. What the hell was going on with them after all this time? I watched the snow, a blizzard now. The outside world was completely white. The buzzer rang again, insistently. If I were alive, I would get up and go down into the cheerful dining room and have a happy dinner. I watched the snow. Again the buzzer rang.

I checked the work chart. I had written the first chapter on the novel of the Roman Empire and ten pages of notes for the novel on the twenty-fifth century. At that minute I decided I would write about the future.

Again the buzzer rang, long and incessantly. I locked the

doors of my workroom and descended into the house and into the dining room, and entering it, I gave a sigh of relief.

They were all there. The children nearly grown and ready to leave. Valerie pretty in a housedress and apron and her lovely brown hair pulled severely back. She was flushed, perhaps from the heat of the kitchen, perhaps because after dinner she would be going out to meet her lover? Was that possible? I had no way of knowing. Even so, wasn't life worth guarding?

I sat down at the head of the table. I joked with the kids. I ate. I smiled at Valerie and praised the food. After dinner I would go back up into my room and work and be alive.

Osano, Malomar, Artie, Jordan, I miss you. But you won't do me in. All of my loved ones around this table might someday, I had to worry about that.

During dinner I got a call from Cully to meet him at the airport the next day. He was coming to New York on business. It was the first time in over a year that I had heard from Cully, and from his voice I knew he was in trouble.

I was early for Cully's plane, so I bought some magazines and read them, then I had coffee and a sandwich. When I heard the announcement that his plane was landing, I went down to the baggage area where I always waited for him. As usual in New York it took about twenty minutes for the baggage to come down a chute. By that time most of the passengers were milling around the carousel into which the chute emptied, but I still didn't see Cully. I kept looking for him. The crowd began to thin, and after a while there were only a few suitcases left on the carousel.

I called the house and asked Valerie if there had been any calls from Cully and she said no. Then I called TWA flight information and asked if Cully Cross had been on the plane. They told me that he had made a reservation but had never shown up. I called the Xanadu Hotel in Vegas and got Cully's secretary. She said yes, that as far as she knew, Cully had flown to New York. She knew he was not in Vegas and would not be due back for a few days. I wasn't worried. I figured something had come up. Cully was always flying off to all parts of the United States and the world on hotel business. Some last-minute emergency had made him change course and I was sure he would get in touch with me. But far back in my mind there was the nagging consciousness that he had never hung me up before, that he had always told me of a change in plans and that in his own way he was too considerate to let me go to the airport and wait for hours when he was not coming. And yet it took me almost a week of not hearing from him and not being able to find out where he was before I called Gronevelt.

Gronevelt was glad to hear from me. His voice sounded very strong, very healthy. I told him the story and asked him where Cully might be and I told him that in any case I thought I should notify him. "It's not something I can talk about over the phone," Gronevelt said. "But why don't you come out for a few days and be my guest here at the hotel and I'll put your mind to rest?"

Chapter 52

When Cully received a summons to Gronevelt's executive suite, he put in a call to Merlyn.

Cully knew what Gronevelt wanted to see him about and he knew he had to start thinking about an escape hatch. On the phone he told Merlyn he would be taking the next morning's plane to New York and asked Merlyn to meet him. He told Merlyn that it was important, that he needed his help.

When Cully finally went into Gronevelt's suite, he tried to "read" Gronevelt, but all he could see was how much the man changed in the ten years he had worked for him. The stroke Gronevelt had suffered had left tiny red veins in the whites of his eyes, through his cheeks and even in his forehead. The cold blue eyes seemed frosted. He seemed not so tall, and he was much frailer. Despite all this, Cully was still afraid of him.

As usual, Gronevelt had Cully make them both drinks, the usual scotch. Then Gronevelt said, "Johnny Santadio is flying in tomorrow. He wants to know just one thing. Is the Gaming Commission going to approve his license as an owner of this hotel or are they not?"

"You know the answer," Cully said.

"I think I know it," Gronevelt said. "I know what you told Johnny, that it was a sure thing. That it was all locked up. That's all I know."

Cully said, "He's not going to get it. I couldn't fix it."

Gronevelt nodded. "It was a very tough proposition from the word 'go,' what with Johnny's background. What about his hundred grand?"

"I have it for him in the cage," Cully said. "He can pick it up whenever he wants it."

"Good," Gronevelt said. "Good. He'll be pleased about that."

They both leaned back and sipped their drinks. Both preparing for the real battle, the real question. Then Gronevelt said slowly, "You and I know why Johnny's making a special trip here to Vegas. You promised him you could fix it so that Judge Brianca would give his nephew a suspended sentence on that fraud and income tax rap. Yesterday his nephew got sentenced to five years. I hope you have an answer for that one."

"I haven't got an answer," Cully said. "I paid Judge Brianca the forty grand that Mr. Santadio gave me. That's all I could do. This is the first time Judge Brianca ever disappointed me. Maybe I can get the money back from him. I don't know. I've been trying to get in touch with him, but I guess he's ducking me."

Gronevelt said, "You know that Johnny has a lot to say about what goes on in this hotel, and if he says it's important that I let you go, I have to let you go. Cully, you know that I'm not in my old power position ever since I've had that stroke. I had to give away pieces of the hotel. I'm really just an errand boy now, a front. I can't help you."

Cully laughed. "Hell, I'm not even worried about getting fired. I'm just worried about getting killed."

"Oh," Gronevelt said, "no, no. It's not that serious." He smiled at Cully as a father might smile at his son. "Did you really think it was that serious?"

For the first time Cully relaxed and took a big swig of scotch. He felt enormously relieved. "I'll settle for that deal right now," Cully said, "just getting fired."

Gronevelt slapped him on the shoulder. "Don't settle so fast," he said. "Johnny knows the great work you've done for this hotel in the last two years since my stroke. You've done a marvelous job. You've added millions of dollars to the revenue coming in here. Now that's important. Not only to me but to guys like Johnny. So you've made a couple of mistakes. Now, I have to admit they are very pissed off, especially about the nephew going to jail and especially because you told them not to worry. That you had the full fix on Judge Brianca. They couldn't understand how you could say such a thing and then not come through for them."

Cully shook his head. "I really can't figure it," he said. "I've had Brianca in my pocket for the last five years, especially when I had that little blond Charlie working him over."

Gronevelt laughed. "Yeah, I remember her. Pretty girl. Good heart."

"Yeah," Cully said. "The judge was crazy for her. He used to take her on his boat down to Mexico fishing for a week at a time. He said she was always great company. Great little girl."

What Cully didn't tell Gronevelt was how Charlie used to tell him stories about the judge. How she used to go into the judge's chambers and, while he was still in his robes, go down on him before he went out to conduct a trial. She also told him how on the boat fishing she had made the sixty-year-old judge go down on her and how the judge had immediately rushed into the stateroom, grabbed a bottle of whiskey and gargled to get all the germs out. It was the first time the old judge had ever done this to a woman. But, Charlie Brown said, after that he was like a kid eating ice cream. Cully smiled a little bit, remembering, and then he was aware of Gronevelt going on.

"I think I have a way for you to square yourself," Gronevelt said. "I have to admit Santadio is hot. He's steaming, but I can cool him off. All you have to do is come through for him with a big coup, right now, and I think I have it. There's another three million waiting in Japan. Johnny's share of that is a million bucks. If you can bring that out, as you did once before, I think for a million dollars Johnny Santadio will forgive you. But just remember this: It's more dangerous now."

Cully was surprised and then very alert. The first question he asked was: "Will Mr. Santadio know I'm going?" And if Gronevelt had said yes, then Cully would have turned down the deal. But Gronevelt, looking him right in the eye, said, "It's my idea, and my suggestion to you is that you tell nobody, not anyone, that you are going. Take the afternoon flight to LA, hook up to the Japanese flight and you'll be in Japan before Johnny Santadio gets here and then I'll just tell him that you're out of town. While you're en route, I'll make all the arrangements for the money to be delivered to you. Don't worry about strangers because we are going through our old friend Fummiro."

It was the mention of Fummiro's name that dissolved all of Cully's suspicions. "OK," he said. "I'll do it. The only thing is

I was going to New York to see Merlyn and he's meeting me at the plane, so I'll have to call him."

"No," Gronevelt said. "You just never know who may be listening on the phone or who he may tell. Let me take care of it. I'll let him know not to meet you at the plane. Don't even cancel your reservation. That will throw people off the track. I'll tell Johnny you went to New York. You'll have a great cover. OK?"

"OK," Cully said.

Gronevelt shook his hand and clapped him on the shoulder. "Get in and out as fast as you can," Gronevelt said. "If you make it back here, I promise you that you will be squared away with Johnny Santadio. You'll have nothing to worry about."

On the night before Cully left for Japan he called up two girls he knew. Soft hookers both. One was the wife of a pit boss in a hotel down the Strip. Her name was Crystin Lesso.

"Crystin," he said, "do you feel in the mood to get thrashed?"

"Sure," Crystin said. "How much will you knock off my markers?"

Cully usually doubled the price for a thrashing, which would mean two hundred dollars. What the hell, he thought, I'm going to Japan, who knows what will happen?

"I'll knock five hundred off," Cully said.

There was a little gasp at the other end of the wire.

"Jesus," Crystin said. "This must be some thrashing. Who do I have to go in the ring with, a gorilla?"

"Don't worry," Cully said. "You always have a good time, don't you?"

Crystin said, "When?"

"Let's make it early," Cully said. "I have to catch a plane tomorrow morning. OK with you?"

"Sure," Crystin said. "I assume you're not giving me dinner?"

"No," Cully said. "I have too many things to do. I won't have time."

After hanging up the phone, Cully opened the desk drawer and took out a little packet of white slips. They were Crystin's markers, totaling three thousand dollars.

Cully pondered on the mysteries of women. Crystin was a

good-looking girl of about twenty-eight. But a really degenerate gambler. Two years she had gone down the drain for over twenty grand. She had called Cully for an appointment at his office, and when she came in, she had given him a proposition that she would work off the twenty grand as a soft hustler. But she would take dates only directly from Cully with the utmost secrecy because of her husband.

Cully had tried to talk her out of it. "If your husband knows, he'll kill you," Cully said.

"If he finds out about my twenty-grand markers, he'll kill me," Crystin said. "So what's the difference? And besides, you know I can't stop gambling and I figure that over and above the fee I can get some of these guys to give me a stake or at least put down a bet for me."

So Cully had agreed. In addition, he had given her a job as a secretary for the food and beverages officer of the Xanadu Hotel. He was attracted to her and at least once a week they went to bed together afternoons in his hotel suite. After a while he introduced her to thrashing and she had loved it.

Cully took out one of the five-hundred-dollar markers and tore it up. Then on a sudden impulse he tore up all Crystin's markers and threw them in his wastebasket. When he came back from Japan, he would have to cover for it with some paperwork, but he would think about that later. Crystin was a good kid. If something happened to him, he wanted her to be in the clear.

He passed the time cleaning up details on his desk and then went down to his suite. He ordered up some chilled champagne and made a call to Charlie Brown.

Then he took a shower and got into his pajamas. They were very fancy pajamas. White silk, edged with red, with his initials on the jacket pocket.

Charlie Brown came first and he gave her some champagne and then Crystin came. They sat around talking and he made them drink the whole bottle before he led them into the bedroom.

The two girls were a little shy of each other, though they had met before around town. Cully told them to undress and he stripped off his pajamas.

The three of them got into bed together naked and he talked to them awhile. Kidding them, making jokes, kissing them occasionally and playing with their breasts. And then with an arm around their necks he pressed their faces close together. They knew what was expected of them. The two women kissed each other tentatively on the lips.

Cully lifted the more slender Charlie Brown, slid underneath her so that the two women were next to each other. He felt the quick surge of sexual excitement.

"Come on," he said. "You'll love it. You know you'll love it."

He ran his hand between Charlie Brown's legs and let it rest there. At the same time he leaned over and kissed Crystin on the mouth and then he pressed the two women together.

It took a little time for them to get started. They were very tentative, a little shy. It was always like this. Gradually Cully edged away from them until he was seated at the foot of the bed.

He felt a sudden tranquility as he watched the two women make love to each other. To him, with all his cynicism about women and love, it was the most beautiful thing he could ever hope to see. They both had lush bodies and lovely faces, and they were both truly passionate as they could never be with him. He could watch it forever.

As they went on, Cully rose from the bed and sat in one of the chairs. The two women were becoming more and more passionate. He watched their bodies flow around and up and down each other until there was a final climaxing of violent thrashing and the two women lay in each other's arms quiet and still.

Cully went over to the bed and kissed them each gently. Then he lay down between them and he said, "Don't do anything. Let's just sleep a little."

* * *

He dozed off, and when he awoke, the two women were in his living room, dressed and chatting together.

He took five one-hundred-dollar bills, five Honeybees, out of his wallet and gave them to Charlie Brown.

She kissed him good-night and left him alone with Crystin.

He sat down on the sofa and put his arm around Crystin. He gave her a gentle kiss.

"I tore up your markers," he said. "You don't have to worry about them anymore, and I'm telling the cage to give you five hundred dollars' worth of chips so you can do a little gambling tonight."

Crystin laughed and said, "Cully, I can't believe it. You've finally become a mark."

"Everybody's a mark," Cully said. "But what the hell. You've been a good sport these last two years. I want to get you off the hook."

Crystin gave him a hug and rested against his shoulder and then she said quietly, "Cully, why do you call it thrashing? You know, when you put me together with a girl?"

Cully laughed. "I just like the idea of the word. It just describes it someway."

"You don't put me down for that, do you?" Crystin said.

"No," Cully said. "To me it's the most beautiful thing I've ever seen."

When Crystin left, Cully couldn't sleep. Finally he went down into the casino. He spotted Crystin at the blackjack table. She had a stack of black one-hundred-dollar chips in front of her.

She waved him toward her. She gave him a delighted smile. "Cully, this is my lucky night," she said. "I'm ahead twelve grand."

She picked up a stack of chips and placed them in his hand. "This is for you," she said. "I want you to have them."

Cully counted the chips. There were ten of them. A thousand dollars.

He laughed and said, "OK. I'll hold them for you, someday you'll need gambling money." And he left her and went up to his office and threw the chips into one of his desk drawers. He thought again of calling Merlyn but decided against it.

He looked around the office. There was nothing left for him to do, but he felt as if he were forgetting something. As if he had counted down the shoe in which some important cards were missing. But it was too late now. In a few hours he would be in Los Angeles and boarding a plane for Tokyo.

In Tokyo Cully took a taxi to Fummiro's office. The Tokyo streets were crowded, many of the people wearing white surgical gauze masks as a guard against the germ-laden air. Even the construction workers with their shiny red coats and white helmets wore the surgical masks. For some reason the sight of them gave Cully a queasy feeling. But he realized that this was because he was nervous about the whole trip.

Fummiro greeted him with a hearty handshake and a wide smile.

"So good to see you, Mr. Cross," Fummiro said. "We'll make sure you have a good trip, a good time in our country. Just let my assistant know what you require."

They were in Fummiro's modern American-style office and could speak safely.

Cully said, "I have my suitcase at the hotel and I just want to know when I should bring it to your office."

"Monday," Fummiro said. "On the weekend, nothing can be done. But there is a party at my house tomorrow night at which I am sure you will enjoy yourself."

"Thank you very much," Cully said. "But I just want to rest. I'm not feeling too good and it's been a long trip."

"Ah, yes. I understand," Fummiro said. "I have a good idea. There is a country inn in Yogawara. It's only an hour's drive from here. I will send you in my limousine. It's the most beautiful spot in Japan. Quiet and restful. You have masseuse girls and I will arrange for other girls to meet you there. The food is superb. Japanese food, of course. It is where all the great men of Japan bring their mistresses for a little holiday and it's discreet. You can relax there without any worries and you can come back Monday completely refreshed and I will have the money for you."

Cully thought it over. He would be in no danger until he got the money, and the idea of relaxing in the country inn appealed to him.

"That sounds great," he said to Fummiro. "When can you have the limousine pick me up?"

"The Friday-night traffic is terrible," Fummiro said. "Go tomorrow morning. Have a good rest tonight and on the weekend and I will see you on Monday."

As a special mark of honor Fummiro walked him out of the office to the elevator.

It was longer than a hour by limousine to Yogawara. But when he got there, Cully was delighted that he had made the trip. It was a beautiful country inn, Japanese style.

His suite of rooms was magnificent. The servants floated

through the halls like ghosts, nearly invisible. And there was no sign of any other guests.

In one of his rooms there was a huge redwood tub. The bathroom itself was equipped with all different makes of razors and shaving lotions and women's cosmetics. Anything anyone could need.

Two tiny young girls, barely nubile, filled his tub and washed him clean before he got into the fragrant hot water. The tub was so huge that he could almost swim in it. And so deep that the water almost rose above his head. He felt the tiredness and tension go out of his bones, and then finally the two young girls lifted him out of the tub and led him to a mat in the other room. And stretched out, he let them massage him, finger by finger, toe by toe, limb by limb, what seemed each single strand of hair on his head. It was the greatest massage he'd ever had.

They gave him a *futaba*, a little hard square pillow on which to rest his head. And he immediately fell asleep. He slept until late afternoon, and then he took a walk through the countryside.

The inn was on a hillside overlooking a valley, and beyond the valley he could see the ocean, blue, wide, crystal clear. He walked around a beautiful pond sprinkled with flowers which seemed to match the intricate parasols of the mats and hammocks on the porch of the inn. All the bright colors delighted him, and the clear, pure air refreshed his brain. He was no longer worried or tense. Nothing would happen. He would get the money from Fummiro, who was an old friend. When he got to Hong Kong and deposited the money, he would be clear with Santadio and could safely return to Las Vegas. It would all work out. The Xanadu Hotel would be his, and he would take care of Gronevelt as a son would a father in his old age.

For a moment he wished he could spend the rest of his life in this beautiful countryside. So still and clear. So tranquil as if he were living five hundred years ago. He had never wished to be a samurai, but now he thought how innocent their warfare had been.

Darkness was beginning to fall, and tiny drops of rain pitted the surface of the pond. He went back to his rooms in the inn.

He loved the Japanese style of living. No furniture. Just

mats. The sliding wood-frame paper doors that cut off rooms and turned a living room into a sleeping room. It seemed to him so reasonable and so clever.

Far away he could hear a tiny bell ringing with silvery claps and a few minutes after that the paper doors slid apart and two young girls came in, carrying a huge oval platter almost five feet long, it could be the top of a table. The platter was filled with every kind of fish the sea could provide.

There was the black squid and the yellow-tailed fish, pearly oysters, gray-black crabs, speckled chunks of fish showing vivid pink flesh underneath. It was a rainbow of color, and there was more food there than any five men could eat. The women set the platter on a low table and arranged cushions for him to sit on. Then they sat down on either side and fed him morsels of fish.

Another girl came in carrying a tray of sake wine and glasses. She poured the wine and put the glass to his mouth so that he could drink.

It was all delicious. When he finished, Cully stood looking through the window at the valley of pines and the sea beyond. Behind him he could hear the women take away the dinner and the paper wooden doors closing. He was alone in the room, staring at the sea.

Again he went over everything in his mind, counting down the shoe of circumstance and chance. Monday morning he would get the money from Fummiro and he would board the plane to Hong Kong and in Hong Kong he would have to get to the bank. He tried to think of where the danger would lie, if there were a danger. He thought of Gronevelt. That Gronevelt might betray him, or Santadio or even Fummiro. Why had Judge Brianca betrayed him? Could Gronevelt have engineered that? And then he remembered one night having dinner with Fummiro and Gronevelt. They had been just a little uneasy with him. Was there something there? An unknown card in the shoe? But Gronevelt was an old sick man and Santadio's long arm did not reach into the Far East. And Fummiro was an old friend.

But there was always bad luck. In any case it would be his final risk. And at least now he would have another day of peace here in Yogawara.

He heard the paper wooden doors slide behind him opening up. It was the two tiny girls leading him back to the redwood tub.

Again they washed him. Again they plunged him into the vast fragrant waters of the tub.

He soaked, and again they raised him out and laid him on the mat and put the *futaba* pillow beneath his head. Again they massaged him finger by finger. And now, completely rested, he felt the surge of sexual desire. He reached out for one of the young girls, but very prettily she denied him with her face and her hands. Then she pantomimed she would send another girl up. That it was not their function.

And then Cully held up two fingers to tell them he wanted two girls. They both giggled at that, and he wondered if Japanese girls thrashed each other.

He watched them disappear and close the frame doors behind them. His head sank on the small square pillow. His body lustfully relaxed. He dozed into a light sleep. Far away he heard the sliding of the paper doors. Ah, he thought, they're coming. And curious to see what they looked like, whether they were pretty, how they were dressed, he raised his head and to his astonishment he saw two men with surgeon's gauze masks over their faces coming toward him.

At first he thought the girls misunderstood him. That comically inept, he had asked for a heavier massage. And then the gauze masks struck him with terror. The realization flashed through his mind that these masks were never worn in the country. And then his mind jumped to the truth, but he screamed out, "I haven't got the money. I haven't got the money!" He tried to rise from the mat, and the two men were upon him.

It was not painful or horrible. He seemed to sink again beneath the sea, the fragrant waters of the redwood tub. His eyes glazed over. And then he was quiet on the mat, the *futaba* pillow beneath his head.

The two men wrapped his body in towels and silently carried it out of the room.

Far across the ocean, Gronevelt in his suite worked the controls to pump pure oxygen into his casino.

Book VIII

Chapter 53

I got to Vegas late at night and Gronevelt asked me to have dinner in his suite. We had some drinks and the waiters brought up a table with the dinner we had ordered. I noticed that Gronevelt's dish had very small portions. He looked older and faded. Cully had told me about his stroke, but I could see no evidence of it other than perhaps he moved more slowly and took more time to answer me when he spoke.

I glanced at the control panel behind his desk which Gronevelt used to pump pure oxygen into the casino. Gronevelt said, "Cully told you about that? He wasn't supposed to."

"Some things are too good not to tell," I said, "and besides, Cully knew I wouldn't spread it around."

Gronevelt smiled. "Believe it or not, I use it as an act of kindness. It gives all those losers a little hope and a last shot before they go to bed. I hate to think of losers trying to go to sleep. I don't mind winners," Gronevelt said. "I can live with luck, it's skill I can't abide. Look, they can never beat the percentage and I have the percentage. That's true in life as well as gambling. The percentage will grind you into dust."

Gronevelt was rambling, thinking of his own approaching death. "You have to get rich in the dark," he said, "you have to live with percentages. Forget about luck, that's a very treacherous magic." I nodded my head in agreement. After we had finished eating and were having brandy, Gronevelt said, "I don't want you to worry about Cully, so I'll tell you what happened to him. Remember that trip you made with him to Tokyo and Hong Kong to bring out that money? Well, for reasons of his own Cully decided to take another crack at it. I warned him against it. I told him the percentages were bad, that he had been lucky that first trip. But for reasons of his own which I can't tell you, but which were important and valid at least to him, he decided to go."

"You had to give the OK," I said.

"Yes," Gronevelt said. "It was to my benefit that he go there."

"So what happened to him?" I asked Gronevelt.

"We don't know," Gronevelt said. "He picked up the money in his fancy suitcases, and then he just disappeared. Fummiro thinks he's in Brazil or Costa Rica living like a king. But you and I know Cully better. He couldn't live in any place but Vegas."

"So what do you guess happened?" I asked Gronevelt again.

Gronevelt smiled at me. "Do you know Yeats's poem? It begins, I think, 'Many a soldier and sailor lies, far from customary skies,' and that's what happened to Cully. I think of him maybe in one of those beautiful ponds behind a geisha house in Japan lying on the bottom. And how he would have hated it. He wanted to die in Vegas."

"Have you done anything about it?" I said. "Have you notified the police or the Japanese authorities?"

"No," Gronevelt said. "That's not possible and I don't think that you should."

"Whatever you say is good enough for me," I said. "Maybe Cully will show up someday. Maybe he'll walk into the casino with your money as if nothing ever happened."

"That can't be," Gronevelt said. "Please don't think like that. I would hate it that I left you with any hope. Just accept it. Think of him as another gambler that the percentage ground to dust." He paused and then said softly, "He made a mistake counting down the shoe." He smiled.

I knew my answer now. What Gronevelt was telling me really was that Cully had been sent on an errand that Gronevelt had engineered and that it was Gronevelt who had decided its final end. And looking at the man now, I knew that he had done so not out of any malicious cruelty, not out of any desire for revenge, but for what were to him good and sound reasons. That for him it was simply a part of his business.

And so we shook hands and Gronevelt said, "Stay as long as you like. It's all comped."

"Thanks," I said. "But I think I'll leave tomorrow."

"Will you gamble tonight?" Gronevelt said.

"I think so," I said. "Just a little bit."

"Well, I hope you get lucky," Gronevelt said.

Before I left the room, Gronevelt walked me to the door and pressed a stack of black hundred-dollar chips in my hand. "These were in Cully's desk," Gronevelt said. "I'm sure he'd like you to have them for one last shot at the table. Maybe it's lucky money." He paused for a moment. "I'm sorry about Cully, I miss him."

"So do I," I said. And I left.

Chapter 54

Gronevelt had given me a suite, the living room decorated in rich browns, the colors overcoordinated in the usual Vegas style. I didn't feel like gambling and I was too tired to go to a movie. I counted the black chips, my inheritance from Cully. There were ten of them, an even thousand dollars. I thought how happy Cully would be if I stuck the chips in my suitcase and left Vegas without losing them. I thought that I might do that.

I was not surprised at what had happened to Cully. It was almost in the seed of his character that he would go finally against the percentage. In his heart, born hustler though he was, Cully was a gambler. Believing in his countdown, he could never be a match for Gronevelt. Gronevelt with his "iron maiden" percentages crushing everything to death.

I tried to sleep but had no luck. It was too late to call Valerie, at least 1 A.M. in New York. I took up the Vegas newspaper I had bought at the airport, and leafing through it, I saw a movie ad for Janelle's last picture. It was the second female lead, a supporting role, but she had been so great in it that she had won an Academy Award nomination. It had opened in New York just a month ago and I had meant to see it, so I decided to go now. Even though I had never seen or spoken to Janelle since that night she left me in the hotel room.

It was a good movie. I watched Janelle on the screen and saw her do all the things she had done with me. On that huge screen her face expressed all the tenderness, all the affection, all the sensual craving that she had shown in our bed together. And as I watched, I wondered, what was the reality? How had she really felt in bed with me, how had she really felt up there on the screen? In one part of the film where she was crushed by the rejection by her lover, she had the same shattered look on her face that broke my heart when she thought I had been cruel to her. I was amazed by how strictly her performance followed our most intense and secret passions. Had she been acting with me, preparing for this role, or did her performance spring from the pain we had shared together? But I almost fell in love with her again just watching her on the screen, and I was glad that everything had turned out well for her. That she was becoming so successful, that she was getting everything she wanted, or thought she wanted, from life. And this is the end of the story, I thought. Here I am, the poor unhappy lover at a distance, watching the success of his beloved one, and everybody would feel sorry for me, I would be the hero because I was so sensitive and now I could suffer and live alone, the solitary writer making books, while she sparkled in the glittering world of cinema. And that's how I would like to leave it. I had promised Janelle that if I wrote about her, I would never show her as someone defeated or someone to be pitied. One night we had gone to see *Love Story* and she had been enraged.

"You fucking writers, you always make the girl die in the end," she said. "Do you know why? Because it's the easiest way to get rid of them. You're tired of them and you don't want to be the villain. So you just kill her and then you cry and you're the fucking hero. You're such fucking hypocrites. You always want to ditch women." She turned to me, her eyes huge, golden brown going black with anger. "Don't you ever kill me off, you son of a bitch."

"I promise," I said. "But what about your always telling me you'll never live to forty? That you're going to burn out."

She often pulled that shit on me. She always loved painting herself as dramatically as possible.

"That's none of your business," she said. "We won't even be speaking to each other by then."

I left the theater and started the long walk back to the Xanadu. It was a long walk. I started at the bottom of the Strip and passed hotel after hotel, passed through their waterfalls of neon light and kept walking toward the dark desert mountains that stood guard at the top of the Strip. And I thought about Janelle. I had promised her that if I wrote about us, I would never show her as someone defeated, someone to be pitied, even someone to be grieved. She had asked for that promise, and I had given it, all in fun.

But the truth is different. She refused to stay in the shadows of my mind as Artie and Osano and Malomar decently did. My magic no longer worked.

Because by the time I had seen her on the screen, so alive and full of passion I fell in love with her again, she was already dead.

Janelle, preparing for the New Year's Eve party, worked very slowly on her makeup. She tilted her magnified makeup mirror and worked on her eye shadow. The top corner of the mirror reflected the apartment behind her. It was really a mess, clothes strewn about, shoes not put away, some dirty plates and cups on the coffee table, the bed not made. She would have to meet Joel at the door and not let him in. The man with the Rolls-Royce, Merlyn had always called him. She slept with Joel occasionally, but not too often, and she knew that she would have to sleep with him tonight. After all, it was New Year's Eve. So she had already bathed carefully, scented herself, used a vaginal deodorant. She was prepared. She thought about Merlyn and wondered whether he would call her. He hadn't called her for two years, but he just might today or tomorrow. She knew he wouldn't call her at night. She thought for a minute of calling him, but he would panic, the coward. He was so scared of spoiling his family life. That whole bullshit structure he had built up over the years that he used as a crutch. But she didn't really miss him. She knew that he looked back upon himself with contempt for being in love and that she looked back with a radiant joy that it had happened. It didn't matter to her that they had wounded each other so terribly. She had forgiven him a long time ago. But she knew he had not. She knew that he had foolishly thought he had lost something of himself, and she knew that was not true for either of them.

She stopped putting on her makeup. She was tired and she had a headache. She also felt very depressed, but she always did on New Year's Eve. It was another year gone by, another year that she was older, and she dreaded old age. She thought about calling Alice, who was spending the holidays with her mother and father in San Francisco. Alice would be horrified at the mess in the apartment, but Janelle knew she would clean it up without reproaching her. She smiled thinking of what Merlyn said, that she used her women lovers with a brutal exploitation that only the most chauvinistic husbands would dare. She realized now that it was partly true. From a drawer she took the ruby earrings Merlyn had given to her as a first gift and put them on. They looked beautiful on her. She loved them.

Then the doorbell range and she went and opened it. She let Joel come in. She didn't give a shit whether he saw the mess in the apartment or not. Her headache was worse, so she went into the bathroom and took some Percodan before they went out. Joel was as kind and charming as usual. He opened the door of the car for her and went around the other side. Janelle thought about Merlyn. He always forgot to do that and the times he remembered he looked embarrassed. Until, finally, she told him to forget about it, relinquishing her own Southern belle ways.

It was the usual New Year's Eve party in a great crowded house. The parking lot was filled with red-jacketed valets taking over the Mercedes, the Rolls-Royces, the Bentleys, the Porsches. Janelle knew many of the people there. And there was a good deal of flirting and propositioning, which she courted gaily by making jokes about her New Year's resolution to remain pure for at least one month.

As midnight approached, she was really depressed and Joel noticed it. He took her into one of the bedrooms and gave her some cocaine. She immediately felt better and high. She got through the stroke of midnight, the kissing of all her friends, the gropings, and then suddenly she felt her headache come on again. It was the worst headache she had ever had, and she knew she had to get home. She found Joel and told him she was ill. He took a look at her face and could see that she was.

"It's just a headache," Janelle said. "I'll be OK. Just get me home."

Joel drove her home and wanted to come in with her. She knew he wanted to stay hoping that the headache would go away and at least he could spend a nice day tomorrow in bed with her. But she really felt ill. She kissed him and said, "Please don't come in. I'm really sorry to disappoint you, but I really feel sick. I feel terribly sick."

She was relieved that Joel believed her. He asked, "Do you want me to call a doctor for you?"

And she said, "No, I'll just take some pills and I'll be OK."

She watched until he was safely out the door of her apartment.

She went immediately to the bathroom to take more Percodan, wet a towel and wrapped it around her head like a turban. She was on her way to the bedroom, going through the doorway, when she felt a terrible crushing blow on the back of her neck. She almost fell. For a moment she thought someone concealed in the room had hit her, and then she thought she had hit her head against something protruding from the wall. But then another crushing blow brought her to her knees. She knew then that something terrible was happening to her. She managed to crawl to the phone beside the bed and just barely made out the red sticker on which was printed the paramedic number. Alice had pasted it there when her son had been visiting them, just in case. She dialed the number and a woman's voice answered.

Janelle said, "I'm sick. I don't know what's happening, but I'm sick." And she gave her name and address and let the phone drop. She managed to pull herself up on the bed, and surprisingly enough she suddenly felt better. She was almost ashamed that she had called, there was nothing really wrong with her. Then another terrible blow seemed to strike her whole body. Her vision diminished and narrowed down to a single focus. Again she was astonished and couldn't believe what was happening to her. She could barely see beyond the stretches of the room. She remembered Joel had given her some cocaine and she still had it in her handbag and she staggered to the living room to get rid of it, but in the middle of the living room her body was struck another terrible blow. Her sphincter loosened, and though the haze of a near unconsciousness, she realized she had voided herself. With a great effort she took off her panties and wiped up the floor and threw them under the sofa and then she felt for the earrings she was wearing, she didn't want anyone to steal the earrings. It took her what seemed a long time to get them out, and then she staggered into the kitchen and pushed them far back on the roof of the cabinet where it was all dusty and where no one would ever look.

Still conscious when the paramedics arrived, she was dimly

aware of being examined and one of the medics looking in her handbag and finding her cocaine. They thought she had overdosed. One of the paramedics was questioning her. "How much drugs did you take tonight?"

And she said, defiantly, "None."

And the medic said, "Come on, we're trying to save your life."

And it was that line that really saved Janelle. She went into a certain role that she played. She used a phrase that she always used to scorn what others value. She said, *"Oh, please."* The *Oh, please* in a contemptuous note to show that saving her life was the least of her worries and, in fact, something not even to be considered.

She was conscious of the ride in the ambulance to the hospital and she was concious of being put in the bed in the white hospital room, but by now this was not happening to her. It was happening to someone she had created and it was not true. She could step away from this whenever she wished. She was safe now. At that moment she felt another terrible blow and lost consciousness.

On the day after New Year's I got the phone call from Alice. I was mildly surprised to hear her voice; in fact, I didn't recognize it until she told me her name. The first thing that flashed through my mind was that Janelle needed help in some way.

"Merlyn, I thought you'd want to know," Alice said. "It's been a long time, but I thought I should tell you what happened."

She paused, her voice uncertain. I didn't say anything, so she went on. "I have some bad news about Janelle. She's in the hospital. She had a cerebral hemorrhage."

I didn't really grasp what she was saying, or my mind refused the facts. It registered as an illness only. "How is she?" I asked. "Was it very bad?"

Again there was that pause, then Alice said, "She's living on machines. The tests show no brain activity."

I was very calm, but I still didn't really grasp it. I said, "Are you telling me that she's going to die? Is that what you're telling me?"

"No, I'm not telling you that," Alice said. "Maybe she'll recover, maybe they can keep her alive. Her family's coming out and they'll make all the decisions. Do you want to come out? You can stay at my place."

"No," I said. "I can't." And I really couldn't. "Will you call me tomorrow and tell me what happens? I'll come out if I can help, but not for anything else."

There was a long silence, and then Alice said, her voice breaking. "Merlyn, I sat beside her, she looks so beautiful, as if nothing happened to her. I held her hand and it was warm. She looks as if she were just sleeping. But the doctors say that there's nothing left of her brain. Merlyn, could they be wrong? Could she get better?"

And at moment I felt certain it was all a mistake, that Janelle would recover. Cully had said once that a man could sell himself anything in his own hand and that's what I did. "Alice, the doctors are wrong sometimes, maybe she'll get better. Don't give up hope."

"All right," Alice said. She was crying now. "Oh, Merlyn, it's so terrible. She lies there on the bed asleep like some fairy princess and I keep thinking some magic can happen, that she'll be all right. I can't think of living without her. And I can't leave her like that. She would hate to live like that. If they don't pull the plug, I will. I won't let her live like that."

Ah, what a chance it was for me to be a hero. A fairy princess dead in an enchantment and Merlyn the Magician knowing how to wake her. But I didn't offer to help pull the plug. "Wait and see what happens," I said. "Call me, OK?"

"OK," Alice said. "I just thought you'd want to know. I thought you might want to come out."

"I really haven't seen her or spoken to her for a long time," I said. And I remember Janelle asking, "Would you deny me?" and my saying laughingly, "With all my heart."

Alice said, "She loved you more than any other man."

But she didn't say "more than anybody," I thought. She left out women. I said, "Maybe she'll be OK. Will you call me again?"

"Yes," Alice said. Her voice was calmer now. She had begun to grasp my rejection and she was bewildered by it. "I'll call you as soon as something happens." Then she hung up.

And I laughed. I don't know why I laughed, but I just laughed. I couldn't believe it, it must be one of Janelle's tricks. It was too outrageously dramatic, something I knew she had fantasized about and so had arranged this little charade. And one thing I knew, I would never look upon her empty face, her beauty vacated by the brain behind it. I would never, never look at it because I would be turned to stone. I didn't feel any grief or sense any loss. I was too wary for that. I was too cunning. I walked around the rest of the day, shaking my head. Once again I laughed and later I caught myself with my face twisting in a kind of smirk, like someone with a guilty secret wish come true, or of someone who is finally trapped forever.

Alice called me late the next day. "She's all right now," Alice said.

And for a minute I thought she meant it, that Janelle had recovered, that it had all been a mistake. And then Alice said, "We pulled the plug. We took her off the machines and she's dead."

Neither of us said anything for a long time, and then she asked, "Are you going to come out for the funeral? We're going to have a memorial service in the theater. All her friends are coming. It's going to be a party with champagne and all her friends giving speeches about her. Will you come?"

"No," I said. "I'll come in a couple of weeks to see you if you don't mind. But I can't come now."

There was another long pause if she were trying to control her anger, and then she said, "Janelle once told me to trust you, so I do. Whenever you want to come out, I'll see you."

And then she hung up.

* * *

The Xanadu Hotel loomed before me, its million-dollar marquee of bright lights drowned the lonely hills beyond. I walked past it, dreaming of those happy days and months and years I had spent seeing Janelle. Since Janelle's death I had thought of her nearly every day. Some mornings I'd wake up thinking about her, imagining how she looked, how she could be so affectionate and so furious at the same time.

Those first few minutes awake I always believed she was alive. I'd imagine scenes between us when we met again. It took me five or ten minutes to remember she was dead. With Osano and Artie this had never happened. In fact, I rarely thought of them now. Did I care for her more? But then if I felt that way about Janelle, why my nervous laugh when Alice told me the news over the phone? Why, during the day I heard of her death, did I laugh to myself three or four times? And I realize now perhaps it was because I was enraged with her for dying. In time, if she had lived, I would have forgotten her. By her trickery she would haunt me all my life.

When I saw Alice a few weeks after Janelle's death, I learned that the cerebral hemorrhage came from a congenital defect which Janelle may have known about.

I remembered how angry I was when she was late or the few times she forgot the day on which we were supposed to meet. I was so sure they were Freudian slips, her unconscious wish to reject me. But Alice told me that this had happened often with Janelle. And had gotten worse shortly before her death. It was certainly linked to the bulging aneurysm, the fatal leakage into her brain. And then I remembered that last night with her when she had asked me if I loved her and I had answered her so insolently. And I thought if she could only ask me now, how different I would be. That she could be and say and do whatever she wishes. That I would accept anything she wanted to be. That just the thought that I could see her, that she was someplace I could go to, that I could hear her voice or hear her laugh would be the things that could make me happy. "Ah, then," I could hear her ask, pleased but angry too, "but is it the important thing to you?" She wanted to be the most important thing to me and to everyone she knew and, if possible, to everyone in the world. She had an enormous hunger for affection. I thought of bitter remarks for her to make to me as she lay in bed, her brain shattered as I looked down upon her with grief. She would say, "Isn't this the way you wanted me? Isn't that the way men want women? I would think this would be ideal for you." But then I realized she never would have been so cruel or even so vulgar, and then I realized another odd thing. My memories of her were never about our lovemaking.

I know I dream of her many times at night, but I never remember those dreams. I just wake up thinking about her as if she were still alive.

I was on the very top of the Strip, in the shadow of the Nevada mountains, looking down into the huge, glittering neon nest that was the heart of Vegas. I would gamble tonight and in the early morning I'd catch a plane for New

York. Tomorrow night I would sleep with my family in my own house and work on my books in my solitary room. I would be safe.

I entered the doors of the Xanadu casino. I was chilled by the frozen air. Two spade hookers went gliding by arm in arm, their heavy curly wigs glistening, one dark chocolate, the other sweetly brown. Then white hookers in boots and short shorts offering pearly white thighs, but the skin of their faces ghostly, showing skeleton bones thinned by chandeliered light and years of cocaine. Down the gauntlet of green felt blackjack tables a long row of dealers raised their hands and washed them in the air.

I went through the casino toward the baccarat pit. And as I approached the gray-railed enclosure, the crowd in front of me broke to spread around the dice pit and I saw the bacarrat pit clear.

Four Saints in black tie waited for me. The croupier running the game held up his right hand to halt the Banker with the shoe. He gave me a quick glance and smiled his recognition. Then with his hand still up he intoned, "A card for the Player." The laddermen, two pale Jehovahs, leaned forward.

I turned away to watch the casino. I felt a rush of oxygenated air and I wondered if the senile, crippled Gronevelt in his solitary rooms above had pushed his magic buttons to keep all these people awake. And what if he had pushed the button for Cully and all the others to die?

Standing absolutely still in the center of the casino, I looked for a lucky table on which to begin.

Chapter 55

"I suffer, but still I don't live. I am an X in an indeterminate equation. I am a sort of phantom in life who has lost all beginning and end."

I read that in the asylum when I was fifteen or sixteen years old, and I think Dostoevsky wrote it to show the unending despair of mankind and perhaps to instill terror in everyone's heart and persuade them to a belief in God. But long ago, as a child when I read it, it was a beam of light. It comforted me, being a phantom didn't frighten me. I thought that X and its indeterminate equation were a magic shield. And now having remained so prudently alive, having passed through all the dangers and all the suffering, I could no longer use my old trick of projecting myself forward into time. My own life was no longer that painful and the future could not rescue me. I was surrounded by countless tables of chance and I was under no illusion. I knew now the single fact that no matter how carefully I planned, no matter how cunning I was, lies or good deeds done, I couldn't really win.

Finally I accepted the fact that I was not a magician anymore. But what the hell. I was still alive and that's more than I could say for my brother, Artie, or Janelle or Osano. And Cully and Malomar and poor Jordan. I understood Jordan now. It was very simple. Life was too much for him. But not for me. Only fools die.

Was I a monster then that I didn't grieve, that I wished so much to stay alive? That I could sacrifice my only brother, my only beginning, and then Osano and Janelle and Cully and never even grieve for them and only weep for one? That I could be comforted with the world I had built for myself?

How we laugh at primitive man for his worry and terror of all the charlatan tricks of nature, and how we ourselves are so terrified of the terrors and guilts that roar in our own heads. What we think of as our sensitivity is only the higher evolution of terror in a poor dumb beast. We suffer for nothing. Our own death wish is our only real tragedy.

Merlin, Merlin. Surely a thousand years have passed and you must finally be awake in your cave, putting on your star-covered conical hat to walk through a strange new world. And poor bastard, with your cunning magic, did it do you any good to sleep that thousand years, your enchantress in her grave, both our Arthurs turned to dust?

Or do you have one last magic spell that can work? A terrible long shot, but what's that to a gambler? I still have a stack of black chips and an itch for terror.

I suffer, but I still live. It's true that I may be a sort of phantom in life, but I know my beginning and I know my end. It is true that I am an X in an indeterminate equation, the X that will terrify mankind as it voyages through a million galaxies. But no matter. That X is the rock upon which I stand.

ABOUT THE AUTHOR

MARIO PUZO was born on Manhattan's West Side in a neighborhood known for decades as Hell's Kitchen. His first books, *The Fortunate Pilgrim* ("a minor classic" NY *Times*) and *Dark Arena,* brought him critical acclaim, but it was publication of *The Godfather* in March, 1969, that catapulted him into the front ranks of American authors. *The Godfather* is available in a Signet edition.

More Bestsellers from SIGNET

- [ ] **LEGEND** by Frank Sette. (#J8605—$1.95)*
- [ ] **THE INFERNAL DEVICE** by Michael Kurland.
  (#J8492—$1.95)*
- [ ] **THE MAN WITHOUT A NAME** by Martin Russell.
  (#J8515—$1.95)†
- [ ] **MANHOOD CEREMONY** by Ross Berliner.
  (#E8509—$2.25)*
- [ ] **DEADLY PAYOFF** by Michel Clerc. (#J8553—$1.95)*
- [ ] **.44** by Jimmy Breslin and Dick Schaap. (#E8459—$2.50)*
- [ ] **NATURAL ACTS** by James Fritzhand. (#E8603—$2.50)*
- [ ] **THE HONOR LEGION** by Edward Droge. (#J8657—$1.95)*
- [ ] **THE DANCER** by Leland Cooley. (#E8651—$2.75)*
- [ ] **CARRIE** by Stephen King. (#J7280—$1.95)
- [ ] **NIGHT SHIFT** by Stephen King. (#E8510—$2.50)*
- [ ] **'SALEM'S LOT** by Stephen King. (#E8000—$2.25)
- [ ] **THE SHINING** by Stephen King. (#E7872—$2.50)
- [ ] **KRAMER VERSUS KRAMER** by Avery Corman.
  (#E8282—$2.50)
- [ ] **VISION OF THE EAGLE** by Kay McDonald.
  (#J8284—$1.95)*

* Price slightly higher in Canada
† Not available in Canada

To order these titles,
please use coupon on the
last page of this book.

SIGNET Books You'll Enjoy

To order these titles,

please use coupon on the

last page of this book.

Recommended Reading from SIGNET

☐ **MIRIAM AT THIRTY-FOUR by Alan Lelchuk.**
(#J6793—$1.95)

☐ **SHRINKING by Alan Lelchuk.** (#E8653—$2.95)

☐ **AMERICAN MISCHIEF by Alan Lelchuk.** (#E6185—$2.25)

☐ **SONG OF SOLOMON by Toni Morrison.** (#E8340—$2.50)*

☐ **THE GREEK TREASURE by Irving Stone.** (#E8782—$2.50)

☐ **THE AGONY AND THE ECSTASY by Irving Stone.**
(#E8276—$2.75)

☐ **CLARENCE DARROW FOR THE DEFENSE by Irving Stone.**
(#E8489—$2.95)

☐ **PASSIONS OF THE MIND by Irving Stone.**
(#E8789—$2.95)

☐ **THE NAKED AND THE DEAD by Norman Mailer.**
(#E7604—$2.25)

☐ **THE ARMIES OF THE NIGHT by Norman Mailer.**
(#J7829—$1.95)

☐ **MIAMI AND THE SIEGE OF CHICAGO by Norman Mailer.**
(#J7310—$1.95)

☐ **THE EBONY TOWER by John Fowles.** (#E8254—$2.50)

☐ **DANIEL MARTIN by John Fowles.** (#E8249—$2.25)†

☐ **THE FRENCH LIEUTENANT'S WOMAN by John Fowles.**
(#E8535—$2.50)

☐ **INSIDE MOVES by Todd Walton.** (#E8596—$2.25)

* Price slightly higher in Canada
† Not available in Canada

To order these titles, please

use coupon on next page.

Have You Read These SIGNET Titles?

☐ **FLASHMAN** by George MacDonald Fraser.
(#E8009—$1.75)†

☐ **FLASHMAN IN THE GREAT GAME** by George MacDonald Fraser. (#J7429—$1.95)†

☐ **FLASHMAN'S LADY** by George MacDonald Fraser.
(#E8514—$2.25)†

☐ **THE SWARM** by Arthur Herzog. (#E8079—$2.25)

☐ **EARTHSOUND** by Arthur Herzog. (#E7255—$1.75)

☐ **THE DESPERATE HOURS** by Joseph Hayes.
(#J7689—$1.95)

☐ **LOVE, LAUGHTER AND TEARS** by Adela Rogers St. Johns.
(#E8752—$2.50)*

☐ **SOME ARE BORN GREAT** by Adela Rogers St. Johns.
(#J6707—$1.95)

☐ **THE HONEYCOMB** by Adela Rogers St. Johns.
(#E7605—$2.25)

☐ **THE SEVEN WITCHES** by George Macbeth.
(#E8597—$2.50)*

☐ **THE SAMURAI** by George Macbeth. (#J7021—$1.95)

☐ **FOR THE DEFENSE** by F. Lee Bailey with John Greenya.
(#J7022—$1.95)

☐ **THE DEFENSE NEVER RESTS** by F. Lee Bailey with Harvey Aronson. (#E8317—$2.25)

☐ **DRAGONS AT THE GATE** by Robert Duncan.
(#J6984—$1.95)

☐ **THE LONG WALK** by Richard Bachman. (#E8754—$1.95)*

* Price slightly higher in Canada
† Not available in Canada

THE NEW AMERICAN LIBRARY, INC.,
P.O. Box 999, Bergenfield, New Jersey 07621

Please send me the SIGNET BOOKS I have checked above. I am enclosing $_____ (please add 50¢ to this order to cover postage and handling). Send check or money order—no cash or C.O.D.'s. Prices and numbers are subject to change without notice.

Name _____

Address _____

City_____ State_____ Zip Code_____
Allow at least 4 weeks for delivery
This offer is subject to withdrawal without notice.